These stories are works
incidents are fictitious and any ......
locations, or events is coincidental.

ISBN: 978-1-998763-10-8

THE COMPLETE
BUMPS IN THE NIGHT
EDDIE GENEROUS

1.   BURN   9
2.   LITTLE HOUSE ON PRAIRIE STREET   17
3.   CRYSTAL-LYNN   30
4.   WHAT'S HE DONE NOW?   47
5.   OFFERING ATLANTIS   53
6.   RICKY'S GOT A KNIFE   66
7.   DAYTONA 500   71
8.   RISEN GREY FLESH   78
9.   RIGHTEOUS HUNT   89
10. THE DONOR   98
11. BLACKTOP EXECUTION   102
12. DELIVERY   110
13. A GREAT HAND   121
14. THE REMATCH   129
15. CLASS OF MEMORY LANE   138
16. SHE'S IN YOUR HEAD   154
17. YOU'RE IT   159
18. A BOWL AT A TIME   167
19. JIMMY   175
20. SURVIVOR BUFFET   180
21. WRONG NUMBER   191
22. PATHS TO OCEANIA   207
23. HUNGRY   216
24. TREASURE   222
25. EASTER TREAT   230
26. LEAVE A MESSAGE   236
27. THE BRIDGE HOME   239
28. BIG BAD BRENDA   254
29. RANDI   265
30. LARRY CARMICHAEL'S HANDS   273
31. CRYING WOLF   287
32. CLAW MARKS   294
33. APOCALYPSE BADGE   298
34. SWAMP LUCK   308
35. INGRAINED   316
36. POOL SHARK   332
37. DEEP WOODS MURDER   335
38. MY MONKEY   345
39. JOE ADAMS, JOE ADAMS   354
40. THAT NAME GAME   377
41. TENDER   385
42. BUGS   388
43. SOON   391
44. MANHUNTER   395
45. WELL-CIRCULATED CASH   399
46. GOLDEN CALF   403
47. OVER HASH BROWNS   405
48. THE CLUB   409
49. THAT SMILE   412
50. FELINE FEEL   416

51.	THE SLEEPOVER	422
52.	THE BURDEN OF BREATH	423
53.	EYE FOR AN EYE	427
54.	THE TOWER	430
55.	TOILET MANNERS	432
56.	COATTAIL	439
57.	HEROIC OFFERING	443
58.	KITE STRINGS	450
59.	JACQUES	453
60.	JUST A TASTE	459
61.	SERPIENTE BRUJA	462
62.	THE CONDEMNED MAN	466
63.	NO RETURNS	470
64.	FORESAKEN MEMORY	471
65.	CHESTNUT ANNIE	476
66.	NEVERLAND	478
67.	ANDI PANDI	482
68.	BARRY'S HAND	488
69.	BULLSHIT CHRISTMAS	493
70.	A BIG SURPRISE	496
71.	A LITTLE WARMTH ON A COLD NIGHT	499
72.	WHEELS ON THE BUS	510
73.	GIN HAZE	522
74.	TIBBYTOWN BUFFET	526
75.	THE DREAMLAND ROOM	532
76.	THE RUT	541
77.	FREEDOM DREAMING	548
78.	NIGHT OF THE LESSON	564
79.	THE FRANCHISE	571
80.	HARVEST QUEEN	580
81.	COME STRAIGHT HOME	596
82.	DESCRY ONE	600
83.	SHOOTING STAR	606
84.	AROWANA	627
85.	DEVIL BOY	639
86.	THE THINGS	673
87.	THE SECRET TO LIVING FOREVER	681
88.	VISITORS	684
89.	LITTLE CANDIES BEHIND LITTLE DOORS	698
90.	JOHN, AMY, AND THE LONG WAY DOWN	709
91.	IT'S JUST A HOUSE	729
92.	PRECIOUS MOMENTS	734
93.	BETWEEN	742
94.	WARNING SYMPTOMS	752
95.	DEATH GAME	757
96.	DICHOTOMY GROUNDS	768
97.	SUMMER SINGALONG	781
98.	THE MILKENING	793
99.	NOBODY THERE	796
100.	WHEN YOU NEED IT MOST	

INTRODUCTION

I suppose there are a million addictions worse than writing fiction. And addicted I am. If I go too long without writing something, I become irritable and difficult to live with; when I'm in the middle of writing something, and I'm liking it, I feel light and easy. Writing is my happy place—I know, I know, I'm supposed to complain, supposed to say it's difficult and painful, but it's simply not for me. Especially when it comes to short fiction.

Ideas come at me faster than I can keep up with; the good ideas linger, and the bad ideas disappear inside a day or two, unwritten. 100 is a big number, especially for a single volume— really, this is eight books in one—that I can't argue, too many stories perhaps, but as the saying goes, *better out than in*. And compiling a huge volume feels a bit like letting out a good ripper; these are stories I don't have to worry about again, they've grown their wings and taken flight—sometimes an editor asks to reprint, sometimes it's a movie/TV producer sniffing around, but those are good problems, found money. Many have been published in small magazines or anthologies, many yet are seeing light for the first time.

This collection represents about a third of the good short fiction I've written over the past nine years. The older entries have been rewritten, sure. They needed the work. The plots remain as they were, but the delivery is much, much smoother.

Not all the rough edges were polished out because I'm far from perfect, and each of these stories represent a piece of me.

The dread-inducing to the raunchy to the suspenseful to the spooky to the comedic, all parts of the greater me.

Likely, this is why I have such a good time writing, part of the reason anyway. Likely, this is what scratches my junkie's itch, doling myself out for you to read.

Maybe there's something that will scratch an itch for you within these pages, a sinister need to experience the darker shades of weird.

With all my heart, I hope so.

Eddie Generous
October 2022

BURN

(2015)

The stairs creaked beneath Todd's steps as he cursed the stupid old house.

"Mom? Dad?" he whispered into the pitch-black basement.

The only light available was an orange flame emitted by the mini, Bic brand lighter he wielded. Outside the home, a storm thrashed the countryside. The power was out when Todd awoke to the cackling laughter coming from the main floor. By the time he climbed out of bed and retrieved his lighter from its hiding spot in his sock drawer, the laughter had become conversation.

It was just him and his parents way out there. His mother was a lawyer and his father was a surgeon. They were older than most other kids' parents, older and wealthier. They joked that once they saved up five big ones that they were moving to smack in the center of nowhere to live the stress free, simple life of country folks. Todd didn't believe it until they snatched up the roots from the life he'd known for ten years and plopped the family into a strange, disconnected world.

At first, it was pretty cool having all that space. There was a trail into the forest that came up on a clearing and a giant stone. The giant stone had a gnarly tree growing right out of the middle of it. It was probably the coolest tree Todd had ever seen. There was also a pond and a big hill he planned to make full use of come winter and snow.

Of course, the fascination with the detached place waned quickly and Todd wondered about internet speeds and lagging behind his old friends when it came time to enter one of the many virtual worlds they'd routinely traversed. He was not alone on that front, his father wondered about similar issues.

Todd had begun to question the realities of country living. Sure, there was the trail through the woods, the pond in the backyard, and the big hill, but where was the connection to the world? At such a distance, human contact became difficult. Todd's father had craved solitude and once he got it, he wondered how close the neighbors were, *five miles, ten?*

Todd's mother was adamant about sticking it out, working through the kinks of change. As they always had before, Todd and his father caved.

Steamy summer days passed and the house boiled. Todd's mother began to understand the discomforts of country living. The original settlers knew a hell she could hardly fathom. Problems she wanted never to understand or relate to, even in a slim sense.

It was only that morning that she declared that the house would go back on the market, and they'd return to the city with their gadget loving tails between their legs. The first sprinkles of rain began as she spoke and the shower picked up gradually as the day progressed.

Todd listened with relief as his parents got through to the moving men and the realtor that listed their as of yet unsold brownstone. The listing switched and the country plot and house hit the market. The city dwelling would take its relieved former tenants in only a few days.

The successful calls ended there. The cellular service was shaky from the moment they'd arrived, and the ever-building storm cut off the wireless connection. Todd's father used the landline to make one more call and had it drop before he and his former partner in practice traded goodbyes.

Todd's father whispered with mock fear that it was as if the country wanted to keep them right where it had them. They all joked about the so-called simple life and into the night watched choppy, buffer-ridden videos online. The rain battered incessantly on the tin roof. Lightning danced and thunder drummed a roll.

At 9:30, more bored than tired, Todd went to bed.

It really wasn't a wonder he awoke so easily after a few hours upon hearing voices downstairs. The real wonder came when he got to the main floor and the voices seemed to come from deeper in the home.

The basement.

As nice as the old house was, the basement took rustic too far. Muddy floors and jutting, whitewashed stone walls coated in thick grey webbing. Weepy cracks and breezy gaps. That wasn't all, to Todd it *had a vibe*. A creepy place, Todd's parents laughed at him when he voiced the opinion, joked that he was too much of a *city boy*.

This was forced humor. The adults avoided the basement just as the boy had. They felt that vibe.

So what were they doing down there in the middle of a storm?

A vibe wasn't a real threat, not to Todd and he swung open the door to the basement and felt the cool breeze on his face.

"Mom? Dad?" he whispered and cleared his throat as he stepped down the creaking stairs, then called out, "Mom! Dad!"

No voices returned, but there was chatter just beyond the whistling wind and dripping rainwater.

Creak. Creak.

"Mom?"

Creak.

"Dad?"

Creak. Creak. Splash.

Todd's foot fell into cold water. The basement flooded. The voices ceased.

"Mom? Dad?" Todd said and swung his arm around in a gentle motion. Not gentle enough, his thumb slipped and burned on the hot steel safety guard. The lighter fell and plunked into the water at his feet. "Dammit."

Splashing sounded all around the basement as if two-dozen rubber-booted kiddies kicked at puddles.

"City boy lost his light!" a shrill voice screeched through the darkness.

"Who's there?"

"City boy, city boy, too late to run home!" several childish voices cried in unison.

Todd turned and sprinted blindly up the stairs, screaming, "Mom! Mom! Mommy!" as he moved.

The voices fell away behind him as he flung open the door to the main floor. It was dark, but not as dark as the basement. Lightning outside flashed and he caught strobe visions of the kitchen.

"Todd? Todd? Where are you?" Todd heard his father call for him.

Todd's heart pattered toward the safe, warm feeling of a parent nearby. "Dad!" he shouted and shuffled in near blindness toward his father's voice. Out of the kitchen and into the living room. His father's shadow faced the dining room, lightning flashed. "Dad!"

The man spun toward his son and opened his arms. "Oh son. It's all on you now," he said.

Todd held his father tight as he could. "What is?"

"It's all on you now, son. You're the man of the family."

Todd's arms fell slack. "What?"

The man pushed Todd out to an arm's length. "City boy, city boy, too late to run home. This place is damned and your father's gone cold!"

Lightning flared and Todd peered at his father. The man's eyes had been sewn shut with thick slimy twine. His mouth spilled viscous black liquid around the words.

"Dad?" Todd cried.

"City boy, city boy!" Todd's father began screeching, his skin peeling from his scalp down, the wet bone and muscle beneath glistening under the heavy staccato crash of the electric storm beyond the walls. "Too late to run home!"

Todd reefed backward as his father began a horrific cackle.

"No Dad, no!" Todd stumbled and rushed toward the front door. He was ten, plenty old enough to hop in one of the cars and tour back to the city. To hell with the law. "Mom!"

The door swung open and banged against the porch railing. The rain had drowned the yard under three feet of water. In the sky, white bolts flashed sideways in layers of circular currents of light, shining down on the mucky property. Humps popped about the wet surface like frogs emerging from beneath lily pads. Filthy children in ancient garb splashed forward, their collective voices forming perfect terror.

"City boy, city boy, too late to run home. This place is damned and your father's gone cold. Dead but the one called…"

Todd felt a hand on his shoulder, wrenching him backward through the door. He screamed and flailed, fell wetly on the old hardwood.

"No, please!"

"Shh, Todd. Something's happening, come on."

"Mommy?"

"Yes, come. We've got to hide, someone's in the house and the power's out… Oh hell, I don't know what's happening!"

Todd's mother pulled him to his feet and then quickly up the stairs. They rushed into the master bedroom and Todd's mother slammed the door. She began dragging the dresser sideways. Todd fumbled in the dark, helping her with a push.

"Mom, Dad's dead!"

Todd listened to his mother's quiet sobbing. He put a hand on her back.

She mumbled something into her palms.

"What?"

"Dead…dead but the one called Burn," she whispered.

"What did you say?" Todd rubbed her shoulders, cool and damp from the rain.

Todd's mother rose and stepped away from her son. A thump landed on the door and rocked the contents of the dresser. The old dresser was heavy, only the stuff in the drawers moved.

"I said, dead but the one called Burn."

"I don't understand," Todd said, fear bubbling up his throat.

Outside, the spinning electrical currents lowered around the house like a halo and shined white light through the window. The heavy drapes did little to dampen the tenacity of the glare. Thumps landed on the door again. Thumps pounded the walls. Pictures fell and voices filled the air.

"City boy, city boy, too late to run home. This place is damned and your father's gone cold. Dead but the one called Burn. The master has risen for your turn."

"Mom!"

Todd put his hands over his ears and watched his mother stride to the window. She swung the drapes aside, the light pouring around her silhouette was nearly blinding. The pane shattered and the woman turned. She held a shard of glass between her palms.

"City boy, city boy, too late to run home," Todd's mother sobbed as she joined the chorus of voices from outside the room. "This place is damned." She ceased her chant while the others continued. The glass pierced her chest and crunched against ribs. Blood drained in a shower down her pajama shirt. She resumed her chant as she dug: "Burn. The master has risen for your turn."

Todd stumbled back and fell to the floor at the sight of his mother wrenching her heart from her chest and then biting into it as if it was an apple.

"Mom, no!"

The woman quickly toppled into a fleshy heap, lifeblood seeping into the cracks of the floorboards. Behind Todd, the dresser screeched across the floor and the walls around him began to crumble. Children stomped a wet parade. Mucky footfalls pattered in the blood that had begun raining down from the ceiling.

"City boy, city boy, time to meet Burn!"

Todd covered his face and brought his knees tight to his chest. The chanting voices washed away, as did the splashing and the patter of the blood rain. Still, he didn't dare open his eyes.

In the quiet, he heard heavy steps approach him. Todd balled tighter.

Thump. Thump. Thump.

"Welcome home, Todd," a deep voice said.

Thump. Thump.

The footfalls drew away and Todd remained so tight that his knees touched his chin. The heat at his core began to rise until sweat bubbled on his face and still he refused to open his eyes. Todd wanted to cry out for someone, or something. A figure or figures, he didn't recall which, it was receding...

Until...

It...

Was...

All...

Gone.

After a time, the heat no longer burned him and the terror wasted away. He opened his eyes.

—

"I could've sworn this place was off the market," said the man in his three-piece Armani suit, red Gucci loafers, and a gold Rolex timepiece.

The realtor smiled. "It was and then poof, the owners disappeared and never came back. I guess they'd called their agent in the city and told her they were done with the quiet life. Only lived out here a little while too. The agent passed it off to me."

"Couldn't hack it, huh?" asked the woman in a striped black

and yellow Stella McCartney dress, floppy Flora Bella hat, and Dolce slippers. "We're really looking forward to slowing down. Live the simple life, ya know?"

"And the privacy," the man added. "Isn't that right, Kite?"

Kite, a nine-year-old girl grimaced. She worried much about leaving the city for this grungy old house. The whole place gave off bad vibes, but nobody ever listened to her.

The realtor led the trio through the home, and from his spot between the floorboards, Todd whispered with anticipation, "City girl, city girl too late to run home."

LITTLE HOUSE ON PRAIRIE STREET

(2021)

He'd forgotten to bring a towel to the gym. Sweat sprouted and trickled from his hairline as he pulled his hands into the sleeves of his coat, avoiding direct contact with the door handle. Two fat drops streaked down his forehead as if targeting his eyes and he squinted hard against the salty sting as well as a strong gust of cold winter wind. Blindly, he shuffled toward where he'd parked.

The lot and walkway were smokey ice. One step, two steps, three steps—his right foot shot out from beneath him and he thumped backward, hard against the slick concrete, gasping and shaking. Blood bloomed through a rip in his coat where his elbow nailed the cement lip of the sidewalk. He couldn't move more than a tense vibration, could only blink at the sweat in his eyes and the snow falling on his face.

"You okay?" a voice said, a young man by the sound of it.

"Yeah. Think so."

The young man had him by the armpits and was pulling him up. "The ice is all the way around the building; deadly, huh?"

The gym building also featured a bank, a cannabis store, a Panago Pizza, and forty-two apartment units. The young man had been sitting there out in the cold for a while. His many boxes and reusable grocery bags all had an inch-deep layer of snow riding atop them like cake frosting.

"What are you doing out here?"

The young man had turned down his face to speak into the collar of his jacket until he backed away a few feet. "Got evicted for updates, but my new place isn't ready for a week. Was supposed to be ready last week."

After bending to pick up the keys and the small backpack housing his gym gear, he assessed the damage to his elbow and his coat. "That's kind of crazy. You..." he trailed, his mind falling behind his mouth. "You need a ride someplace?"

"Nowhere to go and I had to do first and last and a deposit at the new place. I have twenty bucks that has to last me three weeks. Boss cut my hours way down."

"Oh, shitty." He assumed the pandemic; it had been very hard on a good many people. He reached into his coat pocket and withdrew his wallet. There was a ten and a five in there, he thought about which to give and decided to give both. "Maybe you can get warm for a few minutes," he said and held out the cash.

"Uh, okay." The man accepted the cash.

After a nod, he was in his car, his elbow really singing at the gentle rise in heat. He started the engine and pulled away. He didn't live far from the gym, probably should've walked, but the weather had been crazy all week.

Out of the parking lot, he immediately stopped for a red light and put on his left turn signal. The snow was really coming and the heat emanating from his body had the windows fogging. Across the intersection was a stubby dead-end street and snow had spackled the backside of a stop sign, something about the way it looked gave room for a memory, but rather than letting the thought climb up and take hold, he switched the signal and took a right through the red. At the parking lot's other entry, he hooked another right.

The man sat with his boxes, snow piling around him. The driver's side window came down.

"I have a garage. It's a lot warmer and drier than out here...couple sleeping bags you can use, too?" It came out like a question, almost a plea, but it cancelled any guilt he'd started to feel.

The man looked at the back of the car. "Okay, pop the trunk."

—

"Thanks, eh," the man said.

They'd spoken little, but the man had said his name was Lawrence and he had nowhere to stay because he'd only been in town six months—which was why he had no friends—and had moved from far out east. Lawrence had come right to the coast because he'd never seen an ocean, and he stayed because he got a job at the Staples store, though they'd recently cut his hours back to part-time thanks to the virus. The failure to match up the availability of the two apartments was simply bad luck.

"Well, uh, knock if you need to use the washroom. I'm going to lock the door," he said.

"Makes sense," Lawrence said.

After the deadbolt slipped home, he hurried through the kitchen and past the living room to the washroom. He needed a shower. As the hot water pattered, guilt began festering anew. He lived alone and had a couch in the living room and even a spare bedroom—though it was about the size of a walk-in closet. Still, anywhere inside the house was more comfortable than the cracked cement floor and cob-webby walls of the garage.

Once dried and dressed, he hurried back to the door. The deadbolt slipped in reverse and he switched on the light. Lawrence was amid his stuff, wrapped in a sleeping bag, his nose gone Rudolf red.

"You won't kill me in my sleep if I let you inside?"

Lawrence blinked at him in a way that suggested he might've already fallen asleep. "No," he said.

"I'm not gay, so it's not like..."

Lawrence shook his head. "Yeah."

"Okay. You hungry?"

"Nah, I had crackers and things from before," Lawrence said.

"Okay. The couch is pretty comfy."

"Thank you. I don't know if I'd do it, if I were in your shoes I mean," Lawrence said as he kicked out from the sleeping bag. "So, thanks."

—

Only one day until the weekend, he left behind the hapless Lawrence and parked in the library lot because work had its demands. Lawrence handed over his driver's license as a sort of guarantee, the only piece of collateral available that fit into a pocket. And he'd hold that and go to the cops if something happened. A skid-steer piled the several inches of snow from the night before, revealing a good deal of ice upon the lot's asphalt. He guessed the library would be slow today; was almost always slow since COVID arrived.

At 9:15, the call came in that Eileen, his co-worker, couldn't make it. She lived out of town, up the mountain, and had gotten much worse weather. Feet of the white stuff had piled overnight.

"No worries, so far the only person who has come in was a teenager b-lining for the can. Stay safe."

"Great. You in tomorrow?" Eileen asked.

"Nope."

"When do you work next?"

"Wednesday."

"Lucky," Eileen said. "See you then."

The conversation ended and the library remained stilled for a couple hours until he went to the washroom and discovered the young man had not departed, was in fact sleeping next to one of the toilets in a stall. A sad whistle escaped his lips. The snowmelt around those sopping grey Adidas and the cuffs of the kid's blue jeans...he could only shake his head. He did his business quickly and left without a word to the boy.

Once into the hallway, he stopped and backtracked into the can. He withdrew the wallet from his pants pocket and found he had a five and a ten. He placed both bills on the floor by the kid's legs, having to reach under the stall door to do so.

The next time he entered the washroom, after lunch, all that remained of the boy was a mostly dried puddle of salted water and black road grime.

—

"So, you from here?" Lawrence said.

"No. I'm like you, came from out east."

Lawrence nodded as he chewed. He'd found a roast in the freezer and texted to ask if he could make it for supper. A great idea. "I guess I should've...I don't know, practiced my people skills in college."

College was probably the best time to do it. He began to think of his own time at college, but Lawrence continued.

"I don't know. I got in a dorm and everyone in my hall was ESL and I just played online poker and..." Lawrence sighed. "Hope this isn't too much info, but I'd had these huge plans of starting new and becoming someone else. I was going to get laid, like how it is in every movie where a guy goes off to college, but college wasn't like that for me. I freeze up...I've never even kissed a girl. I'm twenty-three and never kissed a girl. How sad is that?"

Plenty sad, but there was nothing to say.

"I even went to therapy for a while and the therapist tried to suggest I was gay and then maybe I was trans and then maybe asexual. All these things had to do with my *true self* not getting to live. He tried to get me to blame it on everyone but me, so I stopped going," Lawrence said, eyes pinned hard on his empty plate. "Accountability is important."

The openness was uncomfortable and got him to thinking about his own life and how he'd wound up being a thirty-five-year-old bachelor himself, but the thought stopped as he gazed out the window and to the street. The boy from earlier was out there, huddled up, walking.

"That kid was in the library today."

Lawrence turned. The kid had stepped from his view. "What kid?"

"There's a homeless kid." He kicked out his chair and stood, started toward the door. Lawrence followed him, even as he slipped on his shoes.

"...fuck outta here!" the neighbor on the corner shouted as the kid spun from the doorway and rushed to the bench at the bus stop across the street. The neighbor slammed the door.

They stepped back inside and Lawrence said, "That's tough, huh?"

He nodded. That kid was soaked earlier, if he spent the night outside, that wet, he'd be dead before sun-up. "I'll be back," he said and grabbed his coat.

"I'll start dishes," Lawrence said, and then switched on the TV to listen to the news.

———

"I thought she was waving to me," the kid said and swiped a sleeve beneath his nose. He was doing a good job not crying, but he hadn't yet warmed up. "I went over because of that. All I said was can I sleep on your floor and that guy flipped out. I thought she was waving to me and I knew I was gonna die if I sat on that bench any longer. I'd seen the sign for Prairie Street and decided I never been on a Prairie Street and started walking and then I had to sit again because of my feet."

They looked at the kid's feet. He'd taken his shoes and socks off, and the skin looked like oatmeal—grey, pebbly, puffy.

"What were you doing out there?" Lawrence said, not accusatorily only curiously.

"I ran away," the kid had his face turned to his hands, which sat in the lap of his dirty jeans. "I ain't going back. I ain't getting hit no more."

"It's okay. You can stay. We can figure this out." Standing, he took the kid's coat, inside was the name Nathan in black marker on the tag. "Nathan, is that you?"

The kid nodded. "They get us all the same coats and we have to write our names... If you're gonna call the cops, I'll just go now."

Lawrence grimaced at this.

"No way. Just asking. I'm going to fetch you a change of clothes and wash all this. I won't call anyone."

"He's a good one," Lawrence said.

—

The typically silent home was suddenly lively. He'd slept in and had only awoken when Lawrence and Nathan were laughing. The TV was on YouTube and they were watching fail videos. The noise was a bit much and he decided after breakfast, he'd take a walk. He needed to think this through. It was one thing to invite a couple stragglers into the house for a night or two, but what did he do with them long-term? And how had they become his problem?

"Hey," Lawrence said.

"Hi."

Nathan nodded and then said, "I can go whenever."

He put out a hand. "Go where? It's okay. Y'all eat?"

—

He left the house. He had on a toque, mittens, and his cat-print face mask. Immediately he felt better in the quiet. Nathan and Lawrence were easy to get along with, but they both had baggage, both triggered questions in himself that were simply beyond him to answer. The biggest being why was he doing this?

The chill had the path at the sea wall mostly empty, but he left his mask up because it kept his teeth warm. Out in the water, sealions bobbed and watched him—more dog-like than lion-like. They caught up a few times, never losing sight of his movements for long. If it were warmer, he might've sat, let the simple wonders of wild animals take his mind away.

The walk to the end of the sea wall and back took only half an hour so he detoured further and stepped into Kingfisher Books. He had dozens of unread books at home, but it was something to do.

The bell jangled overhead. The curmudgeon at the desk didn't turn to look at him. He never did.

In the mystery aisle, he began scanning the titles. Among the letter Bs was a single title stuffed upside down, written by an author named Joanne Fluke. *Blueberry Muffin Murder* had a blueberry skull face in the center of a muffin on its cover. Too cutesy for his taste. He put the book near where it should fit with the Fs and browsed for something more in tune with his preferences: Block, JCO, Westlake, maybe Abbott or Flynn or Harding or Gran or Langan.

He left emptyhanded after burning half an hour. He'd come to no conclusions beyond that he liked the cover of the Fluke book and that getting a cake might be nice. He hadn't had proper cake in probably ten years.

—

Though he had Nathan's health card as collateral, he trusted Lawrence more, so when Lawrence said he could go to the store too, pay for at least part of the cake or the pizza, he quietly asked him to stay behind and keep an eye on the house.

The streets were eerily barren of traffic and there were three employees and one other customer in the FreshCo grocery. He stepped to the baked goods display counter and grabbed a round layer cake.

"Need candles?" the woman at the till asked from behind her mask and a clear wall of Plexiglass.

"Candles?"

"Not a birthday cake then?" she said.

He shook his head twice and withdrew his debit card. He rolled to the Panago and gave his name to the employee manning the counter. The two medium pizzas were ready and boxed. He paid with his debit again, the entire trip so far taking less than ten minutes. When he turned to leave the pizza shop, the world had gone mostly white.

"Holy," he said and then stepped outside.

Huge flakes drifted lazily from the sky like volcanic ash. So much so that he blew off the pizza box before he closed the car door. Wipers on high, he crept to the street. He tried to recall if he'd ever been out in these bad of conditions and thought maybe, one time, way back—he had to slam the brakes as a flash of navy blue bolted in front of his car. He hadn't stopped in time and the figure fell from view on the tail of a thump.

He kicked open the door after putting the shifter in park. In front of the bumper, splayed out was a small pale boy in a bathrobe several sizes too big. He had no shoes on.

"I'm cold," the boy said, whining it out, hitching into a sob.

"Holy," he said and tried to help the boy up.

"Don't touch me!" the boy shouted, clutching the robe tight to himself.

"Do you need a ride somewhere?"

The boy began sobbing harder. "I-I-I got nowhere!"

The snow was so thick he could hardly see the shape of the big house on the corner of Prairie Street and Joyce. Better to take the kid home than to get in an accident on the way to the police station, or further yet, the hospital.

"Get in. We'll figure it out."

The kid had no questions and seemed to know, almost instinctively, that he had to ride in the back seat—cake and pizza up front.

—

Nathan played kid to kid and got the nine-year-old to open up immediately, doing the old, "My name's Nathan and I ran away, too. What's your name?"

"Ben."

"How come you ran away?"

"My uncle. And my mom. She works the nighttime shift at the restaurant and my uncle babysits me and he always makes me take baths and I don't want to anymore," Ben said.

"Your uncle makes you take baths? In front of him?" Nathan

said, incredulous.

They were in the kitchen, sitting around the dining table. Ben had on borrowed sweats but did not want to give up the bathrobe. They'd all eaten some pizza.

"He rubs my wiener and makes me rub his and I doh-doh-don't wanna! You can't make me go back!"

"Hey, maybe let's stop—"

Lawrence cut him off. "Nobody's taking you anywhere. I had a bad uncle, too, nobody's taking you anywhere."

Nathan punched his leg. "Fucking bullshit! Look at this kid, somebody always fucking with innocent little kids! It fucks them up forever!"

Ben went on crying. Nathan went on yelling. Lawrence went on making promises that weren't really his to offer or keep.

He couldn't listen anymore and retreated to his bedroom. Everything about these people was too horrible to think about and he refused. He'd let them stay, but only in his home, not in his head. He crawled into bed and withdrew his cellphone. He brought up Prime and put on one of the recommendations: *Do You Know the Muffin Man?* that Fluke book still on his mind. He made it through the first twenty or so minutes, the voices beyond his door boisterous and emotional, but he fell asleep anyway.

—

"What's your story?" Lawrence said.

In bed, he sat up and looked around. Three sets of eyes banked the light coming through the window above him.

"What?"

"We told you ours, what's yours?" Nathan said.

"Be fair," Ben said.

He licked his lips and sat up further, draping one leg out from beneath the covers over the edge of the bed. "What?" he said again.

"What's your story? You know why we're here, but how come you're here? Alone in this house, taking in strays, how come?"

Lawrence said.

"Yeah," Nathan said.

"Yeah," Ben parroted.

"Why do you need to know?"

"It's important," Lawrence said and flipped the light switch. "You have to face your demons," his voice continued, but it came from Ben's little mouth.

"No...what?" he said, his foot touching down and his other leg sliding to the edge of the bed.

"Demons," Nathan's voice said from Lawrence's mouth and then, in a voice that belonged to some hidden place in time, all three mouths moved in unison and said, "Demons."

He popped up then and backed to the wall. He still had on jeans and a sweater but had removed his socks while he slept. "What is this?" he said.

"What's your story?" the trio said together, as if choreographed. "What's your story? What's your story!"

"I don't have—no!" He burst forward and slammed a shoulder into Nathan before continuing out of the bedroom.

"Face your demons," the trio said.

No time for much of anything. He slipped into his slippers and pulled open the door to the startlingly cold night air. The snow had slowed, but the damage was done—big lazy mounds covered everything.

"What's your story?"

They were right behind him. He didn't have his keys. He jumped and attempted to run, kicking aside great clumps of snow, trying to gain distance.

"Face your demons, ----," Lawrence said, the final word undefinable.

Once to the street, he could almost really run. His mind was frantic, panicking over...what? Their request or the trick of their voices?

"Demons!" Ben said. "You can't run forever, ----."

He shook his head, taking a left off Prairie Street and onto Pacific Avenue—the route to the ocean.

"Demons!"

He started down toward the sea wall, brain too busy to take him somewhere useful. The crashing waves and the heavy winds seemed to call him, seemed to conjure, and a memory began unravelling—

"Demons!"

They were right in front of him, coming at him fast. He slipped on the gravel as he put on the brakes. His hand plunged into cold, cold snow. "I took you in! Why are you doing this to me?"

"You can't outrun us! Just tell!" Nathan's voice said, monster truck match loud.

"What's your story?" Ben shouted then.

He got to the street again and there was Lawrence in front of him, walking calmly toward him.

"Face," Lawrence said.

No good. He turned right, and down from a snowy backyard came Nathan.

"Your," Nathan said.

No better.

"Demons," Ben said from right behind him just before he reached out and grabbed him by the arm.

Worst of all.

He broke left and raced to reach a rusty ladder atop a shed that led to an unmanned lighthouse. He leapt from the higher ground, clearing a four-foot gap, and coming down on top of the shed. Hands and feet on the freezing rungs, he climbed. Anything to be away from those voices, that demand.

The trip to the top was short. He pressed his back against the cold wall of the lighthouse and rubbed his arms. The town was grey from there, totally devoid of color, all but the little house he'd purchased on Prairie Street. That yellow paint shined in the dark and he understood then that was because that home was his sanctuary, or at least it had been until he invited these—

"Face!" Nathan called from midway up the ladder.

One step, two steps, three steps, four, he stopped. Coming around the walkway was Lawrence.

"Your," Lawrence said.

He gasped and spun, almost bumping into Ben.

"Demons!" Ben said.

"No more running," Nathan said as he crested the ladder. "Face your deeeemusss."

"Deeeusss," Ben said.

"Usss," Lawrence said.

Two options: do what they said or...he climbed onto the railing and leapt down onto the snow-covered gravel fifty feet below. The fluffy white padding helped, but it did not let him off unharmed.

—

"Says he doesn't remember," the paramedic said to the nurse working the emergency overnight shift.

"Okay. Maybe he hit his head. Drugs?" the nurse asked.

The paramedic teetered her head left to right, right to left. "Could be, but I don't know."

"Okay, I'll run a tox'," the nurse said.

The paramedic held out a wallet. "Name's Benjamin Nathan Lawrence. I already called it in. No priors."

"Benjamin Nathan Lawrence," the nurse said as he typed it into the computer. "How'd you find him?"

"A man on Pacific Ave. heard him through the closed window, shouting about demons. When he stepped out to check, guy was doing a nosedive from the old lighthouse."

The nurse nodded. "We'd be doing a psyche eval' anyway," the nurse said, looking at the license set on her clipboard. "Benjamin Nathan Lawrence," she said then through a sigh and then stood. "Okay."

CRYSTAL-LYNN

(2018)

Robinson was born from his mother's asshole. Really. It was one of those winter nights when sleet came down like elephant piss. The roads got sloppy quickly, and as if on doomsday cue, Loretta Walker's water broke four weeks before her due date. Robinson was coming despite the fact that she was home alone, the roads were closed, the lines were down, and the power flickered in a tease.

Of course things could always get worse.

Head like a melon and body doing the limbo instead of a nosedive, Robinson's forward motion began tearing at Loretta's flesh. Sixteen and scared as hell, Loretta panicked and tried to run out of her boyfriend's bungalow to the neighbors' place. Not six drippy, waddling steps into the process, Loretta's ankles were right about where her hairline should've been, her noggin an inch from the chunky, thirty-year-old cement of the driveway...and falling fast.

The landing sent a ripple. Loretta's skull cracked. Her pelvis shattered. Robinson kicked and squirmed, booting and scooting and boogying his way down.

In a daze, Loretta recognized that she was too wet, was too damned wet and burning something fierce, despite the weather. Her vagina and asshole had become one big nasty smile—intestine prolapsed and jutting like a fat tongue from the bottom corner. It was six minutes before Robinson was free of the muddied mess of his mother's birthing package and only seven minutes until Loretta bled out.

After an unmatched DNA test, Robinson went into the

system and up for adoption—turns out his mother took more suitors than just the forty-nine-year-old mill worker she'd come to call her boyfriend. Quickly, Robinson found himself the brother to three older sisters and son to a mother and father. Gary Toase was treasurer and Karen Toase was in the midst of planning a mayoral run.

She'd never say it aloud, but Robinson was the icing to her cake during that short campaign season.

—

"What if I paint it for you?" Gary counteroffered Robinson's demand of a new, Jeep-style Power Wheels for himself. "That one's good yet, Stacy hardly used it." The one Gary referred to as *that one* was a pink-on-pink Barbie Corvette.

Robinson, being the sole adoptee and, by default, least important child, he only received new stuff when the girlish hand-me-downs couldn't be butched-up to a satisfactorily male version. He stamped his foot but did so at half-speed—acquiesce speed.

Nine minutes later, Gary returned from the garage. "Don't touch it until tomorrow."

Robinson had big expectations that crashed as soon as he went to the garage to see the sloppy, brush stroked black Tremclad layer over top of the original pinks. Downright shitty was this effort.

"I hate you! I wish my real parents were here to beat you up!" Robinson shouted into the kitchen where Gary stood by the fridge and Karen sat at the table with Stacy, Becky, and Candace, mooning over the Sears Christmas catalogue.

"Hey, if you ever get a hold of your dead mother, see if she can't tell us who your real daddy is, maybe he can take care of you awhile." Karen didn't even lift her eyes as she spoke. Robinson had served his purpose and she'd been master and commander of Everly Hills for nearly six years.

Tears fell and Robinson ran to his room upstairs, stomping

along and swiping sturdier items from shelves as he went. Mad, but not mad enough to break stuff, knowing he'd get a basement timeout if he did ruin something. Basement timeout was the pits because the fruit cellar was full of murky jars and spider webs, and he had to sit extra still to avoid stirring any arachnid attention his way.

Three minutes after flopping face down on his bed, Robinson was in dreamland. Typical five-year-old fashion.

—

He dreamed of the Barbie Corvette, but not pink-on-pink and not half-assed black, but blue with silver accents and chrome rims, woodgrain dash with a blue leather seat. He saw the souped-up battery that rose like a hood scoop air-intake.

—

"Dad, can I try to paint Stacy's car more better?"

"I'm your dad again, am I?" Gary took a breath and turned away from the twelve-inch Magnavox kitchen unit that lived next door to the roll top breadbox. "You want me to buy you some better paint?"

Robinson nodded.

"What do you say?"

"Please."

"Please, what?"

"Please, Dad, can I get some real good paint for Stacy's car?"

Gary looked back at the TV. "We'll see. You do your chores and ask your mother if she has any extra chores, then we'll see about paint."

—

Robinson carried the small cans of paint, the brushes, and the heavy clothes they'd purchased in bulk from the hardware store. Gary dragged a flattened chest freezer box. He saw the box empty in the hardware store and knew the best way to go about letting the boy paint was to give him a disposable workspace.

—

Robinson exited the enormous box when Karen called him to supper. He wore the bulky painting clothes and yellow dishwashing gloves that rose to his elbows.

"Leave those in the box." Karen pointed in Robinson's general direction. He stripped the gloves. "No, everything. I don't want paint all over the house."

The girls came to the door to watch Robinson strip down to his underwear. He turned to toss his pants over to the box.

"Ewww!" Candace and Stacy said in unison.

"Skid marks!" Becky said, pointing.

Karen scrunched her face. "Put on clean clothes before coming to the table."

Robinson stomped in past the female Toases, but didn't knock anything from shelves or make any extra noise. The urge was gone. Working on the car was strangely soothing.

"So, you get it all painted up yet?" Gary asked, they hadn't waited and were half-finished supper by the time Robinson made it to the table.

"No."

"No? Why not, you were out there for six hours." Gary spoke around a mouthful of string beans.

"I only got the black paint *off*." Robinson ate with purpose.

Gary laughed. "My guess, you'll wish you left the black paint."

Robinson shook his head. "Nuh-uh, Crystal-Lynn's gonna be beautiful."

"Who's Crystal-Lynn?" Karen frowned, cut up fish stick hovering an inch from her mouth.

"The car."

"You named my car Crystal-Lynn?"

Robinson spied Stacy hard. "Not your car no more."

"It's stupid and you're stupid." Stacy folded her arms over her chest.

"Shut up, shitter." The words were out of Robinson's mouth for one second before the girls started shouting and Karen had the boy by the ear, dragging him towards the basement steps.

"You sit there until bedtime, mister." Karen pointed into the musty fruit cellar and the overturned five-gallon pale that facilitated sitting.

Robinson went without argument, scowling.

———

"What can we expect? Whore mother, anonymous father." Gary folded back the comforter and slid in next to Karen. He'd only just freed Robinson from punishment, told him to finish his supper, which had sat on the table for four hours.

"I wish we'd never bothered."

Gary lifted his left eyebrow, as if to say, think you had enough humanitarian points to tide you through the campaign? I don't.

"Just go to sleep," she said and turned off the lamp on her side of the bed.

"That little bastard better go straight to bed after he's finished eating."

———

As if hearing the man, Robinson flipped off the ceiling, scarfing down the cold, hard fish sticks from his plate as he walked towards the garage door. He went to the box, pulled back the flap and sat behind Crystal-Lynn's steering wheel, knees against the once again pink dash.

———

Robinson was in the box for a third straight afterschool evening since he'd stripped the black paint away. Over and over he'd opened the paint can, only to close it again. Popping the lids was a lot of work for him, but he couldn't push his hands any further. Something was wrong and he didn't know how to fix it. Couldn't ask for help, couldn't wing it, no, he needed to be more than he was—an idea he'd never be able to formulate into words, but understood at his core.

"Robinson, come on. Bedtime."

Upon hearing his father, the boy leaned forward, said goodnight to Crystal-Lynn and exited the box.

"How do you not have it painted yet?" Gary was in a good mood, ruffled Robinson's short brown hair. He'd met with an old high school friend—and recent divorcee—named Genie and they danced the clumsy but wonderfully different dance of sexual strangers. "You want me to give you a hand?"

"No. I wanna do it." Robinson didn't have to change his clothes because there was not a speck of paint or paint thinner on him.

—

"Where are we going?" Becky asked from the shotgun seat of the van.

Gary had picked them up, but the route home had become abnormal. "Uh, going to check out a new store." Genie mentioned she had a thing for carnival glass and Gary happened to see the old proprietor placing a carnival glass lampshade in the window of a new store the exact moment he drove by that morning.

"What new store?" Candace had a finger up her nose. She'd waited an hour to dig, never did that at school, booger mining was social suicide.

"Stop picking. It's called Essential Artifacts. It's full of antiques and fancy stuff, I think, so don't touch anything. I want to have a look in case I see a good gift for your mother, which also means you can't tell her we came in and especially can't mention if I buy something."

The girls were not the ones to worry about, smart enough to follow the justification offered, but not smart enough to question any follow through if the purchased object never showed up at home. Robinson was not as smart, often had slips and spoke out of turn.

Inside, even the carpet felt expensive. Gary turned to Robinson. "I want you to stand by those display cases and see if you think anything would grab your mother. But don't move from there. Got it?"

Robinson nodded, eyes already wandering over the fine woodwork accents, the antique wallpaper, and the looming brass light fixtures. Dozens of small tables littered the space, each carried a minimum of one item and all had a paper price tag dangling on a white cotton string. Strangely, it was easy to follow his father's direction. None of that stuff was for him. It was mom stuff and dad stuff and stuff like dolls for girls, but not the ones to play with, just the ones to look at.

The display case was no different. Porcelain junk and collectable spoons. Barf. Robinson put his elbows up and draped himself on the counter, wishing for something cool, a video game, a Ninja Turtle, even sports books would do. Even better...

"Hello, boy. I'd bet you like cars."

Robinson lifted his head. A rail skinny woman in a denim jacket and a white Coca-Cola t-shirt stood across the case. A pin on her chest read ACQUISITIONS. She wore jeans two shades darker than her jacket and brown cowboy boots that came up almost to her knees. "Maybe."

"Maybe if it's the right car I bet." He nodded and she continued, "I got just the thing. This is my aunt's store and I help her out sometimes, but she don't like putting out the cool stuff. You stay right there, and I'll be back."

Intrigued, Robinson did as told. Across the lobby, Gary spoke to a white-haired woman in a skirt that ran past her knees, boxy black heels, and an ivory blouse with pearl buttons. She looked about as stuffy as a nun during service. His sisters were before a case, ogling weird old dolls with big eyes and dated attire. He didn't hear the woman in denim return.

"You look like a Corvette man." Her breath was cold in his ear. "What do you think of this?"

Robinson let the woman put the shiny double flags in his hands. Her palms—also cold—brushed against his wrists during the hand off. The thing was heavy in a way that went beyond the physical and it was electric, buzzing pleasantly.

"I don't got money." His voice was a drone; all his, but like a facsimile.

"I don't want money. Around here, we deal. You get what you want and I'll see what's leftover to take."

Robinson nodded, this would be perfect on Crystal-Lynn.

"One thing, this has to be our secret. You can't tell your folks."

His hand tightened on the emblem and he turned to offer her his word, but she was gone.

From across the room, Gary waved Robinson to follow him and the girls. Gary was emptyhanded. The girls were emptyhanded. Robinson slid that precious piece into his pocket.

—

"That kid still out playing with Stacy's car?" Karen asked from behind a beat-up Sue Grafton paperback. She'd been out at yoga class, as well as on a fuck date with a house inspector she'd hired via the city to check dozens of different properties, and came home spent, and lay down on the couch.

The girls were in the basement, watching TV and surfing on their iPads.

Gary was in the kitchen straightening things out, tiptoeing around Karen because guilt had come to make him paranoid. He needn't have worried, Karen assumed Gary suffered from erectile dysfunction because the last time they tried to have sex he couldn't get it up. "Yes, I suppose. So I'm thinking I'd like to go out with Dennis Rusk and Georgie Cobb, bowling. They're in the league. I was thinking I might see if I'm any good, join up."

Karen tutted. "Bowling. Tonight? How's supper coming?"

The lasagna had sixteen minutes left on the timer.

"Yeah, tonight. Eat in about twenty-minutes."

—

The lasagna was still steaming when Robinson came in from the garage. He'd long finished painting, so he no longer had to parade around in skidded-skivvies. Instead he wore jeans and a plain white t-shirt. He had the left sleeve rolled up over a box of Nerds. From under the bathroom sink, he'd found Karen's ancient hair products, and slicked back his hair until it was like a shell, let a curl dangle at the center of his forehead.

"Who are you supposed to be?" Stacy sneered as she spoke.

"Yeah?" Becky added.

"Yeah?" Candace seconded.

"Ain't no shitters like yous," Robinson whispered.

Gary was by the stove grabbing the toasted garlic bread from the oven and Karen was at the counter, mixing a fresh jug of Minute Maid.

"Mom!" The trio of girls were so on point that if shouting was swimming, they could've been synchronized Olympians. "Robinson called us shitters again!"

Gary straightened up, bread in hands, cheese drooping over the edges, scent filling the room with wet mouths. He looked at the boy.

Karen did not look. "Where'd you hear that? Shitter. That's a bad word and a stupid one at that. Say it once more and you'll be in trouble, mister."

Robinson kicked out his chair. "Shitter!"

Gary calmly set the bread on the table. "Karen, bring Robinson." He stormed through the kitchen towards the garage door.

Karen suddenly had the boy by the collar of his shirt. The Nerds fell from the sleeve and spilled onto the floor. There were only a dozen or so left, so the mess was limited. They stopped in the doorway.

Gary had pulled the Corvette Power Wheels from the box. The dream had been Robinson's map and he had the most perfectly deft hand in the history of paint detailers. The blue sparkled, the silver shined, the upholstery almost looked real rather than clever paint. The woodgrain, hell, he didn't recall how that got there, but boy was it *sharp.*

The car looked so good that Gary paused midway through the punishment. "Incredible." Impressed, but not impressed enough. He hit the button on the wall and the roll-up door rolled up. Snowing outside, but he hadn't driven the minivan inside. The fob on the chain came out of his pocket and the lights flared once.

Robinson didn't understand. He stared at his perfect job; stared at Crystal-Lynn. The snow-covered van started and began approaching. Gary had the window down and head poked out to aim his wheel.

The boy got it then, tried to fight Karen's hold. Her grip was too good. The smile on her face was horrible.

Not as horrible as the crunching plastic.

"No!" Robinson howled like a wolf on a full moon night.

—

Gary wasn't home yet when Robinson awoke from the nap he'd inadvertently taken after sprinting to his room without supper. He had an idea. An impossible idea. It had come from his dream and he knew the difference between good dreams and bad life, but this dream felt too good to ignore upon waking.

Quietly, he snuck past his sisters' rooms, past the T in the hallway where the light from his parents' room shined. Down the stairs, quiet as a dead mouse, he went to the shelf by the door and took his mother's keys. The doors locked from the inside, but he saw how he could do what he had to do.

He took a deep breath and slicked back his hair. If this next part wasn't true, the dream was just a dream and the denim lady hadn't actually given him any orders. He opened the garage door, it was dark, but he saw well enough, and stepped to the long box. Gary had pushed it up against the wall after he'd swept up the broken plastic of the Corvette.

Robinson swallowed a lump and pushed inside. Dark, until the electric lights flared and the Power Wheels—fine enough for a Detroit auto show—revved its little engine.

"Crystal-Lynn, baby."

Robinson got behind the wheel and exited the box.

—

"Mom?" The trio of girls stood in the light shined through Karen's door wearing matching princess jammies. Karen had fallen asleep awaiting Gary's return. "Mom?"

She opened her eyes, glanced at the white alarm clock with pale blue digits. A sound like electric bees buzzed around the main floor. "What's that?"

"Robinson's not in his room." Stacy pouted, offering a suggestion to answer who made the noise.

"Ugh." Karen flipped the blanket off her legs and rose. She wore blue pajama pants and a white tee. "Robinson!"

No answer.

"Robinson!"

Again.

"Robins—!"

The lights died and the buzzing grew louder. The girls screamed. Karen scoffed. Thumps joined the buzzing as it moved up the stairs. Suddenly the girls had wrapped themselves around their mother.

The buzz zipped as loudly as it had gotten yet before trailing away and going silent.

Three different blips sounded as the home's power returned—one being the fire alarm, one being the unset burglar alarm, and the third being the automated home safety system. The outage was either a short grid glitch or an issue localized to their fuse panel—for which the safety system automatically rebooted.

"Let go," Karen said when the girls' grip refused to let her legs do leggy things. At the door, the girls like a gown train, Karen looked into the dim hallway, left and then right. Nothing unusual, that she could see anyhow. "Robinson?"

She stepped out and moved towards the stairs. The main floor was dark as it got in town, and in winter, with snow banking the streetlamp shine, that was only mostly dark. However, there were shadows.

"Robinson, are you down there?"

She took the first stair, then the second and third. Hardwood, cool on her bare skin. The girls smacked little feet behind her until they again made contact.

"Robinson, if you don't answer me, you're grounded until college!"

A single, half-second buzz sounded from the floor behind them. The foursome turned. Karen scanned without moving. That noise was familiar, but it had been too long since she'd last heard it to place the origin.

"Robinson?" She moved Becky and Candace so she could put her right foot up a step. Moved Stacy then to lift her left foot. She hadn't planted it yet when the buzz zipped in full form.

The blue and silver Corvette came into view and Robinson was a regular greaser behind the wheel, his knees up by his elbows. "Shitters!" He looked wild as he barrelled towards the staircase.

Stuck: *up or down?* Karen sealed two fates in the moment of indecision. Robinson drifted around the newel post at the top of the banister and gunned it down the stairs. The first contact was with Stacy, then Karen. They flipped back as the Corvette launched over them, letting them tumble in an unimpeded mass. Becky's skull cracked on the third from bottom step as Karen kicked for a footing and Candace's C1 and C2 vertebrae became crunchy goop at the bottom of the mound on the main floor. Her tongue lolled and her eyes danced the herky-jerky.

Karen screamed. "No! Girls?"

"Mommy," Stacy whined. She'd landed on top and was right as a reindeer on a roof, aside from being scared.

The buzzing was somewhere in the kitchen, but turning,

coming back to the living room. Karen was bent over Candace, trying to shake her awake.

"Mommy!"

Robinson sneered in the lamplight coming through the windows and leaned hard to his left. The right wheels lifted and he steered into the back of the couch. When the rear right wheel made contact, the little car seemed to blast off, rocketing towards Stacy, who stood on the last step, above her mother and sisters.

She ducked as Robinson drew close…just as he hoped she would. He landed on her head, foot on the brake, foot on the gas. The rear wheels spun and wrapped her hair around the axle. He lifted his left foot from the brake pedal and shot up the stairs before Karen's angry, swiping arm could smash the source of Stacy's wails.

For three stairs, Stacy became a tin can behind a rented wedding limo. Then her body snagged and her scalp detached with a moist thup. She screamed a new scream. This one seemed about a half-octave away from shattering glass.

Robinson had already careened up the wall as if riding a loop-de-loop and was back facing his mother and flesh-bald sister.

"You little fucker." Karen charged, blind with fury.

Robinson connected with her shins and sent her back. Her right elbow went red with Stacy's blood as she and the girl fell down the stairs.

Robinson hooted.

Robinson rolled on.

In the kitchen, he popped the pack from his shoulder, no longer Nerds, instead he had a pack of Export A—the Green Death. He stood in the car and pulled out a kitchen drawer, rooted until he found a pack of matches. He popped a cigarette into his mouth and drove at leisure to the foot of the stairs where Karen was stuck, in the middle of weeping and raging emotions, as well as a pile of girls.

"Hey, Ma, what's the haps?" His voice was snarling, teasing.

His mouth smiling.

"You fucking cock sucking whore-son piece of...!"

Robinson's smile soured and he withdrew a match. "Smell that?"

"...shit motherfucker. I'm gonna wring your fucking—!"

Robinson lit a match, touched it to the tip of his cigarette, and gunned the gas all in the same breath, tossing the lit match over his shoulder towards the kitchen with a final fuck-you-ma flair. The explosion behind him was coming fast, but Robinson was ready and had a route all mapped out.

—

Genie had dumped Gary and he ended up at the bowling alley after all. Drinking. Alone. He knew well enough to avoid the garage door because it squeaked and decided he'd try the back door. His key wouldn't go in, and not thanks to the drink. He squinted and looked closer.

Someone had broken a key in the lock. Grumbling, he trudged, off the porch and towards the front door, the one only Jehovah's Witnesses and political campaigners used.

Same thing. "What the fuck?" he said and started towards the garage.

A crackling lifted his gaze to the incredible light coming through the bay window. A half-second later, the bay window shattered and a tiny Corvette flew through.

He jumped back. "But I crushed that."

"Hey there, Daddy-o." Robinson sucked on the cigarette and then flicked it at his father.

The drink kept Gary's mind blank. He didn't have a second thought about the car, didn't wonder about his family, and didn't consider beating this shithead pup to a pulp. Instead, the salvation instinct kicked in and he tore out the short lane and then westbound.

"Help!"

Robinson snarled his upper lip's right side and buzzed

Crystal-Lynn. A little game of cat and mouse, at least for a block or two.

Nipping his father's heels, Robinson grinned as he drove. Gary was panting and jumping to avoid the front bumper of the little car.

"Why are you doing this?"

Robinson huffed. "You tried to murder her. You tried to kill her, pea brain. You ain't my dad no more. I hate you!"

"I've always hated you." This was the truth, drunk or sober. Gary Toase hated Robinson since the day they brought him home.

Robinson slowed and fell into a rolling stop, watching as his father took a sharp right on the path by the river that shortcut onto Main Street. Stupid. Robinson shook his head and decided to finish things.

Crystal-Lynn buzzed the war cry of a thousand killer bees as it bore through the semi-packed snow. Robinson was again on Gary's heels, but this time it was for keeps. He smashed the man's right anklebone, causing him to hop and howl. Robinson rolled further into the man's path and he stumbled sideways, bouncing on the gulley wall. He might've been able to stop himself from going further if he wasn't so drunk and if the path hadn't been so slick with snow. If. If. If. He continued down, dropping seven feet onto the frozen creek.

"Owwww, goddamn you."

Robinson stood, got as high as his tippytoes, and saw Gary rise. He had a bloody mouth, was covered in snow, and looked a bit like a hobo, but seemed mostly fine.

"Ha, you can't get me down here, you cun—ah!" As if someone kicked the feet out from beneath him, Gary's body went horizontal for one heartbeat before he landed on the ice again. The crack from his initial landing left the surface not quite sturdy enough for a second touch. "Help!" he managed before falling through and disappearing. A single backsplash breached, but nothing of the man.

Robinson shivered, finally noticing the cold. He considered lighting a cigarette for warmth, but didn't have the same interest in them he'd had only seconds earlier. He thought about home and wondered what he'd do.

Didn't need to, it was already mapped out.

Beyond his control, the Power Wheels Corvette rolled down Main and turned left onto Willow. Every building was dark other than the loading dock door at the side of Essential Artifacts.

The woman in denim waved and leaned inside to hit the button to roll up the door. "Glad to see you got your part of the bargain in one piece."

Robinson was nervous. His body wasn't listening to him, wouldn't let him out of the car. He rolled inside and she closed the door.

—

It was like waking without going to sleep. Robinson walked lighter after the change. Most of his worries evaporated and best of all, he didn't have to go to school anymore. Instead, he played with all the stuff in the back of the store that was miles bigger than it appeared from outside. Part of that, he guessed, was because sometimes he was just so small.

Small enough to walk up someone's nose he figured.

"Robinson. Oh Robinson, you're needed." The voice was booming and suddenly, like sleeping without ever being awake, he was in his skin again, the size of a whole boy. "There you are. We have a girl out there with a bad family. She won't talk to me. Needs a kid's touch. Give her this." The woman in denim—her name was Lela Cunningham—handed over a pair of silver boot spurs.

Robinson took the spurs and his body walked away from the other empty people—boys, girls, men, and women—who stood in rows at the back of the store, unmoving until called upon.

A passenger, looking out the windows that were his eyes, he

said, "Hey," upon reaching the girl.

She had pigtails and a pig nose. "Hi." She swiped her hand over her upper lip and nostrils. Her eyes were puffy and teary pink.

"If you can keep a secret, we can make a cool deal." Robinson held out his hand.

The girl took his offer, her expression brightening.

"But you can't tell your parents."

The girl looked across the store at her mothers and brothers, sneered and said, "Okay."

WHAT'S HE DONE NOW?

(2022)

The laugh was huge, the punishment was swift.

"Pavel!" Mrs. Newman had her little hand spread wide, impulsively covering as much as she could of the image.

"I didn't mean it," Pavel Khabibulin said.

Mrs. Newman charged at the boy, and said, "If I hear 'I didn't mean it' one more time, I swear," the familiar dance beginning anew.

Pavel shuffled on his tippytoes as Mrs. Newman pulled him by the ear to the room currently acting as the school's office. Due to a burst pipe over the Christmas holidays and the subsequent renovations, Saugeen Hills Elementary School had been moved across town to the ancient orphanage that had been taken over during WWII, used as office space for a series of classified assignments, and kept up, though empty of function, by the federal government since then. The building was tall and skinny, redbrick with bars over the windows. Inside, the wallpaper had water spots and tobacco smoke stains.

Mrs. Newman wasted no time with courtesy or pleasantries and barged into the principal's temporary space. The man pulled a piece of nicotine gum from his mouth and tossed it in the waste basket beneath his desk, then adjusted his glasses before sighing.

"What's he done now?" Mr. Hooper said.

Mrs. Newman released Pavel's ear and gave his shoulder a shove. "Talk. Tell him."

Pavel put his head down and said, "I drew a wiener on the board behind the big map."

Mr. Hoover pulled a face, somewhere between anger and

biting back a laugh.

"I won't have him in my class for the rest of the day," Mrs. Newman said. "That lewd, horrendous image..."

Mr. Hooper huffed; the onus now on him. "All right. Okay." He looked around the office as if he might find an answer. "All right. He can do in-school suspension the rest of today and tomorrow." His eyes flashed with a solution. "We'll go see Mrs. Skinner."

Pavel moaned.

Mrs. Newman grinned.

Mrs. Skinner was the librarian, and at the temporary school, there weren't even any books to look at, not unless you counted government junk from, like, a million years ago. Mr. Hooper pushed the boy along the dreary halls and down the stairs, into the basement. The building was always so quiet, something about the walls ate sound, making it feel very un-school-like.

"Mrs. Skinner?" Mr. Hooper said once they entered the room of seemingly endless rows of shelves featuring countless dusty, non-descript, pale brown boxes.

The woman popped out from behind a shelving unit. "Hi," she said.

She was petit and younger than most of the teachers. She loved books, like, love-loved them. She wore a denim dress with a flowery shirt above. Around her neck was a peace medallion. Pavel's Mom called her a hippy. Pavel's dad called her a cutie— but only when his mom couldn't hear. Pavel thought she was just another nerd teacher, always trying to trick kids into learning something boring and pointless.

"Mr. Khabibulin here will be assisting you the rest of the day and all of tomorrow," Mr. Hooper said, nudging the boy into the stuffy room. "At lunch, he can either be sent to my office or eat with you. He is to have zero opportunities to distract his classmates."

"I see," Mrs. Skinner said. "Well, come on then."

Pavel waited until he heard the principal leave and then said, "What is all this crap?"

"*This crap* was all classified military communications, up until last year. Fifty years since World War Two means it's available to the public."

"So?" Pavel was sullen and bored already—most of his personal energy seemed to come directly from other students, he leeched it like a mosquito leeched blood.

"So, your insight might just prove helpful. Khabibulin, eh? Do you read Russian?"

"Maybe," Pavel said, non-committal. His parents had raised him bilingual; he read Russian as well as he read English, both at a higher level than most of his classmates, which was part of the problem with his behavior.

"Thought so. We need to find *bitching* things in these boxes. I'm preparing a series of assemblies about what our town did during the wars. Might write a little book someday. Now, I know what I think is bitching, for a book, but I need to know what you think is bitching, so I don't bore your fellow classmates to death during assemblies. Get it?"

Pavel knew this trick, using risky slang to get a kid to do something. He folded his arms over his chest.

Mrs. Skinner mimicked him, adding a tilted head to her folded arms. "Maybe I'll even get you to help me present it at the assemblies."

He stopped breathing a moment. All those eyes on him... "Okay," he said.

—

Thursday morning, after his in-school suspension had ended, Pavel was nearly late to class on account of it being Taco night the supper preceding. When Mother Khabibulin's tacos wanted out of the guts, they weren't going to be denied. He hurried into the room about five seconds before Mrs. Newman strolled in reading a piece of paper. Too bad. He was thrumming, absolutely had to tell the other kids about the stuff he'd found with Mrs. Skinner.

"Quiet," Mrs. Newman said though the class was already quiet in anticipation.

Pavel looked around, thinking about all that crazy crap he'd read and who he'd tell first—either when they broke into work groups or at recess. He made fists under his desk, trying to calm his breathing.

And crazy crap was an understatement. By 1942, that insane loser, Adolf stupid 'stache Hitler, and his evil Nazi scientists were trying to find magic ways to win the war. It was no secret even then, so then the nut-case Stalin started looking for counter-magic for the Soviets to use. The Allied radio interceptors caught a bunch of the communications and transcribed it in Russian. Some of it was so wacky that Pavel ached with desperation. Not a soul on the playground would ignore this stuff. He bit it down and grabbed hold of his legs beneath his desk; after he gave his classmates a sample today, he would share it in front of the whole school with Mrs. Skinner.

Mrs. Newman sat behind her desk without looking and immediately popped up, the paper she was reading flying from her hands as she jerked to her feet. "Pavel Khabibulin!" She pulled a golden thumbtack from her butt and held it toward him. "Office!"

"I didn't—"

"Office!"

Within two minutes, Pavel found himself back in the basement with Mrs. Skinner, a plan forming as he shuffled through more intel. He'd fix that awful, old bitch, Mrs. Newman.

—

Friday morning, Pavel got to the classroom early for the first time in his short school career. He'd loaded his backpack the night before with stuff pilfered from his mother's cupboards and the attic where they kept his dead grandparents' junk. He got busy setting up based on the intercepted Soviet communique. The candles and chalk lines didn't even look out of place at the front of the room. The stink from the herbs and ashes was big enough that he felt this might work.

Grinning in anticipation, he sat quietly behind his desk, book and pencil sitting pretty, as if he'd taken a place setting course. From down the hall, he heard the bustle of the first students. He closed his eyes to keep calm.

The spell he'd found was meant to create super soldiers for Mother Russia, but the supposed outcome sounded plum funny. A thousand times already he'd imagined Mrs. Newman's stupid face if it worked.

Pavel's classmates whispered as they walked through and around the strategically placed candles and their dancing flames. Most instinctively avoided walking over the chalked shapes on the floor. Pavel remained silent, incantation on a yellowed sheet in his breast pocket.

Mrs. Newman came in, frowning at the scene. "What the heck is this? Pavel?"

The class went quiet. All eyes on him.

"Ugh, you're nothing but—" she huffed, leaning to blow out a candle.

Pavel cut her off, reading aloud, "O velikiye bogi lesa, ya umolyayu vas sdelat' etu zhenshchinu voinom vashego tsarstva, ibo mnogo krovi budet prolito i prineseno k vashim nogam. Preobrazi yeye! Preobrazi yeye!"

"Pavel, you will—!" Mrs. Newman began but the words caught in her throat. She stiffened and the heavy scents of feces and urine filled the room. Her pores began to widen, and thick fur sprouted free.

Some students gasped, some cried, one fainted, one screamed. Pavel's grin slipped to about 70% wattage.

Mrs. Newman lifted her arms. Blood oozed from her hands where claws had forced their way out, sending her red painted nails clattering to her desk. Bones snapped as her jaw elongated, her gums stretching like strung out and slobbery Hubba Bubba. Great teeth forced her dentures from between her darkening lips, clunking them to the floor.

More students began to scream. Pavel swallowed, grin gone, no proof it had ever existed. He looked at the sheet for a reversal spell.

Not a word to fix things.

What he'd read had essentially asked the gods of the forest to transform Mrs. Newman into a beast, offering all the resulting blood she could take as sacrifice. For some reason, Pavel thought she'd turn into a rabbit or squirrel, maybe a raccoon.

Mrs. Newman's body grew larger and larger, her humanistic moans becoming a steady growl. Her eyes glowed red as the Red Army's crest. She bent forward, looking like she weighed a literal ton.

"Uh oh," Pavel said, staring down a Russian grizzly bear.

Mrs. Newman let out a great, wet growl as she pushed aside desks, coming his way. He swallowed, looking again at the page, wishing against reality that he'd missed a magic word to switch her back. Students screamed and ran. The fire alarm rang out. Pavel kept his eyes pinned to the 53-year-old piece of paper until a fantastic, horrible claw sliced the page in two and his gaze locked with the new and improved Mrs. Newman.

"I didn't mean it," he whispered.

OFFERING ATLANTIS

(2014)

Scent came first and it reeked of familiarity and incongruity, as if to say, *I know you and you don't fit here.*

Her past disappeared from mind and she opened her eyes to find her clothing gone, her skin damp, the green mossy floor below her soggy and soft. She tasted salt on her lips. Her fingers ran over skin that was not her skin.

Gone. She'd shed everything unwanted, rolls and ripples thanks to sweets and aging, indulgence and laziness. There was always tomorrow when the urge to exercise arose.

No matter, young again and better than ever.

She smiled at a perfect being; a goddess, approaching—her flesh glistening under the white sky, glow akin to a ceiling fixture passing through a child's fort of bed sheets and pillows. The air was a perfect temperature for nudity and comfort. And yet, the atmosphere was salty and harsh, carried the smell of somewhere else.

The concern of how she got to that mossy floor fleeted, unimportant. Her past was imperfect, her present was nothing short of perfection.

"Lily, Lily, we're so glad you've joined us." The slim goddess of fitting proportions stepped forward with her hands out, welcoming.

In a flash, she recalled her name—birth certificate stated Lillian Rebecca Eastwin. She attempted a *thank you*, but coughed and choked on the water pouring from her throat. A rush of panic flowed through her body, she couldn't speak, couldn't breathe.

"Easy, Lily." The woman smiled and Lily calmed. "In time,

you'll ease, in time you'll be one of us. Let go."

She wanted to say that she was already one of them, the perfect bodies scampering around the damp meadow, children in the summer of their existence, but she couldn't. She ran her fingers over her perfect body and the glistening skin shimmered, the ripples and rolls were back.

"Oh Lily, poor Lily." The goddess shook her head as she stepped away to take the arm of a man, tight and trim muscles wrapped his entire pale frame—another god to accent the landscape.

She wanted to scream at the departure, tried to even, and she spewed water and bile. A lunch of brown cocktail and burning horror. The air around her cooled and the meadow disappeared, the gods and goddesses aging, their flesh greying, wrinkling and rotting before the thick fog consumed it all. She felt another lurch from within and tried to hold on. It burst around her hands, through her lips and out her nostrils.

"Shit. Thank you, thank you," she heard a mannish voice say, her body rocking, his arms around her. The past came back in a rush. He was Brian, Brian Harvey Bester, her fiancé. "I thought you left me."

Lily opened her eyes and her heart ached for the other place. The world around her was cold and dim, grim in every aspect. The harsh salty scent fit in suddenly.

Brian looked like a drowned rat, his stylish hair tight to his head as if painted, his clothing tight to his body, showing the imperfections he'd collected over the years. Levi's jeans and a t-shirt bragging ownership by the Nike shoe company. She felt her own wet clothes, felt the contours of time and dessert, through the cottons and recycled polyester, she hated what she felt.

Tears streamed from her eyes, cutting ruts through the salt stains over her cheeks. "What... Where?" she begged between shivers and sobs.

"It went down, I don't know about any others. Don't you

remember?"

It was there for her acknowledgement. She recalled the ship to Alaska, many hours before arrival in Juno, she remembered the fire and remembered the lifeboat, remembered the screams, remembered the sinking wreckage, remembered the bodies bobbing along, it was all there, but what of the mossy floor and the perfection?

Didn't he know about the other place?

"The others, the beautiful...?" She stalled her question, spying Brian with suspicion, he had to know and he'd stolen it from her, stuck her in the middle of a fog perhaps two hundred kilometers from shore, *on a, on a what?*

Reading her quizzical expression, Brian explained, "When the boat went down, you went under. I got you and swam until we beached on this rock. Oh...I'm just so glad, glad that I still have you." He squeezed her tight.

She decided that he couldn't know of the other place, he loved her and she loved him, despite their faults. Reality was all coming back. Brian's body felt good against hers, and she held firm, the memory of the other place disintegrating in the dim light of the real world, a topic specific dementia.

The fog sat a heavy coat over everything, permitting, but just barely, sight of the edges of the rock and the splashing water a foot below. An oversized home plate, five-sided, flat and safe so long as the weather remained calm.

They called out but received no returned calls.

Brian spoke in a ramble, dwelling on luck and thanks, imagining a world without *his Lillian*. What would his life mean had she died? Lily wanted to remind him that beached on a rock, hours from the coast, and possibly five hundred kilometers from a civilization was a peculiar state to feel thankful or lucky over. In fact, it felt nothing short of precarious, nearly hopeless.

She'd lived the first eighteen years of her life on Haida Haanas, divvying her existence between the islands of the archipelago. At the best of times, the weather could turn harsh and bring sheeting rain in tiny wet bullets for days, sometimes the fog stalled life for a week and even in July and August the temperature could turn to near freezing—didn't even touch on the potential for torrential oceanic activity. She didn't feel lucky or thankful, she felt as if she awaited the executioner.

The light behind the fog fell, offering only insight to which way they peered into nothingness.

Brian's hand slipped and he dropped back. "Sleep, sleep," he cooed. She thought it impossible, but the near drowning stole her energy and left behind an empty shell.

She slept, dreamed of perfect black.

A voice cut through the abyss in a way light and shape could not. "Lily, Lily."

She listened, she knew she might place the voice if only she saw a face, but no light entered, solid shadow filled the eye of her dream. "Who's there?" Her body grunted in Brian's sleeping arms.

"You let him steal it from you."

"Who are you?"

"I know you love the beauty, love our way, love us," the voice said, her tone light and playful, teasing.

"Who are you?"

The voice clicked a tongue against the roof of her mouth, unimpressed. "Need you see again, Lily? Don't tell me you've forgotten us."

"Please, I need it," she said, the memory coming back, soft, warm, and beautiful.

"You disappoint."

"Please, please, I need to see. Please!" Begging, petty and childish.

"Wake up!" Brian shook the shivering body. "You're having a nightmare."

She opened her eyes to dim fog and gentle rain, her heart broke. Brian was not what she wanted, she wanted...*what?* The memory faded and she sobbed, Brian did his best to appear brave and heroic, but his tears added to the wet drops falling over her head and shoulders.

The sun rose behind the blanket of fog, though rain continued its soft torture. Once settled into wakefulness, Brian spoke of foods and drinks, what he'd enjoy most once someone rescued them. He was from the south, the mainland.

Death off the coast wasn't on the tip of his people's tongues as it was in the fishing communities surrounding Lily's childhood. Every autumn her class shrank in number, even with one or two new faces who came with their fishermen and fisherwomen parents. The oceanic elements of the summertime, often enough coupled with inebriation, took islanders young and old. Life beyond the coast was a game with higher stakes and the boys and girls, men and women, saw the value in playing. Enough tempted the waters and survived for the long run, examples set for the rest.

Lily now saw her future as another on a long list of dead at sea, but Brian felt safe on that home plate and increasing his anxiety by drawing attention to likelihoods was of no interest. They would probably die out there. There'd be a memorial; people would cry and people would move on.

Thinking about death didn't help the strange sickly feeling in her exhausted belly; she joined Brian in wishes for food and drink. *Man, I could go for a...* It reminded her further of a feeling, imperfections thanks to a little bit too much of the good things.

"Enough about food," she said, solemn, flattening her back on the rock, thinking that if the temperature held around twenty centigrade they would not freeze.

"What in the hell do we talk about then, the weather?" Brian was wrought and pained. The stresses of his life to that point were not nearly enough practice to conquer the current match.

"Shh, please." She shook her head. Arguing was worse than talking about food.

Brian, angry, stood and stepped away to the tip of the stone. He dropped to the edge and stared into the water. "Better?"

She didn't answer, but the weather did. The rain ceased and she smirked at a thought. She turned to face the water, not because she didn't want to look at Brian, but because her shoulder ached from sleeping on the hard surface.

—

"Lily, you're back. We knew you'd come. He can't keep you forever, not unless you want that," the voice said, for a moment Lily thought she had it placed, but it slipped through the fingers of her mind.

"I'm his fiancé, the wedding's next summer, I'm... Who are you?"

"Such a disappointment."

"I'm sorry, I really am. I'm usually so good with names." Lily wondered if it was a name she sought, or a face, or even a person in the traditional sense.

"I never told you my name, but that doesn't mean I won't."

It seemed of utmost importance that she know, as if putting a name to the voice would bring about a cure to the anxiety and sickly feeling lodged in her gut. "Please, you have to tell."

"Do I? Do I really? You just told me that you don't want us, you don't want to be with us, of us, you told us that you want him."

"I do, I want, I want—" Lily's voice cracked like a cranky pubescent. "I want both."

"Oh Lily, it doesn't work that way."

"Please!"

Lily's eyes opened and she found Brian's arm wrapped around her waist, his stomach, hips, and thighs spooned against her back, ass, and legs. It made her want to vomit and she didn't understand why. She slunk from his warmth and a smile came to her face, but died as her lips cracked and opened tiny vertical chasms.

She wondered if dying of thirst was worse than drowning.

She walked to the furthest western point of the rock to watch the orange hue fall behind the heavy fog. She looked around the rock floor for a dip. Water puddled to her left and she bent and crawled for a drink, silently praying it wasn't splash collection. Lapping like a cat, it was fresh rainwater and her cracked lips soaked and stung. A bitter heaven played in those grooves. That puddle had to last for two and she left it for Brian in case the rain staved all night.

She lifted and straightened. It felt good, despite the expulsion of much needed energy, to move and stretch out the thousands of aches and pains about her body. The slight glow remaining was better for her face than her back and she turned, closed her eyes, and replayed memories. It started in the true familial sense of memory but moved quickly to movies and books, remembering clips and scenes to pass time. Somehow, it didn't feel a waste to kill what might be her final hours, days at most, with a life already lived.

"Did you drink some of the water?" Brian asked from behind her.

The sound of his voice jarred her from a feeling, something built and amassed mixing observed entertainment. "What? Oh, yeah. Did you?"

He nodded. "Better save some in case it doesn't rain more." Silence became burdensome after thirty long seconds. "I'm sorry I got mad before. I'm stressed. I'm not used to the water stuff like you...well, pools and swimming, but not this."

Lily crossed, dropped gently onto her seat and held him. "I'm not used to this either."

"I know, I didn't mean anything."

They held each other as the sun fell away completely. A breeze came through, growing stronger and stronger as the moon settled. The fog lifted and the typically bright white stars sat on the wrong side of what had to be heavy clouds. A crack jarred the universe and these clouds let go their payloads.

Brian grabbed onto Lily, they shivered under the cold rain and chilling atmosphere. "I'll never let you go," he whispered into Lily's ear, his head pressed against her head.

She swallowed a heavy feeling. "Shh."

They entwined, legs between legs, arms over and under heads, and abdomens tight together. Waves crashed upon their tired, sore, freezing bodies and Lily once again touched on thoughts of death. It carried a weight beyond her capabilities and she closed her eyes. Sleep refused her plea, but the voice rode the rain beyond her dreamscape into her ears. "Lily," it said in choppy pitter-patter. "Love us. Be one of us."

She didn't respond, couldn't without alarming Brian.

"He wants to keep you away, forever."

Lily shook her head, she wanted him to keep her, she wanted freedom from his arms and legs, she wanted the voice to stop, she wanted it to reveal itself and engulf her existence until the end of time. Tears joined the rain on her face. Waves crashed and they shook with each impact.

"Lily, be one of us."

She whispered, "How?"

"You know."

She vibrated in disagreement, Brian's hold loosened and repositioned over and under her head. Minutes became hours under the awful conditions.

"You can't be with both." The rain slowed and the wind whipped, the voice trailed on the cold air of the night. "Be one of us."

Brian's body shook and he sobbed. "I can't do—!"

Lily held him tight against her. "Can't what?" she asked around the whistle of the wind, the din of the waves.

"I can't do it, we're going to die!"

"Shh, Brian, shh." She rocked him.

Not so hard to absorb the surf's barrage, the wind blew and

dried one side of both of their bodies. Wordlessly, Lily stood and positioned herself on the other side of Brian, let the cold wind dry the dampness. It had already been a long night when the gusts slowed and the clouds overhead drifted to release the stars.

Brian slept. Lily sat up and stared to the sky. The constellations swirled and begged, *Lily, join us, be one of us.*

She averted her gaze and peered out to the black water around her, listening for activity, fish or perhaps a whale. Her grandmother said the killer whale carried mixed omens, messages harbored within its eyes.

Lily welcomed any distraction from her chilled skin. Crawling to the tipped lip, she stopped to lap water from a dip in the stone—it held much of both sources salt and fresh—and then continued to the edge.

Out there was perfect blackness. Breasts, stomach, and hips cushioning, elbows down and hands under chin. The water carried residual effort from the storm, waves splashed against the rock's edge and Lily watched the visage of a reflection dance on the Pacific.

Recalling a voice, but losing the words, retaining only bits of the sentiment. She was to be part of something, some perfect love. "Brian's love," she whispered to the black waters, "of course."

"Poor Lily," a voice crooned quietly through a mouthful bubbles that rose to the surface. A fat white fish swam back and forth inches from her face, beckoning her attention. The fish leapt from the water, rose two feet or more, and dove back down with little break in the surf. "Poor Lily," the voice sounded again and more bubbles floated.

Lily expected the supernatural power, also expected that she slept and dreamed of the voice that quelled the aches and sickness in her belly, dreamed the fish, hopefully dreamed it all. Perhaps she was at home in bed.

She watched, but the fish did not rise again and she leaned

over to stare into the oceanic abyss. Almost as if boiling, bubbles rose in a patch two feet from Lily's nose. A face lifted, bright eyes below the surface, reflecting the moon's shine, teeth smiling in great contrast to the dark water and her brown complexion.

Lily covered a cry with her hand and looked over her shoulder to find Brian still asleep.

"Lily, with both is impossible." The smiling face under the water did not move her lips.

The memorable feeling came back bit by bit with each break of wave. The comfort, the perfection, the gods and goddesses. They wanted her and she wanted them, to be one of them. It's what it was all about, everything leading to the clarity.

"Tell me," she said to the Pacific.

The face continued her smile and arms lifted from sides, out of the water and reaching until pulling Lily down. Her face entered the ocean and her lips met those of the goddess from her lost memory. She inhaled the knowledge, tongued tongue, lips, and teeth.

She could not be Brian's anymore, shed her chains and accept a moment's freedom, trade it all for new shackles of beautiful perfection. Her body quivered and she reached deeper to the goddess, leaning further into the depths.

"Freedom first, Lily." The voice spoke life into her body and she jerked from the water to stare down at the fat white fish.

She knew what had to happen, but not how to go about making it so. The fish swam from sight, glowing, revealing a shelf below the water's surface. Bright as if spot-lit, the bone handle shined. Lily reached and felt the smooth surface, ran her fingers over the handle to a jagged stone blade.

"Lily?" Brian called.

Lily jerked back from the water once again. "You're awake."

"What are you doing?"

"I tried to pet a big fish." She smiled. She wrung her wet hair in her hands. She started to crawl toward Brian, bone-handled dagger safe on the shelf below the surface.

She snuggled into his arms. "You still love me, right?" he asked.

"Of course, I do. What made you think I didn't?"

He laughed a little. "I had a dream, a fish told me you wanted me gone. It was a strange dream."

"My grandmother always said you can't trust a fish." Lily turned her brows tight to center, disbelieving the image in her head, to murder her future husband was a preposterous notion.

"The fish said you'd say that. The fish also told me you cheated, told me about a beautiful woman that you planned to leave with after I'd gone."

"Where am I going?"

Brian held tight against Lily. "The fish said under the water... Atlantis maybe."

"Sounds like some dream." She looked into his eyes. "I love you."

"And I love you, Lillian Eastwin. Better get some sleep, if the fog stays off when the sun comes up, I expect we'll do a good deal of jumping and yelling."

That sounded too hopeful, but she nodded and nestled in deeper. He felt good.

—

Lily awoke to find the sun out and the fog lifted. She crawled to the tip of the rock and reached into the water for the dagger. The coldness sent goosebumps over her flesh, but she continued down despite the feeling.

The dagger slipped at her fingers' touch and slid from the shelf—caught up only a foot lower. She pushed deeper, agonizing to feel the dagger. She took a heavy breath and then glided below the surface.

"Reach, Lily, my Lily, our Lily." The voice came from all around her.

Her finger felt the dagger's handle, but it slid down further.

Float falling like a deadly feather. She edged her body, reaching down, down, down. The slow tease. The weapon moving always just beyond reach. Lily let her body drop into the ocean.

"So close, Lily."

One foot, two feet, three, five, she dropped deeper, stretching out.

"Reach, Lily."

The voice seemed to whisper directly into her ear and she spun her head to find the speaker. Hands wrapped around her throat and laughter surrounded her. The pale eyes and dying flesh of a dead goddess begged intimacy and permanence. Lily screamed and swallowed water, the goddess' long black tongue emerged like an eel, seeking entrance between tightened lips.

She swallowed more water as she attempted another scream.

Clarity poured into her mind amid the profound uncertainty. It was all so obvious, she, it, the goddess wanted everything, wanted her. Wanted her soul, the easier of the two. Brian's love a burden if Lily died making his soul an easy pick. She would go first, he was to be the second domino.

Lily slashed out against the hold and the eel tongue stretched over her tongue and along her throat. She could no longer tell up from down, subsumed in terror and salt water. Life fluttered and flashes of the perfection glinted in and out, no gods or goddesses, just sad souls trapped in world on the other side of the surf. Beyond the flashes, Lily watched as grotesquerie stole the deceitful aura around her goddess, a demon of rot and temptation.

She blinked hard and the perfect plain settled over her. The others twitched and exhaled as if sucking in on her last visit. Bellies flopped, rolls rolled, dimples and ripples surfaced, smiles dropped and tears fell.

"Welcome, Lily, enjoy your..." the voice trailed.

"Help!" Lily shouted once and tried for a second, water and blood sprayed from her mouth. The perfection blinked back and then decayed further, the voice became a trembling cry of anger.

"You're...one of us...now, Lil—No!"

Another gush leapt from her lungs and she coughed.

An angry groan and growl filled the air and the void blinked back for one, two seconds and then faded away with jumbled cries.

"Thank you, thank you, oh Lily." Brian cradled his fiancé.

"She'll be all right now," the man in the rescue services life jacket said as he stumbled back from the slow-moving body between the wet seats of the red and yellow rescue vessel. "Hold on, an hour and a bit to shore."

Lily sobbed and the memory of perfection washed away on the broken surf in the speeding vessel's wake. She climbed upright, needing to see the water.

"Why did you go in?" Brian whispered into her ear. "Did you see her too?"

RICKY'S GOT A KNIFE

(2019)

Before he came to live with her, Delilah Jackson thought having her fifteen-year-old stepson in the house would make her feel safer, normalize her some.

Offering to help him unpack, she saw the big knife and the handgun—when she protested, he showed her the pellets for the gun, and she was so relieved, she forgave the knife. Ricky Donner was expelled from his last school for threatening a teacher—his birth mother was dead and his father, Delilah's ex, was at the end of the proverbial tether. He begged, pleaded, paid off her credit card and car loan, added monthly stipends to the mix, and finally she'd agreed, but it proved tough. He was distracting and sullen, at times outright disobedient. Her schedule and calendar had become a mess of forgotten appointments and days late into work.

It did not help that Facebook was alive with the news and accompanying footage and photography of the sliced and diced teenagers. The first was a thirteen-year-old girl, found outside Knucky's Tap Room. The owner said the girl came in and ordered a martini, he then said he laughed and told her to get home before the babysitter got in trouble. That was the last anyone saw of her.

"Where do you think you're going?" Delilah hurried over and put her hand on the door before Ricky could open it. Thursday night was not a night the boy should be going out after ten o'clock, not if he wanted to live under her roof.

"Out." Ricky folded his arms over his chest, he wore a button-up plaid shirt, a bandana around his neck, and his knife in a sheath on the belt of his Levi's. "Goin' out."

"No, you're not. It's Thursday and you have school in the morning."

Through the door, on the street, the chanting of the brigade reached Delilah's property line and passed in a crawl. The brigade began patrolling after the ninth teenager showed up dead with a slashed throat. Ben Anderson was an eighteen-year-old with sights on enrolling in the armed forces. This death set the town to frenzy and the cops threw up hands, told the media they needed diligent citizens with open eyes.

"You worried someone's gonna get me?" Ricky leaned in tight, his breath smelled like Cheetos and cola. "You worried about little old me?"

Delilah wasn't about to voice what she worried about concerning Ricky, instead she said, "School, in the morning. You ain't going out!"

"Oh yeah?" Ricky massaged the handle of his knife, crudely, almost as if it was an extension of his manhood.

Delilah pushed him back after snaking her foot behind him— a move she saw a boyfriend use a few times when she was still a doe-eyed high schooler in a cheerleader's skirt. He flopped hard and she bent forward, stuck a finger in his face. "You will mind me, Ricky." His name slipped like a snake's hiss.

"Whatever," Ricky said and rolled over, stomped up the stairs.

It was only an hour later that Delilah was in bed and she heard the telltale squeak of a second-floor window. She shook her head. The kid was stupid if he thought she didn't know the sounds of her home, and he was stupid because as a teen he saw himself untouchable. Like he could do any old thing and not be caught up, not die. Delilah shivered beneath her sheets and tried to sleep.

At 3:00 AM, she kicked from bed, certain Ricky should've been home by then. As had become her norm, she picked up her cellphone and checked Facebook. Twelve minutes earlier, police discovered a thirteen-year-old's body behind the pavilion at Aberdeen Park—just up the street. She sat down and the light of her phone died. Dark silence consumed her for three minutes before the sound of a key in a deadbolt rattled like cannon fire.

Delilah stood and stepped to the staircase landing, poised with a hand on the light switch. Shine slipped up the stairs into the hall from the kitchen fixture. She listened to the tap run and then the fridge open. Two minutes later, after the lights clicked off, footfalls swished up the carpeted steps.

Ricky reached the top, cellphone flashlight app guiding him, and Delilah hit the switch. The boy blinked against the change. His shirt and pants were soaked—like they'd been scrubbed—and he had a slice of cold pizza in his hand.

"You're grounded," Delilah said and then switched off the light before returning to her room.

A door slammed and a voice penetrated the thin wood, "You're not my real mom!" it said.

Delilah shook her head, thinking he was apt to get himself killed going out and—then it came to her, and she had to voice the idea, finally, give it room to breathe. "Killer," she said.

At 6:30 AM, she called in sick. At 7:30, she drove her car around the block. At 7:40, she crept into Ricky's bedroom while he slept and picked up the long, bone-handled knife. At 7:41, she climbed into the bathroom closet and waited.

She had hours to think before Ricky got up and stood at the toilet. She wondered how she'd been so blind and stupid. She wondered how much of it was actually her fault. She wondered if this singular act was enough redemption for what she owed, given what she could've stopped weeks ago.

Ricky finished pissing and flushed—with the seat up—and left the bathroom. The time wasn't right, not yet. Minutes later, he came back in with his cellphone. A video likely accompanied the pornographic audio coming through the speakers, but Delilah tried not to hear *anything*. The shower ran after the sex sounds ceased. The shower curtain drew back. The shampoo bottle farted. Delilah turned the door handle and stepped out silently.

The grip on the knife tightened and she moved toward the opaque shower curtain. Ricky had his hands in his hair, his back and ass to the spout and to her, as he massaged his head. Delilah took a single large step, grasped the curtain, and yanked it back. Ricky turned and she swung.

Blood showered over Delilah. She blinked it away, disgusted by what she was seeing as the flesh she cut continued tearing around his neck until his body sunk to its knees and the head floated on air. Ricky's eyes changed then, shimmering an intense red like the Horsehead Nebula she'd seen on The Documentary Channel. Blood dripped from his neck as the head swung around to her left. She trailed with her eyes and the hand holding the knife.

"What do you think you're going to do with that?" Ricky said, laughter in his voice.

Delilah swallowed, terrified but brave, and said, "Same...same thing I did to your mother."

Ricky's eyes widened and he slashed out his razor tongue as Delilah dove into the bathtub, plunging the bone-handled knife into the heart of the prone body. Ricky's decapitated head gasped and then fell.

She looked up at the running showerhead and wondered how many people this demon spawn had killed and dined upon over the years. She wondered how many she saved from future fates. After dispatching Ricky's mother, she got close to Ricky's father, had to know if it passed into the offspring, and thought she had known when the boy seemed okay.

Delilah reached up to turn off the water. "Maybe it was puberty," she said, thinking about how Ricky was so normal the six years she'd known him, right up to his thirteenth birthday when she and Ricky's father parted ways.

Delilah loaded the head into the tub with the rest of the

body, stripped, and went to bed for a few hours. When she awoke, she got to taking care of Ricky. At sundown, she dug a hole in the swampy field behind her home. In a few days, she'd call the police and Ricky's father, give them both the story of a runaway. Thinking on it, she didn't even need to feign sadness when he never showed up—real mothers lose children, stepmothers gain a renewed slice of sanity.

"And your little murder spree is done," Delilah said as she patted the shovel over the damp soil.

Inside, she showered, eyes scanning for specks of blood and seeing none. Before she climbed into bed, she checked her phone. Another body had been found, a fourteen-year-old girl.

"Hmm," she said and peeled back her covers. She got in and hit the light, thinking, thinking, thinking. She turned the light back on. She swung her legs and opened her bedside table's drawer. She looked at the monthly pill dispenser. She squinted at the full number eleven and then looked at her phone. It was the ninth...had she missed nearly a month? She reached deeper into the drawer, pulled out the two large, orange, prescription bottles—Clozapine and Clonazepam—and began refilling the dispenser with the psyche ward doctor's voice in her head, "Keep these up, and you'll never need to see me again."

DAYTONA 500

(2019)

Lance Bowman Jr. was in pole position behind the pace car, knowing his time had finally come. The voice in his ear, Gary Burns, crew chief of the number 99 LINTrax car, spoke of glory and great battles and, "Right there, remember that spot, because right there is the bullshit that ain't gonna happen twice."

They'd painted over the scuffs on the third wall at Daytona International Speedway from last year's 500, when Lance took a bump at the exact wrong moment and found the nose of his Toyota staring down the immovable barrier.

"Damn right it won't happen again," Lance said and smirked.

The pace car veered to the pit lane coming off turn five and feet hit mats in forty high flying, rolling beasts of the NASCAR racing series. Lance immediately slipped into the space, forcing the car starting second to ease off the gas.

Gary laughed in his ear. "It's yours, five hundred miles and it's yours!"

Lance Bowman had won two of the first three races of the year and finished fourth in the third after miscommunicating a corner on the second to last lap and having to slow to half his pace. Those races mattered in the grand scheme, but nothing mattered like the Daytona 500.

For six straight years he'd finished top five and for the last three, he'd finished second. Over and over, somehow that sonofabitch Walter Daytrip came up with enough surge to hold on in those final corners, leaving Lance with a good share of the prize money and a ravenous, all-encompassing sense of failure.

"It's mine this time," Lance whispered and barked a single

laugh.

—

The crowd was drunk and ferocious. They'd fed on blood all day, cheering the loudest when the middle of the pack tangled metals and cement, effectively separating the hopefuls from the hopeless. It also put Lance a lap ahead of all but four other cars.

Three of them were regulars, but the fourth was a rookie and he hadn't yet finished a race since joining the circuit...after the first race saw the horrible *accident* take the life of Walter Daytrip.

"That kid's having a good race, huh?" Lance said into his mic during the last pit stop—the kid, Buddy Johnson III pulled in right on his tail.

"Not bad for a rookie, but I'll bet you six boxes of Girl Scout Tagalongs he'll be behind two laps by the time the checkered comes out," Gary said.

Lance huffed. "I ain't taking that bet, only way it won't come true is if he smucks and can't finish."

"He ain't finishing, doesn't have the heart or the will to do what needs to be done out there."

To this, Lance nodded.

—

Forget permanent banishment from the sport, what they'd done—if discovered—would've put them in prison. Twenty-five to life was a tall risk, but the Daytona 500 was a tall reward.

Two afternoons before the season opening Advance Auto Parts Clash, Walter Daytrip was coming onto the first corner during his first lap of qualifying and found his gas pedal stuck to the floor—that's what he told his crew chief the moment before the number 11 Pringles car burst into flames.

Sad day for his family.

Sad day for race fans.

Sad day for the world of sports.

—

"He's still there," Lance said glancing into his mirror at the nose of Buddy Johnson III's Ford emblem above the front bumper.

"Don't worry. You know well as I do, the championship laps are where the real men prove themselves and that kid ain't nothing but a boy," Gary said, sounding a touch less confident than he had one hundred ninety laps earlier. "Now you got nothing at all to worry about, behind him is Denny Daniels and he's got a solid mile to catch up, so you keep on and you've got this. This one is yours. Yours!"

"You're damned right," Lance said, ticking off another lap in the lead. So far he'd fallen behind twice during the early pit stops, but recovered in natural course. In total, he'd led one hundred seventy-six laps, meaning holding on would not only give him the biggest prize in NASCAR, it topped King Richard Petty's record for laps led.

—

Lance passed under the flag stand and glanced to the mirror. He blinked and shook, had to jerk—just a touch—around corner number one.

Gary's voice came over the air, "Easy there. What's going on?"

Lance tried not to look in the mirror but needed to look in the mirror. What he thought he saw, in all logic and reality wouldn't be there when he looked again, but what if it was?

"I thought I saw something. There a sticker coming off the kid's car or something?" Lance said, eyes hard on the hot asphalt ahead of him.

"Uh, nothing I can see. Why, he got something loose?" Gary said.

Lance rounded the third corner and gave a glance back to the car behind him. Nothing, just a car. He exhaled a pent breath and spoke as he took the fourth corner. "Nah, guess not." His eyes tipped back up to the mirror a moment before sliding into the fifth turn. He blinked, couldn't look back, not yet, not until the round straightened before him. "You sure there's nothing?"

"Just focus on the race...he's coming on your right." Gary

sounded worried, truly worried.

Under the white flag, Lance looked to his right and saw the kid, pulling neck and neck. The kid was looking forward, tinted visor down, but on the back, hanging onto the spoiler like a surfer about to stand up to a wave, was a white, eight-foot silhouette in the shape of a man, helmet on his head. It toodled the fingers of its free arm at Lance.

"You don't see that?" Lance shouted.

"Calm down," Gary said, smooth and easy, though phony, "don't see nothing. Pitch her hard into one and yank it back up once straight. If the kid's still in the way, he'll learn how the wall tastes. This is the man's lap and he's just a kid. This is yours! Yours, goddammit!"

Lance nodded and did as told. Buddy Johnson III eased off to avoid the wall and fell back. Lance kept nodding, a sneer forming. He hadn't seen anything, it was the jitters, he was about to...the white silhouette rose and surfed on the back of the kid's car.

"You don't see?" Lance screamed into his helmet mic.

"Talk to me. See what? What's going on out there?"

They rounded the third turn and the kid brought his front bumper tight to Lance's rear end.

"There's something on the kid's car! You got to see it! It's huge!"

Gary exhaled a heavy breath. "Sure, now pay attention. One more mile and this is yours!"

Lance squeezed his hands and peeled his eyes from the mirror as he entered the fourth turn. Whatever was going on back there had nothing to do with him. Whatever that kid was trying to pull—Lance's rear end thumped a few car lengths from the fifth and final turn.

"Ah! Christ! Christ!" Lance shouted. "It's on the car! Fucking...it's Daytrip! He's on the car!"

"Lance, breathe. This is yours!"

Lance didn't hear, was too focused on what was obvious then.

The massive visage had a colorless face beneath the helmet, but there was no mistaking the lopsided smirk.

"Oh Christ!"

The huge Daytrip ghost waved and then pointed to his left.

"Hold on! Hold on!" Gary screamed. "Watch your right!"

Lance was on the home stretch.

"It's yours! It's yours! Just hold on!"

Lance shook his head, said, "Nononono," as Daytrip's ghost leaned hard to the left, dragging horrible, stretching fingers down along the asphalt.

"What are you doing! Don't ease! Foot on the gas!" Gary was livid and Lance finally heard him.

"I'm pushing! It's Daytrip!"

The checkered flashed and Buddy Johnson III took it by the length of his hood.

—

"See, right there. I wasn't letting up, Daytrip's ghost was on the car," Lance said, pointing to the video on the monitor in the trailer. Nobody on the team had said a word to him since the race finished, but finally, Gary said, "Go to the hotel. Get some rest. Next year. There's always next year."

Lance could hardly believe it. Sure, the after images didn't show the ghost, but he didn't expect that, not really. Ghosts don't film, if they did, more than just people looking for them would catch them. And sure, it was a big explanation to swallow, but it had happened and if they all wanted to stay on his team...

"Fuck you all," Lance said and stormed off.

—

In the hotel, he took a shower and donned the room's robe. He sat on the bed and opened the laptop. He'd missed two Skype calls on his cellphone already but wanted to call back on the bigger screen for a better look.

It rang twice and the camera drank in a dim image. He saw his wife's face, her jaw moving as if talking. Then his son popped in, silly cowlick rising like a skateboard ramp.

"I can't hear you," he said. "And turn on some lights. I can't barely see you either."

His wife nodded and a light flashed so brightly that his computer screen flared like a sunspot.

"Whoa," Lance said. "What's going—" He swallowed.

The room glistened in a fresh coat of gunky blood. Bits of bone rose willy-nilly like haphazard stucco. His wife's head and his son's head floated on two colorless arms. Daytrip's ghost smiled in the middle, clacking their jaws.

Lance shook his head. "No. No. No!" He slammed the laptop closed. "You're dead, you fuck! You're dead!" He pulled his cellphone from the nightstand and the charge cord, dialled his wife. It rang and rang. "Come on, pick up." And rang and rang and rang. He hit end and slammed the phone down on the bed. "No, they're just not home. No..." But he'd called her cell.

Lance flipped open the laptop and redialed his wife's number. There was no answer and after two rings, the default unavailable announcement popped up.

"This isn't happening," he said and lay back, put a pillow over his face.

—

It was full dark when he awoke with a start. He blinked. It hit him all over, he'd lost another Daytona 500, and then, *oh god.* He pulled his laptop close, woke it up, and...there was a knock on the door.

He waited.

Another knock.

He croaked, "Who's there?"

The figure didn't say a word. Instead, knocked again.

Lance curled under the blanket, sending his laptop crashing to the floor. "Go away!"

The knock landed once more.

"I said, go!"

The knock landed a final time before the digital lock buzz sounded and the handle clicked open, bringing in scents: burned gasoline, hot rubber, and spilled blood.

RISEN GREY FLESH

(2022)

Scott Shockley broke through the Livingston boot room, then kitchen, and thudded heavily down the stairs. In the cramped basement, John Livingston and Dan Boiling sat on a loveseat pushed tight against the stairs while Melissa Spencer sat in a beanbag by the laundry room door.

"Guys! Guys!" Scott said and then sniffed hard as he swiped the back of his hand beneath his nose. "You ain't gonna believe it!"

John and Dan kept their eyes pinned to the TV screen where they were guiding Zeke and Julie through the *Zombies Ate My Neighbors* landscape. John was tall—for a ten-year-old—and skinny, pale as printer paper but for the two rosy blotches on his cheeks. Dan was short and even skinnier, olive toned.

Melissa looked up from the issue of Cracked she was flipping through. "Hey, Snot," she said and then returned her attention to the pages. She was short and frumpy, tanned complexion—in the initial, awkward throes of puberty.

Scott wiped the back of his hand on his shorts. "Guys, listen!" He was a little taller than Dan, wider than all of them, and had peach toned skin that was currently sunburnt on the nose and beneath the eyes.

On the TV, the characters entered the doors that appeared and the level end screen tallied their points. Dan tossed his controller to the floor and Melissa immediately snatched it.

"Guys, you won't believe it!" Scott shouted, vibrating all over.

"You finally fingered your sister?" Dan said.

"Fuck you, man." Scott swiped his hand beneath his

perpetually runny nose—allergies all spring, summer, autumn, and a cold all winter.

"Watch your mouth," John said, eyes on the *Pyramid of Fear* level he and Melissa had entered.

"Who's swearing down there," John's mother said from the top of the stairs.

"Snot," John said.

"Oh, Scott's here?" she said and said no more.

"So, did she smell like fish? When I fingered her, it smelled like sardines," Dan said.

"Fuck you," Scott whispered. "But, so, I went to visit my grandma—you know, at Abbeyfield—and she wasn't in her room, so I went to the dining hall and she wasn't there, then I went to the tennis court—"

"You're not gonna tell us you fingered your crippled grandma?" Dan said, pulling a face.

"Man, fuck off," Scott said.

"Why'd you need to see her? Was her purse gone?" John said.

Scott visited his grandmother because she was senile and gave him ten bucks every time he came, calling him Shawny, his dead uncle's name.

"Yeah, so I had to find her," Scott said. "So anyway, there's like a library, but it's in the basement and you need a key to access the elevator and the doors were locked. I didn't think she'd be down there, but where else? So I go around the side and look in the windows. It's all dark and there's one of the nurses, butt naked..."

John paused the game and suddenly all eyes were on Scott.

"...she's got like fifty candles lit on the floor, I think there was a pentagram there too, maybe drawn in blood, and she's reading from this huge book. And then I saw my grandma, stand up from her wheelchair, her eyes flashing mega-bright light before she fell back."

Scott's grandmother hadn't walked in the ten years he'd been alive.

"Bullshit," Melissa said.

"Did you see the nurse's tits?" Dan said.

John said nothing with his mouth but his eyebrows were hiding behind his bangs.

"Yeah, but that's not it." Scott sniffled hard. "The nurse is a Satanist, or whatever, and she's doing something to my grandma."

Dan popped to his feet. "Nobody fingers Scott's grandma but me and Scott!"

Scott growled and launched himself over the couch. Dan caught his weight, pivoted, and tossed him onto Melissa. She shrieked and pushed Scott to the floor.

"John, get your Polaroid, we're gonna see some titties," Dan said.

John didn't move. "You know it's bullshit."

"So, his grandma'll give us all ten bucks," Dan said.

John stood up.

—

"How come she can't live there?" John said.

They were passing the Cartwell Retirement Home, which was one block closer than Abbeyfield House. Elderly were being wheeled, walked, steadied in en masse through the double doors. A young woman in all black was carting a box from the trunk of her Pontiac up to the entry, scowling as the foursome passed. She got inside and bent—assumedly to set down her box—before locking a deadbolt which was faintly audible across the now silent parking lot.

"What's her problem?" Melissa said.

"She needs a good fingering," Dan said.

"Why is it always fingering?" Scott said and then sniffed, swiped, wiped.

Dan had no response to this.

The evening was calm, little traffic on the street and virtually no foot traffic around them—the odd person stood here and there in a laneway. The air was heavy and hot, the sense of an impending thunderstorm seemed to grow stronger by the minute.

The parking lot at Abbeyfield House was almost empty—only an Audi sedan and a Chevy station wagon remained. The building itself seemed dead. Scott led the way to the squat window where he'd seen the naked woman and his grandmother in the basement. They crouched and peered into the dimness below. There was his grandmother, in her wheelchair, alone, surrounded by candles and a glistening symbol on the floor beneath her.

"Holy," Melissa said.

A strange squeak sounded from the basement. The woman Scott had seen earlier stepped into view. She wore a bathrobe now and was pushing a little old man in a wheelchair. She knelt before him, he nodded and pulled what appeared to be a crucifix necklace up over his bald head. The woman kissed his mouth gently before rising. She opened the robe and tossed it aside. The man held up what appeared to be a carving knife, the blade and handle resting flat on his palms. The woman accepted the knife as the man tilted his had back, revealing his throat. The woman kissed him once more before leaning on his forehead and forcing the blade into the flesh of his neck.

"Jesus," Dan said.

The blood geysered out and the woman knelt, letting it shower her, making her naked body shine amid all those shadows.

Dan nudged John and John lifted his camera. The mechanism within the Polaroid sounded like a gunshot in the silence of the evening, the flash like a solar flare through a telescope. The woman didn't seem to notice. She began swiping the blood around the floor anew.

"She's gonna kill my grandma," Scott said, pouty.

"We'll get the police," Melissa said.

Scott began shaking and sniffing. "No!" He took off running toward the front of the building.

John, eyebrows high as they went, looked to Dan in askance. Dan nodded and the pair took off behind Scott.

Melissa whined, "Shouldn't we get help, from an adult?" as she trailed behind them in a jog.

Inside was empty as it looked from outside. Everything smelled like rubbing alcohol and potpourri. Scott took the same route he had the first time he'd come, leaving off visiting his grandmother's room. He tried the door to the stairs, reefing and grunting. No movement. He then ran to the elevator and began stabbing his index finger into the button above the keyhole. The light behind the button didn't even acknowledge him.

"Where is everybody?" John said.

Scott spun and pointed a finger at Dan. "If you fucking say it..."

Dan put his hands up like the victim of an armed robbery.

Winded, Melissa leaned on her knees. "We should call the police."

John reached out and tapped the keyhole beneath the call button. "Bet there's keys in the office."

They all turned and looked back the way they'd come. The office was a square room that jutted from the khaki-colored walls by the door. There was a door around the side and a window up front. Scott ran to the door.

"It's locked!" He began yanking wildly.

John and Dan went around front while Melissa stood back, watching helplessly. Dan positioned himself at the small window and reached his arms and head through, Supermaning his body as John lifted his legs. He landed with a soft thump onto the carpet on the other side before popping up and looking around the room, ignoring Scott as he panted and whined and sniffed as he tugged frantically at the door.

He began rifling drawers. From the third, he snatched a bag

of Werther's Original candies. He immediately gave up his search and tore open one of the individually wrapped caramels as he stepped to the door. He dropped the wrapper as he reached for the door handle. It didn't turn.

"Snot, screw off a minute," he said and tried again once Scott ceased his useless thrashing. It still didn't move. "Okay, continue."

Scott pounded on the door anew as John and Melissa stood at the window, watching Dan eat candies and open drawers.

"Maybe you should call—" Melissa started but was cut off.

John pointed to across the space. "Hey, any of those work?" he said.

On the wall next to the door was a mounted key box with the door lazily open. Dan started over to them, popping a third candy into his mouth as he went. The light switch was directly below the box and he flicked it.

"That's better," Dan said as he took a handful of keyrings from little hooks. "Here."

He tossed what remained of the Werther's Original bag at the window, sending the crinkling candies in their wrappers all over. John reached in through the gap in the window and plucked two candies from the counter. He unwrapped both and put them in his mouth.

Dan found the key that opened the door and swung it wide as he stepped out of the way. Scott tumbled into the office, landing on his hands and knees.

"Ow!" Scott said, his cheeks wet with tears, upper lip shining with mucous.

"Rugburn's the worst," John said as he started toward Dan who was walking to the elevators.

Melissa watched them go. Watched them rifling through keys until they had the correct one. Watched them enter the elevator. She waited a handful of seconds before hurrying into the office to use a phone. Emergency services was programmed into the speed dial options, according to the tiny slip of paper in the tiny window. She hit the button, and as she waited, she unwrapped a candy.

—

The elevator dinged and the doors slid open. The boys stood a moment, letting their eyes adjust to the dimness beyond the bright box. The basement was a mix of storage—rows upon rows of steel chairs on stacks, tables on flat carts, and oxygen canisters large and small—laundry, and library. In the vacant space between where the library and laundry areas touched was Scott's grandmother, the bloody, naked woman—who was currently chanting something unintelligible to three slumped figures in wheelchairs.

Scott started running. Dan and John carried on behind him, only slower. John snapped another Polaroid of the scene and the woman kneeling on the floor. She twitched subtly at the sound or the flash, or both, but did not quit the ritual.

Scott's grandmother again stood from her wheelchair, eyes glowing whitely. She then levitated three feet and floated there, her flesh seeming to droop in abnormal long swatches of flesh.

"Look at that," John said, coming to a halt, snapping another picture.

"Maybe you better not!" Dan shouted a moment before Scott lowered his shoulder and barreled into the naked woman from behind. At the same moment, Scott's grandmother flopped to the hard floor below. The smack was wet and meaty.

The woman screamed, rolling with Scott before straddling and pinning him. He put his hands over his head as she began driving fists into his face.

"You," punch, "stupid," punch, "little," punch, "motherfucker," punch.

From the floor, the old woman said, "Shawny, what are you doing here?"

The woman quit punching, huffing, her breasts heaving as

she looked from boy to old woman and back. "You're not one of them?"

John hurried around the side to get a front angle of the woman's bare chest, and, inadvertently, the lifeless faces of two slumped figures and a third face barely clinging to life, oxygen mask over his nose and mouth. He had the sticky carving knife in his lap.

Dan stared, slack-jawed and with an intensity matched only when facing off against difficult video game bosses.

The woman climbed up to her feet, shaking her head. "You damned kids."

"What're you doing to my grandma?" Scott moaned.

The woman looked back at him. "Saving the goddamned world, you little bitch." She then stepped to the old man with the oxygen mask. "Third time's the charm, eh Phil?"

He nodded, tears spilling down his ancient cheeks.

"What are you doing to my grandma!" Scott wailed crawling toward the old woman, smearing the pentagram painted on the stone floor.

"Kid, there's a lot you don't know about your grandmother. Thankfully the senility didn't touch the destiny she knew would come eventually," the woman said. "Now, all of you, go away. This can't wait."

Dan suddenly vomited onto the floor around the word, "Boobs." As he leaned on his knees, he tried to speak further and could only get out the word, "Finger," between dry-heaving gags.

"Destiny?" Scott said from the floor.

"Run along now, Shawny, Mama's got to do this," his grandmother said.

"Grandma?" Scott said.

The naked woman came over and lifted the old woman onto her wheelchair. "I got to redraw the symbol—fuck! You all just get the hell out of here! Now!"

John hurried over to Scott and grabbed him. "Lady, you're

bananas," he said, dragging the boy along.

"Look around! They've taken the others. Every granny and grampy in care is gone. They took them and if I don't summon Chukas before they do, you'll wish you were Phil here," the naked woman said, charging back to the old man in the oxygen mask.

Dan stumbled in reverse to stand with the others as the old man lifted the knife on his palms. The naked woman kissed him gently, accepted the knife, and then pinned his head to get at his throat. The blood cascaded over her and she crawled like a monkey to redraw the pentagram before taking her spot on its edge with the huge, leather tome.

She began reading aloud, the words foreign and meaningless to the boys, and yet carrying a weight that confessed their strength. After less than a minute, Scott's grandma stood on her useless legs, her eyes open and glowing white. She then began to float. The woman continued speaking. Scott's grandma began to spin, her nightie burst into a fast and hungry flame, almost instantly revealing the wrinkled landscape beneath. The woman began chanting. Scott's grandma spun faster, her flesh loosening until sloughing off in great swatches that plopped wetly to the floor. Suddenly she was a deep red mass, her body painting blood polka dots around the space.

"Eww," John said.

Dan sat down, panting, eyes still glued to the naked woman. Scott covered his face. The old woman's wheelchair crept forward two feet before bolts began pinging and the steel of the chair began to reshape itself into an oval.

The woman stood and started chanting something different. She then clapped her wet palms against her chest and shouted, "Rise and be silent, demon!"

The ovular steel conglomeration slapped onto the old woman's head, stilling her airborne spin. The wire from the wheelchair began to tine into the muscles of her fleshless face.

The bloody woman's smile lit the scene with premature

celebration as she continued to chant.

——

Melissa led the two cops into the basement after locating another set of keys that would make the elevator go. The doors opened and the cops broke forward, firing immediately at the naked woman. Three of twenty-nine rounds sent hit their target, one of which went into her heart. She gasped and dropped onto her face. At the same moment that the shot shut her up, the skull trap that had once been pieces of a wheelchair clattered down. Scott's grandmother dropped with a tremendous, sticky slap.

"Grandma?" Scott said, looking at the skinless, old woman...the obviously dead, skinless, old woman.

——

The cops sent the foursome upstairs to call the station and report the need for more bodies.

"I just called, and the cops said to get more cops," Melissa said into the phone.

The boys looked like dalmatians, swap black for red. All were sucking on Werther's Original candies.

"You're at Cartwell?" the switchboard operator said. "We sent everyone there already."

From outside, the faint echo of gunshots played upon the air.

"No, Abbeyfield," Melissa said.

"It's happening there, too?" the voice said just before the connection ceased.

Melissa hit the emergency services button again, but the dial tone was gone.

"What do you think she meant?" John said, looking at the pictures he'd taken. "About saving the world, or whatever."

Melissa dropped the phone and plucked a candy of her own from the desk. She then joined the boys in the foyer. "Nobody's coming...something's going on at Cartwell."

"She was summoning a demon so someone else couldn't, isn't that what she said?" Dan said, totally back to his normal self.

"I gotta tell my mom Grandma's dead," Scott said and took a step toward the double doors that led to the mostly empty parking lot.

Shadows began filling in, blocking the light. The doors opened and five geriatric men shuffled through, their balls swinging pendulously between their legs.

"What the—" Scott said before one latched onto him and brought his hungry jaw down onto Scott's throat. "Ow!"

The other fogies shuffled at their version of high speed. John turned to run. Dan grabbed Melissa and tossed her to the floor at the feet of the cannibals. The boys got only a few steps down a hallway before windows began to shatter around them at the force of wrinkly, liver-spotted hands. One hand grabbed John's camera, twisting the strap, whiplashing him backward out a window, into the waiting arms of possessed elderly.

Dan was knocked sideways by John's foot, into several hands; busy digits hooked, scratched, fingered his eyes, nose, and mouth, peeling back the skin leaving behind a screaming, muscled skull.

RIGHTEOUS HUNT

(2016)

Through a grimy, dust-caked window, a yellow cloud hovered inches from the cracked street. Moving forever, driven by malicious intent, hungry for the great grandchildren of the few survivors of the species.

Shoes Lee stared through an ancient black rubber gas mask handed out to every member of his former community. That was back in the times before a cloud took his people and turned them into sour meat.

It was chance that put him in an old diner. It was sense that kept his mask tight to his face while he hunted.

Diners were good for hope. The symbols of yesterday tomorrows flashed often, sometimes accompanying the *messages*. Toilets were better than diners. Picnic tables were all right too. High school locker rooms were the best. His father told him the story, passed down from generation to generation and sideways from boy to girl, from boy to boy, from girl to girl, from all the walls to all the survivors.

Sometimes the walls did talk, but one had to know how to listen, be willing to hear. Other hunters surviving the clouds spray painted markers:

Starshine Eyes

Yesteryear Dawn

Forever is tomorrow and tomorrow is the past

Those were the good hunters, leaving messages for others seeking the majesty of the *Star*.

Bad hunters set out signs and lay in wait:

2 true inside!

No hunter could turn it down. To be a hunter was to seek, to carry the torch of hope to take things back to the before times.

Shoes sat in a booth and stared around him as the yellow cloud crept into the diner. There was no chance to work, or rest, or eat, he had to sit and wait. His gloved hand pressed tight over the recent fish twine seam holding flaps of flesh together behind his leather pants.

Three rises and falls of the moon before, back when he had a friend in the cold world, Shoes came upon a painted *Half-Star*.

"What do you think, Boots?" Shoes looked down to the black and brown mutt wearing a canine gas mask over his snout. "Boots, pay attention."

Boots, a mutt with Doberman genes heavy in his pool, looked up to Shoes. The dog was up for anything, but well behaved and eerily sensible for an animal.

Shoes stepped closer.

"Seems okay but stay behind me."

The *Half-Star* in fresh red paint next to the door carried the message: Iron Survival

It was enough, secret wording only a hunter knew. It was a clue no hunter dared deny.

Shoes was not new to the hunt nor to the games wrought hunters played. He stepped up the crumbling cement stairs of a three-storey red brick building, once a specialty school for children with behavior issues. Standing aside of the fallen tin overhang, he pulled the heavy steel door and waited, listening.

The silence was full and welcoming.

Shoes looked over both shoulders and down the avenue in both directions. The air was clear, the sun had barely risen, a beautiful day, all things tabulated. He lifted his mask and took a deep breath of the fresh air outside and then one from within the former school.

There was stale smoke from a fire many days gone. The floor carried no slip nooses, no bear traps, and no tripwires.

"Come on, boy. Stay close."

The man entered and the dog rushed ahead.

Through the first hall, he followed the signs to a set of stairs and he again lifted his mask. The smoky scent was nearer, but no newer.

"What do you think? Go downstairs?"

The dog whined agreement, barking not an option within the mask.

Dim down the stairs, Shoes ran his light over the vast empty hallways and playing over the walls, seeking direction. A black *Quarter-Star* covered the entire upper-half of a door, the small placard behind the paint reading, *boys' change room.*

Predictable.

The message came to children and teens when their parents didn't listen. In the times before, the youth caught messages while the adults ignored or pushed aside the impending trouble. Arriving long in advance of their time, the messages transcribed onto walls and tables, carved, drawn, painted and seen as graffiti were so much more. Auditory mathematics of the universe dumbed down for the use of anyone willing to seek.

Those in power and those once aware, misplaced the necessary balance and the first yellow clouds appeared. Mother Earth wanted Her planet back from the undeserving and unaware occupants. Humanity had wrongfully assumed themselves gods of the kingdom.

That was then. Years upon years into the past. The people died but the messages remained.

Shoes pushed open the door and lifted his mask for a whiff. There was a new smell, something odd. Chemicals, a pine scented cleaning agent. Odd, but not enough to keep him away from the supposed double messages within. He let the dog enter and then flashed his light around the smallish room. There was an arrow above the shower area, past the benches and hooks. Shoes followed the dog, slowly, training his flashlight on the stony floor. He entered the shower and saw the red paint.

Mask over his face, he did not smell the heavy, close by reek of six hunters doused in concentrated floor cleaner. A red arrow pointed to a corner and Shoes stepped forward absent of caution.

Boots found the stacked bodies behind a shower curtain and investigated. The dog did not have the understanding or the voice to convey what he saw.

Shoes' light fell onto the old message, carved in a circle around the familiar ovular blue bird peering at chains:

No weeping on the day of execution

Shoes' heart thumped in his chest. It was a truth, a message carried on for centuries, awaiting a hunter to collect and then perform. Licking his lips behind his mask, Shoes retrieved his notebook from his battered brown leather satchel.

He wrote in pencil, *21. No weeping on the day of execution.* His hands shook with excitement and he shined his light over the room looking for more paint and found it. Another symbol. A different artist, but old, likely from the same era of behaviorally inept students.

"At the center, your eyes, my eyes," he read aloud.

It was another real deal step to the old world brought to life. As he transcribed the message into his notebook, Boots growled.

"Give me your collection," said a gruff and yet high voice, raspy and savage. "Hand it over or this mutt gets it."

Shoes turned to see Boots held by his collar fur and the rubber strap of his mask. A machete held tight to his ear. The figure with the machete was a small woman, small but hardened with time. Bald and scarred, wearing a green gas mask and bulky leathers, made for a woman numerous sizes larger than the current wearer.

"Hand it over or your dog dies!"

"You know it does not work that way. There is no redemption for thieves and murderers."

"Shut up and hand it over!"

"Fine," Shoes said and held out his notebook.

"On the floor, back over there." The woman nodded in the direction of the shower enclosed by a curtain.

Shoes edged that way after dropping his notebook, feeling sympathy for this hunter. There was no hope for her. Once she collected enough, it would take her nowhere.

"What happened that you—?"

"Shut up, how many do you have? How many?" she shrieked.

Boots growled and tensed.

"Twenty-two with these two."

"Twenty-two," she whispered. "Better than the others. This'll take me away. I'll know heaven! I'll know everything! You can watch if you like. Watch or die, your choice."

No choice, Shoes dropped down to his knees and begged for his dog. Counting days was difficult as it was. He did not want to consider his existence without his only friend.

"Ready the floor. I know you have the sacred fixtures."

"Yeah, okay. Let Boots go, please. He's just a dog."

The woman pressed her knife to the dog's throat. "Ready the ceremony and you might both see tomorrow!"

From his satchel, Shoes took out the chalk, the bag of sand, and the five candles, one for each point of the *Star*. The emblem centered the open stone floor. He lit the candles and set them in place. The sand circled all, and Shoes watched as the woman stepped into the middle, grip still tight on Boots. The dog had eased and cooperated well enough to save his hide.

Her knees held tight against Boots' head to free a hand. She scooped up Shoes' notebook, cleared her throat and read.

Shoes mouthed along with his earned collection, knowing all by heart, even if she stole all she would never take the words unless she ended his life. He heard the latest addition and lowered his eyes as she dropped his notebook and retrieved a slip of paper from her pocket to read from other stolen messages.

He hummed so that the ill-gotten words did not soil his

mind. Two minutes passed before the woman screamed.

"It's all junk, lore! There's no return! A game, a game to lose!"

Boots, jarred by the sound, leapt forward. The frantic woman chopped the machete down on the dog's neck. The dog fell, moaning and whimpering. The sounds echoed from the soft tile walls.

"Boots!" Shoes shouted, his eyes burst into salty showers.

"All junk!" The woman charged, swinging the bloodied blade.

Shoes stumbled back through the curtain, falling onto the decaying pile of dead former hunters. He felt a dead man's knife slice into his thigh. The pain burned past the grief momentarily. His hand jammed into his pack and he brought forth his revolver. Ammunition had become unreliable, dampened and dried dozens of times within the seemingly limitless boxes on former shop shelves.

Shoes squeezed four times before he found an active round. The round jumped and slapped a tiny, wet hole through the woman's forehead.

Shoes rolled from the pile of carnage and crawled to Boots. The dog lay panting and draining. Shoes pulled away the mask. The dog bled out in the arms of his only friend. Shoes held on through the night and come morning, he buried the dog and the murdered hunters in graves under the small patch of grass near the school's entrance.

He left the woman on the steps leading up, a lesson to other evil souls looking to darken heaven and putrefy the *Star*.

For two days and two nights, Shoes lay in the long grass next to his only friend in the world. Bodily need moved him on. Shoes continued on streets unfamiliar to him looking for dried food. Onion powder or ground oats, something not sullied by animal or mold.

It was then that he stepped into the diner, a place called *Flash in the Pan.*

Sitting in the diner, as the cloud rolled by, Shoes wondered if it was worth anything without Boots by his side. He considered the final sentiment of the frantic locker room murderer. Others had questioned his path, questioned his hope and effort, questioned his religion and questioned the *Star.* Many laughed at the hunters, the packs living in their hapless communities, doing nothing to bring about better days, just existing, procreating, gathering junk, ignoring the knowledge, and dying ignorant of the universe around them.

"Maybe they're right, what do you think, boy?" Shoes asked to the empty diner. Shoes lifted his hand from his leg, an idea blooming on his mind. It was all a mistake, the writing in his notebook, words scrolled on tables, symbols painted on walls. There was no return and no hope for the world. It was just graffiti.

He rose from his seat.

"Who do you think you are?" he asked himself, standing at the diner door. "What is tomorrow and the day after, alone, looking for a myth, words taken out of context? What is it all? Just stuff jotted by kids, no path no—" he paused for a deep breath.

A thought, a sad whim, entered his head and proved difficult to shake. He put his hands on his mask. One breath of the cloud without the filter was enough to sicken him, two breaths was enough to send him sprawling for days and three, four, five, six, a dozen, somewhere amid those breaths, spelled his end.

"No *Star,* no yesterday tomorrows, not without you, boy."

Tears dripped down onto the interior of the mask as he rested his head against the door while attempting to work the nerve into the act. The necessary strength to give up and face the true unknown of death.

Somewhere, deep down in his mind, Shoes heard Boots whine, heard him growl, felt the soft rubber of the dog's mask nudge his hand, looking for affection. It was so real and so close.

"I can't do it without you, Boots!"

A bark filled the diner and Shoes spun, dropping his hands from his mask. There was movement behind the counter. A thin black curl wagged above.

"Boots?" Shoes whispered and limped away from the door.

He stepped to the counter, leaned on a stool and looked over. There he saw the soft black curl again. It rushed away, into the kitchen.

Shoes raced after the tail that had to belong to Boots and yet couldn't. Boots was gone, dead forever. And still, what is forever but a promise from the past?

The curl turned a corner and Shoes limped faster, his heart banging on his ribs. He came to a closed door. It was the only option. Dogs couldn't open freezer doors, especially not dead dogs. And still...

Shoes pulled open the door and called into the darkness, "Boots?"

A bark filled the small space and Shoes froze in place, watching a great blue light carve a star out of the darkness.

Beneath it, in the very order he'd collected over the years and the very order he'd copied them in his notebook, the lines formed:

1. Come with me,
2. Fly high, fear no freaks

And on and on, all the way to the lines he inscribed from the school locker room walls and then beyond to the unknown.

21. No weeping on the day of execution
22. At the center, your eyes, my eyes
23. There is nothing to give
24. There was nothing lost

And still, it continued, on and on until the fabled finish.

30. Take me there, take me away!

Shoes Lee lifted his mask and cleared his throat. He had to read the phrases aloud, knowing, only then, that the rest was for show. The ceremony was unnecessary. Speaking the words had made this so utterly obvious and a smile crept to his lips while he read. It was the power of the message left behind; it was always the power behind the words.

Two-thirds through the list, his heart seemed ready to burst and his vision wavered as the hungry yellow cloud from outside followed him into the freezer.

Boots, back in full doggy form, encouraged the man with a nudge. Shoes read on, faster and faster. On his twenty-eighth message, he felt his body vibrating at an unfamiliar frequency.

At the twenty-ninth message, the yellow cloud seeping into the freezer filled his chest.

"Take me there, take me away!" he said and it all ended as far as the world knew of Shoes Lee and his noble search.

THE DONOR

(2022)

"We're going on a bear hunt," the father sang.

"I've got my binoculars," the daughter sang.

Sunlight had yet to fully breach the horizon, but it was wise to get the fishing lines in before dawn. The father couldn't say why, but that's what he'd always been told, and it sounded right.

"I'm not scared," the father sang.

"I'm not scared," the daughter sang.

She was six, and she and her daddy went fishing in Toe River every Sunday morning come summer vacation. It was their time, where they bonded, where he got to know her and where she wanted only to be with him and to impress him.

"Uh oh, there's a big river," the father said in baritone.

"Can't go over it," the daughter sang in response.

From the left-hand ditch, a bull moose stepped out onto the road looking big as a skyscraper. The father jerked the wheel to the right and bounced off the gravel road. The daughter screamed. The father slammed on the brakes, and the tires cut great divots in the swampy grass of the embankment. The truck pitched forward. The father slammed his head the moment the truck began to roll. The passenger's side crinkled over a boulder hidden along the edge of the big river, plastic and metal amalgamated with flesh and snapped bones. The daughter screamed in pain. The father started to come to as the truck began sinking. They found bottom about fifteen feet from the surf.

"Daddy!" the daughter wailed.

"Shh, shh," the father said automatically and then looked

around. The windshield was cracked and leaking. "Oh, no," he said, more there now. There was only dimness around him—the interior light was yellowy and so weak that it might as well have gone out.

"Daddy, I'm stuck!"

The father unbuckled his seatbelt and climbed over the center console of the truck. Bad. The truck seemed to be biting her arm, holding it in place while a piece of steel drove through her bicep.

"Daddy, it hurts!"

"It'll be oka—" Cracking glass stole the father's words as a bigger stream pushed through. He maybe had a minute, probably less. And his daughter? What was his life without her? He couldn't just let her die. The glass cracked again and a fresh leak sprouted.

"Daddy, please!"

To save himself was to let her die. Drowning, aside from perhaps burning, could it get any worse?

"Dadd—!"

"Hush, now! Close your eyes, hun. And keep them closed." The father reached back for the tacklebox and flung open the lid. He grabbed the inflatable boat fender he sometimes used when fishing around especially weedy shorelines. He gave it a single pump from the aerosol cylinder—the floater instantly resolidified.

Water started coming in through the floor and around the doors.

"Daddy, I'm cold," the daughter whined.

"Are your eyes closed?" the father asked.

"Yes."

Another crack bellowed like the final warning before blastoff.

"Good." The father reached into the toolbox for the filleting knife. "Keep your...ugh...eyes...closed. And...this...will...taste...funny...but...you...breathe...it." Finished cutting, he got busy with the next step, even as his vision blurred and his fingers started to disobey him.

—

"Say, look at those tracks," the mother said to her son. She was snacking on trail mix as they rolled leisurely along the barren back road.

She was fifty-two and he was twenty-seven and every Sunday they went out for brunch. They were running a bit late, but that was okay. Sundays were made for lollygagging.

"What's that floating?" the son said.

Not far from where the tracks stopped, floating in the still water, was a bright orange boat bumper.

"Better call someone," the mother said as she pulled to the shoulder.

The son jumped out and began a high-stepping jog through the muck. The closer he got, the more curious the bumper looked. It had something hooked to it. Something pale pink and sprouting outward softly, slightly coiled, like a pig's tail. He then looked into the water.

"Mom! There's a truck down there!"

"Oh, Lord," the mother said, she had her phone to her cheek, baggy of trail mix in her other hand.

The son tossed his wallet and cellphone behind him, and before he could give his mother a moment to object, he dove into the cold water. That pale pink...thing—tube?—reached all the way down and inside the truck. He put a hand out and touched it. Rubbery, but not quite. More like flesh...and a peanut...and two corn kernels?

He got to the broken window of the truck and looked in. He exhaled all his held breath in a scream. There were two people inside that truck. One man and one girl. The man had been gutted, his large intestine puddled in his lap next to his stomach and a couple indistinguishable fleshy shapes. His small intestine...it had been removed and attached to the floater. The other end, the girl held it to her lips. She was so small and helpless but sat stoically in a pink cloud with her eyes closed, using her father's intestine like a snorkel.

The son kicked up to the surface for a breath, veering as far as he could from that stretched organ. It took him a moment to recalibrate. He then swam to the shore where his mother awaited him.

"Well?" she said. She had the Ziploc baggy of trail mix. She often ate when she was nervous. It gave her hands purpose.

The son watched the baggy and felt his guts spin. She plucked out a peanut and popped it into her mouth. He began to vomit into the swampy grass and black mud.

BLACKTOP EXECUTION

(2022)

Jim Nixon swallowed a leaden ball as he stumbled forward at the guards' insistence. The rubber of his prison-issue boots was sticking to the hot, hot asphalt below. This was it; this was how it all ended. He fought back tears, didn't want to give his parents the satisfaction of seeing him cry.

"We ain't got all day," one of the guards said and gave Jim a nudge forward.

—

Backpack loaded of everything he had worth saving, Jimmy hurried out the farm laneway toward the highway. He couldn't take it anymore. His father screaming and pulling his ears and pinching his legs. His mother walloping him with wooden spoons, belts, even a cookie sheet when nothing else was handy. Being seventeen and graduated meant he didn't have to take their crap anymore. Never again.

A Peterbilt rig pulled over and the driver shoved open the shotgun door while leaning on the seat, and said, "Where ya heading?"

The answer was anywhere but there. It wasn't easy, and the $700 he'd saved didn't go far in the city, but he found a job. After a handful of years, Jimmy had become Jim and was staring his future dead in the face.

Unfortunately, the cube truck was out of his budget by about half. With that truck, he could quit working the appliance delivery job and become the master of his future. Anything a body wanted moved, he'd move it.

"Thinking of taking out a loan," Jim said to his girlfriend,

Megan. "I swear, it's like being back on the farm, that numbskull Wayne yelling at me all day."

They were sitting at the rusty and peeling Formica table in the dining crevice of their one-bedroom apartment. Megan was pushing macaroni noodles in red sauce around her plate, eyes on the motion like it was the Moon Landing.

"Something wrong?" Jim said.

Megan took a deep, deep breath. "I'm pregnant," she said, exhaling the breath around the words.

"Oh."

"Twins."

"Oh, oh no," Jim said and rubbed his scalp. He needed that truck now or he'd never get it. His savings would fly away on baby stuff and he'd be stuck under that sonofabitch boss until Kingdom Come.

Unless...

"Hey, Jason, it's Jim." Jim had taken his cellphone into the bathroom so Megan wouldn't hear him—she'd already kiboshed the idea of buying his own truck, starting his own company, building his own future.

"Jimmy, what's happening?" Jason said. Jason was Jason Nixon and was Jim's older brother by four years. He'd stayed on at the farm, until their parents sold. Jason got his inheritance early.

Jim did too, but of course, his was $0.

"Had an idea. Want to go into business together, as partners?" Jim said, and despite that it meant he'd have his own business, butterflies of worry began to bounce around his guts.

—

"Get the lead out," Jamie said as he leaned against the wrought iron fence of a customer's new home. "I tell ya, that kid is lazy as a housecat."

Jim had to clench his jaw not to yell at his brother. From day one, Jamie had acted like he was in charge because he was older, had in fact, acted very much like their father used to on the farm.

Once everything was loaded into the home, they were back in the truck, rolling to Jamie's to drop him off; the truck sat nights outside Jim and Megan's apartment. Jim had cooled down but had to say something.

"You know you aren't the boss of this operation."

Jamie, in the passenger's seat, blew out a puff of steam from his vape pen. "Somebody's got to be."

"Nope. Partners. Means starting tomorrow, we do equal lugging."

Jamie huffed. "Lazy Jimmy, always trying to get other people to do his work."

"My name's Jim, and if I recall correctly, you spent half the day trying to impress the customer while she spent half the day trying to stay upwind of your bad breath."

Jamie dropped the vape pen to his lap and spun in his seat. He grabbed Jim's thigh with a vise-grip pinch and twisted. "You always were lazy."

Jim grabbed Jamie's hand and slammed the brakes, the truck rocking and rattling as straps and empty boxes tumbled about the cube. "You pinch me again and I swear to god."

Jamie sat back in his seat. "Way I see it, this operation's nothing without me. You couldn't buy the truck on your own. You can't move a couch on your own. You'll never get nothing going on your own. You ran away from the farm 'cause it was work and you gonna run away from this for the same reason."

That night in bed, it hit Jim. His brother didn't want to work at all. No. He wanted to make Jim miserable enough to quit and then sell the damned truck, thinking he'd get all the money. Jamie was a dumb hick, just like their daddy, and he wasn't going to beat Jim, no matter what dirty tricks he pulled.

—

Three weeks later, after Jim spent most of the evening loading the truck for a customer's move the following day, he went looking for his brother. They'd been only a block from the apartment where Jim and Megan lived, and five minutes into loading, Jamie had said, "Jimmy, gotta shit something fierce. I'm gonna run to your place."

Nearly every day there was something, usually it was the need to sit on the can; Jamie had pulled that trick all through their childhood. At lunchtime, Jim rode the whiny elevator up to the ninth floor. The door was unlocked and as soon as he opened it, he heard Megan's familiar high-pitched panting. He stepped into the hallway and saw into the bedroom where his brother had his pregnant girlfriend bent over the new mattress they'd had to buy because since carrying all the extra weight, Megan noticed the lumps and springs in a way that kept her awake.

"Pinch me! Harder!" Megan howled.

Jim backed up, too shocked to do anything else.

—

The following morning, with a truckload of household items, they rolled toward the customer's new home. Jamie was taking huge, crunchy chomps from a Granny Smith apple. "I was thinking," he said around a mouthful, "we sharing so much in the business, might as well share Megan. I think she'd be up for it."

Jim began to tremble from his center outward but said nothing.

Jamie tossed the apple core out his window. "You listening?" He reached over and pulled on Jim's ear the same way their father had. "Talking about expanding the business."

Jim didn't shift, didn't try to pull his head away. "You planning on paying for one of the twins, too?"

Jamie immediately released the ear and put both hands up before him like he was in the middle of an armed robbery. "Whoa, now. I don't want none of that."

As was his norm, Jamie helped with the big, awkward things, and spent the rest of the day gabbing. At one point Jim had heard him say, "He's my little brother. It's a favor to him that I hired him," to the very man who'd set up the appointment with Jim in the first place.

While carting four cartons of books into the huge living room, it hit him: the only logical thing to do about Jamie was to kill him. He'd have the whole truck, the whole business, and his whole girlfriend. With that settled, he instantly felt better about his future.

—

To get away with murder, one needed to plan, needed to act with a clear head, needed to eliminate themselves from the suspect pool.

Anger was a thick red fog as Jim pulled up the laneway to the modular home where Jamie lived. There was no yard, only gravel. The home was located on a parceled section of land that had originally been part of the family farm—their parents had set it up for Jamie even before they retired from farming. Trees surrounded the building and much of the laneway. Such a private, intimate setting to commit murder.

In a flash, Jim felt every pinch, ear pull, and nasty thing his brother had ever said. He put the truck in park in front of Jamie's home.

"Wait a second, those people didn't want a whole box of DVDs. Guess since we're partners, we'll split it down the middle," Jim said.

"I call dibs!" Jamie said and popped from his seat to rush back into the cube behind the truck. He began kicking and tossing empty boxes. "Where the hell—ow!"

Jim had grabbed one of the clamping straps from the fridge moving cart and had latched it onto Jamie's ear. Blood oozed as the teeth of the locking, gator-like clamp took hold. Jim's face broke out into a wild, gleeful smile.

"What's wrong," he began cranking the winch handle to reel in the strap, "don't like your ear pulled?"

"I'm bleeding, cut it out!"

"Okay," Jim said, and instead of helping his brother open the clamp, he turned the handle as fast as he could.

Jamie screamed as he fell, his face tight to the fridge cart. Jim backed away a step as Jamie continued to scrabble against the hold. The flesh around the bottom of his ear had torn, revealing a gap big enough to host a human eyeball. Jim looked around the dim cube and found his next tool.

"Get this off me! Please, Jimmy!"

Jim snatched up a twenty-foot strap and played out the entire length. He then ringed one of the hooks through the middle belt loop at the back of Jamie's pants—the man had ceased screaming and was fingering around the clamps, feeling for the release, finally having some of his wits back. Jim dropped the other end of the strap by the big door and then sprinted through the cube to the driver's door and outside. He stepped down and around back. It appeared Jamie was just about free.

For now.

Jim took the second hook and attached it to a hole on the inside of a tire rim. Jamie had freed himself and was sitting in the back of the cube, unaware a second act was underway.

"Jimmy, you just about ripped my fucking ear off."

Jim got back into the truck and looked over his shoulder at his brother and said, "Oops," before starting the truck. He pounded the gas after putting it into drive. The strap wound quickly and launched Jamie out the back, pulling him ass-first into the spinning wheel. His screams were intense, piercing. Jim did three big ovals in the lot in front of the home before stopping to check the progress of his brother's murder.

"Jimmy," Jamie gasped, dusty and bloody and busted all over.

Jim bent close to his brother. "What happened?" he said and before the man could answer, Jim stuck an index finger into the now accessible ear canal. "Say, does that hurt?"

Jamie was wailing, his voice banking off the surrounding trees and echoing back. Jim sighed and got back into the idling truck. He put it into reverse and crunched over his brother, the variety of snaps sending warm and fuzzies all through him. He killed the engine and got out, smiling widely enough to make his cheeks ache.

Then he heard them. Sirens.

Then he saw a drape shift within the house. Megan.

—

Trying out new things was the only way to keep the world from going stale. Nobody wanted to see rockets blast off anymore. Nobody cared about great leaps in medicine anymore. Nobody gathered to watch a death penalty play out anymore.

Or they hadn't.

"Jim Jacob Nixon, you have been tried before a judge and found guilty by a jury of your peers. Do you have any last words?"

"This is wrong," Jim said, trying to keep the acid in his guts from streaming up his throat.

"Kill the bastard!" Jamie Nixon Sr. shouted.

The crowd, and what a fine crowd it was, cheered.

"Jim Jacob Nixon, for the crime of murder via motor vehicle, you have been sentenced to suicide by motor vehicle."

Jim peered out at the slightly curving bridge with no guardrails or shoulders. It looked hot and sticky, but not sticky enough to help him make it. If he managed to clear the mile stretch, his crime would be forgiven, but dammit, the bridge wasn't even as wide as the buggy convertible he'd be driving. His wheels would be half off at all times; still, it was possible.

"Come on, then," he said, nerving himself up.

Once to the buggy—four wheels, an engine, a seat, and a steering wheel—he saw the drop beneath the bridge. It had to be 300 feet, maybe more. The guards put him behind the wheel and uncuffed him.

"Hey, wait," he said, kicking around, discovering there was no gas or brake pedal. He shook his head. *Fuck.* Maybe he could do it, just maybe—"Hey!" He brought his hands up, trying to fight the guard pulling the hood over his head and clamping it to his coveralls. "I can't see!"

"That's the point, you lazy shit!" Josephine Nixon shouted.

Much of the big crowd laughed.

The guards stepped back and the buggy immediately began rolling forward. Jim put his hands on the wheel and tried to envision the bridge, thinking, *if there's any fairness in the universe, I'll make—*

"Nonononononono!"

DELIVERY

(2022)

Charlene Wainwright sighed after hearing her much older husband's voice play through the intercom speaker in her private den. She'd been fixing herself a cosmo while flicking through Instagram posts on her iPhone.

"Coming," she said as she held the TALK button.

—

Dallas Farrish had only the insulated Domino's Pizza bag in hand and his wits in his head. The prepaid order was a little odd, but the tip included was fantastic enough that he didn't ask any questions. He simply hopped onto his scooter and zoomed across the city and into the crumbling, poorly lit industrial section. Industry had abandoned that part of the world back in the '90s, leaving behind nothing but urban blight.

Dallas was twenty-six, he had five semesters of a college degree in zoology, had been kicked off the state gymnastics team for substance abuse—marijuana—and had been working as a delivery man for Domino's Pizza for four months, feeling unmoored and cheated by life. Pot was legal in half the civilized world, almost, probably.

Every day he thought about quitting the pizza delivery gig and leaving town for someplace in need of an agile zoologist with just not quite enough education. And never had he thought more about this than he had tonight.

He'd passed through a gated area after speaking to a faceless man via a rusty intercom device at a security gate. The gate closed behind him as he buzzed onward, into the hanger-like building. Once inside, spotlights lit, and a huge garage door rattled down behind him. All around him were food and package delivery vehicles...and the bones and uniforms of their drivers.

"Uh oh," he said and then hushed up when he heard the first growl.

Ambling from the shadows was a woman with grey skin and blood crusted around her mouth and hands. She was naked and one of her breasts had been torn clean off, revealing blackened muscles and veins and arteries that pumped a viscous golden fluid, which oozed from some of her pores. The woman's eyes were pearls in a sea of gore.

"That's a zombie," he said, and didn't need most of a zoologist's education to make that distinction. He withdrew his cellphone—no bars. He turned to his right and saw a group of five boys shuffling nearer, looking very much like the woman. "More zombies."

Fight or flight: something an educated person had once labelled human instincts when facing danger, but that smarty pants hadn't considered zombies. When it came to zombies, it was fight *and* flight. He'd seen enough TV and played enough video games to know you can't outrun enemies forever, some of the undead had to become reconstituted dead along the way.

Dallas made a quick sum and counted nine zombies total, not quite an invasion, not a horde, but give them a little time and enough delivery people and, maybe. And just what in the hell was somebody doing inviting delivery drivers—this was not the time for that question.

Now was zombie time.

Nine zombies was bad, but the location wasn't so bad. The building was a hollowed skeleton, all angle iron and uncovered beams. None of it would play nice with the flesh of his palms, but the option was much nicer than the alternative.

Dallas popped off his scooter, letting it clank heavily to the marred cement floor, and reached into his insulated bag. Large pie, mozzarella, sauce, double peperoni, double sausage, double ham...the kind of thing someone feeding zombies might order. He palmed the box and ran for the woman zombie as it appeared no zombies trailed her. One on one was the kind of fight a fit young man could win. His free hand flicked open the pizza box lid and he slammed the pie into the growling woman's face before front rolling beneath her reaching hands. He shot out a donkey kick from behind her and sent her reeling. She came to a stop against another zombie—a huge, hairy man. The pizza must've clouded the undead scent because this great big man sunk great big teeth into the woman's forehead.

"Yikes," Dallas said and switched his attention.

While those two were in an insatiable tango, seven others were trudging in his direction. Dallas looked left, right, up, and higher up yet. Atop a steel beam was the girder skeleton of a second floor—the floorboards were gone, leaving behind a series of makeshift monkey bars. A long chain hung from the ceiling and was affixed to the beam. The end featured a hook big enough to total a Mitsubishi Mirage with a single strike.

Dallas jumped up from where he'd knelt since front rolling and donkey kicking, and sprinted toward the beam, narrowly skirting one outstretched set of hands.

Did undead fingernails keep growing?

His sneakers slid on the cement floor before he thumped into the beam. An *oogh* sound rose from his chest and leapt from his mouth. Wits intact, he reached up and latched his bent fingers into the backside of the beam. It was inch-thick T-bar steel. He pulled with his arms and kicked his feet as if pedalling against gravity. There, dangling, he played monkey for ten seconds as the zombies formed a trailing line, as if trying to do Dallas a favor.

"Mindless," he said, the word breathy but hopeful.

Once he passed the latched portion of the chain and the enormous hook, he wrapped his legs around the beam—the steel biting painfully into his flesh—and hung upside down. The hook was so heavy he had to squeeze his thighs in a way that made his muscles threaten to give out as he worked at the chunky bolt that was currently keeping the chain from dropping.

Dallas grunted, "Let go, you son—"

The hook released and the heavy steel worked like a wrecking ball as it swung at the small horde. It missed all but one, clipping that boy in the shoulder and sending him flat. The chain swung by and then arced back, this time completely on target. Five zombies shot out to the sides like bowling pins while the one closest to center rode the hook like a ski lift. It smashed into a postal truck, making a black and gold gore smear up the side of the clean white panel wall.

Only one zombie had arisen after the beating, but others would soon stand, and the pizza eater might've cannibalized one zombie and done him a real' handy favor, but was still playing for the undead side, as proven by growling up at Dallas. A second zombie stood, this one missing an arm, gold ooze spurting free— obviously a zombie's heart still beat. A third, this one simply smashed and crawling along, but not useless.

Dallas drank in the scene and put three steps together like an airborne floor routine. He flipped over on the post he'd clung to, straining his back as close to flat as it would go before grabbing hold and kicking out. He regained his upward motion and shimmied higher. Once almost to the thirty-foot ceiling, he leapt toward what appeared to be plumbing pipe about twelve feet away; just big enough to hold him and just small enough to get a good grip on.

His aim was perfect, but the pipe crumbled beneath his weight before his momentum even halved. The goal had been to get enough impetus to reach the postal truck, then slip inside and hope for keys, before finally smashing through the big door, but that didn't happen. He came crashing straight down, rusty bits of pipe still in his hands.

"Agh!" he moaned after nailing the cement—the fall had been about three yards to the floor from the busted pipe. He rolled off his back and pushed to his feet, despite the pain. He scanned the room and recognized he'd need a weapon before he could even imagine an escape route now.

The sonofabitching things were moving, were in fact almost upon him, stinking decay and drooling mouths, blood crusted and single-minded. On the floor by his feet was an Amazon package. With no other option, he scooped it up and tossed it at the closest zombie's face. The skinny woman didn't move to block it. With her momentarily blinded, Dallas slammed out his foot. The zombie tipped back, but not as far as Dallas had hoped. He'd been going for a second round of zombie bowling, pinning them, giving him an opportunity to jump over them, but they were upright and coming for him and all he had for comfort was a cinderblock wall behind him.

It hit him again: who ordered the pizza?

He broke to his right, sneakers squeaking beneath him. There was a shadowy space under a stairwell, and he had to hope for the best. He thumped heavily against a wall he'd anticipated coming a little deeper into the shadow. Behind him, their breath blowing the hair at the back of his neck, the zombies closed in.

"Dammit!" Dallas shouted and turned swinging out elbows and feet as he continued in reverse until his butt hit something solid but moving.

A door.

He turned once again and sprinted blindly. The floor disappeared beneath him. His hands scrabbled for purchase of anything while his legs readied for a landing. Another wall came at him through the darkness and his fingers found a ledge. The zombies that had chased him pitched down into the hole with great streaming growls.

Dallas didn't hear them land.

Before he had a chance to consider what was below, he popped his feet up to his hands with an experienced jerk. He straightened, his face to the cool wall. Hands up, he pawed around for something, anything. There was nothing. He shuffled on his toes to the right, hands steadily feeling for hidden opportunities or pitfalls. Above him, he discovered another ledge, a wider one. He gripped it and began pulling himself up, realizing at that moment, unless the other drivers of those delivery vehicles were revered gymnasts—at least formally—they were zombie chow...or chow to whatever lurked at the bottom of the pit below him.

He stood and suddenly had scads of space, comparatively. Not far above him was another ledge, above that, the red of what he hoped was an EXIT sign. Up he went.

———

Edgar Wainwright II, retired General turned private contractor, had first suspected his wife of infidelity three years ago—they'd been married less than four—but he hadn't had any proof until having a nineteenth security camera installed in his mansion, one his wife, Charlene, did not know about.

He hadn't seen much beyond an ass pumping and his wife's legs and arms sticking out as if she'd been shocked into orgasm. However, there were other bits and pieces that came together— obviously Charlene had warned her lover about the cameras and where to stand to avoid showing his face, even his clothing; it was dumb luck that this newest addition to the security system had only caught the act, not the actor.

The deliveries dated to well before the sex, but he couldn't be certain which of the drivers had been delivering their package into his wife. The solution became simple once the possibility couldn't be narrowed down. That rung of the social ladder had always been expendable anyway.

———

The sound of night was almost as welcome as the red light from the EXIT sign. The door closed heavily behind him and he reached back, playing his fingers across the smooth, handle-less steel. Dallas swallowed down a fresh sampling of fear. He was outside, right? All he had to do was find a road, right?

"Where's the moon then?" he whispered, and as if replying, he heard the crack of thick wood. He put his back to the door and moved sideways, this time to his left. There was a wooden crosser board at the small of his back. Despite the sheer darkness he fully understood that he hadn't made it outside, no matter the change in atmosphere and soundtrack.

Snap!

He spun and faced the wall, feeling for another crosser of wood. He found one at his eyelevel. He gripped it and brought his feet up, the toes of his sneakers pressing against a surface that was stiff and yet subtly moveable. The first thought was smooth sheet metal.

Not twenty feet behind him—though sounding even closer—an incredible roar rang out, like a tiger, but much, much bigger. And he would know, tigers were one of his favorite cat breeds. Blindly, he scrambled higher, assuming the crossers would be there at regular intervals.

His head struck the ceiling, nearly toppling him. Below, the big, roaring beast scratched at the wall, claws playing nails against chalkboard. Dallas winced as he reached one hand up to pat the cool ceiling. Twice as regular, the crossers were there, challenging him to monkey-walk upside down.

"Then what?" he whispered, even as he slipped out of his shoes. This kind of operation demanded the use of his toes. "Then what?" he repeated as he put the burden of his weight on his fingers and toes.

The growls and roars were accompanied by scratching claws, slight rhythmic changes in volume, as if the beast was circling, perhaps even jumping. Each animalistic cry pushed Dallas to work a little harder.

Something touched his back and he gasped; certain he was caught. It didn't move. He reached behind him. A branch. He was in an animal enclosure, the scene painting itself in his mind. He lowered his feet, crouching, testing the branch without releasing the ceiling.

"Okay," he said when the branch bore zero sway.

The direction of the roar changed. If there was a branch at the ceiling, there was a trunk at the floor. That was bad math. Dallas let go his right hand and reared back. He punched blindly upward. Solid, but sprinkling something down upon him. He punched again. The cuts on his knuckles burned. That burn was a beautiful possibility. Glass. He punched three more shots, the beast breathing not five feet below.

Silence reigned and Dallas knew the beast was about to pounce. One hand wasn't doing it. He lowered his left hand and made fists just above his head, launching himself up. The glass ceiling shattered, shards raking along his arms. As he passed onto the rooftop, something nipped his right foot.

"Shit!"

He began sliding in his socked feet like grease on a hot skillet. Overhead the moon played down, banking off the tinted surface below him as he slipped, his cut hands and arms squealing on the glass as he streaked toward the edge of the building. His toes slammed into an eavestrough gulley and he spiraled sideways, his right elbows slipping into the gap heavily, painfully. His body tried to jerk over as bones in his right arm cracked, the sound ringing through the quiet industrial block.

"Agh!"

He kicked and swung, slamming his body against gravity to keep from flying over the side. He glanced down into the shadows around the building to a collection of golf carts. The drop to their stiff canopy rooftops was only ten, twelve feet. A doable amount.

Dallas turned, his legs dangling. He was about to jump when a cat-like shriek rang out. The animal had made it to the roof and was scrabbling against gravity with its incredible claws.

"Smilodon," he whispered—sabre-toothed tiger to the layman—and dropped to, and then through the canopy roof of a golf cart.

Within seconds the beast crashed after him. There was a tunnel amid the row of machines through the crushed framework and Dallas took it until reaching the front golf cart. He felt around the dash for the key, and then between his legs. Behind him, the beast was roaring, likely as much in anger as in pain. The key wasn't there. Dallas looked to the machine to his left, nothing, and then right. Glinting like a rapper's platinum smile was a key in the ignition.

Dallas shuffled. The roof caved in above him as he turned the key. The engine lit and he floored the gas pedal. The cart slammed backwards. The beast rocked, tumbling into the tight gap between rows. Dallas turned the direction handle and the cart jerked forward. He glanced back, the beast was galloping, easily moving as fast as the cart.

"Git! Bad kitty!"

The beast leapt, slamming the rear of the cart hard enough to stop all motion. Dallas flew through the open front like a cannonball against a high fence. Woozy, mind in a fog, he pushed up and began to climb as the beast wrestled the cart and its humming engine. The fence kept going, and despite the agony, Dallas kept climbing, his eyes on the beast until razor wire sliced into his forehead.

This would be tricky, but far from impossible. Careful and steady, he picked handholds and footholds. He decided right then and there he was going to quit delivering pizzas.

—

Charlene found Edgar in the theater room. Huge on the screen was the image of a man in an Amazon delivery uniform looking terrified, surrounded by ghoulish freaks.

"What's this?" she said.

Edgar waggled his eyebrows. "I know you've been fucking one of the delivery—" he put up his hand, "don't argue. I installed a fresh new camera in the bedroom, under the bed, pointed at the dresser mirror."

"Oh?" Charlene sipped from her cosmopolitan.

"It's why I had to kill them."

Charlene's eyebrows pushed about as high as they went.

Edgar hit play on a remote and got right into the clip show. One after another, men eaten by zombies, a giant tiger, a fucking sasquatch. Charlene clenched all over seeing it. She knew her husband was into weird military stuff, but this was too much.

"One of them? Or was it this fellow?" Edgar said and switched the video source.

A Domino's Pizza delivery man rolled a crummy dirt bike into a warehouse. The zombies converged, but unlike the others, this man was a damned acrobat. Edgar sat in one of the fifteen seats of the theater. Neither said a word, and when the time came, Edgar used the remote to change camera sources—many of which were in night vision.

Charlene laughed nervously when the man and a massive cat escaped from view through a hole in a roof.

Edgar sneered at her. "Which one was it?"

Charlene leaned on her knees where she sat, and smirked. "None."

"None?"

"Not a one. I knew you were losing your mind, so I had cameras of my own installed."

"What?"

Charlene nodded. "I even asked your guys to clip in a porn scene—an amateur, hidden camera thing that would mimic the angle of your latest installation."

"No."

Still nodding, licking the cosmo from her teeth. "That's right. I even had your old friends from the DOJ monitor things for me. I knew you were going senile, but this," she pointed to the screen, "this is totally fucking wackadoodle."

Edgar looked at the screen. "No." His right hand rubbed at his head and neck. "No."

—

Dallas spent the night in the hospital and awoke to find his bill paid, alongside a note that read,

Sorry for your trouble, hope there's no added charges tacked on my payment.

If you're interested in meeting me, shoot on up to 2340 Cranberry Street, and wear your uniform, I fancy a man in uniform.

Char Wainwright

Dallas thought for a moment. Char at 2340 Cranberry, that was the horny housewife who had a thing for deliverymen. He'd been there once, it couldn't hurt to visit again...he still had the Domino's shirt, pants, and visor.

A GREAT HAND

(2014)

Looking at the right bower, king, and ten trump-suit, and then two off-suit aces would usually put Breanne Lockstadt into a jittery fit trying to conceal her giddiness. On top of it all, she didn't pick the suit. Hell, her partner didn't even pick it. She was looking at a euchre and only three tricks away from victory; no doubt now, she and her partner, Lizzy, had another game in the bag.

But Breanne looked grim, didn't feel good. The cards played out. Breanne and Lizzy took the game with authority, and at least Lizzy was happy.

"What in the hell did you make it on?" Jerome asked his partner, Freddy.

Freddy shrugged. He had a thing for Breanne, which was the point of the four of them getting together. You put four divorcees with adult offspring in a room eight straight weeks with an expectation, something would happen eventually. Winning was so far from the point here.

Jerome and Lizzy had tried their luck, went to bed twice, found it incompatible without a goodly dose of cognac, which meant the door was open should the group take to quicken the drinking during the shuffle.

"What's wrong with you?" Jerome said to Breanne.

They'd known one another since they were kids; he used to watch her sometimes when her parents went out on Saturday nights. It was Breanne's idea to get card games going, maybe find some matches along the way.

Now, though, she was off in her own world, had been most of

the night. Even in victory she hardly paid mind to the scene before her.

Jerome snapped his fingers. "Hey, wake up."

Breanne looked at Jerome with a sad and icy eyes. "I'm going to ask you something and I want you to be as honest, as honest as you could possibly be."

He smiled. "Shoot. I could never lie to you." He tossed a wink at Lizzy.

"When you hit that kid with your car—"

"Whoa now," Jerome said; suddenly things weren't so funny.

"Just, please, answer this."

He lowered his head, Lizzy and Freddy watched Breanne, enthralled.

"You'd been drinking, that's no secret, though the cops didn't say anything...it was a different time." She spoke vacantly, her gaze distant. "But you were masturbating while you drove. You'd just left Rosy Kisses, you'd had a lap dance, tried to pay the girl to blow you. She wouldn't. You offered her three hundred for a handjob, but she just laughed. You got three more lap dances and left the building with a hard on and only one option." Her eyes settled on a bald patch the size of a hockey puck budding on Jerome's scalp.

He blinked. "I never said—"

"But I'm right, right?"

He dropped his head back down, staring at his wrinkled fingers.

"I am right, aren't I?"

"How could you know?" His sadness was palpable.

The accident had been more than a decade ago and he'd moved on. The kid he'd hit didn't get to, but accidents happened and it did no good to ruin his life, so he'd called his brother who worked with the mayor and gave a statement to his cousin in the police department.

"I saw it. I saw it back when you used to babysit me. I didn't recognize you, not until later, then it all came back. I saw it, I never told anyone. I see things and I saw you. Now, tell me, did it happen exactly like that? It's important." Breanne was emphatic.

Jerome seemed to consider his options; it was out there now. He nodded, a weak smile playing on his lips. "I guess you're the only one who hasn't seen my dick, Freddy. Want a peek?"

"Huh, well, that just about ends my night," Lizzy said, her expression a mixture of revulsion and anger. She'd known Jerome only months.

"Wait, we're not through," Breanne said, she reached out a firm hand and sat Lizzy back into her chair. "Lizzy, promise you'll answer honestly."

"I have nothing to hide," Lizzy said, smug.

"Fifteen years ago," Breanne started, and Lizzy's eyes grew wide, "you met a man named Earl, after college. We hadn't seen each other for a couple years. You met Earl and he knocked you up, it was all happy. Earl had a good job and you stayed home getting bigger and bigger. You dated Earl out east, you knew he was married at first, but you thought it was done. At eight months pregnant, Earl explained that he had to get back to his real family, that he loved his wife, it had been just a trial separation. That's what he called it a trial separation, I'm right, aren't I?"

Lizzy's jaw dangled, she snapped it shut; her eyes burned fire, but she didn't answer, didn't need to say a word.

"You got depressed, started drinking like crazy. You wanted to kill the baby in your belly, but the baby came. You and Earl had that whole meatless, hemp clothing, hippie thing going, and you had an unlicensed midwife rather than a doctor. She helped you, she was Spanish, an immigrant; you and Earl thought you were helping the poor by hiring her—before he left you. She came and you delivered a boy and you saw Earl. You saw Earl in his jaw and ears, in his nose and fingers, you saw him in those eyebrows threatening to bush right up even fresh out of the oven."

"Stop," Lizzy said, venom dripping from that monosyllable.

"Wait, I'm right so far, I'm right. You lived in Melvin, out east; nobody had seen you in years. Out there with Earl and then with the baby. You fed the baby cough syrup until it didn't move and then you took your compost bin, filled a bag. Put the baby in the bag with the lettuce ends and apple cores. You put four more bags over it and then you drove all night, north first, then east. You put the bag into a Burger King dumpster, put it inside a bag of garbage to be sure and then you drove home. Here home. You came back. I'm right, right?" Breanne seemed sadder the more she spoke.

"I don't have to listen to this. It never happened, you're a liar and I don't care for it," Lizzy said, her show unconvincing.

"You got a tattoo on your hip, it's tiny, but it has the initials H.C. inside."

Jerome pointed. "She does, too, I've seen it!"

"So what? It means Hobart Carol, my great grandfather," Lizzy said.

"Why would you get your great grandfather's initials on your hip?" Freddy asked, his face pulled askew.

"She and Earl were going to name the baby Shine if it was a girl and Haven if it was a—"

"Heaven!" Lizzy shouted and then covered her mouth a moment before she fled from the room.

The trio listened in silence as Lizzy's engine roared into life beyond the carport's screen door and peeled away down the street. Breanne had created an impasse, she looked at Freddy, and he waited. She'd only recently met him.

"Well?" he asked, visibly shaken.

"Yeah, what about Freddy?" Jerome said.

Breanne shook her head slowly.

"Goddammit," Jerome said and stood, pushed his chair under the table. "If you two don't mind, I'm going to drink myself into a stupor and try to remember how to live with myself, and I'd rather do it alone, so..." he said, trailing with purpose.

Freddy shot to his feet. Breanne was reluctant but followed.

"I'm sorry, Jerome," she said and then took her leave.

Freddy had played the gentlemen up until that moment, holding doors and taking arms. They got into his car without ceremony. They sat a moment, unmoving, before Breanne took his hand. He quickly snatched it away.

"Don't worry," she said, "I probably would've seen it by now, if there was anything to see, I'd have seen it."

"Just as well," he started the car and backed out onto the street.

Breanne lived on the north side, fifteen minutes from Jerome's bungalow. Tears flowed down her face, and she rubbed her hands on her legs continually. Freddy finally looked at her and quickly pulled over.

"Easy now, easy now," he said, rubbing her back.

"I have to do something, and I need you to drive me. I'll lose the will if I have to drive myself. Please, it's important," she said after she'd finally managed to slow her gasps.

"What is it?"

"I can't tell. I just need you to drive me. You need to drive me to Twenty-four Elgin Ave."

"Why though?"

"I promise, I'll tell you everything, but after."

"Who lives there?"

"I'll tell you after, this is important, please." She took his hand again. "Please, Freddy, I need to go to that address."

Freddy let go of Breanne's hand, looked over his shoulder, and U-turned across the four-lane street. It was barren; traffic usually was after dark at that end of town. The closer they got to Elgin, the thicker the traffic grew. It was a moderate-income area, moderate leaning to lower.

"This one," Breanne said. She pointed at a home with chipping yellow paint on plastic siding, a roof with patches of moss growing over many shingles.

"This one?" Freddy stared in confusion at the slummiest building on the block.

"I'll be back in five minutes," Breanne said, her voice quavered. She leaned over to kiss Freddy.

Freddy watched through the passenger's side window. Breanne walked up to the door, fished through her purse a moment, and then opened the door. Then she was gone. Freddy sat up straight, a helpless manikin in his own automobile.

"What are we doing here?" he said under his breath.

A few minutes after she'd gone inside, the answer came in two loud bangs. Lights ignited in many of the neighbors' homes and Breanne jogged out the front door.

She hadn't even got her legs inside the car before she shouted, "Drive! Drive, damn you, drive!"

"What did you do?" Freddy said.

It was all over her face, the message in the blasts, the tool of her crime still in her hand, black and shining under the streetlights. She said nothing. Silently, Freddy drove five minutes before he pulled into a dark parking lot running along the pier. The place was busy with vehicles, their lights playing by like it was any old night, like Breanne hadn't just committed murder.

"What did you do?" he said.

"I had to. I've known for years, but I couldn't do it until I knew what I knew was true. But I saw and once I saw, I knew. I saw the face and it all clicked. I've known for thirty-five years he would do it, but I just couldn't, not until I was sure. Part of me weighed the values and no matter what, it couldn't match, I mean..." Breanne cried into her hands.

"What? Who?" Freddy rubbed her warm back.

"He was small when I first saw it, and I didn't recognize. I thought maybe I was just imagining things. But, but then that man, the man with all the changes in mind. I can't remember his name, I'm all fuzzy, he's a senator or something." Breanne shook, her entire body head-to-toe vibrated.

"Albert Milton?" Freddy said.

Albert Milton was the next big thing. Prime Minister someday, maybe, likely. A man leaning well left of center. A man who would change how the country treated wealth and poverty, ownership and retribution.

"Yeah, he was going to kill him, I saw it. I saw it when he was just a baby."

"Who?"

"My son, my Eric, my son. I thought if I did things differently over the years, gave him extra love, put him in better schools, put him first, put him before everything... Walter left me because Eric needed me, but it didn't work and I tried to say he wouldn't, couldn't. But he told me he was planning a trip and the memory, the vision, it clicked again. I saw the sign with the name, date, and time. Eric was taking a vacation, staying at the same hotel and I knew, oh god I knew."

"Knew what, you're not making—"

"Knew he was going to kill Milton. My son, my little Eric, was going to kill Albert Milton." Breanne lifted her head, tears streaming her face, cutting lines down the grooves of her wrinkles.

"So, you...?" Freddy fished.

"I had to; I had to, for the good of everybody. I killed him. He was bad. No matter what I did, he was bad. I tried, oh god I tried," Breanne said, her words falling into wet sobs.

Freddy pulled the car back out onto the street. Breanne continued to wail while Freddy drove. Now and then, she glanced through a window, sizing up their locale.

"I can't believe it. You're insane," Freddy said, matter-of-factly.

Breanne lifted her face, eyes hard out the shotgun window. "I lied to you earlier. I saw something the day we met."

He turned in his seat, agog. "What?"

"It was like the others, and I want you to know I don't hold it against you. It's as much my fault as it is yours. Just move on after it happens, it's for the best for me anyway," she said as she rolled down her window and dropped the pistol onto the street.

"What are you talking about?" he stared at her, his foot to the mat, only a block from the police station.

"Just move on, it's for the best. I really liked you, you know?"

Freddy was too consumed to notice the red light he was burning through. In the middle of the intersection, a police cruiser crushed the passenger's side of Freddy's car.

The knock was jarring, his ears rang and his body thrummed. In the seat next to him was Breanne. Glass pebbles sparkled on her shoulders and in her hair. Her brain glistened in the emergency lights through the huge crack in her skull. Her eyes were dead, dead, dead.

Freddy swallowed, very much alive, with a fantastic explanation to give the cops whenever they asked for a statement. But, god, would they believe any of it?

THE REMATCH

(2019)

The deep fryer scent gets lonely on a day off and somehow that makes it stink doubly; partly, maybe, it's the day-old-ness of the grease, or maybe it's the lack of the pizza oven or the popcorn machine, or even the missing aerosol disinfectant shoe spray scent that has the overall smell awry. The quiet vacancy of the bowling alley is equally off-putting, though in sound and sight rather than scent.

The Patricks came second place last year in the league championship.

It had been good sort of league, fair and competitive, a point solidified by Patrick Morrison's brother, Corey, being the owner of the joint. Though I guess a fair outcome was the one thing that had gone out the window last season, at least in the finals. For the first time in fifteen years, The Patricks were up for the Slam-O-Rama Cup against The Smiling Skulls—a group of bankers and advisers who'd never had a team before and only really showed up as contenders come playoffs.

To hear Patrick Marlowe tell it, the ref was basically accepting cash right there on the spot, claiming line violations and awarding The Smiling Skulls what amounted to two mulligans because of unforeseen distraction: "Gave'm re-shoots 'cause the crowd was hyped!"

I didn't tell that I was there.

There, but not in the league. Four years ago, I'd come to town for a spot at the local graphics shop as a layout and design guy. Bowling has been my game since I was ten and my grandpa took me to the alley two towns over and had me rolling balls that seemed as big as watermelons.

"Smug as you can guess and slick as grease," Patrick Shelby told me the same Saturday afternoon the offer had come. "Especially that captain they have."

Shelby had come up to me after I'd finished the third solo game in a row—high that day was two-sixty, so I was rolling—and he asked if he'd heard correctly that my name was Patrick. I told him yeah and he filled me in on a series of events that I knew already but was polite enough to let him tell.

The crowd was big, drunk, and loud on the day The Patricks and The Smiling Skulls went head-to-head for bragging rights and a name on the trophy. The crowd was on The Patricks' side almost wholly, and I'll admit, at first, I was rooting for the underdogs. Though to consider it in afterthought, those bankers weren't really underdogs, cheating or not, the world was pushing for them. They wore matching Dexter The 9 shoes in black and red—retail close to four hundred a pair—Nike Dry-Fit pants in charcoal, black custom H5G shirts with the SS logo embroidered in Red on the front right breast and their names stitched on the left, and the logo huge on the back. They all had fine, pale brown leather ball bags—customized with The Smiling Skulls logo patched small on the side—and Brunswick Quantum balls that looked like milky planets, influx while rolling. They were thin and clean cut; in their twenties with blond and dirty blond hair, trimmed short and styled with gel. They looked like they could model for a university date rape warning pamphlet. And to top it off, they were okay all season, but killing it in the playoffs.

But the time had come and Patrick Morrison threw thirteen strikes in a row—going back to the first round of the playoffs—before the match started and opened up The Patricks' run with a fourteenth consecutive winding knockout toss that crashed a symphony every bowler knows by ear. I remember thinking he should've been pro throwing with that much boogie on it.

Then the oddities started to go on and to the crowds' defense, they cooperated with the red-faced, sweaty, old referee who was actually voicing issues.

Even with the bull calls, The Patricks were only nine pins shy of taking the championship in the final frame. Of course, Morrison was up, his streak had continued and he was about to bury The Smiling Skulls and earn his first championship.

The crowd fell to a hush. Morrison lined up his shot, gaze like a panther's eying an easy kill.

He started into the delivery and then out of nowhere, someone sounded off an air horn and the ball jumped straight for the gutter as it left Morrison's hand.

Everyone looked for the culprit and then to the ref—he'd given Bobby Bannon, the captain of The Smiling Skulls, two re-do shots for noise coming from the crowd. The ref wasn't moving, just sweating and waiting for the next shot.

Morrison shrugged it off and smirked. This was his, that much was blatant in his expression, in the way he carried the ball. Like he knew his destiny. Like he'd seen the outcome written in stone.

He lined it up, licked his lips, and threw the most perfect shot in the history of championship shots, but just before the ball reached the pins, the ref blew his whistle.

"Toe over the line," the man said and turned to the newcomers who'd just stolen the championship.

Everybody else, me included, looked to Patrick Morrison's feet. His toes were back a few inches, but I supposed, at the time anyway, that he could've, maybe, lost track of where he was.

The crowd was crickets aside from the hooting young men. Then Patrick Simpson's voice rang out, "Somebody call a doctor!" Morrison was on the floor, twitching.

That was two months before I joined The Patricks and exactly ninety days before I showed up at the Slam-O-Rama on August 3rd. A sign written in magic marker stated the alley was closed that day for maintenance.

I stepped inside and everything looked normal, just un-busy.

Patrick Shelby, the new captain after Morrison's passing, told me every year, a week before the new season started, the finalists from the season prior had a fun match. I got there last of my teammates, but long before the first of The Smiling Skulls arrived and that same red-faced, sweaty, old ref.

"Ready for another beat down?" Donald Kearns said to me, obviously not noticing that I was new and had a blank yellow shirt instead of a team shirt. I recognized his face, not only from the alley, but also from the paper; he sold private commercial mortgages. Rumor around town was that he also laundered money, but people always talk.

Moments later, a man named Peter Harper and a man named Watson Hillman came through the door in their team colors. It was a couple minutes before the ref showed up and a few more minutes before The Smiling Skulls started texting their captain.

I'd sat under the lane four scoring monitor, shoes tied and ready to toss when the owner, Corey Morrison, went over and said, "You ready to start?"

"Bobby's not here," Watson Hillman said.

Corey sneered. "I got shit to do, put him last. He can hop in when it's his shot, once he gets here." He turned then and stared down lane three.

Shelby got up, tossed, left the seven standing, but cleaned it up with his next throw. Kearns looked to his teammates, stood, and absolutely slammed a strike—a shot he was lucky he didn't split between the seven and the ten. A shiver rode my back and, baby, it was on.

—

I'd shot fourth and eighth, and to my credit, I was the only Patrick throwing strikes. So Shelby whispered to me that I was also going to be throwing the tenth frame.

I shrugged, but I was pretty pumped about it.

Watson Hillman stood up then, looked to his teammates as if

hoping to delay longer. Their captain still hadn't answered any text messages and that had them sweating. He was obviously their best and they'd left as many open frames as we had, though were still up by two points.

When none of his teammates said anything, Hillman grabbed his milky white ball, his initials inlaid in gold by the finger holes, and started to his position. He closed his eyes, kissed the ball, and tossed. There was hardly any flare, like a good rookie might throw—kind of shot that gets lucky about half the time, but if there's a split, he's probably screwed. He wasn't, the pins crashed and Shelby hopped up. A grin had spread and I just couldn't figure it. He was having a pretty mediocre match and we were getting further down every time he threw.

Up, ball in hand, he hardly paused and hooked from right to left with way too much drift, leaving the one, three, five, six, nine, and ten standing. He stood by the mechanical ball return. His ball burned up from the dark recesses of the machine and along the rubber track a half-minute later. He spun on his shoes, almost like a dance move, almost like he was giddy to lose, and pumped back without eying and knocked down everything but the king pin.

I tried not to look at him, but I was a little frustrated.

One of The Smiling Skulls actually hooted.

Kearns was having a good game and nearly totaled us with a strike. I whispered a thanks to the strong and firm ten pin still standing. He cleaned it and I stood.

I was going for my personal turkey—though it didn't really count that way as there'd been a ton of crap shots between my two—so I took my time. I eyed and envisioned and exhaled a deep breath. I wound back and knew instantly that I'd put too much on it.

I closed my eyes and listened to the lackluster crash.

It could've been worse. A lily is doable, it's not the coffin nails of a seven-ten, but you still need to rely on a messenger pin to bounce one side to the other.

"Look at that sour apple," one of The Smiling Skulls said.

I went to the ball return to wait, not acknowledging the uncouth sonofabitches on the other side of the aisle.

The ball return was a steel hump that jutted from the waxy floor. The paint is obviously refreshed often—an inoffensive tan hue in high gloss—but the track is sometimes slow and the design reveals its age.

My ball returned and I readied myself, psyched myself, and began.

The air horn sounded and I barely managed to keep hold of my ball. I spun and sneered at those high finance buggers. They tried to look innocent and confused, but one had his hand in his ball bag. I turned to my teammates and they all wore grins. I couldn't figure it. This was it, if I didn't clean up and then strike, we had to rely on at least one gutter ball from the opposition and that wasn't likely.

I faced the lane and took a deep breath. I threw quickly so as to put off the timing of anymore interruptions. Muscle memory was my only hope and my body knew what it was doing. The drift carried my ball from center-right to far-left, smacking the outside of the seven pin and sending it on an expedition, into the five, into the ten.

It was my turn to hoot. My ball burped from the return and the air horn sounded as I was in mid-delivery, but I'd been expecting it and was still riding the high from crushing the split. The crash was Beethoven and the groan following from the other side was Mozart.

We were up, though not exactly safe, in the last frame and I could be happy about my game. My eyeballs burned into Kearns who was having the best game of his teammates and was there therefore tossing the cleanup round.

"Hey, where's my ball?" he said.

The Smiling Skulls looked over and I looked over, but I don't think any of my teammates bothered. They sat there grinning.

"Hey, buddy, send out my ball!" Kearns shouted this down the lane.

"Oops, coming right up!" Corey Morrison shouted, obviously somewhere in the pit.

The ball return seemed to chug then and we all turned to face Kearns as he had his hand out to stop his ball. The burp was wet and a subtle, unusual pop followed. Kearns stood dumbly for a couple seconds, his hand blocking Bobby Bannon's wide-eyed, severed head.

"No fuck, no fuck," Kearns mumbled and draped his body over an empty seat—cushioned, molded plastic—before falling to the floor after a loud *thwack!*

From where I was, and by the way he'd turned, I could see into his head. The bone was glaringly white amid the reds and the pink meat of his brain.

Kearns' eyes rolled and his tongue jutted in and out of his mouth like a snake in slow motion. "Oy-oy-oy," he said. "Oy-oy-oy."

The blood from the wound had sprayed and dripped through the ball return track and onto the fine waxy hardwood beneath. My gaze left the hole in the skull and zeroed in on those tiny splashes, not fully comprehending.

Kearns' *Oys* fell away into mumbles.

A moist thump pulled me from my reverie and I looked up to Corey Morrison wielding a bloody bowling pin like he was a caveman taking a bride from one of the trashy pulp movies from the 'sixties. The second shot with the bowling pin was what stopped Kearns, dislocated his jaw, made his eyes all whites.

My teammates grabbed for anything, one Patrick reared back a glass beer stein, another Patrick had his can of shoe disinfectant—his index finger on the trigger—another Patrick hefted his ball above his head like a gorilla with a stone. The young men didn't know what to do, they were on their feet, arms raised, jazz hands-ing and saying "Nonononono." I was utterly dumbfounded. The wails and the blood, the wet smacks and the crunching of bone. Corey Morrison kept shouting, "This is for Patrick! This is for Patrick!" and Kearns' face became a chunky smear like a melted ice cream sundae with all the fixins.

Watson Hillman became my next focus as the scream that left his mouth was high and shrill. Patrick Simpson had the shoe disinfectant aimed and was firing a sudsy wash over the kid's face. Patrick Marlowe cocked the heavy glass beer stein behind his head and thumped it three times off Hillman before it shattered. He used the edge and started cutting the unconscious figure while Patrick Simpson disinfected the wounds.

The broken glass also activated Peter Harper and he hopped the row of seats and started for the door. "Where the hell he think he's going?" Patrick Shelby asked and reared back with his bowling ball—a sparkly Brunswick that had seen a lot of throws—and pitched it overhand. Twenty feet from our lane and twenty-five feet from the locked exit, Peter Harper flopped face first with the impact of the ball to the back of his head. "Steeeeerike!" Shelby shouted and broke after the fallen man. He began slamming Peter Harper's head into the hardwood floor until crunches joined the smacking sounds.

Silence followed and The Patricks, one-by-one, turned to the ref, who'd been silent, wide-eyed, and shaking ever so slightly at the lip of lane two. My new teammates converged. Corey Morrison dropped the smeary bowling pin he'd held and opened the casing for the ball return—any screws holding it together had obviously been pre-emptively taken out. The steel clanged as it fell. He then grabbed two junior balls from the community-use racks and whipped them down the gutter of lane four. He did it twice more and then turned to me briefly. The look was ice cold and I gripped the underside of my seat, petrified.

"No, guys...they paid me...I needed—no!" My teammates had the ref like a torpedo, his arms pinned at his sides and his legs pinched together. "No! Goddammit! No!"

They carted him to the ball return that had just begun rumbling, activated by the balls Corey Morrison had tossed. The ref pleaded until he screamed, the scalp of his balding head peeled free in the gears like leather. The patch covering his cranium rolled along the track like it was business as usual.

The ref screamed one last time until the bone finally lost to steel and began grinding through the machine. It reminded me of those first bites from a bowl of Corn Flakes. The machine stalled then and short-circuited, sending out three flashes of blue before a greasy smoke floated on air.

Corey Morrison and The Patricks all looked at me then, and I gazed around the room, stupidly. All that remained were four mush puddles and bodies to go with them...and a head still on the ball return track. I swallowed and they walked slowly, eyes burning into me like they were slasher creeps. My heart began dancing triple time and I tried to speak. Shelby grabbed a duffle bag from the floor and pulled out a box from within.

"Guys. Guys." I'm not sure if I actually said this or just mouthed it. "Guys."

"We can do this one of two ways. That way," Shelby nodded at the ref's corpse, "or this way." He tossed the blood-smeared box at me.

—

It's been seven months since The Smiling Skulls disappeared and the round robin round of the playoffs are about to begin. The decision I'd made to keep my mouth shut comes to mind now and then, guilt-tinged, but when I think about opening that box and seeing my moniker on that The Patricks' shirt breast, I know I made the right choice.

We're good, maybe not good enough to pull off a championship, but if we get on a roll, you never know.

CLASS OF MEMORY LANE

(2018)

8:52 PM – Seven Minutes Late: Denise and Glenn

"What are we doing here anyway?" Denise asked.

She and her boyfriend Glenn were in the basement of the long closed elementary school, catching vibes of yore, stomping down memory lane on a flashlight glow. They were on their way to the classroom where they'd all first met, feet smacking on a spilled sticky liquid left by the main entrance.

Back before the north side caved in, there was another door that put half of the basement on the ground level, right by the doors to the kindergarten class. That side was no longer accessible, but someone before them had peeled back the boarded doors of the main entrance. They'd also spilled that damned tacky mess.

And of course, the others arrived before Denise and Glenn.

Glenn was a man who did not leave the house without his hair and clothing coming *correct*. Leather jacket, tight Guess jeans, N.W.A t-shirt, ankle-high brown leather boots, and his hair tight at the sides and puffed up top beneath a mousse shell.

Upon meeting Glenn, most people assumed him gay.

He took it as a compliment.

It was too dark in the dusty old school to see his attire and he'd become pouty about Denise's mood. Annoyed boredom was catching.

"Just a little bit, okay? Those were five pretty informative years for all of us," he said.

Denise held the flashlight. The old wax on the stone floor had only a modicum of luster left in its finish. It banked the glow in a soft yellow swatch. The door to the kindergarten classroom yawned ahead about twenty feet away.

"I hardly remember anything before the fifth grade," Denise said.

He didn't either, but he loved nostalgia, loved how cool it was to be nostalgic about the 'eighties. There were three *Stranger Things* t-shirts in his closet and he didn't really like the show that much. He'd never admit that because it was cool and fun. And he'd bought that book, *Ready Player One,* and fully intended on reading it, eventually. Maybe even before the movie came out. Once, he even sought out a used copy of *It,* but decided against reading it since it was so damned big. *It* was before his time anyway.

"So, history remembers you."

"That doesn't make sense."

"Oh get over it. We'll have a few beers and head out for something a little livelier. Just play along for now," Glenn said, hushed as they came to stand only a few feet from the door.

Through the halls, blown debris and loose sheets of paper collected at the edges where walls met floor. The walls were soft stone and barren. The cork ceiling was off and on gone, animals and dampness deteriorating in a strangely particular manner. Wires like veins came and disappeared overhead. Denise didn't shine the light up there after the initial look.

The wires seemed to move in the shadows and something moving aside from their party was not something she cared to consider.

Glenn was no better. Three times already, a shadow brought a scream to the base of his throat. Luckily, it had yet to leap free.

"To hell with livelier, after this I'm going home, sitting in the tub, watching something featuring Yummy Gosling, Yummy Hemsworth, or Yummy Idris. Might even lock the door."

"Girl, you nasty," Glenn said, sassy. There was a time not so long ago that he'd have promised to break down the door and be all the Yummy that she needed, but relationships changed and sparks quieted. Sometimes it was just easier to let doors close and lock.

Denise snorted, withdrew nothing.

They rounded the doorway and stepped in. There were candles at the center of the room, but no other people.

The room itself seemed so very much smaller. A four-tiered down-step separated the toy area from the learning and nap area. The big blocks, the toys, and every little chair was gone. The teacher's desk remained against a far wall, bare, unlike every active kindergarten teacher's desk in the history of kindergarten teachers' desks.

"Hello?" Glenn said. "Robbie? Vin? Sarah? Susan?"

"Anybody here?" Denise shouted. A tinny, dull echo surrounded them.

They stepped down and to the center of the room where the candles sat as well as a cooler and then a grocery bag of beer cans. The beer was Moosehead, meaning Vin was somewhere near.

"Where are they?" Denise asked.

Glenn understood then. He whispered, "Be ready. They're gonna scare us, pop out of nowhere, grab us, try to get us shitting our pants."

"Hmm."

Denise waited a moment longer and broke into a driven jog. There were washrooms in the kindergarten room, reasonably so. They had tiny toilets and short sinks. She swung open the girls' room. It was empty. She crossed the seven-foot gap and swung open the boys' door. It was also empty.

"Hmm," she repeated. Glenn was on her heels, following the swath of light.

"Where else?" Glenn whispered.

Denise paused, swinging the light over the big, mostly empty room. On the far side was another door. A closet if she recalled correctly. Being back in the room didn't trigger forgotten memories as Glenn had suggested it might. Maybe the darkness held them prisoner, but probably they were gone, like so many other meaningless days.

"That's a closet?" she asked.

"It's the boot room where the hooks are, don't you remember? Brad Macklin told me Santa wasn't real in there and I lied and said Santa was real because I'd seen him. Brad said it was my dad. That was wrong because I made it up in defense of my beliefs, hadn't seen a thing."

"The way your mom gets about Jesus?" Denise said and started across the room.

"Something like that, I guess, but different. Jesus and Santa Claus aren't quite the same thing, are they?"

"Aren't they?"

"Ugh, I'm not getting into this again." Glenn clung to a minor belief in Christian lore, while Denise, though raised neck deep in it, scoffed outright at the notion of anything omnipotent, especially a power using humanity like playthings.

"Text your mom and tell her to ask God where everybody is," Denise said.

"No, thanks."

They took the four gentle steps up to the toy level. The floor was hollow and thumped as they walked, despite cautious feet. Denise tried to turn the handle; it wouldn't move. She smiled and knocked.

"You in there, Little Pigs?" Denise said.

Down the hall, footfalls charged towards the room. They squeaked wet, rubber voices.

"Hey!" Glenn shouted.

The door opened.

"Get in here and shut the fuck up," a voice hissed.

Denise shined her light. There was blood on Robbie's cheek, running freely from a gash beneath his right eye, the red a stark contrast to the chalk powdering his flesh.

8:20 PM – Twenty-five Minutes Early: Sarah and Robbie
"Why are we here so early?" Robbie asked, annoyed by the silly idea of paying homage to their collective kindergarten classroom. Sure, there were some good times in elementary school, but who even remembered kindergarten?

Sarah and Robbie were an item in middle school and then high school, split once Robbie went to college and Sarah stuck around town to wait tables and procreate with an older man named Gus. Gus was gone, with the kids, and Sarah reverted mentally. She looked to take back the years lost to mothering and Gus, boring turd that he was.

Robbie came back to town after his job at the Yellow Pages moved to Texas, as well as his co-worker girlfriend. He wasn't interested in anything with too long horns or hip holsters on civilians. He and his girlfriend were more a relationship of convenience, so there were no tears when she stayed on.

It left him an unemployed technical writer and editor, renting a home not far from where he grew up, taking in his options, freelancing contracts from folks all over the English-speaking parts of the globe. It also let him re-spark an old flame.

He foresaw regretting this in the future but was having too much fun to focus on that now.

"The basement, remember?" Robbie said as Sarah took a turn toward the sixth-seventh-eighth grade wing.

"We've got time, come on," Sarah said and pouted out her ass as she turned up the shadowy corridor, cellphone flashlight app shining the way in a great swatch of blue. She wore a skirt perhaps a half-size too tight for her frame. Still, she had a great bod for a woman who'd pushed out three kids, great bod for any woman in her mid-thirties. "I want to take a trip down memory lane."

Robbie had no idea of what she was talking about. He followed nonetheless. Sarah entered the second to last room on the right side of the hallway. It was a former eighth grade homeroom.

"Coming?" Sarah said as Robbie cleared the doorway. She was in the office and supply closet at the front of the room. This was one of the few rooms with a teacher's office and that was because it was also the senior science room. There were gas hook-ups at the two-seat tables and three sinks up the center aisles.

"Remember that time?" she asked and then disappeared.

Robbie did not recall at all.

Through the door, into the moldy, chalky atmosphere of the office, Robbie felt hands dig fingers into his hips.

The flashlight app pointed at the ceiling from a shelf against the wall. The room was no more than five feet across and double that long.

Robbie turned as directed and his ass planted on a desk. His pants came open and he got the just of it then, still did not fully understand. His cock came out and Sarah's tongue entered his mouth. His hands found flesh beneath her shirt and bra, rubbed the hard pebbles at the center of areola fields. She then backed up, crouched, and did what she did: wet vigor, spitting often, squeezing balls, tracing edges, and constantly in multiple directions of motion.

The first time she'd done this, he came in forty-nine seconds.

He was more seasoned now. Plus, she knew when to stop so they could continue rather than leave her damp and unfulfilled with a mouthful of salty man-milk.

"Remember yet?" she asked.

Robbie said nothing.

"This isn't quite as hot. Remember how we waited till Mr. McGuinness left and we came in here. We could hear everyone in the hall and teachers talking through the wall and I sucked you and you came everywhere."

Robbie still didn't say anything.

"Remember, baby?" she said.

He laughed then. They were dating when she was in Mr.

McGuinness' class and there was a rumor that his girlfriend blew a couple guys over the years, but this was the first time he really believed it.

"What's so funny?"

"That wasn't me."

"What?" She sounded hurt and suddenly uncertain.

"That. Wasn't. Me."

"Ah, fuck. You sure?"

"Yep."

"Oh, sorry," she said and slipped his cock back into her mouth to mount a full-on apology blow.

Playfully vindictive, every time he got close, he thought of the poster for the film *Bowfinger*. It was a trick his buddy used in high school when he didn't want to seem like a premature ejaculator. It made him smile and shake with every remembrance of Eddie Murphy's spectacled eyes and upturned lip revealing braces. It was more the memory of his pal than the image that kept him from release.

Finally, after enough time for the flashlight app to drain the battery, he let his mind and body meld. His fingers twined into Sarah's hair, directing the rhythm before exploding into her mouth. Worm-like, his slobbery, quickly receding erection slid free as Sarah began shaking and kicking.

Objects fell from the shelves. Something warm splashed over Robbie's bare thighs. He hopped down from the desk, yanked up his pants, and pulled his phone from his pocket.

"Sarah?" he said, shining a touch screen in her direction.

The glow illuminated a figure hunched over Sarah, the chalk dust on the air, and the reflective blood spilling onto the cement floor.

"Holy shit!"

An arm came up and struck Robbie in the face as he charged forward. Something hard sliced into his cheek. The pain had him jumping sideways, sending more chalk and bug-eaten textbooks toppling. A chalk box broke open over his head.

The arm slashed out again and Robbie felt a burn seep out from his thigh as the blood oozed. He reached blindly for the door. His cellphone was somewhere on the floor. Hand found knob and he was out.

There was more crashing behind him. There was no time to stop and the heart wasn't there to fight. He broke down the hall toward where he'd entered and where he'd parked the car.

Footfalls clapped on the stone floor behind him, matching his pace. He turned to the door and a figure illuminated from behind the glass swung the door outwards. Terrified by this silhouette, Robbie turned down the hall. Being away from town for so long, he had no idea the north end had collapsed and he was effectively cornering himself.

Upon discovery of the collapse, he entered the kindergarten room to seek assistance from his friends. There were candles illuminating the center of the floor. There was a grocery bag that appeared to house beer cans. But there were no people.

8:31 PM – Fourteen Minutes Early: Vin

Parked two spots down from a late model Buick SUV, Vin licked his lips, glanced at the clock, and decided he'd best have a toot before entering. It had been a while since he'd known these people and wasn't sure what they'd think of him powdering his nose.

Bump tapped onto his hand, he snorted. Magic exploded on the front of his mind for about two seconds. He tapped a second bump, freshened his second nostril.

He looked at the baggy under the streetlights and decided to pocket it. The original plan had been to go in clean, have a few beers and pretend to be a happy, adjusted adult. Maybe they weren't squares.

He grabbed the bag of beer from the passenger's side floor. He'd purchased a six-pack and one tall can but drank the tall can on the way to the school. It was absurd how nervous he was to be around these people again.

The school was dark, something he hadn't expected. He lit a cigarette with a scuffed Zippo lighter and left the flame dancing to lead the way. The school was a place he'd never forget. His favorite times occurred at school, back when he was better than normal and cool as Alaska. From kindergarten all the way to grade thirteen, he was one of few kings. The big fish in a little pond notion died in college. He dropped out after the first year, but life at home had changed, people were disappointed and unfriendly. Thankfully, his inheritance allowance was enough that he'd never need for anything so long as he never needed for anything too extravagant.

Staying in a cozy level of inebriation was well within his snack bracket.

The school was quiet as his feet carried him, without fail, to the place where life was first good. He opened the wooden door and closed his Zippo. There were candles in the middle of the room on the low portion of the floor. He took the wide steps slowly.

"Hello?" he said, smile widening. It felt like magic to be back.

A full three-sixty suggested at least temporary aloneness. He withdrew the paper packet of white powder from his pocket, tapped a bump onto his hand and snorted. His head rocked back. The bump had been more of a mound. Still, despite a natural blockage in his left nostril, an anatomical function beyond his knowledge, he liked symmetry and snorted another helping.

This time when his head rocked back, it did so at the exact moment a weighted noose swung and encircled his throat. Vin was too high to understand for the first five seconds as his feet rose from the floor. As the high settled into the norm, his swinging body lashed and writhed. He was suspended no more than a foot high. Muscle pounding overtime, cocaine-assisted cardiac arrest set in long before the snapping bones in his neck mattered to his airways.

His bowels rushed into Calvin Klein boxer briefs via a relaxed sphincter. The rope let go, and Vin dropped like a released marionette. The tall figure in a black hood dragged the body into the hall and then a closet next-door to the kindergarten class.

8:45 PM – On Time: Susan

Honda Odyssey parked next to what had to be Vin's Cadillac coupe. A pain to get a sitter for the kids since it was Saturday and her husband had men's league bowling followed by men's league drinking. In the end, she paid the neighbor kid, a nerdy computer whiz who wore Star Wars shoes, thirty bucks for the night. This was not the prime choice for the informative ages of five and six, she didn't want her kids believing in all that crap, but she was out of choices. They were naïve and had trouble separating realistic TV from the nature of the world. Besides, all that space stuff and science fiction stuff and horror stuff was garbage.

She had her purse and in it, among forty-nine other objects, was a flashlight on a keychain. She fished it free as she stood just outside the doors. She dressed in blue jeans and a long-sleeved shirt, both from Old Navy.

It was a bit of an annoyance to be out of yoga pants on a Saturday night.

Through the doors, she saw a man running in the dark. Sprinting as if being chased. Susan shined the light to her right and then left. She saw nothing and then rolled her eyes. This was a thing, that man was one of the party and it was his job to give rise to her hackles. Well, good luck. She wasn't a child.

"Nice try!" she shouted.

To her right, footfalls approached. She turned the light again. There was a tall figure, shadowy in a black shroud. Thin shoulders suggested this could be a man or a woman, though the height certainly suggested a man. In the shrouded individual's hands was an archaic fire axe. There were a handful of them in the school, stuck behind glass, ready for an emergency since the 'sixties.

"Ooh, scary. Who is that?" Susan said.

The figure drew closer, cocking the axe like a baseball bat, ready for the pitcher's goods.

"Grow up," Susan said. The axe swung into her chest. The shrouded figure drew tight as the blood drained, pinching the flashlight pointed to the ceiling. "Who are...who...?"

Susan wheezed and pawed at the gaping wound over her chest even as the figure dragged her body into the shadows of the long hallway.

8:58 – Underway: Denise, Glenn, and Robbie

"You're fucking kidding," Denise hissed.

"Shh!" Robbie said, fingering his wound. It was like a giant canker sore, impossible to leave alone.

"No, but for real?" Glenn whispered, terrified.

"For real. I assumed it was you who set this up, but was it?" Robbie asked of Denise.

"I didn't even wanna come!"

"Shut up!"

"Calm down," Glenn said.

Beyond the closet door, a tinging rang out. It sounded like a hammer, but the acoustics of the hallway and then the tiered room made it seem much softer and yet vaster. The trio kept quiet while the noise polluted the horror with impending dread. That hammering was akin to Death knocking on the door and all felt it.

It stopped.

Denise said, "Who else said they were coming? I talked to Vin and he said—"

"Why did you talk to Vin?" Glenn asked, his attention peaked. Denise and Vin had a fling a year before Denise and Glenn married. It was a subject they'd pretended to forget over the years.

"Now's not the time," Denise said.

"Are you fucking him?"

"Jesus Christ," Robbie said.

"We'll talk about this later."

"Now!" Glenn shouted.

The drop ceiling fell apart above them, showering chunks. Denise spun the flashlight in that direction. A figure fell into the closet with them. Glenn screamed a high and wild cry as he pawed into the dark for the door handle.

Robbie grabbed onto the arms of the tall figure, pushing hard against a wall where coat hooks jutted out at three feet. The figure grunted, dropped a heel onto Robbie's toes. This released the hold and the figure lifted a hand.

The tip of a plastic clay knife broke through the cotton of Robbie's shirt, the flesh of his chest, and then between his ribs, into a lung. He coughed. The short knife jammed in again. Blood erupted with the next cough.

Robbie latched onto the figure. It was all he could do as the knife slammed in and out, sounding much like a wet zipper rising and falling.

Glenn stumbled and Denise passed him, shining light toward the mostly closed exit. She arrived first, swung it open, and eyes gawked at her. Glenn screamed again seeing the faces of Vin and Susan. They'd been pinned at the shoulders, conjoined. Each had one arm stretched and tacked at the wrists. The same went for their feet, one ankle each nailed in place. Meaty roadblock.

"Who would do this?" Glenn said, his voice was so high and unsteady that Denise wanted to kill him her damned self. "What're we gonna do?"

"Shut up, you pussy! You wonder why I fucked Vin? Listen to you!" She charged into the bodies. They budged. She backed up and went again. The flesh tore and the bone crunched, the corpses leaned like a hammock. She reared again, ignoring a fresh banshee wail from Glenn.

Through the ceiling, the body of a woman fell. Her skirt rode high and her blouse flapped loosely. The weight of this carcass toppled Denise. Glenn recognized her immediately. It was Sarah Jones. She'd once given him a ham-handed tug that lasted for nineteen minutes and amounted to nothing more than a blistered knob and balls so blue they'd strike jealousy in Caribbean waters.

The flashlight was on the ground. Denise began to whine.

The shrouded figure dropped. Glenn jumped, crawling toward the light. He grabbed it, swung it around, and watched the shrouded figure pound a brass doorstop in the shape of a greyhound into the head of his wife.

Another shrill scream left his lips. Blood danced on the light like rubber boots in a rain puddle.

"Why are you doing this?" he wailed, backing up to a wall, skidding his ass on the dusty carpet. "How could you do this?"

The figure stopped and turned. Lowering the hood, the figure revealed her face. It was vaguely familiar.

"How could *I* do this? You all did this to yourselves," the woman said.

Her voice linked two memories, much more recent than anything that went on at school. It was a self-help seminar he'd gone to a year earlier. The host was a man named Kane. He had salt and pepper hair, wore a headset, designer duds, Rolex watch, Prada loafers, and spoke with the authority typically bellowed by autocrats and mayoral offspring. Kane said the only way to be anything moving forward was to conquer everything holding you back.

This was the same hocus pocus junk he'd heard before, but it always puffed up his mental well-being for a couple months after the fact. Kane had held a question session and this lanky woman named Elizabeth stepped forward and asked how one goes about conquering when the demons holding her back had been there since she was very small. His answer was loud and unwavering.

"Exorcise those demons at any cost!" he'd shouted, shaking this Elizabeth by the shoulders.

"You're name is Elizabeth, right?" Glenn asked.

The woman stepped closer. "You've never called me that before. Never!"

"I've never spoken to you. You're nuts!"

"How dare you." She withdrew a cross from the folds of her robe. The long end came to a point like a double-duty vampire hunter's stake. She lifted the weapon over her head in a two-handed grip.

"No, wait. You, can't! Who are you?"

"You don't remember me?"

"I do, but it's only because I saw you last year at Kane's seminar!"

"Monsters never recall their prey. What if I said the name Lizard Breath?"

"Lizard Breath?"

The woman's voice took a teasing tone. "Lizard Breath smells like poo. Lizard Breath drinks her pee. Lizard Breath has a dink."

"What in the hell are you talking about? You've lost your mind." Glenn had no recollection of chanting those very words to a girl named Elizabeth who had to be homeschooled after kindergarten because a small group of children drove her to the five-year-old equivalent of suicidal with their relentless taunts.

"No, I'm just getting it back. I will conquer. I will exorcise! Demon be gone!"

The cross stake drove down into Glenn's head. The crunch was mighty and the flow of blood pumped like a geyser for two heartbeats. Soaking Elizabeth's already damp and sticky robe. The flashlight rolled from of the shaking hand of the fresh corpse.

8:59 AM – Two Days Later: Elizabeth

"You're right on time," the smiling woman from behind the glass said.

It was raining outside and Elizabeth had taken the bus across town to get to the high school. She'd recently passed a train-from-home course in first aid and medical treatments designed for those looking into becoming a nurse or a paramedic someday, or if more school was too much, a first defender in public health for youths—school Nurse being the colloquial title.

The class president of the thousand head high school was in the office dropping off an envelope to be sent to the Prime Minister, demanding the banning of oil use by 2025 (petition signed by eight hundred students). She looked at Elizabeth and smiled.

"Everybody, this is Elizabeth Soames. Our new nurse," the receptionist said to those over her shoulder.

"Lana, you're down that hall, walk with Ms. Soames to the nurse's office, would you?" the principal asked, popping her head out of an office doorway. "Nice to see you again," she added to Elizabeth.

Lana skipped out from behind the desk and stood next to Elizabeth. "Shall we?"

Elizabeth wore a warm glow emanating from within. This was new. This was different. People were never nice, this felt like a...a rebirth.

Lana asked four bored questions about Elizabeth's post-secondary education. Elizabeth answered and stopped once at the open door. The janitor was inside leaning over the sink, looking down the drain.

"Nice to meet you," Elizabeth said.

"Nice to meet you too," the president said, grinning the kind of smile that offers teacher an apple and finishes the year valedictorian. She stepped away but stopped and turned. The smile on the class president's face widened as she looked at the rain-doused woman. "Frizzy Lizzy, 'cause your hair. That's a fun name."

Elizabeth's cheeks burned. She touched her naturally curly hair, made a mess by the rain, thinking that it wasn't a fun name at all, not even a little.

"That'll stick, for sure," Lana skipped away.

Elizabeth watched her movements, etching everything about this demon to her memory.

SHE'S IN YOUR HEAD

(2019)

"Man, think of all you've got going for you. The dream job for one. Not an even trade for a life, but the damned payout covered that mansion you live in. Besides, you have Debbie now. You might not see it, but Sandy was a total...easy...you know...man, you have to move on," Dirk said, he had an arm draped over his best friend's shoulders, a pair of empty beer pitchers on the table before them.

"Easy? Bullshit. You always hated her...it's not the same with Debbie, I thought now that she's pregnant and we'll have—"

"Really? Even more to celebrate. And easy's putting it nice. Man, she got in your head and let everyone else in her—"

Jason shivered, gently, and reached for a mostly empty beer glass. "You didn't know her how I did... It's not the same. Some love is irreplaceable. I had a ring in my pocket and everything, man."

"I know, but your life is like fucking charmed since then! It's because you weren't married to Sandy, didn't come to learn all the shit she did. You never learned...never even got the chance to get bored of her, so you got snakebit by a girl—one you shouldn't have trusted in the first place—and formed this idea about love—"

Jason struggled out of the booth, knocking an empty pitcher to the floor. It bounced hollowly before crashing and shattering by the worn New Balance sneakers of a waitress named Jewel. Jason stepped on a shard, slicing up through the heel of his sandal, but he didn't stop. Didn't stop when Dirk called out to him. Didn't stop when the waitress said, "What the fuck?" He simply charged on, into the warm August night.

—

The ambient glow of the computer screen seemed to heighten his state of inebriation and he swayed dumbly where he sat. Debbie was off visiting a friend in Victoria until morning, so Jason had the entire house to himself. Four bedrooms, two bathrooms, a rec room, a den, a kitchen, but he stuck to the office, lingering over the last Facebook conversation he'd had with Sandy.

Banal. Empty. Pointless. But it was there and he read the love between the lines. He began to type.

I was gon ask you you know???

Had a ring.

Sandy will you marryme???

I miss you

Why can'twe be togther????

I want so bad!

Merryme!

I love you!!!!!

—

Jason dreamed of Debbie, dreamed she walked next to him on the sidewalk where the air conditioner dropped. The same air conditioner that had struck Sandy and killed her. Blood oozed from Debbie's ear and a black and pink crack split her forehead.

"Jason?"

He shook, she couldn't be talking, she was dead.

"Hey!"

Her mouth moved like fat, rubbery slugs, loaded up on blood, wriggling and plumped to the verge of bursting. He tried to tell her no, he loved her, even if she wasn't Sandy.

"Wake up!"

Debbie rose, stiff as a vampire, and began shaking him.

His eyes opened and Debbie was nudging him gently. "Hey," he said and rubbed a tendril of saliva from his lips. Memories of the dream flittered and all that he had crashed over him like a wave: a perfect life. A. Perfect. Life. And Debbie, she was perfect too.

"Were you here all night?"

He didn't glance at the sleeping computer, didn't look around to the office to clue into exactly where he'd passed out. "I'm sorry if I'm distant sometimes. I love you so much."

Debbie smiled. "You're drunk."

Jason grinned then and shrugged. "Maybe a little."

"You want breakfast or to sleep some more, like in bed this time?"

"Breakfast. I mean it, though, I love you so much."

Debbie leaned in and kissed him. "You stink," she said and turned to head for the kitchen.

Out of habit, Jason nudged the mouse and awoke the computer. He blinked a handful of times before recognition set in.

Someone had responded to his messages with Sandy's account.

I know you were.

I know you did.

Of course I will. I've dreamed of when you'd ask me.

I miss you too.

We can be together.

Soon.

I will, silly boy!

I love you too!

And then as this information began to register, the checkmark disappeared and the word TYPING took its place.

That bitch think she's taking my spot?

This is how you do me, you fucking dog!

Jason swallowed a heavy invisible ball and closed his eyes tight. It had to be residual booze affects.

Debbie screamed and the power clicked off with a beep from the fire alarm. It clicked back on with another beep. The computer began restarting.

"Debbie?" Jason said, getting to his feet. Clumsy and lightheaded, he put a hand to the wall and rounded the door, moving into the hallway. The closer he got to the kitchen, the heavier the bacon smell became. The sizzle sounds were there, but there was something else, something underneath it all. Like squeaking. He sped up.

Debbie was on the floor, her legs jittering in a way that spelled disconnection from the brain. The toes of her right foot screeched against the linoleum.

Jason hurried, stumbled, and fell to his knees. He began shaking her before lowering his ear to her mouth. Nothing, she wasn't breathing. He got up and spun, the scab of the glass cut in his foot flaked away and left a smeary trail. He scanned the kitchen, eyes dancing frantically over the surfaces. Debbie's phone was on the counter, plugged-in to charge. He dialled 911, then pressed the warm device to his face.

It stank. He pulled it away and noticed the burn marks. As if hot to the touch, he tossed the thing into the sink. It had shocked her. It shocked her and she wasn't—a great splash showered onto the glass of the door that connected the kitchen to the deck.

"What the fuck?" he said and then screamed as he stomped to the door, "Help!" He pulled it open and said it again, "Help!"

The water on the deck swished gently and a tadpole-like creature wriggled close to him. He stumbled in reverse and tripped over the doorframe, his eyes glued hard on the thing. It was coming right for him, he tried to kick himself away, but the thing was faster and it—turned. It skirted the counter and slipped up Debbie's cheek, between her open lips.

"Dear god," Jason mumbled.

Debbie began blinking and rolled over. "Hey there, silly," she said, her voice not her voice. Her voice belonging to a ghost.

Jason screamed, but not over Debbie/Sandy. Something was attacking his foot. He brought it to his chest just in time to see another little creature disappear into his wound. The pain jolted and he grabbed his calf. The thing flowed, its back lifting flesh like a sea serpent cresting the surf. He grabbed his thigh then as the pain intensified and drew higher. It got to his hip, and he screamed all over again as terror sweat and pain sweat burst from every pore. The thing was in his side, then taking his ribs like obstacle course pylons. Jason punched at his abdomen, wailing. He gagged as the thing broke into his chest, up his throat. He slammed his head on the linoleum when he felt movement in his sinus. When the thing reached his brain, he quit screaming.

Jason/Sandy looked at Debbie/Sandy and smiled.

From the office, they heard his phone chirp. Naturally, they got up and went to answer the text. It was from Dirk, asking if they were cool.

Reading the memories lodged in that wonderfully accessible grey matter inside Jason's skull, Debbie/Sandy said, "Easy, huh? Better invite him over," as they patted their pregnant belly.

Jason/Sandy pouted their bottom lip and typed.

YOU'RE IT

(2018)

The girl stomped, her sneakers scuffed grey by gravel dust, toes hued green by grass, treads mucked with dog shit and pebbles. The campground was miles away. The trail wound to the right and she darted left, into the thick brush. If anybody looked, they wouldn't find her route.

She'd taken off for good this time, maybe join a carnival or become a rock star's roadie.

Through the prickly foliage and beneath the swatch of fallen fir trees, the girl powered onto *someplace* else. Her parents were such jerks. They deserved to be mad. They deserved to cry over her disappearance.

They'd refused to buy her the iPhone 7, so she refused to be their daughter.

Ancient iPhone 6 pulled from the pocket of her jeans, she checked for bars—none. She stomped harder, pocketed the phone, and tugged and snapped the three rubber bracelets around her right wrist. She peered into the dense flora surrounding her. There had to be a road soon, *had to be.*

Onward, there was a great rock hill. She skirted the edges rather than climbing. Beyond the rock was a clearing. No trees, no rocks, no general obstructions. Cellphone in hand, she sought service. Still nothing.

"Hey!" There was a boy in the middle of the clearing.

He waved from about fifty feet away. A warning bell told her to be wary, she'd seen pictures on Facebook and Twitter, read the memes about girls who got molested and murdered.

"Hi," she said and stepped closer.

"What you doing way over there?" the boy asked.

The girl had stopped thirty feet short of reaching the boy. He looked a few years older. He wore a straw hat, a flannel shirt, and faded blue slacks.

"I'm walking. Who are you?"

"Blake, who are you? Come closer, I can't hardly see you."

The girl took five more steps.

"I get it, smart to be 'spicious about strangers. Why you walking out here?"

"I'm teaching my parents a lesson. They think they can run my life. They have lots of money for stupid camper trips but are being cheap about the iPhone Seven."

The boy nodded, he then chuckled. "I got no clue what you're talking 'bout. Come closer."

Here was a bumpkin. The result of hanging around campgrounds instead of the mall. Still, he wasn't ugly and had hardly any pimples.

The girl took five more steps. The boy stayed put.

"What's that?" the girl asked, pointing at the stake driven into the grass two feet behind the boy.

"That? Hell, that ain't much of anything. Sometimes I sit on it, that's all. Why don't you come closer?"

"I am closer."

"All right," the boy said and added, "Look, why don't you come closer so I ain't got to yell?"

She took three steps.

The boy put his hands up. "Fine. Fine. You like singing songs?"

"What songs?"

"Oh I don't know. How 'bout I'm a Yankee Doodle dandy / I'm a Yankee Doodle do or die...what?"

The girl turned her face to her feet, embarrassed for the boy. He was a bad singer and the song was dumb as it got.

"Don't know that one? How 'bout *Take me out to the ball*

*game / Take me...*what now? You got to know that one."

"I should go," the girl said.

"You'll come back though, right?"

"I don't know." The girl had already turned away.

"I hope so. Hey, you didn't tell me your name!"

There was something *funny* about a boy in a field, singing those old songs, dressed like a homecoming scarecrow, so she hurried. Still, it took twice as long to get back to the park as it had to leave it.

Her mother was in the trailer, husking corncobs. "You cooled off yet?"

The girl sneered and said, "*Cooled off yet?*"

"Guess not," the mother said.

—

Each site had a private fire pit, but the girl's parents liked to mingle and dragged her to the larger communal pit at the center of the grounds. A fire blazed. A dozen people sat in collapsible canvas chairs basking in the heat, glow, and atmosphere.

"That's when Blaine the Insane crept into the neighboring houses and slit every throat like he had a to-do list!" Lisa, the campground manager, said. She was rum-stinking and somewhere between forty and ninety. Her face was puffy, her nose was red and angry. She had yellow teeth and thin lips. "True story, we had our very own serial killer."

"Then what happened?" a little boy asked in a frightened hush.

"Some say Blane the Insane is out there somewhere, still stalking."

A mother yanked the scared boy from the fire, flipping off Lisa.

For the next hour, the men and women around the fire drank beer and wine, discussed barbeque recipes and TV shows. The children sat bored, looking into their phones.

The girl Google searched Blane the Insane and found nothing.

—

"We can't go home now. We've got the camper for a month and…"

The girl heard her father no further and charged back through the woods, only subconsciously aware of where she headed. Through the greenery, the sticky pine needles, beyond the chirping birds and the busy squirrels.

"You came back!" the boy shouted, bouncing to his feet.

"Why are you out here?" the girl asked, the idea that he was there both times was doubly weird. Though, she was glad to see him.

"I like to hang out here, what are you doing here?"

The girl stopped ten feet from the boy and hung her head. "Stupid parents. I wanna go home and see my friends. I already missed a party."

The boy clicked his tongue. "I get ya. Sometimes parents ain't nothin' but trouble."

"Exactly." The girl lifted her head. "Is that why you're out here?"

"I reckon that's part of it. How come you sit so far away?"

The girl shrugged.

"Oh. Hey, want to play a game?"

"What game?"

The boy scratched his head. "Uh, what about tag?"

The girl scoffed.

The boy scrunched his face. "What, you too old for tag?"

The girl got to her feet. "I've gotta go."

"No, wait, what's your name?"

"Why?" The girl had become cocky, she wondered if this boy like-liked her or something.

"I want to know. You know my name. It's Brock. You got to tell me your name."

"You said it was Blake."

"That's right, Blake Brock, I got two names. What's your name?"

The girl turned away. "Bye, Blake Brock."

———

"Where were you this time?" the girl's father asked.

The girl shrugged and withdrew her phone.

"Sorry it's not what you're used to," her father added as he cracked a Coors Light.

There weren't ten kids in the entire campground and most of the other kids she saw were *way young*. Other than the boy in the field. Other than Blake Brock.

———

"Stupid name," she said as she thought about him for the hundredth time that evening. She and her mother sat breaking the tips off green beans.

"What's a stupid name?" her mother asked.

The girl cast a nasty glare at the woman.

"Fine... You know, if you don't start acting like a human being, we're taking your phone. Consider yourself warned."

"You can't, it's mine! I'm not handing it over"

"Don't need the phone. You're on the family plan. We can have your service paused."

"That's not fair."

The mother's eyebrows rose and her mouth puckered. "Stop acting like such a little bitch and it won't happen."

The girl's jaw hung slack and she saw red. She imagined running a blade across her mother's throat, just like Blane the Insane from the story.

"Fuck you," the girl hissed.

"You're one spoiled brat." The mother began busting the beans at break-neck speed.

Within an hour, the spot where the bars typically were said *No Service*. She still had the park Wi-Fi, but that wasn't the point.

All night she plotted, flippantly, the demise of her parents. In the morning, she knew what to do; she'd hide out, maybe with Blake Brock, until they learned.

At first light, she crept from bed, packed her knapsack, and left. They'd learn.

—

"I'm so glad you came back," the boy said. He sat on the grass in front of the post that reached two feet above ground.

The girl plopped down five steps away. "My parents are assholes."

The boy nodded, solemn in thought.

"What about your parents?" she asked.

The boy grinned at this. "They're gone. I'm solo."

"Really?" The potential for adventure danced in the girl's head like dreams of sugarplums in the heads of old-timey cartoon orphans. "Where do you live?"

"Old house over the ridge." The boy nodded back over his right shoulder, toward the open field that fell into more bush.

The girl plucked grass. "I wish I could do that."

"I don't know if you'd like it. Might be better for older girls."

"I'm super mature."

"All right, that why you won't play games with me?"

The girl shrugged.

"How about this, we play tag and then you can come back with me."

"Tag's for babies."

The pair stared until the girl averted her eyes. The silence went from awkward to comfortable. The girl watched the clouds. The boy watched the girl.

The girl's stomach grumbled.

"I got cookies at the house, if you're hungry," the boy said.

The girl sat up. "Okay."

"But you gotta play a game."

"Ugh, fine."

"Good! Finally...okay, first, you got to tell me your name."

"Chloe."

The boy tried it out. "Chloe. Chloe. Never heard that one

before."

"So what?" The girl was snippy, *hangry*.

"So nothing, come here. Come close. You can start. I'll run, you chase, got it?"

"Fine," the girl said.

A voice inside questioned why he wanted to play tag. Why did he need to know her name? Why was he always out there? Why did he always want her close?

"Come here and put both hands on the post?" he said.

"Why can't I just stay here and close my eyes?"

"The rules!" The boy was hectic in gaze and frantic with excitement.

"I don't know, maybe I'll just go back instead."

"Don't be such a jerk. You said you'd play if I gave you cookies, Chloe. Chloe."

The girl rose and brushed grass from her butt. "Maybe I'll just go back."

"I thought you wanted cookies."

The girl shrugged.

The boy said, "I thought you wanted to be away from your mean parents?"

"I don't see what playing tag will do for that."

"You ain't mature! No wonder your parents treat you how they do. You're just a little brat, probably."

"Am not," the girl barked.

"Prove it." The boy folded his arms over his chest. "Come close and put your hands on the post."

The girl stomped over to the stupid post, put her hands on it, and closed her eyes.

The boy touched her back. His hand was cool and damp. "Tag, Chloe, you're it!"

He broke away. The girl turned around, suddenly in the spirit, took two steps, and fell flat on her face. Pain jumped up her ankle. She looked down. A chain, weightless and yet firm, shimmery like a rainbow, attached her to the post with about three feet of range.

The boy stood a few yards from the new prisoner. "Don't worry, time will scoot on by after the first few days. They're real hard. Easier after the long sleep."

"What's happening? How'd you...? Blake Brock, you gotta help me. There's a chain, how's there a chain?" Panic and confusion heightened her tone.

"Name's Blane. Calm down, in a week you won't even much mind."

"A week!"

"I'll say *hello* to your parents, if I see them. Say it right close up."

"No, wait! Come back! I don't wanna play!"

The boy started along, off toward the campground, whistling an old-timey tune. Chloe watched, stretching out as far as the awful ethereal chain allowed.

A BOWL AT A TIME

(2015)

Who loves choco-choco-chocolate strawberry, marshmallow, cookie, doughnut breakfast surprise?

The advertisement had aired for the last few weeks and Prime Minister Dunham smiled at every chance she had to catch it. Tonight, it ran during the evening news commercial breaks. There was peace in the Middle East, announced for the third time in as many decades. It never lasted, but soon enough the troubles were to be a thing of the past.

Who loves choco-choco-chocolate strawberry...?

The prime minister bobbed her head along with the tune coming from the small television in the back of her black-on-black stretch limousine; windows tinted for the additional privacy. More often than ever before, the United Nations demanded meetings with the powers of the world. The P.M. never really took them seriously, but it was part of the job. As a group, they were beyond weak: all talk and no action, all while standing in the way of progress.

Her eyes remained trained on the television; a national campaign tweaked to perfection. A personal achievement she was proud of assisting. The singsong opening began slowly once again, *Who loves*, and then raced, *choco-choco-chocolate, strawberry...?* the voice slowed again, *You love...* over and over the jingle pounded the sentiment as happy boys and girls danced around the screen chasing super-sized ingredients, flashing to scenes of toothy faces smacking vibrant sugary balls floating in brown-hued milk.

The commercial almost made her forget about the U.N.

meeting. It let thoughts of terrorism, human rights, Third World governing, *blah, blah, blah*, all float away.

What the United Nations refused to acknowledge was that it all came down to capitalism, the lifeblood of *proper society*. The mindset that separated the lazy and uneducated from the wiser, upper classes. Capitalism wasn't an option, it was the only way, and forcing it around the globe was the next step to peace. Remove power from the monarchies, dictators, and churches, once that was done, she'd help separate those willing to work from those expecting society to carry them from birth to death—excluding those born into wealth, they were exempt because they were the beautiful bounty of capitalism's touch.

...doughnut breakfast surprise is an essential part...

The commercial really was catchy, a jingle like the old days, a jingle meant to attract parents and children alike. After the commercial ended, P.M. Dunham hit mute. She didn't need to listen to understand the television programs around the commercials. Flipping stations, still muted, she hoped to catch the commercial again elsewhere. It had spots on all the stations—minor to major, local to national to international—during cop dramas, trailer park sitcoms, and paternity test shows. Across the UK, Canada, Australia, the US: BBC, CBC, The Seven Network, Fox, and so on. And that's only English! French, Spanish, Mandarin, Malay, Portuguese, Arabic, Bengali, Russian, Hindustani, and more heard the tune in one form or another.

This thought made the P.M.'s grin widen.

The car slowed and then stopped. A door in the rear opened and a red-faced man with a slim build and stark white hair crawled into the limo.

"Madame Prime Minister, sorry if I kept you waiting. I seemed to have misplaced my mobile." Tony MacIntosh nodded as he spoke, forcing brevity in the form of a grin. He was the opposition leader of the country's coalition government.

"I only just arrived." Dunham said. "How's Cheryl, the kids?"

She continued to flip with the remote, bouncing past the news stations. There was something serious coming down in Scotland and Ireland, Eastern Canada, and a few cases in Iran. "They doing well?"

She didn't care about his family, and no doubt, Tony knew this. The P.M. had a single-track mind like that of a freight train behind schedule.

"Is this about the sudden deaths?" he said, ignoring her question.

Within the country, 702 sudden deaths in just two days but centralized to twenty-five cities. According to news sources, although many in the medical fields refused to comment, there were several thousand more knocking on the Grim Reaper's door.

"No room for pleasantries?" she said, one eyebrow raised.

"Fine, they're fine," he said. "You mentioned the plan again, what is it? By tomorrow there might be as many as a thousand casualties with—"

The P.M. lifted her hand. "Shh, listen to this commercial, I love the jingle." She raised the volume, nodding and smiling with the song.

Who loves...?

Tony listened for twenty seconds, visibly fuming. "I need to know what you—"

"Zip it," Dunham snapped.

... An essential part of your child's...

"Is this a joke, Madame Prime Minister?"

Dunham shook her head. "You never did listen. You know, the beta test had a perfect score?"

...available at all Aldi, Tesco, No Frills, Food Basics, and Essentials stores. Chocolate Breakfast Surprise is a Kingdom Oil company.

The P.M. muted the commercial and turned to receive a curious look from her forced comrade in policy. Kingdom Oil funded most of her side of the race, of course they did it through dummies and subsidiaries. Had to do it that way to keep the bleeding hearts and tree huggers quiet. Kingdom Oil paid the way home for Dunham and the conservative, Bluebar Party.

"Since when is Kingdom Oil interested in breakfast cereal? Which beta test?" he said, his face pulled tight toward the center.

"It's the plan. It's how we'll fix capitalism, it's how we'll fix the global society; a sustainable world for future generations," Dunham said, proud and firm.

"Cereal or testing?"

"They're one and the same, but not just cereal. Cereal, cakes, ice cream, pie, chocolate milk, fudge topping, cookies, many items. Even some for those without a sweet tooth: wieners, frozen pizza, TV suppers, potato crisps," Dunham said.

"What?" Tony, expression tighter now.

"The world's population has hit eight billion, four billion of them live in dire poverty, another two go without any sustenance on a very regular basis, why is that?"

A trick question. Tony shook his head in minute strokes. "Because the planet can't sustain populations based on where they sit on the map, which means, we have to offer aid, lots and lots of aid."

"Right across the board," Dunham said.

Tony's visible consternation smoothed out. They'd never agreed on what to do about the poor and hungry.

"You're going to switch your stance on aid?"

"Not just me, we're having a global hand-out party. All the big dogs. Only a few said no. Sweden, Italy, Mexico. But with this lineup, a few naysayers won't ruin the plan. The world is going socialist for a tick to further the capitalist agenda. We're fixing the world!"

The commercial began again on a different station and Dunham raised the volume, but only so loudly that she heard it as background noise. Tony frowned. It didn't matter if Tony cared, didn't need his opinion.

"How will this round of aid change anything? I understand by having everyone on-board, it increases the numbers of fed mouths, but—"

"Every single mouth will have food, guaranteed, for one-year, minimum. Even in the wealthier countries, the new brands will offer food at extremely competitive prices, but only at certain stores. It's something the poor can have that the upper classes can't."

"I don't understand, won't this cost—"

"The cost is short-term for everyone. It will end all future aid requirements beyond devastation—disasters happen, no helping that, but the beta test proved in the future we'll have less to worry over." The P.M. nodded along to the jingle as it concluded. She hit mute on her remote once again. "It will be a perfect capitalist society and on a global scale. Every mouth will forever have food and water."

A pipedream. "Sounds great, but it can't work. Even with the food cloning and genetic propagation there is no way the planet can sustain the growing population." As Tony spoke, his stomach hitched onto something, a prickle, a thorn. He winced.

She shrugged. "The plan is foolproof."

"Does it have to do with this beta test?" he asked, his hand kneading his sore tummy.

"Aha! The beta test, that's the answer right there. Of course, we of our little group will keep it all hush-hush, we'll even cry once the new super-strains of pneumonia and cancer begin to trim the planet's fat. That is after the sudden deaths have finished lobbing off the rotten parts. We'll all marvel over the wide-spread infertility. We have already designed fundraisers and media campaigns calling to action the scientists of the world to discover the strange changes," Dunham said. "Don't worry, it will only affect certain links in the chain, the ones spoiling things for those caring about the future of capitalism."

"I don't understand, what do you—?" He groaned.

"Sore tummy?" she said. "I can get the driver to stop at a drug store."

Tony's eyes widened. "You're going to poison the aid!"

"Ha, took you long enough and not just the aid, cheap food, sugary and fatty items that the gluttonous lower classes inhale like oxygen. Prolonged use of any of the Kingdom Oil, Bulzar Pharmaceuticals, RimRoil Mining, or Atlantic Pacific Engineering brands will ensure one of three things: sudden inexplicable death, rapid-action cancer of the stomach, or irreversible infertility. In fifteen years, the population will be back down to four billion, imagine it. We'll use all the resources we want, get stinking rich, and never run out." Dunham was proud as a peacock.

"You did this? The others know about this and joined? This plan, this is a massacre, genocide!"

"Genocide? Massacre? The real massacre is letting the stupid population spawn like rabbits. They're trying to kill us all, kill humanity. They would succeed if it wasn't for people like me, people willing to do what it takes to rescue the planet from starvation and decay. Global warming has nothing on food shortages; trust me, the planet has been here for millions of years and will spin millions of years after we're gone. Global warming only affects current inhabitants, the planet will persevere."

"You can't do this!"

"I'm saving the life on this planet! Open your eyes, Tony!"

"Open my eyes? All we have to do is tax the wealthy, they're the polluters, they're the real—"

"No, they're the useless by products of a broken system."

"You can't do this! I won't let you! I'll tell—" Tony stalled, another prickle had him bent forward, hands on his middle.

The ride from his home to the conference hall on Holloway should've taken only fifteen minutes. It was evening and the traffic was sparse, the lights outside the limo's tinted windows even sparser. They ridden almost half an hour already.

"Where are we?"

"Tell me, Tony, how does your family like the bounty from the Rotary International prize? Breakfast foods for a year, correct? Chocolate spreads, cocoa tea, fudge flavored coffee, chocolate chip breads, and cereals for the kids. Sounds like a lovely prize to win. How long has it been since you've been enjoying that specific prize?" The P.M. smiled.

Tony looked up at her.

"You are one lucky ducky, one ticket purchased, and bingo, you won. Of course, the real winners of a prize like that are the Rotary club and those they help around the community."

"You didn't," Tony whispered.

"I read the results from the tests," the P.M. said, voice now cold as the arctic.

The doctor had said it was the strangest thing, there had to be a mix-up with the ultrasounds and tissue samples, it was like looking at the stomach of a man seconds from death, his guts a festering cave of malignancy. There was another appointment set for tomorrow.

The motion ceased, seconds later Tony's door opened. The sky was dark and starry, the moon a sliver. Tony looked at the stairs leading into his home.

"Go inside, be with them. You'll have no outside contact, but none of you will make it long. Tony, you've never been much of a leader, but you seem good to your family. Go be a good father and husband, go while you're all still around."

Two darkly clad individuals wearing automatic rifles stood on the stoop outside his front door. They had driven around in circles giving her time to gloat, time to express herself like an ambitious Bond supervillain. Really, it's what she'd become. A character from a book, a movie, something so sinister it seemed impossible.

"I'm dying, my family's dying," he said, finally.

The P.M. shrugged. "You've been in the way, but politicians are like comedians, there's always room for the *straight man* until

THE COMPLETE BUMPS IN THE NIGHT / 174

there isn't. Go be with your family. The beta testing has proven perfect, there's no getting out of this, no miracle cure. People like me have always taken charge in crisis and people like you always need shoved aside when the time finally comes."

Tony gazed around him, the P.M., the television with the horrid advertisements, the man outside the car door, the figures on his stoop, it was hopeless, it was over. He coughed and stepped out of the car. The Prime Minister increased the volume on the television.

Who loves choco-choco-chocolate, strawberry, marshmallow, cookie, doughnut breakfast surprise? You love, choco-choco-chocolate, strawberry, marshmallow, cookie, doughnut breakfast surprise. You do, you do, you do...

The door closed and the driver returned to his seat. The limousine pulled away and the jingle faded into the night. Tony started up his steps and opened the front door of his home for the last time. He ignored the dark figures and their rifles.

Be a good father and husband.

There was nothing left to do but that, maybe eat a bowl of cereal. Chocolate Breakfast Surprise was a treat like no other.

JIMMY

(2013)

The snow faded in a perfect circle, forming a small icy ridge that carried meltwater away from the flames. Jimmy could no longer hear the screams or cries, the awful shrieking little Susan made as she tugged hard against the door. Now, the family was quiet and the only sound was the flames as they licked their way up the frame of the home and congealed the cheap plastic siding into blackened, bulbous humps.

Jimmy didn't mind the sounds or the smells; it had happened before.

The Johnsons, Karen and Fred, their children. Luke and Bradley, and that scruffy mongrel, Duke, they didn't scream when they went, not quite. Splashes of liquid rat poison in their hot cocoa; cocoa was good to mask the taste of just about anything. A few squeezes of the bottle for each of the kids, a few more for the parents, and a good helping for the dog. Jimmy hated the dog most of all.

He assumed they'd go peacefully into the dark abyss of death—what was the point of poison if it didn't make the chore easy? The poison sickened them, had them thrashing and clawing at their throats and tummies. Jimmy had to work quickly, disconnecting the phones, switching off the lights—he didn't need any nosey neighbors seeing—before finally locking the doors from the inside.

When would people learn that the real dangers of the world came from within?

Writhing and squirming and choking and gasping, their pleas fell on apathetic ears. Jimmy stood above the family watching; he didn't mind, it wasn't the first time he'd been forced to kill.

Ralph and Virginia Robinson, they didn't have any kids, not until Jimmy came around. They'd screamed, they'd begged, they'd thrown themselves against the door. The Stanley deadbolt held. It wasn't so hard to get them into the fruit cellar, the little room with mud walls and foggy jars of ancient preserves sitting on all the shelves. It wasn't so hard at all. They'd made him go down there all the time and he'd tested the deadbolt by throwing his own body against it while spiders and creepers investigated his being: into his shirt, up his shorts, all over his body, all because he refused to eat broccoli.

One night, after turning up his nose at some greens, Jimmy noticed a small billiard ball-sized hole in the wall of the cellar, which let in the light from the swinging—it seemed forever swinging—bulb hanging from the ceiling of the basement proper. It gave Jimmy an idea.

Ralph used much of the basement to work on small engines; he'd just fixed up a Briggs and Stratton off an old riding mower. It was dirty and a little rusty, but it would work.

"Did you guys ever notice that shiny handle sticking out of the mud wall? I think it's a really old box or a chest, maybe it's worth something," Jimmy said, playing the role of a surprised and thoughtful innocent.

Ralph and Virginia, always on the lookout for easy money, scurried to the basement; forgetting *Wheel of Fortune* and their bowls of Orville Redenbacher to chase into the basement.

They screamed just as he'd screamed, thumping against the door after he'd closed it and locked the deadbolt behind them. The garden hose went firmly in place through the hole in the wall, the other end fitted over the exhaust of the engine. Jimmy tugged the pull cord with all his might, all his hate, all his broken heart.

First pull: the handle of the recoil dug into his palm, the engine not even sputtering. Second pull: a light sputter. Third pull: nothing but pain in his fingers and hand from the hard handle as the cord suddenly seemed out to get him. He stamped his foot as the Robinsons wailed against the door.

He was missing something...the squishy yellow bubble, the one he'd seen Ralph push to make the engine start. Jimmy gave it three quick jabs. Fourth pull: the engine roared to life, chugging a bit now and then, but doing the job.

The fruit cellar door barely moved, even with their redoubled attacks. *Good door, good Stanley,* Jimmy thought over the banging and the screams. So much noise, followed by so much silence—aside from that purring, sputtering, shaking Briggs and Stratton, of course.

Jimmy didn't mind, he'd heard it all before.

Swimming pools could be very dangerous things, deadly in fact. Jimmy had tried to be a big boy, a strong boy, but he cried for days once he got put in that home.

It wasn't his home. His home was with his mommy.

Jimmy had been under the care of the Jacobs for two weeks: a new mom, Margaret, a new dad, Scott, and a new brother, Stevie. The family was much nicer than the Robinsons, but Jimmy didn't know that yet. Every moment of the day they tried to include him; the perfect family, always together, always loving, but never his mommy.

Jimmy could still remember Margaret's scream, "Jimmy, no!" as he stood poolside, while the entire family floated and bobbed in the big cement tomb.

"The wheels on the bus go round and round, round and round..." sang the childish voices from the giant silver boombox. Jimmy held it up, the power cord running to the wall like a rat's tail. He tossed it in as the family struggled to get out. The music ceased and Jimmy whisper sang, *"The bodies in the pool float upside down, upside down, upside down."*

Jimmy always liked that song; his mommy used to sing it to him. He unplugged the boombox and tugged it out of the pool by the extension cord. He took a plastic paddle and swung at the eject button—he didn't want a shock—until the button clicked and he could flip the player over to retrieve the CD.

The bodies still floated only feet away, all still looking like at any moment they might flip over and yell, "Surprise!" but Jimmy knew they were dead, he didn't mind, he'd done it once before.

Jimmy watched as his mommy and her new boyfriend, Eric, downed beer after beer. "Go to bed, you little punk," Eric had whispered. "Your mommy and me need some privacy."

The crawlspace under the stairs, so dark, so inviting, Eric wouldn't find him there. *Why does mommy need another guy around anyway? She has me,* thought Jimmy as he lurched out of the crawlspace and stepped carefully through the hallway to his mommy's bedroom.

Creak.

Jimmy paused, hoping not to be heard. He waited, terrified Eric would get up and give him another spanking, like the time he knocked over the ashtray.

A light moan joined the *creak creak creak.* Jimmy popped his head in the door. Eric was on top of Mommy, her eyes were closed and she was moaning in pain.

The hand covering Jimmy's mouth enveloped his scream and any air trying to find its way to his lungs; he wriggled to free himself from the hand before he realized that the hand was his own.

He's killing her.

Jimmy, unable to hold it all in, let out a peep, the tiniest peep and Eric turned to face him. Jimmy's mommy didn't move.

"Get out!" Eric screamed.

Jimmy ran, his feet burning against the carpet as he skidded to a halt. "Maybe I can save her," Jimmy said in a half breath, the kind he took when he knew he was in big trouble.

There seemed to be no answers, everywhere Jimmy looked he saw nothing helpful. His toy box? No, there was nothing there to stop a big scary man like Eric. The bathroom? Nope, nothing there either. The kitchen? Oh, yes, the knives, one of those would stop Eric.

The world ceased to exist beyond the hallway as Jimmy walked gently over the carpet and toward his mommy's room. Snoring had replaced the other sounds. Eric was asleep on his back, no longer killing Jimmy's mommy.

Mommy, are you okay? Jimmy asked somewhere deep inside his mind.

The sleeping, or rather passed out, woman rolled onto her side.

She's alive, Jimmy thought as he ran around to Eric's side of the bed, the side that he used to sleep on when he'd had a bad dream, the side mommy used to cuddle with him on and where she'd tuck him in: Jimmy's side.

No precision needed.

Stab.

Pull.

Stab.

Pull.

The blood pooled everywhere. It was hot and scary. Jimmy ran to wash his hands and face, his mommy rolled over and clutched the knife that sat deep in Eric's chest. She screamed, fueling Jimmy's little feet upstairs and into the bathroom.

It should have worked. It should have been just Jimmy and Mommy again. No Eric, no other mommies, or daddies, or sisters, or brothers, just Jimmy and Mommy.

Now, Jimmy stood outside the Johnson home, the fire trucks and police cruisers racing to the scene of the gruesome human incinerator. They were too late, the whole family was dead and Jimmy wondered if he'd finally get to be with mommy again.

He knew where she was, or at least had an idea where. A lawyer told Jimmy that his mommy was going away, incarcerated for homicide, wherever that meant. Jimmy didn't know, but he knew if he tried real hard, he could get there eventually.

SURVIVOR BUFFET

(2019)

The flight attendant in her smart pantsuit and ascot pushed the drink cart along the aisle as if everything were business as usual. A storm flickered on the night sky through the windows. Nearly all the seats were empty.

"Drink?" she said, stopping at a pair of occupied seats on either side of the aisle. To her left was a man in a suit, collar open, tie loose. To her right was a man in a navy uniform.

The man on the left said, "I guess just a ginger ale. You have any of those cookies?"

The flight attendant began digging into her cart before handing off the cookies and then cracking a can of Canada Dry. "And for you, sir," she said to the man on the right as she poured.

The man in the uniform grinned. "Oh, I wouldn't say no to a Heineken." He leaned close, as if conspiring. "Uncle Sam's footing the bill—or whatever's the Canuck equivalent."

Playful, but in that way that can only be professional, the flight attendant winked. She handed off the cup of ginger ale as the lights flickered and the plane dipped. She stood still a moment, as if deciding whether the plane was going to cause her to spill. Ten seconds passed. As if someone hit play on her video feed, she resumed motion and began pouring a beer into a plastic cup.

"Best not waste any," the man in the uniform said, still trying to flirt.

"I'll do my best," she said and handed the cup off before continuing along the aisle with the cart. Elbows poked into view from three seats in the next two rows. Before she had a chance to lock the wheels of the cart, the lights died and the plane pitched forward violently.

—

"One-two-three-four-five-six-seven," Stephen Barnes intoned to himself as he pressed his weight into his co-worker's chest. He leaned in, pinched her nostrils, and blew between her lips. Funny, but not so funny, he'd imagined pressing his lips to her lips about a million times. He pulled back and began compressions again. "One-two-three-four—"

Hailey Thompson—like Stephen, a correctional officer from Kingston, dressed in a blue guard's uniform—made a choking noise and spewed close to a liter of brownish water. She then began whining and Stephen draped his body over hers, squeezing.

"Thank God," Miller Marshall said, another from the prison, making a skinny shadow over the pair, in his left hand was a slim grey rope attached to a semi-deflated life raft.

The four of them dripped Pacific Ocean.

"Yeah, thank god," Sidney Hughes said. He sat beneath a coconut palm on the waterlogged seat cushion he'd swum behind after escaping the cracked hull of the downed plane. He still had handcuffs on his wrists, as he was scheduled to until back behind heavy bars and thick walls.

The extradition order was part of a friendly deal between Canada and the Ukraine. They'd give up Sidney, the Canadian Cannibal, Hughes in exchange for happy thoughts during the next trade deal. The Canadian prison guards met Sidney in Australia—where he'd briefly continued his serial murdering and ingesting—with orders to escort him home for a one 1,000-year residency in Kingston Penitentiary. He'd killed and eaten fifty-nine people but had managed to wiggle his way out of the country during a transfer between Ottawa and Kingston. The guards involved in his escape had moved to the gen pop within Kingston themselves.

"Shut up," Stephen said.

"Or what?" Sidney smirked.

They'd been in the air for about three hours when the engines cut out and the plane slammed into the ocean—the pilots, though both dead, did a hell of a job lessening the impact.

"Is anybody here?" a voice called from down the beach.

Miller put a hand above his brow to shadow the light. There, way down the beach, was the pretty flight attendant—now looking like a drowned cat—who'd been pushing a cart when the plane began its unscheduled descent.

—

The courtroom was wood on wood all over: the walls, the desks, the jury box, the floor, the bench, and so on. The jury was visibly shaken by what they'd seen and heard. To avoid a circus, the judge ordered the court to be vacant aside from people directly associated with the case, leaving but a small crowd at the back of the room. The defense council in their wigs and gowns sat in their seats, looking pale and defeated.

The prosecutor, dressed the same as the defense, stood behind a pulpit, sneering as he spoke, holding a fine fork and steak knife. "Sidney Charles Hughes had these utensils on the mantle of the home he'd rented. He kept them in a place of honor. He kept them in a place that was visible, somewhere that he might remember and relive. Ladies and gentlemen, this knife, this fork, these are the very tools Sidney Charles Hughes used to murder Gloria Darri and then dine upon her flesh. Raw. He cut her throat, holding her to the floor with his knee against her back until she bled out. He then sat in that very hot blood and began to eat. He ate from her breast, her cheek, her eye, and eventually, he opened her up and devoured her heart. I could go on, but I won't...this case makes me sick to my stomach."

Sidney Hughes indiscreetly licked his puffy lips as he watched and listened to the sum of his crimes revisited.

—

"You motherfucker," Hailey said through clenched teeth. Her

knees dug into the beach sand next to the destroyed body of a second flight attendant. The corpse had floated to shore the night before and her flesh was almost entirely intact.

It had been, then.

"You disgusting motherfucker," Hailey said.

Sidney held his cuffed wrists out before him. "I didn't do that."

A fist slammed into the back of Sidney's head, and he flew forward, flopping onto the flayed corpse.

"No laws are gonna save you out here, sicko," Miller said.

The flight attendant named Clare, who'd survived the crash, looked at the body of her once co-worker, visibly horrified. "He did this to her? Who could do that?"

Sidney rolled over and looked up at Stephen Barnes. "Better stake a pig's head," he said and turned sideways to kiss the skinless thigh of the dead flight attendant. He licked his lips. "Salty."

"Get him off her!" Hailey said.

"How could he do it?" Clare said.

"This crime ain't mine," Sidney said, smacking his blood-pink lips.

—

They made camp under one of the huge trees that covered the small island. Inland about five hundred meters from the beach, the tree they chose had a trunk thicker than the length of a pickup truck. Bulbs like breadfruit circled the base, fell from the lowest branches—they were high enough that any features of the branches were indistinguishable. Miller had patted it with his palm, absently telling the others about the summer he worked as a lumberjack—or rather, as a laborer to lumberjacks.

Night was warm and the ocean breeze was melodious, playing them into easy sleeps. During the day, they stayed near the beach. There was a freshwater creek that trickled by the camp and the bulbous fruits falling from the trees proved edible, though not overly appetizing.

By the third night, they'd begun to accept that they might be on the island for a while. The SOS sign in rocks would help, but the Pacific was the biggest mass on the planet.

"Might pay to do some investigating, deeper in, I mean," Miller said.

All but Clare and Sidney rumbled agreements. Clare sat, blank-faced like a beaten waif while Sidney watched the trees. That afternoon, he'd used his cuffed wrists to strangle two pelican-like birds. They'd eaten them at sundown, retreating from the beach where the rats amalgamated to feast on night insects and washed-up sea life.

"Bet there's a cat or something in here," Stephen said. "Probably came from the same place as the coconuts and the rats. Ships from way back, whenever, would stop in to check stuff out. They toss some coconut shells. Rats jump ship. Cats follow the rats."

"Hmm," Hailey said, eyes closed, picking a hunk of cooked bird from between her teeth. "Miller, you might be the one to save us."

"I caught the birds," Sidney said, feigning offense.

"So what? Miller figured out the fire, you motherfucker."

Miller was the only one with his cellphone still in his pocket once their floating party reached land. Too soaked to work ever again, he took it apart gingerly, used the cracked glass screen to magnify the midday light against a mound of coconut shell hair and the plastic battery.

"Should be happy I'm sampling the avian menu...and not my favorite." Sidney licked his lips. "Been a long time, too long."

"Shut the fuck up, motherfucker," Hailey said and threw a breadfruit melon across the fire.

Sidney let it hit him and eyed the woman.

—

Hailey's screams awoke the camp come sunup.

Sidney was on the ground bleeding, hands to the side of his head and cheek. "I didn't do that!" he whine-screamed the words. When he first arose, he'd been smirking, his expression curious.

"You sick motherfucker!" Hailey was livid. Miller held her back. She had a fresh rock in each hand. The first one she'd clocked off Sidney's head had rolled into the shadows cast by the great tree.

Stephen Barnes was a corpse by the smoldering coals. His clothing was gone, as was his skin—from the bottoms of his feet to his scalp, gone. He was pink and white, the colors of his veins playing about him like flair. He looked like an anatomical diagram of human muscles.

"How could I do that?" Sidney didn't dare get up.

Clare stared up into the big tree they'd camped beneath, chewing absently at coconut meat.

—

"I say we go investigate...because what if it wasn't him?" Miller whispered to Hailey.

"Can't leave him with her," Hailey said.

Both looked at Clare, who was still peering up at the green limbs and dangling fruit bulbs.

"I have an idea," Miller said.

Together they tied Sidney to the huge tree where they'd camped as the two surviving guards moved to the beach, dragging the fleshless corpse with them. After a short discussion, they pulled the body into the ocean as they had with the washed up flight attendant's remains.

"You know, I don't get it. How'd he do it?" Miller said.

They'd arranged more rocks into an SOS shape on the beach—the tide had washed their previous attempt away.

"He's sick. Probably used a stone. Probably knows how to do it like—"

Miller cut Hailey off. "I helped my uncle skin a deer once. Skin doesn't just slide off...even if Hughes has some trick, it's a ton of work. Like hard work, yanking cutting, yanking cutting, and you gotta have them hung to make gravity help... Well, that's how my uncle and me did it."

"Let's go ask him then. That motherfucker did it somehow."

"Unless there's something out here."

"We should kill him." Hailey picked up a smooth shell and fired it into the ocean.

"One of us will watch him all night. We'll go in shifts. Like normal."

Hailey shook her head. "Fuck that. Let's tie him to a tree down here."

"But the rats." Miller grimaced, thinking.

"Too bad."

———

"You stay here, okay?" Miller said.

Hailey nodded.

Miller pushed a trail into the thick flora, watching his feet and the forest floor as he walked. There had to be a sign of something else—Sidney hadn't done what Hailey was so certain he had, something else was on the island with them. The only heartening thought was that the something waited until Stephen was asleep before it had killed him.

Miller paused a moment upon hearing the tinkling of water before increasing his pace and chasing the sound. The pond was small but look deep.

Sweaty and dirty, Miller stripped out of his prison uniform. He paused a moment, glancing around, then whispered, "Cannonball," before running ten steps and leaping forward with his knees held tight to his chest.

The water was cool and silky. Miller rubbed everywhere, washing away sand and salt and days' worth of grime. He paused while floating, his hands in his hair. It felt like something was watching him. He scanned the sandy shore before locking eyes with the biggest damned frog he'd ever seen. Big as a housecat and had rubbery lime flesh.

"Are you poisonous or edible?" he said, knowing this couldn't be the island's predator.

As he dressed, Miller watched the frog spear insects with its pale pink tongue. It hardly had to move, it almost seemed as if the bugs wanted to be eaten.

"See ya later, froggy," he said before heading back toward camp.

The frog made a noise like an electric squeak toy and Miller turned as that pale tongue lashed out and clung to his forehead. Miller had no options, numbed motionless, soundless. After a few seconds, the tongue retracted and yanked Miller's flesh away with a wet *ssslurp* sound. What remained were bloody muscles, white bones, and blue veins. His organs spilled out and his heart thumped itself from his chest, dangled around where his naval had been.

The frog's throat had become huge, like it was smuggling a library globe.

———

"Miller didn't come back. There's something. We need to watch out for each other," Hailey said to Sidney, her expression and tone unlike anything she'd offered the man before.

"What?" Sidney said.

Hailey took a step left, revealing Clare's flayed corpse where it leaned against a stone. Her dead head remained tilted skyward.

"There's something here," Hailey whispered.

Sidney tried to lift his cuffed wrists. "Undo me."

Hailey shook her head.

"Look, we only survive if we stick together. You can't let me die in these cuffs."

Hailey shook her head again. "I think we should take the life raft."

Sidney leaned in close to her face. "Uncuff me or we both die."

"How do I know you won't kill me?"

"Because then I'm dead and I have no lookout. We need to work together."

———

The sun was almost down. They'd fashioned spears and dragged Clare's body to the beach, spent the rest of the day gathering wood. It had been hard work and Hailey was visibly beat.

"I'll take first watch," Sidney said.

Hailey yawned, nodding. An indeterminate amount of time later she awoke with her hands tied and Sidney cutting into her ankle with a sharp rock. She wailed and tried to thrash, but he'd put his knee across her knees, and she couldn't move.

"You motherfucker," she said, the words playing free like a hiss.

Blood darkened the sand and within a minute, she passed out again, only to come to screaming in pain and looking up at Sidney. He had a clown's smile of blood and was munching on her uncooked foot.

"Hey there, tasty," he said.

"What have you done, motherfucker?" Hailey said where she leaned against the trunk of a huge tree. Her face was lumpy with great red and purple blotches. Her lips were split, and a swollen gulley ran down the back of her head. She was alive, felt the compounded pain she'd missed when she'd slipped into unconsciousness while Sidney carved away the flesh of her left foot.

"You're delicious," Sidney said. "I really mean that."

She spat. "How'd you kill Miller and Stephen?" She spat again, great black-red globs.

Sidney smiled. "You flatter me," he said. There were two spears close by his side. "Unfortunately, I don't have time to slice you up and brine you before I go."

"Go where?"

"This island has an apex predator, and I don't what to be its next meal."

"You're ins—" Hailey's face drooped after a jolting forward. Her expression tightened as she leaned back. Her face smoothed and then split down the middle, blood splattering out before oozing down. In a blink, her entire skinsuit was yanked away.

Sidney popped to his feet. He grabbed the raft and one of the long, flaming sticks from the fire—forgetting his spears. He charged down the beach toward the water, shaking sand out of the raft. The ocean was calm enough to give him hope, and he pushed in with the raft. Whatever had snatched all those skins, he did not want to test it.

It proved impossible for him to climb inside with the lit stick, so he doused it in the ocean, smoke rising in the moonlight like a soul departing its flesh. He tossed the stick into the raft and them pitched himself backward, into the raft himself. The bottom of the raft was deflated, but the big ring around him was stiff and holding air.

Quickly, making distance from the shore, was what appeared to be a three-foot tall frog. Sidney scrunched his face. At least it wasn't the predator. And as large as this frog was, he was glad he didn't have to meet whatever other oversized creature might've dwelled on the island. He turned his back a moment and tried to use the stick like a paddle—thankfully, the tide was headed out— while his legs lazily motorboated over the back end.

Ahead, the big frog rose through the surf, its eyes shining wetly beneath the big moon.

"Pretty risky, going into the ocean, don't you think?" he said to the thing, his pace slowing a modicum. There was something eerie about this whole situation—did frogs even go in saltwater? He shot a look out behind him. "Hmm," he said.

Behind the raft were four more massive frogs. They began squeaking an electric cry that sent a tingle into Sidney's skin. He looked forward again, dozens of frogs popped up upon the surf. In a pack they swam gracefully to the raft.

"Hey," Sidney said as the raft began to turn, losing ground, and heading back to shore.

He swatted at the frogs with the stick. One frog lifted its face and lashed out at Sidney, hitting the raft. In no more than two seconds, the raft disappeared beneath him like a club performer yanking away a tablecloth. He fell into the water, his knees hitting rough sand and his head momentarily going under. A scream erupted from his throat. There were dozens of the huge frogs.

He popped up and tried to run. The frogs watched him for several steps, until he made it back most of the way. Only his calves and feet remained below the surf, when the first tongue lashed out, then a second, third, fourth. Sidney's motor activity continued beyond his lulled brain as the tongues pumped poison into his bloodstream. He ran against the hold, and kept going, even after his flesh separated like rubber puzzle pieces. The vacant-eyed man reached the beach, fleshless, and pitched forward. He lay still, feeling the intense agony of being eaten alive, but unable to do anything about it.

From the ocean, the frogs converged, swimming and hopping, some swallowing the bits of flesh they'd taken. As a group, they dragged Sidney inland, sand playing into the man's open eyes, clinging to his sticky body.

Over the following day, the frogs gathered the corpses and dragged them into the high, high trees to let them fester, putrefy, and bait all manner of food to the deserted island.

WRONG NUMBER

(2021)

The view from behind her locker door was painful. Robyn and Jessica stood next to Connor and Tade, touching their biceps and giggling into their ears. Natural, casual, perfectly easy.

Robyn spun her head as if possessed by sudden rage. "What are you even looking at, Camel?"

Everyone at school called Larissa Hamilton Camel because of the humps, the bumps, the acne pebbling the surface of her face. Everyone called her Camel because she had nobody to defend her.

Larissa slunk back behind her locker door and began fiddling with her phone. No texts. No DMs. No SMs. Not even a spam email.

"What's a camel need with a phone?" Jessica said as they walked directly behind Larissa. The boys had their arms over the girls' shoulders.

Larissa bit down a retort: *at least my ex-boyfriend didn't show everyone the nudes I sent him.* Though she'd had to bite it down, it wasn't exactly hard. She only wished she had an ex-boyfriend, only wished she looked hot enough to send and receive nudes. After Jessica's ex spammed all the cool kids' phones with the pics, Jessica turned around and did it right back to him. As if it were staged.

She'd trade getting ogled for going unnoticed, in a heartbeat. Sometimes she lay in her bed, holding entire conversations with the cool kids. In her head she was one of them and dated Tade and giggled in his ear and felt his biceps and swapped nudes with him. In her head, it wasn't just her well-meaning dad who said she was pretty. She closed her locker and started down the hall, catching nobody's eye.

—

Adam Howser was killing time in the public bathroom at the law office where he was a junior associate on the rise. He'd been batting flirty texts off and on with a woman named Lisa. She was a barista at the Starbucks on the corner a quarter mile from there—a quarter mile plus forty-one floors down to ground level. He wasn't a player, wasn't a ladies' man, and it was only recently that women had begun to notice him. He'd had two girlfriends in college, though never anything serious. Now, thanks to his gym regimen he had washboard abs, a cut jawline, and arms that strained the fine fabric of his pricey suits.

The bathroom door opened. In the mirror's reflection he saw his boss holding open the door, chatting at someone passing by. Adam hurried to a stall. He stood, phone in his hands, peering into the cleanish white bowl below the hard black seat while he listened. His boss went into the stall next to his and opened his pants with a metallic jangle—that sound seemed to call to memory the women who'd come in to paint the office, including the partner bathroom. He should've foreseen that this bathroom might not be the safe space it was nearly every other day.

A whispered fart blew next-door. Adam was about to leave when his phone vibrated in his hands. There was a message from Lisa the barista.

I'll show you mine if you show me yours

Beneath the message was a shot of her bra strap.

"Hey," Adam's boss said. "You still over there?"

Adam jumped at the sound and his phone slipped from his suddenly slick grip, clanking down onto the seat before falling into the bacteria-laden drink.

"I could use some TP, if you're still there."

Adam yanked open the toilet paper dispenser and pulled out the huge one-ply roll. He handed it below the partition and then took off his jacket, began peeling his sleeve back. His silver phone with its blank screen faced up, sending bubbles, creating a gentle shimmer on the water.

—

Larissa faced the painted cinderblock wall as she pulled her t-shirt over her head. Behind her, another girl in the change room said, "Think you ought to shower?"

Larissa didn't dare get naked in front of these girls. She was almost always the first one in and out of the changeroom. There, she always slipped her shorts up from a sitting position, always turned away to change her shirt—that wall had never once made fun of her. She had pimples on her back and shoulders, sure, but not as many as she had between her breasts and not nearly as many as she had on her butt cheeks.

"I'd wash constantly, like every chance I got."

"Camels don't need to, her humps are full of water."

"More like full of gross."

"We're just looking out for you."

"Yeah, you need to wash more and maybe then you wouldn't be all pimples."

Maybe if you stopped making comments and let me live, I would! Larissa swallowed tears alongside the comment as she waited for the others to leave. The conversation eventually ceased, as did the nearly constant aerosol hiss and steady burping.

"Everybody says it's better after high school," Rebecca James said, a pudgy girl who hadn't let any stereotypical notions of beauty keep her from having a steady boyfriend. He wasn't even a loser or a nerd.

"I know," Larissa said. Rebecca was cool adjacent, so if nobody was looking, she was sometimes nice.

"But there's like a year and a half left, so don't you think you better shower?"

Larissa focused heavily on her sneakers, thinking, *how about you lay off the French fries and Kit Kats.* Of course, she said nothing because Rebecca was confident and wore the kind of clothes that accented her curves. Larissa would kill to be that way.

"Nobody likes ripping on you. You know that, right?" Rebecca said before leaving.

Larissa waited a ten count before saying, "Liar."

—

Adam slipped off the bench and began wiping up as he watched the expansion and then contraction of his swollen biceps. He'd gone hard because he had shots to snap. He'd wasted the better part of an afternoon moving his iPhone contacts and files to his new Samsung, all the while thinking about what he'd send Lisa.

The goal was hot, so hot she'd send it all…or better yet, meet him somewhere. To look his best, he hit the gym. He hurried to the bathroom shower combo after working up a sweat and locked the door. He dropped his shorts and closed his eyes. For a couple weeks now he'd been running scenarios where he climbed in behind the counter and took Lisa every way she wanted to be taken. Running through his favorite fantasy, he snapped a shot of himself, swollen everywhere and sopping wet.

He sent the pic.

You like?

He began working at himself and snapped another shot.

Want to help?

He put his foot up on the toilet seat so he could arch his back and flex his abs. He ejaculated and the white ooze carved a path between the muscles. He took the shot.

Show me how this makes you feel. Make you wet?

The phone went to the counter and he limbo walked over to the shower, trying to keep from spilling anything. While in the shower, he heard the rumbling vibration of his new phone acknowledging an incoming text message. No longer in a rush, he luxuriated in the steamy water, rubbing his muscles. There was no way that wasn't her, hitting him up, there was no way what he sent didn't make her hot. He shampooed his hair and scrubbed his feet. Feeling clean was a huge part of feeling sexy and he needed to be sexy because up until the last six months, women like Lisa the barista were wet dreams.

He dried off and slipped into the Oxford shirt and the suit slacks he'd folded and stashed in his gym bag. He then loaded his dirty clothes and shoes into the bag, delaying himself the beautiful surprise. Ready, he picked up his phone. He opened the three messages, drinking in the photos in backward order. They were extremely close-up, but all the way right.

—

Larissa bubbled. She reached her locker with maybe the first smile she'd ever worn into the school. Robyn said something in passing that Larissa didn't catch.

"What?"

Robyn spun on her heels, weighed Larissa top to bottom and then let their eyes meet. "I said you should lay off the donuts. Don't want to have to change your name from Camel to—"

"Screw off," Larissa said and flipped Robyn the bird.

"What did you say?"

"You heard me, you no ass toothpick."

Robyn's jaw dropped. A cough escaped her throat as she burned away in a huff.

Larissa had changed. She had a sexy new boyfriend who texted her steamy photos late at night—of course her reply photos were borrowed from Pornhub, but he really seemed to like them. He'd suggested they meet up, but until then they could text, and OMG, he was crazy! Just to keep up she had to Google search sexy text messaging and cribbed flirts from strangers, but it was working. So well that she'd purchased a Cosmopolitan magazine from the ampm down the block from her house—the cover teased a sext with a 99% success rate. She could hardly wait for this Friday—

Her cellphone pinged.

Hey, Lisa! Pervert's deposition no longer necessary tonight, want to meet up? Maybe show me some of that beautiful young flesh?

Little mistake, must've autocorrected Larissa to Lisa...still, her heart flew into overdrive and her hands shook so much she couldn't answer until after she took six deep breaths.

Yes where???

The warning bell rang. She ignored it; let the little people with their meaningless relationships rush about like fish in a river, she had a man who loved her.

At your work?

Here, another small mistake, but it had no bearing on their relationship. She simply had to remind him.

Don't work

As she awaited his reply, she felt eyes on her and looked up to see Mrs. Harding giving her the silent business. She opened her combination lock one-handedly, keeping her focus on the screen.

You pick.

The locker came open and she unshouldered her pack as she considered it. She'd have to sneak out, so the closer the better. She swung shut her locker just as the second bell rang.

Mrs. Harding came from behind and attempted to snatch the phone from Larissa's sweaty grip. "Now is the time for learning." Mrs. Harding yanked, and Larissa let go a low growl in the back of her throat, a primal sound. "You'll get this back at the end—"

"Everybody knows," Larissa said.

Mrs. Harding's eyes got huge, and she reeled her hand away. "Knows what?"

"You know." Larissa sneered over her shoulder as she took five regular steps before running toward her class. She'd seen that done on a prank show and it almost always worked because everybody had secrets. The halls were empty and most of the doors were closed. She replied and just before she swung open the door to her room, his reply came.

Cool. 8. I have a white Tesla...don't even need to get a room, could just let the car drive while we check out the backseat.

"Oh. My. God," she said and then looked at her classmates and the teacher. A few cooler girls sniggered while the teacher frowned. She was never late, so he said nothing as she pocketed her phone and sat.

———

Adam had parked in the lot next to the ampm Lisa had suggested. If she lived around there, it was a pretty wild commute across the city. There had to be ten Starbucks between the two points, but what did he know?

He knew to bring condoms.

He knew to pack champagne.

He knew to stash toys.

He knew to keep the toys and champagne and condoms hidden until he was sure she was up for it. Though the way she talked...dammit, she had to be up for it. Up for almost anything.

In the evening gloom and stretching shadows of the lot, he watched people come and go and with every tall, slender figure, his heartrate increased. It had been a tough day. He'd been distracted, and too often pulled up his phone to retrace their interactions. His mind eventually wandered to her personality: was she looking for more, did real relationships start out with tawdry texts and dick pics? His mind had drifted there again as he watched out the window, ignoring the frumpy shape heading his way.

Then he saw her—maybe?—crossing through the glow coming from the glass front of the convenience store. She paused and pulled out her phone. Adam smiled and flicked on his headlights. The woman looked up almost the same moment his passenger's side door opened. The frumpy figure fell into the car. She wore a cheap black hoodie, but enough of her face was revealed to show she was a teenager. Not a pretty one. Not one of those Lolita ones. Just an awkward girl riddled with acne, backpack between her knees. The zipper was busted, and a safety pin held the two halves together. In the fading interior light, he saw two things within the bag: a wad of pastel purple cotton and part of a spine from a fat textbook. An eleventh grade Science book.

"Can I help you?" Adam glanced sidelong out the window and the woman had departed the light of the ampm. "What...?" He didn't know what else to say.

The girl took a breath. "I'm a virgin."

"So? I don't...so?" Adam was shaking away distracted cobwebs.

The girl reached into the muffle pocket of her hoodie and withdrew her phone. "I love you."

Adam's phone pinged on the dash. He scooped it up.

A message from...Lisa?

I luv u

Adam gasped. It pinged again.

My dad will be wild when he sees my first bf has a Tesla

"BF?" Adam scrunched his face, drinking in the girl, understanding what had happened. "Oh, god. That was for someone else. I didn't mean—"

"You're so funny."

"No, those messages were for Lisa."

"I can be Lisa."

"No. You can't." His thoughts spiraled. This girl was young with a capital Y and what happened to grown men who messed with young girls?

Not two hours earlier, he'd discovered the truth behind his free afternoon. He'd been working for a family, trying to avoid court, but they were willing if it came to that. The accused was a thirty-year-old man and he'd been in an online relationship with the plaintiffs' fourteen-year-old son. The accused was a pillar of the community, an executive for a mutual fund company, a deacon at his church, married, soon to be a father, and now a vegetable, unable to attend the disposition.

He'd shot himself through the mouth and into the back of his brain. He was either a hebephile, or he looked enough like one that it wouldn't matter if a different truth ever came out.

Adam saw himself then, sweating on the wrong side of the table. What had he said to this girl? And those pics, could it get any raunchier?

"We're in love," she said. "We have a connection. I know you feel it."

Adam shifted, feeling the blood draining, possibly spilling from his feet. He swooned and clutched at the fine leather of the car. Eleventh grade, that was what, fifteen? Sixteen?

The girl had begun crying a little, as if finally understanding. Maybe he could talk to her and she would listen, like an adult. Maybe—

"If you don't love me, I don't know what I'll do." She waved her phone gently.

Adam watched it, thought of snatching it. But she seemed to sense this and stabbed the phone down between her thighs.

"You love me, right?"

Adam saw it then. There was no coming back from even a remotely plausible accusation. He'd sent a child pornography and had received pornography back—he should've suspected something when it was so close!

"You tell all your friends about me sending you messages?"

The girl paused. "No."

"Oh?" Adam could drive her home and he could trick her phone out of her hands long enough to delete anything incriminating; she didn't know his name.

His phone pinged as he sat in thoughtful reverie.

I don't need friends I got u

The phone pinged again.

Mrs. Adam Howser Larissa Howser lawyer wife someday???

She was nuts. An idiot. But she had the ingredients and

recipe to ruin his life. No. He wasn't about to be the guy other lawyers called the perv client. He'd overcome too much, worked too hard.

"How do you know my...?" he whispered, but the answer was obvious. His cellphone was his work phone and two minutes of Googling would reveal his identity.

"I'll do all the stuff we said," she said.

Adam inhaled deeply. "Okay." He swallowed, pausing, thinking, thinking, thinking. "Okay. Let's party. Tonight." He push-started the car.

"Oh. My. God. Nobody's going to believe some hot guy and me partied."

"Have to go to Vegas to do it."

She batted her lashes, trying to look sexy but looking more like she had low cognition and a case of Tourette's.

"I'll go anywhere with you."

"Hey, yeah, good, let's party a little. Champagne and a fun pill." Sometimes before a big case or meeting, he couldn't get to sleep. His doctor had prescribed him Lunesta. He'd gotten a refill two days earlier and forgot to take it out of the glovebox, noticed them when he'd stashed the extra condoms.

"Oh. My. God. Yes."

Adam set a course for the autopilot, and once they were moving, got to gingerly opening the Dom Perignon. "There's a pharmacy bag in the glovebox. Grab it for me." He didn't even want to reach across her. (*Fifteen!*) He readied two glasses and swapped the girl—this Larissa fool—a drink for the bag. Using his teeth and free hand, he opened the bag and withdrew the pill bottle. "You know, since we're celebrating, we should do it in style. Three pills each."

Larissa held the glass up to her face and frog-dipped her tongue into the champagne. "Fizzy," she said.

Was she even fifteen? Adam handed off three pills and set the bottle aside. He made a fist like he held pills too and then clinked her glass. "Cheers," he said and put his empty hand to his mouth and then drank, washed down those imaginary pills. He forced a smile when the girl showed him that she'd swallowed the pills by sticking out her tongue.

Seven hours later, he was exhausted, covered in sand, but home and could rest easy about the girl.

—

Larissa didn't understand. She was cold, her mind muddy. How had she ended up in the desert, and where was Adam? They'd been together, riding in his car, Vegas bound, to party and then, nothing. She didn't have her backpack or cellphone.

"Adam? Mr. Howser?" she said and then swiped her sweater sleeve beneath her nose where a steady trickle of mucous ran to her upper lip.

She decided to walk, and since the sun promised warmth, she picked that as her direction. Quickly, she came to the conclusion that there must've been an accident. That scared her. Not quite running, not quite jogging, her feet picked up pace as they cut over the hard sandy floor. Ahead, a giant boulder loomed like a curtain, and beyond it would be the modern world, and Adam. She closed her eyes, saw a mangled car and an unconscious man. Bloodied, oh god, she had to save him.

She did begin running then. Her chest burned and her legs felt like rubber, but she continued pushing until she reached the cold, cold rock. She leaned against it with her shoulder and had to drag her limp noodle body around the rough edges to see beyond.

Nothing. No wreckage. Only sand

Except, distantly, a rock wall rose and she knew then that after the accident she'd been so woozy she stumbled along, into the desert. Beyond that rock wall would be the world, and her love.

—

Adam awoke, bolting upright in his bed. Holy god, what had he done? He kicked from the fine sheets with the high thread count that the pretty woman at the home décor store had picked out for him. His feet hit the faux hardwood flooring of his rented condo and his hands went to the sides of his head. He squeezed, as if pressure would waylay his guilt.

"You had to do it," he whispered.

He'd emailed into work when he got home just before sunrise that he was sick and would miss at least a day. Before, that might've been a problem, but now, he could Zoom meet and go over files from home. Nobody wanted sickness spreading through the office, even if it was only a cold or a bout with diarrhea.

"You had to," he said again, trying to convince himself.

But was her life worth so much less than his? Was his hard work so much more valuable than her immature youth? Had to be. She was going to ruin him.

His hands fell to his sides and he took his first step with a fresh perspective. "Had to do it," he said, *knowing* this was the absolute truth of the matter.

———

Larissa was so hot and so thirsty. The sun beat down on her mercilessly. She'd taken off her sweater and wrapped it around her hips so that the hood flopped and whumped against her thighs. In the daylight, she no longer imagined the world beyond the rocks, though at night, her mind had played a million games.

Vultures swung lazy circles in the air high above her and when the sun went down, she heard coyotes. Spiders crossed her path. Snakes rattled behind rocks and she veered to avoid them. Two full days gone, and here she was on day three. Her lips had been licked raw and sand clung blackly to the weeping pads of degradation, and in the corners of her eyes, and in her ears, everywhere that moisture remained.

She sobbed off and on fairly steadily, no longer thinking of Adam in that constant way she had since receiving that text message, but thinking instead of her bed, her parents, the refrigerator—though Adam was never far from her thoughts. When she cried, no tears fell; her body knew to conserve that moisture.

The world had become yellows and reds. Sand and rocks and sun and sun and sun against her plodding motions. "Please," she moaned and leaned against a rock with her face, basking in the coolness of the shadow. She remained there against the rock so long that her legs tried to give out and her cheek brushed roughly against the stony surface. "Daddy, come get me," she said and pushed upright to resume following the sun. She always followed the sun, because the sun eventually got where it was going and so would she.

Five steps out, she pitched forward and landed hard against the baked desert floor. She touched her forehead. It had dried out. The acne wasn't smooth, but the pimples were receding as her body devoured the grease.

Now she got it. Adam wanted her, but she had to get pretty first, had to stop being a camel. He'd come for her once she was no longer Camel Hamilton.

A voice in the deep, deep darkest recesses of her mind hissed, *in the desert, a camel's a good thing to be.*

—

Tyler and Chelsea Hamilton opened the door of their home to the two officers in slacks and button-ups shirts with ties. They both looked somber, the kind of expression that said you aren't going to like this.

"Hello, Sir, Ma'am. We just need something cleared up here."

Tyler waved an arm to the detectives, welcoming them inside. They remained on the stoop.

"This will only take a second."

"Okay," Tyler said.

"Larissa, she was in the eleventh grade, but according to her birth certificate—"

"Oh, that!" Chelsea said. "In the second grade, she was out for recess when this troublemaker kicked a basketball. She was maybe thirty feet away, but it hit her in the temple and she fell down. She seemed fine, then halfway through the next class, she fell unconscious. She remained in a coma for sixteen months. When she came to, she was—"

Tyler cut in. "Soft in the head."

"Right. So rather than causing her any undue aggravation, once most of the physical therapy stuff was down to only in the evenings, we enrolled her in the second grade at a new school. The principal knew and so did most of the teachers, but we didn't need—Larissa didn't need the other students to know that she was older."

The cop with the pad of paper nodded as he listened. "So, we had it right. She is eighteen?"

"Yes, but mentally she's about fourteen. Does it change things? That she's not a minor?" Chelsea said, a fresh round of tears budding.

"Not for us, just clearing up an oddity."

—

Larissa had no way of knowing she'd been out there for five days, but she had. Her feet kept pushing her on during the day and at night she slept. The sun would lead her. The sores around her cracked and blackened lips were dirty sphincters that sucked in sand. Her acne was all gone now, and she knew she'd lost weight. She pawed at the loose flesh at night, and it made her smile because soon Adam would come for her. She'd be the exact woman he needed.

"Adam." Her voice was gravel in a cement mixer. "Mrs. Adam Howser."

Her feet kept going and she kept on following the sun, now and then thinking that the redundancy of the desert shapes was creepy, unaware that she'd been moving in a great oval since she'd awoken. Unnoticing of the solitary footfalls brushed into the hardpan sometimes only feet to the left or right of where she walked.

—

In the police station, a woman behind a computer shouted, "Found him!"

She'd been scanning similar images of the face for days, pretty much ever since they returned from Larissa Hamilton's locker with the printed images of the naked man. While she looked at millions of possible matches offered up via internet searches of social profiles in the area and then businesses, the two detectives assigned to the case had put together a few things. The pictures had been printed at the ampm near Larissa's home the morning she disappeared. The night she disappeared, she'd been milling around the ampm for more than half an hour, consuming three liter bottles of water to the great interest and fascination of the clerk on-duty. But then she was gone. Thirteen vehicles came and went during that time, but the lot camera did not pick up any license plates.

The detectives took the information and burned it to the address listed for a one Adam Henry Howser while two plainclothes officers headed to his office. He lived in a new high-rise with black glass and shining copper embellishments everywhere. Upon reaching his door—and after he didn't answer—the detectives decided they heard sounds of a struggle coming from within and demanded the superintendent let them inside.

The stink came first. The visual came second. Adam Howser lay on the floor, his legs stretched out from the doorway of his bathroom and into the hall. The moment the detectives reached him, they discovered three things: one, he'd taken whatever was missing from the empty prescription bottle next to him; two, he'd been dead for at least four days; and three, he wasn't going to tell them where he'd stashed the girl.

"Maybe there's a note," one detective said to the other.

—

In the wee hours of the morning, Larissa discovered she'd been walking at night, as if guided. Her feet fell and lifted, moving her onward, without the sun's direction. And this was good because she saw lights and a town. The desert became faded asphalt and she bubbled with newfound energy.

She'd made it so long because the others were right, she was a camel. Camels cross deserts and come out the other side.

In the gloom, that light drew bigger as the sun overhead continued to climb. She wouldn't follow it any longer, not when the ampm just ahead was a true beacon—besides, hadn't the sun already done its job, bringing her this far?

She'd worn holes in her shoes and her face was more weepy sores than it was even flesh, but she'd finally made it. Upon reaching the automatic doors, she paused and then stumbled on in when they opened. She ignored all else within and swung the cooler door. So much water! She grabbed an Evian and twisted away the pale pink lid. The cool moisture against her cracked mouth was a symphony of angels playing heaven upon her flesh. She emptied that bottle and reached for another.

"You okay?" a voice said.

She ignored it and twisted a blue cap off a Fiji bottle, slugging hard on the silky water.

"You okay?" The voice was high, harsh.

Larissa dropped the empty bottle and grabbed a bottle of Smart and twisted away the clear cap. The bottle went to her lips.

"You okree!"

Startled, Larissa turned. The clerk had a hideous, wrinkly red face. His eyes were little beads in his pinhead skull. Behind him, the wall of tobacco products began tumbling, revealing endless yellows and reds.

"You okree, kree!"

Larissa put the water up to her lips again and closed her eyes.

"Kree! Kree!"

That wasn't a vulture, it was a man, and if she didn't look and kept her eyes tight closed, she was inside the ampm, not roasting on the desert floor.

PATHS TO OCEANIA

(2014)

Frizzy grey hairs rose in jagged strings that poked to the sky, as if dancing on electricity. The scalp of Trudy Christian was an act of anarchy. Trudy herself was a local poet of some notoriety. She stood out front of a Royal Bank, day after day, with a petition and a hollow plastic megaphone. Fat plastic buttons rode both lapels of her ancient denim jacket, suggesting all sorts of far-left things, including a few that expressed her disagreement with a recent amendment tacked onto the already alarming anti-terror bill.

"Stop Big Brother!" Trudy shouted. "Miss! Miss, do you want the right-wing, oil obsessed nut-jobs peeping behind your doors to ensure you're thinking the correct thoughts?"

It was a Tuesday. Michelle Mansfield turned her gaze briefly to the sky as she huddled into herself to avoid the loud woman. Trudy frowned.

"I'm not the one to fear! I'm not the one in question!" Trudy shouted, megaphone at her side.

Michelle was close enough that the loud voice sent a shiver of alarm down her back like the Grim Reaper was playing her spine like a xylophone. That woman was a damned menace. Sophisticated society was a place of reasonable tones and volumes. Shouting was archaic, dangerous.

"I never said a thing," Michelle said. Although, inwardly, she did worry about the government's peeping. "I can't sign," she added as she scurried along.

Michelle had worried a great deal about the bill when it first passed. She wasn't the only one. There were many riding a wave of public outrage. The outrage fizzled as it tended to when the silver-tongued politicians suggested that the bill only looked into *them* and never into *you*. The bill was for *your* protection. If *they* had nothing to hide, *they* had nothing to fear. *Them and they* never being *I* or *us*. *They* were a group so unlike *we*, most accepted the explanation and moved onto other worries.

Most, not all.

Those who refused the easy explanations met trouble during tax season. General problems fell like raindrops in the face of immediate, personal trouble. This kind of behavior, everyone knew it happened, though never mentioned it...lest it be them next year.

Michelle did not buy it and was glad she'd played the quietly wary citizen from the beginning, never speaking out and never signing a petition. Women yelling on the street were begging for trouble.

"Hey, Doc. You catch Trillah last night?" Lily Waters asked as Michelle stepped into the reception area of her office.

Michelle smiled. A quick scan of her internal database of names found Trillah. She tried to keep up with the usual shows, but most simply didn't hold her attention. Michelle's husband didn't like those shows either. His distaste arose because the shows were cheap. She didn't like them because they seemed a glimpse of the future. He didn't share her fears about governmental nosiness and saw no correlation between feeding the public shows about constant, everyday observation of house members and the government's constant, everyday observation of citizens.

"Not last night, no."

"Well, Trillah convinced Cotton and Robbie into a threesome and then halfway through, they basically kicked Trillah out of the bed. Scandalous!"

Michelle waggled her eyebrows. She made it through but one full episode of *Hormonal House*, for educational purposes. She didn't recall Robbie or Cotton.

"That show's just a bit racy for me," Michelle said and hung her jacket in a small closet.

"Oh, you prude... Anyway, your nine cancelled as did your three. Early day, maybe?"

"Maybe," Michelle said and slid the key into the lock on her office door.

Once inside she flipped the bolt paddle closed, silently. It wasn't easy keeping up the routine with Lily. It wasn't easy performing the ruse that was work either.

Some patients still came into the clinic, but Michelle had created many of the appointments herself, masking her voice over the phone, and then again the day of to cancel. Cancelled faux appointments gave her a chance to think. Most times she was thinking about where she'd be in two years—hopefully free of prying eyes—and the truths she'd stumbled upon. Sometimes during hours of emptied schedule, she thought about the breakdown of her relationship. This was secondary. Her hubby did not believe a word she'd said about her discoveries.

So, there she had it, they weren't a perfect match. Craig Mansfield told his wife she was *being crazy.* Always with a smile. The suggestion was that she needed help, not exactly joking, still smiling. He didn't understand the truth. Or worse, he did.

Michelle sat down at her desk and hit the power button on her computer. There were steps to keep things looking normal on the outside. To stay on the acceptable side of things, Michelle opened a window in Chrome and let the digital signal from King FM 98.1 play. Mozart kept up a normalcy and offered comfort. She didn't think they could hear thoughts, but technology moved so fast.

She opened her email and responded where necessary, the messages vapid and distracted. Being a podiatrist mattered little to her anymore. Most lives weren't going to be worth the hassle of existence soon. Of course, she never said so. They'd make her go away if she said something so uncouth.

Who are they?

No answer existed to that one, not a cut and dry answer. Nothing was that easy. It didn't matter whom; it mattered that they existed and actively sought. At some point, she'd done something that put her on their radar. Some dumb slip up. Long stressful nights had stretched painfully. It was making the mask hard to keep in place.

She leaned back on her chair and looked around the office with a heavy breath. The idea was to appear eccentric, not paranoid. Little sticky-post reminders clung to most surfaces. An absent-minded doctor, some *daffy woman*. Every note had its purpose. Looking at them now, they certainly were kooky, a regular topic of conversation when real clients had appointments.

The light overhead flickered and she gasped, quickly turning her gaze from the fixture back to her desk. Someone had fooled with the office last night; of that she had no doubt.

It all began with the webcam built into her monitor. It glowed green one day, only a web browser open on her computer. Whoever watched hadn't disabled the telltale light—a mistake or a warning shot? She steeled herself, thinking, thinking, thinking until she got it and wrote a note: *Pay dues Tues.* She placed that sticky note over the camera lens, and there it had stayed for the last six months.

Try ginger latte, was the second. It fit over a dark grain in the wood of her door. *Stop by school with donation*, the third. There was a stain seeping through the paint on the wall opposite her desk. The fourth through sixteenth found chinks and cracks, here and there. Covering the interested eyes was nothing more than a delay in the inevitable, and still, it made her feel better.

It was unreasonable to post a note on her light fixture. Too obvious. They'd see her from then on. *See this.*

She put a finger in her nose and then reached a hand up her skirt to adjust. Nobody knowingly under a watchful eye would do either. She was careful, clever, but there was no doubt she'd have to accelerate the plan. There was so much to give up.

It was time to go back to roots she'd never known. Times long before the birth of her or her mother. She thought she'd miss her television. The pleasure of a movie. *Everybody* knew that the television watched and listened to them. And they'd accepted that when smart TVs became dirt cheap, and who could turn down a brand-new TV at rock bottom prices?

Manufacturers apologized for the intrusion, though never rectified the invasion. Individualised advertising interests, *nothing more*, they promised. The anti-terror committee piggybacked on the tech in every home. After TVs came the phones, and the phones were the true gateway into lives.

"Not mine," Michelle mouthed.

The phone on her desk buzzed.

After a breath she answered, "Yes?"

"Yeah, Robert Wilkes just called, he said he has to stop by later. He has questions about..."

Lily continued but Dr. Michelle Mansfield was already off the phone and rooting through the hidden cubby of her desk for the small pistol she'd placed there. Nobody just stopped by. There was no client named Robert Wilkes—*was there?*

Didn't matter. The time had come. She unlocked and swung open the office door.

"I guess there's...Doc?"

Michelle raced out of her office and into the building's lobby. Two men in black suits stepped up to the glass doors to enter. Michelle spun around on pivoted heels, hurrying toward the rear doors. She wasn't certain that they'd come for her until their steps followed her from the front lobby to the rear exit.

The back lot was a series of cement boxes and alleyways. The scenery leant assistance to the getaway. This was the easy part. Around a chest-high wall, a row of air-conditioning units ate the space and offered her the perfect cover.

She heard a door open behind her.

Once amid the clunky, energy-guzzling boxes, Michelle heard the door close. Male voices rumbled in the silence. She didn't catch their words, but knew they were agents pretending to be smokers.

Michelle cut out onto a sidewalk. Trudy Christian remained on the street, yelling. Michelle finally saw her for what she was. Those names on that list would receive extra attention. How could they be so stupid? How could Trudy Christian be so sneaky?

That's probably not her real name and she probably didn't write that book of poetry.

Michelle had been so, so blind. She lowered her gaze; above the so-called Poet was a lamppost, a camera was hidden next to the bulb.

Michelle put her face down and charged on by. She entered a parking garage where she rented a space under an assumed name. The garage accepted cash and her lack of identification with trepid reluctance. This came as a positive sign. Subtly paranoid was harder to fake than utterly spooked or completely comfortable.

The white panel van's paperwork stated that it belonged to a Lincoln Dollard. Lincoln Dollard had a licence and insurance, he also had a cemetery plot. He'd resided in that plot for close to a year already. Michelle paid five times the van's value to acquire it with the information intact. The seller was a patient's aunt, a pregnant, amphetamine addict named Monica. Eager to sell, the junky was no fool.

It was difficult to keep a moderate pace. Running brought attention she did not need. It was some comfort to slide a hand into the pocket folded behind her skirt pleat and feel the solid pistol grip. Even a doctor could kill...when she needed to.

She drove east three hours and stopped in a small town appearing a few overdue notices from collapse. They had a single store which had gasoline and food. Most importantly, they accepted cash. There was food at the final destination, but that was another three hours east and she hadn't eaten much breakfast.

The old-style flat screen hanging from steel brackets high on the wall was a comfort. This was a model produced years before the first Smart TVs.

"Maybe you can find one of those old windmills or some bootleg solar panels," she said to the dusty dash of the van.

A nice thought. One not easy to follow through. It was the kind of activity generally deemed sneaky and anti-government. Something to monitor. What are you hiding? What's wrong with the power grid? She didn't need that particular flavor of attention.

She took two gravel roads from the cracked and baked highway asphalt—she was a long way from anywhere worth being. She pulled up the lane. Dusk settled an auburn cast over the open land as Michelle stepped into her new life at the old farmhouse.

—

The strange woman paid a lease for five years, cash up front. It was a dream deal for the young Gilmour family, having trouble keeping their operation afloat as it was otherwise. The thankful husband and wife spotted Michelle's van and decided they would drop by with gifts the following morning, a welcome basket of preserves and fresh baked goods. The main house was more than a kilometer away, door-to-door. Across a flat field and over a privacy fence of short trees it was but a half of that. It was a warm night and to save on energy, the Gilmours slept with all the windows open. At about midnight, a muffled bang echoed over the fields.

"Was that a gun?" Hannah Gilmour asked from next to her husband in bed.

"Probably Zeke saw a cy-oat," Felix Gilmour said.

—

Craig Mansfield took the call first thing in the morning. He'd been a wreck all night when Michelle didn't come home. It had been eight months since she accused him of being one of them. Whatever that meant. He'd tried to get her help then, but she was a grown woman, and now she could leave him if she wanted. It was her right.

He was on the phone, his butt resting on the counter as his extremities refused to cooperate. "It says what?" he said.

"You can come out and see if you like. It's not pretty though," said the uncomfortable voice on the far end of the line. "Looks like it's her last words, er, whatever."

"I'll come. I'll come." He hung up. "Oh, Michelle."

Craig called into work and then sped off toward a small community he'd never heard of; a spot where his estranged wife leased a farmhouse unbeknownst to him. Where she blew half her head off and then finger-painted a message on the floor just before she perished.

Paths to Oceania.

"What does that even mean? You helped so many, how didn't you see that you needed help?" he mumbled as he pulled into the laneway.

There was an officer awaiting him. Big in the shoulders, a blocky head, a push broom moustache, a cookie-cutter cop.

"She's in the living room. Straight through the kitchen," the cop said, pointing in through the open door.

"Thanks."

Craig stepped inside.

Paths to Oceania. Oh ,Michelle, what does that mean?

He walked through the kitchen. There was a wall of canned soups and beans. A stock ready for a long stay. He swallowed hard. She was so, so much worse than he'd seen. Paranoid, delusional, how had he missed that she'd fallen so far from reality?

He flicked the living room light switch and saw the blood. In the center of the barren room was a reddish stain stretching over a threadbare rug onto ancient hardwood. She'd shot herself, like the cop had said, and with her dying motions wrote a message with the blood: *PATHS TO OCEANIA.*

Too much, by far. He leaned against the wall and cried quietly. Wallpaper roses of different shapes and sizes rode over an off-white background. Ugly wallpaper, new and yet in a foregone style. Someone had already picked at the paper, seemingly at random and all over the room.

"Was it you, honey?"

Absent fingers scratched at the paper, peeling away a strip. He looked at the pale wall below, rubbing the bit of paper he'd torn between a thumb and finger.

"Paths to Oceania?" he whispered, glancing down at the paper in his grasp.

He looked back to the wall. The pale surface shifted and rolled. An eyelid peeled back and revealed a glassy eyeball. It stared at Craig Mansfield, and he stared back. The empty living room came alive with moist movement, tiny damp clicks of eyes opening from beneath fleshy lids no longer hidden by the rosy wallpaper. Hundreds of eyeballs watched him.

"No," Craig Mansfield whispered shaking his head gently.

He licked the glue-side of the torn wallpaper and stuck it back on the wall. Out of the living room, through the kitchen, and away from the scene. Like most, what he didn't care to recognize, he could ignore. Those eyes were on somebody else. They weren't looking at him, there was no reason to look at him.

HUNGRY

(2015)

From the beginning, Baby Kashmir couldn't get enough of that delicious mama's milk into her round baby belly. The child's lips had swollen from constant sucking, and Sophie's nipples had become raw and bloody, cracked like dry heels.

Something was wrong with the kid. She was so, so hungry.

Sophie sat in the waiting room with the tiny bundle sucking away at her exhausted, pebble-like nipple—couldn't get blood from a stone, but pink milk found a way to flow.

Time for a switch. Kashmir's lips popped from her tit with a farty suction sound. Only the little boy with his nose red from wiping and cheeks green with sickness watched the transition. Kashmir wailed until the new mammary mass found her lips. Sophie rubbed the baby's bulbous belly until the nurse called her name. That belly was the main cause for her worry, that and the hunger. The baby came out like a Buddha, gut enough for two or three babies.

The doctor laughed at her concerns.

Asshole.

He then humored her by taking Kashmir's blood. They'd know if there was an issue in about a week, until then, *look how big she's getting!*

The blood came back fine.

"Maybe she's just fat?" Tai said, husband and father. He tickled under Kashmir's chin as the chunky baby sucked on a bottle.

Sophie shook her head. Tai was always so quick to take the easiest route and never faced the issues straight on.

"Something's strange. It isn't normal. Listen, it's like a well in there." Sophie lifted the baby's shirt and tapped on the hard belly. "Hear that?"

It sounded a little like a drum full of water.

Tai took Sophie's pale hand in his and kissed her knuckles. "There's a word for this. Empty nest, postpartum something. It's making you see things that aren't there. Kashmir's just a great, big baby!"

This wasn't postpartum anything.

—

Kashmir cried often in the six months since she'd been home, but this was different. The shriek that pierced the air wasn't surprise, or hunger, or fear, or annoyance. It was pain.

Sophie leapt from bed. Tai followed close on her heels. The nursery door swung inward at a kick. Baby Kashmir gripped the rails of her crib, her hands at her sides as she lay on her back.

"Arrrggguhhh!" The tiny baby made the un-baby-like sounds. "Arrrggguhhh!"

"Kash!" Sophie screeched and rushed across to the brown bundle swaddled in white sheets below the veiled canopy.

Kashmir wore her *I'm takin' a dump* face and Sophie saw the massive slope of belly nearly flatten as if steamrolled. The white sheet was instantly drenched. The dampness crept up the cotton, seeking with dark tendrils of moisture. The baby began a normal, everybaby wail.

Afraid of what she might see, Sophie held the blanket but couldn't pull it back. Tai, unnoticing of issue looked at the wetness and laughed.

"Like a flood! The levy failed! Good baby!"

He grabbed the blanket and lifted to reveal a pink mess, a torn diaper, and a cord stretching out to the bottom of the crib. He was smiling, obviously didn't care to recognize it for what it was.

"Kash must've ate some string," he said even as Sophie took a step in reverse.

Kai grabbed onto the cord and followed it down below the crib. Sophie continued until she'd backed to the door. It was insanity. She was losing it. Postpartum one thing or another. Had to be it, because that thing coming out of Kashmir looked just like an umbilical cord and that was impossible.

"It just keeps going!" Kai said, glee in his tone.

He crawled under the crib. The heavy oak unit, a gift from a friend, handcrafted and weighing just shy of two hundred pounds.

"How the—?" The bottom half of the crib fell onto Kai's neck, crushing him. He made a single wet gargle noise after the crash.

Sophie's fear was washed aside. She launched forward for her daughter. She grabbed the suddenly light little thing, feeling the sticky amniotic fluids instantly clinging her nightshirt to her flesh. Kashmir continued to wail. The pain sounds returning.

"Arrrggguhhh!"

Sophie backed up from the crib with her child pressed to her chest. Kai's legs convulsed with death's rattle. For a moment, all was horrifically calm.

Sophie swallowed, was about to call out to her lump of a husband when a tiny figure rushed from his side and into the shadows. Postpartum hallucination? Sophie ran to the door.

As if snagged on a nail, she jerked back in a whiplash. She charged onward again and then yanked back again as if on a tether. She refused to look at that umbilical cord—that impossible umbilical cord. She put her head down, grunting and running. Something fought her momentarily but gave up a mucky sounding freedom as a purple placenta slung across the nursery and thwacked against the pale pink wall at the far side of the room.

Sophie made for her bedroom. She slammed the door and jumped into bed, cradling Kashmir tight. Murmuring into the crying baby's scalp, "It's okay. It's okay. Shh. Please, Kash, shh."

Next to the bed, the red light on the telephone base lit. Sophie knew then that she'd imagined everything, and Kai was on the phone. Ordering in some emergency service like it was Domino's.

Sophie put a breast to Kashmir's mouth and the baby sucked, silenced by a lactic consolation. Wrought mother picked up the telephone and put it to her ear.

"I'm hungeee, Dada," a high, infantile voice said.

"Your mama will feed you till I get there," a smooth as jazz timbre came over the line.

Sophie gasped.

"Sophie?" that smooth voice said.

"Hungeee, Mama. I'm coming for yeeew."

Sophie threw the phone and covered a scream threatening to leap from her lips. She waited in the dark, Kashmir tight to her chest. The seconds mounted but she didn't wait long. The bedroom door creaked open a few inches. Sophie gasped. Little wet footfalls pattered on the hardwood.

"Mama, I'm so hungeee. Maaawmaaaw!"

"No, don't, you're—" Sophie stopped mid-word as that voice from the far end of the line clicked, triggering recognition.

The doctor. The fucking doctor who'd assisted her and Kai. His sperm or her egg...something wouldn't spark, not until the doctor stuck that tube up between her legs and squirted in some *magic beans.* He laughed when she went back to talk to him after her general practitioner congratulated her on finally conceiving.

The sheets at the end of the bed tightened as the little thing climbed. In the moonlight shine pouring in through the window, Sophie saw the glistening wet face floating beneath a tuft of hair. Little lips smiling.

"Meee sooo hungeee!"

The thing rushed between Sophie's legs. It was fast, too fast for Sophie to wrench her body away, not with Kashmir latched and feeding. The thing was on her, and Sophie stiffened. It started toward her second breast.

She could feed both. Sure. She had two breasts. Feed it and then somehow get away from it. In the blink it took to make this assumption, the thing grabbed onto Kashmir. Sophie felt the second wet detachment and screamed.

"No!"

Sophie's fingers wrapped around the skinny homunculus, slimy with familial goo. She found the umbilical cord and wound it around the neck. She pulled tight, tight, tight. It gargled against the fleshy rope. Sophie latched a hand onto its head as it tried to clamp its horrible baby teeth down on Kashmir's doughy cheek.

"Gramma, noooo!" The reaction was of surprise and scorn amid the sucked breaths and burbling moisture.

Sophie's fingernails drove into the soft, baby-cooked skull as she wrenched on the slick umbilical cord. Kashmir screamed then and Sophie wondered if she screamed for her child. The thing thrashed as its little brainpan lifted beneath Sophie's fingers with a crunchy pop.

The thrashing stopped.

Kashmir cried.

Sophie panted.

She wiped her hands on the bedsheet and held her child. It was over. Kashmir found a nipple once again and Sophie leaned back. She closed her eyes.

———

The sun was up.

No.

Not the sun. The light was on overhead. Kashmir was a weighty hotbox on her chest, sleeping. The other thing was gone, but the mess remained. In the chair by the closet door—the chair she used to put on socks when she was pregnant because it had become nearly impossible otherwise—the specialist she and Kai had hired was crying into the ragged, bloodied bundle.

"You killed her," he whispered.

"Get out!"

The man sneered, rose, and left with his bundle. To Sophie's surprise, she heard the front door close. So simple. It was truly all over. Sophie kissed Kashmir's head and two tears dropped to the baby's scalp.

"All done."

In the hallway, she saw shadows scurrying. From the corners of her eyes, things jerked and approached. She bent and kissed them away, Kashmir's fine hair against her lips, her eyes closed, baby held tight against her. Those shadows couldn't be real.

It was over.

It was over so long as she never opened her eyes to the awful little things climbing on her bed.

"Sooo hungeee," a hot little voice whispered into Sophie's ear.

"Hungeee," another hissed from between her legs.

TREASURE

(2015)

The sand got stuck under my toenails, down my shorts, and between my ice cream sticky fingers. I remember it so clearly that it might as well have been only seconds ago. The sun baked us, my back warm, but safely under guard of goopy white cream. Knowing my mother, likely SPF 60. Down the beach was a man with a metal detector.

"What's he looking for?" I asked my mom.

"Treasure."

"Like pirate treasure?" I said.

My mom laughed and explained about dropped items: rings, watches, coins. I asked if we could get one, a metal detector—though by the time the words were out of my mouth, I knew we'd never have one. My parents didn't have the excess for such a frivolous whim; groceries didn't buy themselves after all.

I watched the man with his detector. He wore a straw fedora, a grey tank top that didn't quite cover his considerable gut, red short shorts, and black Velcro sandals. He went by without even looking at me; he looked at my mother a second—she wore a two-piece bikini—but he didn't linger, obviously not interested in her kind of treasure.

It was then that I heard a whisper. Even now, I can't tell if it was imagination working from intuition or if the thing really spoke to me, heard my wish of treasure for myself.

"Caspar, treasure, real treasure, this way, Caspar."

I looked to my mom; she heard nothing. I crawled on hands and knees to the water's edge.

"Dig, Caspar."

The sand underhand cooled the further the deeper I dug. My mom asked, "Whatcha lookin' for Cas?" but I didn't answer, partly because I didn't know and partly because I couldn't look away from the hole I'd dug. Not for a second—look away a heartbeat and the treasure's snatched up by someone else.

Finally, almost shoulder deep, there it was, white with red ends and black dots. A trill played into me, and I wanted to scream with joy.

If only I'd left it there. I used to imagine digging a deep hole and posting up like a sentinel, armed with a machine gun, guarding the treasure so that nobody dared touch it. But how could I know that at first. This guilt...it was not my fault and still I couldn't shake it.

My mouth opened and an intense feeling hushed me. The thing went into my pocket, and there it stayed, that voice repeating, "Don't let them see. Don't let them see."

Only minutes later, Mom told me to jump into the water, get all the sand off me, time to go. No argument, I got in and rinsed off. After, I followed my mother in her teeny peach tone bikini to the car.

Mom towelled me dry and made me drop my trunks in the parking lot, assuring me that nobody wanted to see my dinky. She always called it a dinky. I quickly stepped into dry shorts and a tee shirt. Mom snatched my wet shorts before I had a chance to grab for my newfound treasure and pitched them into a grocery bag. We rode home and all I could think about was my treasure.

Once home, I offered to take all the wet stuff into the house. Mom smiled and quickly draped a tee shirt over her top after she'd pulled shorts over her bottom. My dad didn't like the peach outfit unless he was there; she liked it enough to defy him.

The neighbor twins yelled across the yard, but I ignored them and I ran to the laundry room with the bag. I searched my pockets, and for a long moment, I thought it was gone, dropped along the way somewhere, lost forever...*if only*. But there it was, cold in my hand, and heavy, no longer smooth. It looked like a painted rock, nothing special, but then I began to think about the shape, wider on one end, red on the tip, black specks all over.

The doorbell rang and I listened. Mom yelled for me to come. I looked back down at the thing in my hands. It did not change, and yet I saw something different in the shape: a firehouse Dalmatian. Stupid red hat and all. Now the thing looked almost alive, and I desperately wanted to show my mother, show the twins who'd obviously come by, but my voice caught and the treasure returned to my pocket

The twins were in my bedroom. They'd gone to the afternoon matinee showing of *The Little Mermaid*. The ads for it had been all over TV and I'd longed to see it, if only because by and by everyone else had seen it. The twins hum-sang the songs. A pang of angry jealousy struck me in a way it never had before. I'd been to the movies three times in my whole life. The twins went a couple times a month!

As quickly as they came, the twins left. There, alone in my room, I rolled the treasure around in my hands. It changed again but didn't; the Dalmatian's fire hat shifted into red fangs.

"What did they want?" Mom said from my doorway.

I closed my fists around my treasure, hiding it. "They went to see *The Little Mermaid*...can we go see it?"

"Sorry, Cas, that's beyond the budget."

I flopped around, putting my back to her were I lay on my bed. Treasure in my hands, black, white, and red swirled and I saw a crow with a bloody beak.

At the supper table, my dad wore a great big grin as my mom dished out Kraft Dinner. "What do you say? *Days of Thunder's* playing at the Millmount."

A movie. Anything at the theater was a big deal and my foul mood drained to nothing...until my dad said, "And, Caspar, you get to play with the neighbors," as if that was some fantastic consolation. My fury boiled. I felt the treasure in my pocket and the trio of shapes and colors swirled in my mind. It was changing but not changing again: a red van with black tinted windows and a white licence plate.

The neighbors lived just across a small patch of grass. As soon as I got there, the girls started in on Ariel and how I had to see the movie.

"That's enough, girls," their mother said.

We watched wrestling—an adult choice that I actually agreed with—and while the Hulkster shook and yelled a greasy song of anger into Mean Gene's microphone, I rubbed my treasure.

Finally, it began.

I heard what the others did not. Through walls and windows, through the night's sky, getting closer with every second, the growls and the howls. I looked around the dingy living room, brown shag carpet under my knees, the twins in the corner by the window playing with dolls, and their parents on the couch, close enough to the table to reach the cans of High Life. I covered my ears. Those sounds came so close, but nobody noticed. On the TV, the Hulkster lay out cold thanks to a Jimmy Hart steel chair.

With a jarring din of violence, glass showered into the living room from the broken window. The girls screamed as the Dalmatian shook broken glass from its coat. The twins' parents shouted as the dog's head split into two, the flesh between stitching itself back together as it remolded into double the trouble. Snapping and growling, the two-headed beast lunged at the twins.

"Get away!" the twins' mother shouted.

The twins surely would've died had their near-drunk father not taken a surprisingly sober aim with the shotgun he kept in the closet by the door. The boom sounded and the Dalmatian whimpered once prior to dying in a heap of unnatural monstrosity.

I chanced a peek.

Twin soup in blood sauce, hold the faces.

I don't blame them for forgetting that I was there, leaving me in front of the mess and the dead dog as they rushed to the hospital with their all-too-quiet girls bleeding rivers and breathing in short little sips.

My parents had locked the door when they left, so I sat on the cement step outside. The treasure had become a rock again. So young and accepting of wonders, my mind didn't make the connection between the Dalmatian I saw in the rock before and the thing that attacked the neighbors.

Hours slipped, and I sat. I slid from my spot and huddled myself into a ball on the lawn. It was cool, but I felt fine, safe, even protected. I slept eventually. Some time later, a car pulled into my driveway. It wasn't Dyna the Chrysler Dynasty.

I gazed up at a man in a dark blue coat and slacks as he rushed around to the passenger's side of the white car. The man opened a door and helped my mom out. She had a crutch and a sling, a bandage over her head. I couldn't move, she could hardly move and for a second we all stared at each other.

"Have you been out all night," she said. Before I could answer, she added, "Your father's dead, van hit us. Didn't even get to see the car movie."

The man hushed her—I guess she was in shock—and they stepped past me and to the door. He helped her inside and shook his head at me, sympathetic.

Just Mom and me for a couple days. She didn't get up to much until the second night. She trudged around in a frantic drag and swagger, demanding every window open, getting rid of Dad's scent so we could move on. Weird and frantic, but how could I know what she really needed? I was a kid. I didn't know what she was thinking or why. I was sad too, though not too sad.

My mother began scrubbing the walls. In the distance, I heard a bird cry out. It came closer and closer. Mom dropped her sponge and bent to retrieve it from behind the couch.

"Screee!"

Mom lifted her chin in time to see the enormous crow buzz through the window and swoop down from above, not enough time to protect her face from the first pecks. Unlike with the two-headed dog creature, I wasn't afraid of some damned crow. I hovered and I grabbed onto its pointed feet, pulling it away from Mom's face.

The crow stared me down with something too knowing to be natural. "Screee!"

I nearly dropped the thing but managed to keep a grip. "No!" In a swooping arc, I slammed the bird against the coffee table hard enough that I heard a series of cracks. Quickly, the bird was a dead thing and Mom was shouting for me to call for an ambulance.

Paramedics arrived and took us both. I slept on a couch in the nurses' break room while doctors worked on my mother. I got to see her the next morning, but she'd never see me again, never see anything again.

For the first time since finding it, I'd left the treasure at home, but I never forgot about it, it felt like a missing limb until I'd slept. There is no doubt in my mind that I'd left it at home. But when I awoke in the hospital, I found the treasure in my pocket.

We took a taxi back this time. Treasure in my hands where I sat on our couch, Mom dozed on painkillers next to me while listening to the television. She didn't hear me leave. I walked as far as I dared, through town and to the quarry. With no ceremony, I reared back and threw the rock, threw it with every bit of strength I had. It clunked and bounced way off in the distance. My heart ached for it. But I felt better. With every step closer to home, I felt better.

Mom called to me in a faraway kind of voice, "Cas, get ready for..." she lost consciousness, and I assumed the next logical word was *bed*. I did. The next morning, the treasure was under my pillow like a prize from the Tooth Fairy.

I'd dug up the treasure, it was mine, and I was its.

For the rest of the summer bad things happened: the twins came home from the hospital with skin-grafted faces under bandages and a cuddly puppy. The puppy hated me though, snipped at me; I reached into my pocket and felt a sharp-edged puck. Words formed that I didn't recognize until later. The puppy got into poison—stuff called Coon Doom.

I knew but I didn't. The janitor lost a foot in an accident after he gave me trouble for drawing on the wall near my coat hook. My teacher broke her hip, hit by a runaway bus without a driver inside—she'd given me the business over a snowball fight on the yard. Little accidents plagued everyone that caused me grief. Three bullies died after falling through ice.

By age ten, there was no more fooling myself. I took a ride on my bike a day before the start of fifth grade. At the pier, I felt in my pocket and pulled out what appeared to be no more than a colorful rock. I slung that thing into the ocean water, slung it as far as I could—just like when I'd gone to the quarry. By the time I got home, the thing was in my pocket. It was only a test, and I was not surprised by the outcome. I tried burning it, but that did no good. I mailed it to an address in South Africa, no return address, and still, my treasure appeared on my doorstep in a different package. Post-marked from Russia.

I cried for days, I told my mother, she politely asked me to stop yanking her chain. It was all my fault and I knew it. By the time I was fourteen, the grief wore a hole in me, and I decided to end it all. I'd seen enough movies to know about slitting wrists in comfortable bathtubs. Ready and willing I stared at my treasure and took the razorblade out of the cardboard package. I sliced and the blood spurted, I felt good for the first time in a long time. I slit the second wrist and smiled at the stupid thing; I was going to win. The water became crystal clear. My wrists, clean of damage. I shrieked and tried again, the razorblade melted into a soft puddle against my flesh.

"No, damn you!"

Mom knocked on the door. "You okay, Cas?"

I said I was and drained the tub. It just wasn't fast enough. Speed and strength. I needed it to happen so quickly and profoundly that the treasure couldn't reverse it.

In town, the highest building was the defunct lighthouse. It sat in the middle of a parking lot near the banks and the fairgrounds, now a museum. I paid the dollar and climbed to the top level. I didn't think, didn't hesitate, I sprinted and pinioned over the handrail. I heard a scream from above as I fell, but it only took a second. The world slipped away in a black mass of heat.

Only seconds later, I awoke looking up at a young man. He laughed and said, "Holy smokes, he's fine!"

Mom was mad when she heard the news. "Promise me you'll never do something so reckless again."

"Okay," I said.

That night, I felt the treasure's weight in my pocket. I pulled it out and it rolled like loose rubber in my palm, shifting and changing and swirling. Now, my treasure was a face, a face like my dad's face was, but not the same, had hints of my mother.

It was me, me of the future.

It smiled and opened its bright red lips to say, "Accept me and be happy for my bounty." I blinked and it was a stone, just a stone.

For years I'd pondered the message until I got it.

Married and divorced, I no longer have an ex-wife and her lover didn't know what hit him. I climbed the corporate ladder with relative ease, a lot of accidents and *random* violence going around. I haven't had even so much as a speeding ticket.

Accept me and be happy for my bounty, it said that, and I did, I am.

Grief is one of those things that can eat a man up, but only if he's looking at it from the wrong angle. There's always a sunny afternoon for every dark night.

EASTER TREAT

(2019)

"Ain't that a corker?" Debbie Ransom said as she peered through the sweaty window overlooking the fluffy white gas pumps. "Can't say as I've ever seen so much snow this late in the year."

It was Easter Sunday and better than two feet had dropped since noon on Good Friday. Ricky Ransom was at Durham Fuel with his Aunt Debbie because his mom was on a trip with her new boyfriend and his dad was in court-ordered rehab.

Even with the terrible weather, the place was steady busy. Tim Hortons and Durham Fuel were the only places open on holidays—Tim Hortons closed for Christmas, but the Ransoms were generational atheists and happy to reap the monetary benefits of being the only game in town.

Atheism was a convenient way to live. They got Sundays free if they wanted them and it didn't keep them from seeing the good side of religious holidays, everybody liked gifts at Christmas and...

"Say, why don't you tuck your pants in your boots and head over to that big old church, the Lutheran one, just a block that way," she gestured over her shoulder with her thumb, "on Rocton, do a little egg hunting and bring us back some treats?"

Ricky looked at his aunt and then looked at the counter—Snickers, Mars, Aero, Caramilk, Kit-Kat...you name it, she had it. "Why don't you just have one of those?"

Debbie turned from the window and grinned. "*Hippety-hop, hippety-hop, Easter's on its way.* Bunnies and eggs. Something about it...usually I hold back a couple eggs, but Barry must've put them out when we sold the rest."

Barry was a twenty-something going nowhere fast. Had him a ninth grade education and two kids with a girl still three years shy of the legal drinking age—nineteen in British Columbia. He grew a beard from his neck, thick and long, and had patches of thin pubic-like hair on his face. He wore eyeglasses that he must've picked up at the serial killer superstore, and he thought Debbie didn't know that he went into the can at least three times a shift to rub one out into the toilet. She never complained because if he was rubbing them out at work, maybe he wasn't making more babies at home, and maybe it would stave off him asking for another raise. He already made two bucks above minimum at $6.50 per hour.

Debbie's eyes glazed and she licked her lips. "Something about biting into rabbits and their stupid eggs. Can't say as I know why, but there's something...takes me back, nostalgia. Wait 'til you're forty and anything that takes you back to your single digits is gold. *Hippety-hop, hippety-hop, Easter's on its way,*" she sang again.

Ricky thought she was crazy. He was nine and couldn't wait to be grown. He'd be done with school. He'd get a fly ass car. Marry a hot babe. Could be if he got good enough, he might be a Hartford Whaler like his hero Ron Francis.

"What do you say?" Debbie said.

Ricky twisted his face a bit and looked out the window. "Nah, too stormy."

Debbie was about to argue, but the bell on the door chimed and she turned to see the familiar Ski-Doo jacket of one of the Thompson boys stalk over to the *Ghosts 'n Goblins* arcade box next to the milk cooler. He had his hood up and snowmelt dampened blotches in the black and yellow of the jacket. Usually he had his twin brother with him. They had matching everything, but weren't fraternal.

The game started up and the bell jingled again as the door opened for Marty Hatcher.

"What do you say, Marty?" Debbie leaned her elbows on the counter.

Ricky thought it could be that his aunt had a thing for this Marty fella, way she pushed her boobs at him over the scratch tickets.

Marty kept going toward the coffee counter, shaking his head. "I just come from the egg hunt and—"

"Did you bring me a treat?"

"Geez, you ain't had the radio on or nothing, huh?" Marty dumped powdered whitener into his coffee as he spoke.

"No, why?" Debbie straightened her spine, looked over at Ricky, briefly, before looking back to Marty.

Marty had on a bulky brown Carhartt coat and huge black snowmobile boots that rose almost to the knees of his stained, but clean looking, Denver Hayes blue jeans. He slurped as he turned around. "Place is on fire and people were talking something 'bout the pastor going crazy, but Gary Wellman says the pastor been sick and some guy they hired via the phonebook was 'sposed to put on the bunny suit and hand out the chocolates. People looked nuts when I drove by so I parked at the end of the block, watched the fire and listened to the radio. Wild."

"Wait. What?"

Ricky looked at his aunt. Her face was all scrunched with confusion. He felt saliva tickle at the corner of his lips and snapped his jaw closed. Usually, stupid little Durham was the definition of boring on his visits.

"Dozens are dead. Mostly kids. Some parents too. Real mess, if it weren't for this snow, bet you'd a seen all the ambulances and cop cars, at least heard'm." Marty took another sip from the coffee and felt in his pocket. "Oh, but I do got one of these eggs...since you said you like'm." He held out a Cadbury Egg wrapped in foil and started over to the till.

Ricky watched the gap close, and beyond it all, he saw the Thompson kid lower his hands from the game controls as he stiffened.

"Oh that's so nice—oh, hell, dead?" Debbie seemed stuck in between: like wanting to flirt, but also wanting to reel from the news.

Marty reached the counter and blocked Ricky's view of the Thompson kid. But Ricky still heard him. "Eeegg?" he said, all gravel and goo in his throat. "Eeegg?"

Marty spun, obviously hadn't known the kid was in there. The motion put the kid back into Ricky's sightline and he gasped. Debbie gasped too.

The Thompson kid was facing them now. He had smeared blood all over his cheeks where the whiskers had forced their way through. His mouth and nose had gone fuzzy pink—more blood, by the looks of it. His front teeth bucked a full inch over his bottom lip and his eyeballs seemed way too big for the sockets, like spotting an orca through the ice fishing hole you cut at your favorite pond. His hands weren't hands, but were paws with sharpened nails. The fuzz covering his skin was charred black.

Ricky wondered how in the hell he'd played the *Ghosts 'n Goblins* with hands like that, but the thought passed the same second the kid bent forward and broke toward the till in a kicking, four-limbed sprint. As he moved—like lightning—the hood came down and two long white ears sprang up from his head.

Marty's legs didn't budge an inch and the kid put those big teeth into his wrist, biting into the Cadbury egg as well as taking the man's hand. Marty shook his arm over his head, spraying blood all over the store.

Ricky was nodding, stupidly; he could relate. One time he was making a birdhouse from a kit and smucked his thumb with a hammer, did that same thing with his arm since it hurt so much.

The kid went out of sight a second, but popped up in a froggy—check that—bunny-like leap. "Eeegg!" that gravelly, syrupy voice said. "Eeegg!" The teeth then sunk into the closest thing Marty had to an egg left on his person: his skull. His eyes rolled and the blood washed down. His corpse remained upright until the kid jerked back and the top of Marty's skull popped off with a wet *thwupt!* The coiled pinkish grey mass underneath seemed to try to jump free from the brainpan.

The Thompson kid and Marty both left view, beyond the counter, and Debbie and Ricky looked at each other with saucers for eyes. "In the back!" Debbie said and waved for Ricky to get through the door by the VHS rental wall.

Didn't have to tell Ricky twice, his boots were squeaking on the stone tiles, but Debbie gave him a little push anyway, and then took one step to follow before stopping to scream. A great, hot splash landed on Ricky's shoulder and neck, a bit on his cheek and ear too. He looked back and the kid was bouncing his head with his mouth stretched wide, punching holes into Debbie's scalp with those damned bucked teeth.

Ricky's jaw dropped as acid crept up his throat, in the back of his mind he heard: *hippety-hop, hippety-hop, Easter's on its way!* He tore through the door and swung it closed.

A flimsy door with a flimsy lock. He waited there for ten seconds before he heard "Eeegg," as the door thumped.

"Nuh-uh," he said and spun around, made for the employee and after hours exit. That door was silent, didn't have a bell or a beeper, and for that he was thankful, figured maybe he'd get away and the freak kid wouldn't put the pieces together in time to catch him.

Outside, the heavy snow made the world sound dull, but he still heard screams and sirens. This was all wrong and it wasn't even his town. If it wasn't for his stupid mother and his drunken, deadbeat dad, then he'd never—

"Eeegg!"

Ricky took off like a rocket and ran for his aunt's house two blocks away. The snow was thick and heavy on the street and the cold air nipped at his lungs, but he kept up the sprint the whole damned distance. He circled and went in through the back door.

Inside, he flipped the light switch, but nothing happened. He crossed the living room, dropping great clumps of snow onto the shag carpet as he went. He pulled the phone receiver from the wall, the long cord banging against the paneling. The number for the police station was on a square of paper Scotch taped at eyelevel. He spun the dial all seven digits and waited.

It did not ring.

He pressed down the plunger and listened to the dial tone.

"Okay. Okay," he said, wheezing. He'd just screwed up the first time. He dialed again and waited.

It rang and rang and rang.

And rang and rang.

And rang.

The back door wheezed open and Ricky heard, "Eeegg."

Then another voice, "Eeegg."

And another, "Eeegg."

He dropped the phone and mumbled, "Hippety-hop, hippety-hop, Easter's on its way."

LEAVE A MESSAGE

(2014)

Monica Henry opened the door to hear the final ring from her telephone.

"Dammit," she said as she listened to the dial tone, the message service had already picked up. She waited a minute and then checked the message, nothing. The caller ID had only zeros. Fiona Plum across the road and Lynn Templeton next-door both said the same thing was happening to them, from the ID with all zeros.

Monica shrugged it off. "Probably just one of those captain's calling cruise bullshitters."

The call really wasn't something worth worrying over, not in a place like Portman Lane: a gated community with handpicked residents and 24-hour security.

—

Robbie Arnott cradled his phone, put down the recorder, he already knew that message. He wished some of these women would change their recordings.

Outside, he heard a child yell happily. He pushed aside the blinds and zoomed with his telephoto lens. He snapped shots of two little girls, one little boy, and two mothers, one of which he hadn't gotten enough pictures of to perfect a likeness. Not yet, but he was close.

He'd taken pictures for his whole life, but he rarely left home, sometimes to the store, but mostly things came to him. The internet was wonderful. He'd lived in Portman Lane back when it was still called Oriole Circle, but then more rich people moved in and they gated it off. He only lived there because his parents left him the house and all the money when they died. Robbie didn't work, not professionally.

The newish woman strode along the sidewalk near his window and Robbie snapped off a dozen more shots. "Good enough to start," he said. He'd still have to look up her phone number, but there was time; worthwhile things took time.

He left his window and stepped into his shop. He had industrial machines to work with the leather, and made molds and shaped the pale skin, tinting it with dye to match the people outside his window. He smiled as he worked into the afternoon, often taking peeks at his collection of shots. His fingers ached for a break and he dialed a number, holding the recorder to the earpiece, ready.

"Hello," a voice said and he waited. "Who is this, I'll call the police." The woman then hung up. Robbie hit the replay button and listened. Someday he'd figure out the voice stuff on his computer, until then he worked with what they gave him.

He rose from his seat and stepped through the kitchen to the basement door. He flicked the lights and a replica of the neighborhood came to still life. Men, women, children, and pets all stood full-size and uncanny in likeness.

Robbie waved, the happy dolls of Portman Lane smiling, he tugged on a plastic ring from behind a replica Monica Henry, the string followed and the voice bounced around the lifeless diorama.

"You've reached the Henry house, we're unable to take your call, please leave a message."

Having her speak to him was honey for his soul. He pulled the cord behind Monica's son's head. "Trick or treat! Thanks mister."

He pulled the cord behind a good representation of Fiona Plum. "Who is this? Stop calling here! I have a friend at Bell, you can't hide your number from them." The string reeled into the head.

Robbie raced around his basement community, pulling cords, listening to the chatter, thinking the computer sound program was so complicated that he might forget about it, maybe just get some real people-dolls, they can say all kinds of different things and he'd hardly have to sew them at all.

THE BRIDGE HOME

(2014)

Mrs. Gramble's house seemed to lean toward the school's east end—cracked and yellowed vinyl siding, wasps' nests caking the roof's overhang at the corners, the shingles gone to moss. Mr. Gramble had looked after the house while Mrs. Gramble tended to the flowerbed and the trees. Mr. Gramble was dead, the house was on its way, but the flowerbed and the row of dogwood trees next to the sidewalk thrived.

Dogwood, red and stiff, slim branches with soft innards beneath hard exteriors. Many old timers liked them for switches.

"What does Stevie Borden have to do with my kingdom?" Mary Fischer asked Tommy, her only son. She wore a wide billowy dress and powder makeup, hair done-up high.

"Your Majesty, please pass the taters," William Fischer said. He wore a jester's outfit, goofy hat, goofy shoes, rosy red cheeks.

The family sat around a thrice handed-down kitchen table that had never left Hudson. It was a Fischer table, and these Hudson Fischers never left because home was a new world every day.

Mary passed the taters. "Mine jester, art thou going to entertain in mine boudoir this evening?" She lifted her eyebrows almost to her hairline.

William Fischer swallowed and looked down at his son. "Should her majesty allow me."

"But, Mom, what do I do about Stevie?" Tommy's hands were fists wrapped around a fork and a knife. He had marks all up his arms from the bully using dogwood on him.

—

Five days of peace, not a welt, confidence soaring, Tommy walked quickly out the backdoor of the school. There weren't any dogwood trees on the north side of the playground, this helped, but so did going unnoticed.

Tommy was four years younger than Stevie's thirteen. Stevie and his father shared a squat trailer and a welfare check. A mannish boy. He had a full beard and his muscles rippled under his shirt. Stevie let the other kids at school pay for his lunch.

He didn't thump the ones who paid him.

Tommy's parents refused to give him money, so he had to be crafty, which was why he scooted out the backdoor and had begun keeping to the library at lunch. The library was also where he came to love Miss Mogely. She was a history teacher for half the kids—the lucky ones—and was the most beautiful woman he'd ever seen.

Tommy walked quickly, imagining touching her boobs, running his hands through her hair, kissing her subtly lipsticked mouth.

"Dick stain switched his route." Stevie stepped out from the shadow cast by one of the old bridge's beams. It was a covered deal, wide enough for two lanes of traffic, but only used for walking these days. "Think you're smart?"

Twenty years earlier, the mill and the bridge leading to it, became redundant. Both fell to slow decay. The mill had a rusty construction fence circling it and no trespassing signs which hung crookedly. The building itself had boards over the windows and chains on the doors, winos inhabited the place every winter. The bridge had gone grey but could easily hold the weight of foot traffic.

"I'm talkin' to you, dick stain. Think you fooled me?"

Tommy passed Stevie and then swish, swish, swish, three bright red welts surfaced in less time than it took for Tommy to whirl around. He cried out and Stevie flipped the switch in his hand, fat side threatening, snap, snap, snap. Tommy's hand rose and his knees buckled. Stevie had never given him the fat side on the neck before. Damp and hot, he touched the wound. Blood spotted his fingers.

"I got to catch you up. We missed what? Five days?" Swish, swish.

Tommy rolled into the fetal position.

"Ever hear of compounding interest?" Stevie laughed, flipped the branch again and snap, snap, snap. The dogwood broke over Tommy's head.

"Stop it!"

"Shut it." Stevie kicked Tommy in the gut and then looked around on the bridge for a new tool. Metal glinted from between boards a few feet away.

Stevie started off and Tommy took his chance. He broke for the park by the mill. Stevie stayed behind and swung a broken car antenna around the air, a glow blazed and died at his whim.

"Get you yet, pussy!" Stevie shouted and though Tommy was fifty feet away and feeling safer, he didn't doubt it for a second.

—

Mary's father stopped by unannounced for supper. He was a writer for The Weekly World News and lived in a cottage east of Hudson on Thimble Lake. The paper mailed him twenty strange photos a month and he made up stories to fit, attributing accounts to *sources say.*

"What the hell happened to you?" Despite thinking them nuts, Barney Lancaster played along with the suppertime games. He wore a green wig and grey paint on his face, grey apron covering the rest of his body.

A family of trees.

Tommy shrugged. Some of the welts had swollen to split. Paint covered most of it.

"You have a bully? You know about this Mary?"

Mary looked up from her plate. "Did someone carve their name in your trunk?"

Sometimes Barney wanted to shake his flakey, weirdo daughter. He looked to his son-in-law. "William, you're not doing this are you?"

"I am but a tree!"

"Forget the game a minute. Look at him. Someone's putting a wallop on him. Who did this to you, Thomas?"

Tommy shrugged again—snitches got stitches.

"Tell me, I mean it."

"Your creaky branches are ruining our night," Mary said, rustling her leaves.

Barney ignored her, squinting at Tommy. Then it hit him. "It's a goddamn Borden kid, ain't it?"

Tommy didn't shrug, couldn't move or he'd breakdown.

"Barney, this talk is very un-tree-like," William said.

"Bordens are trouble. Remember those wannabe gangsters?"

William rolled his eyes, they'd all told the lie to each other so much it became a truth. "That was just an accident, everybody knows that. Craig Borden didn't even get charged."

Barney shoved his plate across the table, it clanked against a gravy boat and a pitcher of iced tea. "Accident, bullshit."

—

"It's Tommy." A low whisper, his hand over the phone and his mouth. "Will you tell me about the accident?"

"Mary and William know about this call?"

Tommy paused, he didn't like lying, especially not to his grandfather. "No, sir."

"Good, they have their heads up their arse holes."

Twenty years prior. 1994. Summertime. Three local boys had spent entire days leaning on the nose of an old Cadillac Brougham. They wore white tank tops, fake gold rope chains, and baggy Dickies, hanging low so their boxer shorts puffed out like crinoline on a prom dress shoulder.

Story went, they sold enough pot to cover the gas in the car and a few cans of spray paint. Wezzide Boyz started showing up on walls and signs all over town. The chief took the boys in, slapped wrists, handed out fines, and things settled for a time. Soon enough *Wezzide Boyz 4 Lyfe* and *Bordenz eat cox* started appearing. Cops seemed to mind this less and none of the locals complained.

Still, the act caught attention. Late November and warmer than normal, winter had only just begun poking through the autumn vale. The river wore a layer of ice like frost. The Wezzide Boyz parked their Caddy a few feet from the bridge. The windows cracked, smoke poured out alongside the rumblings of DAS EFX. They'd been out painting again, this time they gave the rusty rims of Craig Borden's lifted Dodge a splash of color.

The Dodge's engine was loud enough that it crept over *bum-stiggety-bum stiggety pa-rum-pa-pum-pum*s, but by the time the Wezzide Boyz noticed, the huge Dodge bumper was about to make contact with the back of the Caddy.

—

Halloween came around and Tommy felt pretty good; Stevie seemed to have disappeared. He had to dress-up so often that he decided to go simple for Halloween and wore a bed sheet with eyes cut out. For most of the kids, the order was to be home by 8:00 PM and that was fine. Tommy didn't have a curfew. His parents were having a jungle night.

Tommy and his friends parted ways at the school. They lived to the west and didn't have to take the bridge. Rather than rushing back, he sat and inhaled goodies.

Snickers.

M&Ms.

Doritos.

"Save some for me, dick stain." It was full-dark and the moon rode low behind clouds. "I didn't give you permission to eat my candies." There was a swishing sound, like a dogwood switch, but firmer.

Tommy couldn't yet see Stevie and jumped up, leaving the

candy sack behind. He tore toward the park, stuffing the bed sheet into his pocket. He didn't get far when he met the open arms of a smiling boy named Buford Vroon—Buff to Stevie and his friend's.

"Gotcha, ass face." Buff wrapped his arms around Tommy.

Tommy shot out a knee, connected with testicles. Buff squealed and dropped. The swishing got closer. Swish, swish.

On the third swish, Tommy cried out. "Owee!" The old car antenna hit Tommy right in the eye. He dropped.

Swish.

Swish.

Tommy tried to roll away from the pain, the laughter. He couldn't. Buff got up and punted Tommy in the gut. There was a hollow sound and then Tommy wretched up a soggy orange mess and pissed hot gold simultaneously.

The running stream caused more laughter. "Pussy boy pissed." This voice belonged to Val Roudin. His parents were Russians a decade landed in Canada.

Stevie rolled the wheel on his lighter and lit a cigarette. "Eatin' all my candy." He clicked his tongue.

"Take it," Tommy begged and then appealing, "You got my eye, please."

Swish.

Swish.

"That's enough, don't ya think?" Buff said.

"Only getting started." Stevie swung the antenna over his shoulder four times, aiming for the light flesh in the dark of night.

Tommy moaned.

"Stevie, come on man, he's had enough." Val lowered his gaze, peered into the abyss between the slats of wood underfoot.

Buff put his hands into his pants pockets.

Stevie took a long drag from his cigarette and exhaled as he spoke, "You're just pussies." Swish. Swish.

"You're nuts," and "Fuck this," turned the trio assault into a one man show.

"You're both dick stains!" Stevie shouted as the other boys started away.

Swish, swish, Tommy's body didn't flinch. Stevie kicked Tommy's side.

"Wake up, pussy!"

Tommy didn't. Stevie shortened the antenna and shoved it into his pocket. The smell of vomit and piss was so strong it made Stevie gag.

"I know what'll wake you up." Stevie lifted the small boy onto the sill. The water beneath the layer of ice rolled gently. The bed sheet from Tommy's pocket snagged on a nail as his body dropped. His unconscious form splashed and thunked.

—

Four weeks passed, the river froze solid and snow lined the streets. Nobody had seen or heard from Tommy since Halloween.

So when Tommy showed up on his familial doorstep, all were surprised, but didn't question it much. Only his grandfather pressed him, but he was so happy, he didn't press very hard. Tommy had no explanation for the absence, only recalling the smoky car and the three boys who'd dropped him off.

"Who were they?" the old man asked.

Tommy simply smiled.

—

"Dick stain, where ya been hiding?" Stevie followed Tommy onto the bridge.

"Leave me alone."

"Don't be like that. We're old pals, ain't we?"

Tommy quickened his pace, stomping through a light crusting of snow that slickened the wood floor. Stevie kept up, feeling around his jacket pocket for the broken piece of antenna. He found it and began to pull it free.

"Hey, Tommy, you all right, homie?" a voice called from the

bridge's entrance, just beyond the cement parking blocks enforcing the strict no vehicle policy.

"You fuckin' with Tommy, bro?" another voice added.

Stevie stopped and turned. A long brown Cadillac with shiny chrome rims sat idling, some old rap track played low in the background.

"How about you dick stains mind your business?"

Stevie turned back to Tommy and he'd taken off like a bullet into the park. "You scared away my buddy," Stevie looked over his shoulder, "you—" The Cadillac was gone.

—

The news was all over school the following morning: Buff was dead. Found on the sidewalk, never made it home after yesterday's final bell, his throat bruised and marked, a fat imitation-gold rope necklace had choked out his airways. The police questioned everyone that might've or should've seen something, but nobody saw a thing.

Losing Buff ruined part of the half-formed plan in Stevie's head, but he thought he'd make do yet. He could just see the little bitch stripped naked and left in the gym for the seventh grade girls' class to come in the next morning.

At lunchtime, Stevie warned Tommy that he'd catch him after class.

—

Tommy was different. He told Miss Mogely in the library what Stevie said. Miss Mogely called Craig Borden and demanded his son be picked up immediately. Sent home like any other troublesome bully would be.

At home, things were different too.

"That scary Borden man called." William was in drag, sequins painted beneath his eyes while he sat at his desk, translating a repair manual to be sold in Mexico. "I wish you wouldn't pull us into your problems."

—

At school, Tommy smacked at a licorice, potato chip, and chocolate cookie lunch. Stevie strolled up to his table. Four boys scooted away in fear. Stevie picked up a cookie, took a bite, dropped the cookie and spat a gooey wad of melted chocolate and softened doughy mess, it oozed onto Tommy's head, slow like a sticky cow patty.

"Not a healthy lunch, dick stain."

"So?" Tommy shook off the chewed cookie. He attempted to stand. Stevie pushed him back down onto his seat.

"Where do you think you're going?"

Tommy looked around the cafeteria for help. The room usually loud with life, was quiet as a funeral. Miss Mogely walked past the entrance and then reversed. She had a box in her hands and tears dampening her cheeks. Like a bull, she entered the cafeteria.

That morning, she'd stepped into class to find a note on her door and a substitute in her chair. The principal wouldn't look at her, gave her the story that they couldn't function with the threats and possible scandals. "I don't believe that you're in a sexual relationship with Tom Fischer, but I can't deal with the media."

Miss Mogely spent her morning on hold with the union. She was too new and they suggested they'd assist in finding her a better placement, so long as charges weren't filed.

"You let go of him you little prick." Miss Mogely dug her pink nails into Stevie's arm.

"Hey, hey, don't touch me, you twat!"

"Eat it, Borden."

"My daddy'll—"

"Your daddy'll what? Make up some garbage? You worthless little prick, your daddy's just trash."

"You can't—"

"I can and will. You got me canned, so I'm just a woman doing her civic duty."

Tommy's lunch remained on the table, but he'd disappeared during the confrontation. Miss Mogely let go of Stevie's arm.

—

Stevie called Val nine times before he got an answer. Val was rich and had his own cellphone. There was good news, they had a third man back and they were going to make it look like Miss Mogely and Tommy were fucking. Forget Hudson District, she'd never work as a teacher again, anywhere.

"Where've you been?" Stevie demanded when the lines finally connected.

Some weird old rap came through and then the sound of laughter before the lines disconnected. Stevie dialed again and got the automatic mailbox voice.

Stevie figured Val was being a pussy and told his father. Craig hadn't thought they'd need the other boys anyway—a good father-son project.

Craig had typed two notes. Short and to the point, one of which begged for Tommy to join Miss Mogely at the school after hours.

—

The next morning, seconds after Stevie slid the note into Tommy's cubby, students flooded the hallway. News of another death electrified the masses. Someone had spray painted Val's face and throat; drowned him in red and black Rust-Oleum.

—

At the hardware store, Barney learned of the murders and had a couple theories. The paint had to be from an ancient can, the shade of red wasn't available anymore, the texture rubbery, an older recipe. Rust paint had advanced great leaps over the last couple decades. That was lead-based shit.

At the grocery store, folks explained the flakes of gold coming from the gold rope, it was surely cheap, but nobody recognized it. Barney thought he would've liked to have seen it, if only for the sake of interest.

Since in town already, he decided to pay a visit to Mary. She was usually at home, both she and her husband. They'd become shut-ins after a payout and worked sparingly. They'd been involved in some medical trial and, due to negligence, they'd be susceptible to a host of permanent skin maladies.

When nobody answered his calls, Barney searched rooms methodically, entering as he came upon them. He opened their bedroom door after he'd been around most of the house. Both William and Mary lay in bed, wide-eyed and pale, dressed as half-assed tinfoil robots. The blood drying on their chests was highly out of character.

Barney stumbled, shaking his head until the sight diminished, slightly. He dialed the police and explained the scene as best he could. At the station, he filled out a report.

He went back to the house to wait for Tommy.

—

Miss Mogely found a note on her car, begging for help from Tommy. He wanted her to come to his home. Strange, but he'd had it hard and perhaps he'd started the rumor that got her fired, could reverse the flow of the deed—she doubted it was him, but hope sprang eternal for easy answers.

Hands seemed to fire from the bushes out front of Tommy's house. A man shouted *Hey!* from near the sidewalk. A cloth went over her face. As she crumbled, she heard the words *You're the fuck's granddaddy* and then a pained moan.

—

Tommy never believed the note, but he wasn't going to let Stevie get him anymore, it was time for a stand. It's why he came back in the first place; he knew that now.

Stevie and his father got to the school only minutes after Tommy hid in the shadows cast by a big oak tree. Craig Borden walked ahead of two figures, both hooded. He'd tied their hands and knees tight so their motions were small. Stevie brought up the rear of the party with a baseball bat in his grip.

Tommy remained silent.

The note had directed him to the gymnasium. So whatever they'd planned, it would go down there. He made his way around the back.

Miss Mogely, gagged and tied, took center stage quite literally behind a basketball hoop on the assembly platform. In the shadowy wings, Barney leaned, dazed, against a painted cinderblock wall.

Tommy took this in and let the cracked door close against his forehead. He inhaled a deep breath to build up his nerve. He pushed through the heavy double doors into the gymnasium. It was dim but for a bright spotlight on Miss Mogely's struggling frame. Tommy raced forward, getting to the foot of the platform, looking up and then hearing the swish through the air.

"Dick stain!" Stevie was gleeful as he swung back for a second strike. Tommy had fallen, but did not feel any pain. That part of his life was long gone and he'd been faking it for some time now.

Another thwack hit.

Tommy stiffened on hands and knees, a grin forming on his face.

The lights died on the stage.

"What the hell?" Craig Borden's voice was close.

Barney heard the question and attempted to open his eyes against the swelling, couldn't tell if he'd succeeded in the pitch-black room.

"Dad?" Stevie asked, car antenna in his hand, but no longer poised to strike.

"Microphone check, microphone checka." The sound came from somewhere within the gymnasium. Everywhere it seemed, being loud as it was.

"Dad?" Stevie asked, fear in his voice.

"Tiggety-time to get buck wild!"

"Dad?"

The song stopped. The sound of air releasing in a tight

stream hit the quiet alongside particles of otherworldly spray paint.

"Believe that's mine, homie," a voice said very close to Stevie's ear, the car antenna wrenched from his hand.

"Dad?"

"Who you think you're fuckin' with here?" Craig said through clenched teeth. "I'm Craig-fucking-Bor—!"

"We know." The voice breathed a cold breeze into Craig's ear. Craig swung around with a roundhouse punch, finding nothing but air.

"*Wezzide Boyz!*" The words came from in front of the stage. Two bright beams spot-lit the action. The sound pumped and pounded. Miss Mogely attempted to scream, but the gag muffled most of the sound.

Craig got it then, so did Barney.

"Dad?"

The car revved behind the blinding lights. Stevie looked to the ground. His victim gone. Two more sets of laughter expelled from the wings of the platform. Craig stumbled forward. Half-drunk on confusion and Budweiser.

"Dad?"

The car revved. The music intensified, though was not as loud as before. *"Microphone check, microphone checka."*

The trio of young men pushed Craig to his knees.

"You're dead!" Craig yelled from the high gloss basketball court. "You can't be here!"

Hands came down onto Craig's arms and he attempted to wrench free, but for the first time since he faced off with his own daddy, he wasn't the strongest bully on the playground. In two lightning heartbeats, he found himself in the backseat of a 1980 Cadillac Brougham with a burgundy interior. It reeked of lake water, rotting meat, and weed smoke.

"You're dead!" Craig shouted to the figures moving him like he was stuffed with cotton.

"Wezzide!" yelled one.

"Boyz!" yelled another directly after.

The third yelled, "Come on, got something for you!" He grabbed Stevie.

Stevie fell into the front seat and felt a smallish body push in behind him. He lifted his head. Tommy grinned and revved the engine. His face paling and losing shape. Shades of green and black festering around his nose, eyes, and mouth. "Who's the dick stain now?" Tommy threw the chrome shifter into reverse.

The car backed out of the gym, slamming the heavy doors wide open and punching a hole through a classroom wall. Bricks tumbled free in a dusty wave and suddenly they were outside.

The closer they got to that old bridge, the more Tommy's face seemed to melt into carcass. The Wezzide Boyz were worse, nothing but bones and eyeballs and tongues. Just enough to rattle and laugh and stare.

Stevie begged the corpse to his left, doing his best to ignore the nodding, cackling skeleton to his right.

"Dick stain! Dick stain!" Tommy screamed. "I ain't scared of you anymore, Stevie!" His tongue flapping loosely as if replaced by a land-bound fish. His foot pounded the accelerator and the skeletons all rapped along to the beat. Craig whimpered and Stevie outright sobbed.

"'Cause we're, jussumenthat's on the mic."

The front end struck the concrete blockade and launched the heavy car into the air as if hitting a ramp, time slowed but the song continued.

"...we're jussumen..."

The heavy car roared through the night, bright as a comet soaring on the atmosphere and landing with a thud, a creak as the wood distressed, a crack as the wood voiced trouble, and then a crash as the entire bridge crumbled.

—

Miss Mogely watched this through the ruined wall. She

attempted to scream and found her voice gone. Barney had gotten himself partly free and put his hand on her back, knowing Tommy was long dead, even before the night played out. Every so often there's a good reason for ghosts to return.

"But Tommy!"

"Gone," Barney said, "for now, anyway."

BIG BAD BRENDA

(2022)

Harper leaned away from Rory's lips, a slim trail of saliva connecting them for six inches before snapping and disappearing between the two. Rory gave Harper's ass a playful squeeze.

"I need to go," Harper said as she shimmied down from Rory's lap.

She was 4'11" and Rory was 5'11". The difference was less than what she'd gotten used to over the last five years.

"Don't want big, bad Brenda to get suspicious," Rory said, smiling though no humor played in the joke.

"She's already suspicious." Harper stepped to the dresser mirror and adjusted her clothing before bending to snatch her panties from the carpet. "See you Thursday?"

Rory nodded, pitching his hips forward to lift his pants and boxer shorts over his ass so he could zip his fly. They were in his house, the only place Harper dared to see him for fear that Brenda might catch them.

"I promise you, I'll take care of her soon and we'll be together for real. It's just, you have to ease into things with her," Harper said.

"Yeah. Yeah."

Harper leaned in to plant a fresh kiss on Rory's mouth. "Promise."

—

"I'm home," Harper said around a piece of spearmint Excel—chewed to hide the beer scent.

She slung her purse over the back of one of three mismatched dining chairs around the kitchen table. She stepped into the living room. The TV was on, but nobody was watching it.

"Brenda?" she said and got halfway through a turn before a grip on her hair yanked her backward. "Ow!"

"How could you do this to me?" Brenda said, her voice whiny and yet fierce, baritone. She had a body to match, standing 6'7" and weighing close to 350 pounds. "And with a *man?*"

Brenda slammed Harpers face into the stiff, though padded, top of the couch, sending one of her front teeth backward 3 millimeters and her eyeteeth into her tongue. Blood gushed and burst from her mouth like a popped water balloon.

"I don't know why you make me do it! You're mine forever, I'll never let you go," Brenda said before tossing Harper across the room into the corner of the wall separating the living room from the hallway. Her forehead thumped and she dropped in a heap. "You can't treat me like this, don't you know how much I love you?"

Harper moaned, looking through one eye from where she lay to see the treads of a size 13 Timberland boot coming straight for her face. Her final fleeting thought before being knocked unconscious was that Brenda had stepped on a piece of candy and that it might get stuck in the apartment's carpet.

—

It was the following Monday before Harper could get away to see Rory, though not at his house. Under those white, white lights, surrounded by white linens, the man looked like a plum on a pillow. His entire face was purple with bruises and his left arm was in a cast.

"Oh, Baby," Harper said, pouting it out.

Rory huffed. "She hit me with a bat," he said, speaking carefully so as to keep from re-splitting his lips. "I didn't stand a chance."

"You didn't call the cops?" Harper said.

Rory swallowed and shook his head gently. "I work for the city, remember? I see those guys all over. I don't want to be the guy known as the guy who got beat up by a girl. Even if it was by the Amazonian bitch."

Harper had her eyes on her hands. She took a beating, had bruises all over her face and had to make an emergency visit to the dentist, but looked much better than Rory. "She's not Amazonian...that's a mean thing to say."

Rory laughed a single bark before the pain of opening the wounds on his lips soured the moment. "I don't give a shit where she's from."

"It's...people have called her that, and lots of other stuff, her whole life."

"Like I care. Look, I love you, but I can't do this again, so maybe—"

Harper rushed to his bedside. "No, I have a plan. I just need your help. It's the only way. She's so miserable, we'll be doing her a favor."

"Oh yeah?" Rory said, not sounding convinced.

"We just have to wait a month, cool it off with one another. No phone calls to our usual cells, nothing."

Rory tilted his head. "You actually have a plan?"

—

Brenda picked up her vibrating phone. There was a text from Harper: Hey baby can you run those gifts over to the school and drop them in the bin? They're supposed to be in today.

Brenda glanced through the window of the ground floor apartment they shared. The snow was really coming down outside. She then looked to the bench by the door. There was the bag with the two gifts inside. Her phone vibrated again.

Before 9.

Brenda growled. It was 8:37 AM. The school with the toy drive box shared an alleyway with the apartment building, so it would hardly take three minutes, but the effort, the immediate effort was one grade A pain in the rear.

Fine, she texted back and pushed to her feet.

It took ten minutes to get herself ready and dressed for the weather. She took the backdoor out of the apartment building and sidestepped a big, green dumpster. The wind whipped and an engine sound rumbled. It was the kind of cold that made her wish she lived in the south somewhere. She pulled her hood tight by the drawstrings and carried on, head down, eyes on her feet and the glassy asphalt below.

She had no time to react when the garbage truck came barreling down the alley. It struck her and sent her sprawling, landing on top of the toys. The truck didn't stop. A tremendous scream launched from her cavernous mouth as the heavy wheels drove over her foot, leg, and hips. The wheels began to spin, dragging her deep beneath the weight of the garbage truck until it regained its grip and bounced over her corpse, and then repeated.

"Stop," Harper shouted as she waved, leaning to the driver's side so Rory could see her in the mirror.

Harper knelt and pulled at Brenda's shoulder to get her on her back and be certain the woman was dead. It wasn't easy, but she got her flipped. Brenda's face had been flattened, her eyes were abnormally spread and her long tongue lulled from her mouth, making her look bovine.

"Ugh," Rory said upon rushing back and seeing his handiwork.

This was the only way; Brenda had sworn that Harper belonged to her and nobody else, and always would. Harper believed it, and after the beating he took, Rory believed it— running the bitch over would just be icing on the cake.

Now came the dirty bit.

"I told the guys I was test driving this, I can't have it out all day," Rory said. He was a mechanic for the city and the truck was in for a simple oil change, but he'd written a work order concerning a strange rumble that did not exist.

"Which end?" Harper said.

"Help me get her top in; the bitch is too heavy to do all at once."

Harper inhaled deeply through her nose and helped carry out this piece of her plan. They got Brenda up, her back bent over the lip of the tail on the dumpster bed. Her eyeballs drifted apart, as if she were spying both her assassins at the same time.

"Hold her there," Rory said before hurrying around to her big boots—now twisted backwards and misshapen, leaking blood around the eyelets and tongue.

He hefted her the rest of the way in, and she landed with a hollow thunk. He grabbed a lever, a steel gate grinded into action, forcing the corpse into the belly of the truck. Harper grabbed an armload of snow from the top of a discarded box next to the apartment building and tossed it onto the bloodstain, as well as the toys in their smooshed and ruined boxes—a Cabbage Patch doll in a bull costume and a remote-control tank.

After a quick kiss, Harper rushed back to the apartment to set a scene and Rory did a quick dump of several half-full dumpsters before returning to the shop with the truck.

—

Brenda had nobody aside from Harper. Harper made a show of asking around Brenda's gym and the women's shelter where Brenda had worked, stating that they'd broken up, and Brenda had been taking it poorly. After a week, she called the police, suggesting that sometimes Brenda got in bad mental states—"just ask her doctor"—and demanded that someone check her apartment. They did and immediately got back to Harper with questions concerning the breakup and questions about Brenda in general. Brenda had a record, had been institutionalized as a youth in juvie and as an adult in jail and then on the psych ward of the hospital.

"What did her apartment look like...I mean, like did she clean it out? I'd only moved out on the second."

The cop whistled. "It doesn't look like she left with any intention of coming back, any intentions at all. I can't really say more."

In the crime section of the paper, a single, brief paragraph was paid to ask for information on a missing person named Brenda Lee, describing her height and weight and formerly frequented whereabouts.

Harper stayed nine days in a WYMCA before moving into Rory's home on the outskirts of town—her stuff had already been there since the day they'd murdered Brenda. Days and nights they assuaged each other's guilt, and with each passing day and night, they felt less and less bad about what they'd been forced to do.

"She left us no choice," Rory said for the umpteenth time as they sat before a crackling fireplace, sipping wine while the December winds screamed beyond the walls.

—

Christmas Eve ticked over into Christmas. Though it was childish, and she knew it, she couldn't shake the excitement she felt every year. When she was a child, she'd gotten so excited for Christmas, it made it impossible for her to sleep and come sunup, she got sick to her stomach, had her vomiting on the gifts her parents had given her.

She didn't puke anymore, but she didn't get much sleep either. From beneath a curtain no heavier than a doze, Harper sat up fully awake. There'd been a strange thump in the living room; a soft sound, like a thrown pillow. Following directly after was the unmistakable sound of a log shifting in the fireplace.

Had it reignited?

Had a bird fallen down the chimney? A raccoon?

A clatter. One of the utensil drawers being rummaged through. Harper began shaking Rory. His heavy breaths snapped twice before continuing on smoothly. She shook him harder.

"Rory!" she hissed.

He opened his left eye and looked at her. "Wha?"

"There's someone in the house."

He closed his eye. "You're dreaming."

"No. Listen."

Neither moved, neither breathed for a five count. Soft, padded steps rushed along the hardwood. Rory opened his eyes and sat up. He reached for the lamp on his side of the bed— Harper's side didn't have a table or lamp. The room lit and the pair squinted, listening for more movements. A jingling set of rattles rang off a moment before a crash. Obviously, according to the cacophony, the Christmas tree had been brought down. Rory and Harper both kicked from bed simultaneously, though Harper waited for Rory to pass through the bedroom door before following him.

Rory reached the end of the hallway and flicked the living room light switch without entering. "Tree's knocked over," he said and stepped around the couch. He stopped in the middle of the room.

As if going station to station, Harper stepped to where he had been standing and waited. "What?" she said, scanning the space for interlopers. Her eyes locked on the fireplace and the mess of ash on the floor next to an overturned RC vehicle.

"Looks like a monkey in socks or something came down the chimney," he said and knelt next to the tree. He began lifting it gently.

Harper came around the couch and picked up the RC car. She quickly recognized it as the same one she'd purchased for the toy drive...the toy drive that put Brenda in the alleyway.

Rory lifted the tree higher when he saw no signs of a hidden animal. Balls pinged against the hardwood as they dropped, bouncing about the room. Harper watched one roll beneath the couch. Amid the shadows and dust bunnies were two sets of eyes: a beady black set and a doughy blue set. The face beneath the eyes grinned. Little hands palmed the floor and the doll—a Cabbage Patch Kid in a bull mask, the same damned Cabbage Patch Kid Brenda had been carting alongside the RC car—pulled itself out from beneath the couch. Harper was struck silent.

"Hopefully it climbed back..."

The doll bolted on stubby legs, its soft feet tapping gently on the floor.

"...out the chimney and we—Ow!"

The doll had leapt, latching onto Rory's bared ankle. The rubber mouth stretched wide, revealing two rows of glassy looking teeth. It bit. Blood gushed and Rory dropped as his Achilles tendon rolled up beneath the flesh of his calf like a slap bracelet. The red-face doll began climbing higher, traversing his hip onto his abdomen.

"What the fuck!" Rory shouted, the words tumbling free in a torrent of panic.

The doll—Harper recalled its name being Bull Briggs—was gnawing at his bare stomach. He punched and pulled, rolling over Christmas decorations, each exploding into little smatterings of glass.

"Harper!"

"She's mine, prick!" the little doll said in a squealing voice before it jerked its face back down to take a fresh chomp of the man's soft belly.

Blood burst free as if the thing had bit into an overripe plum. The hot, hot blood laser-targeted Harper's agape mouth, hitting her tongue and uvula. She choked and gagged, but it was enough to bring her from terrified reverie. She looked around wildly, her eyes stopping on the fruit cake platter and knife left on the coffee table from their evening snack. The knife was small with a hooked end.

"Fuuuck!" Rory wailed, squeezing the doll's head uselessly as it twisted and jerked with a mouthful of flesh between its teeth.

Harper charged, snatching up the knife as she went. She fell onto Rory to quell his motions and give her a better target. She sliced the knife in a downward stroke, running from rubber to cotton. A fluffy white injury bloomed. The teeth let go.

"Why do you make me do it?" the doll said.

Harper ignored the familiar words and pressed the hooked tip deep into the rubber head before pulling it backward. The steel pierced the rubber and the doll's arms and legs flailed wildly. She continued pulling, splitting the head like a melon.

The doll ceased all movements a moment before Rory tossed it across the floor, knife stuck in the rubber. It came to a stop against one of the couch's legs.

"How bad is it?" Harper said.

"What in the fuck?" Rory said, holding his wounds.

He didn't know what the gifts were she'd purchased for the gift drive, didn't know Brenda's words by heart, and therefore didn't have the pieces to fit the puzzle together. Of course, Harper did.

"Brenda."

"That doesn't make sense," Rory said as Harper helped him to his feet—mostly just the left thanks to the torn tendon.

"And a killer Cabbage Patch Kid does otherwise?"

Together they shuffled to the kitchen, Harper flicking the light switch along the way. The wounds weren't particularly deep. Tea towels would do until they could get to the hospital.

"There's a crutch hanging in the basement doorway, from when I broke my foot," Rory said, the words laced with pain.

Harper crossed the kitchen to the basement access. She pulled the string on the overhead bulb and there, alongside a broom, was the aluminum crutch. Turning from the door, she had to pause, wide-eyed, terror renewed for another episode.

The knife with the hook end had risen. Its wooden handle had split. It was walking toward them like a doubly peg-legged sailor. It picked up speed and Rory looked over at the sound. Once to the unofficial border separating kitchen and living room, the knife launched, spinning on air. The split wood the knife had used for legs entered Rory's eyeballs like darts.

"Ack!"

He spun from the pain, his back nailing the fridge. He stepped into the middle of the kitchen, still spinning, tugging on the blade like it was a handle, blood pouring down his arms and cheeks. The knife came free on a great reefing yank and then flew across the kitchen, into the freezer. Harper shot over and slammed the door before attending to the current love of her life.

"My eyes! I'm blind! I'm blind!"

"Shh, shh. I'll call for an ambulance."

Rory's phone was on the kitchen table. She snatched it up and plugged in his four-digit code—8008. She hit 911 just as the freezer door burst open and a frozen turkey began shaking itself free of its plastic wrapper. Every motion crinkled and snapped.

"Nine-one-one, what's your emergency," a feminine voice said as the cellphone dropped from Harper's grip.

"What is that?" Rory wailed, his head jerking back and forth, not unlike a turkey.

The frozen turkey leapt down from the freezer and charged Rory's helpless body. The turkey climbed Rory's abdomen and he tried to push it away, but without being able to see, he couldn't get any kind of grip.

"Brenda, stop!" Harper said.

The frozen, headless turkey paused on Rory's chest, seeming to look at Harper for about two heartbeats before Rory turned sideways, hands on the frozen bird. It slipped free and dove into his open mouth. It jerked and writhed, slick as raw bacon. Rory tried to pull it out, but it refused him, sliding deeper, stretching out his throat.

Harper slid on her knees, latching onto the turkey's back legs. As had Rory's, her hold failed. The turkey—all 5.5 pounds of it—worked down Rory's throat. Harper shoved away as Rory began flailing, bones snapped, fluids gargled and bubbled, his hands and feet slapped convulsively at the floor. After five more frantic seconds, his body ceased all movements.

Harper watched him, knowing he was dead and that she'd

never be able to explain—the flesh of his stomach burst out in a wash of gore that painted her face pink and brown. The turkey climbed out, as if being birthed. It turned to Harper, freezing her as if caught by a tower gunman's spotlight. Slowly, each step squeaking and slipping, the frozen turkey walked toward Harper.

"Brenda," Harper whispered.

At the sound of her voice, the turkey fell, de-animated. For a half-second Harper wondered if it was over. Then her head snapped back at a tremendous blow, knocking her unconscious.

—

Harper came to, crouched at the Christmas tree, her hands busily unwrapping presents.

"Good morning, sleepy head," her lips said, but those were not her words, and the moment after she thought that, her lips added, "Of course they're not. They're mine."

Brenda. Brenda was in her body. Harper tried to scream, but it was ineffectual, pitiful, with no mouth, she simply couldn't. The struggle was useless.

"I told you, babe, you're mine forever, I'll never let you go," her lips said as she tossed aside a nice scarf Rory had bought her as a Christmas present.

Though it did no good, Harper wailed silently, thrashed motionlessly, prayed hopelessly that this would end.

"Forever's a long time," Brenda said with Harper's mouth.

RANDI

(2013)

The sound of her mother's voice made her cringe: "Raaaaandi!"

What kind of parents looked at their newborn daughter and said, *Randi, she looks like a Randi?*

Inconsiderate jerks.

Randi. Randi. Randi. Randy the Macho-Man Savage, Randy from that trailer park show, Randy the giant simpleton who handed out samples at the grocery store, his neck always needing a shave and his gut hanging just below the bottom of his shirt. And then her, amid weird those men.

"Raaaaandi!" shouted Claire, Randi's mother.

Randi squeezed her fists tight in irritation, turning her attention from the Farscape re-run on the TV. Her name hurt her with the cool kids, but the current cool disinterested her anyway; if the *Teen Wolf* didn't involve Michael J. she didn't care. And she'd tried to fit in. She'd tried to care about the things the kids at school cared about.

A girl named Dodie once called her a freak and said, "Normal people don't care about all that old junk unless their old losers."

Randi didn't pause, didn't give her brain time to catch up to her flying fist. Two-day suspension.

It didn't seem fair and it didn't seem funny that kids got to yap and she couldn't defend herself. It shouldn't have surprised anybody that she sat at the office for kicking Dodie's ass, but they still acted like it. Life was like that. Some kids ruled and some kids drooled. Randi, queen of the droolers.

"Hey, Randi, get your ass in gear," Claire said, coming halfway down the staircase of their split level home.

"What?" Randi said, face in a bunch.

Claire clenched her jaws. "I told you, we're going to the store. Now move your ass."

"Why can't I stay home?" Randi asked, already switching off the television and standing.

"Because you're not twelve yet."

"Fine. God, you treat me like a child." She drag-assed toward the stairs, going maybe a twentieth of her top speed.

"Christ almighty. Move it!"

"I'm coming. I have to pee first. Even people in prison get to pee."

Claire made room for her daughter to scoot past on the staircase, rolling her eyes as she did. "Everything is a hassle with you."

"I didn't ask to be born!" Randi said, running now.

After lifting the toilet seat, she stood facing the mirror. She didn't have to pee. A nice patch of red little pimples dotted her forehead, not helping her cause at school. She scrubbed at them with an Oxy pad. The commercials said they worked, but she had yet to see much improvement. She inspected her teeth. For years she'd had crooked, cartoon hillbilly teeth, and now that she finally had her braces removed, they left little yellow indents. She brushed her teeth nine times the evening after the dentist visit.

"Why can't I at least have that normal?"

After flushing the toilet, she emerged from the washroom, her mother stood outside the door, tapping her foot impatiently. "Ready?" she asked, wide-eyed, arms folded, attitude at wholesale prices.

It was Randi's turn to roll her eyes. She went out to the car— another source of anti-cool. The Bolton family paraded around town in matching Nissan Cubes: one silver and one blue. Claire drove the silver one. Randi figured they had to be the ugliest cars in the world, and it didn't make sense that anyone would want one, let alone two.

It was a quarter to 5:00 PM. The streets were lively, though far from packed. Gig Springs was the home to 1,023 residents at last count, so even when the streets seemed crowded, a body might stand every ten feet. Above town, a low mountain range snugged up tight. Below town were winding roads that led to more interesting places.

Randi scanned the familiar faces as they rolled toward the grocery store. Dodie Deiter was on her way home and turned to make eye-contact with Randi as Claire pulled up to a stop sign. Dodie's long, pink tongue shot out and wiggled. Randi looked at her mother who watched Mr. Ellis, an elderly crossing guard, help three small children.

Coast clear, Randi stuck up her middle-finger.

"Randi!"

"But mom she..." Randi started in her whiniest voice, trailing in futility.

"Zip it."

Randi looked back at Dodie. A big smile stretched ear to ear and began to blacken. Her cheeks followed. Her long red hair singed, shrinking as it melted and turned to ash. Her clothing burned, taking on a charcoal hue.

Randi gasped. It had been years since she imagined a person she knew dead. Mr. Gilmour, her second-grade teacher, she'd seen him blue, his eyes bugging, his wrinkly body naked. Blood oozed from his head, collecting in a strange hovering halo.

Randi bit it down.

That night Mr. Gilmour slipped in the shower and cracked his head on the faucet. It wasn't until after the fact that she told her parents. They politely asked her to knock it off.

She closed her eyes. She saw Dodie like that because she hated her guts, surely.

Their Cube pulled into the grocery store lot. Stewart's Valu was the very last building before the steep hill out of town. Such a nothing place to live.

Randi turned to say something to her mother as they stepped inside the store; instantly, her mother's face blackened and her hair and clothes ignited. Her skin seemed to drip from her skull like candlewax.

"Speed it up. I have to make pies for your brother's fundraising thing," Claire said, yanking her stunned daughter along.

The image slipped away and Claire returned to normal. Randi scanned the small crowd of shoppers, they all looked fine. She rubbed at her eyes as she walked, following close enough to bump into Claire's butt when she stopped to inspect the produce.

"Watch it."

Apples and blueberries in the cart, Claire and Randi rounded a corner away from the outer aisles of the L-shaped store. Randy, the dim-witted giant, approached with cheese samples. Randi screamed. The skin on Randy's head peeled and blackened to reveal a charred skull beneath his scalp, his bushy eyebrows ignited, his eyeballs burst, the liquid steaming off him. His shirt lit and his mouth opened, flames shot up his throat.

"Randi! What's gotten into you?"

"We have to leave. People are burning. Please, Mom!" Randi covered her face with her arms.

"You little shit," Claire whispered. She took the keys from her purse and pressed them to her daughter's chest. "Wait in the car."

Randy extended his hand to Randi. "Cheeeeese saaample?"

Randi shook her head. Avoiding looking directly at anyone, she ran to the vehicle and for the first time since they were purchased, felt thankful to be inside the Cube. She watched through the window, none of the shoppers were burnt. Not a one.

—

Claire tossed the bags in the backseat and swung open the driver's door furiously. Randi looked at Claire, her face lit, the flames shot out from her collar and engulfed her hair.

"Why are you always doing something?" Claire said.

Randi didn't answer, in fact, she said nothing all the way home.

The Cube parked in the driveway and Randi shot inside and down to her room. She lay on her bed, listening to the house above her. Her father, Gary, had come home.

"Your daughter is being extra. She had a fit in Stewart's. I wish she would just be normal," Claire said.

"A fit?"

Randi heard no response and covered her head with her pillow. She heard nothing for several seconds until her little brother shouted, "We're going to Pizza Hut?"

Inside a minute, Neil's little feet played down the stairs and he banged on Randi's door.

"Open up!"

"Fuck off," Randi whispered.

"We're going to Pizza Hut!"

Randi popped from bed in a fury when he opened the door, but before she had a chance to yell at her brother, his skin blackened and his hair lit, just like the others. The flames crawled around his body looking for flesh to engulf.

"No!" Randi squeezed her brother tightly for the first time in years.

"Let go," Neil said.

She did.

Neil bolted away.

Randi watched his absence, knowing she was going crazy.

"Come on!" Claire shouted.

By the time Randi made it up, the family stood on the landing, her father's back to her. He turned and gave her a wide smile, his teeth browned and his lips melted away from the hot little Chiclets in the front row. The flames jumped out from beneath the Lions cap he wore, dancing downward over his abdomen. She held in a scream and shook her head in five violent strokes.

"I think I'm getting the flu or something," she said.

"You know what Aaron Geddy told me?" Neil said, ignoring his sister. "Randi means having sex."

"Neil," Claire said, scolding.

"No, it means horny," Gary said.

"Gary!"

"What's horny?" Neil asked.

"Ask Aaron Geddy," Gary said, grinning.

Randi stamped a foot on the linoleum by the door. "Dad, I don't want to go!"

"Too bad," Gary said, and petted Randi's head.

His hand shifted to her back and pushed her out of the house. The family jumped in the blue Cube and headed toward Pizza Hut. Randi continued to stare at her knees, she didn't want to think about what she saw—because what if it came true, and it came true because she was thinking about it?

Pizza Hut sat across the road from Stewart's Valu. Gary parked; the Cube's nose pointed at the grocery store.

"Do you want me to run over quick and grab the sugar?" Claire asked. "You can get a table."

"I was thinking of making a family night of it; movies and snacks after pizza," Gary said. "We'll all go."

"Randi can stay at the car." Claire tossed *the look* at her daughter. "She's embarrassed me enough in there for one day."

"Right. Randi, you protect the car."

Randi lifted her head to watch her family cross the street, smoke rising from their scalps and the collars of their shirts. Suddenly stifling, she got out of the Cube for air. The other faces on the street appeared normal, for the most part. Herbie Calvert, the car salesman at Romello Nissan, smiled at Randi. His face blackened and burned, but this time Randi continued to watch him. He crossed the street and went into Stewart's Valu.

Shifting from foot to foot, Randi began to whimper. Who knew what it meant...and what if she only imagined envisioning

Mr. Gilmour before he died when she really only imagined it after hearing the facts? That had to be it and now her brain was just trying to freak her out.

Dodie strolled up the block with her mother. Her mother was window shopping, bending forward to peer in at a display. Dodie stuck out her tongue again. Randi saw it roll back and fall to ash. The Deiters continued on and walked into Stewart's Valu.

No way she could wait another second. Randi looked left and then right before stepping a foot onto the street. An orange glow lit, like a second sun, this one coming from straight north. Her hands stole her attention. Flames licked and peeled away flesh. She jumped back, tripping over the curb and landing hard on her butt.

The smell of gasoline and barbequed meat filled the air, but there was no smoke. Randi began to cough, looking around to see if anyone else could smell what she smelled.

"Are you all right little one?" Milton Dickens asked, a man she knew from church.

"Don't you smell it?" Randi said, a smoke puff following her words.

A loud horn sounded, air brakes screamed, and then a raucous scratching noise rang out. Randi turned her head and saw that second sun for real this time. A double-haul tanker truck raced down the hill; moving about triple the speed-limit. Slamming on the brakes didn't help. The wheels skidded and the truck bullied through a grassy field. Moving faster and faster as it continued its decline.

"The store," Randi whispered. "Oh god no."

It was no good, the truck slammed through the heavily windowed wall at the rear of Stewart's Valu. Screams of terror filled the air and the truck's tankers doused the building and lot in a gasoline shower.

Silence reigned for two seconds before the screams began anew...*Boom!* Stewart's Valu quickly became a black smudge on the pavement. People ran around frantically, their backs and faces aflame; just as Randi had foreseen.

Boom!

The second explosion came from somewhere within the store, showering Gig Springs' downtown with charred body parts and blackened produce. Randi continued to watch. An old woman went running by, her hair on fire. Milton chased after her. A shadow slashed by overhead a moment before a fleshy thump sounded on the roof of the Cube.

"It was your job to watch the car," Randi said, the words hollow.

She pushed upright and climbed onto the Cube's hood. The roof had a crater, and centering the crater was Neil's head. Blackened, burnt, singed, blistered. The head rocked around as Randi moved. She slinked her body as close as she could and looked at her brother's face, his expression agape. The raging fire danced in the reflection of Neil's eyeballs.

Randi watched it flicker and sway, thinking now that it was only her, she could probably change her name.

LARRY CARMICHAEL'S HANDS

(2018)

Probably I was the only one who looked away when that scream continued. Ginger had bent the pinky finger of the brown leather glove on Larry Carmichael's right hand and the crack was nearly as great as his wail. That anguish had me cringing, half-eaten bologna on white bread floating a few inches from my mouth. I understood immediately. My guess, it took a second for everyone else to clue in. The pain spun him. The whites of his sclera showed double and his dilated pupils darted around the room like fireflies.

That was in the eighth grade. I met Larry in the summer after third grade.

My mother had this thing about vulnerable people. She was a helper—even when they didn't want or need her kind of help. She used money to manipulate situations in ways people couldn't refuse, and when she saw Larry at the front of the church with his big leather gloves on, she zeroed in. She left me and Dad with Kerry Sutter and his son Douglas—I think Dad sat us there for me, Kerry Sutter's brother played in the NHL and I was a hockey maniac.

The meet and greet stuff after church lasted about an hour and in the final lingering minutes, my mother came over to us and informed me that I was going to spend the afternoon at the Carmichael house, and more specifically, with the weirdo who wore the big gloves in the middle of summer. They had this shitbox Ford that smelled like engine grease. There was Larry's mom, Larry, and two of his siblings. I sat in back with the siblings: Jessica and Darren. Larry sat up front because of his hands. Jessica looked out her window and Darren grumbled and looked out his window while Mrs. Carmichael explained about Larry's gloves and why he had to wear them. That's how she did it too, as if the gloves came first.

Turned out, Larry had a rare medical condition called Osteopotiri, which translates roughly into bone glass—I got it then, I was a piece to one of my mother's grand charity schemes.

"He wears the gloves to protect his hands. It's a birth defect. The bones in his hands are made of glass. He has to be very careful."

I held in everything: questions, remarks, facial expressions.

The trip was no more than twenty minutes and she told me about how kindergarten and the first grade were "For other kids. Boys and girls without gloves." She'd quit her job and homeschooled Larry—Darren grumbled something about their old car and their old house in the city, but Mrs. Carmichael ignored him and kept on talking. "He tried regular classes for the second grade, but the children were mean."

At this, I clued into something else, too: this kid was a loser. I tried to say something, I don't remember what, but Larry started talking with an angry whine, "What's with the gloves? What's wrong with you? What're you some kind of freak?"

"Well, are ya?" Darren mumbled and this time Mrs. Carmichael told him to shush. Before we even made it to the old side of town, she told me about the cost of the gloves and how expensive the treatments were and how the government didn't cover cosmetic diseases.

"We've argued to the moon. His bones aren't cosmetic!"

The walls were closing in on me. This whole situation was wrong and weird, and I was stuck. There was a minor relief when we cleared the outskirts of town. Barns and sheds, mostly red and mostly faded, passed by the windows before Mrs. Carmichael took a left onto a road with a number for a name. She took another left up a short lane that dead-ended at a tall farmhouse, rough and ramshackle as a fixer-upper parody.

"Here we are," Mrs. Carmichael said.

Jessica turned to me. "We used to have a nice house in Richmond," she said and climbed out. I waited a second for Darren to get out after Mrs. Carmichael opened Larry's door.

Never on that whole trip did I expect to like Larry, but when we got to his room—after his mother helped him put on slimmer, more dexterous gloves—he carefully withdrew a padded binder of hockey cards from a shelf. Immediately, I forgot about the gloves.

The cards were older, but not old enough to have real value. "They were Darren's mostly, but some were Mike's. He's at work. He got a job doing hay. He's in high school."

I was nodding and flipping through.

"Mom and Dad get me a pack every two weeks. Before I came around, we had more money," Larry said and I looked up, trying to be polite or something, but he was reaching for another padded binder. He sneezed twice opening it. "They always get me..." His face scrunched and he sneezed again. "...these ones Dad got from one of his friends." The cards were from the '70s, but dog-eared and creased and stained and musty, worthless but cool as hell.

On the last page before I switched to look at the real old cards, I pointed to Dirk Sutter and said, "His brother goes to our church."

The three Sundays following, I was at camp. I didn't see Larry again until school.

—

Larry was in the other half of third grade, but his presence reached through the walls. First thing, first day, the PA squeaked and the principal explained about Larry's condition, and how we should play nice, and welcome him and his siblings, Darren and Jessica, into our school. By first recess, kids were calling Larry Pussy Hands.

When we made eye contact in the hall, I looked away.

—

Mom bought Larry middle of the road protective gloves. I guess there's tiers of protection and treatments for Osteopotiri. But since there weren't any celebrities with it and nobody did concerts for it and it was so rare, help was expensive and difficult to find. My mother told my dad and me all this at supper one night after Larry showed up at school with new gloves—still clumsy and awkward looking. Dad nodded and I did nothing. When Mom asked how Larry got along at school, I said he was in the other class.

—

The next year, Larry was in my class and sat at a desk by himself while the rest of us sat at tables. Some teachers were as bad as the students—worse, because teachers knew better. Mr. Nixon hated Larry and made him wipe the chalkboard with his gloves instead of the brushes. "Get used to it. It's about all you're good for," Mr. Nixon would say, or something thereabouts, and the mean kids would laugh. Nobody defended him.

Larry did as told and never complained.

Now and then, my mother made me go home from church with Larry, sometimes she even drove us and stopped in at Hank's Collectables and bought us boxes of hockey card packs to open—which I let Larry keep all of, like an apology. He never mentioned that we didn't talk at school and that almost made it worse.

—

High school was in the bigger town one over. Bryce Angus invited me for a Friday night sleepover and I rode the bus home with him. He took the same bus as Larry.

Larry sat alone in the seat behind the bus driver. When the driver wasn't looking, students threw food and spat wads of chewed paper against the back of his head. Larry did nothing, and I did nothing when Bryce chewed up a page corner and spat it through a straw.

In penance, I went to Larry's the following Sunday afternoon. His father was home, but still had on the company shirt he wore to sell chainsaws and lawnmowers. The TV aired an evangelical program. A man in a white suit stood before women in burgundy robes. He started screaming, "Abominations! These devil diseases! It's not just AIDS! You've got poor babies born of sin, reminding us that Satan is real! Kids with bad hearts, weak legs, glass for bones! These kids are sent by Satan himself to destroy our race!"

Larry's father turned to us then and said, "Maybe he's got a point."

There was nothing to say. People all over believed this kind of thing about Larry's bones.

"If I had good hands, I'd play hockey," Larry said as we sat in his room. I watched him sort through the big box of cards I brought him from home. "You ever play hockey?"

"Of course," I said and then burned with embarrassment. Larry had hand-me-down pictures of people having fun and the rest of us simply had fun.

This time was different from other visits. Sad and defeated, he sat in his bedroom, staring out the window, maybe imagining a place where normal children played and where he was one of them.

My mother told Dad and me that insurance companies refused coverage, doctors treated Larry like a curiosity, Larry's parents did not take Larry anywhere with too many stairs, and that she was doing her part to help them out.

—

When I saw them, I stopped dead. Hope had sprung and at fifteen, Larry made a public friend. She smiled and talked to him over lunch hours. She asked about his gloves and the hands beneath. She knew, but wanted to understand how it felt. He couldn't tell her because he didn't know. He had no comparison.

He told me all this, gleeful and uncaring that I only associated with him one Sunday a month. Sometimes I sat near them in the cafeteria, trying to understand this girl.

"I want to see them," she'd said between tater tots.

He took his gloves off for Ginger and she held his hands, gently.

"They don't look no different." She massaged them while he closed his eyes. "They look normal."

He shook his head at this and the gloves went back on.

She clung and people called them girlfriend boyfriend. They weren't, according to Larry, but he wanted to ask her. I even encouraged him and he laughed at me, shy and embarrassed. Ginger was not pretty and sometimes she smelled too much like Irish Spring soap. Her hair was stringy. She had more freckles than not-freckles. Had beady lobster eyes.

A match made somewhere, if not in Heaven.

—

"That's not even my real name, stupid!" Ginger shouted.

It was the first day of eleventh grade, a Tuesday, lunchtime, in the cafeteria and happening before an audience.

"It's a stupid nickname. How'd you like it if I called you Pussy Hands?"

Larry Carmichael had been Pussy Hands since he came to our school, but never to Ginger—never to Tiffany.

He apologized. By that Friday, she was again yelling at him in front of everyone. "I don't even think you got it. I think you're trying to get sympathy." Ginger grabbed Larry's pinky finger.

He screamed and we all turned to see. I knew before the rest and I looked away. My heart raced and Larry just kept screaming. There was nothing he could've done, couldn't even push her away if he wanted.

I couldn't save him anyway and he stood there, still, but screaming. None of us knew Osteopotiri typically stayed in the hands, but not always. In rare cases, the syndrome mutated and travelled, it was possible the shattering of a finger might send a tremor, destroy something in his arm or shoulder, maybe a rib.

I visited Larry one night in the hospital—he had to stay for three weeks. Painkillers and therapy for the following eight months. Larry's parents sold their house again because Osteopotiri wasn't covered.

Mr. Carmichael said to my mother, "Government insurance doesn't cover freaks," and she nodded while opening her checkbook.

—

He stayed out of school for a year after that. Larry's siblings started going by Mrs. Carmichael's maiden name. I would sidle up and ask about Larry, but they'd come to hate him and pretended to not hear me.

Larry returned for the twelfth grade, so as to achieve a proper diploma. Mrs. Carmichael thought if he had a diploma rather than a home-schooled test score that he'd find a better job. She wanted him gone.

He hardly grew and the same gloves my mother bought him were the same ones he still wore. Those gloves protected his hands against bumps, but left him vulnerable to everything else. The gloves broadened the bull's eye on his back. He resorted to an old habit and circled the librarian between classes.

By then Ginger had grown into her freckles and beady eyes. She had a boyfriend and she grinned when passing Larry. I saw it all and my heart concealed my shame in silence. I could've been his friend, at any time. I could've stood up and did something real for him.

One day there was a new girl named Jeannie who was a couple grades behind us, and Larry harbored some deep down hope. She came to town from the city. She wore gloves. They were black sequined and more shapely than the brown leather gloves he wore. They were wonderful and expensive looking. They were everything that his gloves were not, and still, they were gloves. They were the same.

I was in the library skipping class to catch up on an assignment about Henry VIII. I saw him staring and saw the pretty girl look his way. She was with the jocks and cheerleaders in their school team windbreakers.

Jeannie walked toward him and I could almost read his mind. There were two sets of glass-boned hands and they were about to come together. He looked at her like she was the answer to all the questions: did she have any scars from stitches and surgery, would their lips feel right and perfect together, what about his tuxedo next to her prom dress, handsome new gloves, what about Larry finding his place and a mate and all the happiness afforded to regular kids?

My god, the pre-emptive embarrassment I felt.

"Nice gloves, those from Walmart?" Jeannie said.

"No."

Wal-Mart never sold specialty gloves; couldn't buy them in bulk.

"*No*," she mocked and the chorus of acceptable young adults snickered behind her. "I want you to stop looking at me. You're a creep and you're poor. We're not the same."

His face went so red it turned purple. His hands clenched, as if he'd willingly break his bones on her face to prove how much the same they were.

I doubt she ever spoke to him again and I doubt he ever imagined the boutonniere he'd pin to his chest that would match her prom dress.

—

After graduation, I screwed up. College was too fun and I drank too much, so my father made me get a crappy job to understand what life would look like without all my privilege.

My foreman at the yogurt factory was a guy two years older than me who had dropped out and somehow passed his GED test while being a complete and utter idiot. I was ready to quit and promise to do better at school, promise anything my dad wanted, but then Larry Carmichael started and Larry had a way of making me forget myself.

My foreman told me the manager had a daughter with Osteopotiri—a girl who happened to wear black sequined gloves and was in her final year of high school. The manager was understanding and sympathetic of Larry's plight. He forced all of Larry's coworkers, me included, to watch a thirty-minute video about the glass under his skin. It was paid time, so nobody complained. Not about the movie.

We all had to pull a little extra because Larry was to load the lids and press the kill button only, nothing else. I guess a man with glass hands is a good man for the right task. The spinning and rushing of lids on machines. He was careful where others were not so careful. Men and women—hungover, high, plain tired—lost track of fingers and then lost fingers. Not that I ever saw that, but people talked and showed off nubs like party gags.

—

Maybe it was my fault. For the first time ever in public, I said hello to Larry as I was leaving the lunchroom and he was just coming in. He smiled and waved. Around a corner was the men's change room and I heard the conversation. Larry had worked up the nerve to talk to one of the other guys. Larry had to know we all watched the video and maybe he thought that made people care, maybe it was just me acknowledging him; like, *hey, your hands are not your fault and you're the same as them everywhere else*.

"Fuck off, Pussy Hands. You ruined gym class for a whole year."

Larry said nothing that I heard and I stumbled back to the doorway to listen.

"Just fuck off, freak."

Larry whined then, "Gym class? When we were kids?"

The way he put it, that perspective, I sank against the cool wall and closed my eyes. It would never stop.

"In the fourth grade?" Larry said then.

I tried to shout. People had to be sensible, it was so long ago. Couldn't they let it pass? Couldn't they be nice?

"So what if it was? Pussy Hands."

Nobody said anything else and I got back into my white coveralls and white rubber boots.

—

I waited after work the next day. "Hey, Larry!" I shouted and he turned, but didn't quite smile, did not wave. "Want to hang?"

"Okay," he said and I drove us to his apartment after grabbing a sixer of Moosehead. The place was sad and grungy. He opened the lobby door and the staircase door with his back. His apartment door demanded his hands and he was gentle as ever. Slow. Methodical.

There was a stained chair that looked like it came from the lobby of a defunct '90s doctor's office. It sat next to a window. He had a computer and a TV, but the chair seemed to be the important spot. There was a park outside and I imagined him alone, watching people with dogs on leashes, and kids running free, and fathers and sons playing catch. Then I imagined his glass bones with calcium fortitude. He'd be such a different person.

The adult gloves were better. He'd used a VISA to buy a pair made of slim Kevlar that sunk onto his hands like a second skin.

We drank the beers and he asked me all about college and I explained how bad I screwed up and then he told me about how my mother stopped talking to his family once there was a second kid in town with Osteopotiri.

—

My two weeks' notice went in eight shifts earlier. The manager left on that same day and they brought a new guy through. He'd managed a plant out east that closed a month prior. He was fat and had a huge moustache—most of the managers did; we had to wear hairnets and beardnets, but they all had moustaches and no nets for them.

"Gloves get in the way of work. Take them off," the new manager said.

I was sweeping up by Larry's station. Larry told the manager *no* and then explained why he couldn't take them off.

"How long have you worked here?" the manager said.

Larry told him how long.

The man grunted and walked away.

People saw and people talked. A factory is a miserable place and people need to let out their anger somewhere that won't cost them their livelihoods.

The following morning in the change room, the new manager stood in front of Larry and said, "You're still here? Didn't I fire you? Oh, wait, no. Can't fire someone for being weak and holding up the line."

That same voice, the one who accused Larry of ruining gym class, said, "He holds up everything."

Morning passed. The lunch buzz was two minutes away. I was dicking around because it was my last shift—turned out it was Larry's last shift, too—pushing a broom not far from where Larry worked. The final two minutes were mostly automated. It was up to Larry to load the last of the lids and then hit the kill button after the others left.

Larry stacked the lids into the tubular steel frame that shook them down one at a time onto the liter pails that followed on the conveyor. I watched, waiting for him to finish and then we'd go to lunch together. Larry eyed the lids, hand over the red button, ready to kill that part of the line—nothing fully shutdown until Friday night.

Factories are loud places, and I had my plugs in. I'd swung my broom a couple times, looking at the floor, so I didn't see or hear the men coming. Three of them grabbed and lifted Larry by his feet. I looked up then when Larry yipped and began shouting.

"No, wait! No, wait!"

The cruelty was one thing, but the method was overkill. The bones in his hands were hollow glass. They didn't need to tip him upside down and guide his hands into the gears, didn't need to keep pushing until his gloves caught and dragged him into the machine like bunched cloth.

Larry screamed, steady then, and the men ran as his flesh and bones triggered an automatic shutdown. There he sat, crouched forward, knees on the hard floor, arms jammed to his shoulders, mouth wailing into the rubber surface of a conveyor system.

I dug into my jeans below my coveralls and found my phone. I dialed 911 and ran toward the quiet of the change room.

Paramedics removed him a few minutes after noon and I followed in the car my parents bought me for graduating high school. The nurses and the doctor kept me up to date on his condition. They asked about his family and I told them who they were. An hour later, I asked a nurse if she got a hold of anyone and she said they refused to come.

"Said they can't pay another Larry bill."

I spent the day and came back the next morning. A nurse let me in to see him first thing. Larry was high and furious. I told him not to get excited, told him the cops had been called, told him he'd be able to sue and never have to work a day in his life.

"Yeah, and what am I supposed to do with my time then?" he said and I had nothing.

The doctor entered and I stepped back to a wall, giving them all the space they'd need. She was youngish and sad looking. She carried a manila folder; Larry Carmichael typed on a white sticker. They traded greetings. She asked obligatory questions and he answered.

"I see you've had corrective surgery and extensive therapy before." Larry agreed that yeah, he had. "This is much worse than that." He nodded. "That's not all."

My head went into my hands, the guy had never caught a break and it just got worse and worse.

The doctor took a deep breath and exhaled before saying, "The Osteopotiri has mutated." The doctor withdrew three black and grey images from the folder. "It's rare and unfortunate—"

"Incredible," Larry whispered and I straightened, started over to him. She held the scans of his chest so he could see—light grey lines spider-webbed over an ovular mass. "Is that *my* heart?"

"As I said, it has mutated."

"Jesus," I said, unable to move closer or away. The sight had me rooted. He had a glass heart. A fucking glass heart!

"That's *my* heart?" Larry asked again and she closed her eyes. He smiled. "It's beautiful."

The doctor didn't seem to hear. "The only real option we have is to install a prosthetic," she said. "And we have to do it as soon as possible."

"No."

"No?"

I covered my mouth.

"You can't change this, it's exactly right," Larry said.

"But you're a heavy cough or sneeze away from the glass shattering and, and then that's it." The doctor was firm.

"I don't want you to do anything."

"I think the morphine is clouding your judgement."

"No, it's not."

The doctor left and I said, "Man, Larry, you got to do something."

He looked at me then and said, "*You* have to do something. Finally. For the first time. *You* have to do something."

My mouth was dry and sticky. He'd kept track how I'd kept track.

"I need you to go to Hank's and get me the oldest pack of cards he has."

It was so unexpected that I didn't question him, and I certainly didn't understand. Hank's was about five blocks from the hospital and I paid three hundred bucks for six packs of O-

Pee-Chee from 1975. I didn't know, I thought the more the merrier, like we were kids again, opening hockey cards.

Larry was giddy at seeing them and said, "Open them where I can see them. Do it like your arms are mine."

Next to him, I was hardly looking, just doing because I owed him and I didn't understand and he loved hockey cards. Really, I was doing because of everything I'd never had the nerve to do.

"Closer."

I moved the cards to under his chin and flipped from one player to the next. There were ten cards and I made it through the first bunch quickly. A cement-like stick of off-pink gum fell onto his chest.

Larry was breathy, agitated, and said, "Next one, and flip them too, so I can read."

As I did what he told me to do, unsealing the brittle glue and peeling away the wax pack to reveal the first card and another stick of gum, a memory came to mind: his binder of old cards and how they always made him—

Larry sneezed three times in quick succession, and it sounded like someone dropped a vase on linoleum, soft but final.

He exhaled a final breath as tears streamed from his eyes. I stepped in reverse, cards falling from my hands onto the floor. That was that, and I'd finally done something real for him.

CRYING WOLF

(2017)

A gentle golden glare seeped through the cracks around the frame and the even freckling of vent holes. It was a tight fit and it smelled of sweaty gym gear and wet sneakers, which made absolute sense since it was a locker.

An indeterminate amount of time had passed and Jordie's ears suggested that maybe it was safe. Maybe there never was any real danger. They'd done a stupid thing, but possibly not a dangerously stupid thing.

"Or a janitor's playing a trick," Jordie whispered with a voice hardly more than a breath.

—

Only a few of them knew about the basement. Only a few of them knew about a classmate searching for Saku. Nobody really thought it was more than a tale big kids told little kids to give them shivers. That was until Oland went missing and left clues behind that suggested only one thing.

Neighbors saw Oland enter the school on a Saturday. It would be weird if it was anybody other than Oland, but Oland was a nerd and the teachers and janitors let him hang out in the library on weekends. Funding for the Whitewell town library had run dry and it had closed down just a year earlier. Oland lost his haunt and the heads of the school took pity on him.

The police investigation came up with *nothing*.

Jordie and his friends never liked Oland until he went missing. Suddenly it was as if someone stole a piece of their group when that boy who never really belonged disappeared.

—

Jordie put his ear to the cold steel door and pondered the likelihood of what he thought he heard and what he thought he saw from the corner of his eye before he kicked into gear and sought the shelter up the stairs, down a hall, into a change room, and behind a locker door.

Screaming. Growling. Wet snaps. Moans for help.

It was just a gag. It had to be a gag.

———

There were clues the adults ignored. Oland had three books on loan when he disappeared: *Wolves in Canada*, *Truth Behind the Myths*, and *The History of Whitewell*. Oland's BB gun was gone and so was his lucky meteorite, according to his mother.

None of them, not Jordie, or Willy, or Jasmin, or Vanessa believed the stupid, shiny, magnetic rock was from space, not until he disappeared anyway. It was Josie who suggested space rocks were magnetic to metal and intangibles.

Ya know, like it can find stuff people can't see.

They'd all nodded, knowing this was so. It was obvious then.

———

"Stupid," Jordie whispered. It had been *a real long time* since he heard anything and with every dozen seconds, it became clearer that a janitor played a trick and scared everybody else away. Of course, there was no Saku the Wolf and if there was, Saku wasn't living in the basement of the school. "Stupid," he said a little louder and felt into the back of the handle mechanism that opened the locker door.

———

Willy was the troublemaker of the crew and he had detention Friday after school. He'd made a mess of ketchup and chalk. Although nobody saw him do it, everybody knew it was his handiwork. An outline like old cop movies, but huge, on the cafeteria floor. A ten-foot man-shape splayed out with a white outline while ketchup-blood smeared all over the chest and head.

The janitor made him get a brush and mop from the

basement. That was where he found Oland's rock.

The books, the BB gun, now the rock? Saku's got him, probably ate him... We'll be heroes when we kill that stupid dog.

—

Jordie was all for it, in theory. He didn't really believe a mystical wolf somehow tracked down and followed one of the original settlers of Whitewell, not all the way from Finland. That was impossible. Dogs can't swim across oceans, dogs can't fly, and not even the most supernatural beast can teleport. He went along with the search for Oland because it was just something to do.

The locker door clicked and Jordie suddenly had second thoughts. He pulled it tight back and stared at the glow around the frame. What if there was a giant, kid-eating wolf out there and what if his friends were already dead?

"Just wait, probably nothing, just wait," he moaned, his head leaned against the steel door.

—

They'd set out just after supper, wanted to be sure they'd get in and be alone, supposing the window Willy opened around the back of the school was still open at all. Jordie figured, or maybe hoped, it wouldn't be.

It was and they entered. Willy had led the way to the basement. The stupid stone that may or may not have been Oland's space rock leading him. To Jordie it was like the Ouija game and how you always knew somebody moved the plank of wood, not ghosts, not spirits.

There was a wooden crate that had no business in the school's basement and Jordie suddenly felt a chill. He scoffed at the others checking out the box and meandered back toward the door and the stairs.

—

"Just some janitor playing a game," Jordie said a little louder, puffing himself up. "Not no damned Saku." The steel handle clicked and the door opened an inch. "Guys? Guys, you out there?"

—

There was the sound of rusty hinges and Jordie felt his heart drop. He'd stepped back to the staircase door and turned the knob. It was all crap. It had to be.

What's that? Vanessa had asked and then Jasmin said, *Like a statue or something.*

Then Willy screamed and there was a wet snarl. The girls whined and Jordie peeked back, thought he saw blood and a long snout with bright white canine fangs.

—

"Just your imagination and a stupid, jerk-face janitor playing a trick," Jordie said and pushed open the door to peer around the locker room.

—

The moans and snapping, lapping like a dog at a water dish, Jordie heard this from a distance as he ran. At the time, it was all so real and his only hope was to get away and hide from Saku. The Finnish hunter wolf existed and was in the school. Stupid Oland disturbed him and then stupid Willy made the whole crew disturb the thing as well.

Not me though, Jordie had whined, tears in the corners of his eyes when he first hid out.

—

"Not me though," he said stretching his back. "Didn't scare me though!" Heavy stomps, he crossed the locker room and swung open the change room door. "Didn't scare me!" he shouted into the vacant hallway.

—

From inside the locker, he'd heard the clickity-clack of claws on the waxed stone floor. Those sounds drove icicles into his veins. The meat of his heart threatened to dance itself to death and his cheeks burned hotter than ever before.

—

Into the hallway, Jordie strode, slowing himself to prove his bravery. It wasn't just the janitors. His friends were in on it too. They wanted to give him a scare because he was the youngest or maybe because he had red hair, who knows. It didn't matter because he was onto them.

"Screw you guys!" he shouted, swinging open another heavy door.

Saku the stupid wolf. Dogs can't swim across oceans. Can't fly. Teleportation was TV crap.

"Stupid jerks," he added gathering his bike from the wall at the south end of the school.

The other bikes remained and it was obvious the joke was still on. Jordie huffed and hopped on his Supercycle. See if he'd hang out with them again, yeah right. Their kind of friendship, he didn't need that, no way.

Jordie lived only a block from the school and was home in just minutes. Closing in on twilight, Jordie slunk to his bedroom. His father was in the living room watching the game between the Eskimos and the Tiger-Cats. His mother was in the office on the computer, playing a game.

He switched on Facebook and instantly, a message popped up. It was from Willy's mother, asking if Jordie had seen him.

"Pfft."

They thought he was stupid. They didn't fool him. It was surely Willy on his mother's account.

Another message popped up, this time from Vanessa's mother.

Hey Jordie, you see Ness?

Out the window, sirens roared. Cop cars zoomed up the street and stopped abruptly somewhere near the school.

"Nice try. You guys'll get in real crap making phoney nine-one-one calls," Jordie said.

Another message popped up, Willy's mother again, Jordie, are you there? You weren't at the school, right? Tell me you weren't.

"You know I was, dick!" Jordie shouted as he typed.

The landline began to ring.

Something crazy going on! Corina Tanner posted alongside a picture of an ambulance and cop cars outside the school.

Corina Tanner was a high schooler that babysat Jordie sometimes. Not likely someone in on the joke.

"Jordie, Willy's mom is on the phone! She wants to talk to you!"

"Okay, Mom!" Jordie scooped up the telephone next to his keyboard, knowing it was one of the girls pretending to be Willy's mother.

"Tell me he isn't at the school!" a loud, adult voice screeched into his ear.

Holy crap, this is nuts! Corina Tanner posted another picture from through her window of paramedics pushed away from the school by the police, gurney empty. One officer had the yellow tape roll in his hands, about to tie off the front entrance.

"Tell me!"

Jordie dropped the phone and rose from his computer desk.

"It's impossible, dogs can't swim 'cross oceans...Saku couldn't smell that far anyway...Saku's not even real. No real wolf could hunt like that, no way."

Behind him there was a rattle, clothes fell from hangers in his mostly empty closet, and a hockey trophy teetered and fell from his dresser. Faintly, Jordie heard a breathy growl.

It was just a game. A big hoax to really get him. Saku wasn't real.

"Enough," he tried to shout but hardly wheezed.

The growl grew louder and Jordie closed his eyes, ready to concede.

"Okay, okay, you got me!" he whined.

There was a wet slapping, chop licking.

"Saku isn't real, nothing could track someone down over an

ocean." Jordie shook his head, unwilling to peer upon his bedroom or anything lurking therein.

The slopping sound drew closer and it hit him, the block from the school was a much shorter distance than crossing an ocean.

He opened his eyes and whimpered, "Saku, please, no."

CLAW MARKS

(2022)

"At least your mother can finally rest," Peter said to his daughter, Rita, and his sons, Philip and Fred. "She was sick a long time and now she's resting easy."

Rita was the eldest at fourteen, and the only one of the trio who fully comprehended that their frail, emaciated mother had passed on to where she was never coming back from. Philip was four and Fred was only three. Even with the news coverage, the videos of bodies lined up in hospital hallways, in makeshift treatment centers in mall parking lots, in black bags and mass graves, it didn't quite hit home to them.

They did, however, understand that they must, at all costs, stay away from the glowing green moths that had appeared some three months and 600,000 deaths ago. The moths landed on people, secreted an enzyme, and flew off to mate, eat, or find another victim. Since last week, they'd been spotted and had claimed lives on every continent aside from Antarctica. The public had begun to fear sundown. As if enacting a self-regulating curfew, they stayed in nights, which was when the moths crawled from beneath soil and tree bark to pass on their poison.

"But she's coming back, right?" Philip said, eyes red from confused crying.

Peter clenched his jaw to keep the quiver in his chin from moving to his tear ducts. He'd cried more in the last five days than he had in his entire life. The survival rate was 71% for those infected by the green moths, those who'd contracted the Green Death. Philip and Rita had both whipped the sickness, but it dug into Isabelle, loving wife and mother, with insatiable hooks that weren't appeased until reducing her to a waif and ghost of her former self before ultimately devouring her life. The boys had seen her go into the coffin and had watched the coffin slip underground, but it was obviously too much to comprehend, or perhaps simply too much to bear.

"No. She can't come back. She's dead," Peter said, his voice soft, the words so hard to accept, even three days after the funeral and burial.

In their shared room, Philip and Fred climbed into single beds. Peter moved to Fred first, tucking him in and ruffling his hair before doing the same with Philip. He shut off the light, leaving on a rubber Spiderman glowing redly from a power outlet. He left the door open and headed to the living room.

Beat, Peter said, "Don't stay up too late," to Rita who was posted on the couch with her cellphone in hand. He shuffled to his room and stripped to his underwear before sliding onto his side of the bed, careful not to sully Isabelle's side. He would eventually, but he wouldn't do it on purpose.

He dropped off to sleep after only minutes of lying on the lonely mattress. From there, visions of Isabelle's wasted form plagued him. She asked over and over, "Why? Why would you do this to me? Why?" He had no words for her, only tears and supplicant hands, moans audible on both sides of his conscious.

"Daddy! Wake up!"

The cries stole him from the hellish dreamscape. Rita stood over him wide-eyed with a twisted expression, breaths panting, her right hand waving her cellphone.

"Look! Look!" she said.

Squinting against the brightness, he looked at Ian Hanomansing's familiar face where he sat behind a CBC news desk. "Tonight, reports have been confirmed, and potential for the reach of this confirmation is catastrophically large. Adam Alda showed signs to an ER doctor and mortician to be deceased, a victim of the Green Death. As autopsies have been outlawed for assumed deaths resulting in moth poisonings, there was no way to know his body had gone into a coma so deep it appeared, even to modern medical devices, that he was dead." The screen shifted to show a boney man with puke green-hued flesh.

"Thankfully, when I awoke, I felt better than I have since I first got sick. I guess my family was slow getting here and I was in a drawer longer than normal. I hate to think of all those who've been buried and..."

The man continued speaking but Peter heard no more. He got to his feet, flipping the light switch as he raced to his closet. He stepped into heavy slacks and pulled a grubby t-shirt over his head.

"I want to come. You're going for Mom, right?" Rita said. Her face was a canvas of tear streaks and puffiness.

"You stay and watch your brothers."

"But—"

"Mind me, Rita...please."

Eight minutes later, he was in the cemetery with his shovel and a flashlight. He wasn't the only one. All over people were digging and weeping. He'd worked thirty years on a construction crew, and though he didn't use a shovel much these days, it wasn't as if he forgot how to be efficient. The sod came up easily; after that, Peter pushed himself like he hadn't pushed himself in decades.

—

Rita was still up when he returned home. She was stress eating ice cream out of the tub. "Mom?" she whispered. "She didn't wake up?"

Peter sat on the bench by the door to slip out of his filthy sneakers. "No," he said, trying to shake the image of the clawed rips in the casket lining and blood streaks and broken fingernails and the agonized expression on Isabelle's dead face. "She was...she was dead when we buried her. She didn't suffer."

Rita pouted her bottom lip. "Okay...I wish she could've...I

imagined her screaming and trying to dig her way out...I'm sad she's gone, but..."

"But happy she didn't suffer?" Peter said. That Isabelle suffered a terror of unequaled torture, for what appeared to be many, many hours, was his burden alone to bear. He stood and wrapped his arms around his daughter, squeezing her tightly, eyes closed to the burning of a fresh batch of tears welling in his sockets.

Rita gasped. "Dad, there's a moth in your collar."

Peter opened his eyes, and for a heartbeat saw the silk lining of his casket surround him, saw the blood and broken fingernails from his panicked terror, saw his end drawn out in slow horror. Saw what Isabelle must've before she suffocated, alone and hopeless underground.

APOCALYPSE BADGE

(2015)

Peering through the frost cracked glass of a stalled camper, Tore sought life and found none. Light snows began nineteen days earlier but coated most of the country with two meters in the last forty-eight hours. True preparation was impossible for the dropping of the mercury. Those with the skills discovered life after the frost.

Forever winter began and Tore was in a small market, gathering with a grin. He'd left Norway in the spring for a warm vacation after an especially hard winter back home. Canada first, coast to coast, then down to the States. He wanted to see that world Hollywood so anxiously spread.

One month into the vacation, already onto the west coast of Canada, the snows began. It was his luck and he'd gone to the market to gather in a way familiar to him. Storms came and went, hunkering down was in the Norwegian blood. Born with skis on their feet, the elders joked and then their children and grandchildren joked.

Tore had taken a room in a small cottage belonging to three Californian hippies who'd moved to Canada some eight years prior. They feared the snow. Tore told them not to worry and that he had enough experience in the snow for twenty lifetimes.

They were right to fear the snow.

Spider webs worked through panes of glass and Tore gazed at the ever-spreading frost, an ache in his lungs taking root. There had been generators putting along after the initial sudden freeze that knocked out the grid. When the true cold set in, those generators lasted exactly four seconds.

The air bit at the lungs like fire, crystalizing moisture and killing from the inside out. It was a theory of cold familiar to Tore. In the homeland, there were tales of the freeze that would bring about the new ice age. These myths had apparently never reached the isolated greenery of the southwestern coast of Canada.

When the flash of cold hit, thousands stuck outside died in seconds.

Working silently, Tore moved deeper into the market, caught enough of what was happening beyond the building to think. No time to confer with the panicked shoppers. The basement was smallish given the size of the building above, but it was completely beneath the flash-frozen crust. The venting passed through the floor and into flimsy silver ductwork. It would do. For a time. A woman donning a manager's tag shouted at Tore but quieted the moment he turned his cold blue eyes and shaggy beard onto her.

It was only two minutes after Tore readied the basement that the boy burst through the front entrance of the store, bringing the biting cold in with him. He was dead before his face hit the hardwood floor. The screams began and micro-pandemonium ensued. The cellphones that worked just minutes earlier found no signals. People were dead in the street. Seized engines crowded the asphalt.

Smoke poured onto the main floor from the basement as Tore began burning what was on hand. Although he hadn't planned for every possibility, he had planned for Labrador and permafrost conditions on the northeastern coast. The expectation was that Tore wouldn't need his winter gear the remainder of his trip, parka, mitts, and boots and now was thankful for their availability. He had dug them out from the trunk of his rental car at the first sign of snow, smiling then at the locals having a fit over the sudden chill.

Tore returned to the main floor and carried with him

unquestionable authority. The people in their flimsy windbreakers raced with armloads of goods from the shopping floor. There was a fire burning in a steel bin on the basement's cement floor, the vent work spreading heat and smoke.

Tore moved the deceased boy from the doorway. He'd been running most likely. The gasping breaths were gasoline for the burning cold. Closed but not locked, Tore scanned the frozen world hoping anyone that needed warmth would find them. There was food and heat in the market, enough for several weeks if necessary. He grabbed two bags of campfire wood from the pile at the doorway and returned to the basement.

Within four hours, three more locals wandered in, fingers failing and tears frozen in waves upon their cheeks like built up lake surf. Six men decided, if dressed well, that they should go out to find help. Tore did not like this plan and remained quiet. He'd done his part.

Three local teenagers poured into the basement wailing and scabby with gaping and oozing cold sores on their cheeks. One of the teens died within an hour. The six men did not return.

On the fourth day, the locals who did not care for Tore's insistence that they wait out the storm and that they limit the fire and food consumption, took a vote. Tore was not a local. Tore was to go.

"You can't tell us what to do, you're not even Canadian," one man said.

Pleas reached his teeth, but the proud man refused to open his mouth. The rabbit lined hood of his parka lifted and he stepped outside with plastic grocery bags filling his pant legs.

The first test was of time. A steel wristwatch older than he was, worked to monitor the available minutes. Tore walked slowly for nine minutes the first go, then broke into a home and lit a fire, three flash frozen corpses huddled on a couch next to him. On his second measure after warming himself next to the dead couch potatoes, Tore walked for sixteen minutes before stepping into a woodshed. To seek out life, to exist amongst others was a task worth driving toward.

Thirteen days after the locals in the market forced him away, Tore felt ready to settle in somewhere and decide the value of a life alone on a world too cold for comfort. He'd walked his absolute limit that afternoon, twenty-four minutes, and pushed through the door of a used bookstore. If nothing else, there was easy fuel for flames lining the walls, and he had a loaf of bread to toast in his pack.

Once through the semi-barricaded door, Tore recognized the signs of life after the storm. "Hello?" he called, accent thick.

No voice returned to him. He followed the path cut in the snow blown in through the cracks in the street-facing wall. Without considering much of anything beyond hope, he swung open a door and felt his feet rush from beneath him.

"Oogh," he said.

Flipped, his hood brushing on the cold floor, Tore cast a glance up to the snare trap hanging from the ceiling. He then looked about the room of shadows of the lifeless space.

The first strike landed on the back of his head so unexpectedly that he didn't make a sound. The second strike caused him to blurt a Norwegian curse. The third strike quieted his thoughts.

The headache was profound when consciousness stormed his grey matter. Tore rocked with his foot to the sky. A fire burned before him, warming his chilled body. Behind him the door had closed. The building, with all those books as extra insulation until they became fuel, would warm better than anywhere he'd been in town.

"Hello," he said, a shadow moving beyond the bonfire light.

Tore attempted to curl up but did not have the strength to reach his foot and dangled silently—it would not be long before permanent damage occurred. He stared for the movement he'd seen and could not catch it, could not hold it. There was nothing, it was almost as if a ghost had caught him.

"There are no ghosts, Tore," he whispered in Norwegian.

A book flew from a shadow and landed on the flames. Tore peered into the blackness and wondered if his affirmation was true.

"Hello?"

Another book landed on the flame, its source from a different corner. Tore closed his eyes to imagine a world where ghosts were impossible. Another book flew to flame from a different angle. It was suddenly so obvious. Ghosts had brought about the frost, the snows trailing their entry like bridal trains. The ghosts had taken the world and enjoyed toying with the meat.

"Kill me if you are to kill me," Tore said in his native tongue with as much dignity as he could muster, dangling by a foot.

Another book flew.

"Please."

Another book. The flames grew and Tore finally saw the tiny eyes draped in shadows. Bulbs glinting the musty orange flames back at him.

Not a ghost. This was a demon and Hell had frozen over building a bridge to an Earth of frost-fried greenery.

"Draug," Tore whispered recognizing the gaze of a *returned walker.*

Tore covered his face and prayed silently to a God he wasn't certain carried any weight in the frozen world. He pushed up with his arms to relieve the pressure on his foot for as long as he could without looking at the monster in the room. Relieving the pressure was a tangible act, something he could do to better his situation without dealing with the demon before him.

Arms sapped, Tore once again dangled on the painful snare. Tears slipped along his forehead, into his toque. He closed his eyes and wished for mercy.

—

There was no way to be certain of how long he'd been out, but when he opened his eyes onto the chilled piece of bread on the floor beneath him, he knew he'd been unconscious. The bread was hard and stale in his hands. He hadn't eaten since, twenty-four minutes before he entered the Draug's bookshop.

"Is this how you enter flesh? Is this to be the vessel of my undoing?"

A book flew from a shadow. There was a scurry and another book flew from another shadow. Again, over the floor, feet swished, and books flew. It was an act of something pretending to be what it was not. There was something in those shadows, playing up its size.

In English he said, "I am Tore Olimb. I mean no trouble."

"You are a rabbit!" a high voice squealed, and two books took flight, one right after the other. The flames climbing, revealed a small face surrounded by blackness. "You are a rabbit. I am not hearing you talk!"

Tore took the bread, grabbed onto his pant leg, leaned as far upright as his energy permitted and ate it. He then fell back painfully and stared through the dimming light at a child's face.

"I am Tore and I am people, not rabbit."

A book flew over the fire and struck Tore in the chest. It was a moderate volume on Canada's horrific Residential Schools, like-new condition.

"Rabbits! Do! Not! Talk!"

Two more from the Canadian non-fiction section struck Tore and he winced—both were in hardback. Mordecai Richler, *damn his long wind.*

"No, they do not. Therefore, I am not a rabbit," Tore said. It was hard to speak. The blood in his head had begun to feel like lead. "I am a people. Let me down."

No book flew and the eyes backed into the shadows.

"Hello, child?"

The eyes returned and a telephone book landed on the fire, green tinged flames rose.

"I catch the rabbits. I bat the rabbits. I skin the rabbits. I reset the trap. You are a rabbit because you are in my rabbit snare."

Tore shook his head. "Rabbit snares take wrong catches. I am a people like you."

"Why can't you talk like normal then? Maybe you are a smart rabbit!"

The information was too much to willfully comprehend. She had said she skinned the rabbits. Tore wheezed, "The rabbits, were they big as me?"

"Very big winter rabbits. Jackrabbits, I know because I am the Chickadee-Dee-Dee!" Her voice cracked over the quiet room.

The greenish flames had gone from the small fire as the phone book had become ash.

"Are you saying that you are a bird?" Tore pushed against the floor to relieve the pressure on his foot.

"No!" she laughed. "I am the Chickadee-Dee-Dee. I have all the badges and the certificates, and I'm only ten. There are no more so I am *the* Chickadee-Dee-Dee!"

"You are a..." lacking the English, "Spiederforbund?"

"I am the Chickadee-Dee-Dee!"

"Okay, yes. I am not a rabbit though. I am...on vacation in your country. I am people like you. Not a bird or rabbit."

A book flew across the cold space. The flames flickered.

"Will you let me down?"

Two more books flew. The flames grew and Tore recognized the barrel of a small rifle. The child had done as her brags suggested. Merit badges and certificates for a *Chickadee* level Girl Scout proved invaluable during the frozen apocalypse.

"You are not a rabbit. You are maybe a bear."

Tore shook his head somberly. There were worse ways to die.

"What kind of bear are you? It is best to be vigilant in the presence of mother bears," the girl said as if reading lines.

Tore whined, "I am no bear. I am a man—people! Please, I am in pain."

"It is important to take care not to attract bears as they can be hazardous to camp and person. You are a hazardous bear and that is why my batting did nothing on your rabbit head because your rabbit head is a bear head."

"Dear God, rescue me," Tore whispered in Norwegian.

"That! Is that bear, do you have languages? Can you talk to koala bears and panda bears, or do they have different languages from you? The brown bear I should think, you are not a grizzly or a black bear."

"I am not a fucking bear!"

The girl squeezed the trigger and tumbled back from the recoil. Her aim was wide by several feet. She began to cry. Tore closed his eyes again, no more loud pleas, no more growling like a bear.

—

Books began piling at the edge of the fire, thrown from the far side of the room.

"Do you suffer?"

The girl was closer than ever before and Tore drank in her height. Four-foot-nothing, a body hidden beneath puffy layers of tundra ready Gore-Tex.

Unthinking, Tore said, "Yes, I suffer greatly."

The girl stepped into the shadows and retrieved the rifle. "It is of the utmost importance to ensure no animal suffers at the hand of a Scout. Animals used in the case of Scout survival should be treated with dignity and compassion. Make the kill quick and painless."

"I am a man!"

"You are a bear, and you suffer. I will show you compassion."

The rifle was only feet from Tore's chest. The girl leaned down and steadied her bearings. She squeezed the trigger, making Tore wince. Nothing happened. The rifle had a bolt action. The girl studied the tool.

"Please, do not. I am people. Not bear or rabbit, not even bird or dog...I do not suffer...I am..." A familiar image popped into mind, two words he'd seen over and over since coming to Canada. "First aid! I am in troubled need of first aid!"

The girl continued to fiddle with the rifle, yanking the bold back, sending the spent casing air bound.

"Cleanliness is of the highest importance when dealing with open wounds. A Scout can make an educated judgement concerning the nature of injury and take the steps necessary while applying proper first aid."

The rifle lifted and the girl steadied herself.

"You do not shoot people in need of first aid!"

"Of course not, but you are a clever bear, and you will maul me if given the chance. I will show you compassion."

A last chance effort, Tore swung both hands at the book fire and flung flaming pages at the girl. Startled, she jerked back and fired. The shot ripped into Tore's shin. He screeched. He roared. He growled.

The girl cried out, "Chickadee-Dee-Dee!"

The bolt expelled the spent casing and another round dropped home. Adrenaline raced through Tore. He rocked his body upward, reaching for the snare. Cold, tired, swollen fingers latched onto the rope. Quickly the shots jumped from the rifle. The frantic girl screeched again, calling out her rank, her war cry, her apocalyptic title. The first shot missed. The second shot bit into Tore's hip. He growled all too bear-like as his body swung downward, failing half the way, nearly free.

"I am a people ! Do not shoot!"

"I'm showing you compassion! Chickadee-Dee-Dee!"

The bolt clicked back, but nothing hopped into the chamber.

"I...! Please...! I am lost hiking and need first aid!"

The girl was crying. "Bears live where they are, they do not get lost. You are a bear and I have to show compassion."

There was a wooden Cooper baseball bat leaned against a bookshelf. The girl picked it up and cocked it.

Beyond the backroom, into the cold showroom, a door opened, and voices approached. Men called out.

"Rabbits," the girl whispered. "My snare...my snare..." she whined.

"Leave me be and I will scare away the others," Tore said.

The girl ran away, into the shadows as the door swung open behind Tore and bumped into his back. Uncertain, the vacationer played dead.

"Buddy! Geez!" a voice shouted. A light flared over the room in an ovular glow.

Tore squinted at the man. "Please, help me."

"Hold tight, buddy, who put you up there? Is he still here?" asked one of the two men.

"A girl, Chickadee-Dee-Dee. She has a baseball bat and a small rifle, but no shots."

"Chickadee?"

An Arrow cut through the frosty air, hitting with a sluicing cry. The quiet helper of the pair gargled, blood blooming from a hole in his throat. The flashlight beam spun in search of the assailant. Two books dropped from a pile and the light shifted to chase them.

The girl was clever. Another arrow whizzed from several feet away from the fallen books and the man dropped, struck dead as the upward arch took the arrow through his eye and into his brain.

Chickadee-Dee-Dee emerged with a crossbow pointed. "I show compassion. It is necessary to show compassion to bears."

Tore nodded once before sending out a great, bellowing roar.

SWAMP LUCK

(2015)

Just one of those things, an item to scratch off the bucket list.

I'd always loved dinosaurs, spent weeks in both Alberta's badlands and Montana's badlands, went to museum exhibits all over the continent, scoured articles and journals, but it was as if I was missing something. Late for the show, I suppose. The life wasn't in those bones anymore and I wanted a thriving, shaking, scratching, biting view of the great beasts. An unreasonable urge, but matters of the heart rarely are. Reasonable, I mean.

I even tried on the Jurassic Park movie when it came back out in 3D—hell of a lot of fun, but not what I needed.

"Pard a da reason de's still 'round, is de smarts," said a man with the right arm of his shirt noticeably empty of extremity.

He spoke of the alligators. You see, I thought the alligators were to be my link, the living snapping, snarling dinosaurs I so eagerly sought. The man leading our little pleasure cruise into the swamp was named Big Tuck. He spoke broken swampy slang, smoked roll-your-owns—amazing what he managed with one hand—and had a general reluctance about city dwellers. That included me, it also included the East Asian couple snapping shot after shot on their Nikon Ones and a clueless New Yorker and his two sons. The boys looked bored enough to toss each other in just to see what would happen. Big Tuck was extra stern with them as he explained loss. Said he once had two arms. Said he once had a brother. Violent demise was a sad swamp reality, and the remnants of the Cretaceous Period weren't exactly against helping with the effort.

"Big'un dat got ma arm, he'd still out dare. Cetus, he more

den fiddeen foot, weigh 'bout de same as a truck." Big Tuck swung his stub and his existent arm with the same enthusiasm. His loose cigarette showered embers onto his alligator hide vest. "Got ma brudda en me when we's skippin' rocks off de shore."

Now, Cetus—See-tus, named after the ancient beasts of Greek and Biblical mythology—was just the kind of beast I wanted to see and I asked Big Tuck if it was likely. The man paused and then shrugged. Cetus was old and the old ones get that way by staying smart. There's something very respectable about that if you ask me, of course, I had no idea of how smart they really were. It's one of those you've got to see to believe kind of things.

We'd been out on the boat, a pontoon, for much of the day, we'd seen a bunch of little gators, but nothing that pounded home the prehistoric bloodline. I'd hoped from the moment of hearing his name that Cetus trailed behind, perhaps scouting, hoping for a proper meal of a tourist.

The two boys started tossing bits of their pack lunches— sandwich crusts and then potato chips—in an effort to drum up action. I thought a gator would have to be as stupid as it got to snap at such obvious danger, and I was right. The water stirred a moment before a goodly splash had us wide-eyed.

A babe, no more than four feet in total, snapped up the chips. We all rushed to the side. Big Tuck warned about throwing food, but the boys ignored and kept on tossing. The little gator came back and snapped again, but didn't rush back down, just waited and spied the surface.

A stupid move for a creature in a dog eat dog environment. Even a tourist could've nabbed him if natural selection hadn't come along and showed its teeth. Bubbles came first and then a swish and then a great wave. After that, I saw the jaws and those teeth, another gator just about swallowed the young gator whole.

Amidst our oohs and aahs, Big Tuck jumped to his feet and his face went pale. "Oh sweed Lordy!" he screamed and throttled down on the accelerator.

Pontoon boats could be slick on the deck and I hadn't much considered my footwear from a traction standpoint, mostly just for moisture resistance. My big green rubbers slipped and I found myself on the wrong side of the boat in the time it took to blink. I flailed stupidly, everyone screamed, and Big Tuck swung the boat back around once he'd noticed my unplanned evacuation. "Hold on!" he yelled—as if I had other plans.

The bubbles returned, and I jerked around, kicking my feet to keep afloat, but the big gator head didn't come up. No sense looking down, it wouldn't have stopped anything had I seen it coming. Teeth sunk into my life jacket and the waist of my Levi's. Piss leaked and I swallowed a mouthful of swamp as, despite the awesome buoyancy of my life jacket, I went down like a rocket. Only shapes in the muck, but I saw enough to know I was face to face with what I'd always wanted.

I knew it when I felt his body against mine. Cetus. He could've cocooned me with his pale belly. He spun, I recognized a definite start point and remained conscious of one full revolution, but after that, it blurred. The act melded together my entire understanding of life and death; I saw what keeps certain beasts around for millions of years—in one fashion or another. Intelligence, it's always a factor, but there's more than that.

We spun and spun, my lungs began to fill and then the world slowed as my soul crept from my body. I looked back and every second happened in minutes, slowing further and further, almost pausing for me.

Metallic clicking carried easily and light poured through the murk around me. When I turned my focus, I really experienced that light. I figured it was the afterlife; folks who die and come back talk about *that white light*. So I went, walking on the muddy floor, I didn't hear any welcoming voices or encouraging serenades, just that clicking.

I stepped through and my eyes adjusted.

Took a second even after. Had to shake my head and blink a few times. That light had led into a small waiting room, like a doctor's office or a dental clinic. There were two lines, one said *New Arrivals* and the other said *Rematches*. I stepped forward to an officious looking box with a sliding glass window. There was a figure, back turned, in a tall office chair. I cleared my throat, got no response, looked around the room, the *Rematches* line was long, there were a dozen or so people of all manner of sizes and ages wearing the same annoyed look on their faces.

There was something about the whole thing I did not like, part of me wanted to go back out and try my luck in the murky swamp water, but when I looked, the door was gone, dry-walled over like it never really was.

I cleared my throat again and still got nothing.

"Ding the bell, dickface," said a young man smacking chewing gum at the front of the *Rematches* line.

Turned back around, I looked and saw the little silver bell. I tapped the button and the chair spun at the sound.

It would be the understatement of a lifetime to say that what I saw startled me. I was about ready to hide in the corner and start sucking my thumb as I rocked to and fro, tugging on my hair and scratching away at my eyes, but I didn't. Something about all the elements together had me in a smooth state of shock.

A small alligator wearing red lipstick, fake eyelashes, and a gold watch on its wrist—ankle? What I assumed to be a she looked at her watch and pointed one of her tiny upper legs toward a seat. I didn't move and the secretary gator shrugged and picked up a nail file. She sharpened her teeth with it and I watched until a door opened at the front of the lines next to the box.

A small boy stepped out. He looked furious. "Exy-lem, what de hell is dat?"

"Xylem, young man, those X words are tricky," an older man said. He was at the back of the line.

"It's stoopid, triple ledda stoopid!" the boy said and stomped to stand behind the man in the *Rematches* line.

The secretary cleared her throat and pointed to the door with the nail file. I stepped forward, past all the sneering faces in line, and through the open door. It was dark and a spotlight shone down on a chair. No choices there, and even with legs like cement, I moved.

A voice boomed as if from all around me, "Sit, please."

I did and the spotlight grew. I saw the Scrabble board and then I saw my opponent: larger than life, Cetus. He smoked a pipe and winked at me. The gesture was big and wet. A grimace stretched my face and I tried to speak, but nothing came except for a whispered gasp of air.

"Loose rules, no slang or names, but places and types of supper welcome. First one to one hundred wins. If I win, you go to the rematch line. If you win," he gave a double *ha ha,* "you join your body. Don't beat me first go, your body probably going to die. Just a warning."

Reeling, I gulped down my nerves and watched as Cetus reached into the satin bag for his letters. He handed the bag over—I had to do most of the reaching—and I took my tiles with hands shaky enough to roll dice.

I hadn't played Scrabble in years, and the last time I had, I'd lost by a bundle. I remember thinking it was all about luck.

"House goes first," he said. Every time he spoke, it felt as if my head might cave in through my ears. "I'll start light and give you a chance." He took a puff off the dark wooden pipe between his teeth and I watched his tiny limbs put down the word DOILY. It was worth thirteen points and I thought if that was his version of going easy, I was damn well doomed.

I hadn't even looked at my letters yet. Cetus pulled five letters from the bag. My brain started working some and I thought about the clothing and the language out in the waiting room. It was Hell or Purgatory! That fate scared me as nothing had before.

"Time's a wasting."

I forced myself to look at the board and then my letters and then the board, I almost hit the roof. My fear washed away with some luck. "Zoic," I said as I placed the tiles.

He grunted. We both did the math. The Z found a triple letter score.

"No more Mr. Nice Scales," he said and quickly slid four letters onto my Z: AGAZE, thirty-five points, same as my ZOIC. "You need to pick your letters before I do."

I stuffed my hand in the bag hoping for some tile gold to go along with my K, A, N, J. I pulled two Es and a B. Somewhere, someone smiled on my hand and I went to work: YANKEE, double letter on the Y and double word under the first E.

We did the math again and Cetus' grunt became a small growl. I thought one more word like that and I had the game— like it was easy-peasy lemon-squeezy.

Cetus fished his letters and then I got mine. It took a few seconds, but then he looked up at me with a grin, smoke billowing through the spotlight's shine. You've never been unnerved by a happy face 'til you've been eye-to-eye with a gator with good tiles.

"V, E, X, E, D, vexed, double word score."

The second E fell onto the sweet spot below the word YANKEE. My tiles made me want to cry. Like full-grown-ass-man blubbering.

"Tick, tock," he said.

I bit down and put what I had after I'd gathered a handful of vowels to go along with my consonants. There are better words, especially since I hit another double word score, I know, I've checked since, but I put COPE on the end of AGAZE and the battle felt a whole lot closer.

Right then, I was up, but by only three. My hand went back into the bag. Cetus wore an expression that was a lot less humored or confident. Twenty-points from killing me dead, he shook his jaw subtly. Three shy of victory. DOWDY ran horizontally from his vertical DOILY, the double letter score just not enough.

Relief washed like swamp water. I needed only sixteen. My tiles seemed to spin beyond recognition. I no longer understood English or board games. The pressure crushed me and forced my mind back to past games, flipping through my imagination, picturing things that may or may not have ever happened during a game of Scrabble. I saw my siblings, my parents, they taunted and laughed, *three letter word, huh, good luck with that one!*

"Quick, I've got the finishing touch," Cetus said, smile in his voice.

What I had wasn't enough, but I'd run out of time. I put down a J and a B around the O in cope. I was done, my body would die and I'd be in the waiting room at the back of the line. It wasn't hard to imagine my parents crying over my empty casket after I'd just imagined them laughing at my stubby word choice. I then began to imagine eternity.

Cetus slumped and I lifted my head and waited for him to take his turn. "Well?" I said finally.

"Been many years since I lost first round, was a stupid boy that got lucky with the word quiz," he said. So sad and angry, I didn't understand until I noticed my B fell on a double word score.

"I won? I won!"

He growled, grunted, and then softened, "You did, now get out before I eat you."

For a second I wanted to shake his hand, but those claws...instead, I tore out into the waiting room. Everyone looked at me: anger and frustration and jealousy. It was like smiling during a wake. Still, I didn't really care enough to force a complete emotional check. The door was back and I raced for it.

"Hey, you dare, ya ev' meet a boy named Lil' Tuck, ya tell'm I ain't wanna skip no damn rocks in de firss place, shud be him in'ere."

A huff left my lips and the door sucked me through like a vacuum and shot me back into my body. The physical form Cetus took let go of me. The big gator winked and swam off, the bubbles staying in view long after he'd gone. It was only a second before I found my way to the lighter shades of muck. I heard the yells and the engine coming to a stop, it was the surface world.

My chest sodden as my clothes, Big Tuck eyed me suspiciously as the others pulled me onto the pontoon; it was there, the knowledge, but something more, the stuff making up the gods and demons of the universe. Big Tuck knew about it. Even as I choked out muck from the swamp, I saw as much.

After I'd puked all there was to puke, I lay on my side and said, "Your brother says it should be you in there."

The other tourists gawked at me like I was a pickle slice in a toaster, but Big Tuck shook his head. "He still dare." This wasn't a question—a solemn statement. "He jus' ain' god de luck. S'times ya jus' ged lucky. Quiz god me." He tapped his head with the only index finger he had left.

No argument from me, so I nodded. Sometimes you just get lucky.

INGRAINED

(2016)

James imagined a starter home of their own, with a furnace just like the clunky green unit in the basement. James set down his toolbox and looked out the window, thinking that a furnace would be a pricey update. He imagined putting in a new system, watching his wife pay, and the thought made his heart ache.

The snow started sometime in the night and the heat had pumped off and on since—so far so good.

The world was all new and a husband might eat the bread his wife brought home, but that didn't mean it was easy. There was a word for a man like him. That unspoken title echoed in his head as if taunted by schoolchildren, *Househusband! Househusband!*

James rubbed his jaw. A few more inches out the window and he'd have another task on the list. Another that carried no monetary value. He inhaled deeply and exhaled, breath fogging the little pane of glass next to the door. An old fingerprint came into view and he used the cuff of his flannel shirt to wipe it away.

He turned and looked at the freshly unpacked home. The place had more room than they were used to and it made their accumulated stuff seem inadequate. Three weeks and it felt far from normal. All day at home when he was used to being elsewhere.

The midday sun streamed through the living room blinds, dust particles hanging on the air made the house seem aggravatingly unclean. There was a scent lingering, not exactly bad or dirty, a lived-in scent of others. The past dwellers clinging alongside those dust particles like gassy ghosts. The hues fruity and sour.

The furnace pushed these scents around rather than away. Cleaning the ductwork was another job for James, one he'd already popped onto the list.

He picked at the arm of the couch and pictured his father and grandfather accepting what he had. James worried about his pride without ever admitting the cause of his anxiety. There was a job and one that paid well, but it wasn't his. It belonged to his wife, Leanne.

His father wouldn't have lived like that and scoffed at anyone who did. His grandfather might've laughed in a man's face who stayed home while his wife went to work, questioned that man's manhood.

Moving to the new place for her work meant Leanne alone paid the bills. Oh, he'd find something, eventually. Maybe. It wasn't easy and was getting harder all the time.

Before they moved and made the idea a reality, it brimmed with promise. They'd dreamed where her education might take them, the vacations and cars, the toys and a home all their own. While she furthered her schooling, he worked and with that work knew the great pride of contribution. Deep down he always assumed she'd be number two, he'd wear the *pants*, because...just because.

Househusband! Househusband!

Man earned the meatier share. Man protected that share. Woman pitched in to help, mostly with the family, the nurturing, the hugs, and the bandages.

James shook his head and punched his hip, trying to cast away the feeling. Equality didn't have set jobs and he loved his wife. The move was good. Her job was great. A career.

As if affronting a household law, James was without income and his wife didn't need a protector. Worse, she didn't mind at all that he wasn't either. He agreed and smiled when she'd explained it over the phone to her mother.

Thankfully, James' parents were a decade underground.

When they moved, the world came at him in a flood. The small house needed work. It kept him busy and if he got most of it done quickly, he might equal Leanne's wage with the effort. Those first few months anyway. The owner had placed an advertisement online the same week Leanne accepted congratulatory handshakes of the new future. The ad stated an interest in swapping work completed for housing. Renovations in exchange of a year's rent, *some expenses covered. Must have own tools.*

Before the move, James had had a job. Hated it the four years he'd been there. This while Leanne sat in campus classrooms, learning to better their collective fate. The money dreams were fun, but the reality cut, and the voice inside whispered revelations until it was time to shout.

Househusband! Househusband! Real men earn real money!

The unfinished basement was the first chore. It involved the heaviest lifting, but came together with the least mental strain. The room was a fleshless skeleton, pink fluff under plastic, like guts in need of muscles and meat, drywall and paint. Wires ran without obstruction and came down with ease. The new walls received updated lines for modern needs.

At three past noon, James had glanced at the cracked face of his cellphone and stopped for lunch. Bell hadn't yet come to fit the home with an internet router. Tuesday *between eight and one*, they'd said.

Grumble in his belly, he scrolled through meagre updates on his Facebook page while he heated a can of Campbell's chicken and rice on the stovetop. The new life wasn't far from their past. They'd moved an hour away. It was a lonely mess. James had never been so far for so long from his friends and family. He'd become a spy, snooping through social site profiles with equal parts nostalgia and boredom.

Before, he'd *liked* maybe a handful of updates a week. Since the move, he did that much a day and then some.

Bubbles bounced in the soup and he dumped it into a large bowl. Crumbled nine crackers over the broth. The digital tuner atop the television accepted signals from four stations. James settled on the CTV news, blowing on his soup while he sat on a couch found amid the free listings on craigslist. It was nice enough but had worn armrests and a big tear in the back. He'd tried to sew it, but it triggered his anxiety and he did the *man* thing, pinning the flaps together, running a seam with Gorilla Glue, and pulling the pins once it dried. It would just rip again, but he couldn't sew it, couldn't.

Househusband! Househusband!

The couch wasn't a keeper. A decade plus a year if they stuck to the loan schedule. They could get a better couch then, sooner if James finished the renovations quickly and found a job—doing something, anything, just so a paycheck featured his name.

The troublesome voices in his head never went so far to state a woman's place in life, but suggested, surely, that there was *a man's place*. A man's place affects a woman's place, but not immediately and not intentionally.

Househusband! Real men earn real money! Real men provide food, shelter, and protection!

Such thoughts were disgraceful, felt—

Househusband!

"Stupid," he muttered.

He sipped back the final bit of broth and rice from his bowl, then killed the power on the television. Before returning to the basement, he took a flathead screwdriver and two tiny screws and swapped out a cracked light switch plate. He then scooped up his phone. One last refresh to social media. Nothing new, it was as if he needed some bit of hope, a job offer, a windfall, something.

He dropped the screwdriver he'd pinched beneath his middle finger into the toolbox before he stepped into the kitchen, bowl and spoon in one hand, cellphone in the other.

The bowl and spoon clanked in the sink. The cupboards were

ugly wood, shiny and cheap, something not on the list, but if the house were his... Outside, a gentle rumble rolled in the lane. It was a private place with a private driveway, stubby wide coniferous trees offered peaceful solitude and a buffer between property lines.

Just as likely to block the neighbors from seeing the rental house as it was the other way around.

A Ford Expedition cut over the crystalline world. This was not a Bell van and James did not recognize it. Curious and somewhat annoyed, he stepped onto the porch in just his shirt sleeves, his breath puffed and he squinted against the cloudless sky

Most of the homes in the area were newer and much bigger than the rental. James wondered why the owner kept the home, why he didn't build afresh, a mansion or a timber-frame, something big and pricey, like the neighbors had. The little place stuck out in its *lack*. Stuck out in the fact that it didn't actually stick out. It was small and old. It did not scream for attention and did not promise anything more than the most assumable homey attributes.

Country guitar twanged through the windows of the vehicle. The music reminded James of his old job. That made him tense. He held one hand at his eyebrows to shield the sun and the other at his side, cellphone still in palm.

A wave of gravel dust and powdery snow plumed in the Expedition's wake until it stopped right where Leanne usually parked. A radio call filled the air for a moment when two doors swung open before the engine ceased: "...hits you know and—" The driver's door opened, followed by other doors, and one at a time, three men stood.

There were cracks in the chrome-coated bumper and rust patches blooming through the paint on the nose where gravel chips went unattended. The men moved closer—shadowy silhouettes under the blazing sun—one smoked a cigarette, he dropped it.

"Can I help you?" James asked.

The driver and apparent leader stepped forward with a hand out. James swapped the cellphone from right to left, unthinkingly, and shook the offer. It was soft and greasy. The men had a sweet scent that carried below the odor of smoke, heavy on the crisp air.

"We stopped by to welcome you to the community. I'm Geo, and that's Liam, and that's Roddy." The man nodded over his left shoulder and then right shoulder.

They were youngish men, early thirties, Geo obviously the eldest. All three wore clean, collared button-ups, two blue and one pale orange, beneath heavy canvass Carhartt jackets. Faded blue jeans and off-brand boots fashioned to imitate Sorels. To James they looked like down on their luck farm insurance salesmen in need of a meal. Skinny and soft.

"Hello, I'm—" James started, but was cut off by Geo.

"I bet this place sold at a steal."

James looked over Geo's shoulder, unsure if the man meant it offensively or he just had odd manners. "I don't know." This was an honest answer. He nearly added that it probably had, the owner bought it to eventually flip, once James made it more liveable.

"Nah, you wouldn't. So what do you do?" Geo asked.

"Right now, I'm just fixing up the place, needs a lot of work. We moved here for my wife's job."

"Ooh, a kept man. Househusband, what's that like?" Geo grinned, his teeth yellow with too dark gaps. Before James could answer, Geo swung out a hand. "I'm just playing with ya. It's how the world is and people need to rely on each other. And who better to rely on than the one ya married, am I right?" Geo squeezed James' forearm as the two others nodded.

Looking at them together, his eyes settled enough to drink in their features better. It struck, a total *a-ha* moment.

Grown brothers.

"I suppose you're right. Can I do something for you fellas?"

"We only stopped in to greet ya, but if you're offering, a coffee would be mighty nice of ya," Geo said.

"Coffee maker broke, but I've got some lemonade." James wondered why he added the second part, *why offer anything?*

"Whoa, and you got out of bed?" Geo's grin stretched. "Nah, lemonade would be great."

It was a surprise when James heard the three men follow him inside the home. He'd expected they wait outside. Upon running back over his offer, he decided they'd done nothing out of place given that it was winter. If anything, offering lemonade when there was frost on the ground was out of place.

"A table and a hutch would sure look nice right there." Geo pointed to an empty corner of the kitchen as he wiped his boots on the mat. The floor had indents from where furniture once stood.

"Maybe, someday. I've got to tear up this linoleum and put down some nice wood. Going to class up the place, I guess." James said this as if in defense—the home was rough and he would make it better, *promise.*

The men were in the kitchen, still in their jackets and boots as James reached into the cupboard looking at the tall glasses and deciding on the shorter ones. There was work to do and short glasses equaled short offerings, equalled short delays.

"This linoleum don't even look all that old, but I guess some people have rich tastes, some people have all the money in the world," Geo said.

The other two grunted.

James poured the lemonade from the pitcher into four glasses. A problem. There was offense intended, these men didn't seem as if they lived in the neighborhood at all. The nice houses and the aging vehicle didn't fit together. These men wanted something.

James drank back his lemonade in three quick gulps and put

his glass into the sink. "Look, is there something else I can do for you guys? I have a ton of work to get to, as you can maybe guess."

James turned his back to the men, his left hand still on his cellphone, his right on the handle of a knife Leanne had used to fix her pack lunch before she left that morning. This was an instinctive clutch like a child's grasp on a teddy bear.

The quiet brothers slurped their drinks.

"No, sir, just saying hello. We'll get right out of your hair. I *can* see you've got lots of work to do." Geo tilted his glass to let the cold lemonade slide down his throat.

The brothers followed suit and Geo led the way to the door, boots clomping. Hearing them, James let go of the knife. Once they were out, he'd lock the door. There was something odd about these brothers, something unnerving in the way his politeness let them in and had to assume nicety, even when appearing otherwise.

At the door, Geo turned back and held out a hand for another shake. James took the hand. Geo squeezed tight.

"Hey, you know that fella?" Geo pointed down at a small pile of mail.

James looked at the table and the tension washed away. He'd had them almost all the way out and maybe they knew the rightful owners of the mail that refused to stop coming. Maybe they'd get rid of it for him.

James set down his cellphone and scooped up the pile, let go of Geo's hand. He flipped through. The first three were to a Roderick Duguay, the fourth to a George Duguay, and the fifth to a Liam Duguay. A connection blazed, finally. The names and the scent, they didn't belong in the area, not anymore, not neighbors at all. These men used to own that home and were up to...what?

James looked beyond the envelopes to the table by the door. His cellphone was gone.

"What do you want?" he asked and lifted his eyes.

"Ya shouldn't a did what you did, Billy boy." Geo swung a

heavy fist that landed on James' left cheek. The crack sent a momentary blackspot over James' mind like a solar eclipse, rattling his teeth and rocking his head back in a whiplash jerk.

Then the trio rushed him. The rumbling footfalls of scurrying boots thumped like beats on a plastic drum. James was falling. The unmistakable sound of toolbox clatter chased him down.

The blackspot disappeared and he looked up at five arms. The sixth didn't reach toward him at all. It had reared back, above a head. James wasn't sure which brother. A hammer swung as James groped at those reaching arms.

The blackspot was different after the wet strike landed. It was like a burn on a movie reel, stalled on a single frame.

James exhaled what was in him in a huff and felt those hands, but the world was too bleary to make out much. The color differences and the movements, but nothing to distinguish.

"Took our home!" a voice shouted.

The hammer came down again. James' world shook loose and that blackspot spread until he fully lost connection.

On the ground, the world came back. In and out, under a thick brown shroud, blipped voices around him laughed, calling him *Billy, Bill, William*. He heard them and wondered why they said that and what it meant, was it a slur? A colloquial name for...what?

A foot pounded James in his gut, pain flashed, and his body coiled tight. Another foot made a great sinking shadow for two-tenths of a second before landing on his temple.

Out and back. The quality of light coming to him was better than the last time he'd awoken, but James didn't connect any of that. Didn't know he'd been out, only knew that he hurt all over.

Two coherent thoughts fluttered above the pain. Firstly, he was thankful, almost ecstatic, that Leanne wasn't home. What would they do to her? They might do unthinkable things, things maybe worse than dying.

The second thought was of a man named William Pire.

William Pire had handed over the keys when they'd signed the rental agreement.

"Robbed us, motherfuckin' shit bag!"

Billy, Bill, William.

Another foot landed and a rib cracked. The sound was dull on the outside. On the inside it was a blow horn. His bent back straightened and a fist connected four times in quick succession. The blackspot was a blanket then, swaddling him until his world returned to a muddy ocean.

The ocean cleared after an indistinguishable sum of time. Heat pattered onto James' face and laughter filled the room.

"Ya like piss, Billy boy? Pire, what is that some fuckin' French name? Come here and think ya can kick good people out their homes?" Geo screamed these things as his urine ran over James. "You and that mortgage cunt? Don't think we don't know ya was in cahoots from the beginning, sign us up and make it so hard to pay, then snatch the place!"

James took a breath and opened his mouth, tasting piss and blood. He wanted to tell them, *no, it's all a mistake. I'm just a renter, basically a contractor. I'm not the one who put you out,* but the words remained locked somewhere behind the broken teeth and the swelling in his throat. *I'm just a Househusband, fixing up the place. I don't own shit!*

The piss stung in James' eyes and smelled just like it tasted. It didn't matter. He knew he was dead. The piss was just one of the final sensations of his existence. At least Leanne was safe at work. Leanne was young, and attractive, and smart, and she had a good job.

She had the tools to move on. Didn't need him anyway.

Consciousness was a tug o' war and he was punch drunk clinging to the rope until it disappeared from his grasp. Out again.

James' head was harder than he'd ever imagined possible. Not that he ever thought about how much abuse he might take and still come out of it.

Pain, bright as the sun, flashed over the blackspot. He blinked and rocked forward, sending aches into overdrive. He moaned into a puddle that reeked of piss and shit. A world where he reeked of piss and shit.

New trouble. Pain came from his right hand. Beyond whichever brother it was who lifted his arm, he saw that they'd brought over one of his toolboxes—could tell for sure because of the shape and the color: a bright yellow rectangle. Another shot of pain flared and James attempted to yank back his arm.

The Duguay men wailed, laughing as Geo worked. James squinted and grimaced, looking down to the end of his arm. Something didn't make sense, until it did and Geo snipped another of the fingers from James' right hand.

James convulsed and tugged. The men weren't letting go.

One digit at a time. Red geysers sprouted and slowed as quickly as they came. They let go and James looked at his hand, a stump of oozing gore. He attempted speech.

"Shut up!" One of them landed the hammer on the top of his head, as if swinging a croquet mallet. That blackspot was all-encompassing and delivered him once more from the pain and humiliation.

Time passed. Wading through the thick brown reality, James awoke to a quiet room. Certain he was a ghost and ghosts were deaf. He looked around, tried to float. It had the same outcome all the times he'd tried to use *The Force* as a kid.

He and his body remained tied. No floating.

The sun had fallen and he thought of his wife again, long before he recalled the brothers. *Was there an accident? She's home late, oh God don't tell me...*

Househusband can't protect his wife!

There was a potluck at the office. It was a monthly thing that didn't include spouses. It was nothing to worry about, nothing bad. There was no accident. She was out eating meatballs, and fried tomato hunks, and little wieners on toothpicks, drinking box wine from a plastic cup or a can of Diet Coke. They'd make jokes and tell stories until one of them drank too much and crossed a line.

James moved his arm. The pain reminded him of the brothers and what they'd done to him. He opened his eyes as wide as possible. A distracting brown smear teased, clinging to an eyebrow. It was a foggy view, but it was something, and he wasn't dead. He needed to call Leanne, needed to call her and tell her what happened, keep her away, keep her safe.

Calling for an ambulance wasn't such a bad idea either.

He put his right palm flat and tried to push. Pain screamed through the numbness. He slipped on sticky, wet linoleum. The thud of dropping sent his head spinning. A new moan erupted from his chest. There was blood everywhere, so much that he thought it couldn't possibly all belong to him. Then, if it did, how did he get it back inside?

There, next to the fallen set of shears, were his fingers. He looked at his hand and then down to the arrant digits and back to his hand. At the tips of his knuckles were blackish, clotted, sponge-like stubs. He used his left and pushed himself into a sitting position. His head was groggy and swaying on a loose neck, as if wedding guest wasted.

James wanted to move, had to move, but decided he'd sit for a moment, wondering if they'd come back. He'd surely die and they'd want a finished job. You can't almost kill a man and stop, not when he knows your names.

A breath wheezed free, whistling out at the end. He was a dead man. There was no way to see it otherwise. They left for a break, maybe just to get coffee, but maybe to wait for Leanne.

Did I mention Leanne?

Of course you did, househusband.

Luckily, they'd left his legs alone and he could push. They were heavy, but functioning. James leaned up from a wall to his feet, dragging his head as he walked, bloody piss smeared over the wallpaper.

He groped at the door with fingers that weren't there. Pain shot like lightning, and he tried his left hand.

The doorknob had transformed into a safe's wheel, spinning but without the combination, he'd never get the door open. *Click. Click.*

"C'mon," James mumbled, a reddish saliva bubble formed and popped as he wheezed. His words sounded more like "Muh-mon."

He closed his eyes and thought about Leanne. He had to protect her from this. They'd be back and he had to warn her, tell her to drive and drive and drive when they returned...maybe they hadn't truly left. It's possible they lay in wait, wanting more action, more violence, another victim of misplaced retribution.

The doorknob eventually took pity on James and turned. It was dark outside, but it was obvious that the big Ford was no longer in Leanne's spot.

How far had it gone?

James still wore his sneakers and stumbled, teetering, nearly falling through the open door. His cellphone lay in pieces at his feet on the cement porch. The hope to call someone vanished, and really, he hadn't figured they'd leave his phone. This was a game and games had players. Outsiders could only obstruct a game in progress.

James crawled, blood dribbled from his lips into the snow, filling in a boot print. It had snowed an inch at least. Soon he'd have to shovel and...he was a dead man and dead men don't shovel.

He lifted his head and looked into the blue night, studying the shadows for unnatural shapes. Men shapes. Ford Expedition shapes. Hammer shapes. One of them would come, as if stepping from a movie cover in the horror section at Walmart.

Lights flared at the end of the lane. They were bright and

huge. The brothers had come back. Of course they'd come back. They'd waited until he got up.

"No," he moaned, thinking, At least you won't get Leanne too. You came back too early. Hurt me, I know you will, but go away after that.

The vehicle approached slowly, as if worried about the fresh powder. The lights grew, joined by the rumble and grind of Death rolling over gravel.

"Leanne," James whined, wishing she was there, but so glad she wasn't.

Househusband! Can't provide! Can't protect!

Those brothers would do so much worse to her. A flashed image: her naked and strapped to a wall. Them with cocks out and knives and the hammer. But they'd spun it around on her, maybe tie her to a table and bend her over.

Leanne.

The violations James bore from the brothers rode outside the hardened shell of his body. What they'd do to her would run deeper, they'd touch her in places she'd never be un-touched. They'd cut and ruin and then they'd get to the real pain.

Would they kill her or leave her...or keep her?

"Go'way fucks," he mumbled and spat blood. "She ain't here, you can't have her." None of these words sounded like words. These were wet and incoherent gobbledygook.

The lights bathed him on the cold porch, the radio played, lower than before, yet audibly. He needed them finished with him before his wife returned. She'd need protecting and he wasn't up for it, better to sacrifice himself and send them on their way.

He crawled out and down the first step, tipping and falling over the second. "Hurry up, if you're comin'," he said. Tears welled in and on his puffy eyes.

That light ate his sight and he leaned over, falling to his side. Let them kill him quickly and be gone. The vehicle had stopped. A door swung open. It was over, any second they'd come upon him.

They'd just gone for a snack, a coffee break even, there was still work left to do.

"James!" a voice screamed.

James shook his head, tried to rise, tried to wave her away, and then dropped into a heap.

No, Leanne, no! They're coming back! Who will protect? Who will provide?

"Run," he mumbled.

She couldn't be there. They'd be back. She couldn't be there. The things they'd do to her. He wasn't up to task. He couldn't live with what they'd do to her on his watch.

"Leanne, no!" he howled to the moon watching over his head.

"What happened to you?" Leanne cried and cradled her husband's bloody body as she rooted into her purse for her phone. "Who did this to you?"

Her hands hurt so good on him. He tried to warn her, but his mouth had become mashed potatoes in gravy.

Leanne.

She squeezed his head and the blackspot invaded. He fought it. Blinks of a brown halfway place, blinks of reality. Blink. Blink.

"You can't be here," he whispered. "There's bad brothers and they'll come back." The words had no middles, no pauses, mostly vowel sounds.

"Shh. Shh." Leanne rocked him like a baby. Her tears fell onto his smattered face.

Lights flared out in the yard. James saw them rolling toward them, heard the radio call from an open window. They'd come and do horrible things.

Not a man. You can't provide. You can't protect. You're no man at all. Househusband, they've come back and you can't do jack!

"Run Leanne! Leave me!" These words joined frantic movements. The only thing Leanne understood was the panic.

Why didn't she get it? They were back and would do things

and he couldn't protect her.

She hushed him, sobbing. "They're here now. I'm here now. I've got you. You're safe now. I won't let anything happen to you. I'll protect you, nobody's gonna do a thing."

She didn't understand the torment they'd perform on her. They'd finish him off and do unspeakable things with her soft, beautiful body. They'd exploit her femininity.

"Run away," he said, garbled, blood bubbles forming on his puffy lips again. The shadowy silhouettes approached through a blinding flashing red and white glare. "I can't protect you!"

"Shh, you're safe. I won't let anyone hurt you anymore. I'm here. Everything will be all right. I'll make sure of it. I've got you. I've got everything," Leanne whispered and then let go when the hands came down onto her, cutting into this new vehicle's glow.

Leanne did not argue and stepped aside to let the paramedics do their job.

POOL SHARK

(2019)

Grown-up, manly. The smell of those places had me intent on playing it cool, trying to look like I belonged. It was all grey clouds and aftershave and chalk dust. That's how the pool halls smelled before the government nixed lighting up in public spaces. Probably for the best, but I do miss that smell. Sometimes when I close my eyes in the dark of night and breathe deep enough, I can catch it.

I miss my dad too. He first took me to a pool hall when I was six. I sat on a stool, sipping fountain Coke, watching him rack and collect, rack and collect. He was so smooth, even when he was playing rocky.

He used to say, "Sammy, only thing you gotta watch out for is a pool shark," and he'd grin at me, the eye teeth pointed like wolf fangs.

One time a drunk woman yelled at my dad after her boyfriend gambled a necklace the man had bought her and lost. She said, "You're nothing but a shark," and he grinned that grin. The boyfriend cringed and folded into himself, ashamed.

We used to go on the road, most places the same as the last. Sometimes we had to run, but always my dad won. Until that last time when I learned what to watch for, the real pool sharks.

Mom was gone by then and Dad had to make double to keep the house. He was always talking about 26% mortgage rates, and that we had to keep winning or we'd lose it all, and how it's pretty fun anyway, the thrill of the big win. I wasn't worried. I thought nobody could beat my dad.

Eleven days after my tenth birthday, we went to this real

classy joint. A private place. It had neon signs and Elvis on the jukebox. It smelled like fine cigars instead of cigarettes, and halfway through the first game, my dad was whispering and looking over his shoulder real funny at me. A minute later, he was behind on the table and he came to me with just three balls left, two of them his and it wasn't even his shot, and he said, "Sammy, you know I love ya, but these are our moneymakers, so it's gotta be you." He wiggled his fingers as he spoke.

I nodded, felt proud because I didn't get it. Didn't understand that Dad was using me in the bet. It had never gone like this before, this had to be part of a ruse. So the other man, the guy who owned the joint, he looked down at the cue ball and the eight ball and just shook his head. He was bald, but on purpose bald, and had strong arms and big hands. He was light brown and wore a beaded necklace with a shark's tooth dangling.

He exhaled and followed through just as smooth as buttermilk and the eight fell into the pocket while the cue spun tight circles, hardly going anywhere at all. My dad was looking at me out of the corner of his eye and he whispered, "I'm sorry, Sammy, but it can't be me. It's how we live."

Naïve as I was, I just said, "It's okay, Dad. You'll beat him next game."

See, Dad lost lots of first games and second games, that's how he got guys betting. Trick them into thinking they had a chump with money to burn.

"Sure," Dad said.

The man leaned against a wall and pressed a button, and a gentle dud-dub bathtub sound came from near the pool table. It was like those quarter-a-play tables, with the pockets all closed off, but it didn't take a quarter to play. Never did in private places, and this place was as private as it got.

"One of you gotta rack 'em," the man said.

"That's you," Dad said.

I got down off my stool and wasn't thinking much, moving on

instinct. I went to the table and did how I always did when I approached from the side and put one hand in a corner pocket and one in a middle pocket. They felt empty, but I'd seen the balls go down so I reached a bit deeper.

That's when I learned about pool sharks.

I tried to reef away as soon as I touched water, but those razor teeth had both my hands. My wrists were free above the table, but the small sharks that had clamped onto my flesh were too big to fit through the pocket holes. I screamed for my dad to help me, but he wouldn't. The owner stared down my dad like he was mad at him. I yanked and yanked and yanked and screamed and screamed and screamed. The blood was spraying and running. The felt of the table turned black and I finally fainted.

I woke up in a hospital with bandages over my nubs. Dad wasn't there and I never saw him again.

That man who owned that table was a tough one. Maybe the best. My father was foolish, but I don't think he was a fool. But there's always guilt. My guess, he doubled down, but used his own hands, or his head.

Then again, maybe he's still out there, swimming in safer waters, spots where pool shark is only an epithet.

DEEP WOODS MURDER

(2018)

The absurdity of it. Ranger Higgins decided to let the insane complaint slide. It was the same monster in the woods crap he'd heard for years: evil frogs, screaming trees, ravenous flesh-eating squirrels, and so on. Malevolent crows weren't so different. In fact, they were somewhat disappointing in their normalcy.

This girl was obviously high: pupils dilated, sweaty, and pale as a ghost's reflection. Tripping hard, jumping at the squawking in the trees. She wore an ankle-length dress, a loose billowy tank top, beads in her long, braided hair. She fit the description of a user long before she opened her mouth and complained of avian tormentors. She hadn't cared for Higgins asking over her sobriety and stormed away.

Once she reached the forest floor, he yelled, "Go sleep it off!"

He sat in his chair at the top of his rangers' station reading a Nick Cutter paperback about hungry boy scouts. Probably that would be the last he heard of her or the birds. He hoped.

Minutes became hours. The forest was strangely quiet, but he didn't notice until he heard the scream a good distance from the station. Crystal clear, no natural soundtrack accompanying the cry.

First thought: *broken leg.* Second thought: *damn, it's quiet.*

Higgins watched over a parcel of forest forty square miles that rested just about five hours from any kind of population. There was the odd community between the forest and the city, but none of any size or importance.

If it was indeed a broken bone, he'd have to call for a helicopter. He clipped a radio to his leg and headed out to find the source of the cry. Beyond the station, not a bird chirped, not a branch snapped, the woods were riding a deadly lull and it sent a chill up Higgins' back. He called out and then listened. The injured individual had gone silent.

"Dammit."

A series of snapping branches called his attention.

"Help, they's back, those danged crows! Ya gotta help me!"

Higgins watched as the woman raced up the stairs, her dress was gone, torn at the waist. She had cuts all over her arms, legs, face, and scalp. She also had some thorns and leaves in her hair.

"Come on." Higgins spoke under his breath where he waited at the top of the station staircase. "Did you hear that yell?" he asked, didn't have much patience for a tripper that literally tripped and fell into a thorn bush.

"The crows is everywhere!"

"Calm—"

"Ya gotta help me! We gotta get outta here!"

Higgins rolled his eyes, he had six more days until someone from the busy world took his spot and he could spend a week in civilization, just enough time to tire of it. He loved the outdoors but needed a reminder of why every few weeks and got it when he returned to his small apartment in downtown Tammany. He lived above a pizza parlor, sometimes the scent drove him insane with hunger and other times it just drove him insane.

It never took long to recall why he preferred the wilderness. But for the trippers, of course.

"Listen, there's somebody else out there. I heard him yell. You wait here for me to get back. There's a living area and cot, sleep off the dope and then we can talk."

The woman opened her mouth to argue but closed it and stepped inside.

"Clean those cuts before you get blood all over the sheets. You can borrow some pants, there's lots of first aid stuff in the toolbox there." Higgins felt his leg to ensure he had his travel aid packed in his pocket. It would do little good beyond a cut or to dull the pain of a broken bone, but it was something.

He walked in the direction of the cry and then followed a less enticing sound the rest of the way. That was bad for two possible reasons. Firstly, the man who cried out was dead and secondly, any time a mountain lion sees a man as a meal that spelled trouble in the ecosystem. There was too much food around to consider something the size of a man as dinner.

"Shit," he mouthed. It was indeed a mountain lion.

The sight was awful, but the meal was focused, letting the ranger backpedal unharmed from the lion with its blood red beard. No sense sticking around to watch. He broke into a jog once he got a good distance. He imagined the lion stalking him, on his heels, ravenous after getting that first sweet, sweet taste of humanity. His mind reeled. Was it chasing him? He heard those steps behind him and they crept closer and closer, soon he'd feel the playful nips and the... He slowed, took a deep breath to push away the fantastical fear.

The forest opened, unveiled itself like the perfect Christmas gift and he drank in all wonderful bits of civilization. He got to the top of the staircase leading to the rangers' station and let out a relieved breath. Leaned against the greyed railing, his vision shrank, and he again saw just how bad things could have been if—

Caw!

He looked around, located the crow. Just a crow but it was the first bird he'd heard all day and that was an almost unbelievable thought.

Caw!

On his other side, another crow. He considered the woman's complaint. The crows watched him and he recalled the chase, or the chase he imagined. He gave another glance to the forest floor. The lion hadn't followed him home.

"You two, stop squawking at dope heads. Pain in my ass."

Inside, Higgins lifted the receiver to his radio comm and waited, the connection buzzed. "Park services," a feminine voice said, she seemed light-years away.

"This is Ranger Higgins, over at station oh-four in Koronae Park. I have an emergency. A dead man and a wild cat." Higgins enunciated slowly to ensure understanding.

"Heart attack?" the woman asked, the sound of her typing fingers came in over the line.

"No, I said a wild cat, not heart attack."

"Really? I'll put in a request, stay put. That's serious. Hmm." Her fingers clacked. "You should have help in about four hours, maybe a little less. The pilot will be in contact with you at the ranger station as he gets closer. Update us with any changes. Hang in there."

"Roger that. Over." Higgins cradled his receiver.

He opened the door to the living area and checked in on the girl. She hadn't borrowed pants, but she'd covered the dozens of cuts with bandages. She slept, drooling onto his pillow, her leg swung over the blanket. She obviously needed the rest. Higgins returned to his watch, closing the door behind him.

He wasn't prepared for an angry cat, not at all. He picked up his paperback and tried to read but couldn't focus. The lion was a scary thought, a scary lingering thought.

Every hour or so, Higgins stepped back outside. There was no lion, but there was—

Caw!

A ten count the first trip.

Caw! Caw!

Twenty the second and close to fifty the third. Fat crows. Seeing them was enough to chill the veins, it was probably how the girl found herself in the thorns, stumbling scared and high and completely out of her wits.

The radio com buzzed minutes after 9:00 PM, full dark was still an hour away.

"Hello, Higgins, oh-four, Koronae," he spoke automatically.

"Hear you've got a bad kitty?" Voice amid a heavy static.

"Uh, yeah. E-T-A?"

"Half an hour. I've got a rifleman, we'll take up the night and get the body and the cat out of there in the morning, supposing the cat's still there...guess that goes for the body too."

"Right. Over."

The connection ceased and Higgins sunk back into his chair, and tried again to focus on the ravenous boys in the paperback. Knowledge that the chopper was close softened his world and let him drift off.

"Hey, hey, Higgins."

Higgins felt the hand on his shoulder and woke. "Oh hey." He lowered the leg rest of the recliner, looking up at the pilot, Kennedy. Behind Kennedy was a man named Milne. "Were those creepy crows still out there?"

"Didn't see them. You think we'll track this kitty or will it take off?" Kennedy asked.

"Your guess is as good as mine." Higgins scratched his chin.

Caw!

"Jesus, there's your crow. Got one in your apartment." Milne laughed as he set down his rifle on the table.

"No, don't—" Higgins started to warn Kennedy about the sleeping woman and not to disturb her, but he pushed open the door and flicked the light switch.

"Jesus, shit!"

Crows covered the bed. They were big and seemed to shimmer in the light. Blood dripped and glistened from their beaks. They squawked and raced to the floor, aiming toward the open door.

Cawcawcawcaw!

"The feet are blue. What's with the bump out the back of their heads?" Milne seemed entranced.

Caw!

The crows hopped closer, a few taking flight.

Kennedy slammed the door, the crows croaked angrily, pecking at the wood, thumping over and over as they flew senselessly into the barrier.

"Something's wrong here!" Kennedy shouted over the din.

"Something's wrong big time!" Higgins said. Something about the size of those birds and the shapes of their heads reminded him of a bit of folklore his grandfather once tried to pass on to him as fact.

"I think we should call in some professional bird types!" Milne shouted.

The shape of the woman was a fate none of them wanted to meet. Higgins nodded and picked up his com. The radio was dead. He rooted through a drawer for a cellphone. He turned it on and had no bars. He looked to the pilot and rifleman. They both pulled phones from pockets and shook their heads. Higgins gulped a ball of leaden fear and suddenly he missed his lonely apartment in Tammany, missed all the concrete, the smog and the pizza smell, wished his grandfather never told him that story about the enormous bird from the times before man, the one still lingering in Canadian wilds—*not too far from right around here.*

"The chopper has a radio!" Kennedy suggested.

Higgins led the way. Bright yard lights shined down on the staircase and the area surrounding the tower. Not a crow in sight, they still moved as quickly and quietly as was possible. The breeze rustled an unnerving swish in the trees, footfalls although gentle, seemed like hammer strikes, and the breaths came in out of their chests like the achy wheeze of a first-time mother with a breaching baby.

Caw!

The call came from behind them, and they ran. It seemed ridiculous to run from crows, but they all saw what had happened, what those bastards had done to that woman.

Milne slowed loading his rifle as he jogged.

"Come on!" Kennedy cried over his shoulder.

Caw!

The calls seemed to sound from everywhere: *Cawcawcawcawcaw!*

Higgins stopped feet from the chopper. "Impossible!"

Red eyes the size of baseballs burned through the dark night. A four-foot bird hopped forward into the light. The back of its head jutted to a point. It was so much like the thing his grandfather had described it made Higgins shake. But it was different.

"Down!" Milne shouted and aimed.

Caw!

Higgins flopped to his belly. The massive crow shimmered and Milne dropped his arms and smiled. The crow flew over Higgins. Kennedy watched, stupid and frozen, as the man-size crow lifted Milne by the head and swung his body until the two parts detached. A shower of blood rained for one second as the body fell. Milne's legs worked for two steps before the headless man toppled.

Caw!

The monster opened its wings and Higgins rose to his knees, locked in the wonderful shimmer of the crow's feathers. It reminded him of a rainbow; one with the peaceful, beautiful flicker of a fish caught under the summer's sun. Higgins smelled the river behind his childhood home, felt the breeze, felt the warmth of his father's hand on his shoulder, heard his grandfather's voice, but couldn't make out the words.

They'd fished all day and it was perfect.

His mother was there too, she would cook the fish so long as somebody else cleaned them. Higgins took a fish head from the discard pile and chased his mother. She'd screamed, he'd giggled and knew exactly when to quit. It was better than perfect. Mother, father, grandfather, even Scruffy the mutt. A memory emboldened and perfected with arms wide open, embracing for—

The shot rang out, the giant crow's head exploded in a bomb of feathers and gore.

Cawcawcawcawcawcaw!

"Let's go!" Kennedy tossed the rifle and ran for the chopper. Higgins felt drained and a little sad that he lost hold of the vision. It was better than life. Better than ever.

Caw!

Thump, thump, thump, normal-sized birds pelted the windows of the helicopter, light and harmless against the heavy, pressure-resistant glass. Wordlessly, Kennedy flipped switches and hit the ignition. The helicopter roared. The engine's din drowned the avian cries.

Kennedy and Higgins took off. Higgins considered the moment he fell victim to the shimmer and recalled Milne's face just as the bird wrenched him into the sky, before his neck tore like taffy, stretched until it stretched no more.

"They hypnotize!" Higgins yelled.

Kennedy didn't turn his gaze. "Take a nap. We'll be back in no time. We'll get them to send out a fucking exterminator, the goddamn army, everything they got!"

Higgins didn't think he could sleep, but the rock and sway along with the constant drone of the propellers slid him from reality by little bits.

After what seemed like a handful of blinks, Higgins looked around and saw the bright lights of the city.

"Good morning, buddy," Kennedy said with a smile.

"We almost back?" Higgins stretched, yawning, feeling much better.

"Yes, sir."

The helicopter was long enough to transport a body, meaning there was a good deal of space behind the seats. No body this time, but there was a cooler next to the empty gurney. Higgins eyed it.

"Why don't you grab us some Cokes?" Kennedy kept his eyes

forward.

Higgins shrugged and slid the cooler toward him. He opened the lid looking for red cans, seeing only red eyes.

Caw!

Higgins screamed. The crows pecked at him, rocking him back and forth.

"Hey, wake up, wake up!" Kennedy had his hand pressed firmly against Higgins' shoulder attempting to slow his motion.

Higgins opened his eyes. "Oh God...I had a dream about crows." He looked behind the pilot's seat, no cooler, he was thirsty, but it was a relief to see nothing there.

"Just another ten minutes or so." Kennedy's hand returned to the controls.

"Imagine if those things found their way to the city. They could kill off thousands, no trouble, hypnotize them and peck them to death."

"Or rip their heads off."

"Or rip their heads off, Jesus."

The men finished the trip in silence, considering what would happen if those birds found their way into the real world. Higgins kept thinking about his grandfather and that story. *What did he call the bird things?*

They landed on the roof of the hospital. The moon was pale in the sky, the cloudy darkness left behind in the forest. The propellers slowed to a stop. Higgins was weak and shaky. He swung open his door, felt lucky to be alive.

"Just imagine," Kennedy said as they walked across the wide rooftop, "the damage they'd do."

Higgins turned back and looked up to the moon. A cloud drifted in and smothered the light. "I don't want to imagine." He watched the cloud shuffle and lower with tremendous speed.

Kennedy stopped and turned back to see why Higgins had stopped. "What is it?"

Cawcawcawcawcawcawcawcawcaw!

The cloud bombed, beaks aimed at the rooftop, hundreds of massive crows had followed them out of the wilderness. It was impossible and horrible and the most terrifying thing either man had ever seen. The mass of birds drew closer. They worked as a singular killing machine, perfect in formation, perfect in hunger. They surged forward. Higgins put his arms over his face.

Caw!

They'd found lunch.

Higgins ran.

"Oh G—" Kennedy made it four steps closer to the door, his right boot rolled an extra yard, a good portion of foot intact, a mist of hot blood floating on the air like a fog. Higgins reached for the door handle. His grandfather's voice cleared, finally offering up the forgotten word, screaming it in his head: *Thunderbirds!*

Caw!

The door opened but a crack. Then Higgins was gone. One filthy tube sock and the third of a hiking boot left behind.

Caw!

MY MONKEY

(2021)

Boots. He could hardly believe he'd forgotten the damned boots. The solar train had reached the depot and the senior class of Covington High filed out as Mr. Davis, one of six teachers chaperoning the environmental placement trip, shouted that they had fifty-two minutes and that they had to be at the bus station around the corner by noon. Most of the students made for the quarter block of fast food joints.

"Damned boots," Jacob Wymark hissed as he stormed up the street, hoping for a Walmart or K-Mart or Target, something. "Damned hell ass boots!"

Ten minutes passed and he saw nothing helpful. The train and bus stations were in a rundown part of the city, mostly industrial, but some businesses and office spaces remained like lingering spirits. He needed boots and he needed them cheap. They sold boots at the tree farm, but he'd priced those out already. Timberlands, sure they did right by the environment, but they wouldn't do right by a seventeen-year-old, two nights a week stock boy. Not financially.

"Goddamned shit ass boots!" he shouted.

An old lady with blue hair wearing a hemp smock and vinyl duckies laughed at him while she squinted at an ancient iPad. "Yeah, fuck them boots!"

Jacob grumbled and broke into a jog. Time was short and there was no option to hit the fields in his shoes—safety rules. And if he didn't hit the fields with his classmates, he couldn't graduate. He needed to graduate just as badly as Earth needed more trees planted, garbage collected from the ocean, or recyclables sorted and processed.

There'd been collective relief amongst the student body that his graduating class had pulled tree planting, it was almost exciting by comparison to the other options. But the boots, the damned boots! He'd picked up a pair at Mark's, on sale even, and they were in his bedroom at home. Useless.

He pulled his phone from his pocket to check the time. It was already twenty to twelve. "Shit. Josephine, find depart—" he hissed into his phone as he broke around a corner and slowed, then whispered, "Thank Christ."

Value Village. Not his optimum choice, he wasn't nearly cool enough to pull off shopping for boots second hand, but it would do. He hoped.

The place smelled like dirty socks and toe jam. Old people milled through the aisles like zombies. Mothers dragged toddlers by tether shackles. Hip local girls on spare periods flicked through ratty t-shirts and laughed over hologram videos projected from their phones. Jacob tried not to look at them, hoping it would go both ways, and b-lined for the boots and shoes lining the wall next to the washrooms. He let out a huff and started rolling leather and cotton tongues to read the sizes.

The first six pair were too big, the next three were too small. "Dammit!" he shouted and the girls and the old people and the mothers and an employee pushing a rolling cart all looked at him. He flushed and yanked his phone from his pocket. He had eleven minutes.

The employee parked the cart next to Jacob and peeled open a huge box. Boots. Dirty. Worn. Stinky. Boots.

Jacob didn't wait, couldn't. He dug in. The employee gave a half-hearted "Hey," but said nothing further.

Like a lighthouse in a hurricane, Jacob found a pair of Terra work boots: size nine, yellow leather, brown laces, steel toes poking through at the tips, and a good helping of crusty maroon stains, but good otherwise. The price was $15 and Jacob sprinted to the tills, thumbing open his banking app as he went.

—

"Mr. Wymark, glad that you could join us," Mr. Davis said, voice carrying in a bellow.

Jacob shuffled onto the bus, scouting for an empty seat, a blush burning hotter and hotter as he passed fifty-seven laughing, grinning, smirking faces. The only open seat was a single over a wheel well and next to the toilet. He flopped down and the bus started away in its near-silent electric hum.

"Nice boots," Anya Sevigny said from across the aisle and then bit her lip to fight a laugh while her crew cackled around her.

Jacob forced a smile. "Yeah. I forgot my boots and had to buy these."

"Where from, skid mark, some homeless guy?" Mike Horner said and then swiped a meaty slap across the top of Jacob's head. Mike was the best wide receiver in the province and Anya was his cheerleader girlfriend.

"You got skid marks," Jacob whispered, not really moving his lips, pretty much not really saying it at all. Which was wise, he didn't need anyone rehashing how he got that nickname in the first place when it was really only Mike Horner who ever said it anymore.

As quick as they came, the insults ended and the cool kids got to watching videos and scrolling social feeds on their phones' holo-displays. Jacob let his eyes draw up to Anya for a moment before jerking them away—nothing like a Band-Aid because this kept hurting.

One day in the eighth grade, Anya Sevigny appeared like an angel. Mr. Burnside, the history and science teacher, sat her next to Jacob and for four periods, they became friends. Every day since, he'd dreamed of becoming more.

It was like all the bad teen movies. She was cool and hot and smart. He was lame and pimply and only knew what an A looked like because of the alphabet. She was popular. He spent Friday nights playing WoW+ like some old head dweeb. She touched anybody she wanted, hands, hips, lips, arms, chests, whatever. He hadn't had anything resembling a physical relationship since his grandmother's cat finally died when he was in the ninth grade.

Jacob's guts rumbled as he sat back, unshouldering his pack and setting the boots on the floor before him. The plan had been to eat at the last stop, but now he'd have to go four more hours until they reached the tree farms. He withdrew his phone and made quick work of scrolling feeds. He had zero notifications across six applications and no emails or text messages. Not that he expected anything, but he couldn't *not* look.

His guts rumbled again and he pocketed the phone. What he needed was a distraction.

The bus bumped over something big enough to bounce around the passengers, sending a joyous trill through the students, as well as knocking the boots sideways into Jacob's ankle. He hadn't even tried them on. After a quick glance to the cool clique, he turned sideways in his seat and slipped off his sneakers. He had to loosen the laces of the boots, but his right foot slipped in, snug, almost perfect. He repeated with the left, but something blocked the passage. He lifted the boot into the light and tipped it back. A furry ball with red, white, and black wires poking from one end rolled to the heel. He squinted.

At first he thought it was a dead rodent.

But the wires?

He reached in and pulled out the object, let it fall into his palm. It was a little grey hand with three fingers. The fingers were curled in tight...until they weren't. Jacob's eyes went wide as the hand—no, paw—unfurled in his grasp. He recognized it then. When he was a kid, many of the girls in his class had robot monkeys in pink tutus. The monkeys responded to their names and could fetch small, pre-programmed objects. They also hugged back and made kissy lips.

My monkey. My monkey. Wherever I goes, she goes. My

monkey. My monkey, the jingle popped to mind like brain cancer.

Someone had torn the monkey's paw off and dropped it into the boot, but why? Before he could come up with any kind of plausible idea, his guts grumbled for a third time, louder than ever, and he thought, *wish I had a Whopper.*

The bus bumped and jounced again. Jacob squeezed his hand tight so as to not lose the paw, though the left boot fell from his lap. The bus began to slow then and students started groaning. Seconds after that, Mr. Davis stood and said, "We have a flat. Stay put unless it's an emergency." He then followed the driver out the door.

As the students began bickering and whining, Jacob looked out the window. A Burger King, not fifty feet away.

———

As he finished the fries from the bottom of the bag, Jacob tried to pry the first finger of the little paw open, but it wouldn't come. "Must've crushed it," he said and let it be, dropping it into the breast pocket of his t-shirt.

"Didn't save any for me? That's rude, skid marks." Mike loomed over Jacob. He had his phone in his hand. "You're lucky I have business of my own to attend to or I might've had time to teach you a lesson about sharing."

Once Mike stepped into the toilet, Jacob whispered, "Dick."

"I heard that," Anya said without turning toward Jacob.

Jacob flushed pink and cowered into himself, thinking, *I'd love to see somebody sharing that medicine Mike dishes out with him.* Something scratched at his chest and he put his hand over his pocket, but didn't pull out the paw, was too distracted to do so.

———

Mike sat in the little john with his pants around his ankles, his genitals tucked down between his thighs. He held his phone and the holo-display was open to the latest issue of *Sonic & Tails vs. Cthulhu.* He began the routine push.

To his left, a warning light blinked red five times before the words CLEANING MODE lit in blue on the tiny screen. Mike scrunched his face, curious, for about a second before the tremendous suction began from beneath him. He tried to stand, but found his backside sinking and his scrotum stretching instead. He screamed and forced his powerhouse legs upright as the warning light began blinking anew.

"Mike?" someone shouted through the door.

Mike didn't hear, all his senses had amalgamated at his sense of touch, his sense of flesh torn free in a great, agonizing swatch. "Ug-ug-ug," he mumbled as he half-turned to see his ass, dick, and sack driven down into the little stainless-steel toilet bowl. "Ug-ug-ug," was all he could say as blood began pooling on the floor, soaking his pants and sneakers.

"Mike?" The hands attached to the voice began reefing on the locked door.

An automated feminine voice said, "Prepare for antibacterial." Water began rushing from the wall seams before sputtering and banging in the hidden water-work pipes.

Mike blanked, starting to fathom the world of his body and—

Feces and urine and blue cleaning agent blasted from the pinhole seams. Mike tried to cover his face and then his injuries, but the pressure was too great. He fell onto the toilet, conking his chin off the flush handle. His flesh and manhood disappeared as Mike slipped unconscious as human waste coated him like spackle.

——

The bus company put the students and faculty up in a Best Western for the night until the following morning when a new bus would arrive and they could continue up to the future tree fields. Most students slept two or three to a room. Jacob had to share his room with Mr. Davis.

"What's that?" Mr. Davis said, after shutting the door on the room service bot that had brought up their supper. He set the trey on the desk in the corner.

"Oh, uh, a paw. It's from one of those My Monkey pets, remember?" Jacob held the paw out. Two of the three fingers were curled.

"Are you superstitious?"

"Why?" Jacob looked at his palm.

"Thought maybe you kept it for luck. Or does it grant wishes?"

"Huh?"

"*The Monkey's Paw*, you know, it's a scary story."

"Like on Instagram?"

Mr. Davis simply shook his head. "Grab a plate and then maybe we can find something to watch on TV."

They ate, and Mr. Davis found a football game—of course. Jacob finished his portion of the Chinese food and said he wanted to take a walk.

"Grab a key in case I'm snoozing by the time you get back," Mr. Davis said.

"Right," Jacob said, snatching a key card. He also took his wallet and the pocketed paw. He'd been thinking about wishes, about how he wished for a Whopper and a Burger King appeared—though, strangely, they were out of Whopper buns— about how he thought Mike needed a taste of his own medicine— though he'd gotten much, much worse treatment—and about how two of the fingers curled in, like ticking off points. He was still thinking about wishes when he rounded a corner and there was Anya. She was in a towel, bending over to retrieve a bottle of Coke from a service bot. Jacob slunk back and tried to get a peek up the towel.

Anya straightened and turned, facing him, but not seeing him, her eyes and cheeks smeary with drying tears, her expression disassociated. She'd screamed for Mike when the paramedics carted him out of the bus. Wailed for him when she heard two of the teachers talking about how he might not make it and how if he did, he'd never have kids, even if they crafted new genitals for him.

Without any real consideration, Jacob thought, *I'd love to fuck her, just once.* The paw's final stretched finger curled in his pocket and he gasped. He took the paw out and studied it, wide-eyed, until Anya's door opened again and she shuffled into the hall, still in only her towel, approaching Jacob and the stairwell. She stepped past him and opened the door, slowly, as if it was a great weight.

Almost certain of his chances, Jacob cleared his throat and said, "Anya, you're so hot in that towel."

Like magic, she lowered herself to the cement landing. The lights flickered out in the stairwell. Jacob hurried through the door after her. The shine from the hall revealed a yawning towel and Anya's knees spread apart where she lay flat.

"I've always loved you," he said and got down to his knees, pressed his lips to hers. She kissed back, not exactly passionately, but definitely kissed him back—good and wet. That was it, his wish come true. Quickly, he got to opening his pants and positioning himself. He sucked her breasts as he ran a hand down to feel the warmth between her thighs. "I'll love you forever. You don't need Mike." He pushed inside and gasped.

He came instantly.

He didn't want to seem like a loser, so he kept rocking, finding himself hard again almost right away. He pumped and pumped and pumped and sucked her breasts and her tongue. Her mouth was slobbery and tasted acidic. He wondered if the Coke had spoiled or if she'd eaten some weird cheese off the room service menu. He wondered but did not stop.

"Oh god, I'm coming," he said—almost let an *again* slip at the end.

The hallway door opened and the light flipped on. "Jacob. Jacob," Mr. Davis said, too serious, didn't sound mad at all, more like shocked.

Jacob shuddered as he came, blinking into the light, drinking in the scene. Mr. Davis with his face pale and eyes huge, in his hand was an empty prescription pill bottle. Anya, eyes staring vacantly at the ceiling, lips blue, hair wet and all over the place, vomit trails smearing on her cheeks and neck. The rumpled towel beneath her.

"No, I—no, she—it's..." Jacob trailed, sliding up off the corpse and covering himself with his hand. The monkey's paw dropped out of his pocket and landed over Anya's unbeating heart. Electricity danced between the sprouting wires like the timeless laughter of atoms while the three little fingers stretched open.

JOE ADAMS, JOE ADAMS

(2013)

Mom died.

The process of death was a mess. Having no will doubled that. My siblings didn't even want the house, they just wanted their piece, for all those awful years. Compensation for the horrid job done by our parents—the pain, physical and lingering, emotional and infinite. That's all they wanted, a piece. For the justice of it, I guess.

I wanted the house. I needed the house. For me.

I needed it for me the way I needed air and water. The house was my last granule of hope.

Families built with blood and shared circumstances, but nothing else, turn cold and solidify. Listening to their arguments, I knew they never saw what I had, and if they did see it, they never entered. Through that shadowy crack was my space, my sanctuary. Made me wonder if they couldn't see it, if maybe it was just for me, built on my tears.

Money made me tired. I was sick of working so hard. Cement pads didn't build themselves, so some dumb shit had to build them. Oh, there's more, it's not just pads: walls, tanks, and foundations, but usually pads. I hate pads. My knees took a beating, but I never was smart enough for other work.

Could be worse.

Had been worse.

James, Courtney, Josh, and Cathy thought I'd gone mental. They don't understand why I'd want the old house and I'd never tell them. It was for me. It has always been for me. They talked about the windfall and vacations. I couldn't explain my side because they wouldn't understand. In these walls there's a place I used to go and where I need to be.

When I was little, I pretended I was a pirate. I wrote maps to buried treasure and then followed them, hoping eventually, by some mystical, magical power, I'd find real booty—a piece of me that thinks it's smart, suggests I sought a way out. I've always too dumb for big thoughts to be right, so that can't be it. Sometimes I watch TV doctors and their words come out of my mouth.

I think everybody has that sometimes.

When my pirate phase ended, I became an archeologist, not a stuffy office one, an Indiana Jones kind of archeologist, fighting for what is right and good.

One day, Dad had come home early. I don't remember if it was a Monday or a Tuesday or a Wednesday and I don't remember the month. I do know we hadn't finished the chores. Now, my brothers and sisters were older and smarter, they all had their hiding spots. Courtney and Cathy fit like two skinny storage cubes under the bed they shared, pulled clothes and junk in around them. Josh always climbed into the attic space. I don't know where James went, his hideout was so damned good. That left me standing like a punching bag, every child for their self.

I got to thinking about places I'd explored, but my brain wasn't moving quick enough. My dad was like that giant, *fee fie foe fum*.

Dogs can smell fear, bears too, that's what people say. I think my dad was like that and I wore my fear like a musk, like it was a beacon calling for rage. He always found me. Probably, he found me by all my sobbing and not my smell, but angry dads seem like huge things, great big monsters. Monsters that make kids cry and run and bleed.

Eventually, the kid learns where's good to hide.

Dad called through the house, my mother in the kitchen, hot dogs on a frying pan, corn cobs in a pot of water. She sported a tattered apron that had a rooster on it, and wore a puffy cheek.

"James, Josh, Cathy, Courtney, Joe, get out here. Now!"

The first twenty or so times I heard it, I fell for it, running to stand at attention. I learned, maybe a little slower than most, but I learned. It's how a dog learns when it gets its nose shoved in piss or shit on the living room floor.

My feet moved. Carpets barely make a sound under a little boy's running feet, even with stops and starts. I'd checked most of the house for good spots, but never found that one really great space. When the pressure's off, you don't look for the future, not when you're a kid. You go about life.

Into the bedrooms and bathroom, through the hall and back through the hall.

Finally my memory clicked and I thought of a risky cubby I'd found once before, though never tested against a warpath dad.

When I say I found the spot that really isn't true, it's more like the cubby called to me in a whisper. Even that first time, when the need wasn't there, as if getting me warm on the idea.

With a flicker of hope, I chased after that wispy little voice in my ears, all over the house. I knew where it came from, but I still tried to deny it. There had to be another route. In my sisters' room, they told me to get out, their voices together like a two-headed snake.

"Get in here, now!" My mother was a warning before Dad finally lost it.

"Where the fuck are you!"

Dad's voice made me ignore the worry. He was obviously still in the kitchen when I heard him. His next step would be to go looking. No way I was waiting for that part, not out in the open, so I ran after that whisper and into my parent's bedroom. Tears dampened my cheeks and I refused to breathe. Dad had bad ears for everything but breathing. You could ask him a million questions and he'd never acknowledge you, just turn up the TV, but when he needed to hear, he did.

And sometimes my breath felt like spaceman breath. Like

Neil Armstrong's *one small step for man,* marred by the static of exhalations, *one giant whooping for a boy.*

My socked feet padded and slid off the carpet onto the tarnished hardwood in the bedroom. I slid sideways trying to stop before I got to the closet. The calls to me grew, almost screaming for me to hurry. Dad was in the hall behind me. I heard him so close.

Shoe boxes and a cotton laundry hamper sat at the bottom of the closet amid the shadows cast by the hanging dresses and shirts. Right there almost seemed like good enough cover. "Fuck you think you're doing in there?" My dad's voice made me stone. I had an idea to be so still he didn't suspect me under the laundry and behind the boxes, but I was scared too, scared right out of my mind. So I shook. I always shook.

Into the shadows, I crawled deeper, behind boxes, knowing it was a doomed effort. The closet was miserably shallow and the bedroom door boy-oinged on the doorstopper. Dad shouted again and I turned to face the panelling. That's when the voice came clearer, and I saw with my fingers and pried at the flimsy wood.

Still, I turned away.

The shadows were thicker and better as I pulled the vented doors closed. Truth is, the voice had come to scare me too, and there with the hanging clothes, I could see out, but Dad couldn't see in. Safe, almost.

The voice whispered again, this time I understood the words in a tangible way. "He'll find you, deeper, come deeper, Joe Adams, Joe Adams."

My breath burned my lungs. Dad's shadow moved around the room, he looked under the bed and behind the dresser, only one more spot to check.

"Joe Adams, deeper. Come deeper, Joe Adams."

The reality struck me then. Going to the closet trapped me. Pretty well guaranteed I'd be caught. The door opened and I got as small as I could, hot tears shot from my eyes and my body began to shake. I turned to the wall and I think my next daydream was that if I didn't see him, he wouldn't see me. If I pressed tight against that crack in the paneling, I'd be safe.

Pushing hard. Getting real thin, I squeezed between the wood.

There was a grunt. The laundry hamper thumped. Clothes hangers made that metallic mouth noise on the steel rod. Footfalls moved away and then all I could hear was my heartbeat in my ears.

Then I realized I went through the wall, way more than I meant to. Just hiding my head seemed like enough before. In a panic, I dug my head back out to the closet proper. Dad's footfalls came back around then. This jerked me into the space anew.

It was bigger than it ought to be.

Comfortable enough, I waited.

Eventually, I slid my body out to the tossed hamper and scattered shoeboxes, and then turned; the gap was gone.

Mom had explained imaginary things to me before. The mystery of real and unreal had long washed away, but this one felt so real. Couldn't be though, had to be shadows and luck and my imagination. Stuff doesn't just disappear. The dips in the paneling were normal under touch, but this gap had gone completely. Two feet to my left, I felt a little lip. A crack, I pressed against it and then pulled. The paneling moved—I knew it was hollow, Dad put his hands through it enough, other times a shoe, one time a frying pan—but it wasn't like that. Solid, the thing under hand wasn't as flimsy as the rest of the paneling.

Out in the hall, a voice boomed. I should've stayed and lived in that shadow I'd imagined or hadn't imagined. Tear-wet eyes pressed tight together, a prayer to the voice flitted into my mind. Not words so much as the essence of need.

My fingers groped.

It came back.

But so did Dad. "Where the fuck are you little shits?"

The whisper became whispers; lots of little voices chattered. They were beyond normal words, speaking the same pitch as the terrified prayers in my head.

Fingers in and wriggling again, my hands saw with closed eyes. I wiggled. I pushed. The paneling brushed on both sides of me, almost scraping. More shadows, though different. No great light and no vast darkness called to me. Dad's feet slammed around the hallway again, ordering in the troops, Mom joined him. I hated her, as much as I hated him. Her self-preservation cost us, her choice to wed and bed this man cost us.

Lastly was my leg and I yanked it through the gap. The shadows changed yet again, and before me stood a door; it had a frame and everything. Whatever was there had to be better. It opened just wide enough to shimmy sideways. The door sucked closed behind me.

"Who's in there?" My mother's voice sounded as if coming from a long distance but would catch up in a hurry.

The entire contents of the closet found the floor and I prayed to God and then to Santa and then to Hulk Hogan, all in my head. Then to the voices. Still as I had to be, I waited it out, further behind the closet than could be possible.

Briefly, I figured maybe I was dead.

Is Heaven a hole in the wall when you need to hide?

Leaning against the wall of the cubby, my head should've been just about in the toilet, but nothing was there.

"Deeper, Joe Adams, come deeper."

Disobeying adults put me where I was and proved the usual better option. This was not the same. Soothed and lulled, I'd have done about anything asked.

"Joe Adams. It is better in here, Joe Adams, Joe Adams."

Repetition hits me. Cathy always says it's because I'm childish. Her nice way of calling me stupid. She's a genius. She went to college and wrote a book about turtles on an island. James is smart too. He works for the city, the big city I mean,

Vancouver—designs sewers or something. Josh too, he got me my job. His friends once hired my boss to put in a swimming pool or something. Josh and Cathy went to the same college, but Josh works at a high school. Post-secondary was beyond me, but I finished high school. Courtney isn't so big in society, but she's crazy smart, she drives a school bus and has four kids and the hydro company pays her for the energy she generates with panels and little turbines. She has a cabin in the woods and grows her own food.

Carol told me everything with lots of repetition, especially music, is for dumb people and children. It makes it easier to sell lots when songs get stuck in heads.

Joe Adams, Joe Adams, Joe Adams, the voice had said it three times and I crawled deeper. "Joe Adams, Joe Adams, come on, Joe Adams."

Ahead, a light shined dimly around another door. On a later visit, I measured how far I'd gone, I should've been in the cow's drinking pond up to my chest in floating manure, but instead I was still inside. Somehow.

The first time I opened the door, I expected to find a bedroom, maybe mine, maybe the girls', even for a second, I thought maybe the shed out back.

An orange glow lit a cavernous space. It didn't make sense. It was like I was outside, but I wasn't. The green, green grass seemed unsubstantial, every stone a pebble, and the trees were like those little trees from the *Karate Kid* movies, but taller. Everything lived at a maximum height of about eight feet.

"Joe Adams, Joe Adams." A little voice came from an even smaller man.

Years later, I learned the word homunculus from the TV— that one about the scientists where the guy was Darlene's boyfriend from *Roseanne*. Homunculus, that's what they were.

From about a foot and a half above the little man, my gaze fell downcast. "Do you live in my house?"

The little man's dark eyeballs were shiny, fully void of color. They bulged out some, but other than that, he was just a little man. Appearance wise. Their faces and bodies, everything about them, looked like a shrunken version of normal. The ones I figured to be men had neat, short hairstyles. The women wore their hair long and straight, no mullets or rattails. Most of my classmates had rattails back then, the boys I mean, but Mom told me Dad would rip it out if I ever had one. Same with earrings.

"Your house lives on our world, Joe Adams, Joe Adams."

"What is this place? Are you guys real?"

"Of course, Joe Adams."

"Who are you?"

A few more little people circled around me and I felt like Dorothy in Oz, but without a guard dog.

"No witches here, Joe Adams, Joe Adams," a woman said who'd come around from behind my back.

Knowing my thoughts was pretty scary. It made me try to think only nice things. The one who greeted me first laughed. "You won't offend, Joe Adams, Joe Adams. To answer an earlier question, my name is Gilbert, Joe Adams, Joe Adams."

My face scrunched. The smaller I made it, the better I thought, but it didn't work. "Huh?"

"We are all Gilbert or Genie, Joe Adams."

If nothing else, this oddity had me forgetting my home life.

"Doesn't that get confusing?"

The little man in front of me shrugged. Blips and rises like splashing waves, questions came to me all at once and I had to shake them off. I think if I'd seen it first as an adult I've might gone crazy. Too weird and too mysterious and it all felt too okay to be so damned strange. Then a steam whistle blew, sounding like the ones on old locomotives from movies, and all but the little people in front of me scurried on.

"Where's everyone going?"

"Work."

"What?"

Not that I recall exactly, I'm sure I wondered a million more things. Gilbert answered good enough. "Everyone works, even kids, even babies, even sperm. We fix things, things people don't like to acknowledge broken, Joe Adams, Joe Adams."

"Can you stop saying my name so much? It's confusing. I feel like, oh, I don't know..."

"I'm sorry, Joe Adams, Joe Adams."

An uneasy feeling wore on me. I wanted to go to my room, scary or not, it was home.

"Don't go, Joe Adams. Help us fix broken things, Joe Ad—" He stopped himself short of another repetition.

I smiled and he smiled.

"You don't want to go back yet, it's hard out there, J—"

Gilbert's difficulty had a strangely soothing effect, plus the more I thought about home, the more visions I had of the strap. Staying was the better option. Gilbert nodded then and motioned me to follow him with a wave.

Beyond the thick brush of squat trees, the blue sky above felt so close, for a second I thought I could reach up and grab the sun, but it was still plenty far. Not so warm, not how the Earth Sun is.

Little houses, very much like the houses in town. Uncanny in detail, great models, though not models. "Joe Adams," Gilbert started, cringing as he said it, "we have to fix problems. People cause trouble and it may take years, but we fix it eventually. In some ways it's better to wait." His massive black eyes were on me.

"What broke?"

"Not that kind of problem. Here, a man had his way and didn't want to pay the toll. There's a young girl out there, her mommy affords only the dullest of things, used and tattered things, and eats only from canned-food drive nicety—too many beets and too much creamed corn for a young girl."

"Beets, ugh. Dad makes me eat beets."

"We know what Jack Adams does, Joe Adams."

His knowledge made my eyes tear up, but I held on. I didn't want to think about it and I didn't want Gilbert to know that shame about me. I'd imagined having a good dad, like a TV dad, or like the dads boys in my class had—Chris' dad worked same as my dad, but picked him up from school sometimes and bought him new clothes.

"What'll we do?"

"Don't worry, for the first one you only watch. I want your help with something a little later, a tough one, J—"

He really was doing his best. Hard as it was to keep from scratching your nose in the middle of church when you're supposed to be thinking about Jesus, that's how it looked.

"Just like that. You're my itchy nose."

"You talk funny," I said and regretted it. My big dumb mouth.

We walked a while, beyond the houses and down a trail of red gravel. Looked like brick chips, but more natural. The sky was greyish with the blues, and the world smelled of nothing right then. Each breath was stale in my nose and out my mouth.

As if rising from the soil, a wall of tall doors and staircases stood at the end of the path, red like the ground, but kind of unnatural. Gilbert took my hand and led me to the second floor. The staircase was so skinny I had to climb it sideways.

Next to each door was a keypad and I wondered how he'd remember every code, he grinned and then explained. "This morning I woke up and knew the numbers and what to do, nothing more. Tomorrow I will know different numbers and a different problem, Joe Adams, Joe Adams."

Too busy punching numbers to stop himself, and really, I didn't need to care. One-two-nine-four, my mouth moved with the digits until I figured out it was as long as a phone number. The Gilberts and Genies used telephone numbers to find people. I think, but maybe it was like GPS numbers. But thinking it was phone numbers, suddenly, I didn't feel so out of place.

The ceiling demanded that I crouch to enter and then I had to crawl, just like in my parent's closet. We pushed through the wall at the end of the tunnel, a heating vent popped and gravity shifted.

"Joe Adams, hold on, Joe Adams." Gilbert pulled himself through.

He helped me get onto the surface and I looked back, another mystery. It was so small, I couldn't have climbed out, but I had.

"What are we doing?" A quaver had worked into my throat. This was a home and if it was like my home...

The room sat dark and seemingly lifeless. A few vague shapes rose in shadowy forms. The walls had big paintings, sculptures sat on shelves with the books, and the bed looked about the same size as my whole living room at home. A man snored light breaths.

My eyes adjusted and I understood luxury.

"Fixing things." Gilbert was on the move.

Like a puppy, Gilbert pulled me on an invisible leash, that's sort of how it felt, like I was lesser and couldn't do anything beyond what he got me to do.

Gilbert retrieved a lighter from his pocket. There, in the closet, he set fire to a row of suits. The beeping alarm cried out and Gilbert pulled me to the side of the man's bed. The man jumped up and took two steps toward the door. Gilbert tossed a slipper under his foot. The man flew forward, conking his head on the door jam.

"Is he going to die?" I no longer whispered, things felt too real, too severe.

"No, Joe Adams, it will give enough time to burn something irreplaceable; payment to fix the careless ways, Joe Adams."

Gilbert pointed toward the man's hand. Flames circled and engulfed it. The gaudiness of the home was then fully apparent in the orange light.

The man didn't stir again while we were there. We slid back into the heating vent.

"How do you know he'll wake up?" The awfulness of the act had me shaking, it was ugly, didn't seem like fixing, seemed like destroying.

"The fire department is breaking down the door as we speak, Joe—" Gilbert stopped in the tunnel and looked back in my direction. "You know, it isn't so easy to avoid a name."

Some assuring thought must've flittered because Gilbert turned forward and laughed, giddy and high-pitched. The sound bounced around the tunnel and away, as if the space stretched on forever. He swung open the little door.

"Joe Adams, Joe Adams, Joe Adams."

Happiness that easily attained couldn't be wrong. That laugh, so hearty, I forgot about the burning man.

Nothing about the strange little place had changed when we returned and again I took note of the nearly scentless atmosphere. Gilbert led to the steps and then I followed him down the path and past so many doors, little houses, little staircases. At a seemingly random door, he stopped; each looked exactly like the one before it.

The next one we went through was on ground level. Gilbert punched a number and we entered, crawling into a little wooden tunnel once again, bits of sand sticking to my palms, making tiny indents. Light flickered at the end. Gilbert pushed his way through another doorway.

A television played, a scrambled screen danced shadowy light over the room. We'd come out of a cupboard beneath a sink. It was a tiny apartment, a bachelor. Mother and daughter both slept on a mattress on the floor. Visions of setting mother and daughter on fire filled me with the kind of terror reserved for really good horror flicks.

Gilbert tugged on my finger. "No, Joe Adams, Joe Adams, we are fixers. This place is already broken." We moved toward a patch of linoleum that represented the shoe room.

A heavy hemp purse rested against the wall—brown and

shiny in spots from long use. Gilbert rooted into the compartments. He stopped and lifted a slip of paper free. I knew what it was as soon as I saw it. A Lotto 649 ticket. Gilbert shoved it into his pants pocket. With his other hand, he reached into another pocket and pulled out a different Lotto 649 ticket, identical in condition right down to a thick crease and two bends a hint beyond rolls.

"One hundred and twenty-two thousand." He turned and winked at me. Like that, we started away and he pulled me along, confused but intrigued, to the sink cupboard.

As we crawled, an understanding began to settle in. The burning man was the father and the poor girl in the shabby apartment sleeping on the mattress with her mother was the daughter. It was good, I felt good. Gilbert had a great sort of life, righting wrongs and doling retribution.

We came back into the world of little grass and red stone. Gilbert explained then that I had to go home, but could return anytime I needed to.

"Sorry, Joe Adams, Joe Adams."

The door home was different, old with ornate designs running through the wood. A rotary dial hung nearby. We waited. Gilbert had his hands in his pockets and shifted from the balls to the heels of his feet. Approaching from a shadow to our right, a different Gilbert had a boy of his own.

The boy and I looked at one another.

"Dial five zeroes, Adrian Vos, Adrian Vos."

The boy looked to be about my age, his clothes were ratty as mine. His hair overgrown and greasy. The leather of his too big shoes flaky and scuffed—hand-me-downs if there ever were. The boy was a mirror boy, but his face wasn't mine.

He dialed and the door opened. On the verge of crying, he nodded to his Gilbert and then crawled through. My Gilbert led me to the door then. "It was nice to meet you, Joe Adams, Joe Adams. Come back when you need us, when the tears burn and your heart aches, Joe Adams, Joe Adams."

"How do I—?"

"Five zeroes, Joe Adams. Five zeroes is always home at this door."

The thing inside me that demanded such bravado puffed up my chest and steadied my quivering lower lip. I smiled, but it wasn't a true smile. I wanted Gilbert to feel okay. I didn't want him to know I was scared and sad to go home.

I fingered and spun the dial, sniffling.

"It's okay, Joe Adams, Joe Adams."

Gilbert always knew the truth.

Slowly, wishing the tunnel was endless, I crawled. Quickly, the end appeared. Two heavy breaths entered and then exited my chest. I pushed open the gap and emerged into my parents' dark bedroom. The lights shot on and my father jumped out of bed, taking up his pocketknife as he did so. My mom stood by the light switch covering her mouth.

"Joe?" Dad said as if I might be someone else.

"He's back, oh Jack, our Joe's back." She ran to me, pulled me in tight to her saggy chest.

No words came. Baffled, I let myself be hugged. The impending terror flooded and my guts suddenly felt heavy and wet.

"I have to get some sleep." Dad closed the knife, tossed it onto the nightstand. "You can tell us where you've been in the morning."

Mom let go, reluctantly, and I walked to my bedroom. Josh didn't even rustle as I slunk into the bed next to him. The scents were huge and blooming. Boy smells, pre-pubescent sweat and grime.

My absence lasted much longer than it felt, for three days I'd wandered in the world of little Gilberts and little Genies. For three days my family considered me missing. My mother had even gone so far as to ask the neighbors. My father called the school, said a few more days and he would've called the cops—a big deal since you only call the cops when you're asking for trouble.

My explanation was no good. I started to explain where I'd been and even tried to show my family, but the door wasn't there anymore. This made me look like a liar, so I stopped talking about it.

Life was suddenly better, and still, I wanted to go back. Home was all smells and sneers and un-listening parents.

The next ten days were ten days okay.

Dad went out with the boys on the tenth night and that meant a quiet peace until he stumbled back in the door. Don't know how the others handled it, but I lay awake until I heard slamming. In between didn't exist on nights like that, the only certainty was a drunken father. He might be happy or furious. To find out which? You'd have to wait.

The banging of the door and the heavy footfalls suggested it was angry Dad, and I listened. Maybe I was wrong or maybe he spent his rage different with my sisters. Their door creaked open. A few tiny laughs filled the air and then within minutes, the sounds were girlish squeaks and mannish moans. My pillow went over my head. Kids at school talked about sex. They talked about bumping into girls and having it almost as they walked by, but I think maybe they didn't know what I figured. Sex sounded awful and painful. You can't do it walking by like Aaron Watson had told me.

Tears followed, not his, obviously, whenever Dad left their room. The belt would slide out of the loops of his pants, the tail snapping free from its final hold as he walked. He'd get us, one at a time, oldest to youngest. James' screams shivered up my spine and to my toes and then rode back up to my scalp.

He then came in our room, Josh's and mine, his eyes flashed off the yard light outside. Sobs burst from my chest in anticipation, and Dad would hiss for me to stop being such a pussy. The strap—that's what Mom called it. Josh got puppy small, poking his bum out, we always knew the extra meat could take a thrashing, even if it did make it harder to sit the next day.

Thwap, it said.

"Please!" Josh screamed.

I was so scared, I ran.

Never before had I attempted to avoid those particular licks. Into my parent's room. Mom pretended to sleep, she couldn't sleep through that, impossible, and I sensed her eyes following me into the closet. She didn't utter a peep. Dad burst in and switched the light—it shined through the door slats and around the door itself. Slobber streamed from the corner of his mouth and his eyes bulged, red and angry. He'd lost his shirt somewhere along the way through the house and his fly rested halfway open.

I crawled deep as possible and pawed at the wall. Nothing.

"You shithead."

The closet yawned like a mouth, big, a whale's mouth. The light didn't reach all the way back thanks to the hanging clothes. My eyes snapped shut and I saw with my fingertips. There it was, the gap, nice and easy.

Inside, I let out a strained breath. Dad banged at the wall. "Where the fuck did he go?" The sound fluttered and shifted the further I went down the safe wooden pathway. Again, I made it beyond the house, the property, the region, the province, the country, the continent, the world. I was elsewhere, too far to measure, but close enough I'd find my way back.

The door at the end opened and there was my Gilbert. "Joe Adams, Joe Adams. So sorry, Joe Adams."

That time, hearing the repetition made my heart soar. The way he said my name over and over offered protection. I imagined that it gave me the superpowers needed to travel between the worlds. Gilbert laughed at my thoughts, but I didn't care.

That night, we went to a small house. Rundown, but not horrible. We crawled in through the bathroom closet. Damp clothes rested on the floor like pastel dirt heaps. A yellow nightlight glowed from a hallway. The carpet was hard and thin leading up to the off-white linoleum.

"Joe Adams, Joe Adams, fetch me the tallest toothbrush, the pink one, way, way, way up there, Joe Adams."

The brushes sat in a cradle, well within reach for me. It came out of the porcelain holder with a glassy slip sound and I handed it to Gilbert. He pulled a small vile of fluid and jammed the bristled end inside. He smiled and handed it back to me, I wondered, but didn't need to speak.

"Joe Adams, it's called Halitosis. She's said bad things, Joe Adams. Now her mouth will stink so much, her words will no longer infect, people won't listen, Joe Adams, Joe Adams."

"Is that fixed then?" I worried I'd have to go home before I got that goodie-goodie feeling in my belly.

Gilbert shook his head and I followed him back. Turns out, there's usually an A and a B when dealing with righting wrongs. Through the tunnel and then the little door, into the strange world connected to ours.

Walking for a few minutes took us to another building, this one dipped on the side of a hill and we climbed down the three levels to the bottom floor. Gilbert looked between two doors, squinted and then chose. Number punched, he walked and I crawled into the shadow made by the half-swinging door.

I'd never seen a place like it; it was so small to have that much stuff. Two beds sat in a space without a kitchen. A dorm room, Gilbert explained, and walked over to a desk. Both beds had young women sleeping in scant pajamas, and both stirred, though didn't wake while we worked. It smelled like stale body odor and old pizza.

Gilbert jumped up to sit in the flimsy rolling desk chair. He pulled the golden string under a green-shaded lamp and the room illuminated in double V shapes like an hourglass. My heart thumped. Being somewhere we weren't invited, good or bad reason, made me think about punishment.

Gilbert flipped through a binder. The teeth clacked open like a blow horn shout, but the sleepers hardly stirred. He removed four pages and then replaced them with pages that he'd retrieved from the back of his pants.

"Joe Adams, Joe Adams, a perfect A, Joe Adams. She'll keep a scholarship, Joe Adams, that nasty mouthed woman will no longer poison her mind with failure, Joe Adams."

It struck then and I had one of those eureka moments; that mean woman was her teacher.

Gilbert shook his head.

Wrong.

Her mother. The woman had said bad things, made the girl feel worthless, unfocussed her blooming brain. The facts were good and they made me feel good. We walked back the way we came, to the ornate door, to the stairs up the little hill, to the rotary dial. I didn't want to go, but I knew I had to.

"Joe Adams, most get one visit, but you're different, you have an open pass. Poor Joe Adams, Joe Adams." Gilbert pouted a puffy bottom lip as he shut the door behind me.

Crawling toward the smells of home, I wished I was a Gilbert. Eyes closed and wet with budding tears, my head connected with the panelling wall. I pushed and my knees bounced silently over the soft wooden floor toward my parents' room.

It was daytime, the clothes above me ting-tinged on their wire hangers. The house was quiet otherwise. The room appeared the same, but the door was different. I tried the handle, but it wouldn't move—new lock, a double-sided deadbolt. My knuckles landed dully against the wood. Beyond the door remained silent and I waited.

Eventually, a regular, living commotion filled the home: my brothers and sisters and Mom. My hand pounded again. Nobody came.

Within minutes, big heavy steps echoed through the house

and I knew Dad was home. Whispers followed. Footfalls raced toward me. No time to think, no time to hide, no time to leave the world again. The lock clicked and the door shot open and his fist landed squarely on my right eye.

Down I went, woozy. Dad pounced and dropped his knees into my back, while fists knuckled over me. Every hit numbed and darkened my world a little.

I awoke in my bed. The switch and the strap both stung and left reminders in their own ways, but never like this. Every lungful burned and my bones ached. My face felt puffy and scabby, my right eye was swollen shut.

The physical pain was not everything. He'd put that new lock on his bedroom door and I'd never get back to Gilbert.

Once the flood began, it refused to stop, tears running wild. I cried for my family, but they ignored me, orders from Dad, I'm certain of that. Day became night and there I lay, aching and alone. I had to get up and make my own food, get my own drinks.

On the second night after the beating, I listened to Dad explain the plan for the future, no more school, he had a friend, we'd work for a man moving stone in the bush, $2.50 an hour—much less than minimum, but what could we expect being almost useless kids. My sisters had to work too, but not stone. Their jobs were to work in a kitchen and help serve food, something like that.

I didn't care much for school, so it didn't sound all that bad, but I knew the stone man, met him once, he was just like Dad and he had nine kids of his own, none went to school and all had holes where teeth should've lived. They were mean and stupid, dumber than dumb.

More tears formed like a spring thaw and I sobbed against my yellow-stained pillow. Crying is tiring. Something about sadness, it exhausts like hard labor. So sleep took me again and I awoke to a silent home.

I was hungry, but moving was tough and made me think

about how unfair everything was, until a high voice, tiny and familiar, said my name. "Joe Adams, Joe Adams, can you walk, Joe Adams?"

Smaller than ever, was that voice. I turned, but Gilbert wasn't there. This made me cry anew, my stupid brain making me sadder with hope.

So I'd figured, anyway.

"Look closer, Joe Adams. We are going to fix this situation, Joe Adams, Joe Adams."

My head rocked despite the pain in movement and still nothing. That's when I felt a scratch at my ear and almost screamed. A cockroach sat on my pillow. Instinct had me revolting.

"No, Joe Adams, Joe Adams."

Leaned in, I looked real close at the cockroach. Just a cockroach. Aside from the eyes. Gilbert in roach form read my mind, jumped down from my bed, and waited for me to follow. Laser pains danced through me, but I got steady on my feet. The hallway was a dark throat. I was fearless with Gilbert near, while the door at the end was closed, anyway. I took the handle and turned. It didn't give.

"Hey, Joe Adams!" Like a mouse peep.

My eyes went to my feet and then I saw Dad's pants on the floor, shoved halfway out the door from beneath. His keychain was right there. I took it and my heart screamed as the bolt turned.

Mom and Dad slept, both snoring quietly. Seeing the figure next to the bed almost made me jump. Gilbert, in full form.

"Joe Adams, Joe Adams, I've thought about how to fix this and I can't really figure it, Joe Adams. It isn't my duty, but I feel, Joe Adams, Joe Adams, that this needs fixed." Gilbert stared at my father.

"Can you make him happy?"

Naïve is an understatement, I was plain dumb and too

hopeful. Older you get, the more you figure out about people and changing them or even putting up with them is rarely worth the trouble of it all.

Gilbert shook his head. "Dues owed will be dues paid, Joe Adams."

He reached out a hand and placed it over Dad's chest. The man slept in his underwear, bedsheets down to his thighs. Gilbert's fingers twined in the coarse black forest just to the left of center. The skin worked away, parting like the Red Sea when Moses freed his friends, but nothing appeared damaged. Gilbert pinched a valve running toward the heart, twisting it ever so slightly as he did.

"What's gonna happen?"

"If he keeps happy, he'll live, Joe Adams, Joe Adams."

Gilbert lifted his hand and the chest sealed seamlessly. It was then that we noticed the open and glaring eyes of Mom. Gilbert shot her a look and she fell back asleep.

"Will that fix it then?"

"'Fraid not, Joe Adams, Joe Adams, hearts broken throughout the house. First, James Adams, and then Josh Adams, Courtney Adams, Cathy Adams, Celia Adams, and of course Joe Adams, Joe Adams." He smiled a mouthful of reflective pearls.

Silly to think of me that way. I didn't feel broken, not with Dad being fixed now especially.

"What about Mom?" I didn't even whisper, Gilbert made me feel so safe and right.

"Not innocent, she shielded her face with yours by staying silent, Joe Adams, Joe Adams." Gilbert was more serious than I'd ever heard him. "Up to you, Joe Adams, Joe Adams."

Work made her miserable and Dad didn't make her feel good, but he was fixed, so, I figured if she had a new skill... It really was Dad's fault, mostly. "What if she could use a computer, type fast and sit in an office?"

Gilbert considered this then nodded and reached out, ran his hands over her hands and eyes. His stubby legs took him around the bed. He reached down the front of his pants and retrieved five clipped classified advertisements, set them on the dresser.

"Done, Joe Adams, Joe Adams, the rest is up to her."

It didn't feel as good as some of the others. I knew my mom might just keep on at the factory because even good change is hard to conceive sometimes. Like that saying, you can lead a horse to water.

Two down and the rest of the family to go. Gilbert led the way, he massaged each of my sibling's heads. "Smarts, Joe Adams, smarts, a good brain can fix the future for the scorned and maybe some memory loss to boot, Joe Adams, Joe Adams."

Intelligence, it was exactly right. I never imagined they'd become so smart and perfect, but they have Gilbert to thank and don't even know it.

"Okay, Joe Adams, Joe Adams, it is time. You can be smart, Joe Adams—"

"But I don't want to forget; I can't forget any of it."

"Don't you want a fix, Joe Adams, Joe Adams? You're broken, your heart in particular, Joe Adams." He touched my chest.

"I'm fixed fine."

Gilbert shook his head. "You are too good for your own good, Joe Adams, Joe Adams. Come see me again if you feel bad, if you need a fix, Joe Adams, Joe Adams."

He took me to my bed and I lay down, wincing a little less than before, and Gilbert walked away.

The next morning, Dad took two steps, maybe remembered he was who he was, remembered his life, his family, and how he hated everything, maybe a bunch of things, and died on the spot. Fixed. Two weeks after that, Mom took a desk job at Marshall Insurance, a little office in town. Fixed. Over the years, one by one, my brothers and sisters all took scholarships, so smart, so successful. Fixed. It felt good and they didn't know anything, but

I couldn't tell them the truth, they wouldn't believe me.

I never saw Gilbert again.

Mom finally died and someone had to take the house.

It's my turn now. I need a fix. I've worked too hard and given up everything. Gilbert said I could come back and now I'm back because I was wrong. I'm not fixed, never was; I need so much from him.

That deadbolt had gone unlocked a long time, nobody knew where the key was. The closet was right where I'd left it. Kneeling like a little boy, I checked the wall, felt for the crack. It wasn't there. Unfairness had invaded, it wasn't right. Gilbert said...

The pizza delivery girl came out and I tipped her extra because she said it was a pain to leave town so far. The pizza was okay. I watched what was on the CBC because Mom didn't have any services hooked up and the internet was already shut off.

Morning came and was too bright. The house smelled loud and different. I teetered from my bed. It all felt so big. I scanned around. It changed somehow, seemed clearer. Down, I looked to my hands and gasped, then ran to the washroom. The toilet made for a good foothold and I climbed up onto the sink to see into the mirror. I pert-near lost my balance. My eyes, my eyes were black and big, my head and body so small.

"Joe Adams no more, Gilbert, Gilbert," a familiar voice said, my lips moving.

I clapped once. My fix, the greatest fix, to be a fixer. I ran to my parent's bedroom, to the closet, and found the crack. The tunnel was plenty high for me and my feet burned a trail into the shadows.

Fixed.

THAT NAME GAME

(2019)

ABORT GRANDMOTHERS TODAY was painted in huge pink bubble letters on the laundromat wall across from the theater and next to the parking lot. A pigeon picked at the remnants of a box of French fries while a greasy rat scurried along the gutter with a soiled pair of Fruit of the Looms underwear small enough for a toddler. Unnoticing, uncaring, the street was busy with hooting couples who'd bunched in together as they walked. They leaned shoulder to shoulder as if they might tip without support. Lynell Mosely envied them and hated them. Their happiness was an affront to all she'd gone through, all she was feeling.

The theater had only just let out from its late showing and this throng of couples flowing her way was the result. The rat had taken a turn into the sewer, but the pigeon remained, indifferent to the people jacked up on the sensual horror experience.

Candyman—they always showed the horror movies late. *Candyman*—late because it wasn't just horror, the underlying sexuality was so thick it had people racing to private spaces; those who hadn't fumbled free sticky messes in the back of the theater, where the lights didn't reach and the buzzing of bees swallowed their moans of ecstasy.

Candyman.

This was the third time Lynell had gone to see the film in the last week, but tonight she left early, knowing it was just the kind of thing Ray would be going to. When they were together, all he ever wanted to watch were movies like *Hellraiser* and *Nekromantik* and *Last Dance* and *Howling* part fucking *two*. He had a collection on VHS and Betamax. And as much as they got him going, they got her going, because she'd do anything for him. Anything.

Lynell closed her eyes a moment after casting a glance to the marquee sign and seeing that name gain. Truthfully, Ray wasn't the only reason she found herself drawn to *Candyman*. That actor, that Tony Todd, was repulsive, but enticing somehow. Deep down in the pit of her gut and lower, something stirred at the harsh hum of his words and the electric pulse of that hook. Plus, when did horror movies ever look like somewhere she'd been and have people who looked like the people at work, the people who went to her church, the face in the mirror?

Minus that hook.

Minus those bees.

Minus that demonic sexuality.

Of course.

Her eyes opened and she continued on, careful to avoid a spent rubber and chewed lollipop lying in the path to her car—a blue Chevy Citation. At night, she always did a full loop to glance in the back. Now, she had her hand in her purse on the fat knitting needle she carried, just in case. Mostly just in case, partly because she wished a motherfucker would.

The streetlight high overhead was only a few car lengths down the lot and shined enough thin yellow that she could safely transfer her hand from the makeshift weapon to her keys. There was nobody in her car. Okay. And good. Back at the driver's door, she opened up and fell in, yanking the handle quickly after her—men were sneaks and all they needed was a second to catch a lonely woman unawares. The car was old and rusty. The door's hinges creaked with even a slight shift and absolutely cried out when slammed.

She paused a minute and squinted, inhaling deeply at the familiar scents of Elizabeth Arden Sunflowers, Newport Menthols, and Secret deodorant. This simple act made her feel better. She slammed her hand over the lock knob on her door and felt even better yet.

"Locked for everyone but you," she said beneath her breath.

Lights were coming alive around her from vehicles pulling away and she watched for Ray. Ray and that bitch he was going with. Lynell cracked a window about two inches—much more than that and the glass would shift; someday it would fall, and then she'd have to waste thirty bucks on the repair guy, again. She didn't have thirty bucks to burn on a good week, especially didn't have thirty bucks since she'd had to become a regular every time a new horror movie hit the screen.

But it wasn't as if she could stay home. She cracked the window a hair more, because listening was part of tracking a man, and his bitch, and without risks, the rewards were hardly ever worth it.

"Ray. Ray. Ray," she said, not seeing him among the sea of faces before her.

This was just a fling; Ray would be back, Lynell knew that. She knew it like she knew eventually she'd track Ray to the theater, confront him, maybe dropkick that new bitch right in the mouth.

Faces. Faces. Faces everywhere and none of them Ray. She grunted and shook the steering wheel. Patience wasn't a virtue she harbored.

"Wouldn't even have to kick the bitch," she said. Once Ray saw her again, he'd drop to his knees and beg her. He'd give her the *Lynell, baby, baby, baby* and she'd take it and roll with it, use it like a blanket, a pacifier, she'd feed on it.

More vehicles started and passed by, and she scanned every face for Ray.

Not him.

Not him.

Not even a him.

"Shit," she said as she fished a Newport from the pack in her purse.

Newport was not even her brand. She'd started smoking menthols because of Ray; he'd said it was cheaper if they split packs and smoked the same kind. Getting a carton did save about a buck and a half, but hell, Ray smoked twice as much, meaning she'd had to keep the supply up and she wasn't saving a cent, he was!

And she did that for him because she was a good one. Not like others, not like that bitch he had in her rightful place now.

Lynell exhaled the minty smoke and watched the last car leave the lot. Suddenly it was quiet and the theater's lobby lights and office lights went down, all but the marquee sign. It remained lit like a promise of more steamy terror to come.

She read that word spelled out in yellow bulbs, "Candyman," and got a shiver.

Her eyes rolled to the rearview mirror and she peered into herself. There was a game in the movie, something fun and terrifying in nearly equal parts.

"Candyman," she said and then quickly after, "Candyman. Candyman. Candyman."

She envisioned Tony Todd showing up behind her, leaning in with his hook, grazing her cheek with the sharpened tip; that sexy voice and promise of violence...god, it made her feel funny. Like being stretched every which way. The thing with Ray didn't help, of that she was sure, but something about that monster stood alone like an offering to anyone willing to play the game.

"Candy..." she trailed, licking her lips, finding she was scared. For real scared.

She laughed then and sucked a final drag on her cigarette before tossing it out to the damp asphalt of the lot and rolling the window up. It slipped some and she gently rolled it back down an inch. She palmed the glass and shoved as she turned the crank. It slipped in straight, back where it belonged.

Back where it belonged and by her hand. PROACTIVE popped into her mind like the word of the day, neon and singsong. She took a breath. What did proactive mean beyond what she was already doing? She inhaled deeply through her nose and let her eyelids fall. She saw Ray in Tony Todd's jacket, wearing his hook, wearing his bees.

"Candy—" she started abruptly and stopped just as abruptly. Eyes on her reflection in the mirror. "Don't be such a wimp." She licked her lips again and pretended to check her eyeliner. She settled and looked into her eyes, laughed some more, and then blurted, "Candy—!"

She put her hands to her face, really freaked out, but also laughing still. This was too much and it's not as if it could possibly work. Right?

She stiffened her body and took two deep breaths.

Her gaze fell back to the rearview.

She cleared her throat, twice.

The air suddenly felt thin.

"Okay. Okay. Okay."

Breathed deep.

"Candyman."

She waited and waited and laughed and cried and then said Ray's name five times like he'd pull a Tony Todd *Candyman* and appear from thin air, but nothing happened. She turned the key, yanked the light plunger, and moved the shifter into drive.

As she made it through the quiet neighborhoods, her eyes fell on the mirror more than a dozen times, half-expecting, half-seeing. She laughed more, feeling a bit like a crazy person, laughing that much. She lit another cigarette and a rarely used hamster wheel in the very back of her brain began spinning. She followed its lead and she turned away from her home, away from the other theater, away from anywhere but that one exact place she had to be.

After three right she took a left and departed the busier streets for a shadowy residential area. The apartment driveway she pulled into had four dozen spaces and three yellow speed bumps. She parked in a spot behind the lime green building where Ray lived and looked up to his dark window.

"She in there? That bitch, she in there?"

Lynell knew the woman's name was Kiara, but that was all she knew about her. Bitch felt better anyway, more on the nose.

"That Kiara bitch."

Saying the name made her think of Tony Todd again and in a single rushed breath she said, "Candyman. Candyman. Candyman. Candyman. Candyman."

Nothing happened and she sucked on her Newport like a soother. The idea behind the character in the movie reminded her of a game the girls would play before gym class. Back then she'd thought a boy named Bobby was going to be her forever love and she and her friends would write names on mirrors in stolen lipstick while they tried to conjure a witch.

"Bloody Mary. Bloody Mary. Bloody Mary," she said and then sneered at her reflection, daring it to work.

She'd always been too chicken to try it in school for real, only mouthing the words—because what if it was that *she'd* said it that the witch appeared?—but now she thought, *what if they had it wrong and the movie had it right?* Could be things like that only worked if you did it five times. Five time's the charm.

She inhaled deeply from the Newport and spoke through the smoke. "Bloody Mary. Bloody Mary."

Nothing.

The light in Ray's apartment came alive and she tossed her cigarette out the window before reaching into her purse. The hamster wheel went into overdrive and an epiphany struck her like an electric shock.

She had it, no playing, no games, she had it and soon she'd have Ray all to her damned self. The keys remained dangling in the ignition as she charged across the dark lot toward the main doors. She carried only the knitting needle she'd retrieved from her purse.

Up there in Ray's apartment, that was where she was

supposed to be and someone had to pay, and now she knew how to make it so. The mathematics behind it were so clear now.

At the door, she pressed the button next to the HOOKER label. Ray's label. The line connected and she let off the button.

"Motherfucker, you know what time it is?" Ray shouted.

Oh she knew, but did he know? Did he really know?

"Ray?"

"Shit...Lynell?"

"Ray?"

"Lynell?"

"That's twice, just three more times." Lynell clenched the needle, knowing this would work and knowing why it didn't work the other times.

"What?"

"Say my name. Say it so Kiara can hear it!"

"Lynell, you crazy. I told you to leave me alone."

A sneering smile widened the bottom of her face. "Two. More. Times."

"You need your head examined, crazy bitch."

"Say it!"

"Who's that?" a distant, feminine voice said and Ray replied, face turned away, but audible, "Lynell. I told you 'bout her. We went out for about a year until I got my head on straight, crazy bitch."

At the doorway, Lynell clenched her fist so tightly the skin around the needle turned pale grey. "Once more," she whispered and closed her eyes.

"Tell her to get out of here," the voice, probably Kiara's, said and then Ray said, "Yeah, she don't listen, crazy bitch."

"Say it, Ray, and I'll disappear." Lynell didn't let on that she'd only disappear from the doorstep and then reappear inside his apartment, because that's how it worked when the elements came together. That's how it had to work and she damned well knew it.

"What?"

See, with Candyman and Bloody Mary it failed because she didn't believe it, didn't need it to be true, but this, this was different. Faith was magic.

"Say. My. Name!"

"Lynell, fucking Lynell, Lynell, Lyn—!" Ray had his finger on the button for two more seconds while Kiara's screaming voice filled the apartment's doorway through the little speaker. Upstairs in Ray Hooker's apartment, a knitting needle slammed in and out of Kiara's neck and chest while Ray shouted, "How the fuck did you get in here!"

TENDER

(2022)

Sopping with rainwater and exhausted from the trip, Winston Cahill stomped into the foyer of the dilapidated castle after being let through a door by a ghastly old man with highly pronounced cheekbones in a scruffy grey suit. Immediately, the enticing scents of roasted meat hit Winston and had his mouth watering.

"Please, follow me, sir. The count is about to sit down for his supper," the old man said after taking Winston's peacoat over his right arm.

"Where's my sister," Winston said, demanded it in fact.

The building was as rough on the inside as it was on the outside. The stone walls featured great, haphazard mortar patches. The tapestries were alive with mold. The floors were cracked and going to sand.

The old man paused by an open, heavy wooden door. "Mr. Hackman, Mr. Winston Cahill."

At the head of the table a small man with doughy cheeks and welcoming eyes stood. "Mr. Cahill, it's so good to finally meet you. Sit." He gestured to an empty seat. "Barry, fetch Mr. Cahill a plate."

The old man nodded before hurrying through the small, cozy dining area to a door on the far side of the room. Winston watched him go, then focused on Count Beverly Hackman.

Winston stretched out a battle-scarred index finger at the soft little man. "My sister will not be marrying you."

The count jerked his head backward like a chicken. "Of course not."

This brought a frown to Winston's face. "Oh. She sent a

letter...she said..." The romantic ramblings she'd written really weren't worth repeating.

The count gestured anew. "Please, sit."

Winston acquiesced. "Where's Elizabeth."

"She was feeling under the weather." The count shook his head gently. "I believe I may have broken her heart, though I assure you, I did no more than offer her a roof. I'm not certain it was all a ruse, but she'd told me she was studying castles."

This was confusing, but Winston had to admit, his sister was prone to emotional extremes and sudden, intense captivation of subjects—perhaps that included moldering castles.

"I see."

The old man appeared with a plate mounded with meat and vegetables, smothered in gravy.

"Though I'm not entirely innocent. It's lonely out here and having a visitor was quite thrilling at first, so thrilling I ignored the telltale signs of girlish infatuation," the count said as he cut into the meat on his plate.

Rather than having to suck back his drool any longer, Winston himself picked up the silverware that had been laid next to his plate. The trip was so long, and this food smelled, so, so good.

After swallowing a mouthful, Winston said, "I apologize for coming into your home so strongly."

The count waved it off, too busy chewing to answer. They ate for two minutes in silence. Winston was surprised by the tenderness of the meat, given the state of the castle, he never would've guessed such food could be prepared in such squalor.

Plate more than halfway cleared, Winston said, "Is Elizabeth upstairs then? I should like to see her, and I should think she'd like to see me."

The count took up his goblet, raising it in a cheers; Winston quickly mimicked. "Too Elizabeth," the count said before taking a mouthful.

The fluid in Winston's mouth was not the wine he had anticipated, and he spat—he'd been in enough rough situations in his youth to know the taste of blood. "What is the meaning of this?" he shouted across the table at the count.

"The nutrients in blood are virtually unparalleled," the count said, red lifting the corners of his mouth like a clown's smile.

"Where's Elizabeth," Winston said, rising, his voice carrying, echoing off the stone walls and high, high ceiling.

The count stabbed a fork into the remaining piece of meat on his plate. "Hello, brother dearest," he said, raising the pitch of his voice into mock girlish.

Winston looked at his plate then, all the meat he'd eaten. "No," he said, lifting his head.

The count only grinned while into the room came the old man in the scruffy suit, now wielding a bloody hammer with a head as big as a coconut. Winston took a step to the door he'd come through, but there came an identical old man in an identical suit, this one holding a loaded crossbow. The air deflated from his chest and he tumbled back into his chair.

"It's your last meal, you might as well eat," the count said.

Winston, pliant with shock, looked at his plate, thinking, *she certainly was tender.*

BUGS

(2019)

The men rushed through the sliding doors, boots squeaking on the brilliant white floor, as Dr. Cortez leaned away from the iris reader. Inside, Elizabeth Bezos was on her bed, standing, waving her boney, wrinkled arms and screaming about bugs. Her voice was like damp wood over a campfire. The men in white body suits, white gloves, and bare faces reached for her.

"Are you insane?" Elizabeth shouted, her eyes bulging and red around the edges, brown circling enlarged pupils. She clawed at the hands reaching to grab her. "Don't you touch me!"

"Let's all take a moment—" Dr. Cortez started.

"No masks! You're not wearing masks! The bugs eat the microbes from your breath! They survive on your filth!"

"Come now, Elizabeth, you're having an episode," Dr. Cortez said as the men continued their attempts to take hold of the ancient heiress to a fortune that could've fed every starving mouth across the universe, could've saved Earth before it was too late.

Dr. Cortez stopped then. "Right. Derry, Hans, back away." She then withdrew a white balaclava from her pocket and pulled it over her head. "I'm sorry, Elizabeth, we rushed in as quickly as we—"

"The bugs are growing!" Her face was pale as snow as she pointed to a corner.

The room was polished polymer from floor to ceiling. Only the bedding and Elizabeth's clothing were of fibrous materials. The cracks between the walls and floor panels were infinitesimal. The space was evacu-scrubbed daily. The air recycling system was filtered down to the atom, leaving nothing unwanted.

"Look at that one!" She pointed a long, gnarled digit.

Derry and Hans were trained well. They looked at the doctor where she stood in the doorway, and she simply shook her head. "We'll do another evacu-scrub, Elizabeth. Come down and we'll get this room cleaned." Dr. Cortez stepped to the bed and turned her back to the patient.

Elizabeth climbed aboard to piggyback the doctor. She whispered, "This is unacceptable. These conditions are unacceptable." She yelled then, "I deserve better! Look at that thing! Look at the boils and the oozing gunk! Those claws and the slobbering! They're monsters! You can't put me in a locked room with monsters, it's inhumane!"

Dr. Cortez did not look to where Elizabeth pointed. The deal never changed.

"These conditions! My heart! You can't strain my heart with these filthy conditions!"

Dr. Cortez stalked toward the door, rolling her eyes—the damned princess wanted to talk *inhumane, monsters?*

"I demand better! Don't you know who I am? This is all wrong!"

"Okay, Elizabeth, calm—"

"Why hasn't any of my family come to see me? Why haven't—ooogh, get away, get away!"

Dr. Cortez continued her straight path.

"It's coming! Look! It's horrendous, disgusting!"

The doctor stopped and peered down to her side where Elizabeth had pointed.

"Those teeth! And its eyes, what's that yellow stuff? Git! Git! Don't let it lick me, look at the slime!"

Dr. Cortez sighed and said, "Really, Elizabeth," before continuing on toward the exit.

"What is wrong with you? It's right there, all slobbery and oozing and weeping, and those teeth!" Elizabeth vibrated as she spoke.

"There's nothing there," the doctor said.

"I won't stand for these conditions! Look, another! It's purple and that trail it's leaving behind it...! Look, dammit!"

The doctor grinned gently, but did not look. The description was exactly as it should've been, exactly as she'd had installed, alongside dozens of others. "Elizabeth...there's nothing there."

"How can't you see it?"

"Shh, shh," Dr. Cortez said. "We'll get this cleaned and you—"

"This is unacceptable! My heart! You can't put strain on my heart!"

Dr. Cortez cooed more, as she'd been trained to do. It was all part of the game, the room, the bugs, keeping Elizabeth alive these two hundred years as they floated just beyond the once beautiful planet their ancestors had called home. Elizabeth would survive. For as long as the pain stung, she'd survive. And she'd pay; the doctors, nurses, and orderlies would pretend the alien things were disgusting, weren't released daily into Elizabeth's cabin.

Apocalyptic greed was ugly, but post-apocalyptic wrath nearly made up for it.

SOON

(2015)

The platform was alive with conversation, shouting men and women. The voices roared in languages foreign to the boy. He understood only the tones and the volume. Frightened, he took his papa's hand and peered down at the track, felt the familiar roughness of the palm, worn and crusty tissue from days cutting stone. The man retracted from the touch as if stung, and the boy looked up at his papa, but not his papa. The hand belonged to a stranger. The man screeched, terror on his tongue, and jumped back, untethered surprise in his eyes and feet.

The boy backpedaled with haste.

"Papa?"

The platform was alive with vibrant, swishy swirls on dresses. Arms linked to men anchoring in sensible blue denim and pale khakis.

"Papa?"

There was a familiar figure standing at the center of the platform. The boy rushed toward him, certain here was the lost papa. The place was thrumming and his papa disappeared into a sea of life and luggage.

"Papa!" the boy cried.

Into the folds, enveloped by the soft threads twined, cut, and sewn, he raced, pushing between, squeezing through those awaiting the train.

Some jumped at the childish touch. Some danced full circles before discussing a distasteful notion with their loved ones. Now and then, an old woman or a young child would hold gaze to the boy, registering his existence until letting it wash away. He was not a problem they needed to heed.

The world is full of trouble, Papa says so, the boy thought. Be a good boy, Sabastian, Papa says that too.

"Papa!"

The fleeting hope and determination pushed the boy to the platform edge. He looked down at the dirty men fooling with the track. Faces around him peered as he peered. None of those faces was his father's.

The train was late, the rising voices gave credence to this and the boy recognized the impending timeline. He had to find his papa before boarding.

"Why don't they use the other track?" he asked a woman. She didn't hear and he tugged her dress, pink with black floral swirls. "The other track?"

She glanced down, fidgeted with her dress, and turned back to look where the others looked. Sadness in her expression. Wrinkles around her mouth and eyes from smiling and laughing, but she wasn't laughing or smiling then, nobody was.

"Why don't...?" the boy started again.

The woman shook her head in disgust and turned away.

The boy inhaled, scream preparation, but caught a glimpse of his papa.

The man scurried as if lost himself, frantic, calling out into the crowd. His voice carried. "No! No, he can't be!"

The boy headed to the shelter of the overhanging roof outside the station. He stood on a bench for a better angle. So many people and none minded him...but there he was!

"Papa!" The boy's voice buried, absorbed in the travellers' choir.

"Tanto sangue," a woman said to her companion.

"Foveri ntropi," a young man said to his friends.

"Geez, that's sad, imagine if that was our Peter," a man said holding his boy at his side, speaking to his wife.

The boy ignored these words and jumped down, raced to his

papa. Just an arm's length away, he reached out and caught him by a coat sleeve. The approaching train whistled, and the papa shouted, running for the opening doors, free of the boy's grasp.

"Paaa-Paaa!"

The flow pushed him away. Lost, he plunked down on the wooden bench and watched as every passenger disappeared onto the train. Rain streaked through the quickening dark.

Papa was gone.

The boy sat lonely. Impossibly, he knew that he'd be there forever. To live as an orphan in the shelter of the station house, surviving on half-eaten bags of peanuts and water collected in puddles. He put his face into his palms and tried to shut away this staggering aloneness.

"Sebastian?" The voice was mannish. It was not Papa but was comforting. "There you are, boy."

A man in a pale yellow t-shirt and faded blue jeans held open arms. He wore a Kansas City Chiefs cap—just like the one the boy's papa kept on the mantle. Right next to the picture of Papa and his brother when they were kids.

"Who are you?" the boy asked.

"I'm your uncle, Carl. Your dad and me are brothers."

The boy eyed him suspiciously, tried to reconcile the possibility. His papa's brother died before he was born. "But...Papa!" Suddenly feeling in danger from this man insinuating familial connection.

"Oh, Sebastian, it's okay, yeah? Your papa will be along soon. He'll come real soon, he misses you a whole lot and he'll make it so that he can find you, real soon. The accident didn't get him like it got you, not right away, but soon. See, he's on his way to the store, yeah? Gonna empty his wallet and get a tool to bring him along."

"Where?" The boy got to his feet, ready to run, and yet, just as ready to embrace this man and his wonderfully warm, though confusing words.

"He'll head home, your mom's at work, and he'll leave a note, yeah? Explain everything, the accident, why he got himself a forty-five from the pawnshop. He'll come soon, you be together real soon."

Carl opened his arms. The boy stepped into them.

"Your dad's real sad, but he's coming on the next train, maybe the one after that, too sad not to come."

It was good and the boy hugged Carl tight as tight got.

Carl sat on the bench with the boy.

"Soon as he can't take no more," Carl said. "Maybe, umm, soon as the rain stops, sun-up. Yeah?"

Rain slashed, coming hard, washing away the blood from the tracks.

The boy sniffled, stifling a sob.

"Don't worry. Always rains hardest just before the dawn, yeah?" Carl put an arm over the boy's shoulders.

Legs swinging, the boy watched as the clouds let the first streaks of dawn down onto the station. Soon he'd find his papa. Real soon.

MANHUNTER

(2021)

The boys called it Manhunter instead of Hide 'n Seek 'cause Hide 'n Seek was for babies. They'd started playing around Jimmy's yard, but Bobby said that wasn't tough enough, so they went to an abandoned warehouse over by Bobby's place. When the warehouse got stale, Joe-boy suggested they try the cemetery, but the cemetery had nowhere good to hide, so Gordo said, "Hey, let's try them woods over by Claude's place."

At the mention of Claude, the three other boys groaned. Claude had gone missing, then his father had skipped town, unable to deal with the grief and his mother went crazy.

"Man, just last week Claude's mom grabbed me and did the," in time like a chorus line, the other boys joined in with Joe-boy, *"Claude? Claude, where you been!"*

All four laughed a bit, but it was never funny when Claude's mom ran up and gripped on you like you were an umbrella in a thunderstorm.

So the boys got to walking toward the wood's by Claude's house. The sun was already mostly down, but the boys all had parents too busy or tuckered out to worry where they were. They cut along the quiet streets. The temperature had fallen and most folks had their windows open, doors too if they weren't at work. The further they went, the sparser the homes became.

Bobby put out his had to stop the others from walking. "See that?" he said.

"Yeah, that's her, ain't it?" Joe-boy said.

"What's she doing?" Gordo said.

Jimmy started off in a crouch like he was crossing no man's

land. "Come on," he said.

They'd cleared all the other houses and all that remained were Claude's house and the forest. On the goodly patch of lawn in front of Claude's house, was his mother. She was rail thin and wore a translucent nightdress that revealed the sharp jutting of her bones beneath. She held a dark candle in her right hand and a big white book in her left. She was humming when the boys got to the ditch on the far side of the road.

"Geez, she's one messed up lady," Gordo whispered.

They'd all felt pretty bad about Claude. His family came to town six months earlier and Claude had almost become the fifth member of their group, he even knew the secret window-tap signal. Back then, Claude's mother wasn't weird at all. None of the boys thought Claude was really dead, not for real. Probably he was just lost in the woods and living off berries and mushrooms, or maybe he had a secret yearning to become an actor, or work in a carnival, or tour with a band.

The humming ceased and Claude's mom opened her eyes. "Veni ad me! Et attollat, veni ad me! Infernus et virtus voco ligna silvarum ego mandavi tibi ut detrahet me tergum pueri mei! Veni ad me! Et attollat, veni ad me!" she said and then threw the candle to the grass before her. A brilliant flash of fire jumped, forming a perfect circle.

The flames were wildly bright and revealed the boys' faces in the long grass.

"Claude? Claude, where you been!" Claude's mother shouted and started toward the boys. Her thin nightdress lit on the flaming ring and fire danced swiftly to her long greasy hair. "Claude! Come to mama, Claude!" she said, her arms spread as the flames licked the sweat from her pores like it was gasoline.

The boys popped up and ran for the woods, racing into the pitch-blackness, stumbling and teetering, but never falling. They kept going until the light was but a flicker behind them and Claude's mother's screams were only a memory.

Bobby stopped first and knelt, gasping for breath. Gordo stopped next and leaned on his knees. Joe-boy and Jimmy stopped in tandem and Joe-boy tilted his head way back as if the air was better behind him; Jimmy simply huffed and puffed, forcing words out where he could.

"She's...gone...totally...looney!"

Gordo looked over and opened his mouth to speak, but several snaps rang out. All around them, wood was breaking and leaves began rustling. Flames began lighting, controlled bursts at the tops of snapped off trees.

"They're coming," Bobby gasped and pushed to his feet.

The trees were walking, branches jutting like arms, twigs trilling like fingers. The flames waved against the night like burning peacock feathers, right above carved out eyes that shined a brilliant ruby red.

Scared out of their wits, each boy got to running. Bobby was caught first and he screeched. Joe-boy came next, he wailed and kicked and punched, but it did no good. Gordo fainted when a tree grabbed him and lifted him high. Jimmy made it further back toward the street and sanity, but a dogwood tree reached down and snatched him, spinning skinny branches around his arms and legs like a boa constrictor. The boys screamed and the trees walked. Gordo awoke at the edge of the forest and said, "What the? What the?"

Claude's mother was bright with impossibly red flames that played upon her body like burning Sambuca in a shot glass. "Veni ad me! Veni ad me!" she said.

Jimmy's tree stopped first and flung him. He thumped hard against the lawn and he looked up in wide-eyed terror at Claude's mother.

"Claude? Claude, where you been?" she said and then frowned.

Gordo's tree tossed him next to Jimmy and when he landed all the wind burst from his lungs and he honked like a donkey.

"Claude? Claude, where you been? You're not..."

Joe-boy and Bobby were tossed then, landing side-by-side next to the others.

"Claude? None of you are my boy, Claude!"

A great rustling sounded from the forest and a fifth boy was tossed free. The body was slouched like a marionette at rest, head canted sideways, arms between spread legs. Claude. He was in the same sweater and jeans he'd been wearing when he disappeared, but his skin was grey with big black rot holes. Fat worms wriggled in his hollowed eye sockets. His jaw fell open and a rat crawled out.

"Claude? Claude, where you been?" Claude's mother said.

"Playing in the woods," Claude's whisper hissed out without his mouth moving.

That was more than plenty to see and the boys were back on their feet, hauling butt for anywhere but there. Joe-boy's was closest and they paraded down to his basement where they sat in the dark, staring at the windows, knowing Claude really *was* dead, or at least had been.

Hours passed.

The boys had finally begun to relax.

Then came the signature tapping, their special code.

The foursome looked at the window but didn't dare step close, didn't dare make a peep.

"Guys.

"Guys.

"Let's play Manhunter," a raspy voice hissed like wind through a doorframe.

WELL-CIRCULATED CASH

(2022)

33 years behind bars, 33 years pining and waiting and imagining what he'd do with all that dough once he got free. Now, finally, today was the day Malcom Bridges would be let out of Kent Institution—the maximum-security penitentiary for most of Western Canada. He could eat and drink and piss and shit and sleep and exercise whenever the hell he wanted, especially because he never gave up where he and his partner had stashed the 2.1 million in well-circulated cash.

"Oh, Tracy," he said, thinking of his old partner's deep green eyes, and then of his screw up that left a catalog of evidence against him on her body after he'd murdered her. "Note to self, poke holes in the lungs when dumping a corpse or it'll float." He laughed at this, could laugh now, though it hadn't been funny until he walked through that gate for a final time, his back to the big grey walls that had entombed him so long.

Malcolm stepped off the bus to the street. He had $23 in his pocket, probably only enough to cover a cab out to the old farm— he'd chatted up enough newbies when they came in and read enough online to know the buck didn't go very far these days.

Flagging them down wasn't working—not without an app— so Malcolm planted himself in the middle of the street, waving both arms over his head when he saw another car with that telltale yellow paint. "Will twenty bucks get me out to Red Bridge Road?" he said to the little brown man behind the wheel.

"Barely."

Malcolm sat back and watched the world beyond the window. Everything had changed so much, at least until they hit the outskirts of town. Red Bridge Road looked almost identical to what it had looked like in 1990. The bridge was a little less red, more a rust brown now, and the dusty gravel of the road seemed less traveled.

Malcolm was so excited, he had to keep himself from jogging the three miles from the highway where the cabbie let him out to the farm where he'd stashed all that beautiful cash.

To his surprise and delight, there was a for sale sign at the end of the lane, the ditches overgrown with eye-high weeds, the mailbox smashed inutile. He couldn't help it any longer. It would be dark soon and he guessed the power was off in the ancient barn.

In twilight's orange glow, Malcolm rushed into the basement of the barn. At some point in his time away, someone had whitewashed the stone walls. Likely that even did him a favor and help keep that one particular stone a secret. He found it and began slamming his palms against it to wiggle it loose, making his hands dusty white with cheap, powdery paint.

Not five minutes passed before the watermelon-sized rock dropped from the wall to reveal the hiding place and the Saturday canvas duffle bag hidden within. The bag was packed with denominations from $10 to $100.

"Come. On," he grunted, yanking.

Pap-pap-pap.

Malcolm jerked his head around at the noise. He saw nothing in the dim barn basement, though did note that it was getting dark quickly. He returned his attention to the bag, thinking perhaps he should wait until tomorrow.

Pap-pap-pap-pap.

Malcom let go of the bag and spun fully around with his dukes up. Again, there was nobody there. "Tomorrow," he whispered and bent to pick up the rock he'd wiggled out.

Pap-pap-pap-pap-pap.

This time he didn't have to turn, looking up in time to see the rear end of a llama fly through one of the big doors. He began howling with laughter, knowing he could safely grab the bag.

"Might get spit on," he said as he pulled at the duffle, finally getting it to rise.

Pap-pap-pap-pap-pap-pap.

The sounds seemed doubled up, and much closer. They weren't worth his attention however because the bag was coming.

Pap-pap-pap-pap-pap-pap-pap-pap.

The huge duffle flopped down into the ancient, scentless manure on the floor. Malcolm unzipped the bag.

Pap-pap!

Like an army stamping in unison. He looked up from his work. Ten llamas stood in a row, chewing their cud, looking at him with glowing green eyes.

Pap!

"Git!" he shouted and swatted his arms at the animals.

Pap-pap-pap!

"I don't have any food for you."

Synchronized, the llamas looked at the open bag.

"You wish," Malcolm said, bending to zip the bag back up.

He didn't get it a quarter of the way closed before a parade of *paps* rushed him and head butted at his prone state. He flew against the wall, looking up in time to see four of the animals blast him with their hard heads positioned like battering rams.

It hurt like hell, but he skittered into the corner. One llama followed him: *pap-pap-pap* went its hooves against the soft, dusty manure. Behind this animal, the other llamas were nosing into the duffle bag.

"No!" Malcolm shouted and tried to rise, only to be slammed against the wall by the tremendous strike of the dough-eyed beast. "Git!" he shouted and tried to rise again, and again, and again, after the fifth time, he remained on the floor, cowering in the fetal position, trying to protect himself from the green-eyed bastards. He could hear his fortune being eaten. Could hear his future being ground into papier mâché between the llama's jaws. Could hear the whiny voice of the teenaged manager he'd have at whichever fast-food joint was willing to take a chance on a felon. Could hear—

"Green eyes, just like Tracy," he said and then peeked from behind a protective elbow.

The llama guarding him winked and then spat into his face.

GOLDEN CALF

(2013)

Wailing, arms waving, body trembling. "Help!" she screamed.

The glow of the world bounced off her back, her silhouette casting a dark shadow onto the pale sidewalk as she moved. Behind her, the flames rose.

Bystanders stood at a safe distance, watching…watching what? The flames or the young woman?

"Please, help me!" she screamed, slugging her tired body away from the scene.

The bystanders continued their by-standing.

"Can't you see I need help?" she begged and for a moment, a split second, she thought she'd died and become a ghost. A destiny as sad as the flame overtaking the commune. But no!

Tears rolled down the cheeks of a little girl as she buried her face into the jean clad leg of her father, only the eyes of the teddy bear in her arms still daring to watch the young woman on the sidewalk, wailing, making a scene.

"Please, please, it hurts!" she screamed; and it did hurt. Her skin was of crispy bacon, on the verge of crumble, she fell into a crawl, the cotton of her robe seared into the flesh. "Please Makalee!" she prayed to her god.

"Shut up, you heathen," spat an old woman amid the bystanders, "your lord is but a devil, an ant under the foot of Jesus Christ!" The old woman rushed forward and kicked the burned girl.

"Please!" the young woman screamed and heard the glorious sound of sirens. The police didn't have a stake, worked for the good, didn't have a religion.

The old woman backed away at the firm command of the officers.

"Thank you, thank you," the young woman cried, gentle hands on her arms.

"Up we go," said one of the officers and she rose on battered legs.

"Thank you, thank you, thank you," the young woman rambled as her feet dragged over the cement, the officers pulling her to...to where? The heat rose.

She lifted her face, suddenly too hot again.

"Praise Jesus!" a bystander shouted.

"No!" the young woman screamed.

Her weight pitched forward and the officers' hands left her. She glared at her burned feet, the green nail polish she used just the night before chipped and darkened by flame and smoke. "Where's your Makalee now?" one of the officers asked. The other laughed.

The young woman wailed and bucked amidst the pyre that was once her holy place.

"Okay, okay," the reverend said, waving his arms in a black robe, crucifix dangling around his neck, "we've restored our town, let there be no further speak of saviors or lords, no further speak of truths or histories, unless they are of the one true Lord."

The crowd cheered, "Amen!"

The small girl turned her face from her father's leg. She inhaled deeply and then sang, "*Amazing Grace, how sweet the sound...*"

The bystanders joined in and sang for their eternal souls.

OVER HASH BROWNS

(2015)

The glorious, deep-fried scent of golden hash browns smelled like home, it felt like there was no reason to be anywhere else, and that was the point. Happy students were keen students.

Morgan Samuels had lived his entire life in Elmdale: a small town, close knit, good times, generation after generation. This kept his eyes from wandering to far off colleges. His campus in Elmdale was an offshoot from the main campus branch in Oodena.

He loaded the orange tray and stepped to the checkout till with coffee, juice, pancakes, and hash browns. He scanned the small crowd for a friendly face. An arm flew into the air and a voice followed close behind. "Yo, Samuels!"

Morgan swiped his card and then hurried through the smallish room of mostly hungry young men—a few young women, too—toward the arm and the voice. Terry Perkins was not a local, but might as well have been. Smalltown type, would likely settle in a town like Elmdale after school. Every bumpkin town needed rookie cops.

"How's the jerkin', Perkins?" Morgan asked.

"Too damn regular," Terry said with a smile, his gaze shifted over Morgan's shoulder. "Hey, Day!"

Phil Day jogged across the room with his tray, choices identical to Morgan's. Phil Day was another local in much of the same mind-set as Morgan. They'd gone all through grade and high school together, though he'd gone away for a year to get his final six credits at a military school—his father thought it would help him get a job later on, be a more upstanding face in a lineup of hopeful officers. That's what he told Phil anyhow.

"Wackiest shit ever," Phil said and dropped his tray onto the table. He sat next to Morgan and across from Terry. He spoke just below a shout to carry over the din of forks and knives on plates, voices, slurping, and chewing. "So, you know that wino, he was in town like three years ago? The one with a red face and a goofy smirk, always wore a clean denim shirt to match his pants."

Terry listened without comment or recognition, the question was not for him.

Morgan nodded as he chewed. "Sure, I remember, I figured he'd died. He used to sleep in the park behind the police station."

"Right, well he didn't die and last night I went out to Future Shop," Future Shop being to the east in the small city of Organvilla, "and I saw buddy hitchhiking and I thought what the hell, right? *Be a good guy for once, give him a ride.*"

Both listeners nodded in understanding.

"First off, he wore this cheap suit. It was blue, but not denim, and I thought, *steppin' up in the world.* Wrong! Buddy stank of beer, sweat, and dirt, like mold and cheap cigarettes. So anyway, he flops down into the seat, 'Goin' to Elmvale,' he says. I wanted to laugh. Guy was bombed, but I didn't laugh, not yet, and got back out onto the highway.

"So, you know how last week my brother borrowed my car?" The listeners didn't know this, but Phil carried forward his tale. "Well, he smokes like a chimney and left my ashtray overflowing with butts."

He paused as Darren Murphy, once of Organvilla, relocated for college, slumped down into a seat next to Terry. "Morning ladies," he said, obviously sleepy, his tray had two cups of coffee as well as a double order of hash browns with pancakes.

"Just in time, Phil's got a tale of intrigue going," Morgan said.

Darren made a gesture with his fork to encourage Phil's continuance.

"So anyway, buddy doesn't ask and reaches into his pocket and pulls out a battered dart tin. Then he grabs a rollie and I was about to tell him not to light it, but before I knew it, it was lit. He had these warts and cracks in his skin, his fingernails were fucking green, and he had all kinds of dirt under his nails. Man, I was amazed and disgusted, I mean his tongue ran over those dirty fingers when he sealed his rollie, but still, the whole deal had me hypnotized, or something. He lit and it stank like you wouldn't believe. I'm pretty sure buddy repurposed tossed butts into his rollies."

"Nasty," Terry said.

"Finally, I hit the button to roll down his window and he looks at me, 'Hell ya doin'?' he asks, and I'm thinking *shit, my car, buddy. You don't like it, you can hit the road*, but then I remember he's just some old wino and I'm being a good guy for karma, or something. So, I tell him 'I just like fresh air' and he says, 'I don't,' and he rolls up the window."

"Quite a guy," Morgan said and sniggered. "Fucking winos, eh?"

"I know right? So anyway, he finishes his grodey dart and stubs it out in the ashtray and I tell him I'm going to the college, so I can drop him anywhere along the way. He tells me he hangs out at the top of the hill, right where I'd turn. You know, by the subsidized apartments and that rundown old building next to the old factory and the cemetery?"

Morgan and Terry nodded. That place was like a black eye on the pretty face of the town.

"All along I'm thinking the ride'll be done in just a few minutes, you know, like *Lord give me strength*. We rolled into town and buddy's like, 'Hey, I need my shoes b'fore you drop me.' I'm thinking, *when did I become a wino chauffeur?* But he pointed just past the stop sign, up the street a ways to a house with a sign that said *Mobile Cobbler*. Just then, I felt guilty about everything, about having a car, enough food, going to school, being young, everything, and I parked in the cobbler's lot and watched buddy stagger inside. Once he was out of sight, I started to laugh, and I mean howl."

"Did you leave him?" Darren asked as he moved pancake bits around his plate without eating.

"No, like I said, I felt guilty, but it was still funny. He came out with his shoes in a grocery bag and flopped back into the car. He looks at me and says, 'One more stop b'fore I go back.' I'm like what in the hell? 'Don't got no beers left,' he says. I'm thinking maybe I should pull over and kick Captain Stinky out of my car, like, he's worn out his welcome or sympathy, or whatever, but you know what I did?"

Terry and Morgan both grinned and shook their heads.

"I drove his ass to the store. He came out with four of those liter cans of ten percent sludge beer with the German name, Faxe."

"Think that's Danish," Terry said.

"Then what?" Morgan asked, smacking around some syrup and pancake.

"Nothing, that's it. I took him up the hill and came back here.

"I guess I emptied the ashtray and air-freshenered the hell out of my car. Still reeks." Phil shoveled two folded and dry pancakes into his mouth.

"You ever see that guy growing up?" Morgan asked Darren.

Darren didn't answer as he pushed his breakfast around on his plate, eyes glued to the motion.

"You know the wino, red face, like he's got a permanent sunburn. Used to wear denim head to foot, smokes, sometimes walked around looking for change on the sidewalk," Phil spoke around the mouthful. "In a suit nowadays."

Darren remained silent.

"Hey, wake up." Terry nudged Darren.

Darren kept his head down. "Huh?"

"Well, you ever see him?" Terry said.

Darren looked at Phil. "Yeah," he said and looked back down at his plate, loaded his fork with hash browns. "Next time you see him, just drive past. Dad hasn't been the same since he died."

THE CLUB

(2017)

"The first rule of the Chuck Club is you don't talk about Chuck Club. The second rule of the Chuck Club...?" The voice was high. A whine echoed, trailing through the grimy barnyard basement.

Six boys replied the second rule, words stolen and remodeled under the light cast down by their lord, Chuck Palahniuk.

—

Ellen walked...well, no, not any longer. Ellen waddled to the can. It was after nine and Bobby hadn't returned. She wished he'd stay home more often. Cats weren't the same as people, and since she'd put on big pounds, she'd become a pariah. Loneliness made her bored. Lately, bored made her think too much about food.

The doctor had used the phrase *even out* so often that Ellen wondered if he cared at all. One hundred twelve pounds in the last six months. The exercises, the diet changes, the prescription pills, none of it worked.

Give the new medication a chance to even out, bring your metabolism back into check, the doctor had said.

What did he know?

Nothing, apparently.

Dammit! Her body was out of control and she was too grey to imagine lasting long packing on multiple digits every week. Five-three, one pound shy of three hundred, how did it happen?

There'd been a boyfriend, a job, a figure that hadn't demanded that she lift flesh folds to wash pasty nooks or grime-fouled crannies. How does a middle-aged woman get so fat so quickly?

Ellen rose from the can, flushed, and then stepped onto the

scale. Three-oh-one. Two more pounds since breakfast! How? All she'd eaten were a bag of rice cakes and the diet bars Bobby made for her. And these were the doctor's recipe and tasted something awful.

Tears rolled rounded cheeks, over the spider web explosions of burst capillaries, traversing the mysterious yellowy bruises. It was better to sleep than to face the mysterious misery.

Three little pills popped, Ellen climbed into bed.

—

A door slammed and hushed voices scolded. Ellen opened her eyes, sleep-aid groggy. It was dark. She glanced at the clock, after 4:00 AM.

"Bobby?" Ellen called out, feeling like a turtle trying to work a shell. "Bobby, that you?"

"Dammit, you woke her up," said one of the whisperers.

"Bobby?"

Bobby was thirteen and he'd been trouble for a little while. He'd become anti-social to everyone but to those of his little group of friends. They all wore black. They had shaved their heads to whiskers. They always went quiet whenever Ellen entered the room, back when she was more mobile and could almost sneak up on them.

They always stared at her with eyes she could not read.

They always carried around that stupid book like it was the Bible.

"Yeah, Mom," Bobby said in full volume.

"Who's out there with you?"

The door to her bedroom creaked open and Ellen peered through the darkness at Bobby and his friends standing in the lit hallway. They wore painter's coveralls and rubber boots.

"Bobby?" Ellen wondered if the night dope had her reality out of focus.

"Sorry, Mom, but we gotta do this," he whispered. "You're helping to make a better world."

—

Bobby was the eldest of the group and had to stay strong. In the basement of the barn, beneath the blown-up headshot of Chuck Palahniuk, the warm Ziploc bags of Ellen's fat rested in a pile atop the fat gathered from Gabe's grandmother. They hadn't had to kill Gabe's grandmother to get the fat, just had to dig her up, poke holes in the old skin, and suck it out with jumbo straws stolen from 7-Eleven.

It was gross.

It was very salty.

It was a sacrifice that needed done.

It was a step toward a brighter world where banks didn't come to steal homes, where folks didn't lose jobs because labor was cheaper in Mexico, and where the Scrooged-up summation of what granddaddy saved didn't mold everyone's future.

That book was so good. The movie was maybe even better. It was gospel. It was what the world needed from the youth. It was a pain that the women of farming communities didn't get liposuction.

Too bad.

"How's your mom coming along?" Bobby asked.

Gary, a boy with two black eyes, too small to stand a chance when they fought, kicked at the ancient cow shit underfoot.

"Gary?"

"Slow, she won't eat the bars...but I been feeding my little sister and she's... Soon she'll be real big."

Bobby nodded. "If it ain't one, it'll work with another. Praise the lord, praise Chuck P. and his *Fight Club* gospel."

THAT SMILE

(2015)

If I could turn back time, I would find a way...sometimes I hum that tune, sometimes other things. Tunes an infinite distance away, possibly right next-door. I have no way of knowing. A distance close or far that doesn't matter, like a wall or dome, so high, so deep, I can't climb, I can't dig; *Ain't no mountain high enough, ain't no valley low enough*...another tune I know.

If there's a way out, I can't find it. If I could, I would stop thinking about home. I remember so many things, the differences brighten my memory, the contrast from the here and now to the there and then bring dark clouds.

A Saturday in autumn, the oranges and browns littered the green grass below like freckles on a cheek. I hated autumn. It always meant winter was coming and that I had to wear a jacket. And now, I miss it like you can't believe, don't know any tunes about missing something like a season. I never was a fan of folk or country.

I'm forever reaching for the dials, turn back the clock of my existence and warn my curious past-self.

I was a popular man. Often I wonder what people said about my disappearance, if they missed me. Other times I wonder if hours pass at all between the there and the here. Maybe I'm stuck, aging while my old home moves like molasses through the eye of a needle, never registering my absence. Anything is possible and I know that now.

Because I've seen this place.

This strange place, dusty and cool. The plant life soaks up the liquid until reaching a consistency like sponge; pinks and purples instead of greens and browns. I call it water and I call them plants because they keep me alive; I eat the wet leaves, they taste strange. Nothing tastes like chicken, not even the crawling things or the flying things. Nothing swims. The rain is an off-blue grey.

I guess it's a miracle that this place can sustain me. I'm the only one, me and the bits of debris I've found from my world. Trash engulfed like me, left to waste. It gives me some hope. Garbage keeps me from suicide.

I need to find that spot where I crashed through, but it was as if I fell from a low-flying cloud, like a raindrop and then it was gone. Poof. Leaving me in this place of incommunicable lifeforms.

I've never been one to talk to plants, but I may start.

That last day in my home world, I was a student, I wanted to change my major, but I had only one semester until graduation, so I thought I'd best stick it out. I think if I'd just followed my heart, if I'd done one thing differently, I wouldn't have seen that girl. Hell, if I'd spilled jam on my shirt at breakfast, missed the bus, or watched a video on YouTube that girl would've remained an unsought mystery.

It's always a girl, isn't it?

I saw her and she saw me. She smiled, and I pulled that cord overhead and the bus screeched to a halt. If I hadn't paused, I might've gotten to her before she left, but I stalled and had to rush up the street to catch her.

If I'd known her name, the air and everyone in the vicinity would've heard me. My lungs would've been the bellows of an instantly lovesick, puppy dog heart.

She jogged up the museum steps, a place I'd been a few times before. I chased, paid the toll, and then ran about the hallways of hanging masterpieces and sculpted wonders. After some time, ignoring the beauty around me, I caught a glimpse of her red jacket; she moved to an area designated for employees, beyond the boring still life paintings.

Now, I would marvel to see anything created by another body. Fruits, the shadows left behind by eaten fruits, the brushes painting those shadows.

If I'd just taken heed of that sign: EMPLOYEES ONLY. Through the door, I chased into a long hallway of locked doors, I turned four knobs before I found one that opened. It was a bright room and I sensed a presence. I thought I'd caught up, I'd tell the story, we'd go out for coffee after her shift, maybe a drink, she'd tell me about her last boyfriend, that lug, and we'd kiss.

I called out a half-whispered, *hello*, as I stepped around wooden crates. Some new exhibit. I didn't care what it was, just stuff between the girl and me.

I called out again, *anybody here*. No answer. I thought maybe I'd chosen the wrong room, but then I heard a noise and stepped around a massive crate.

Splintered wood littered the floor. A black egg sat amid shipping straw. It shimmered. I moved closer. My hand lifted and I don't understand why I touched that damned egg. At my chilled finger's contact, the egg cracked open. A blue and yellow yoke spilled out, I backed away; I'd broken some ancient artifact after all.

The yoke chased and grew. The worry of financial retribution fleeted as I backpedaled and tripped over a smaller crate. The yoke leapt like a net and consumed me. My bones shifted and remolded at the yoke's design. I tried to scream, but it oozed down my throat.

And then came the rush. My blood burst into a trillion little firework displays, everything from within found a way out and I evaporated. It's the best I can describe the feeling. I'd become a mist amid the yoke and together we moved back to the egg. A crack echoed—I assume it was actually an un-crack—and then I fell like rain from a cloud, back into my shape, back into me.

If it was at all possible to return, I'd live my life, I'd follow my heart, but I'd check the signs, literal and metaphoric alike, I'd change my major, I'd take a nice smile from a pretty girl and let it be that. But I can't and here I am, somewhere else. The only hope I have remains a stinking reminder of what put me into this mess...but then again, maybe it wouldn't be so bad.

She, the smiling girl, she could step into that room and touch the egg, join me amid the oddity of this new frontier. I would like to see her smile again.

FELINE FEEL

(2015)

The high tune bounced and echoed up the narrow and lengthy alleyway. Samuel Moore liked to whistle while he did his hourly rounds. It bothered the stray cats some, sure, but it was the lesser of the two evils. The dark silence was spooky, meaning he had to whistle to withstand his fear, as irrational as it was.

Whistling was his mobile safety blanket.

Armed with a four-pound flashlight, pepper spray, and a jackknife—that had only ever come out at lunchtime to deal with pesky packaging—Samuel stepped into the darkness. He headed along into the alleyway, to his left an abandoned building—once used by a chemist or pharmacist of some such sort—and to his right, the creamery plant. The milk came onto the lot in long silver tubes trailing behind Freightliners, Macks, Volvos, and BMWs.

Sometimes he quietly wished that there were cows on the lot. A silly thought, and the stink... Still, it would've been nice for the general ambiance. Known beasts making sounds instead of terrifying mysteries.

His job was to watch the creamery for vandals and, as he found out on his first day, it was the feline persuasion that caused most of the damage. He also discovered 99 out of 100 times that mysterious rustling was a cat on the prowl for a treat.

He liked cats and it was a bit of a struggle, both internally and externally, to keep them away. Most camped out in the empty building next door and fed off the milky spillage running into the grates of the back parking lot.

Samuel whistled along with his quickened pace, through the

tight space and then to the front of the building. "All's well," he whispered to the night, taking a few deep breaths to bring his fear into check.

That alleyway had manifested into a thing of nightmares. He'd dreamed that he'd become trapped, forever running in the dark on a never-ending path. Other times he dreamed that he'd lost his light and shrouded figures approached from behind. Sometimes he dreamed that he was still at work, found himself standing in his closet, monitoring it like it was the creamery.

Those were the worst ones.

The front of the building was the face, the show, bright lights bounced from the signs overhead and onto the general population entryway. Moran More Milk—MMM, as in *mmm*— was one of the final parts remaining to a world gone by. Businesses came and went, MMM stuck it out, made it big offering *100% Nut-Free* treats for all occasions before it was common to do so.

Samuel walked slower at the front of the building, it had exactly zero creeps and sometimes a car drove by and gave him something to think about.

It was just after two in the morning, so no cars. He rounded to the side of the building. There was a parking lot with three yard lights and numerous places to hide. Nooks, crannies, and corners that avoided the shine.

There weren't many reasons that a person would come at night and loiter around the lot. During the day, okay, maybe, but at night? No cars to break into. No scores to settle.

But those cats, yes siree bob.

It lightened his steps to know he wouldn't go back down the alleyway for another hour. Like clockwork, every hour, he'd make his rounds of the building. He had monitors to watch the cameras and still had to go out. There were things in the night that a camera didn't see. Plus, cameras didn't react, they couldn't shoo away hungry cats.

"Nothing new on the western fr—"

A metallic crash rattled out from behind the abandoned building. Samuel pointed his light.

"Someone there?"

He approached, readied his lips to whistle, afraid, but doing a good job of hiding it. It felt like such a poor career choice given how squeamish he was about the night. Not that he had a choice. Times were tough and none of the comic book stores had an opening.

Never did.

As he got closer, he heard more sounds, tinny and then guttural, his tension eased. He let his whistle die. It was a catfight and everyone liked a catfight—curiosity being stronger than fear.

He shined the light around some old garbage cans. Two massive tomcats, on their haunches, matted and filthy fur ruffed up around their necks, ears back, mouths open, hissing. One swatted the other and then glanced toward the flashlight and tore away.

"Aw, don't run on account of me." Samuel huffed, gave it a second, and turned. He then saw those vibrant green eyes. "Well, hello." He bent down.

Tiny, perhaps a couple pounds, a bright white kitten sat alone quietly watching Samuel. The kitten lifted its chin to the finger and Samuel petted the soft fur. It seemed awfully clean for an alley cat.

The kitten's face scrunched and it bit down on Samuel's finger.

"Ouch, you little..." He stuck his finger into his mouth.

The kitten shook and its green eyes flared like fireworks on the night's sky just before it sneezed and exploded into a cloud of fluorescent green light. Samuel fell back, startled, the kitten debris covered his body like a bank vault blast pack. Disgusted, surprised, confused, he cried out, wiping away until he recognized that it did no real good.

His clothes were glowing. His finger was still bleeding. He thought about the pharmaceutical remnants possibly still behind the walls of the abandoned building and gulped away an irrational fear.

"What the...? How the...?" he rambled. The connections refused rational contact. "Maybe like *Peter Parker* and the spider...or like *Catwoman*, the Michele Pfeiffer version anyway. What if I...?"

He envisioned himself in a latex dominatrix outfit, long claws, pointed ears, leaping from rooftops. It wasn't a good look for him. He shook his head and rose.

"More like Spiderman," he mumbled.

The key clicked tumblers of the backdoor of the creamery and Samuel resumed whistling. The inside of the building was unsettlingly bright.

He yawned, figured he'd best wash out the cut and brush off the uniform. He took three steps and yawned again, he decided he'd have his third cup of coffee a little earlier than usual.

He washed, brushed, grabbed a coffee from the machine, and returned to his post.

"Man," he said after another yawn, a tear settling near his nose.

The coffee was oddly bitter, not enough cream, though the color was right. After chugging back half the cup, he set it down and picked up the paper, the lifestyle, entertainment, sports, and classifieds all spilled to the floor.

"Dammit."

He leaned off his chair and crawled under the desk to pick up the mess. The next yawn was the widest yet. Suddenly, the newspaper looked like a pillow and the atmosphere under the desk seemed like the presidential suite. With a stretch and then curl, he let his head drop as he balled up.

—

The sound of a door opening startled him and he shot from

beneath the desk, grabbing at the paper as he went.

"Oh, there you are. Quiet night?" Molly asked. She was the daytime security attendant.

Samuel couldn't believe it. He'd slept through most of his shift. He blinked away a lost night and nodded.

"Sure."

"See you tonight then?"

His name was on the schedule. He nodded, folding the paper back into place. An uneasiness overtook him and he rushed away, the brightness outside gave him a headache and he thought if he didn't feel better later he would have to call in sick.

Samuel lived three blocks from MMM.

—

"Morning, son," Toby Moore said, already seated, dipping the corner of his toast into the runny yolk on his plate.

"Mom. Dad," Samuel said, then yawned.

Dini Moore set a plate of eggs, sausage, toast, and hash browns on the table, before returning to the stove to fix her own plate.

"Good night at work?" she asked.

Samuel munched back a sausage in two bites, famished.

"Yeah, I saw two toms go at it."

Toby grunted and Dini started into a story that her friend Patty told her about Sue Ellen down the block. "Her daughter's back from college, you know. Not so pretty, but single and she looks to have good hips—"

Toby laughed.

Samuel grunted. He wasn't listening to her much, didn't give a rat's about so-called childbearing hips. He started into his food. The coffee was finally ready to burst, an immediate need pounding at the gates like the Mongols.

He finished his toast and ran.

Piss stream flowing, he moaned his appreciation.

"What in the hell are you doing?" Toby asked from the back

door.

"Taking a pee, what do you think?"

"In the old sandbox?"

Samuel looked around, his bare feet in the box where he used to play. Something was wrong because peeing in the box felt right.

"Guess so," he said, finished off, shook, and zipped.

"Were you drinking on your shift?"

"No, I'm...I'm just feeling a touch iffy. I think I just need some sleep," he said, kicking his feet behind him to cover the urine puddle. He stretched and shifted achy muscles, as he headed back inside.

"What'd you do to your finger?" Dini asked as Samuel slunk by, dragging his head along the wall—his hairline had an itch.

Samuel looked down at the bandage.

"Kitten bit me," he said.

"Boy?" his father stood in the doorway, almost in the backyard still. "You all right?"

"What?" Dini said and turned to look at her husband.

"He took a pee in the—Now just what in the hell are you doing?"

Dini jerked her head and gasped.

Samuel had dropped his pants and leaned against the wall with his legs spread. He lifted his eyes and spoke around a tongue paused mid-drag over his scrotum, "What?"

THE SLEEPOVER

(2022)

Lilian lay in bed with her eyes closed, unable to fall back asleep. She threw a frustrated fist into the mattress at her side. From down the hall came the endless, chittering giggles from her daughter and the friend she had sleeping over.

For the first bit, Lilian had had to force herself to stay in bed, not wanting to be a mom who ruined sleepovers—her own mother had been one of those types. But now, these hours later, her brain muddied by exhaustion, she couldn't sleep and had no choice.

She huffed and kicked from bed. She stepped quickly, loudly down the dark hall to her daughter's room. Red light poured out from beneath the door. She reached, her mouth opening to release the locked and loaded demand for quiet, and paused, her hand hovering an inch from the doorknob.

Her daughter had gone to a friend's house for a sleepover. The sleepover was happening across town.

"Why don't you come in, Lilian," said a voice as harsh as a frog's croak from the far side of the door.

THE BURDEN OF BREATH

(2017)

Laps around the evergreens and the Douglas firs, pattering sneakers dance over the browned needles and fallen limbs. Chuckles ride the air like birdsong, suddenly natural as the flies, the breeze, the river rushing a half-mile away. Squeaks and shouts, smiles are wide on candy red lips. Kids being kids with the woods as a backdrop.

This energy seems inexhaustible. The rareness of the world outside the concrete and steel is suddenly everything. It's one of very few places a class outing has designs for such exhaustive action.

These descendants of ape show their roots in a foreign embrace uncannily like home. Arms swinging, stubby legs kicking, students of Ms. First-Year-of-Teaching-I'm-Going-to-Make-a-Difference's class hang from the park signs.

BEAR COUNTY

IF YOU SEE SMOKE CALL...

REDSKY PROVINCIAL PARK

It is a day excursion away from class, away from the scents and the traffic, away from the convenience shops and the high-rising glass towers. A day to visit the slow rocketing browns and greens rising from a floor alive with minute lives.

Drink it in, kids! Doesn't it smell wonderful?

The class answered the teacher's call with the grouped din of freed leaves dancing dryly on the wind, of unshackled beasts finding their congenital state of grace, of digital children discovering a world beyond Wi-Fi.

Don't go far! Stay close to the bus! Remember the buddy

system!

Frenzied heartbeats pound quiet rhythms in juvenile chests.

Please, Jessica, don't throw that! Darren, do I have to put you in time out?

Underfoot, the twigs, gravel, grass, and dirt rumbles, breaking and crumbling. A fetid rot odor blooms and sours the sensation of perfection. The woods make no promises.

The students continue their motion, though slowing. Curiosity demanding eyes. The dirt breaks and the trees split and disintegrate while stones rise and reshape. The first tears fall and the most boisterous of the children make demands.

What? No? No!

The flesh animals have turned silent, even the river's rush is dampened as the world cracks and the rocky grind of mystery breaks apart the happy moment.

Don't! Don't hurt her! You can't!

Pants darken with liquid and screams rain horizontal showers of terror. It is in the air, the universally understood wailing of horror.

The crimson seepage from the teacher's throat is a reminder of the safety in the city, of mommy and daddy, of the notion that scary things lurk in the unknown.

This, of the collapsed trees, the cracked dirt, and the liquefied stone, the slender, long-armed forms rise, cast shadows that stretch unholy figures over the forest. There are so many. The long limbs swish and cut the atmosphere upon aerodynamic rhythms.

Too fast for hope.

Hacked, the children topple like felled lumber.

Those surviving the first strikes screech. Those fallen are quickly to discover that life is not all. Slices and toppling. More children fall until the bawling shrinks to a pair of whimpers.

Free of fleshy reins, the fallen overcome the fear and the pain. Aimlessly through the flora and around the long yellow bus, the fleshless students parade.

Tag! You're it!

Nuh-uh, no touchbacks!

Not all see, not yet.

Twins kneel, heads together, squatting below the bus bumper, cradling one another for a modicum of comfort in the presence of violent endings. Janey. Jilly. Two tear smeared faces beneath frizzy black braids peer with great brown bulbs.

What is it?

Classmates' corpses litter the landscape. And these horrible things...wispy green spider web hair, skin of dried tree bark, eyes black as space, and mouths two feet wide with stalagmite bottoms and stalactite tops. Long sharpened stone fingers drip hot agony like paint tipped from a can.

Scary thing, this, said one of the beings from the woods, waving an arm-like appendage over the carnage like a Vaudevillian crier standing before a tent of oddities. *One of you, happy soon.*

This voice is gruff like chainsaw teeth against asphalt, but the mention of happiness is a slaking friend in dry times.

Janey watches the stone arm set upon an arch of destruction. She squints against the truth. The peaked edge places new weight in Jilly's arms following a warm splash of familial plasma.

Hush, the thing coos. Don't cry. Save those tears, infect the world with possibilities, tell them of the wild things they ought to avoid.

Sticky fluid cascades over Jilly as the heft of sisterly skin and bones made inanimate topples her. From beneath the sudden weight, Jilly watches the things return to the wooded shadows, to the stony outcroppings, beneath the crust, pouring as if fluid back into the greys, browns, and greens of the forest.

The student ghosts keep at the dance, no cares for the living, disinterested in a sad girl clinging to a corpse. Not even Janey minds Jilly any longer. This freedom is infinite.

Alone, gathering memories that she will keep forever, that will mar and determine the path of her existence, Jilly's solitary sobs pervade the quiet wilderness while timid critters eye a lifetime of meals awaiting their visit.

EYE FOR AN EYE

(2022)

That motherfucker raped my daughter and got away with it. I don't even know why we're talking here. Y'all didn't give my daughter justice so I sat and waited all these years and got a little justice myself. Eye for an eye. Rape for a rape. See what I'm saying.

What are normal people supposed to do when the system fails so glaringly? So, yeah, I followed her home. For a whole week I followed her home. She has a keypad lock and never tried to hide the code. It was simple to get into their yard, I mean her parents don't pay attention—her mother's never home and her father's stunned from one too many knocks to the head. Getting into the house was tricky, but not so bad. The bathroom window is usually open. The ladder is the same as their groundskeeper's. I brought it in that second night. And hell, they're so light nowadays. Twenty years ago, ladder that big would weigh sixty pounds. Now? Shit. Gotta say, though, craftsmanship ain't the same.

So, I climbed up and inside, simple. Took no effort at all to find the girl's room. The doors were all open...they have cats. I'm a dog man, but my ex-wife had cats, doors always had to be open or you get skritch-skritch-skritch all fucking night.

The girl's room was dark and smelled like spray deodorant. The one corner next to the closet is full dark and I stood there, watching her, listening to her fart and send text messages, that glow on her face blinding her to my presence. I don't know how kids these days get a wink of sleep, fucking phones always right there.

One night, after I'd been there awhile, she sits up and goes, Who's there? She fumbles with her phone long enough for me to slink into her closet. The flash on her phone lit. A bit of me wanted to come out, but her fear man, it was part of the retribution. That fear was honey nut on my Cheerios. After a few minutes, she starts going, There's nobody there. There's nobody there. Man, I had to bite my hand to keep from laughing.

Then tonight, when she wasn't scared and went right to sleep, I guess I got a little tired of the game. Having nothing happen was a backstep, so I went forward. I shut her up with the ball gag I bought at Lasting Temptations, seemed expensive, but, man, did it work. The rest was easy and that sonofabitch father got what he deserved.

The detectives sit wordless, as if waiting for further confessions. When none come and the self-righteous man simply sits back grinning, the bigger of the detectives tells the smaller, Grab the thumb drive connected to the Booth case and your laptop.

What's this then. They have security cameras in the house? I just confessed, but it's justice. It's what had to happen because y'all can't do your job when it's some fancy rich kid who done a crime.

The other detective returns, loading a video from the thumb drive as he walks. He sits the computer on the desk at an angle that all three can see before sitting down himself. He hits play.

Fuck is this?

On the screen is video from more than twenty years ago—evidence sticks around much longer thanks to the shrinking of data.

Cynthia?

Cynthia Booth—this man's daughter—is stumbling around drunk at the tail end of a house party, tugging on Bobby Gorman's arm—Bobby Gorman being the victim's father—and she's saying, Just fuck me, Bobby. You can't dump me like this, just fuck me and remember how good I am. Bobby looks at her, disgust written all over his face, and says, I was drunk, it was dark, and I thought you were someone else. I can't dump you because we were never a thing. Bobby wrenches himself away and leaves the camera's view. Cynthia watches him, sneering, and charges the kid holding the camera. Turn that off and let's go to the room, she says. The camera continues recording as Cynthia has sex with the kid and immediately afterward begins punching herself in the face between shots of tequila.

The one detective lifts an eyebrow while the other kills the video.

I'm guessing your daughter never told you why the charges were dropped.

The self-righteous man sits back blinking and thinking, blinking and thinking, and then says, I just made all that up, you know. I was never even there...never even saw that girl.

THE TOWER

(2014)

Each step, slow, methodical, it wouldn't pay to lose grip, slip and fall, tumble down the eighty-nine steps to the floor at the bottom of the ancient tower. The children played games, princesses, princes, heroes, and dragons. It's a tower so what else.

One step at a time, up: 31, 32, 33.

Those childish voices have long ceased. The games are but a memory bouncing around the dusty staircase. Those sounds live in the walls and steps, organisms trapped for all willing to listen, willing to hear.

61, 62, 63.

Two know, outside the walls, children followed the tragedy; hands of purpose choked the life from throat. A classmate, playmate, deadmate.

It was a game until it wasn't. Prince and princess slay the dragon, barehanded they mastered the dragon. It wasn't a game for Tobias, it stopped being a game earlier and he tried to stop the princess, Jessica, she needed to slay that dragon.

77, 78, 79.

Jessica told Tobias that he couldn't tell, or mean men would take him away, take him away from his mommy and daddy; he didn't want that, anything but that. They lived, the world searched, none suspecting that the children had broken into the useless wing of the library to play tower in the attic. There were so many steps up from the basement, where they'd broken that window, that it truly was a tower.

89, through the door, following his little nose, following a promise in the air, a rat joined his brethren to feast on the dragon, feast on the child, feast on Jessica's twin sister Janine.

Didn't she know? Dragons never win.

TOILET MANNERS

(2017)

The stalls rose to a foot from the ceiling. Pine finished to a golden shine, polished with a slick, seemingly wet waxy sheen. The floor was of pale granite. The toilet paper was luscious two-ply.

Wade felt as if he could spend half the night in there.

He'd lowered his pants to appear a reasonable patron making likely use of the can instead of what he was: an emotionally wrought mess, killing time.

Wade was a capricious sort when it came to thinking about his spot in the world. Sometimes he was man, awaiting the moment to bring the wrath. Other times he was uncaring, not a trouble, to hell with the stressors of life. Mostly, he was a sad sack, paying full attention to self-abasing thoughts and twisted memories.

Délices Rares was the fanciest place he'd ever been and it made him sick. Being there, not the restaurant with its fine scents and sweet wine. It was either that his wife, Gabriela, did not recognize facts or that she just did not care. It began two years earlier and at first, it was for the good. Gabriela, a physiotherapist, worked alone besides her clients, but on the whole, was employed by the province alongside a list of other physiotherapists.

Jamie, a physiotherapist from the mainland, met Gabriela at a conference. They gelled and Wade was happy that his wife had another friend. She needed friends. Wade himself was a loner and mostly fine with the fact or at least, felt resigned to the fact.

A month after the conference, Jamie invited Gabriela on a campout with a few of the *girls*. Wade wished her well and ate a pizza from the freezer, as when he didn't have to cook for two, he didn't feel very much like cooking.

The afternoon following, Gabriela came home excited and red-faced. The *girls* had gone skinny-dipping, like teenagers. They had drinks and told stories. Jamie did Gabriela's toes in pink by lantern light within the canvas of their shared tent.

Stopping abruptly from her tale, Gabriela demanded sex.

It had been a few weeks—the norm—and if camping out put Gabriela in the mood, that was just fine. Hell, he'd schedule the next outing himself.

The sex was dutiful. Two people mashing together toward mutual fluid release, as it always had been.

After slipping off to the can attached to their bedroom and then returning to retrieve their clothing, Wade finally asked if Jamie had a husband.

"Oh, no, she's a lesbian...single either way."

A slow clock worked in the back of his head. On the toilet in the fancy restaurant where his wife, her girlfriend, and another couple sat awaiting apértifs, Wade pondered whether or not it was cuckold if the sexual intruder was another woman.

The restroom door wheezed and Wade listened to squeaky wet steps cross the floor and stop before his stall door. A wide shadow fell and then the figure opened the stall door to Wade's left.

Wade had a sudden pang of embarrassed fear. Bad things happened in toilets. "In fine dining toilets?" he whispered and made dutiful sounds with the toilet paper rolls.

The swishy steps next-door sounded strangely wide, short, barely lifting.

Go away. Go away, Wade thought. Be a spring snowflake and melt, let me alone.

The movement changed directive and Wade imagined an enormous fat man, an old man with a wobbly gait, a small boy with his pants around his ankles holding onto his undies to fight the need until the porcelain bowl was safely beneath him. No matter the make or model of humanity, Wade's private self-commiseration was no longer possible.

He stood, flushed for effect, and lifted his pants, facing the stall wall he shared with the other patron. In the short gap below the partition, a milk crate slid and banged against the finely finished wood. Wade had his hands on his shirttails, tucking them in, but stopped, curious about the movement. The toilet paper roll tink-tinked and swung on a screw sideways, revealing a shadowy hole. The hole was just about big enough for a...

"Holy shit," Wade whispered, his heart pounding, terrified by the connotation.

"Hey, you put something through, and I'll put my mouth on it," a soft voice said, deep. Lips sounding wet, as if salivating while speaking.

"What? No, I'm not gay," Wade said, heart fluttering, pants filling with the notion of a mysterious blowjob, of a tit-for-tat, of working toward evening the field. "I'm sorry."

Tit-for-tat...

There had been tickets for the Canucks and then there weren't. Wade was to meet an old friend in Vancouver to catch up. Walter, one of three men who'd acted as groomsmen about a million years earlier. He called just before Wade made it past the outskirts of town and to the highway. He'd gotten a message from his wife, from the doctor's office. Sad, scary, all-encompassing news.

Wade rushed home, feeling terrible, only to find his wife and her lover in bed in what the kids in high school used to call *scissor action*. Rather than speak up, Wade backed out of the room and drove to the city. He parked at the north end and rode the SkyTrain for four hours before returning to his car and then home. Gabriela was on the couch next to Jamie, they smiled and giggled, made girly jokes. Wade's cowardice at the face of unwelcome change had paralyzed his tongue.

As of lately, Gabriela visited Jamie two nights a week,

sleepovers, *you know the ferry schedule, what a pain in the ass!*

"What's gay about some head?"

"No, but... It's the men's room and..."

"Look, you can't see me. I can be anything you want. Come on, I'm quite skilled."

An image of Gabriela lapping at Jamie as if a dog at a water dish flashed and, to his shock and giddy nervous energy, he let his pants fall. His penis tented the front of his shorts. The shorts followed his pants while his hands held shirttails aside.

"I can't believe I'm doing this... Is it even clean? Are you even clea—? Oh god, yes..." his voice trailed in ecstasy.

A new fantasy played over his mind, Gabriela, hog-tied, tears running. He held a gun to Jamie's head while she slurped and sucked. It was horrible, disgusting, and all too erotic.

The mouth working his manhood received a quick splash and continued, on and on until Wade felt drained, his penis quickly softening.

"I know you're straight," the voice said after a loud swallow, "but, maybe you can suck, just a little. Even just the tip, rim it some, maybe?"

Surprising himself, feeling so good and thankful, Wade replied, "Just a little."

"That's what I like to hear."

Both sides adjusted, the milk crate slid away while Wade dropped to his knees, eyes closed, a parade of butterflies in his guts.

Are you really going to suck cock! Gabriela of his self-conscious, self-abasing scenarios asked.

Sure, what's it to you? he thought back. It's a new world, nothing to be ashamed of!

"You still there?" the voice asked.

Wade reached up and grabbed the semi-ridged shaft, extended his tongue to the tip, his mind filling in blanks where his eyes refused to see. It was odd. The head was concave at the center and the ridge of the head sloped like a megaphone.

You're licking an uncircumcised penis.

It was a shock. He expected the penis to be like his own. The intrigue and fun flooded away, slipping down the floor drain of that fine restaurant.

His eyes opened as he said, "I'm sorry. I can't—What the hell?" Wade leapt back against the opposite dividing wall.

The thing before him, poking through the hole was ghostly whitish yellow, six inches long, and definitely not a penis. On the floor where the milk crate had sat was a globular form, fat and the same ivory shade as the...

Tentacle? Antenna?

"Oh Christ! Oh Christ!"

"Quiet! They'll hear, now do what you're told. Trust me, you don't want me over there."

Wade clicked the latch and swung open the wonderfully finished stall door. The stall door next-door squeaked open as well.

"Your mouth or your nethers," the deep voice said, no longer smooth. "Makes no difference to me and it's going to happen one way or another."

"That's not right, that's not..." fair. One way or another...Tit-for-tat is better than the alternative.

The stall door squeaked closed and the latch clicked.

"Good boy."

Eyes closed, Wade imagined Gabriela and Jamie holding six-shooter pistols with pearl handles and gold on sterling inlay designs to his head. Laughing, their breath smelling of wine and musky pussy. Their skin aflame with post-coital glow and their hair matted from exertion.

Wade felt a stringy splash at the back of his throat.

"Don't you dare stop!"

He didn't.

Like saltwater chalk. Wade, unthinking beyond a

subconscious level, swallowed and burst out of the stall—the thing next-door sighed—straightening his attire as he ran. Wade made it out of the salle de bain in time to pluck the final olive from the dish and spill the last bit of wine from the first décanteur into his glass.

"Did you fall in?" Jamie asked.

"No, there's a glory hole. I was getting a blowjob," Wade said absently. "Then it was my turn, tit-for-tat's all fair, right?"

Laughs all around.

The waiter returned. "Excuse me, we have now located the misplaced entrée and it shall be out momentarily. More sauvignon blanc?"

"Yes, yes," Roger Washington said—one of the couple Gabriela knew from some committee or another. "Best bring two, unless something accents la limace? Bring what suits. How did you misplace an entrée?"

The waiter shrugged. "Big, busy kitchen. I know the very wine for the delicacy," he said and then departed.

Wade drank the wine and then his water, light-headed and confused. Feeling filthy. Zoning away. Abashed, he felt the heat rise within. What he'd done was disgusting, cowardly, insane.

"La limace!" the waiter's voice echoed over the table conversation and Wade drifted from his reverie. Two men set a silver platter on the table and lifted the domed cover to reveal an enormous ivory slug. "The tentacle is said to hold aphrodisiac powers." The waiter grinned at Roger and then at Wade. "And with some," the waiter spied the women, lifting his brows, "a calcium deposit solidifies in the heat of the pot and becomes a precious pearl."

Wade stared at the two-foot slug, boiled now. He felt a sickness rising, a wave of slug ejaculate inching up his throat. He went green.

"Wade, you feeling all right?" Gabriela asked.

"Little slug make you sicky?" Jamie mocked.

Wade dry-heaved.

"Uh-oh," Jasmine Washington said from behind a palm.

Wade lurched again. And again. And once more. Wine, olives, and a single white pearl splashed down onto his plate. The bead pinged against the china and rolled with the puddled ooze onto the fine white linen.

COATTAIL

(2015)

Leonard rolled from beneath the thin sheet atop his bed. He hadn't slept much the night before, so when he heard Tabitha's excitement fill the home like audible smoke, he jerked upright, knowing, just knowing, something horrible had happened.

"Another one! Leo, he got another one!" she shouted. "Oh goodness me!"

She stood in front of the television in the living room. Aghast. Leonard found her with her hands in front of her chest as if ready for prayer, *just say the word*, knees slightly bent, mouth wide and eyes wider. The voice on the television explained the ninth murder in three weeks and the shortest waiting period since the first three days when the sniper took four innocent lives.

"Oh hun." Leonard held Tabitha tight to his chest and rubbed her back. Helpless against exhaustion, he yawned.

"Why does the Lord allow it?" she moaned.

She'd become a shut in, and for the first time since leaving, she felt that her babies in college were safer away from their mother.

"How about I make us a breakfast treat? I bought some of that special bacon. It was on sale and—"

"Look, look! It could've been you!" she screamed pointing at the photos on the screen, the familiar scene. It was the Super Save just blocks from their home. The exact place Leonard did the grocery shopping. "You didn't see any of this last night?"

"I guess I just missed it," he said.

"Oh my gosh, Clyde Syl. You know him, don't you?"

Leonard squeezed Tabitha tighter and groaned.

"That's the guy, right? You knew him from high school?"

Leonard nodded without speaking. A rusty dagger slashed every time that name came to ear. Those horrid memories clinging fast.

Tabitha felt Leonard's body break out into tiny shakes. She knew those shakes; she'd bawled over the close calls, enough to recognize a pig in a sty. "Here. Here," she said, rubbing his bicep.

The voice on the television said several witnesses spotted a white truck leaving the scene, and given the nature of the assault, it was obvious that the sniper struck again. Damned white truck seemed everywhere, like a ghost.

"Okay. Okay now," Tabitha said, cooing the shaking man in her arms. Usually it was Leonard's task to calm her and it was about time he let these murders get to him. "I'll go make coffee and pancakes, and that bacon." She backed him to the couch. He dropped. "They'll get this sonofagun soon enough."

She knew this sniper thing must hit her husband especially hard, being the principal of a school. The sniper had an undiscerning manner. He pegged off victims young and old without reason. How could it not hit hard when Leonard had so many community ties? The next kid could be one of Leonard's students. A little Mike or Jennifer, a hole through their head. *Lord!*

"Soon enough," she said again as she left the living room.

Leonard nodded to her words, his face in his palms. He waited a tick and a tock, waited until he knew she was gone. He let his hands fall and the smile spill. The shaking laughter overflowed and he let it. It felt good to laugh.

"How do you like that, Clyde, you prick?" he asked the television showing the body beneath a white sheet. "Teach ya, don't it?"

31 years earlier, Clyde Syl and Leonard Hammond attended the one and only high school in Bonny, Michigan. Leonard had

his best and first love with a girl named Loretta Tolkers. They were like a two-piece puzzle until a week before graduation when Loretta admitted to taking a liking for a boy named Clyde Syl. A boy she said knew what to do and wasn't so shy about making a move. A boy who would touch her in all the ways Leonard couldn't figure.

Leonard burned at this. He'd tried to make it with Loretta a dozen times and she always pushed him off. Something he'd respectfully accepted. Prom night was going to change everything. He had the room and the flowers and the special condoms he bought, embarrassingly, from the drug store.

That girl broke his heart and Clyde Syl danced on the blackened remains.

It was a pain that wouldn't go away.

Then the answer came.

A sniper ran around the great state of Michigan, ticking away lives with no reason beyond statistics. *More gonna die!* explained the note written on the back of a playing card left behind at the scene. The eighth assassination occurred in the small town of Blissfield just a hop and a skip up Interstate 223.

It was so close and so damned scary. The terror sparked the idea in Leonard. The perfect answer to the question he'd pondered for more than three decades.

The reports were always a bit scattered and in every parking lot there was a white truck. He didn't bother with a note and figured the real sniper wouldn't mind. He'd step up and pinch-hit a terrifying homerun, but hand the credit off to the man who wanted it. Just a misplaced RBI on the scorecard, that's all.

Leonard would never tell a soul. Never admit that pulling that trigger felt so damned good, almost as good as when Clyde Syl grinned at him until he saw the rifle. Sure, that didn't match the modus operandi of the real deal sniper that pegged heads at 50, hell, 100 feet. It didn't matter. The cops wouldn't look into it.

For a moment, Leonard saw Clyde Syl in his tuxedo again,

frilly white ruffles, Loretta on his arm. It was better than sex. Better yet, Loretta Syl could go back to being Tolkers.

"How many pieces of bacon?" Tabitha asked from the kitchen.

Leonard settled his smile and put aside the laughter for later, and answered his unsuspecting wife, "Better just one. Doc says you only get so many chances before it's too late. Best not press my luck."

"To hell with the doctor. There's a sniper and food gives us comfort. Besides, those kids'll need a smiling principal to show them everything's all right. Best way I know to raise a smile is with some sinful eating."

Through the little house, Leonard followed his nose and his ears.

"You're a good woman," he said.

"And you're a wonderful man." She forced a smile, hoping he bought all that surprise. As if she didn't know that old flame flickered and that old pain drove him mad. "Sit and eat."

He nodded.

She turned back to the stove and sneered, knowing Loretta Syl—née Tolkiers—might just be next up on the sniper's list.

HEROIC OFFERING

(2015)

Organ donors are heroes, that's what it said at the bottom of my renewal form. I read it dozens of times while I waited in the DMV line. People always complain about the DMV lines, but on that day, the line moved with speed and grace until back-to-back-to-back grandmothers got to the windows and started yelling—the halt, no fault of the helpful folks behind the glass. The lunchtime crowd groaned in stalemate and I fidgeted with my papers.

I'd checked all the boxes next to the organ donor questions. *Organ donors are heroes*, I read it again and beneath the suggestive hero-line, there were instructions as to where to find the fine print about organ donation. Instead of locating the fine print, I jumped back to the top of the sheet. Big print, all caps, *ORGAN DONORS ARE HEROES.*

I always assumed I'd be too dead to care about my giblets and entrails anyway. It never seemed so heroic to check a box and let doctor's harvest for the greater good.

Organ donors are heroes, sure are.

A week after the DMV visit, I forgot all about my heroic forethought and went on the strangest first date of my short life. 26, I'd had some semi-mature relationships of a serious nature over the years but for whatever reason, to lump onto my parents' disappointment in me, none of them ever moved beyond the *Really* stage (as in, to say, *Really, huh? I'd never have guessed that about you*).

Long before the destructive *Really* stage there's the first date, first date hiking on a mountain trail a first among lifetime first dates. As strange as it was for me, it seemed to fit her, as did her outfit and attitude. Strong, firm, and proportioned for both power and femininity, Sara was an intriguing date. I'd never gone out with a woman that could overpower me without question, but I was game, even excited by the prospect of the new light.

I soon found that the trail wasn't for the inexperienced. Sara grew frustrated and was constantly telling me to keep up. I tried, sweat slickened my entire body as if I'd become a slug; even the soles of my shoes started to sweat.

Team Cameron wasn't up for the task and Team Sara became grouchy and rushed upwards. I told myself that things happen, it's better to know now that things won't work, better than later and yada-yada-yada, but something inside fought against it. I felt my time as an eligible bachelor running short and I wanted to, at very least, give things a valiant effort. *Team Sara, look out, here I come!*

I scanned the rocky landscape upwards and spotted Sara, way up the hill. The ambition to join my date at the top surged and I dropped a handful of quarters into my mental jukebox for a Rocky Balboa power ballad playlist. I imagined myself in a grainy montage pushing my way to the top of the mountain and screaming *Drago!*

I pushed it all right, as hard as my body permitted, I pushed it. I felt good despite the huffing from my mouth and the fat drips pouring from my skin.

"Sara...slow...down...just...a..." I struggled for oxygen.

Sara turned and looked at me with bugged eyes. She opened her mouth to shout, but I didn't hear a word of what she said. I heard tumbling rocks and snapping twigs, I heard my voice, and then I heard the echo of my scream. The trail dropped away; I saw a stream of grey rock face as I dropped the forty feet. The world disappeared.

I awoke and that seemed impossible. I remembered the thump and the rocks, Sara's face; that fall deadly on anyone's account, but there I was, eyes open staring at steel beams running along a whitewashed ceiling. I croaked out a call, but it hardly sounded over the strange beeping machine. I listened, it didn't ping along to a heartbeat like the ones on television, it chattered mechanically and the harder I thought, the more it chattered its electronic language.

"Hello," I wheezed again. I tried to move my arms, feel for something, but I felt nothing. "Please, help me," I tried again; a little louder. I begged with an unfamiliar voice not really mine. The idea made me feel detached; I was paralysed and panic set in. I turned my gaze downward, couldn't see my nose or my cheeks. Paralysed, and my eyes refused long movement. I saw different bits of the room, but I didn't feel my eyes. Never in my life had I wanted to squirm as badly as I did then. I screamed out and heard my voice, but it was distant.

I called out again and again until I heard a door open. "Cameron Honan, can you hear me?" a voice asked.

I screamed out a string of nonsense, though meant to say *yes*.

"Whoa, easy now," said the voice. I didn't feel his hands on me and I didn't feel the bed move, but my gaze shifted and I looked out at a white room with two brown leather chairs and a young man in a lab coat. "There's no need to yell. How are you feeling? According to your chart you took a tumble."

"I feel...I don't feel anything at all," I said. The man laughed. I heard the electronic chatter, but quietly. "I can't believe I'm not dead. Am I paralyzed? Will I make it? Am I a talking vegetable, tell me, tell me!"

"Vegetable in a sense, but not for long," said the man, he turned and left the room.

I watched the door close and the panic bubbled again. I told myself I was lucky and that I should be dead. The man said *not for long*, I'd move again, by God I would. I looked around fighting the urge to scream out.

My cheeks and nose continued their avoidance tactic and I freaked out a bit. I looked down again, hard, and saw nothing but blackness. I looked left, right, and back to the ceiling: no eyebrows, no dangling hair, no nothing. I told myself to calm down. *I'm not Eugene Levy, maybe they're just...*

It was then that I realized it wasn't just paralysis, it was facial deformity, skin grafts, prosthetics, a new rubber me that would need a permanent sitter. I felt sick, but not really. Head sick, not body sick.

"Hello! Please!"

The door opened and the man poked his head in. "Quiet, you're making a bad impression." The door slammed shut.

I thought about Sara and then my footing failure and then the DMV; *organ donors are heroes,* it said I was sure someone parceled some of my body, it had to be, it would explain the vacancy. But that didn't make sense, I needed my body.

"Help me!"

"We're here now, just calm down," the door had opened again and the man in the lab coat stepped aside and let a man and a woman into the room.

They were in the first half of their mid-lives, somewhere between thirty and fifty. The woman had her arms folded; she scowled, wearing a gold leather purse with a small golden triangle where I saw the word Prada. The man was fit, younger than she was, but he seemed worried, scared even. They sat and the man in the lab coat said his farewell and left them in the room with me.

"I don't know about this," said the man looking at his shoes.

"Oren, you agreed. You want me happy, don't you?" the woman said, she had the piercing stare of the kind of creature that ate nails.

"What is this?" I asked.

"Ha, I didn't believe it at first!" laughed the woman. "I'm Monica and that's Oren." She said his name as if it bored her to do so. "Tell us about yourself."

"I don't think I want to go..." Oren mumbled.

"You promised, besides, you already signed the form. I'll have you in jail so fast you'll wonder if I have a time machine. So, Cameron, tell me about you."

I looked at her and I didn't know what to say, but I wanted to talk. I wanted them to stay; I needed them to stay, so I started at the ninth grade and moved through the years. For some reason I really wanted to tell her everything. I saw Oren smiling more and more as I let out the story of me as Monica scowled and grimaced. I got to a story about camping when I saw a UFO and about then how I spoke to an alien in a dream.

"They're not like in the movies, you know," I was saying.

"That's the third time you mentioned aliens," Monica said.

"Don't forget Bigfoot!" Oren began cackling.

"So?" I asked.

"I won't have it," Monica said; she stood and stormed from the room.

Oren mouthed the words *thank you* to me and he followed her. It seemed some kind of social psychological treatment; I thought that maybe the man in the lab coat had decided that I needed to work on people skills after the accident. It seemed the only reasonable conclusion at the moment.

I fought the lonely panic by telling myself it was all steps to recovery. I waited for a return, for anybody. There were people beyond my room. I tried to force away the sound of my machine and listen to the voices in the lobby, but I couldn't make out a word. After a while, I gave up. Shortly after that, the lab coat man came back. He smiled at me.

"Aliens and Bigfoot?"

"So, what of them?" I asked, defensive, closed-minded people always irked me. "Please, just give it to me straight."

He shook his head. "Don't worry, it'll be done soon enough, but you may want to keep all the creature feature stuff inside, not exactly first date material."

"First date? I can't feel my body. Where's my body? You harvested me, didn't you? Is this even a certified hospital?"

"Stop yelling. Gone, your good organs went out, saved some lives, bettered some others, you're a hero."

I felt as if I'd just drowned in an ocean of Alice's tears tipped out of the Mad Hatters' teacup. "I need my organs. I can't live without them." I wanted to cry, but I no longer worked like that.

"Nope, you're right. You can't live, not in the normal sense; all that's left is your conscious-self. But in another sense, you're just fine. Don't need organs, or limbs or eyes for that. But soon enough...just keep that weird stuff to yourself and we'll have you a new body lickety-split."

"Where's my body?" I shouted.

"I don't know, the ground, maybe someone burned it. If you checked all the boxes on your donor questionnaire, your body might've gone for med students to chop up. It doesn't really matter, you couldn't use it anyway."

"But..."

The man looked annoyed. "Look, you checked the boxes. People need all kinds of donors." The man looked at his watch and turned to the door. "Remember, keep that stuff to yourself and you'll have legs again."

I watched him go, baffled. I pondered my existence until the door opened again. Another couple came in. The man was dishevelled and rough. The woman was clean and avoiding touching the man at all.

"One question," she said. "Before you died, were you a stupid drunk that chased college girls?"

"I told ya, it didn't mean nothing," the man said, his words slurred and his voice sad.

"I died?"

"Sure, close enough. Well, did you, were you a drunken horn-dog?" she demanded an answer.

"I'm dead... I can't..." Her question registered somewhere and I had an answer to it, one little thing I could grasp, I had an answer. "No, I don't like the taste of—"

"Sold!" she yelled.

The man wailed.

Because I'd checked those boxes on the sheet stapled to my license renewal, a woman saw the world again through my eyeballs, a boy lived to see his tenth birthday with my one salvageable kidney, a man survived an extra year with one of my lungs, and a marriage side-stepped divorce court because of my consciousness.

I live where that wailing man had, I took his name. Seymour Dieter Pound. I feel bad for the real Seymour Dieter Pound and people like him; I doubt anyone wants his conscious-being, but the man in the lab coat assured me that he isn't alone. There's an entire storeroom full of unwanted minds.

"They don't really get along, but they should've read the fine print on their marriage licence before checking the box and signing their name," said the man in the lab coat the day I was inserted into Seymour's body.

I feel like there's a worthwhile lesson in that.

KITE STRINGS

(2015)

"Half a million hits in just two days! We should go back, what if the kite's still there? Maybe we could convince the guide to follow it or something," Amanda Raymond said, brimming with excitement. The husband's turn at selecting their vacation destination finally seemed a good idea. "It's like our fifteen minutes or whatever."

Peter Raymond shrugged, it was all fine by him, he was just glad that he got to see the African wildlife firsthand before pollution and poachers washed it all away; it was also nice that his wife wasn't giving it to him about the trip being the *opposite of relaxing*.

"Great! I'll call the safari people," Amanda said as she retrieved a card from her wallet and then picked up the telephone in their hotel room. It was an old building with mint green everything as if there'd been a flash sale on the paint and the price was just too good to pass up. Amanda's face lightened as she spoke into the matching minty-colored telephone.

Three days earlier, Amanda and Peter joined a safari group and spent the day touring a sunbaked world of dead and dying things. Amanda complained incessantly: too hot, too dry, too boring, and not at all relaxing. Peter was thankful the other vacationers on the safari spoke German or Dutch and the guides didn't care a lick what they whiny woman said so long as her money was good.

That was before they saw the kite, before Amanda took a sudden interest in the African wildlife and she pulled the camera from her pack to shoot a short video.

"Wow," Peter said seeing the subject,

The others of the group remarked much of the same in their native tongues, the guides watched wide-eyed and silent.

"What? Holy cow!" Amanda said, a camera emerging from her purse on a whiplash motion like a gunslinger drawing at high noon.

She shot while others gawked and spoke in short broken blips of wonder. No more than 50 feet from the battered convertible Land Rovers, a massive lion jogged along the dusty golden world. It was graceful and beautiful; a sight in its own right but that wasn't the surprise. They'd seen several lions, most lazing in the sun, but this one jogged and amazed.

A fire engine red kite fluttered 20 feet above the lion, blue tails flowing behind the red; trailing the animal as if the king of the jungle was also king of the timeless playground novelty. Amanda kept focus and a steady hand as she followed the animal's movements. The kite rode high and mostly smoothly in the gentle breeze until it fell from view as the lion stepped into a valley.

"There's room! We've got spots, I just hope, somehow, the lion hasn't gone off. How do you think it got the kite in the first place?" Amanda asked after she cradled the telephone.

"I assume some brave jokester tied the kite to its paw, maybe with a snare trap. Eventually, those fifteen minutes will shift to him I suppose...or her." Peter smiled, he still wanted to see a few more things while on safari vacation, but he'd gladly relive a day to keep Amanda happy. She only liked vacations with musclebound wait staff, sandy beaches, and drinks with umbrellas poking over the brims.

"Ooh, maybe we'll meet the guy... doubt it was a girl, it seems too stupid and dangerous to be a woman tying kites to lion's paws, more of a young man thing to do."

Peter considered defending his sex, but she was right. Something so stupid and so dangerous was likely a young man.

"What time do we head out?"

"Five!" Amanda shouted and flopped down onto the bed. "Get the lights, we need our beauty sleep, big day tomorrow."

Peter did as told.

———

It was hot and it was dry, the same weather it had been every day they'd been on the continent. Amanda and Peter took a taxi to the garage where the guides kept their Rovers. The guides waved from a door at the side of the garage instructing the Raymonds and the others waiting that they'd be just a few more minutes.

A small girl crossed the street. "Excuse me, excuse me. She passed around photocopied flyers.

"Yes, little one?" Amanda asked in the typical condescending nicety she reserved for children and the especially elderly.

"I'm looking for my brother, have you seen him?"

Amanda looked at the flyer. She soaked in the image and decided not; held the flyer so that Peter could take a look.

"No, I don't think so," he said.

"He's been gone three days." The girl sniffled. "It was his birthday and he ran off. He was so excited about his stupid…"

"There, there," Amanda said, patting the girl's shoulder.

"…gift, he's such a baby. If we ever find him, he's in for it. I told Mom we should've got him the trains, but no, nobody ever listens to me. You don't chase around with toy trains!" she huffed. "If you see him, please call the police. It's not safe sometimes and my little brother's strange."

"What was the toy?" Peter asked.

"A stupid kite, red and blue, stupid and he wouldn't let it go for nothing!"

JACQUES

(2019)

"Bro, man, I don't know," Chase said as he looked out the passenger's side window of the lifted Dodge Ram 4X4.

"It's cool, guy. I've been ordering Red-Rage Ultimate right to his house. Told him to forget food and just Rage and pump iron. It's not like he has to work and if he does, it's farm work so it builds muscle anyway," Scooter said from behind the wheel. He slowed and hit the turn blinker, then slowed a little further than normal given the weather.

"What do you mean he don't gotta work?" Chase was still watching the heavy piling of flakes as they fell from the sky—that and his reflection in the window glass as he flexed his neck off and on to make the cords in his throat bulge.

"His parents willed him the farm. Worth like a million bucks, guy."

"Yeah, but that's not liquid. Those assets are tied up, bro. It's become increasingly more difficult for farmers to mortgage properties given the instability of the global markets, and what a guy can grow in this part of the world ain't worth big bucks." Chase flexed his neck again.

"Guy, I don't know about that stuff. How come you know?"

Chase shrugged, was embarrassed about the night courses he took, was thinking of getting into accounting or finances and thought a good groundwork in both would set him up for a good job a few months down the line. He still hadn't told Scooter he wasn't going to take the personal trainer business they'd started to the next level—you get old, then what do you do? No sixty-year-old personal trainers, none he'd ever seen.

The lights of the truck came onto the little farmhouse at the end of the half-mile long laneway. Something was wrong, something...

"Holy cow," Scooter said. "Look at that, guy." He pointed.

Chase shifted his eyes to the windshield and looked at the home with a toppled corner and a collapsed roof. "Bro, what did that, you think?"

The truck slowed around the bend that wound to the parking area of the driveway and toward the barn and sheds.

Scooter opened his mouth, got out the words, "Guy, I don—" before the truck flipped. Glass shattered and steel creaked. "Guy! Guy!" The interior light had come on, though the engine was dead. The truck had flipped onto the driver's side. "Guy! Bro! You okay?" Blood poured onto Scooter as he shouted at the mangled visage dangling by a seatbelt over him. "Guy?" A hunk of steel stuck out of the side of his throat.

A great snort and then an even greater rumbling growl filled the entirety of the frosted landscape. Freezing air poured into the truck. More snorts. More growls.

Scooter began to look around, but from his vantage, he saw very little. He unclicked his own seatbelt. It didn't retract, simply flopped. He punched at the deflating airbag to shrink it.

The snorts and growls were close, too close, coming from the front end of the truck.

He pushed against Scooter's dangling body, avoiding the steady trickle of bloodletting, and said, "Sorry, guy," and climbed into the backseat. The rear window had crunched out of shape and he had to squeeze sideways to climb into the box.

Heavy footfalls joined the steady rumbling growls and Scooter didn't stand a chance. He was airborne, the truck spinning from the impact. He flew 30 feet before landing in a snowbank.

"Scooter. Scooter," a voice whisper-yelled.

Groggy, but awake, Scooter first looked out to the shining

lights of his truck, saw something huge in a flash before the truck clanged and began spinning again, he then looked up the tree a few feet from the snowbank. There was Ned's treehouse, faded and rough, but still standing. The swinging window had been pushed open and light shined through.

"Get up here," that same voice whisper-yelled.

"Ned, guy?"

"Get up here before Jacques sees you!"

"Jacques?" Scooter turned to the spinning truck and then began scurrying over the packed snow mound to the ladder nailed to the thick old spruce. The trip up was a lot shorter than he remembered and his head struck the trapdoor—which was closed until Ned pulled it open. "What the hell is going on, guy?" Scooter said and darted his eyes around the small space. The nude cut-outs they'd pasted when they were pre-teens were gone, but everything else looked the same. Well, aside from the squat steel barrel in the middle of the floor burning twigs. "Guy, what in the hell?"

"Shh! Jacques."

Ned had a sleeping bag wrapped around him, looking like a nerdy caterpillar. He wore too-big glasses, had an enormous forehead that stretched long and skinny like the top of a pencil, and the width of his chest was about fourteen inches across.

"Jacques? Guy, Chase is dead! Who is Jacques?"

Ned said, "Shh, damn you! I've been up here for four days and he hasn't found me yet. Tell me you have your cellphone."

Scooter frowned and then began feeling his pockets, knowing his phone was in the cup holder of the truck. "Who is Jacques?" he said and leaned into the fire to warm his cold, damp hands.

"Jacques is Dad's...the bull."

"The bull?"

"The bull."

"Guy, it destroyed my truck! How does a bull do that?"

"Got the house too. And the barn foundation. And my truck, pushed it right into the creek." Ned pulled a granola bar from somewhere in his sleeping bag and held it out. "You want one?"

"What?"

"It's salted caramel. I got a crate of them from Costco, but I didn't know where to put them, so I stashed them in the driving shed. I grabbed ten boxes last night. Jacques was busy with one of the heifers. He mounted her to death." Ned shook his head.

"You're telling me a cow did this? And we're hiding up here 'cause of a stupid cow?"

Ned put up a finger. "Cow's a girl that's had a calf. Bull's a male with his nuts intact."

"What?"

"Everybody just calls the whole bovine species cows though, so I guess, yeah. It's a cow, sort of."

Scooter vibrated, hands out, wanting to crush something. Steam was rising from his coat where the snow melted and began to heat close to the fire. "What kind of bull—I mean—what the fuck, guy?"

Ned tossed the wrapper from his granola bar onto the fire. "Well, really, this is kind of your fault."

"What?"

"Red-Rage Ultimate, it tastes awful, but there was so much of it and money's been tight after the auction. I just wanted a good start, you know? Like get a couple cows, a couple heifers, and I already had Dad's bull."

Scooter was still moving in disbelief and fury. "Guy, what the fuck are you talking about?"

"The protein powder, I don't know if you should take that stuff, I mean, I've been feeding it to Jacques and it was cool, but he got huge fast and I was—"

"Wait, guy, what?"

Ned shrugged. "Jacques always ate twice as much as any of the others 'cause he was big, and I had so much of that damned powder...so I fed it to him. He got so big so quick, I thought I'd take him around to shows, but his attitude changed. He's crazy."

"You gave the bull all the protein powder I ordered for you? Guy, that shit is expensive!"

Ned frowned. "I never wanted to get big and I never wanted to join your stupid rec' hockey league—there's not even hitting in it!—so I gave the bull some of the powder."

"You thankless little punk," Scooter said, he couldn't believe it. He'd done this great thing for a dweeby little friend and the guy fed the powder to his cow. "You could get real big. You could get the chicks—"

"I already told you!" Ned popped to his feet, legs inside clunky snowmobile boots like flamingo stocks. "I'm not into chicks. I have a fucking boyfriend online and we fucking play Scrabble and Risk with his friends and we all make fun of meatheads. Getting big, Christ, who gives a shit?"

A snort echoed and then footfalls approached. Ned silenced and fell back into his sleeping bag, cocooned himself. They waited and the stamping feet drew closer and then further away and further away. Jacques snorted and it sounded as if he was back over by the barn.

"You never told me you were gay, guy," Scooter said, all the steam out of him.

Ned pouted his bottom lip. "I tried to give you a handjob in high school."

"You were drunk." Scooter shrugged as if to say, *who hasn't helped a bro out?*

Ned turned and opened the window a smidge and looked around for Jacques. "At least he'll run out soon," he said.

"Run out of what, guy?" Scooter had fallen back into the shadows, sitting halfway on the trap door.

"Red-Rage Ultimate. I stored it in the barn and Jacques sniffed it out. Just lucky nothing else found it... You know what?" Ned stood. "I'm not gonna die up here without a fight."

Scooter looked at the puddled sleeping bag and then up to Ned. "Okay."

"I'm gonna make a Molotov cocktail and have us a barbeque."

"You're going to throw and hit something, guy? Tell me where the gas is and stuff and I'll do it twice as fast and twice as good." Scooter flexed his biceps within his puffy jacket—loose as it was, the material still firmed up.

"Oh...all right," Ned said and re-cocooned himself.

—

Jacques wailed as he ran. The sheer size of the bull nearly stunned Scooter into inactivity, but the great snort brought him around. The thing was as wide as a rhino and stood nearly eight-feet tall. Scooter lit the first cocktail, nailed the beast. It kept coming, burning as it ran. He lit the second and had about three heartbeats to throw it. The gasoline found eyeballs and Jacques jerked and jumped like a rodeo bull trying to buck a rider. Scooter turned then and broke for the treehouse.

Ned was up and jumping. "You did it! You did it!"

Scooter climbed the ladder and pushed into the treehouse. Ned went back to the swinging window and looked out. "He's like Ghost Rider," he said, awed.

Scooter stepped over to the window to watch. "Guy, Chase, guy. He's dea—what the hell is that?" He pointed back at the barn. Beneath the moonlight, five shapes scurried, all about the size of Power Wheels cars.

Ned spun and pressed his back to the wall. "Coons. Coons always get into the granary."

"What?" Scooter whispered, thought he heard him wrong, acted as if he hadn't made eye-contact with the biggest of the raccoons.

It chittered, even seemed to point at the treehouse.

"Why did you send that powder? I never wanted to get big," Ned whimpered these words.

Scooter watched Jacques' slowed circles and the masked bandits making for the treehouse. He said, "Guy, I was trying to do you a favor."

JUST A TASTE

(2014)

"Hey," the girl whispered, "what's your name?"

She peered into the shadows cast over the room. Only pinpoints of light shined in from the hallway, around the steel window where rivets had fallen out or had never been installed. She slept on a mat on the dirt floor, her world was the cell. She'd never had a visitor before, and she wasn't about to let this one sit there without saying anything.

"Please talk to me," she begged, her voice sweet and sad.

"You're bad," a voice said, another child, boyish and familiar to the girl.

"Who are you?"

"Why did you do it, Bea?"

"Why did I do what?" she asked, coy.

She knew who it was now. Someone from her life before the cell.

"You know!" the boyish voice blasted from the shadow, just an outline.

"I didn't mean to." Beatrice lowered her head. She knew what she did, but it was an accident. She'd told them so.

"They think I helped you!"

"You didn't and I didn't mean it! It was an accident!"

"I saw you! I saw you and you meant it. They say we're replaceable, they say we don't matter. They say we're monsters! But you, you're the monster, not me!"

"Please, Walter, don't say that. They'll let us out, they have to!"

Walter jumped at Beatrice. "Why? Mom and Dad say they can

get new ones, new ones of us, gooder ones!" His tiny hands dug into his sister's shoulders.

"I didn't mean it! I was just wondering! I didn't mean nothing!"

"Mom and Dad hate me 'cause of you."

"I'm not a monster! I'm not, you can't leave me here. Mom, Dad?" she bawled out into the dark.

"Johnathon Junior said you weren't the first monster, said that's why they got this room under the house, said there were others that just went away."

Beatrice hadn't thought about the room, she was too young to see abnormalities. Bad parents, a lack of food, a lack of light, a cell in the mud with an iron door, it was all normal, all parents do that stuff and all bad children are monsters, but what Walter said that Johnathon Junior had said...maybe it wasn't right.

"Please!" she screamed.

"Why did you do it?" Walter shook harder.

"I just, I just..." She trembled and wailed, "Mommy! Daddy!"

"They don't love monsters and neither do I!" Walter slapped his sister.

"I didn't mean it. I just wanted to taste it."

"You knew. Monster." Walter punched her.

The strike drove the fear and sadness away in favor of anger.

"I knew and I'll do it again!"

She bit down on her brother's face. And he tasted wonderful. Since she could remember, since she knew how to remember, her parents demanded that no matter how hungry they got, no matter what they saw the travelers doing, no matter what the travelers said, they would not become cannibals.

Cannibals are monsters, they'd say, but she'd never known meat until that traveler gave her a bite and it was so, so good.

There's free meat everywhere, he'd said and smiled a gapped-tooth grin.

It wasn't fair, her parents got to eat meat growing up and she didn't, they spoke with longing, *in the back-then-times you could eat meat and not be a monster. But not now, never again.*

They told of beasts, unimaginable. She couldn't understand, and the traveler showed her meat; that didn't make her a monster, it just made her hungry.

"I only tasted it!" Beatrice screamed as she sucked on the flailing figure she was now biting. "Just a taste!"

SERPIENTE BRUJA

(2018)

"Hey, man, don't I know you from somewhere?"

Ossie Benet turned his back to the hombre sidled up next to him at the bar. This guy had been eyeballing him for an hour before he finally worked up the nerve to approach. Ossie hadn't crossed the border for this. This is the shit he got at home.

"Uh, bootaya, uno," Ossie said, his Spanish horrendous, "and deuce tequilas."

The bartender nodded. A good one. He'd serve you while you had the dough no matter how far into the abyss you travelled, he'd even prop up passed out patrons.

Ossie took his drinks and staggered away to an island table surrounding a rough wooden beam. The place was mostly empty and the man with the guitar modulated his volume accordingly. Ossie nodded in tune and tried not to think.

—

The hothouse piss stink was incredible. There was a steel trough that caught urine and two be-shitted porcelain thrones, fit for the king of Mediterranean Avenue. They sat in stalls without doors. The collected waste ran to a ditch out back. Spanish graffito authenticated the room.

Ossie, scent adjusted, leaned his head forward while he worked at peeling himself out of his pants. Typically, he used stalls, but the drunker he got, the more like his former self he became.

The door swung inward.

"Oh, bendeja," said the mustachioed Mexican that had bothered him earlier. "You look familiar. I been to America, man,

I drive. I know your face."

"Go fuck yourself," Ossie mumbled, his piss stream finally flowing.

"Why don't...?" the Mexican trailed, his eyes tumbling down to Ossie's package. "Shit, now I know. Man, essa perra, man."

"Essa perra," Ossie droned.

It was international news. Greta Benet had married an asshole, a man that used his cock like a teacher's pointer and an authoritarian's hammer. Frustrations and failures came home and Greta felt them in her bones, flesh, and loins.

One day, something changed. Greta changed.

Sleepwalking through life no more, Greta had focus. Ossie had returned to the trailer and thumped her when his flag refused to rise. Exhausted, Ossie sheathed his fists and systematically consumed every ounce of liquor left in their ramshackle abode.

Greta watched while something bubbled to life within.

Ossie awoke to pain and babbled to the 911 operator, "My cock!"

Unthinking, Greta dropped the knife and carried the flaccid worm while running to the bus stop a mile up the road. Rain pelted and washed away the blood. On the bus, eventually, she noticed the prize she'd taken and tossed it out a tiny window.

Locating the penis took too long and Ossie lived his life with a stub and all the fame that came with it.

The judge had sided with Greta. Self-defensive targeting.

—

"Man, you ever hear of Serpiente Bruja?" the Mexican whispered to Ossie.

Ossie turned his head. He'd settled back into a glass from the tap at the bar.

"Fuck off, buddy. Ever hear of that?"

The Mexican shook his head gently, understood why this dude was cold.

"The Serpiente Bruja, she can fix you. Man."

"Fix this," Ossie said, grabbing his groin—an old-life gesture if there ever was one.

"Exactly, man. Don't you want your verga, man? It's dangerous, but it's possible."

Finally, the Mexican had the American's attention.

—

Ossie stared down in the hole. It was a little after 7:00 PM and the sun declined with haste. The Mexican had said it was dangerous, but he knew a one-legged guy that sought out a Serpiente Bruja. An hour later, the man had his leg back.

"True story, man."

The hole was right where the Mexican said it would be. The one-legged and then two-legged man had shown the Mexican after losing a bet. The Mexican figured knowing where a Serpiente Bruja dwelled might come in handy someday.

The sandy yard behind the row of wild shrubbery tipped down like a locker room shower, toward the deep hole.

"You in there, you rotten snake?" Ossie whispered.

The ground hissed as if a thousand snakes hid just below the surface.

Reckless and desperate and wildly drunk, Ossie jammed a hand into the hole. Immediately, he yanked it back. A four-foot, red, black, and gold snake had latched onto his palm. The pain was unbelievable.

"You bastard! Ow-ee! Whore dog!"

Ossie yanked at the thing. This did nothing. Since it was what he was supposed to do anyway, he bit down on the head of the snake. It let go and Ossie continued biting. Fangs tore through Ossie's cheek. He chewed right back.

The head was gone and Ossie dropped the rest of the snake, feeling the swallowed lump pass down his throat like a golf ball through a garden hose. The snake slithered, headless, back into the hole.

Ossie stumbled away.

The Mexican rushed to aid Ossie. The poison from the snake seeped purple tendrils through every vein and capillary.

"Man, you need a doctor. Man."

—

Paramedics carted an injured party that had been tossed outside the hospital through the automatic ER doors. The doctor recognized right away the effects of a coral snake bite. The *twenty-minute snake.*

Help in twenty or dead in twenty-one.

"My cock!" Ossie shouted. His face had blackened, swelled marshmallow puffy, ready to ooze. "My cock! Check my cock!"

The doctor tried to focus on the venom.

"Is it back?"

The doctor injected the anti-venom.

"How's my cock?"

The man was delirious, obviously.

"Is my cock gone?"

Ossie swung his rigid limbs trying to feel for his penis.

"Nurse, watch him. Cover him if he dies," the doctor said. Leaving the room, he mumbled, "Stupid drunk American."

The nurse rushed over.

"My cock, is it okay?" Ossie moaned, slipping.

The nurse, more caring and much greener than the doctor, opened Ossie's pants.

"Is it there?" Ossie whispered, fading.

"Hush, it's fine," she said and for good measure, gave the full handful a squeeze.

Ossie smiled a moment before exhaling his final breath.

THE CONDEMNED MAN

(2017)

From that height, seeing the smoke from his burned shack teased his soul—those lingering grey tendrils that climbed into the blue beyond. This hurt like nothing had hurt before. More than the spikes and more than the lashes.

Closer. Trodden paths ran a trail over the golden grass under the heavy white sun, between the yellowed trees circling round the glade. Closer yet. 43 shadows stretched long fingers onto the overgrown grass and overturned dirt.

Beneath that blaring sun, flesh dripped until the bone sacks fell, men picked over by committee—hideous vultures, crows, and second-class doves. The stench was unbearable to most and onlookers did not linger unless tethered by familial aches, and even then, the smell eventually outweighed the pain. That stink was music to the birds, to the whining dogs that came at night to gawk up at those pinned by wrists and ankles, and the endless buzzing of flies.

Men survived for a time, staked to the crossed planks, eyeing down the hungry ugliness in the light of day. They'd listened to the squawks and rustling talons and fighting mongrels when the night cast darkness over the world, knowing.

They lived until they died, mostly.

Aching, retching, terrified beyond the notion of terrified, the last man felt himself slipping. Delayed executions stretched agony of the declared befitting punishment. That last man cooked, set on high for a crime hard to define. Wrong *thoughts*, notions that carried the burden of unflinching faith, bullheadedness in spite of the throne and the decrees passed down onto the public. The old gods were out and so were those refusing to praise the new gods, the better gods.

The buzzards hopped and bopped, there was always enough to go around at a religious execution. And yet, they acted with impatience and longing. Ravenous beasts.

The last man had faith. He peeled his lids after closing them on the image of the husk of his former home. A cool breeze touched his pre-rotting flesh. He'd dreamed of drinking and eating, but mostly of letting his arms rest.

Time was slow and he looked around for signs of change while his sanity flickered. As if out of nowhere, a boy sat before him, no older than ten, staring up.

"Help me, boy," the condemned man said, his voice like sand against stone.

"You are lucky. There is bad to come for the sons of Zeus and the daughters of Hera. There is more bad to come than you could ever dream in a thousand nightmares. I tell you, in the days to come, more will burn under the sun, pecked by beaks, scorned by lips." The boy spoke with a man's tenor and wore the shadow of a looming corpse to keep from baking himself. His little digits picked at pebbles where he sat amidst the rot and avian life.

"Please, help me."

The boy brushed his hands. Three vultures stood over the shoulders of the last man, perched on the board-work behind and above him. In a diamond shape was that stand, to ensure the man hanged and hanged and hanged; even when nails tore flesh, a man would hang. While alive, at least.

The birds tested, now and then, the constitution of the pre-rotten flesh. The living and the dead are different and birds know patience.

"Don't speak, there's no need. I am here to help you, but I will not touch you. You must do that part on your own."

"I'm nailed, can't you see?" The man's voice croaked as he shouted.

The boy frowned and rose to his bare feet. He wore short leather pants and a long cotton shirt, both clean and fresh. Almost impossibly so.

"It is you who cannot see. Come down from there and I will show you away."

The condemned man shook his head. "Can't *you* see? I am pinned and—" The man paused as an ugly, redheaded vulture drove its beak at his chest. Rustling. Digging. "Help me, boy!"

The vulture knew the choicest meat and burrowed, pushing aside the dripping crimson muscles and the bony cell.

"Shh, it is the way. Now, come down."

The man roared, "See me, blind boy! There are stakes driven into my hands and feet! Can't you see? This bird is—help me!"

"I see, but you do not. Come down, son of Zeus. You are dead. There is no need to stay on that torture stand. This is no place for you now. See? Your home is burned. Your people are dead. Your gods are silent. Come down before the new rulers begin stringing more of your people. It is not a good show and will ache fearsome."

"Not dead yet!" The man was angry, so angry that his arms shot outward. The world rushed at him as he dropped.

The boy smiled and laughed as the man passed through him. These men never understood, not right away, and sometimes not ever.

"You sneaky boy! You will not smile..." the man trailed and then looked up to the vultures dining on his corpse, fighting over his organs.

"Forget this and I will show you away. You are one of the last for a long time. Many more will die, but there will be darkness. There will be horrors in the forever stone of hardened hearts."

The last man's expression sank and tears spilled. For so long he'd fought and prayed to the gods for salvation, prayed to the deities and monsters, to those who grew scales and fur and horns and hooves, but in the end, he'd died a criminal on a bone stand.

"It is better now, for you," the boy said. "The sons of Zeus and daughters of Hera are better off without their skins, better now for one million moons."

The man opened his mouth. His words were a whistled breeze. Those spilling tears rolled against gravity like reverse raindrops.

The boy took the man's hand, facing up to him in the way a son does a father. The boy then inhaled deeply and blew a tremendous breath that smelled of water and fresh grass. The air filled the final man's lungs and he floated, past his corpse and beyond sight of his burned-out home. The boy inhaled even deeper and blew a gale, sending the man to where he would be one of many, among stars and moons, with his brothers and sisters.

NO RETURNS

(2016)

Itsy-bitsy hands, crimson dripping from finger webbing. Emotionless stare. SpongeBob nightie. Feet bare.

"I'm sowry, puh-please!"

Skipping rope held tight, tying a victim to a bed. That mattress was a seepage puddle catchall. Frozen jammies soiled pink, yellow, and brown.

Tiny painted nails dug into hair.

"You did it first," Julie said, sneering at her sister.

"No!"

Julie aimed her little fists. Golden locks yanked a handful at a time to a soundtrack of screams. Payback for Barbie's buzz cut.

FORSAKEN MEMORY

(2013)

Cold.

Wet.

Stinging pain shot into his brain. His back and legs ached. *Where am I?* he wondered. *Trees, but...*

It was different, they were different. A fine netting of moss hung from every limb, running down onto its body, then the trunk, before joining the grass. Icy water ran around his feet, patches of snow hid away from the rain deteriorating bit by bit as the drips fell. It was dark, shadows loomed and crossed, his memory refused cooperation, all he could remember was urgency.

They're after you, run.

He ran. Turning back for a moment, he saw light beams flash through the tall, mossy, snowy, damp, cold forest. An animal growled and barked.

A dog. You remember trees, you remember dogs, and you remember fear, but why are they chasing you?

He ran more, deeper into the forest, following the whipping frosty creek. Just a peek, he turned again. The flashing searchlights drew closer and the angry dogs continued their calls.

Why are they after you? Wait...who are they?

His feet numbed and froze, more and more his fear grew and battered his aching bones and stinging brain.

Who are they? Who, who, who?

A dim light wove its way around the thick forest. Its origin unknown, and yet inviting. Light meant warmth in most circumstances and if they were going to catch him, it might be better warm.

To die without the shakes. Do they really mean to kill me? Who are they? Who, who, who?

The hill might as well have been a mountain of flat rock in his weakened state, but he turned from his watery path to trudge through the little mounds of snow and the yellowy moss. The light called him as fear fueled his body. An old stroller rested midway up the hill, and he paused next to it; what this was didn't register in the functioning portion of his memory.

I should know this. I should know it all. Why, why are they chasing me? Why would anyone want to chase me?

He climbed onto his fours, up, up, up, the light beckoned. His skinny digits stung with cold pain. It wasn't right, everything wrong.

Why would they chase me? I haven't...his thoughts paused looking for a stack of memories. Who am I? No, no, no, who am I? Maybe I've done something, maybe I deserve this.

He slid backward, the hill too wet and too steep. The lights flashed and casted eerie shadows over his aching body. A stream running in the background called out.

The water, follow the water. But why? Could be you're a murderer or a thief or a rapist; they might have every right to kill you.

It didn't feel right; he didn't feel like a criminal. He continued. Splashing feet and paws chased after him, so close the flashlight beams almost touched him. No more than a kilometer ahead, he saw more light and on an almost level plain to his own. He chased it as the searchers chased him.

Everything around him appeared foreign and awful, the cold, the wet, the moss, the snow, the rain, he could remember the idea of atmospheres and he knew about growth and precipitation, but something wasn't clicking. His bare feet made sucking noises with each step through the heavy moss and mud.

Maybe they are looking for you, not chasing you.

A nice thought, but it didn't feel right. He pushed his meager body hard and put a little distance between himself and the pursuers. The light cast new shadows over the forest, strange shapes emerged. Beer cans, a car seat, a wheel-less wheelbarrow, all foreign and unnamable under his gaze.

Where am I? Who cares? Run or they'll catch you. But, who, who'll catch me?

A large rectangular building shaped and formed under the light. Through a floor to ceiling window, he saw the dry world of the inside, warm and inviting. He gulped at the air. He needed the inside; he needed the dry warmth that the light promised through the glass.

A door, oh please be a door.

The forest ended abruptly and his bare feet stung on the hard black ground. He knew the name of the surface, but it wasn't coming. No matter how hard he called, pleaded, and demanded his memory, it all remained in a mysterious untouchable place.

A small wooden porch raised four steps to the glass wall. A silver lining appeared, it was there all along and he just couldn't see it. The hollow wood announced his arrival at the tall rectangular building with the glass wall and the promise of dryness and warmth.

A door, warm, light, rest.

He wrapped his frozen fingers around the handle and pulled and then pushed.

Locked.

No, no. He tugged and tugged.

His pursuers sounded so close and he realized he'd run in a straight, easy to follow line in search of freedom. Although he knew very little, at that moment anyway, he knew this was a stupid thing he'd done. He stomped in anguish. The hollow step below called and offered a solution.

Just as the flashlight beams began to contact the light from the building, failing as they touched one another, he jumped down from the step and pulled it away from the building.

Cobwebs and an animal nest, vacant at the moment, resided beneath the step.

He didn't have time to wonder about the ferocity of the beasts whose home he'd just invaded, and he slunk low. The hollow step dragged nearly noiselessly and he glared from beneath. A small crack gave him a view of his pursuers' movement.

He waited and the shapes formed. At first, he didn't recognize any of it, but as the faces emerged, his memories flooded back to him.

Hairless apes. The fourth stage, the troublesome years.

The men spoke and he didn't understand the tongue. It was all there. They wanted him thanks to a technical difficulty aboard his ship.

The crash.

The idea that he'd run from such a minor life form angered him. They were just a stage, a piece that helped ready a planet for the master species. Most times, they lived and died, but it was Hyphani and for whatever reason the drogens didn't understand their position.

Hyphani... Drogens... Ugh.

On most other research planets bred in the similar pattern of miniature universe creation, the life forms acknowledged their lowly importance when compared with the needs of the planet on which they lived.

Tenants, you stupid things are merely tenants. Hyphani belongs to us and you're not doing it any favors.

He remembered why he was there. A warning signal, one sent from the planet's core, announcing a critical period. The inhabitants refused to follow the easy guidelines and the strong warnings the planet sent. He didn't understand it really, something about money, something about trading resources for power.

An urge to stand and destroy the twenty or so individuals in yellow uniforms overwhelmed him.

Self-important blips...

Hyphani wasn't the first, during his training, a case of a similar nature occurred, but it was rare, such an asinine series of events had to fall into place for a blundering repeat performance. The inhabitants created disagreeing gods; deemed the planet a gift to be toyed with—the only common notion among the gods—and eventually the core failed. That planet, Earth was its name, failed thanks to its tenants and its love of money and its sense of entitlement that followed after decreeing a godlike status of themselves.

Humans, drogens, no difference.

He felt at the side of his ovular skull, a transmission screamed. The drogen pursuers and their dogs fell writhing in pain, holding their heads and pawing at their eyes. One by one, the group of pursuers fizzled into bubbly puddles of gore, and he stepped from hiding to wait for a ride off the decimated planet.

CHESTNUT ANNIE

(2014)

From amid the pine needles, the silvery tinsel, and the tiny white blinking lights, she watched and she listened. This boy had his name on the wrong side of the ledger.

"It better be coming!" the boy shouted. "Mom, I'm serious! If Santa doesn't bring it, I'll scream!"

It was a hard year financially. There was no budget space for big gifts.

"Are you listening?" the boy screeched, "I want a SKELEMAN! DEATH! PALACE FOR CHRISTMAS!"

Chestnut Annie shuddered imperceptibly from her place in the tree. The Big Man was right; coal just didn't send the message anymore and doling out comeuppance to this one was like killing two turtledoves with one candy caning.

—

"Where are we?" the boy whimpered, shivering in the sudden cold.

Only minutes earlier Chestnut Annie had climbed down out of the tree to capture the greedy brat. Clad in the official uniform of the Nutcracker Brigade, Annie stood a mere three inches. A size suggesting weakness; her abilities and will proved otherwise. She shackled the boy while he slept, dragged him from his bed, and stuffed him down into his stocking, which under the right touch became a portal to the frosty familiarity of Santa's Village.

"Kid, your life's gonna be a whole lot different from here out," she said and yanked the boy's shackles toward the open doors of a long steel building. The air from within reeked of sweat and melted plastics. "Welcome to your new home."

"Who are they?" the boy snuffed back tears.

"They're boys and girls just like you...spoiled brats."

"Buh-buh-but what are they doing?" he said, adding in a blubber, "I wanna guh-guh-go home."

"Home? You are home. And as for what they're doing, you don't think Christmas toys make themselves, do you?"

The boy wailed, "I'll be good! I swear! Ple-eee-ease!"

"I'm glad you're enthusiastic; well-behaved boys and girls deserve well-made toys."

NEVERLAND

(2018)

"Promise me you'll stick to this block," Mrs. Halpern said, stern eyes set on the boys—one her own, the other a neighbor friend.

The block in question was once one to avoid, part of the old Balkans Quarter, the kind of place where prostitutes and fortunetellers lingered, while pushers and junkies made their exchanges beneath the shadowy cloak of the buildings. Before it had little by way of streetlights and even less by way of policing.

Gentrification. That's what the TV called it. Mrs. Halpern thought they could call it whatever, it being only two blocks from home, so long as she could take her son trick-or-treating there and get back before she blew the whole night.

"Okay," the boys said in unison.

Dylan was Iron Man. Leslie was Black Panther. They ignored any potential Marvel universe tensions in favor of treat gathering. The boys were both ten and that meant they needed some slack to their tethers when it came to running in the night with sacks, eager for candy. Mrs. Halpern didn't like it but conceded because she'd worked extra hours when Debbie went home sick. Plus, she didn't feel like chasing around after them. Let them go but keep them to the safe spaces.

An hour after they left Mrs. Halpern waiting in her car, they'd visited forty-seven doorsteps. No more lights remained lit directly ahead and they were about to round back but stopped. From where they stood, they could see into the Ford. Mrs. Halpern was asleep behind the wheel. And their bags were decidedly light.

Dylan said, "Let's cut across and do those." He pointed to an apartment complex. They were from the '70s, two of the three buildings were lifeless and boarded up—next up on the city's list of places to beautify and rebrand. The lit building had nine ground floor units, each with its own entrance.

"But your mom said—" Leslie began rebutting.

"But your mom said," Dylan mocked his friend in a nasally intonation. "Don't be such a wimp."

"Fine. Not like she can ground me." Though if she talked to his mother that was most likely the eventual outcome. If caught. "We gotta be quick."

They started off, rushing in case Mrs. Halpern woke up and grew impatient. The other side of the street was much darker than the designated hunting grounds. Down the street, fewer houses had pumpkins out. Hardly any of those places covered their porch beams in fake spider webs. Only a handful even had those cheesy window stickers from the nineties. Some did however, some had all three, and it only took one good one to make it worthwhile.

"Let's just do these five, okay?"

Dylan acquiesced, suddenly not so hot about his plan. This other side was spooky.

They drew up to a defunct convenience store with boarded windows and doors connected to one of the apartment projects. Two lots beyond were the ground floor apartments with lights blazing.

Before they could go any further, a man stepped out of a shadowy vacancy between the former store and a chain-link fence surrounding the second dilapidated building. Dylan gasped and Leslie clenched his fists, the outfit really made him feel the superhero part, at least a little.

"Hello, boys." The man was skinny and tall, wore a forest green tunic, lighter green tights, and a forest green tricorne hat with a red feather accent sprouting like alfalfa. A man in costume, normal as normal got for Halloween night.

Dylan eased, at the understanding that this getup was Peter Pan, like from the ancient cartoon his grandma had on VHS. Peter Pan was a friendly image and maybe too friendly as weirdos came in all shapes and outfits. "My mom's watching, don't get no ideas."

Peter Pan smiled. "Sure she is, but I bet adventurous lads like you know how to duck her rules. I'm a boy myself. I know all about making the rules as I go. Where I'm from, you never grow old, and you get to play all day, forever."

Leslie's face scrunched beneath the plastic mask. "You're not a boy."

"Am too." Peter Pan put hands on his hips—very Peter Pan-like.

Dylan said, "Maybe a pervert, but not a boy. Don't think we don't know about perverts."

Leslie wanted to smack his friend for all his talking...always talking.

"Peter Pan is a boy. I am Peter Pan, therefore I am a boy. The mathematics of it is inarguable."

Not quite, Dylan began to argue, needed to tell this creepo to take a hike. "Like hell you're a—"

Peter Pan wagged an index finger and then floated six feet from the crumbling sidewalk, toes twinkling ever so slightly. "See? And now I'm looking for adventurous playmates. It's fortunate I've found you two. You look just the type."

Warning bells rang and still, both boys knew the kind of fun Peter Pan got up to, and if he was based on a real person... *Wow!* And this guy could at least do a cool trick if he wasn't really...

Suddenly, as if reading minds, Peter Pan floated high enough that neither boy doubted his authenticity. "What they get wrong in the stories is that time moves fast in Neverland. We'd have fifty adventures before your mother could scratch her nose."

Leslie's heart pounded.

Dylan leaned forward.

They almost had to. Think how cool the stories would be. Everyone in class would be jealous. It would be like true magic, hell, maybe they could steal some pixie dust and show it off. Fly circles around the principal.

Peter Pan smiled, drifting toward a dark alleyway. "Come adventure with me, boys!"

The mini-Marvel heroes couldn't help it and ran into the shadows.

—

Nine minutes after she awoke from a light doze, Mrs. Halpern stopped a man in a Peter Pan costume coming from the direction where the boys were trick-or-treating. He wiped at his mouth with a white handkerchief covered in red splotches.

"Have you seen two little superheroes?" she asked.

The man folded the handkerchief—his name monogrammed on the edge, clear as a crystal ball: *Vlad Drăculea*—and put it in his pocket. He then ran an absent finger over his bottom lip to be sure his fangs had receded and then straightened his department store Peter Pan costume. "Sorry, no. Not to worry, they're probably off adventuring. Boys love to adventure."

ANDI PANDI

(2015)

The air was heavy and pungent with hot curry. Thomas, self-aware of his sloppy eating habits, typically ate in the apron he wore while preparing supper. It wasn't his apron and it wasn't Andi's, it belonged to the marriage. Pink edges, multi-colored polka dots with a pink, yellow, blue, orange, and green rainbow draw rope—a color scheme befitting a pride parade. *Aside from all those curry and buffalo sauce stains,* Thomas thought.

A layer began congealing over the chicken curry and Thomas sent Andi a text message. Sometimes she was late thirty minutes, he didn't say much as her high stress position with the securities commission meant she had to argue with lawyers all day. Which earned her some leeway.

That job also meant that he could stay home and paint.

ETA? his text asked.

He held the phone for a few seconds and then plugged it back into the living room stereo. Thomas mouthed along with his favorite parts, swaying and half-stepping, occasionally throwing rap hands, jazz hands, and mime guns at the floor or ceiling along to a new remix of a 'Pac classic.

Still swinging and nodding, he stirred the long-finished food, added a few drops of water from the tap to the rice so it wouldn't burn, and began rinsing utensils.

On random, 2pac made way for Prof who made way for K'Naan. He removed the food from the heat and built himself a plate. Thomas pulled the wire from his phone. The music stopped abruptly. He sat with his plate in front of the television, phone on the coffee table. After a few bites, he sent another text.

Andi Pandy?—a pet name.

No reply. He finished supper, flipping channels until he came to the HBO boxing rerun. The curry warmed his belly and he stretched out on the couch, catching only two rounds before napping.

—

Sweat seeped from every pore, his shirt soaked, his hair wet, in the brief time he'd slept, the evils of the night found him and he dreamed of tragedy. Awake, he shot to his feet, spinning before realizing the living room was not Andi's slaughterhouse. He dropped back down onto the couch and looked at the clock. Nearly 7:00 PM and his wife had not yet returned.

He checked his phone, nothing.

He flipped to his contacts and hit *Andi Pandy*. The phone rang, each rumbling buzz more wrenching than the last. The rings became an amalgamation of every bully, every boss, every smug curator he'd ever known, mocking his tension with laughter.

"Hello, you've reached Andi Riley. I am unable..." Andi's recorded voice started. Thomas did not need the message service, what he needed was...was what?

"Just a dream. She's late sometimes, cool your jets, crazy man," he said and forced a smile.

He went to the kitchen to wrap the leftovers, spilling as he scooped the extra curry and chicken from the pan into a plastic container—not a problem, the apron caught the slop. Once finished, he retrieved two cookies from the jar atop the refrigerator, poured a short glass of milk, and returned to the living room. The third fight of the broadcast featured a Russian and a Mexican, the crowd was only subtly into the action. In New Hampshire, folks paid the prizefight ticket toll to see the local boy, the stuff before the main event was simply fluffing.

The Russian was like a steel bull, most times that kind of will and hard headedness would prime his excitement, but his mind was elsewhere. At the end of the round, he looked up at the wall clock. Tick. Tick. The dream lingered.

With each blink, he caught glimpses of the horror, the bits and pieces of his wife's desiccation. Andi, chained to a wall and sliced through the abdomen. Andi, kept alive to feel the dull blades tear into her face. Andi's screams, her tongue poking out a bloody hole in her cheek.

The announcers on the TV started a fevered play-by-play as the Russian toppled his Mexican opponent.

"Good show," Thomas said as his fingers worked the text screen. He repeated his last message and then restarted his phone, wondering if perhaps he hadn't lost signal and confused the device. It vibrated as it came back to life, no messages, text or voice, nothing.

He leaned back. The announcers discussed the main event. Two Americans, the one from New Hampshire and the other from Texas.

The crowd settled into a collective state of bananas when the bell finally dinged for the start of the first round.

Thomas peeked at the clock. He called Andi again.

He wasn't usually the type to put much stock in omens or feelings, but that dream had a severe and ominous heft, and she wasn't answering her phone. She always answered eventually.

"Sometimes she works late that's all, doofus," Thomas said, the phone in his hand had become warm. He wouldn't let go, couldn't.

Round after round after round, Thomas glanced at the clock. Tick. Tick. He looked then at his phone. Nothing. Not a word from Andi—Andi with the hole through her belly, Andi with the hole in her cheek, Andi stolen away in broad daylight, taken to a slimy room and chained to a wall.

"Dammit!" He dialed again.

Ring-ring-ring-ring. "Hello, you've reached Andi Riley. I am unable to take..."

Ding, end of the fifth round. After 8:00 PM and the sun was sinking. The sixth round began; Texas appeared ahead. The crowd wasn't happy—New Hampshire had a cut above his eye. Blood trickled over the glistening petroleum jelly smeared on his cheek...Thomas saw Andi dancing around that ring, a shadowy man with knives chasing her after her, no jiving or bouncing, dancing or swaying, pure chase, life or death. Andi screamed, the knife sliced through her leg and she toppled...Ding, the round ended and New Hampshire tagged Texas with a jab-jab-hook combo that evened the cut status.

Thomas looked at the clock, two minutes after the last time he'd checked, he dialed again.

Ring-ring-ring-ring, "Hello, you've—"

"Dammit!"

Ding, the seventh round began, and New Hampshire exploded...Andi was Texas, New Hampshire's hands were chainsaws. Andi met the chunking, hunking blades, flesh littering the canvas, and blood spraying a crimson geyser.

"One, two, three, four," the referee said, swinging his arm as Texas got to his feet nodding and waving, "five, six, seven, eight...good, good?"

The fight recommenced.

Andi was fine. Thomas knew it. The fight represented as much, just as his dream foretold her demise.

He dialed, ring-ring-ring-ring. "Hell—"

He hung up on the service.

New Hampshire belted into Texas, his face a puffy pillow, cuts ran over both eyes, Thomas couldn't watch, he dialed and redialed over and over, New Hampshire cut down Texas, those early round body shots so obvious in the middle and later rounds, the arena erupted as new blood and spittle showered; pandemonium, the ringside dinged the ten-second bell and New Hampshire charged into Tex...chainsaws ground into the meat of Andi.

"No!"

Thomas dialed again.

"Wha—!" Andi shouted the half word, but that was all. The call ended.

Thomas jumped to his feet, dialed again. Nothing. Immediately to voicemail.

"That means she's...that means she's turned her phone off. She answered, you nutcase." He smiled a genuine smile and slumped exhaustedly onto the couch. He watched and listened to New Hampshire give his winner's speech.

He felt so stupid about the dream and his calls. She'd been late before. What he saw during the prizefight was something he'd never repeat, ridiculous.

At 9:13 PM a call came to his phone, he didn't check the caller-ID.

It had to be Andi.

"Hey," he said.

"Uh, Thomas Riley?" a man's voice said.

Curious, a twinge worried itself into his belly. "Yes, who is this?"

"My name is Michael Skitters, I did paperwork for Andi."

Did paperwork, did? "Um, all right, so...?"

"There was an accident. Terrible."

"What happened? Is Andi all right?" Thomas' heart thumped and his breath caught.

"She's, she's gone. I'm so sorry. She was giving me a lift to the station and then—"

"She's dead?"

"I'm so sorry." Michael Skitters' speech quickened. "She was taking me to the station, we worked late trying to reconcile some legal loopholes taken by—doesn't matter, she was driving me, she was speeding a bit, late for supper and hungry, said it was curry night—"

"She loves curry."

"Her phone rang incessantly, she didn't want to answer and drive, something about her Bluetooth kicking the bucket, I don't recall exactly, but the phone kept ringing and ringing, she got mad and dug through her purse, finally answered."

"Oh...no, no," Thomas said as the morbid realization dawned.

"I didn't see it either, not really, I was watching her dig through her purse, she was such a nice lady. She missed a red and went through the intersection and there was this truck, oh hell, this truck, a moving cube and it smashed right into us. I broke my leg. The cube exploded its payload, guess it was moving some hunting or supply store, there were knives and chainsaws all over the street..."

Thomas couldn't listen, ended the call, went to the kitchen, and hung up the marital apron.

BARRY'S HAND

(2018)

The aura of catastrophe was palpable. Hanging like fog. The tunnel and the connected street were the scene of endings and of chaos.

In blue uniforms with reflective strips wrapping sleeve bottoms and shins, wearing heavy black boots, and with expressions burying panicked scowls, focused paramedics hurried about St. George Street as pedestrians stood stupefied, phones in hands—some recording the sight, others agog and too stunned to share. 41 calls to 911 had already met the emergency switchboard.

The atmosphere was cool. Summer was over, but the street was busy with stalled life, intrigued and mingling on the edge of the foray. Rubberneckers collecting anecdotes for later: *you wouldn't believe it, but I was there!*

The station had crumbled, casting out a cloud of dust and shrieks like a collapsing barn teeming with swallows. Shimmery shards of glass twinkled on the asphalt in a starry warning. Most of the uninjured survivors and those who were stunned and bloody joined the pedestrians on the fringe, watching the scene unfold to its conclusion. And it was a scene, no doubt. By nature, scenes demanded an audience.

Leaking, dirty, in jeans and a peach-colored t-shirt, one of the survivors sat on the curb in front of a skinny, leafless maple tree, gazing blindly.

A paramedic peered down at those sad eyes and considered the options. He cleared his throat and said, "What's your name?"

A mumbled response. Words missed and then, "… Salimi."

"Are you okay?"

"Am I? Is it? It happened. It was horrible. All the bright light, like fireworks, but not good like fireworks. How can that be?" To Mr. Salimi, it was as if the rupture quaked from the inside out. With vibrant emotion and monstrous power so bold and yet limited, the blast had rocked him like a ragdoll. "People were screaming and I held. I held for life."

A truth had jarred loose within those sad, teary, bloodshot eyes.

"It's all right."

"It's love that makes it different. You know how people say they see their life flash before their eyes? That's true, it happened to me, but the world didn't stop. My feet didn't stop. I kept running, had to."

"Please, just—"

"Please nothing!"

The paramedic looked over his shoulder for help. There was none available, everyone was busy with bleeders and screamers. He took a breath. "I'm sorry, it's necessary that I—"

"I saw it all again in the flash. We met at a wedding. Not together. We played it slow, went for coffees. I studied him online like a predator. He did the same to me. We laughed about it later."

"That's—"

"I held tight and I ran. It was as if I came apart. The world exploded. My heart, the flash. I *saw* sounds. I experienced the *weight* of light. Pain was in me, like bizzip! I held. I held because love conquers. Right?"

The paramedic closed his eyes. Often enough, shock made his job more difficult than anything he'd trained for. "Please, sir, I—"

"Everything barreled, like a train, chuggalugga-chuggalugga. My legs just kept going and I held tight, so tight. Then the flash. I saw our first date. Our first apartment. I lived everything all over. Love is the flash at death. Not life. But I'm alive!"

"Please, calm down. You're bleeding. We need to get you help and—"

"It was the end, but not... A bomb, yes?"

The paramedic whispered, "I think so." Rubbed his temple as he side-eyed numerous others needing his assistance. This man was taking too long.

"It went off. You've never seen me run so fast. There was blood and breaking things and screams. Then the brightness. Love washed me clean." Mr. Salimi tapped a bloody, dust-caked hand over his chest. "I relived the first time he held me. We ran away without seeing the world, hand-in-hand. Love guided me to safety. I saw our wedding day and all of the gold gilded edges. I saw the face of God and *It* was in Barry's eyes!"

"Please calm down, sir...Mr. Salimi."

"The explosions were as much in my heart as out. It was love and I squeezed. He squeezed back. Love survives all!"

"Mr. Salimi, please. You need help and you can't... I mean... We need to take that." The paramedic pointed.

Talal Salimi looked down his bloodied arm to his hand. Fingers entwined with Barry's fingers, palms pressed together, everything missing above a lost husband's wrist. Dust clung to the blood of the stub, and bone and bits of vein stuck out like dead birch trees in a glade.

"He still loves me. I can feel it."

The scene was such a damned mess and there were so many others. There were hundreds injured and this man was not the center of need. The paramedic bent down and touched Talal Salimi's arm.

The harried man looked into the paramedic's eyes as the fingers began peeling back. "But I can feel—"

"Let go, please, Mr. Salimi."

Finally, he did. Barry's hand lay flat against the heartbroken survivor's palm. Talal stared as the paramedic touched the dead man's hand like it wasn't part of something bigger, a piece of a puzzle. Talal felt a gentle squeeze before the paramedic took the hand.

Talal cried through the day in the hospital, cried through the interview with the police, cried that he had not seen the two bearded, white men in heavy coats and red baseball caps leaving backpacks on the station platform, and cried when he arrived home to an empty apartment. The love was not between those walls, not surrounded by selected and collected decorations.

Talal paced the formally shared space, considered joining Barry, resuming love over the edge of his balcony. It was not so far, but if he went down headfirst...

"Come back, I'll give anything!"

In bed, broken inside, but fine outside, Talal drowsed though slept fitfully on the prescribed medication. He did not hear the balcony door squeak open.

Fury conquered and Talal kicked his legs against his mattress, screaming like a toddler until his voice was hoarse.

Five damp taps started across the linoleum toward the bedroom. Still, Talal heard nothing.

"Join him in death," he whispered and considered anew his demise. A parade of macabre possibilities that wore fuzzy, pink, doped-up edges danced the peripherals of his awareness. He could do it and they'd be together again.

The minute tapping sound drew closer and Talal stopped and listened.

Silence.

He kicked the mattress again.

Something tugged on the sheet beneath him and his mind switched as he felt the gentle pressure at the end of the bed approach. It reminded him of his childhood cat, Chucks, and how she jumped up every morning to inform Talal that her bowl was empty.

His breath caught and his heart pattered double time. The thing on the bed, like a heavy spider, had touched his foot, was still rising after that, and tickled up his thigh.

Talal whimpered.

The tiny prattle rustled beneath the sheets, tugging, lifting, settling.

Talal opened his hand at the mysterious meaty prodding, and cool digits found Talal's palm. Fingers entwined.

"Barry?" Talal flipped away the sheet and looked at the hand squeezing his palm.

It was not Barry's hand.

BULLSHIT CHRISTMAS

(2020)

Douglas Swain white knuckles the steering wheel of one of the Greyland County pickup trucks. He's mumbling to himself about the total bullshit of Christmas and the total bullshit of tinsel and wreaths and gifts and goddamned reindeer.

Snow's falling, but the plows have been busy—Christmas Eve notwithstanding—and Swain's having zero trouble maneuvering the exit ramp from Highway #1 back to Jonesville. He's been on the road for six hours already, and over the course of the last month, he's done a different but similar route once, sometimes twice, every day.

Maybe it was the Peanuts' *Twelve Days of Christmas* that got him, maybe it was Mariah Carey or David Bowie and Bing Crosby. Maybe it was just time somebody did something about all the bullshit.

Swain hits the interior light and glances in the rearview mirror to be sure the payload's still in the truck bed. It is. Wriggling and kicking even all these hours later, but it's still there. He flicks the blinker and pulls to the industrial area just north of town. The streetlights cease, but the headlights cut the night just fine. He reaches the padlocked chain-link fence and pops out of the truck.

"Puh-puh-plea-ease," the voice says from the truck bed, so cold his teeth are snap-chattering together. "Yu-yu-you guh-got the the the wrong guy!"

Swain clenches his jaw and says, "Bullshit," more to himself than the man with wrists and knees tied together, a black hood over his head.

Fence open, Swain drives through and pops out again to lock it up behind him. Not that someone's likely to swing by at 11:30 PM on Christmas Eve. Not here where the stink—if you ain't used to it—will burn tears from eyes and tickle the gag reflex. Swain's back behind the wheel and rolls another half-mile. He kills the engine. The yard lights around the waste treatment plant never go out while the grid's up, so he's seeing just fine.

"Bullshit snow," Swain hisses as he opens the tailgate and grabs the man's big black boot. The walkway is under about a foot of powder from just the last twelve hours.

"Puh-puh-please luh-let muh-me go!"

The man's irritating Swain something fierce and he yanks him along the slick bedliner to the soft-packed snow. "I will," he says, "but you gotta cooperate. Now, march."

The man gets up and starts shuffling. They go about forty paces. Swain pulls the man's red jacket to halt him and steps out front to take the lead. He withdraws a keyring and opens the heavy steel door. The stink pounds afresh and the man forgets his plight. "Cuh-Christ! Wuh-what is that?"

"Move it, Santa." Swain's behind and pushing again.

The man starts to tell him all over from the beginning that he's got the wrong guy. Probably wanted the Santa from Lakeview or Springmount, a different mall altogether. Like he hasn't heard the rumors or seen the news reports, like Swain's looking for a particular bullshit Santa.

Their footfalls clang heavy on steel grating and the sound takes Swain back to childhood, when he was ten and his mother just beat breast cancer after enough chemotherapy to pret' near do her in, and his father was behind the wheel, ten days back on the wagon, and there was that drunk Santa, fake beard dangling beneath his chin as he ran the red light in his Toyota SUV and smucked into the Swain family Chevy sedan.

Beat cancer?

Beat drinking?

Bullshit Santa says too bad, gonna die in the street and leave a little orphan named Dougie, oh, but maybe a little extra for your trouble yet...

Swain pulls the drifting half of his conscious mind from reverie and stops the man and says, "Right there's fine," and turns Santa so when he pulls off the hood he's facing Swain.

The man screams and jerks backward, trips—they always do—upon seeing Swain's stretched and shiny face. Time hasn't been kind and his lips pull out around his gums and ridges of stiff flesh hood his eyes. His nose is flat on the end and he grows no hair anywhere on his face. The surgeon was junk, but to be fair, it was the '90s, and an insurance deal, so no bells or whistles included.

The Santa drops into the sewage treatment pool and immediately starts gagging and gasping. He can't kick or wade and he sinks. Swain waits, leaning on the railing next to the opening. It's 90 seconds before the last bullshit Santa rises to the surface.

19 red backs bob like apples in the thick brown sludge. Swain knows none of these men is the man who killed his parents and destroyed his face, but that doesn't matter, when it comes to bullshit Christmas, it's the thought that counts.

A BIG SURPRISE

(2022)

Diane squints as she stumbles. She knows where she was headed—despite the hangdog tequila shots—but the sign before her does not say Orca Drive, it says… "Harvest Lane?" After she speaks, a spicy burp climbs up her throat. "Wrong street. Fucking cabbie," she says as she withdraws her iPhone. It's dark around her, a space where the city seems to butt up against the country.

She is a wealthy woman in designer everything. This afternoon, a verdict had come down on her client like a guillotine's blade. 100 years, no chance of parole. And Diane simply moved on, only shrugging to her client as he was walked away in ankle shackles by a chubby bailiff.

"No bars? What is this, nineteen-ninety-nine?" Diane barks a single, harsh laugh as she drops her cellphone back into her purse.

A laugh returns as if echoed, though that is not her laugh.

"Who's there?" she says as she rifles through her Prada bag for what she calls her American Express, because she doesn't leave home without it. Once she has the pepper spray canister firmly in her grip, she repeats the question, "Who's there?"

Where the country begins, rows upon rows of green corn rise and run infinitely to her left and right. Here and there, stalks begin to sway and ruffle.

"Okay then," she says and turns away from the greenery to the—more corn?

The asphalt beneath her feet is gone, now it's dirt and harvested stalks that have left behind only nubs. Overhead, the moon is huge and red, and she's certain that when she stepped into the bar, it had been but a pale sliver.

More stalks ruffle. She stands in a perfect circle of harvested corn, which makes no sense—how could a combine enter a field, harvest a circle, and then depart without trampling stalks upon exit? Makes as little sense as the city suddenly disappearing. Another laugh rings out.

"Who's there?" she says, like third time's going to be the charm.

Pepper spray shifted to her left hand, she relocates her cellphone within her purse with her right. Still no bars. She takes a deep breath and closes her eyes. "You're drunk, stressed, overwrought. When you open your eyes, this will all be gone."

She opens her eyes; nothing has changed, she's surrounded by corn. She's about to pick a direction to start walking when she notes the sudden appearance of a scarecrow with a rotting jack-o-lantern head. Flames ignite within the moldering gourd and its eyes flash red, red, red.

Once capable of peeling her gaze from the scarecrow, she spins, looking to make distance between herself and it. There, before her is an identical scarecrow—same flannel shirt, same jeans, same tufts of straw playing out the seams, same rotting pumpkin head, same flashing red eyes.

"No," she says, turning and seeing three more suddenly around the periphery of the circle.

Her cellphone rings in her hand, the vibration causing her to toss it away like a hot potato. She chases it, snatches it from amid the stiff remnants of harvested stalks. On the screen, she reads the caller ID: Kent Institution. Doesn't matter. She accepts the call and says, "You have to help me! I'm—"

"Why should I help you, you didn't help me?" the voice says.

Diane recognizes it instantly. It's Willem Morgan, the man she'd failed to defend against the slew of violent and revolting charges he faced for the countless archaic and downright eerie acts he'd committed. It's only now that she makes the connection. The women and children Willem had murdered and tortured showed signs of being harmed at an undisclosed, undiscovered location. A farm. They'd been mutilated, raped, and murdered on a farm before being dumped. Diane had tried to level with Willem about his coming clean with the location, about his making a deal concerning other victims. He'd said it was impossible because the farm, "Exists up here," tapping his temple.

Diane drops the phone and puts her hands over her eyes. "You're drunk, stressed, overwrought. When you open your eyes, this will all be gone. When you open your eyes—"

"You will get a big surprise," five raspy voices whisper tight around her, breaths reeking of vegetable rot, burnt wax, and blood.

Diane doesn't dare look. She'll prolong this surprise forever, if she has to.

A LITTLE WARMTH ON A COLD NIGHT
(2022)

The gentle flickering of light rose from the three burning candles on the floor of the McCarrens' 1928 Ford Model A. Elanor McCarron shivered, an almost steady whine playing up her throat over the last 20 or so miles.

"I'm as cold as I have ever been," she said through chattering teeth.

Theodore nodded, bumbling along the icy, ill-kempt patch of road between Marble Canyon and Numa Creek. He peeled back the stiff fingers of a gloved hand from the steering wheel and pointed through the frosty windshield.

"A light burns," he said before sniffling back against his leaky sinus.

"Thank heavens...is it an inn?"

They'd moved at a steady pace of 23 MPH since sundown. The weather was not only bitterly frigid, but the wind kicked up snow in great white dervishes that had Theodore leaning closer and closer to the windshield.

"A church," Theodore said finally.

"Thank heavens, thank heavens," Elanor said again. "Miriam had bragged about the heater in her husband's Chevrolet, and I had told her a little cold did not bother me, but goodness, if I am never this cold again, I shall count myself fortunate."

The lane leading up to the church had been shoveled. Theodore turned in. To either side of the lane were great swatches of field, the deep snow was lumpy with peculiar ridges. Peculiar until the setting and uniformity performed a mental math equation in both their minds. Neither said it, but both recognized that surrounding the church was a sea of gravestones, buried beneath the season's fluff.

Theodore led the brief parade up the snowy steps. Directly above was a single electric bulb, the only light they'd seen. He took the brass knocker and rapped it against the door with three heavy strikes. The sound was a dull contrast to the wind whipping over the lifeless countryside. Both stood silently appraising the ornate floral embellishments of the door so as to take their minds from the cold. Stained glass to either side of the door remained dim, and yet the door opened.

A withered face on a short frame with white, white hair wrapped beneath a black, black shawl leaned through the crack. It was an old woman. Her eyes were pearly blue and quite obviously blind. "Hello?" she said, stretching the O and holding it, *hellooo.*

"Hello. I am Theodore and this is my wife, Elanor."

"Hello," Elanor said, fighting to still her teeth long enough to get the word out clearly.

"We have been on the road longer than expected, and though I hate to impose, I must ask to come in and sit a spell in the warmth of the church," Theodore said.

Elanor clutched at his arm. What if this woman said no?

"Of course, come iiin," the woman said and took a backward step into the sheer blackness of the church's vestibule.

Theodore urged Elanor through the door. Both moved with light, shuffling steps. Neither could see a thing. Theodore pushed the door closed behind him.

"Pardon me," he said. "Is there perhaps a light switch or a candle?"

Distantly, the voice came back to them. "Forgive meee. It is so rare that we have night visitooors." The old woman had walked surely, moving quickly ahead of their shuffling steps, and was now at the far end of a large room.

Elanor discovered a pew and put her hands on it to sturdy herself. "We?" she said.

Directly to her left, a match lit and another woman, this one big and sturdy in a nun's habit, started toward them with an oil lamp in her hands. The flame touched wick and threw a dim glow upon the small meeting area. A second nun sat in a pew directly to Theodore's left, startling him enough that he jumped at her sight. She was tall, slender, young, and nearly pale as the snow beyond the walls.

"Excuse me," he said.

"Do not be offended if Sister Mary and Sister Agatha don't speeeak. They have taken vows of sileeence," the old woman said from the far end of the church.

"Thank you," Elanor said as she accepted the lamp and the nun headed back to the shadowy spaces.

"Come, this waaay." The woman began feeling around before locating what she sought. "Here, matcheees." She patted a sill by a door before passing through.

"At least it is warmer," Elanor whispered.

"Hush, darling," Theodore said.

Upon reaching the matches, Elanor's lamplight shined on a second, identical lamp. Theodore made quick work. With two flames burning, the simple kitchen beyond the church floor became apparent. The old woman stood before a range, a little flame burning beneath a kettle.

"Would you care for a cup of teeea?" she said.

The kitchen was the warmest room yet. Elanor sighed and set the lamp on the dining table so she could remove her gloves.

"Yes, please," Theodore said.

"Yes, thank you. It is very gracious of you," Elanor said, she then looked at Theodore. Under the enhanced glow banking from the pale-yellow wallpaper, the mess of Theodore's face was suddenly all too visible. She laughed. "You are filthy."

"Am I?" Theodore said, grinning. At the last bit of sunlight, he'd filled the gas tank from a can and worked free two dirty snow chunks that had affixed to the Ford's undercarriage.

The old woman turned to face them. The great lines of her

face starker in the lamplight. "At the end of the hall, the door on the left is the indoor privy."

Theodore shrugged to Elanor before tilting his head, giving her serious askance eyebrows. She waved him away. The kitchen broke off into a hall that spread into another room. The church seemed much larger on the inside than it had looked from the outside.

Elanor opened her mouth to ask about the church, but the whistle of the kettle interrupted her. The old woman felt around the counter for a jar. She pulled it close. She then opened a drawer to her right and began pawing around inside. Her hand reappeared with a large steeping spoon. Elanor winced, wanting to offer her assistance, though not wanting to shout over the squealing kettle. The old woman reached into a cupboard and felt around until discovering the trio of cups with saucers she wanted—all three different—and the pot a different design yet again. Elanor clenched her teeth and squinted with her entire expression, that damned whistle—why didn't she remove the kettle from the heat? The old woman loaded the spoon from the jar before deftly placing the spoon over the mouth of the pot. Finally, finally she reached for the kettle, quieting that cursed whistling. Slowly, and without spilling, she ran the water into the tea pot through the spoon's payload.

It smelled earthy and sweet, a bit like November apples, brown and soft. Elanor turned up her lip. Rather than speak on the scent, she said, "Is this an old parish?"

The woman turned, two teacups rattling on their saucers in her hands. "Pastor Davenport discovered this land iiin..." The old woman trailed off, her hands tipping, muddy red tea spilling onto the linen tablecloth.

"Goodness!" Elanor rounded the table and touched the old woman's forearm.

The old woman wrenched away, flinging the teacups across the kitchen. One hit the floor without damage, while the other struck a wall. The tea splashed a great swatch upon the white paper before oozing down to the pale wainscotting.

"Do not touch me, dew-beateeer!"

"Excuse you," Elanor said, stumbling in reverse. She was suddenly plenty warm enough to continue on her way. "I think it is time for my husband and I to depart. We thank you for the warmth of the church."

She took up her lamp and rushed down the hall. There were three doors at the end. She opened the one on the left. The washroom was cramped—a clawfoot tub to one side, a toilet and a sink a foot apart, almost kissing distance from the tub—and dark. Theodore was not in there. To her right came a rustling.

"Theodore?" she said.

She closed the washroom door to a crack and stepped to the middle door. The knob was cold in her grasp; she could feel carved lines within the steel. Locked. She tugged hard. She attempted five quick jerks, and still nothing. She heard more rustling, to her right yet.

"Theodore?"

She tried the handle and the door pulled open. The light from her lamp immediately shined on the ruddy face of an old man. He jumped. Elanor jumped, nearly dropping the lamp.

"Oy, scared the dickens out of me," the man mumbled. He had no teeth and when his gums came together, it depressed the entire lower half of his face. "What's all the shouting about?"

Elanor put a hand to her breast. "I am sorry, my husband came back to use the facilities, but he is not—did you see him?"

The old man squinted an eye. "Privy's the door two down."

"I am aware. He is not in there, and the middle door is locked."

The old man shuffled out of his room. It reeked of sweat and tobacco, with the hint of something sweet and earthy, perhaps a cup of the old woman's tea.

Though she'd been in the little washroom, she went back and

flung open the door. "Empty."

The old man stood next to her. He was in a nightshirt that stretched to his knees. The top of his head came up only to Elanor's shoulder, and she was no taller than the average woman. He leaned in for a better look around the washroom.

"I sure do appreciate the indoor works," he said and leered a mashed-face grin at Elanor. "Must have gone out to the church." The old man pointed past Elanor.

There was a fourth door; this one on the other wall. She wordlessly pulled the door open and looked out to the empty rows of pews. It didn't make sense...then again, perhaps he'd wanted his pipe. That was almost logical. He didn't know the blind woman was so strange, and he'd simply gone out for his pipe.

"I suppose," she said and started through the church.

The old man shuffled behind her. "Nobody comes out here much," he said. "Never was much of a congregation...but it keeps me fed, so I ought not complain."

A sense of politeness overcame Elanor's mouth as she swung open the heavy door to the vestibule. "Are you the pastor."

The light above the steps continued to glow. Looking outward, everything was visible. The yard was frozen and barren, the edges devoured by thick shadows. The Ford was snow-spattered, but the windshield was clear enough to see the two nuns. One sat behind the wheel and the other sat on the bench next to her. They were rocking, as if taking tight turns. Both appeared to be wide-eyed and grinning.

"I am no pastor," the man said, pushing up close behind Elanor to see out.

"What are they doing?" Elanor said, a whine on her words.

"That your husband's auto?" the old man said.

Elanor now sensed his closeness and wanted to push him back but did not. She then felt hands creep into the pockets of her coat. Fingers prodded the silk lining that played about the areas just above her thighs. The old man pressed himself against her.

"It is a nice car," he whispered, his breath tight to her ear.

She spun, stumbling to the floor, again nearly dropping her lamp. She climbed to her feet before the old man had the chance to close the distance. She hurried back between the rows of pews. This was all wrong and that old man, what was his business here, if not a pastor.

Elanor was suddenly aware that she was now alone, but equally aware that if it came to it, she could surely fend off a toothless old man and a blind old woman. And just where had Theodore gone?

She'd seen him go down the hall. He wouldn't go outside without her. He wasn't in the washroom, and he wouldn't have gone in the old man's room. That left the locked door.

"Locked *now*," she whispered and finished the sentiment in thought, *but was it always?* A tink-tink-tinking played quietly as she pushed through the door into the hall but stopped abruptly. She gasped when she saw the old woman standing in the dark but recovered quickly. "Open that door."

"Which dooor? The old woman said.

"The middle door. The only locked door. Theodore must have gone through that door."

"That door is looocked."

"I know! But someone must have locked it after he passed through. Now, open it!"

The old woman did not move. "I do not touch that dooor. That is the dooor to the graveyaaard."

The sea of bumps in the snow surrounding the church flashed upon her mind. So, so many grave markers, but for whom? It didn't matter now.

The old man shuffled through the door and Elanor took a spinning step away, pointing to the middle door. "Open that door!"

The man's eyes widened. "That door is locked."

Frustrated, Elanor stamped her foot. "No! My husband had to have gone—"

The rumble of an engine played just above the rushing winds, cutting off Elanor's train of thought. She looked past the old man. The vestibule door remained open, and the yard lights remained lit. She hurried by him, bumping him aside. The old man and the blind woman followed Elanor, though did not make it more than halfway across the church floor before Elanor's cry paused them in their track.

"Where are they going?"

The Ford had backed out the drive and was rolling quickly from the church. Elanor jerked away from the sight and charged toward the old man and old woman.

"Where are they taking the car?"

The old woman frowned, and the man bunched up his face.

"Where are they taking the car!"

"Whooo?"

"The nuns!"

The old man laughed. "The sisters cannot drive a car. Your husband must be with them, giving them a *ride*."

The final word came out like a slur, something tawdry and below Elanor's acknowledgement. "Someone better open that goddamned door!" She pushed on, shouldering between the old man and the old woman.

The tink-tink-tinking resumed and although it did not sound like a fist knocking on a door, did not sound like a voice, did not sound like anything she could discern, she knew, *knew* it was Theodore. The sound stopped once she reentered the hallway.

"That door is locked!" the old man shouted behind her. "Only Davenport has a key!"

But it wasn't locked any longer. The knob spun easily in her grip. For a heartbeat, she paused before swinging it wide enough to reveal shadowy stone steps. Davenport, the pastor, he must've opened it. Likely he was lonely and had trapped Theodore with some boring tale or another. From her experience, clergymen loved to chat with strangers. Conversion bidding.

"Theodore?" Elanor said and stepped down into the black maw. It was warm down there, smelled sweet and earthy, like the blind woman's tea. "Theodore?"

A rough stone wall butted up to the landing at the bottom of the stairs and she turned. Her lamp shined brightly over the huge room. There was a carpenter's workbench. Next to it were planks of wood. Behind it were coffins. Elanor moved closer.

"Theodore?"

The tink-tink-tinking sound grew louder and she trailed it, stepping deeper into the room. Beyond the coffins were great slabs of limestone. Future grave markers, no doubt.

"Theodore?"

The tink-tink-tinking was coming from her left and she followed it, eyes on the floor as she stepped around rock debris and chunks of wood. The scent was heavier now.

"Theodore?"

At the end of the room was another set of stairs, cut into the rock. It had to be a storm door. She hurried along, mindful of the floor. She reached the stairs and found that the tink-tink-tinking was now behind her. She paused a moment to drink in the room in her wake, or rather, what she could see of it in the light cast by the lamp.

"Theodore, is that you?"

New sounds played through the storm door. A chunking, clunking sound, alongside heavy breaths. There was somebody out there, but what if that somebody wasn't Theodore?

"Who else?" she said.

She steadied herself, ignoring the tears now cutting damp paths down her winter-dry cheeks. With her free hand, she pushed open the heavy storm door, and was immediately rewarded with a bitter wind that seemed to form icicles in her bone marrow.

"Theodore?" she shouted into the blustery night.

Ahead, flames rose from the ground. A man stood amongst them with a pickaxe that he was using to chunk up the frozen earth. The tink-tink-tinking behind her stopped and she heard faint footfalls. Elanor turned from the wind and shined the light down the stairs.

"Theo—"

What Elanor saw cut the name in half in the back of her throat. The man coming toward her was in a black suit, dusty with limestone powder. His clergy collar was clean and tight. In his breast pocket were chisels and a small hammer. He had a long blue, blue face. Red blood flashed a stark contrast upon his lips, a drip playing down to his chin. He had hideous yellow eyes and pointy ears.

"You must be the missus," he said, revealing two rows of elongated eyeteeth.

Elanor screamed and popped up the stairs, dropping the lamp into the snow, and slamming the door closed behind her. The snow was high enough that she could only follow the trail to the fire and the man digging.

"Theodore?" she said, stopping eight feet short of the oil spilled and burning in perfect rectangles amid the snow. "Theodore?" she said again.

The man with the pickaxe was naked, his flesh pale, almost blue. Elanor recognized him from behind without having to see his face. At the back of her, the storm door banged open. She had no choice, and ran to him, ignoring the burning oil atop the frozen earth.

"Theodore!"

Elanor grabbed her husband and yanked him around. He obliged her effort and peered down at her with eyeless sockets. A chunk had been bitten from his throat. She screamed, her legs giving way, sending her sprawling out of the flaming quadrant.

Dizziness reigned while the cold world fought to burn away the flesh of her hands and cheek, bare against the elements. The world darkened when Pastor Davenport leaned over her and sank his teeth in her throat.

His mouth was so, so cold.

———

Luna reached across the center console and grabbed Ophelia's arm. "Oh my god, you have to stop."

Luna was already wide-eyed. "I know!"

Luna wheeled their 2023 Fisker Ocean SUV into the lot of an old church seemingly plunked down in the middle of a massive graveyard. There were several hundred stones, if not a thousand or more. They were smokey white and begging to be rubbed.

Ophelia gathered the Rubbermaid bin from the hatchback of the Fisker and started toward the gate of the stubby wrought-iron fence separating them from the cemetery. The gate creaked and Luna made a point of playing it back and forth. It was perfect.

"If a cemetery gate doesn't creak, is it even a cemetery?" she said.

Ophelia laughed and set down the bin full of cloth paper, charcoal, rubbing wax, and the cleaning brushes. She gazed out at all the markers.

"Where do we even start?" she said.

A window of the church opened before Luna could answer. An old woman, eyes milky blue leaned out and said, "Would you care for a cup of teeea?"

WHEELS ON THE BUS

(2013)

It wasn't easy being the little brother, especially when big brother was such a show off, such a big shot. Fuck him.

Damp and heavy snow landed and momentarily stuck to the windows of the bus as it cut through the dreary evening. It was a Greyhound, the newest one Larry Slider had ever been in, and that said a little something. Larry knew about buses, riding them anyway.

Dark at a quarter after four didn't hurt his chances. Being as small as possible and as memorable as a Saturday night home alone, jerking it to a skin flick, well that helped too. He chose a corner seat at the back, the one across from the door to the closet toilet, the spot that always managed to stink, even when nobody had gone in there yet. Stink didn't hurt either, it would keep bodies away and eyes averted.

In that plush seat, so new he doubted anyone had even puked on it, he hunkered and tried to listen to his workout playlist. A list he'd put together three months earlier when life had options, possibilities, hope even; hope plausible enough that he might just show his brother that he wasn't a loser.

Born more than a decade prior to Larry, the product of focused copulation, Roderick basked in the warm glow of two supportive and healthy parents in their mid-forties. Niles, Pa, Slider, had a defect hiding somewhere amongst his gooey gene map. The defect didn't show until Roderick was already achieving at law school. At home with Ma and Pa Slider, Larry learned the glorious and colorful world of mental instability in a legal guardian.

Nobody really understood what happened at first, nobody ever found out exactly, but Niles Slider's hens skipped the farm and took the coop with them when they left. The man got loud. Something about mind-reading government officials that had the country's logging crews under control. He explained this to his eight-year-old son. The theory usually surfaced while the pair hid in the dark farmhouse, holding hands in the closet. Larry believed everything his father told him. His father gave him a hat made of tinfoil, both figuratively and literally.

Blocking: a fine hobby for anyone with too much memory and too few birthday cakes or trips to Disneyland. Larry blocked things. Blocking was great...when it held.

—

His closet reeked of mothballs and leather. Larry sat on the floor, balled up tight, as if hiding behind one's own knees offered a reliable form of coverage. Niles let go of his son's hand and stood, it was abrupt and uncommon. Sitting in the closet with his father wasn't abnormal, but silence and a stoppage in physical contact were abnormal.

A string dangled from the ceiling and Niles yanked it. The light lit, bouncing from Larry's tinfoil hat back to his father's eyes. The aging man saw something, felt something, knew something, but Larry didn't understand. He picked up on the fear and acted accordingly—how one ended up in a closet holding hands with his father in the first place.

"I knew it," Niles whispered. "Whoever you are, I want my son back."

Uncertain if his father just lost track, Larry whispered, "Pa, I'm here."

"Liar!

This time Larry didn't know what to do, so he sat there. The fierce glow under that simple yellow bulb made the boy uncomfortable and he balled as small as possible. Niles put on a math-thinking expression. The figures were adding to something immeasurable and insane, no doubt. "Ah-ha!" he said and Larry lifted his head. "You can't get me, if I get me."

Conditioning and age didn't matter, those words didn't sound right. Niles rooted into the pockets of his heavy canvas duster—the jacket he wore every day for the final six months of his life. Larry hoped, somehow, he'd forget the search or misplace his pockets, but no, he found the object of desire.

"You can't get me, if I get me," he said again, and according to the carving knife in his hand, he meant business.

Blood sprayed onto Larry's face like hot cream shot from a cow's tit as his father dragged the knife along his own throat. The man stood tall and lifted his arms, that blood trailing into the shadows beneath his coat. Then he put his hands up as if he recognized the mistake and wanted to reverse it, or at least, to staunch the bleeding. It was too late. The man fell onto Larry.

Three hours trapped, screams muffled by dead, fatherly weight, before Ma woke up and found them.

—

Larry leaned his head against the cold glass of the bus window. It was slow going, but he was out of the city and that was good. They stopped in the next suburb—only six kilometers from A to B—and waited. He watched a woman through the window, shouting at her teenaged son while a man stood next to her, sneering. It took him back to when Ma married Terry Macy and he moved into the loft above the garage.

Terry Macy took the role of father figure to heart and attempted re-enactments of his own childhood. Stand straight, fly right, obey your elders, top of the class marks, or else. The belt had a Harley Davidson brand carved into the leather.

"You little cocksucker!" Terry Macy would say, his balding, vein-ridden head, sweaty and red. "You think you'll ever get a goddamn job without a diploma? Tap dancing Christ, I won't be paying a cent for a loser kid to sit around jerking it to titty rags when he's failing science. You need that course to graduate." He'd suck in a heavy breath and then snap went Harley Davidson. "Why can't you be more like your brother? He doesn't sit around dog fucking." Harley Davidson said...snap, snap, snap. "Lazy losers get nowhere!"

Soon as he could, Larry ran. He stayed in the shelters until a social worker found him and forced him into a group home. The group home was tight and they forced him back to Terry Macy and the Harley Davidson belt.

"Fuck you!" Larry said as he threw a rock through the Harley Davidson shop window, a place out by the movie theaters. He was drunk and wanted the trouble. He waited while the sirens drew closer. He picked up another rock and bonked it off the hood of a cop cruiser.

"On the ground, motherfucker!"

Larry flipped the man off and ate dirt after about two heartbeats.

Only 16, they had to let him go. After processing, a fat faced stinker of a cop dropped Larry off at Ma's house. Terry Macy refused to pick him up from the station, late as it was, but waited in the dark, standing behind the door just inside the loft, Harley Davidson poised and ready.

Terry Macy watched the boy pull off his shirt and then pants. Terry Macy moved. No leather this time. The buckle end, the business end, thwapt in a way that made that leather feel like pinches from Grandma.

Larry screamed and bruised and bled. Two weeks later, he was in juvenile detention for breaking the window of a gas station kiosk and stealing a pack of Player's Light King Size and a black Bic lighter.

—

Larry's stomach grumbled while the bus idled. Only one more town over, but he had to risk it. A bag of jerky and a microwave burrito from the convenience store.

Six hours until the bus crossed into the Yukon. All that space, nobody would find him. He'd become a goddamned mountain man. Life like an Eskimo, it couldn't be that hard.

Behind the till, a small television aired a news feed, he couldn't see the screen but what he heard sank his guts to his shoes. He grabbed two cans of Red Bull from the small cooler next to the chocolate bars and stepped close, leaning around the bin of pull tickets, and tried to make enough noise so that the cashier would turn from the TV before—there was his face, the mug shot taken during his last arrest.

"Don't want no trouble," the cashier said without turning around, "I already called, saw you through the bus window. Don't kill me."

Sirens squealed outside. Larry was in a daze. He grabbed his goods and broke for the door. "Fuck," he whispered as the cold air sliced at his lungs. He couldn't take that bus to the Yukon, but there were other ways, hell, there were other buses. Average looking white dude could get anywhere in Canada—if they didn't nab him right there and then.

—

As a man, Larry liked to blame all of his problems on his past, blacking out the meat and potatoes, yet holding onto the feeling of tragedy. But maybe who he became wasn't his fault. If it wasn't for his father and the man's demented thoughts, he wouldn't be on the run, and his brother wouldn't be blank-staring at a wall from his bedroom floor, dead.

A week earlier, Roderick called Larry, asking if they could meet. It was an odd request. Larry and his brother lived on the opposite sides of the tracks. It wasn't close either, one was miles onto the good and the other miles onto the bad.

But Larry had hope. He could be a better person, could excel like his brother had, given a second chance. Visions of brotherly love and mending the torn relationship, Larry wanted to become close with his brother, his niece, his nephew, and sister-in-law. The visions ventured so far as to create a scenario where Roderick found Larry a halfway decent job, one he could stick out and learn to love for years. Maybe someday he'd buy a house—nothing as big as his brother's, mind you, but a place to call home.

A little after 8:00 PM, a fresh downpour of December rain melted much of the snow. Larry rode from the nearest bus stop and rushed two blocks to his brother's six-bedroom home, looking haggard, but feeling optimistic.

Sitting down in the Slider family den, Larry looked deep into the short glass of expensive rye so smooth it was as if everything he'd ever drank until then was mule piss. He rotated the glass in his hand, watching the ice cubes dance in the amber liquid while he listened, waiting for his chance to burst in and apologize, to accept any conditions his brother might have about fixing a future.

On and on the man talked. He refilled Larry's glass twice. The position didn't come up, the offer to help didn't come up. Hope didn't stick around very long at all.

"Let me get to it," Roderick said as he stood behind the red leather wingback in his study. "I'm looking to step into a bench judge position."

Larry set down his tumbler, blinking. This wasn't about olive branches at all. This wasn't the lucky helping the unlucky. This wasn't a peace pipe, not even a Styrofoam lifesaver tossed overboard to save a drowning man.

"I need you out of my life and somewhere you'll never again get the chance to besmirch my good name. You've proven yourself to be garbage over and over, and I won't allow you to ruin my career with your petty criminal persona."

Larry didn't see red, he saw black.

Larry got to his feet and told Roderick exactly what he thought of the man and his great big house and his stupid fucking judgeship. Roderick, looking a bit stunned—perhaps that anyone would dare—told Larry to get out of his house, city, family, and existence. After breaking his glass and taking a few gulps from the rye bottle, Larry did.

He caught the next bus, entered his apartment, grabbed the bag of cocaine he'd planned on cutting and slanging to kick off his better life, and went upstairs to apartment G. The Cobra .380 was small but looked new enough that it would do the exact befitting damage.

"Watch you with that 'un. Match rounds to Bigsby's deal, if they get 'em. 'Member him?"

Larry did remember and maybe at another time would've said thanks but no thanks to a gun linked to an armed robbery resulting in the death of a counter clerk and two little girls in the wrong place at the wrong time.

Two hours later, he waited outside his brother's home. One light at a time, the place darkened. People always locked the main doors, especially the wealthy pricks like Roderick, but they never seemed to think about the contractor skimping on a chintzy electric garage door opener. A few jiggles, a few tugs and that door tracked backward, allowing Larry to roll in unnoticed.

The alarm on the wall blinked, Larry tried three different sets of numbers until he successfully punched his mother's birthday, disarming the house. The angry, irrational thoughts came back in a boiling flood. The fact that he'd daydreamed his cocksucking brother as some fucking savior was the worst of it. The house was nearly full dark and Larry moved with quiet steps. The first two bedrooms he checked were vacant, maybe waiting for a visitor, possibly another baby, who knew, who cared. The next was the little boy's room, Alexander. Larry loomed over the sleeping figure, beams of light from the streetlamps illuminating his shape beneath the comforter. Larry wasn't mad at Alexander, so he didn't want to see his dying visage. He grabbed a pillow and let off one shot, through the fluff, through the skull, through the bed, and so on.

It didn't go as he'd hoped.

It was too loud.

Susan, Roderick's trophy wife, was the first mole to pop her head out a door. Larry was on the move by then and put two shots into her chest. Blood and silicone burst a second before she went down. Clementine, the girl child, exited her room rubbing at her sleepy eyes. She was a much smaller target, and unsure of how much ammunition he had, Larry strode forward and pressed the hot muzzle to the little girl's forehead. Her eyes widened and she tried to jerk away, but the pop was faster. Her brains and bits of skull blew out the back of her head like a smashed watermelon.

Roderick had to have heard, but the coward he was, stayed in his bedroom. Larry stomped, a madman's grin spreading across his face. His father never had the crazy where it met happiness, but Larry found that intersection and danced in it.

He flicked the light switch after opening the final door, hoping to bask in the glow of his brother's fear. Not letdown. The moons aligned. The man looked like he saw a ghost.

Roderick jumped out of bed and tried to run, three bullets entered his back in a small cluster. Larry almost skipped with joy when he rounded the bed to look at the body. His brother reached up to him, reached for help...just as Larry had. The smile slipped and Larry closed his eyes as he emptied the clip into his brother.

Moving, Larry rummaged through drawers looking for cash and non-descript valuables. Between wallets, piggy banks, and a small wad in the underwear drawer, Larry collected nearly $500. The jewelry looked too good, so good it might as well have a GPS built in. Nobody would buy it, not from him. He took Roderick's credit card though, figured if he used it before anyone knew the man was dead, it wouldn't be a problem. After catching his reflection in the dresser mirror, he decided to borrow some of his brother's clothes, too.

—

Outside the convenience store, sunrise was about ready to roll into the sky, but heavy clouds hung, blocking the harshest of the light. Looking left, Larry saw the bright blue and red flashers rounding a corner, so he jetted to the right. The snow was thick, wet, and slippery. He skidded around a corner, dropping to a knee before he could continue. His right hand stung with cold as he ran as a Red Bull can rolled into the street. He pushed the other can into his pocket, along with the jerky and the smooshed burrito.

Sirens drew closer. Larry focused on a playground in the distance, beyond that, a forest. A car pulled up and parked just down the street from where he ran, he wondered how far he'd get in a stolen car, a lot further than on foot—no doubt about that. He pushed, his chest ached, but the car jerked from the curb, as if also needing to avoid those approaching sirens.

"Prick!" Larry said, the word bookended by gasps. Too busy watching his getaway car get away from him, he didn't notice a deep dip in the sidewalk. He stumbled. His arms flailed and his head nailed a snowy bench. Pain lashed, but it was short lived. He was up. Whipping around the corner next to the stop sign, a school bus, painted dark blue, jerked to a halt on squeaking brakes.

The door swung open. "Holy smokes, buddy, you all right?" asked a smiley middle-aged man at the wheel of the bus.

The sirens sounded as if they called his name: "Laaay-Reee-Laaay-Reeeeeeeeee..."

"They for you, buddy? You'd better get in." The driver was nodding, eyebrows high enough to touch his bangs.

No other options, Larry said, "Thanks," and ran up the slick black stairs.

"No problem, buddy," the driver said as he jerked the bus forward.

Only a few seats remained vacant. Lumpy heaps of cloth rose on most of the brown benches, but six others had passengers. None smiled, all looked beaten and dejected.

"Where's this bus going?" Larry asked over his shoulder as he moved toward a seat only halfway occupied by a heap of lumpy cotton.

"Away from those cops. I'm sure you don't mind that, now do ya, buddy?" the driver said, a few passengers sniggered.

"Sure, but where?"

"It's a secret. You like secrets, buddy?" The smile was Stretch Armstronging the driver's face. "Won't snow where we're going. Bet you'll like that, buddy!"

A young female passenger moaned.

"What, like Florida or Arizona? Where?"

The driver cackled like a stoned witch. "No, buddy, not Florida or Arizona. But out of Canada. Cops won't touch you if you're out of Canada, eh Buddy?"

Guy was nuts, but leaving Canada worked, so long as he could avoid trouble at the border, which was unlikely, but it was a problem for later. He pulled the burrito from his pocket and tore the wrapper. He took a bite and maggots oozed from the opening, pouring onto his lips in a busy scatter. He threw the thing and screamed, spat little white nuggets of life. A man across the aisle scrunched his face.

"Jesus," Larry whispered and wiped his mouth, and then rubbed his head. He felt a deep gash, was surprised when it didn't hurt, even when the road bumped and his fingers prodded accidentally. Larry tried again, "Hey, seriously, where we going?"

The bus driver looked into the mirror and made the key locking his lips gesture.

Larry turned to look through the back window. It was blacked out. The side windows were too, not tinted like he'd thought earlier, but black. Larry stood up and was about to speak, but sat back down next to the mound of white. He tugged at the cloth. It slid and pooled in a heap on the bench seat.

"Are we there yet?" It was a small boy with a battered face and a neck bent so far sideways there was no chance of meaningful connection to the rest of his body. "I think I gotta pee," he said.

Larry popped from the seat then. "What the fuck?" he whispered.

"Hey, buddy, watch the swears, we got kids onboard, okay buddy?" the driver was still smiling that rubber smile.

In the seat behind his, one of the shrouds or cocoons or whatever the hell they were began falling and an elderly lady leaned forward. "What'd ya do?" she asked, her voice playful, but hoarse. She was green and scabby. Yellow shit oozed out from around her eyes.

"What?" Larry said, taking a handful of steps in reverse, up the aisle, toward the driver.

"To get on this bus, what'd ya do?"

Somewhere he missed something. A hand reached out from another white hump and grabbed his arm. There were six fingers, long as knitting needles and nearly as skinny but for the knobby spindle knuckles.

Larry gasped and wrenched free.

"I fed my kids a bottle of rubbing alcohol. Once they passed out, I put 'em in the tub and played *Dunk Dunk Went Kermit the Frog*." The green woman howled laughter for two seconds before stopping abruptly. "You have kids?"

Larry shook his head, still walking backward.

"Hey, buddy, better sit down. You don't want me to tell you again, buddy," the driver said, his smile opening to reveal teeth like barbed wire ends.

"Man, let me off. I don't...let me off," Larry said after he'd turned away from the driver but didn't start back to his seat.

"I will, buddy, but you gotta sit down!"

The way that voice boomed put Larry's shuffling feet into motion. One of the cotton humps began hitching, as if whoever was under there was sobbing. Larry went all the way to the back and tested the emergency door.

"Nice try, buddy!" the driver shouted, tone full of mirth.

Larry fell into an empty seat. "Where the hell are we going?" he shouted and put his head in his hands, prodded the gulley at the back. It was so deep and...was that his brain? Could he feel his brain?

"Bingo, buddy, you guessed it!"

The green woman laughed. "Where the *Hell* did you think we were going?"

The driver bellowed at this and a handful of moans and snivels carried the background tune. Through the front window, a blinding red light poured into the bus as the driver geared down, pulling up to the end of the line.

—

Officers Bitz and Officer Wilson looked down at the body of Larry Slider, a man suspected of murdering his brother's family.

"Don't get any easier than that, do it?" Officer Wilson asked after fetching the wallet from the dead man's pants.

"Looks like he slipped, huh?" Officer Bitz asked.

"I'd say."

"Going full-on, slipped, and cracked his skull off that there bench."

"Call it in, too friggin' cold out out here."

Officer Bitz leaned down close to the body. "Got what you deserved."

"Punched himself a one-way ticket," Officer Wilson said, rubbing his hands together for warmth.

GIN HAZE

(2019)

Yolanda Handler celebrated her fourteenth birthday with her first glass of gin. Discovering a distaste for the liquor—and by extension, her friend Whitney—Yolanda shouted a holy tirade about her suddenly tarnished goodness. Whitney, less drunk by several degrees, instructed Yolanda to shut up or get out.

Out it was. Home was a six-kilometer city walk, five if she cut through the park. This typically took about an hour, but in her liquor slickened state, an hour had come and gone with another three kilometers to go.

The cement park path bent around a field. Yolanda's heart broke with exhaustion. It was as if she'd never been so far from her bed. Across the park was the church. Once there, she still had to turn left down Honeysuckle Avenue, and beyond that, continue a block before reaching her door.

The distance toyed in the realm of lightyears.

Yolanda stumbled into the damp grass off the trail. Shortening the shortcut. She moved outside the touch of the overhead lights, into the shadows. The dewy floor danced beneath her. The gin in her blood had her limbs like greasy rubber.

Already spinning, Yolanda hadn't noticed she was falling until she fell and took a mouthful of grass. "I hate you!" Fingers yanked green strands from the earthen scalp.

Up, she ambled along, forcing a jog that was nearly as much sideways as it was forward. Blackout blinks stole bits until they became chunks. Unconscious on her feet for two shuffled steps, she tipped. She awoke on the ground. Face down in the wet grass again was not a mystery of how, but when.

"I hope you die." Yolanda combed the damp field as her eyes slipped closed once more.

Time passed beyond recognition and her eyes opened. Mouth sticky and tasting awful. Head throbbing. Body numb. Yolanda patted the grass, squinting at a change. Not only were the strands dry, but they were different, shorter and firmer. The drunkenness had dissipated, drastically. She looked left and then right, saw absolutely nothing. Above, far away, was a yellow sliver that might've been the moon.

"Hello?"

Up, pre-gin steadiness filled her legs, though the absence of light left her shaky. Balance was an agreement between the eyes, ears, and extremities. Toe tapping for obstacles, she moved blindly. To her left, there was a moist squishy noise, so she veered to the right. One, two, three steps, her extended fingers met a wall.

The only wall that should exist given her last recognizable location was the church, and even that was a stretch. Beneath her touch was not brick. Here was a surface flat and warm, steel or plastic, free of pores. Slapped palms offered virtually no report.

Yolanda had heard that bad moonshine made a girl go blind. Did gin make a girl go blind? Go crazy?

"Hello?"

The tears resumed. The squishing sound slowed, a handful of chirpy clicks joined in, mostly from her left. But in motion. Nasty, insectile chittering. Shoulder to the wall, she made distance. The bug noises echoed from behind, below, and above.

Fear bubbled. This was the outcome of underage drinking and she'd never been sorrier.

"God, can you hear me? Sorry." She quickened her pace as the things behind grew busier in her wake.

Then the wet sloshing became frantic, she broke into a jog, the wall leaned into her as she leaned into it, and after a dozen steps, the sound was ahead of her rather than behind her, she stalled in confusion and terror, dropped into a crouch, the sliver moon above was the only hope remaining.

That light still existed somewhere was a life preserver.

The sloppy movements continued their approach, from every angle, though lesser so from across the empty space.

"God...Daddy...please?"

The sliver of light dimmed for a half-second before two stick-like objects entered the image, followed by a huge bumpy head and a translucent abdomen that put a green hue over the faraway glow.

The truth struck. Not the moon.

The sounds at her peripherals were too close and she broke as if from blocks at a starter pistol's bark, 14 steps in a left-veering path took Yolanda to the wall at the far side of the room, and her middle finger crunched on contact, it hurt, but the terror was greater.

"Let me outta here!"

The squishy motion was everywhere, the sliver above had vanished behind cloudy activity. Three painful jabs at her face brought her arms up to guard.

She ran, screaming.

To her left, the noise was less.

"Help me!"

She hit wall again.

Things prodded and broke skin.

She spun, hands to the weeping wounds suddenly inhabited by digging critters, she tried to run, but a wave hit her and burrowers created pathways, the chittering teeth tore and swallowed as if her constitution resembled butter rather than fresh, untanned leather, "You got—!" the words choked away as a creature entered Yolanda's mouth and dug a tunnel through her sinus, and squirmed an elastic body into the hard palate.

—

Lights on, the buttoned-down scientists peered into the observation dome. It was similar every time, and though varying the scenery caused differences, it never changed the outcome.

"Much slower in the dark," Dr. Polina Alexandrovna said.

Dr. Richard Bachman nodded. "Further suggests eyes are the prime means of locating nutrients and vessels. Subject Ten lasted the longest by two minutes four seconds."

The body of Yolanda Handler, Subject 10, was a lump above a dark stain in the faux grass. It had been three hours and nine minutes since she'd died and was due any minute to...

"Ho, here we go," Dr. Alexandrovna said.

The body of Yolanda, bloodied, gaping holes in her arms and face, rose to a shaky stance. The slack mouth hissed and chattered from within. The five bugs crammed into her brainpan moved Yolanda as if she was a string-less marionette.

"Remarkable," Dr. Bachman said. "It never ceases to amaze me. It's terrifying."

Dr. Alexandrovna nodded. "Any hard numbers?"

"ROSCOSMOS and NASA are running circles, now they're saying it might be more than twelve hundred *bugs* have escaped. Any word on the news?"

Below, the former Yolanda slammed a fist against a wall. Gazing upwards, seeing through the reflective, tinted ceiling, hungry to infest and ingest.

"Some. I'm not going outside for a while."

Dr. Bachman offered a sickened expression. "I should think not."

The former Yolanda slammed a fist again, mouth opening. "Feed us and you may live." The words came out in bug clicks and chirps but were unmistakable.

Dr. Bachman lifted his brow. "That's new."

"They're learning by committee."

TIBBYTOWN BUFFET

(2019)

Plate in hand, face and neck pouring out from the collar of her shirt like dough waves, the woman said, "You need more shrimp, rings too. If you got 'em." There was no need to await a response. The woman turned from the buffet with a loaded plate.

"Right away, right away," Echo said, scurrying back toward the kitchen. The gentle breeze was pleasant. The uniform breathed better if she rushed.

Through the hot dining floor and through the swinging doors into the cooler portion of the kitchen. It was a trade-off, the heat was lesser, but the grease stink was much higher. There was a clamor of clanking dishes and utensils, thirteen teenaged boys and girls staffed the six stainless-steel sinks around the long wash alley. Grates on the floor let the teens spray blast the room clean at the end of every shift. A fan built into the ceiling kept the temperature at a comfortable cool.

Comfortable workers were efficient workers.

At the far end of it all, were a sliding order window and a kitchen buzzer button. Echo bumped one of the washer boys as she hurried to the buzzer. He dropped a dish and shouted in his native tongue. It was difficult to recall where they'd all come from, especially when many did not last long.

The Tibbytown Buffet paid minimum wage and the employee door revolved. Foreigners almost always. The regional manager accepted the brunt of the incoming resumes at immigration offices. Zhou Wen switched continents and became Echo, met the manager of the Metro Vancouver Tibbytown Buffet chain the same hour she arrived in the country a year earlier.

"Sorry, sorry," she said to the angry boy—tanned skin, dark black hair and eyebrows.

There was no time to feel guilty. Water droplets sprayed as she shrank her arms tight to her body so as to avoid collisions. At the back wall, she pressed the buzzer and the slate window opened. Heat streamed through the gap and Echo jerked her head away.

"Yeah?" asked a man in square wire-rimmed glasses beyond the window.

He spoke with a local accent. Echo learned the difference between Canadian and American accents quickly enough.

"Need bin of rings and bin of shrimps, rings and shrimps," Echo said.

"Shrimps or shrimp, which is it?" The man began closing the window as he spoke to another white-coated cook in the hidden room. The window swung back open; Echo had already turned around. "Echo!"

Spun on a pivot, she peered through the gap in the steel. The food smelled fresher in there. It was impossible to ignore that some magic must go on behind that wall. The mysterious ingredients of the secret sauce.

"Can you come 'round back? We need the shipment brought in, but you can't tell anybody. Dr. Regent skipped out on us and we're swamped."

"Right away, right away."

The idea that all the cooks had doctorates offset any hope that if she stuck around, she might climb the ladder.

"That's a good girl," the man said, but as the window closed a feminine voice from behind the window shouted at the man and the window swung back open. "Echo! I apologize for calling you a good girl. It was condescending and sexist." The window began to close again. "There, you happy?" The window clapped the rest of the way home.

Echo found most Canadians totally odd.

She raced to the dining floor and through the door on the side of the building. A big man from out of town sat with his small wife and their three big daughters at a picnic table. They waved to Echo, probably needing drinks, but she ignored them. If she delayed helping the kitchen, the delay compounded tenfold while dealing with the customers later on.

It was hot outside. Sweat instantly bubbled and dripped from her tight candy orange ponytail. She glanced around the alleyway. Seeing nobody, Echo bent forward and brought the front of her billowy bob dress to wipe her brow. The plastic bracelets clanked on her wrists like gumballs falling from a machine.

At the back of the brick building, next to a steel door with a touchpad lock were the shipment boxes. Rumors abounded about the food at Tibbytown. There were protests by people dressed up in paper bags holding signs. They came and went. They wanted in on the secret. Tibbytown Buffet won a lawsuit that said they didn't have to share trade secrets and since the health inspectors remained happy, they never had to open their doors to public interests.

Besides, the offerings always tasted fresh and perfect, and nobody ever got food poisoning.

Tibbytown Buffets had begun popping up all over the world. Echo knew this from her Tibbytown employee emails. *Bigger than McDonald's,* the manager often promised, *Give us a year!*

Great taste and great value, Tibbytown Buffet often had a line. Customers waited with smiles, complimenting the staff, and stating that it was cheaper to visit Tibbytown Buffet than the grocery store.

How is that possible?

Echo would smile and shrug her tiny shoulders. She had no answer, only the doctor-cooks knew the secrets.

She knelt by the back door and picked up the first two boxes of the shipment. She kicked at the door, twice.

The back alley was too clean to be behind a restaurant. The

dumpsters looked as if they belonged outside an office supply store rather than a buffet.

The door opened and the man with the glasses stepped sideways. He slid a steel ring stopper on an arm to hold the gap.

"Put the boxes over there and hurry. You're letting the heat in," he said and then rushed to a small monitor.

There were two other doctor-cooks in the squat room, both wore white coats and stood by monitors attached to humming stainless-steel machines. Fans blew from the ceiling. The machines gave off tremendous heat.

Echo dropped the first two boxes, her curiosity overloading. Suddenly she was facing the restaurant world's biggest secret.

It was a strange kitchen and the name on the boxes was familiar, she'd seen the symbol once as a schoolgirl while touring the north near the Russian and Mongolian borders.

Yinger Shipin. Protein farms.

They mixed all sorts of things to feed to animals and inmates. According to the government, it was a big help during the droughts. There were rumors that the farms also added deadstock to bulk the nutrient counts. There were rumors that some of that deadstock came from the prisons, but nobody really believed that.

Most people didn't believe it.

Echo gathered two more boxes from outside. It was impossible to take her eyes from the big machines. After the final box, she lingered, fiddling with the doorstop on the steel arm while she watched the monitors. Mostly numbers, but there were some words.

"If you're going to stay a minute, close that door," a frustrated woman said.

"Okay, yes, yes," Echo said.

"You know she shouldn't see this," a man said. He had a long dark face with frizzy grey hair.

Echo thought he looked like a cotton swab.

"She's cool. She won't tell, will ya?" the man with glasses said.

Echo shook her head, twice.

"Better not, trade secrets and whatever," the woman said. "They'd sue you so hard you could serve onion rings for a million years and never pay what you owed."

Overhead, a tub swished liquid and a rushing downward splash slammed within one of the machines. The frizzy-haired man tapped at his touch screen. A light thump followed the sound of rushing air.

"Cool it. Echo, come over here. You said rings and shrimp, right?" This was the man with the glasses.

"Yes, shrimps and rings, shrimps and rings."

The man lifted a bar attached to a stainless-steel wall of the machine. It resembled the industrial dish rinsers the washers used, but there weren't dishes back there, only trays for the food.

"Just watch this, shrimp and rings are both easy, no sauce on them, no extra nutrients." The man with glasses tapped instructions on the screen and the machine beeped. "Oh yeah." He walked to the small pile of boxes and peeled one open. From within, he pulled out a square wrapped in translucent blue plastic.

It looked like twigs, or fruit stems.

"See, we put the compacted protein in here." The man with glasses pointed at the packet and then the machine. He then showed Echo how to load the organic square into the hopper. Unsealing the plastic released the vapor lock and the twigs and stems came alive, though stunted with time. The doctor-cook tapped on the screen three more times. "We use new blocks mostly, but we also make about two protein blocks a night from dishwasher refuse. Do folks like them light or dark?"

Fascinated, Echo answered without thinking, "Crispy, crispy."

"Darker then."

The frizzy-haired man said, "That's what all the ladies say."

The trio laughed. Echo did not.

Through the window of the machine, the mostly dead crickets, spiders, and mantises gave the last throws against impending demise. The machine had started to buzz and light shot into a stainless-steel buffet pan. Building out from the center, she watched a mountain of onion rings form at the ends of the protein beams.

"And that's protein printing," the man with the glasses said. "Now, you'd better go before Wen comes in."

"*You doctors, back to work, and you, what you doing back here, huh? You want me to send you back to China-land?*" The woman had lowered her voice to mimic the manager.

The trio laughed again, and Echo backed away, not laughing, her mind aflutter. She opened the door to the brightness and the hotter heat. The collective reality of the situation made her gag. The only place she could afford to eat since moving to Vancouver was Tibbytown Buffet.

Through the slowly closing door to the kitchen, the man in the glasses said, "Hey, when you came over, you picked your name right? Why did you pick the name Echo?"

Echo turned around—the blood mostly departed from her head—and faced the three doctors who printed the food at Tibbytown Buffet. They looked right back at her.

"Immigrations woman give it to me. I don't know why," Echo said.

THE DREAMLAND ROOM

(2018)

After 9:00 PM, but they had plenty of time; the rules of the house demanded that all visitors be in their rooms by eleven o'clock. Despite an email suggesting otherwise, Laurel, the host of the home, waited by the door to greet Vic and Christiana.

"Welcome, welcome," Laurel said, her arms spread in reveal. She had short, soft, white hair, a skin-and-bone frame, and wrinkles riding her cheeks like fine, silky spider webs. She wore a red velour robe and pale pink slippers—material that resembled cashmere in texture and allure, though made from Chinese synthetics, magic.

"Hello, this is Vic and I'm Christiana," Christiana said, pointing at her husband first and then to herself.

Christiana and Vic were on a minor vacation, the only type they seemed to take, and chose the Poet's Retreat from the list of Airbnb options based solely on cost. They'd only been out of university for a few years and the collective six-figure debt schedule had a ten-year pay-off period. This was as aggressive as their incomes permitted, a few cents more and they'd be homeless. Banks were tyrants, but not quite pillagers.

"That's lovely, you're lovely. I'm Laurel. Please do come in, your room is the last door down the hall. Dreamland."

"Thanks," Vic said and lugged the suitcase behind him.

"Perhaps I'll see you in the morning." Abruptly, Laurel nodded and strode—not simply walking, striding—down the hall with light, swishy steps, and through a door only two up from the door marked Dreamland.

Vic and Christiana arrived with their gathered luggage having discovered two other rental rooms along the hallway: Sorrows Expunged and Emotions Abounded. Both had light shining from beneath the door cracks.

From the room marked Laurel's Room, and before they'd even got so far as to close their own door, came the ululations of a woman deep in chant. Something with a native feel.

"Ahhh, Portland," Vic whispered.

Christiana smiled and opened the door on what appeared any old guestroom at any old split-level home. Which, essentially, it was.

Sleep came easily to Christiana and not so easily to Vic. The Emotions Abounded room shared a wall with Dreamland, and by the sound of it, the wall was hollow. A man spoke to a woman, chatting like old friends or a pair in the midst of courtship, nothing like a married couple. The words were muffled. Vic stared at the shadowy ceiling listening to them.

—

"You look tired, did you sleep at all?" Christiana rubbed cream on her arms.

"Hardly, dude next door didn't shut up until four and then the damned birds started going at six." Vic was looking at his eyes in the dresser vanity: bloodshot and puffy.

They drove downtown, paid for a day parking pass, and walked until they found a suitable breakfast joint. The Poet's Retreat promised breakfast, but offered only plain, all-natural yogurt, unleavened bread, homemade peanut butter, almond milk, soy milk, and a carton of eggs one day past expiry. They needed calories and what was a vacation for if not to pig out some.

Walking for breakfast. Walking to Powell's. Walking back to the car to drop off 17 used books. Walking up the winding hills to Pittock Mansion. Walking through the woods. Walking back to the food trucks. Walking. Walking. Walking.

"There's no way I don't sleep tonight," Vic said when they

finally arrived at the car.

—

Dark, Christiana's breath had changed suddenly to the inhale/exhale of a sleeping woman. Vic envied her and listened to Laurel's chanting. The man next-door was quiet, suggesting that perhaps he was alone, or gone. Vic had not seen nor heard the individual or individuals renting Sorrows Expunged. The Airbnb set-up wasn't really his thing. The quiet, anonymous solitude of the roadside motel was more his flavor, but when the budget dictated one spot over another, he laid his tired head on the cheaper pillow.

Oh but what he wouldn't give right then for a Best Western.

And that Laurel certainly was strange.

Throughout the night, doors opened and closed. Vic counted objects and farm animals and hockey teams and Stephen King books in his head. The Dreamland room was not what the name suggested, or rather, he was not susceptible to its suggestions.

—

"You look like hell," Christiana said.

Vic stared into her eyes. When had they gotten so old?

"I'm tired, what's your excuse?"

Christiana stuck out her tongue. It was a food day. Vic ate and ate. Portland had the kind of smorgasbord they had to have on Mount Olympus.

The goal was a food coma.

—

"I do hope you rest tonight," Laurel said, pouting.

"Geez, is it that obvious?" Vic asked.

They'd seen Laurel only that one time prior and yet she caught his exhaustion with a simple glance.

Christiana stayed awake reading, joining Vic's chorus of sleepy farts, and then giggling and moaning over the bouquet lingering about them like diaper perfume. Lights out, the chanting began. Emotions Abounded was silent but for the whisper of movement. A swishy sound of light steps played along from the hallway.

Vic felt his bladder and knew that if he did not rise to use the communal can now, he'd need to in an hour. If he actually fell asleep, this would be a supreme and ruinous aggravation. Up and into the dim hallway. The swishing motion quickened. The door of Emotions Abounded creaked open as Vic passed. A pale, wispy figure, like a reverse shadow, swept into itself and then disappeared. Just as the chanting and the swishing ceased.

"Losing it," Vic said.

In bed, Vic stared at the ceiling until the birds chirped and he finally fell into a sturdy four-hour sleep.

—

Christiana was still asleep when Vic awoke. She wore wrinkles Vic had never seen. She breathed heavier, wheezier.

"Aren't you observant," Vic mumbled and plucked his cell from the nightstand. It was already after 9:00 AM. "Hey, wake up. Wake up."

Christiana's eyes shot open, pink bulbs strained and icy.

"I'm sleeping more... Twist those blinds better," she said, words thick with grogginess.

Vic did.

"Okay, well, I'm heading out for a couple hours. I'll come back with breakfast."

More sleep would be impossible, even in the pitch-black bedroom—those were truly fantastic blinds.

Vic stepped out of The Poet's Retreat, hearing Laurel's chant rise and fall just as he closed the door. Murder of Poes was an occult bookstore on the western end. It opened at 9:30. Vic wasn't yet hungry and stepped into the climate-controlled shop, moved amid the books, ornaments, art, and ritualistic bric-a-brac. Men and women watched him with cold, judgmental eyes.

Vic expected something along these lines. Murder of Poes was a store for paranoid people, run by paranoid people.

Flipping through an old medical tome that explained the proven value of bloodletting and how to vent one's brain, Vic listened to the conversation over by the till. The men and women spoke of vampires as if real. They spoke of the too trusting nature of the every-human. They spoke of a dark future and the eventual need to rise up.

Vic replaced the tome, felt his belly grumble, and decided on breakfast. The store didn't have the inexpensive kitschy stuff he'd hoped for. It carried plenty of kitschy stuff, but nothing within his price range—he was no collector.

Head down, Vic made for the door and passed a lingering twosome arguing about something vampire related, probably.

A woman said to the man, "Ask him, I bet he's already stepped into it willingly. Ask him."

"Fine. Hey, you."

Vic half-turned and gave a polite grin. He touched his chest with his right hand.

"Yeah, you. You're a tourist, right?"

Vic nodded.

"You staying in a motel or within the walls of a *stranger's* home?"

"Huh?" Vic asked and then said, "Oh, yeah, I guess. Airbnb."

"See! Vampires can't sneak inside, but they'll invite you in, take your money, and your soul!" the woman said.

Vic laughed. Vic left. Vic ordered breakfast to go from a coffee house that fried their own donuts. Vic drove back to The Poet's Retreat pondering the reversed shadow figure he'd seen and the chanting he'd endured. Putting it alongside what the weirdoes at the store said spooked him some. After a moment stuck at a red light, Vic laughed at his trepidation.

———

"Hey, wake up. What's wrong?"

Christiana was pale and seemed almost withered. It was as if she'd aged a decade since the morning, and after she'd already looked decidedly older.

"Sleep with me," Christiana said.

Vic decided it was a trick of light and really, there were three more days of vacation. He could use a nap. After eating both shares of food, Vic lay back feeling the wonderful warmth of full guts.

Minutes in, perhaps an hour, Vic jerked forward to the blaring music coming from beyond his window. For a moment, he thought he'd heard the chanting again before the jazz blared like an especially horrendous alarm.

The racket outside was abrupt, starting and stopping. A single saxophone. Vic rolled off the bed and peeked through the blinds. It was the woman from Murder of Poes, sitting on the hood of a faded red Toyota, her body pointed at the house.

Eventually, she put down the saxophone.

Christiana did not stir.

Intrigued and rejuvenated by the brief nap, Vic left the black room, groping along the dark hallway out to the living area where light poured through pollen dusty bay windows.

"You followed me," Vic said after he'd slipped on his shoes and stepped outside.

He hadn't noticed it before, not under the ugly lighting within the store, but this woman was sort of pretty. In an occult, I believe in vampires, kind of way. Too pretty to follow strangers. She had dirty blonde hair, puffy pink lips, high cheekbones, and the frame of a semi-professional tennis player.

"You're not sleeping much, right?" she asked.

Was it that obvious to everyone?

"Why would that matt—?"

"You have natural defenses. Your ancestors, one of them anyway, must've been from Romania. The Gypsies feel things that others don't. I hear some New Zealanders do too, but that's not really been documented."

Vic scratched at his head. "Gypsies? New Zealanders? Maybe.

No idea. Why did you follow me?"

"To save your life. Airbnbs are the slow boiling plague. I've looked into this place. I didn't play my Sax until I knew for sure. Laurel says she's a poet but is nowhere online other than the Airbnb listing. I don't know who you know, but the ones I know, they're always sharing their godawful poetry, they crave an audience. Not Laurel, no poetry anywhere. It's a deviant and dependent ruse. Also, she doesn't own the place. She's managing the rooms. Another commonality of the vampires."

"Wait, you're suggesting that Airbnb is a vampire front to get easy blood to drink?" Vic asked, incredulous and yet, touching his throat, seeking puncture wounds.

"Vampires don't bite necks. They suck soul years. Tell me, is this Laurel chanting or dancing at night?"

His eyes widened. "Wait a second." He put his arms out, as if to steady himself.

"Is it supremely dark inside? Have you seen cloud-like forms from the corners of your eyes, like flashes, but duller?"

"Hey...what?"

The figure. The reverse shadow.

"Vampires drink sleeping souls."

It came to him then. "Oh geez. This is a come on. I'm sorry, lady. I'm married."

The woman frowned and went back to her car, shaking her head and scrunching her brows. "You're one stupid sonofabitch."

—

Christiana refused to rise. Vic opened the blinds. The darkness suddenly carried the vibes it had when he was a boy: monsters under the bed and demons in the shadows. Beneath the light streaming through the glass, Vic read a copy of *The Snake* by John Godey, a '70s, pulp-ish thriller that gave him a dozen factoids about the black mamba and a twinge of suspense.

"Can't we go eat?"

"Leave me alone!" Christiana screamed.

"Fine. Fine."

Vic left Christiana and headed for downtown. Vic ate chicken shawarma. Vic smiled at the locals. Vic accepted a napkin from a high school girl grinning at him and the blob of tzatziki on his shorts. Full to stuffed, Vic drove to a green space where he parked. Vic strolled until sundown, worrying over Christiana.

—

"Are you still alive?" Vic half-joked.

"Yeah, feeling better too. Just need more sleep."

The chanting began and Vic tried to let it lull him away. Eventually it did.

Awaking, surprised, Vic saw the white shimmer that wore the shape of a young woman. From Laurel's room, the chanting rode high.

"Fuckin' geez!"

Vic backpedaled from the sheets and landed on the floor with a thump. Terrified, he rolled under the bed and waited. By and by. It came to him.

Dreaming.

Obviously dreaming about what the saxophone woman warned. Back into bed, the weary, exhausted man climbed, too embarrassed to smile.

Sleep fought him until sunrise and from there he slept to the rhythmic tones of Laurel's chanting. The blinds were tight. He dreamed of a tomorrow, of a home he and Christiana would someday own, of children they'd have, of ages they'd reach together, anniversaries they'd share.

Vic dreamed a dozen stages of life while sleeping next to his deceased wife. Vic basked in these dreams of a future. Vic's dreams offered an existence he'd never see. Vic's dreamland featured tomorrows forever beyond his reach.

—

"Hello, welcome. Welcome. I'm Laurel," Laurel said. She spread her arms. She appeared to be in her 30s, shimmery blonde hair, clear skin, and shining eyes.

"Thanks," Jane Winter said, 20, exploring America, scheduled to stay at two-dozen Airbnb locations over the coming months.

Next to Jane was a friend she'd met online named Ducky Fontaine. Ducky loved Portland and the idea of sharing homes seemed so much more *human* than renting from corporations like Motel 6 or The Holiday Inn. Ducky was 40 and spritely. Plump cheeks and smiling lips. Her scalp was bald.

"You're new to Airbnbs?" Laurel said.

"This is my first," Jane said.

"I've stayed in a few," Ducky said, "but never for a week. Always only a night."

Laurel nodded. "You're in the Dreamland room, just let me know if you need anything." She turned in her robe and slippers, swishing away down the hall.

Ducky and Jane smiled upon hearing Laurel's chant through the closed door.

"Girl, I love Portland," Ducky said and poked a tickle at Jane's side.

THE RUT

(2014)

The nice way to put it was *in a rut.*

Sandra stepped out of the bedroom where she held telephone conversations with her mother, shaking her head, a glazy filter over her eyes.

"I swear to God, if I hear about Donnie Lease's stupid house one more time I'll scream," she said.

Her husband, Elton, sat on the recliner reading, his typical state of being when he wasn't translating furniture manuals. "Donnie Lease?" A smile tipped the corners of his mouth.

Donnie Lease was the boy who took Sandra to the eighth-grade graduation dance, a formal. He never moved from the small town where he and Sandra both grew up, had a house and a boat, a job at the power plant, one that brought in big bucks—big bucks for an uneducated laborer. Sandra's mother, Eleanor, often reminded her that Donnie was single, had a home, had a boat, made good money, much better money than furniture manual translators made.

"You know, the perfect man I'm letting slip away," Sandra said and flopped onto their couch.

Sandra's mother, Eleanor, blamed Elton for the absence of her daughter. It had been years since Sandra had even gone home to visit.

"Successful adults don't live in apartments," Eleanor had said on numerous occasions over the telephone. "Why won't Elton let you see me?"

The whine in the old woman's voice grated like a loose fan belt. And no matter how often Sandra explained that most of the human race lived in apartments, Eleanor refused to listen.

"She's so damn frustrating," Sandra said. "She doesn't listen to a thing I say."

"That's partly the booze, don't you think?" Elton asked rhetorically.

15 years earlier, just months before Sandra and Elton began dating, Eleanor's husband, Sandra's father, explained his intention to leave the family and join his fancy girlfriend in Australia. Eleanor didn't see it coming; it had blindsided her. Everyone showed sympathy, nobody was surprised that she drank a bit, sometimes liquor could be a handy tool, time's assistant in the healing process.

Time moved on but Eleanor didn't. Stuck in a rut.

The divorce papers, the ex-husband's marriage, the ex-husbands death in a plane crash, none of it helped Eleanor find tomorrow. She drank. She drank and felt sorry for herself more than a decade after everyone else had ceased doing so. No more *poor woman*, no more *poor Eleanor.*

Eleanor never left the small town where she grew up. By and by, her friends came to ignore her, and after she retired from her position at the library, Sandra became her only link to the real world. At first, she went out to purchase groceries, purchase books at the used bookstore, and of course, frequented the liquor store. Eventually grocery delivery came to her small town—which included booze—and she was generally too drunk to read.

"I swear it's been the word-for-word same conversation for the last six weeks. She has no life, none at all," Sandra said, her mood lightening with every passing moment. It was the best time possible. It would be a week before she answered another of her mother's calls.

"It can't be that bad, maybe we ought to bite the bullet and go back for Christmas? Give the old girl some cheer?"

"She's not even that old! She acts like she's ninety. She's only sixty for heaven's sake." Sandra sighed. "It might be a nice surprise for her, but I...ugh."

The week came and went in a flash, as they did and the telephone rang as if scheduled.

"Why don't you visit me? No time for your mother? Why don't you move back this way, they always need therapists in the school board. You could stay here until you found a house to buy, or is that too close to me?"

Sandra stormed out of the bedroom, hands in fists.

Elton cringed. "Maybe you can talk her into doing something, work herself out of her obsession with self-pity?"

"I don't know why she refuses to see a psychiatrist." Sandra dropped onto the couch, slouching like a disgruntled teen forced to stay home on a Friday night.

"He might point out that she's an old drunk, might point out that her marriage falling apart was at least partially her own doing, and point out that you don't want to visit because she's such a needy old bitch."

"Likely, but what do you think going home would really do? She'd just call more and more, encourage her begging. You know, you're lucky she doesn't like you."

"Don't I know it, but maybe we ought to do Christmas this year. It's not as if we have something else on the go." Elton's parents and grandparents spent every Christmas in Las Vegas dropping coins into chrome bandits, didn't care if all, or none, of the kids came along.

"Should I tell her or should we surprise her?" Sandra asked.

"Don't tell her, let's us change our minds last minute." Elton offered a knowing grin from behind a manual for a bedframe with a dozen assembly steps and about a million pieces.

The week went by as it had since the begging of time. Sandra went to work. Elton stayed in to work. Come Sunday, Sandra's cellphone rang at exactly 2:00 PM, the voice on the other end drunk already. Sandra moved into the bedroom and closed the door.

Clockwork.

"This time I'm sure, she's saying exactly the same things every call. The only change was when I accused her of it. She said that I was crazy and went on about stupid Donnie's house—*got a deck, ya know*," she said, mimicking Eleanor's voice.

"Might be better for everyone if you stopped answering the phone."

"Bet she'd have a heart attack if we changed her Sunday routine. She doesn't do anything else all week, drinks wine and plays card games on her computer. It's insane."

Elton had turned his attention back to his booklet. "Yeah."

Week after week went by and every Sunday, Eleanor called. Sandra complained. Elton rolled his eyes. The rut was inescapable, and Sandra didn't have the heart to cut off her mother completely.

"Yes, I love you too, Mom," Sandra said, a replay of a replay of a replay. She had an urge to warn her mother that they might come by next Sunday, Christmas, but fought it.

Sandra came out of the bedroom and flopped face-first onto the couch. A little more than a year earlier, Sandra had had visited her mother. The house was a filthy maze of empty liquor bottles and TV dinner wrappers. Every surface featured a sticky film. Eleanor appeared to be about 50 pounds heavier, 30 of which landed on her head, 10 pounds on her cheeks and nose apiece. The booze had turned her into a bloated pincushion.

—

The following Sunday morning, they got moving. The plan was to roll into Eleanor's driveway right around 11:00 AM, surprise the hell out of her, put a big smile on her puffy face just in time for a tea, but the universe had different plans. Fat snowflakes blanketed the world three hours into the trip, and they crawled along, turning the final three hours into a six-hour event. The radio warned of road closures and the need for extra care. Elton wasn't impressed and drove around three separate sawhorses with blinking orange lights.

Finally, they pulled into Eleanor's at 1:58 PM, according to the green numbers on their dashboard clock.

"I'll actually be happy to be out of this car," Elton said.

"You say that now." Sandra smiled sadly. Anxious, she opened her door, winter bombarded her, as if pushing her away.

Arms loaded, they ran to the door, knocked, and stepped inside without awaiting an answer. The first thing that hit them was the visual state. The home was dark, trash and dime-deposit liquor bottles covered the kitchen floor and table. The grimy film bounced light from every surface.

"You smell that?" Elton whispered, his sleeve over his face.

They waded through the mess.

"Mom? Mom, you home?"

The phone in Sandra's pocket rang.

"No, really, do you smell that? I think the sewer backed into the toilet or something," Elton said before bending to inspect the kitchen sink.

Sandra's phone continued to ring.

"Mom!" Sandra said, worry in her tone.

She pulled the phone from her pocket and followed Elton into the living room. She answered thoughtlessly; chilled, the home was barely above the temperature outside. "Hello

"Hey, it's just me, your mother. You remember your mother..."

"Oh my God," Elton said pointing at the body on the floor behind the couch. He stepped slowly. Sandra pushed ahead of him.

It was Eleanor, her puffy skin colorless and coated with the familiar film. The cordless telephone pinned between her hand and her head. Sandra held her own phone to her face, listening.

"...you know I saw Donnie Lease. He asked after you..."

Sandra hit end, then rolled her mother onto her back. Her eyes were cloudy white and lifeless. Her cell phone rang again.

"Oh, honey, I'm sorry," Elton said, grimacing.

Sandra answered her phone absently. "Hello?"

"Must have got disconnected. I was saying that I saw Donnie. You know he's single, got a house and a boat. You love the water. I also heard from Debbie Clifford. There's an opening..."

"Mom?" Sandra asked her phone.

"Sandy, are you listening? I think you should..."

Sandra screamed and threw her cell across the room. Elton held her tight to his chest. He used his free hand to dial the police with his own cell. The police asked that they lock the door and leave a key somewhere. It was Christmas and thanks to the snow, they wouldn't make it out for a time.

An hour later, they were back on the road, stopping for the weather, having Christmas in a motel room with a bucket of KFC to substitute turkey. The television aired *A Christmas Carol*, the black and white version.

"It doesn't make sense that the calls...how could?" Sandra said where she lay, pants open, belly ballooned with grease gas.

Elton shook his head. "Maybe you're confusing something. I mean, she couldn't—" The telephone on the nightstand rang. Elton answered. "Yes?"

"Elton, is my daughter around? We got cut off earlier...thank you," said the voice of Eleanor.

Elton handed over the telephone, his entire face drooped open on gravity's pull.

Sandra took the phone and listened for the following 39 minutes. The very same conversation they'd had for weeks. Once through, Sandra said goodbye and handed the telephone back to her husband.

"How?" she said.

Elton shook his head, absently popping a cool fry into his mouth.

Three days later, Elton received a call from the police. According to them, it appeared the body had been dead approximately two months. Unfortunately, two of her fingers broke while prying the cordless from her grip. Elton didn't mention the calls, thanked the officer, and explained the situation to Sandra.

That Sunday, no call came to Sandra. The following Sunday was the same and she realized she'd grown to expect them, molded her Sunday around them. She now had nothing else to do with the allotted time. On Monday at work after a wasted Sunday, Sandra explained the situation to a co-worker named Tamara Hutch.

Tamara pointed a slender finger at Sandra. "You're just in a rut. Best to switch things up, get a hobby, leave the house, take a class, anything. Ruts have a way of sticking around if you aren't careful."

FREEDOM DREAMING

(2013)

Chest filled until brimming with delight, Gregg Egan let out a long slow breath. That scent, that amazing scent, streamed from the air freshener the doc used—simply called *Ocean Breeze*. Gregg convinced his wife to buy the stuff once, but he could tell just by the droopy look on her face that it would be a one-time purchase. Fine, he could just drive to the ocean to smell the breeze when he wasn't in therapy.

And he'd needed to visit Dr. Richards twice a week lately anyway—those goddamn dreams again.

Sinking into the lovely black leather couch, enjoying the pleasant Ocean Breeze scent as he did so, he scanned the little office. Everything was as it always was and where it always was. Gregg supposed consistency and familiarity kept the loons from going loony.

For Gregg, his problem seemed to him like there should be a simple solution; hell, they were just dreams after all, but man oh man, were they lifelike. It was as if he could actually touch, actually taste, actually feel the world his brain created when he went to sleep. Creepy stuff too, and always the same place, building on the same themes.

"I'm ready to listen," Dr. Richards said.

Gregg sighed, resigned to his fate. "I had another dream."

"Same dream or different?"

"Not exactly the same, but prison rarely changes. There I was, in that light grey little cell with Flip—the asshole cellmate. He was his usual self. That endless mouth of his..."

"Go on."

"Flip was Flip...for lunch we had meat loaf. I haven't dreamt about meat loaf since one of the first dreams. I'm getting into re-runs, time to cancel the show." Gregg laughed a nervous little chuckle. Back when he'd first dreamed of meat loaf, he'd explained it to his wife, explained all about the prison dreams, but she didn't care. Not an iota.

Dr. Richards remained stoic in his leather chair.

"The other change...I was cheating on you, I guess. I had to see the prison psychiatrist. A small woman. Like, tiny and with a highly defined jawline, but she seemed absolutely beautiful at the time, but now that I think about her, she looked about a six, six and a half. I suppose prison does that to you, even in dreams. Crazy, huh?"

"I wouldn't say crazy. Intriguing, certainly."

"She was going on how if I try, I may fit in more; you know, not get into the fights. She told me that I had to let go of the past and move on. I think I got most of the stuff she said from a memory of you, but one thing was very strange. She wanted to discuss my sexual urges, a lot. She then whispered that murderers turned her on and that if I wanted to, I could choke her and, well, you know," Gregg said, repositioning himself as he spoke.

"Copulate?"

"Right, give her the Charles."

"Give her the Charles? I don't think I've heard that one."

"You know the Dickens, the Charles Dickens." Gregg belted a great laugh. "I thought of that one myself, Doc. So anyways, right after she said that, she motioned for the guard to take me back to my cell. After listening to Flip, being sent to do cleanup, and then coming back to more Flip, I woke up."

"Do you always wake up as soon as you've gone to bed in your dream?"

"No, but typically. I remember the one dream, I was in the prison shower, this guy tried to...give me the Charles, without my permission of course, and I beat him silly. Some guards pulled me off him and I slipped on the tile and smacked my head. I woke up then; there are a couple other times too."

"We will have to get to those next session."

Gregg glanced at the clock. "Geez, time flies when you're having fun, huh?"

"I don't think you're having all that much fun, Mr. Egan, but I do think we'll get to the bottom of this."

———

The parking lot was empty. He looked at his watch, knowing that his wife would have his ass if he were any later than she expected him. Halfway between home and the doctor's office, nestled amid goliaths of steel and concrete and shoddily replanted nature, was the Sundowner. Gregg pulled into the lot.

Walter Burns stood behind the bar, rubbing a rag thoughtlessly, his eyes glued to the television overhead. He was a biggish guy, though teddy-bearish, inviting.

"Walter, my man."

"Well, look who it is." Walter said.

"Where is everyone?" Gregg asked, waving a finger over his shoulder.

"Your guess is as good as mine, maybe they knew you were coming and scattered."

"Ha, very funny. I'll take my regular, but only one tonight. The wife is waiting," Gregg pulled a face, "and if I want to keep my balls..."

"One Stella coming right up." Walter was already pouring the beer.

The Stella Artois tasted fine, so Gregg ordered a second, with a shot of Wiser's Deluxe on the side.

"That's the stuff."

"Rough day?"

"You know how it is: work, wife, sleep, and repeat."

"I suppose I do...did. I'm a single man now," Walter said, fiddling with something glass below the bar.

"She give you the bootski?"

"She would have liked to, I suspect, but I beat her to it."

Gregg took a deep drink. "My wife, shit, but I can't really imagine life without her."

"It is easier to imagine than you think and if you think hard enough about it, life can look pretty sweet."

Gregg emptied his glass. "But who wants to lose half their stuff?"

"I didn't. I didn't lose a damn thing."

"How'd you swing that?"

Walter leaned in. "Can you keep a secret?"

Gregg nodded slowly. "But you'd best pour me another beer."

"Another Wiser's too?"

"Why not?"

Walter glanced around. "Poison, slow and steady."

"Fuck off."

Walter gave a shrug—*buy it or don't.*

"Shit. Did she go to the doctor?"

"Sure. I was a little worried at first, but her family doctor couldn't figure it out and she died while awaiting a scheduled visit with a specialist." Walter stuck out his tongue and rolled his eyes.

"Fuck off." Gregg's expression was full moons.

Walter burst into laughter.

"You ass." Gregg laughed along. "So, what really happened to your wife?"

"Died in a car accident...I cut her brake lines."

Gregg's laughter died when Walter's expression turned serious. "You need another?" he said.

Gregg shook his head.

—

More than two hours late, the side door creaked and the sound gave him a shudder, he could hear his wife cleaning dishes. To get into the house he had to go through the kitchen, had to enter the dragon's den.

"Where have you been?" Janelle asked, not turning from the pan she was scrubbing with a Brillo pad.

"I was at therapy. You know, about the dreams?" Gregg was cautious.

"Yeah, but then where?"

Lie and they'll be pulling your body out of English Bay, or more likely you'll float and become shark food, he thought. "The doc was running late—"

"Liar!" Janelle dropped the pan back into the sink with a sudsy splash.

"Fine," he paused still considering piling on some more fiction, but decided against it. "I went for a beer."

"Figures. Men, all you want to do is drink and carry on like children. Did you ever think that maybe I wanted a break from cleaning, watching the kids, making you dinner? Which is cold now."

She was never like this before she started hanging around all those divorcees: Malice for Men, or whatever MFM stands for.

"I can go for a beer if I like."

"Parenting is a two-person job, although women do all the work. You men. You think I can't do all this without you?"

"I do make all the money." *You are one stupid man,* Gregg thought as soon as the words crossed the threshold of his lips.

"You thankless, no good asshole. Men, I swear..."

Gregg shut down his ears and began imagining cutting her brake lines and poisoning her coffee. *And then you have the kids, alone.* Hell, he didn't even want the damn kids. He never wanted children.

"Are you listening?"

"Of course, dear," he said and stepped toward her, his arms open for a hug, a move that worked in the past.

"Get away from me." She pushed him.

"Fine, I'm tired anyway," he said and turned, letting his arms fall to his sides.

"You're sleeping on the couch.".

Gregg stopped, his feet half on and half off the carpet. "Are you nuts? I have to present to the committee tomorrow."

"Nuts? Now I'm just some crazy housewife, am I? Just because you deny me my little enjoyment, my downtime, that doesn't mean you can keep me from a good sleep. You men are all so self-important."

Gregg spun like a bull top. "Downtime? All you do is sit around all day staring at the kids!"

"Being a mother is the hardest job in the world. I will trade you any day you like, any day, mister." She pointed a long, dish-panned finger at him. "You think you can do what I do? You think you could handle the pain of childbirth? You think you can deal with the menstrual cycle, looking beautiful no matter what, having the public eye on you and expect nothing but perfection? You think you can make amazing meals?"

That little voice in his head tried to save him: *Don't do it.* "I hardly call packet gravy and frozen meat pie an amazing meal. As for beautiful…"

"Get Out!"

One of the girls started to moan from down the hall. Janelle charged by Gregg on the warpath.

—

Gregg awoke with a sore neck, and he was late. "Shit!" He rocketed up and got busy. Only 20 minutes until the presentation, he climbed into his car.

Four minutes to spare, he got to the boardroom and paused, taking deep, relieved breaths. Four minutes, he had time to grab a coffee. The office was strangely dead, despite that he was there earlier than normal. The coffee pot in the breakroom was off, the bit of coffee in the bottom was cold.

"That's not right," he said and returned to the boardroom, peeking through office windows along the way.

He sat and waited, eyes on the clock by the door. 10 minutes passed, then 20, and finally after 30 minutes had gone by until Gregg saw another soul.

"What happened to my presentation?" Gregg asked. "Where is everyone," he added as an afterthought.

Gregg's boss, Russ Gilbert, shook his head gently. "You know, if someone told me Gregg Egan, Mr. Anal-retentive himself, would be late for the biggest presentation of his life, I would have laughed in their face, but here we are. We wondered if you'd died. What the hell happened?"

"I was here on time!"

Mr. Gilbert looked around the empty office and scrunched his face. "Darren ran it this morning? Are you just getting here?"

Gregg looked at his watch. "It's only a quarter to nine? Where is everyone?"

"Gregg, I suggest you go home. Take the rest of the week off. You know, if anyone else, and I mean anyone, did what you did today, I'd can their ass so fast they'd think my father's name was Campbell."

Gregg looked through the boardroom door, through the window of an office door, and to the ever-darkening sky. "I lost a whole day?"

"Go home, come back on Monday."

———

"How in the hell?" Gregg said once back in his car.

The drive home was too quick and Janelle once again got on him about how late he was. His mind blanked, he kicked off his loafers and flopped down on the couch, strangely tired, despite sleeping a day away. His eyes fluttered, even as Janelle filled his ears with hot, hot anger.

The fluttering ceased and his eyes were no longer heavy. The steel frame of a bunk bed came into view. The sound of roll call brought him into full view of the cell.

"Thank god," he whispered.

From above his bed, on the top bunk, the sound of Flip's little body creaked the entire frame. "You crazy today?" he asked.

"Huh?"

"You gonna play crazy again? Get yourself out of work duty. You know you're lucky the screws don't mash your skull," Flip said letting out a little cackle. "Scramble those fucky eggs you got?"

"Hey, Flip?"

"Yeah?"

"Go fuck yourself."

Flip laughed.

Gregg rose, got in line, and awaited instruction. His prison dreams were so vivid, lifelike; he could smell the stale air of hundreds of sweaty men. He could hear the hoots and hollers, the steel-on-steel clanging.

Within a few minutes, he started to wish to wake up. Despite Janelle's endless bitching. Prison was mundane and uncomfortable. The bad food. The sharing showerheads with other men. The monotonous work detail. Then there was Flip, the Janelle of his cell life—this realization lit like a lighthouse beam in a storm. He'd have to tell Dr. Richards during their next session.

"So, this one broad, right? Well, I was at the bowling alley, you know to score some shit? And all of a sudden this broad, and I mean one foxy mama, reached under the table and started givin' me a jerk right there in front of—"

"How about you shut up?"

"Why don't you make me, you goddamn head case? It's a free country."

"It's not a free country and you're a prisoner; you have no rights. Especially in the United States of Egan, but if you like you can attempt a coup," Gregg said watching as the bottom of Flip's mattress rustled.

Somewhere amongst the springs and the fluff, Flip stored his shiv; actually, just a well-worn toothbrush sharpened to a point at the handle, but it would do the trick. Gregg had seen the idiot put it there.

Janelle, Janelle, Janelle, he thought as Flip dropped down from the upper bunk brandishing the shiv.

In the real world, Gregg might have shit in his pants, but in the dream world he was strong. He didn't really feel stronger physically, it was a matter of mind over matter. In his first dream, a man had tried to make an example of Gregg; he was one big bad dude and Gregg was a lamb for the slaughter. The man took his butterscotch pudding, sneering as he did so.

Without a word, Gregg flipped his tray, sending the rest of his food soaring, and smashed the big dude across the side of the head. The tray bent to a point along an edge and before the dude could recalibrate, Gregg slammed the point into his neck. Blood spurted as the guards Hollard and the other inmates scattered like roaches.

Now, Gregg kicked out a heavy foot, landing with a whoosh into Flip's midsection. The would-be assailant flailed and fell to the floor, the shiv slid harmlessly onto the grating of the walkway beyond the cell.

Flip scrambled toward his weapon on hands and knees. Gregg jumped up and planted his foot firmly into Flip's ass. The momentum was a little much, and Flip launched through the railing, nose-diving onto a table where two old men played checkers twenty feet below. His head opened like a punted watermelon.

Gregg leaned over the railing and began to laugh.

Almost instantly, three rubber bullets pelted Gregg's chest. The pain was amazing, he coughed and wheezed, struggling to regain a semblance of his uncaring self, but goddamn those bullets hurt. Footfalls raced toward him.

—

Gregg opened his eyes and remembered his week off. "Damn," he said. To explain to Janelle what had happened, would bring about further abuse, his real life wasn't like his prison dreams, he couldn't slice her open with a cafeteria tray or punt her through railing. Real life wasn't that convenient...was it?

Was for Walter.

"Gregg!"

Gregg didn't answer and attempted to hide with a cloak of silence. Something that had never, ever worked and yet he still tried.

Janelle appeared before him in the living room. "Gregg?"

"Sorry, I was thinking."

"That's right, I forgot, men are incapable of multi-tasking. Tonight, I'm hosting group and you can't be here. I mean not for..."

Janelle continued to speak, but Gregg stopped listening, he thought about the bartender once more. What if he did kill her? What would he do with the kids? Kill them too?

"Don't you have to be at work?"

"The bartender did it," he blurted, shaking his head in minute strokes.

"What?"

"Just kidding. The office is closed 'til ten. Some painters or something..." Gregg said.

"Don't be here tonight, not before...sometimes we chat until eleven," Janelle said before she charged by.

Gregg sat up. He couldn't be around her another second. Not a millisecond.

After a long breakfast at Denny's, Gregg went to the Home Depot, the shrubs in the backyard grew wild without attention, so he needed a tool to fix that. He inspected the little clippers, but they didn't seem manly enough. He went with a Makita chainsaw.

In the afternoon, he went to a matinee at the Cineplex. *Captain Phillips*, the movie was probably pretty good, but once out, he could hardly remember what happened, his mind stuck on

Walter, the bartender.

Bored and aimless, he called Doctor Richards, hoping to tell him about his realization that Flip was his cell Janelle—*even rhymes.*

The phone rang twice before clicking through, Dr. Richards himself answering.

"Why are you answering? What happened to the reception girl?"

"Day off. What can I do for you?"

"Do you have time to see me today?" Gregg winced, knowing this was not the way doctors did things.

"Sure, I have nobody in for the next hour and a half."

Gregg paused, thinking, *Why doesn't he have other clients today?*

"My schedule is open. I've downsized. Planning to move on after I finish up with some things."

"I'll be there in ten minutes," Gregg said and then hung up.

The drive seemed to come and go in a flash, his head so full of everything. Squinting against the sun, Gregg stepped into the office and that familiar scent flooded his nose, that beautiful ocean breeze.

"Gregg, is that you?" Dr. Richards called from within his office.

Feeling so much better already, Gregg almost pranced from the waiting room with long lunging steps. "Hey, Doc, I may not need to talk after all. I feel fine now."

"You're here, why not have a chat?"

Gregg was already flopping down onto the sofa. "I love this air freshener by the way."

"You've said that before. Why not tell me about the first prison dream."

The prison dreams were not exactly where the funny dreams began. There was an arrest dream and a trial dream. As far as Gregg could figure, he was in prison for murder, but nobody ever said whom he'd killed, not that it really mattered.

"My cell was cold and it stank something awful, like a locker room after a hockey game. Nasty. My cellmate—hey, I finally nailed Flip a good one."

"You nailed him a good one?"

"I had a dream last night that I kicked him under a guard railing and onto the floor twenty-some feet below." Gregg sat up and clapped his hands together. "Splat!"

"Interesting, let's go back to that first night."

"Hmm, besides the smell and annoyance, I guess, I guess nothing much happened."

"How did you feel to be in prison?"

"I was scared to death. I knew it was a dream, sort of, but I didn't have the control I do now. I am starting to like being there. I have more control there. In real life, I have a boss, I have a wife, I have a mortgage, I have annoying babies that are forever wailing. I thought I wanted all these things, but it's too much."

"Why don't you tell me about your wife?"

He did, leaving very little out, he explained her transformation from bitchy teenager, to bitchier young woman, to even bitchier mother, and then onto the current stage: super-bitch. From a speculative view, it appeared a very natural progression, one he should have foreseen.

"It sounds like you have no love for her."

"I hate her guts."

Dr. Richards leaned closer. "You can leave her, put up with her, learn to deal I suppose, or you can kill her, and the kids, I suppose."

Gregg squinted, closing his left eye fully. "Huh?"

"Every problem has a suitable answer. It all depends on the individual. I used to be married myself. My wife got in with one of those sewing groups...it led to other things, which left me with only one option."

Gregg sat straight as a nail. "No way."

"Way, my friend. Cops and judges all have annoying wives, they barely bother with wife killers. Look at O.J., he didn't do any real time until he stole something valuable."

This was too much. Gregg's mind swirled. "I have to go." He launched from the couch and barreled through the waiting room, out to his car. Without direction, without notice, he drove. The sky darkened and he found himself driving along the coast. To his right the harbor, to his left the Strait of Georgia. He rolled down the window and inhaled that magic scent. If he could bottle it...he laughed; companies did bottle it!

———

Parked in his driveway were five different cars: two Subaru wagons, one Volvo wagon, and two Volkswagen wagons.

Doc Martin's and Birkenstocks would line the shoe mat by the door. Gregg shuddered. The safe bet was to wait in his car. After an hour or so, his eyes grew heavy, and he nodded off into a dreamless sleep.

Rain dripped down on the windshield. He looked at his dash clock: 9:03. His legs ached when he stretched them out the driver's door. Uncertain of how to deal with what would most definitely be an angry wife.

Janelle was in the kitchen drinking coffee, her free hand holding a bottle up to baby Katy's face. Gregg's other daughter, Mellie, sat at the table, Cheerios scattered all over her highchair tray.

"Where have you been?"

"I slept in the car. I came home and you had your friends over, and I didn't want to disturb you and then I fell asleep."

"Liar!" she screamed, dropping the baby's bottle, causing Mellie to sob. "Look what you've done."

"I didn't—"

"Lying piece of—I want a divorce. You can pack a suitcase and get out."

Gregg started upstairs, uncertain if this was good or bad. The alimony was going to bleed him out, but he'd be away from Janelle.

"Don't forget the third option," Dr. Richards and Walter's voice said in unison, in his head.

His guts swirled violently. He stumbled on the stairs. Behind him, Janelle was shouting something. He threw open the bathroom door, dropped to his knees, flipped up the lid, and began to vomit. Once the hot rush finally ended, he stared into the toilet; there were bits of everything he'd eaten the day before—somehow—as well as some things he didn't recall eating.

He flushed.

The disgusting collection swirled the drain. Afterward, a few dozen kernels remained, spinning, spinning until they stopped, spelling out KILL.

"Kill?" he whispered. "I couldn't... Never."

Gregg flushed again and stumbled to the master bedroom to pack his bags. Janelle stomped up the stairs, then slammed the washroom door.

"You left the seat up!"

Gregg bubbled, laughing quietly as he imagined her ass in the drink. He ran his fingers along the selection of silk neckties, and something clicked. He grabbed three of the ties and walked to the washroom door. He waited. The toilet flushed.

Janelle emerged in wide-eyed surprise.

"You didn't wash your hands," Gregg said through clenched teeth and then swung a heavy fist into Janelle's nose.

Tears poured down her cheeks, blood spurted from her lip and nose, and her body tumbled to the floor. Like an angry cat, Gregg pounced and struck her face two more times for good measure. She was dazed. Gregg wrapped one tie around her mouth to act as a gag, while another tied her hands behind her back. The final tied her feet. As a boy, he'd made all the way to Venturer Scouts. Some skills you just didn't forget.

Not really minding her well-being, Gregg dragged Janelle

down the steps and into the kitchen. He ran outside, backed Janelle's Honda Odyssey into the garage, and lowered the heavy steel door.

Privacy.

First, he loaded the girls into the van and then Janelle, all three sat on the floor in the back. Gregg was giddy as he drove toward the coast, that beautiful, that pure, that perfect smell of ocean breeze blooming larger and larger as his family screamed and squirmed.

He parked on the pier. Waves crashed below, wind blew through his hair, and one by one, he dropped his family into the water. It took several minutes before anyone came around. He smiled at the first officers on the scene, explained what he'd done, and attempted to walk away. A cop jumped him, his head nailing the cement, conking him out cold.

He attempted to move his arms.

"Calm down, inmate," the horny doctor said. She gave Gregg's manhood a quick squeeze and then laughed. "You're quite the killer, first your family and then your cellmate. So dangerous; just how I like 'em."

"They'll let me out once I explain," Gregg said, mentally crossing his two plains of existence. "Just a dream."

"Still on that?" asked the other doctor, a little old man with white eyebrows and a shiny bald scalp. "This boy is cookies."

"Give him a shot. We'll see how he reacts in the morning," she said. "We can't have crazies walking around, it's dangerous, especially if this stud thinks there aren't any consequences to his actions." Her lip trembled as she pressed her weight against his flailing body.

The old doctor stabbed a needle into Gregg's arm. He felt the poison floating into his blood stream and his eyes closed once again. The smell of the ocean was all around him. He was in a waiting room, an office door opened, and a man came out.

"Mr. Egan? My name is Clark Richards." Dr. Richards held out his hand.

Gregg shook it and smiled.

"So, you're having strange dreams?"

NIGHT OF THE LESSON

(2017)

She put her head down and closed her eyes. The cold nipped in chunks. The weather had gotten very bad very quickly. Her parents agreed that she wasn't to stay out past light. Given the incredible snowfalls they'd had recently, that was for the best.

But 14 was an age that demanded freedom and bred certainty of self-indestructability. For a 14-year-old, social standing was of uncompromising importance, so parents could demand any old thing they wanted, didn't mean it'd take.

There was to be a gathering in town and only two miles from the hotel. There were no guests thanks to the season. The recent turn in forecast kept away even the most ardent tundra travelers.

Folks feared snow, so soft, so clean.

Lowa Stratton did not fear the snow. She feared missing a party, missing a first tongue kiss, missing that one true chance to fall in love. She feared what people might think if she didn't trudge through the snow and winds to make an appearance.

It took triple the time, but she made it. Thankfully, once within the town limit, the winds fell off to mere gusts. Out of town, the world was flat and desolate. The road was wide and icy, and straight. No turns or twists, head down against the wind, she had leaned and pushed through the white wall of gale forces.

The shop was a recently abandoned container shed. North of town, on the southeastern shore of Hudson Bay, SentierOmni had built a new shipping and receiving facility, along with dozens of warehouses and sheds. This left *the shop* open for party squatting.

When Lowa arrived, the place was empty. She waited. The

winds picked up. Her cellphone had chilled too far and the juice in the battery had evaporated. Snow blanketed the world through the window, adding several new inches every hour. Her phone had told her it was just after two in the afternoon when it flared momentarily before locking on a still of her background photo and then fading to charcoal in a series of brickwork crystals of color. Two o'clock meant that less than an hour of daylight remained.

The walk home would take much longer, given the accumulation and the wind. Longer still in the early afternoon dark of the 52nd parallel.

It was warm in *the shop*. There were blankets and a couch, but her parents would kill her if she stayed out all night. There was a hard decision coming, but it became easier with each lonely minute. If nobody showed up, then she wasn't missing a party.

Shadows drifted across the cloudy mounds, Lowa lifted her hood, slipped on her mitts, and started back into the frosty world. The town was different in such weather. There were no cars or pedestrians. No moose or bears, it was only her, the diamond-edged snowflakes whipped up from the ground, and the pounding winds themselves. Head down, she aligned her body with the memorized target miles away, and walked.

It was not long before her feet numbed. It reminded her of half-thawed chicken. Her skin existed, she felt it, knew it was there because that's where it had always been. By the minute, it got worse. Nearly absent of sensation, the skin on her feet seemed too soft over ice brick bones. She wiggled fingers to keep the blood flowing topside.

Whenever she looked up, hoping for a landmark, she saw nothing. On and on, the driving gusts pounded against her and the feet beneath her continued moving, despite them no longer feeling as if they belonged to her.

Sundown stole her sense of space and she forced those legs, trudging up what she hoped was the road. Her thighs were chapped beneath her pants. If it were not for the absence of temporary heat, she might've believed the sensation between her legs suggesting that she'd pissed.

She'd been cold before, there were symptoms.

On she moved.

It was not long after the light departed that she experienced the trueness of night creep through the layers of her heavy parka and insulated pants. The drips in her nose crystalized. Breath did the same in her lungs before quickly melting.

There was a chance she'd become another lost teenaged face in a land of lost teenaged faces. She groaned into the breath-damp layers. There couldn't possibly be much further to go. The thought of the posthumous embarrassment fueled her weary limbs.

She imagined the wolves holding a chow line over her body. A mama dragging her away to feed her pups. That would be better than getting lost so close to home, at least people weren't likely to think her too stupid to walk a straight line.

Earlier, Lowa scoffed at her mother's overreaction to the weather, now that voice, those words, rang like a warning siren: *You can't go out in this, don't be crazy!*

The steps became painful and the voice grew louder: *Don't be stupid, you're not going out.*

"It's my life," she mumbled, shivering, reliving.

With sorrowful shattered glass pangs gliding her bloodstream, she lifted her face to search for the property lights around the hotel. Tears froze on her cheeks. It was black, even the snow pushed about from the sky seemed like soot rather than clean powder.

On and on. Cold and tortured.

Lowa stumbled and teetered sideways into the gathered snow. Rolled onto her back and looked up. Snow covered her face and it tasted so pure.

Don't be crazy!

"I'm sorry," she whispered and turned onto her side, recognizing that to rest was to die. Although never truly feeling that, not in an honest sense. Death was for others, older people. "Hot chocolate. Bathtub. Fireplace. Slippers. Bed."

Mentally emboldened by self-promise, she bent her frosty knees and pushed forward. Breath moved in and out of her chest at a higher pace, staying cold within, freezing her lungs. It hurt and still, she pushed.

Don't be stupid!

"I know, I know."

Don't be crazy!

"Got it."

Something jabbed into her leg and Lowa fell backward in pain and surprise. From the ground, she saw light. Miraculous, glorious, welcoming light! Light was love. Forcing her body forward, she sat up and drank in the snow-muddled scenery.

It was the chest-high wrought iron fence—waist-high in the quickly packing snow—that had jabbed and toppled her. Lowa had meandered from the track but managed to hit the hotel property. Her heart leaped and scolding tears rolled, freezing before reaching her chin. She followed the fence from the stretching backyard around to the front of the property.

Light fought the night and won to reveal safety.

Inside: "You stupid girl!" her mother screamed.

"You're grounded until spring," her father said.

"We were losing our minds! You think of nobody but yourself, do you, Lowa?"

Lowa shrugged. "I'm sorry." It was never so close to the end, she saw that now. All along, her brain had overreacted to the discomfort. Sneaking out and getting temporarily lost was hardly a thing to ponder.

The shouts went on until her parents had said enough and slunk off to their bedroom. Lowa waited to hear the telltale slamming of a door before she crept to the family bathroom. She filled the tub and felt her body threaten to break apart as she stepped in. Thawing those frozen bones and harried mind worked like a pumice scrub against any lesson learned during the plight.

Eyes closed, the hot water cascaded her soul with new and mounting relief, never ending, more upon more.

Eyes open. Cold and dark, she was in the snow and freezing.

To rest was to die.

She sat up and screamed, "Mommy! Mommy!"

She got to her feet and trudged, again in her snow gear, again beyond the safety of the indoor world. On and on. Tears rolled and her recently thawed body was again like a meat popsicle.

"Daddy, help me!"

Don't be stupid!

"Please."

Don't be crazy!

Forever it seemed. Pain rode her veins like kite strings to the powerful burden of negativity blooming within her mind. She'd never been so defeated and tired. The yard lights and bath water felt so real a minute ago.

You can't go out in this.

"I'm sorry, Mommy, I won't. Help me! Find me!"

The pain was hard and full. The pain was the only thing she recognized.

She stumbled forward and looked sideways. 50 feet to her left were lights fighting through the snow. The hotel. The hotel and the loving warmth within.

"Don't let it be a dream."

Inside, the shouts raged. Mother and father scolded their frozen daughter.

"Don't you know how many stupid girls die every year?"

"Girls just as dumb as you!"

Lowa waited for the door to slam after the shouting ceased and crept to her bedroom. She stripped down to her underwear and crawled into the cool sheets that worked quickly to normalize her skin.

Safety and warmth swaddled her as if she'd returned to the womb.

Indoors during a storm, that was love.

Maybe she shouldn't creep out against her parents' will...nah, they'd overreacted.

She sobbed happily, wiping snot streaks about her pillow. Pins and needles invaded her flesh as the cold lost its grip. It was the longest night of her life, but it was over. She drifted.

Snow fell on her face and she shrieked. Freezing, she sat up. Dreams of home broke her will...almost. Move or die. It had become real. It had become so damned real. The possibility of real death. Lowa Stratton's demise, it was real and possible and eventual. It could be now and forever.

She was stupid.

Don't be stupid.

She was crazy.

Don't be crazy.

On she went. The snow had gotten so deep. Her exhaustion threatened to put her down, sink her into the depths and bring about consequence.

"Mommy!"

You're not going out.

"I did, it's too late. Daddy, come get me!"

Tears gathered in ice shelves beneath her eyes. Grim and done. Grim and torturous. Her sluggish feet dragged through the powder. On and on.

Light flickered and her heart hardly twinkled. Beaten, she fell forward and crawled. The hotel was there, but it took 20 more minutes to reach it.

The shouts were small. Her mother cried. Her father looked away.

"I'm sorry. I'm sorry, please."

More, as if going through the necessary motions, they barked at the girl. The stupid girl disobeying her parents.

Lowa hung her head and waited for them to leave before she went to her room. Déjà vu was on her. If she was still in the storm dreaming, let her be dead. She had nothing left to fight with, no strength, no will of teenaged self-assurance. She would stay home forever.

The night would take her. The night was a faceless monster.

On a whim, she climbed onto a small shelf in her closet and hid behind her limited wardrobe. The night would take her no more. No, she would stay awake until light and never leave again, not until the ice thawed and the river rose.

She counted minutes, unwilling to sleep for fear that she might awaken outside. And still, it was a long day.

Her eyes fluttered despite her.

Sleep.

She awoke cold.

No more.

Not frozen, only cold. Not really even cold, cool. She heard voices. Opened her eyes and peered through the slated doors of her closet onto the familiar silhouettes belonging to her parents in their parkas.

"Where is she? Not in the tub, where is she?" Lowa's father asked.

"I don't know. I don't know," her mother whispered, tears in her throat. "Maybe three's enough."

"The book says we should go one beyond what we think is enough. She'll never learn to mind us if we stop early, now we have to find her or soon she'll sneak out again, next time there's a party."

"Yeah, but only once more. She was so pathetic when she came back last time."

"Only once more," Lowa's father agreed.

Lowa closed her eyes and dreamed of night, knowing it wasn't the only monster looking to get her.

THE FRANCHISE

(2019)

Knuckles white, back hunched, her eyes bounced from the sunbaked grey asphalt to the speedometer: 160, 170, 180, 190, reaching for 200 kilometers per hour. Two inches away from the speedometer, the little silhouette of an engine was caution amber amidst the plastic charcoal panel. The car rattled. The steering wheel shook. Rachael Matheson's heart had become the snare of a bodily marching band, but her foot remained down.

"Why?" Her words were a moan. The Nissan Micra had a 1.2 liter engine and 79 horsepower. She'd never had the little box above 110KM/H, but now she was on a steep, long downgrade and more than ever, she needed to move.

A love ballad by Adele trailed away on the stereo. A voice followed—light, flowery music in the background that seemed to *smell* like fresh rising dough. "When only the best ingredients will do; feed your soul while you feed your face. Schlop Brothers Pizza." Rachael had heard this ad four times in the last two hours and it made her cringe every time, thinking about the TV spots and the glowing orb of the Schlop Brothers emblem.

Rubber squeaked as she pulled on the steering wheel, skidding through a gentle turn. Tears spilled over her cheeks as she glanced to the rearview mirror. It was blessedly empty but for the trees and the endless mountain range.

Those damned mountains. She'd tried calling her father, tried calling the cops, both had fizzled out. At the next clearing, she tried again. That thought came before the decline, and the engine light, and the goddamned speed. That was before she'd lost the car that was on her ass.

"He's gone. He's gone." Her mouth wasn't fooling her brain. "He has to be gone."

190, 162, 143, 111 KM/H: the hill was steep on the way back up. The phone went from the passenger's seat to her hand and she glanced at the screen. 44 minutes prior, she'd been on the telephone with her father, explaining that it was possible to get home before midnight.

Don't rush, he'd said. *Be safe,* he'd said. *Get a room if you need to,* he'd said. *Ignore the jerk on your ass,* he'd said. *Slow down and let him pass,* he'd said.

The jerk had passed and for nine minutes of small talk with her father, she'd all but forgotten about him. Then he was there, rolling 25 clicks below the speed limit. Rachael was about to tell her father about his reappearance when the trees got too thick and the mountains too full for reception; the call dropped, the Bluetooth cut out, and the radio music resumed from her dashboard stereo—Pink, *Beautiful Trauma*.

On his ass, she waited as long as she could before pulling to the left, into the oncoming lane. She'd sped. The jerk had sped...

Headshake, *kill the memory.* She glanced from the phone to the road.

A call had gone to the cops after the jerk hadn't let her pass. As she spoke to the dispatcher, the car let her fly by, and the cop's words wore the smile of understanding paranoia in some uppity college girl on her way home after exams. That smile had her questioning if she was only stressed and overreacting. That call ended on a scratchy fizz.

Headshake, *not overreacting, not paranoid.*

She glanced to the road, to the rearview, to her phone. Four texts landed as service was hers once again. The phone fell back to the passenger's seat and Rachael stabbed a finger into the telephone button on the dash, quieting disc jockey banter.

"Call—" Call whom? The car was gone. "Dammit." She hit the button and the disc jockey faded in anew.

Phone again in her hand, her eyes shot up and down: up to the seemingly forever climb of the mountain, down to the text from her on again off again, David. If it was more than physical, she'd call him, but she didn't want to sound crazy. Besides, he wasn't much of a listener—more of a suck me, fuck me, text you later guy.

She began typing, her heart finally bump-bumping at the normality of it, adrenaline heavy in her arms and legs, the butterflies of worry in her guts had lost their wings. 19 words in, her body rocked forward and the phone shot from her hand to the floor beneath the glovebox.

In the rearview was the jerk.

"No!" Rachael pinned her foot anew.

When they'd first met on the road, it was light, a couple hours after the atomic family suppertime. Now, the sun had set and made that jerk behind her all the more ominous. Like a breaching shark's fin upon a moonlight surf, the white square on the roof of his car shined.

"Leave me alone!"

A Dodge Neon. Rusty orange paint, black tinted windows, spoiler, gaudy 17-inch rims surrounded by the word Pirelli in white against the black rubber, a chrome intake stabbed through the hood like an upturned nose, and the damned foot-high glowing square—that plastic pizza box—on the roof. It was absurd. That car was a rolling joke. Schlop Brothers meets *Fast and the Furious*.

"Leave me alone!"

The jerk had fallen back when the Micra sped up, but the Micra was built for modern city living, while the Neon was from a time before gasoline was a buck and a half per liter. Coming fast, Rachael tensed, the old adrenaline mixing with new adrenaline, her eyes slammed closed to ready for the impact.

It didn't come. Rachael took a breath and looked in the rearview to see black emptiness. It made no sense. Her eyes fell to the road before her, more nothing. The Micra rocked sideways, the glass of the driver's side doors cracking and falling, shattering between the interior and exterior of the car. The humid air whipped through the openings; openings that let Rachael's screams free.

The jerk was in the left lane. The Neon's window lowered.

"What do you want?" Rachael sniffed and sobbed, foot falling off the gas as she reached the top of the incline.

Inside the Neon, it was shadows and fluorescent blue from an aftermarket stereo. The shape of the driver was a blob, no definition. An arm flipped sideways.

Rachael saw it coming and didn't have time to duck. Her foot slammed on the brakes as red erupted upon her cheek. Hands to her face, she felt the wet mess. Lumpy red shined almost blackly beneath the moon rays that poured through her windshield.

She pawed for a hole, for the source of the gore. Nothing. The smell hit her. Tomatoes, oregano, garlic. Her tongue stretched out. It was fucking marinara sauce.

Next to the gearshift was the Schlop Brothers brand container, red gunk like a frozen wave, mid-leap over the edge.

"What the hell!" Her fists slammed against the armrest and the door, leaving delicious frustration stamps on the porous plastic.

The Neon was gone from sight.

She killed the engine, silenced the stereo, and inhaled deep breaths. Reaching down into the passenger's side, she tapped the floor mat for her cellphone. There it was, hard under palm, she tightened fingers around the device. She sat up and light filled her interior. A horn blared.

She tensed. The little car rocked on a drag backwash of a passing Coors Light 18-wheeler. A breath wheezed from her tight lips. She pressed the button on the right side of her Samsung and the screen lit. Three bars, she dialed 911. It rang once through her speakers via Bluetooth.

"Is this an emergency?" The voice was a woman's, calm, reassuring. Better than the cop she'd spoken to earlier, back before she was sure it was an emergency.

"Yes, someone, someone, a, uh—Schlop Brothers delivery car, he's—my windows are broken and—"

"Ma'am, be calm. Where are you?"

"On the Highway. Highway One."

"What was the last town you went through?"

"The last town?" Rachael racked her brain. She couldn't remember any towns, nothing since the jerk in the Neon ruined her trip. But that couldn't be right. There were many towns, villages, and campgrounds on that stretch of highway. In fact, she should've already been through Revelstoke and on her way to Salmon Arm. "I don't know, it's all messed up."

"Can you drive?"

"I... Yeah. I can drive... It was a Schlop deliveryman. I'm sure of it. It had one of those glowing pizza boxes on the roof. A Neon. I mean the car, not the Schlop light."

"Rusty Neon? That's from in town here. If you're seeing that Schlop Brothers car, then you're likely near Echo. Have you gone past the signs to Echo yet?"

Echo? She'd never heard of Echo, didn't recall it. Then again, there seemed to be a million little burghs on and off the highway, eking out an existence. "Not yet."

"You're heading west?"

"Yeah."

"Keep heading west. I'll send someone out to meet you. Hopefully there's little separation between you and us here at the station. If they don't find you, take the exit into Echo."

"Okay." Rachael keyed the engine and rolled.

The broken window buffeted the air and the call dropped. She leaned over the center console to get out of the wind. The phone went back to the passenger's seat. 50 KP/H, she reached the top of another mountain hump. Four minutes later, the sign for Echo directed her right and she passed a swatch of forest before coming upon an opening. Right there were the bright lights of a police station.

"Thank god." She coasted down a hill and pulled into the parking lot. A thought, she considered calling her father before entering, but decided she didn't want him to worry now that the trouble was behind her.

Pale paneling, pine most likely, covered the station walls. There were two desks with rotary phones and paperwork. A toilet flushed and a woman stepped through a door, stuffing her uniform into her beltline. She was a big woman, tall and thick like an Andrea the Giant.

"You the woman having trouble with a Schlop Brothers' driver?"

Rachael nodded, looking up at the woman.

"Right, let's take a walk. Hard to believe one of them's the trouble. Schlop Brothers...best damned pizza I ever ate; and I've eaten enough of it that I should be bored senseless of it by now. We'll get to the bottom of this. Schlop Brothers is only four doors down."

Rachael felt safe around the woman and followed. Echo was a dead place. The storefronts featured more boards than glass. The signs hung on jaunty angles, the single caution light that blinked orange did so out of tune, and the grass around the sidewalk trees was hip-high and browned. This Schlop Brothers location filled in the space of an old diner. A light on the front of the building was achingly bright, and that familiar glowing pizza box above the door sent an icy caterpillar up her spine.

Beneath the Schlop Brothers sign was a sign the read WEAVER'S in chipped and flaking paint. A remnant. An artifact. Whoever owned the building hadn't modified it much when they switched the business from a mom and pops to a fast-spreading chain. Strange. Dim, there were six booths and a sub-counter with a sneeze guard. A pie display spun dessert options. A retro

Coca-Cola cooler revealed the six types of soda through a glass door—old-timey tall bottles only, the kind with pop tops and once you finished, they'd give you a quarter back at the return depot.

The big officer rang the silver bell on the counter. "Hello?"

"Oh, gimme a second." The voice came from around a corner.

"You got a driver out there misbehaving?" The cop acted as if she hadn't heard the man ask for a second.

"Driver?"

"Yeah, a driver."

The man stepped out. He wore scrubs like a nurse—all white. He had a pin on his chest that read, *Schlop Brothers Pizza,* and beneath that *Sales Manager.* "Rewind, what's happened?"

"Your deliveryman harassed this young lady on the highway tonight."

Rachael puffed her chest; something was happening, and the terrifying mess was finally over. The horror and frustration drained and all that remained was fury.

The man put on a hint of a grin. "Harassed her, like how?"

Light banked off the walls, coming in from the street. Rachael thought nothing of it. The cop did not react to it.

Before the cop could answer, the man added, "Did he grab her ass? *Her-ass,* get it?"

The cop laughed.

The fury took a side route. Rachael blinked. That joke was anything but funny.

More light washed in through the window. The dimness evaporated and revealed huge stains and puddles on the dark-carpeted floor. Spatters covered the walls. She inhaled deeply through her nose. It smelled like tomato sauce.

"Her ass. That's good. Maybe good as her ass." The cop turned and looked at Rachael, licked her top lip, then bit her bottom lip.

Rachael began backstepping, all the way to a booth. Pain shot up as her hip hit a sharp corner. She turned to register her location in regards to the exit, and then scanned for another exit. Her eyes caught on something through the window and the pain in her hip was suddenly so damned minor in comparison.

Three cars with lit squares on their roofs—a Tempo, a Sunfire, and a Sonic—pointed headlights in through the glass. Shine glinted off the nameplate on the cop's chest: *Schlop Brothers Pizza, Security.*

More light poured in. A fourth car, a Neon. The Neon.

"No, but...no."

The man in scrubs lifted a pail from behind the counter by a steel handle. Lumpy red sauce, it was so thick it hardly moved as he lugged and jerked. He hefted the pail and breathed in the aroma. The cop reached around the sneeze-guard glass of the counter and retrieved a large, sauce-smattered pizza cutter.

The pair stepped toward Rachael.

Rachael stumbled again, this time toward the door. She got to four steps away when it opened and a young woman in a pantsuit came through. Her eyes were wet onyx top to bottom and corner to corner. She had chipped glitter nail polish on the tips of her overgrown nails. In her hands were Schlop Brothers pizza boxes.

The woman moved slowly. Rachael spun, dodging a lazy swipe by the cop. The manager in scrubs grunted and lifted the pail high as he could, placing his right hand on the bottom. Schlop Brothers sauce splashed over Rachael's head and shoulders.

There was a door at the back of the dining area. A red exit sign offered her the only hope she had left. The faster she went, the faster those chasing her went. She got there. The paddle was cold beneath her hand and disappeared before she had a chance to push it more than a modicum. A middle-aged man in dirty chef's whites, Schlop Brothers nametag on his breast, had swung the door wide; in one hand he held an open tub of ranch dressing, with his other hand he rooted through a Schlop Brothers branded fanny pack that drooped beneath his moderate gut. He withdrew a squeeze bottle of hot sauce. He tightened his grip, nozzle pointed at Rachael. A red stream spurted out, hit her ear; the scent made her eyes water and nose run instantly.

Rachael spun again and the cop scooped a handful of sauce from the dregs of the manager's pale and whipped it into her face.

"Why? Why?" The words came out through oily red bubbles forming on her lips.

She stumbled, sneakers slipping in sauce. She fell and the deliveryman dropped his weaponry and grabbed her armpits.

"Why?"

The manager stepped forward, grin spread wider than could possibly be natural and dumped a small bowl of spices over Rachael's head. The world went black. She didn't see the cheese that came next, though smelled it; was blind to the dough that came after that but felt its gooey weight.

The last thing Rachael Matheson heard before she was forced into a pizza oven was, "When only the best ingredients will do; feed your soul while you feed the Master."

—

The voice on the stereo was Pink's. The Micra had new windows, but the engine light remained aglow. Rachael's father didn't understand until he was made to understand. College wasn't for her; she had a new calling.

She parked, straightened her visor, grabbed the padded delivery bags from the passenger's seat, and exited the Micra. The music from within the house was heavy and thumping. She stepped up to the front door to hit the bell.

A young woman answered.

"Have your order," Rachael said.

The young woman called over her shoulder, "Pizza's here." She then turned to Rachael with a grin. "Let the guys pay... That smells great!"

Rachael nodded. "Only the best ingredients will do; feed your soul while you feed your face."

HARVEST QUEEN

(2022)

"Oh, so you actually live in the suburbs?" Dennis asked. He was fidgety and shy. This woman was so, so beautiful and for some reason, she'd swiped right on his profile.

"Not quite. I'm a country girl," Maggie said.

"Oh, like on a farm?"

Maggie was so utterly perfect that was difficult to focus.

"Only way to be truly country, if you ask me."

Dennis smiled with his entire expression, inhaling deeply of the coffee scents in the nearly vacant and rundown Starbucks Maggie had chosen, and the sweet perfume, or hair product, or lip gloss she wore that smelled faintly of cola.

"I'm a city boy, through and through. Closest I've been to a farm was a pumpkin patch and haunted house, oh, must've been fifteen years ago."

Maggie tilted her head some, her slender fingers finding his lower thigh, just above the knee, beneath the table. She squinted, her left eyebrow raising. "You don't have kids though?"

Her hand was completely unexpected, and he had to fight off a gasp. The cola smell was everywhere now and his head began to swim. "No, no kids. Only an ex-wife."

He'd said this because it felt like what she wanted to hear— he had two daughters, one 17 and one 18. Dennis would tell Maggie any old thing in the world. She was so far out of his league they weren't even playing the same sport.

"What's say you and I go for a little walk? Find someplace private to chat," Maggie said as her hand rose high enough that she played the top of her middle fingernail against the bulge of his jeans—the bulge at the crotch as opposed to the love handle/gut bulge circling his middle at the beltline.

"Hey, sure." Dennis fought off a nervous giggle. He hadn't been laid in more than a year and a half, had cringed at how his now ex-wife had cringed whenever he'd brought up the topic during those final years of their relationship. Was this beautiful woman really going to let him...?

"What's the end game here, missy?" he said and pushed her hand away. He was overweight, he was broke, he was laid off, and the hair on his chest and back was thicker than the hair on his head. Something was up.

"Oh, I'm sorry," Maggie said. "Forgive me." She put her hands up to her face. "I'm so embarrassed."

Dennis spied her, mostly buying what she was selling.

"I just..." She tittered and shook her head.

"What?" he said.

She waved him off, still covering her face with her left hand.

"No, what?" he said.

She spread her fingers and looked at him, smiling around her palm. "It's a country girl thing."

"What is?"

"Big men."

"Big men what?" he said, now grinning himself.

"Big men make me horny." Maggie covered her face again. "I'm sorry, most guys—and I'm not saying I've done this more than four times, because that's how many dates I've gone on here in the city—want to get into my pants. I just kind of assumed."

Dennis swallowed an invisible golf ball before reaching out for her skinny leg. Still covering her face, she slid down the chair to meet his hand, to push her sensible jean skirt up high enough to give him flesh access at her thigh.

"Let's get out of here," he said.

—

The heat was thick on the air and the air-conditioner inside the

Freightliner was pulling major duty. Maggie was up in the sleeper behind her uncle at the wheel. This was the second time she'd gone with him to the city. Last year was fun because it was different and exciting, but this year had gotten old pretty damned fast.

They pulled into the border crossing line and waited. They wouldn't get to chance it like the others looking to cross in their sedans and pick-ups—they had no choice but to get out of the truck and let the dogs sniff away.

The Mack ahead of them pulled into a stall. "You think you'll do a three-peat?"

"A 'three-peat,' what...oh. No. I'm not in the running this year, two years is enough. I'm going to college," Maggie said.

"You're not leaving us for good, though?" her uncle asked, looking into the rearview mirror.

"No. I couldn't leave home. I just...Harvest Queen's a lot of bother and it means more to the younger girls. On that side, I'd feel like a jerk if I won three times."

"Not sure there's a right girl to replace you. And what's the other side?" Her uncle let off the brakes and pulled into a customs stall. All the necessary paperwork for the 41 head of Texas longhorns he'd purchased down in Nebraska were in a file at the ready.

Maggie covered her face in an act that looked a bit like what she'd done in the Starbucks, sitting next to a man named Dennis, but it was for a wholly different emotion. "You know."

Maggie's uncle had been bringing livestock across the border for decades. He turned in his seat to look at her head on. "Don't ever be ashamed of who you are or where you come from."

A knock landed against the driver's door. Maggie's uncle shifted and killed the engine, gave a wave down to the little woman in a customs official uniform holding a clipboard, and grabbed the paperwork.

"Come on now," he said to Maggie as he pushed open the

door.

Maggie grabbed her purse and located her passport within.

—

The sisters couldn't be more different than they were, not while being only a year apart and having the same parents. They'd lived in the same household, they'd eaten the same food, and their parents had shopped for them at the same stores. Trudy was eighteen. Raven was seventeen.

"He probably killed himself," Raven said, her eyes on the screen of her cellphone as she scrolled the accounts of the beautiful and the famous.

"Jesus. What's wrong with you?" Trudy said.

They were in their father's crummy bachelor pad apartment. It was just like on TV: pastel paint on the walls, cramped rooms, ancient furniture, walkways to everywhere, and a funky pool down below next to a ratty patio set and a dirty barbeque. His car was in his parking space and his wallet was on the coffee table, but he was missing.

"What? Probably found out Mom's dating Jimmy and then found himself a cliff to jump off."

Trudy shook her head. Raven was cold, flippant, and wildly selfish. Always had been. And when she'd turned 16, she grew into her body, was suddenly the girl every cool person wanted to be near. Had a million dates. Had a million friends.

Trudy bent to rifle the junk mail that had been pushed through the slot on the door. No real mail, no hints as to where he'd gone. She dropped the small stack and straightened, pulling her jeans up. She had love handles and no ass—was in fact shaped very much like her father, Dennis.

"Maybe a neighbor knows?" Trudy said.

"Maybe a neighbor knows which cliff he jumped off of?"

"Ugh, don't be so damned horrible all the time," Trudy said and stepped outside.

She looked to her left and then right, deciding on room 219

to her left. The door seemed more inviting, despite being nearly identical to the door of the apartment to the right of her father's; the seven was made of janky yellowed plastic rather than the faux gold of the rest of the numbers. It was just a little weird. A little off-putting. Trudy knocked on 219.

A man wearing an off-white undershirt with large hairy breasts and a bulging gut answered. He held a bag of Vermis brand pork rinds in his hand. "Yeah?" he said around a mouthful.

Trudy leaned away some. "Um, sorry to bother you, but my father lives next-door, and nobody's heard from him in days."

"How many?" the man said.

"How many what?"

"Days."

"Oh, at least a week," Trudy said.

The man shoveled a handful of greasy pork rinds into his mouth and crumbs drifted down like snow to settle in the pelt between his cleavage. "Oh, 'bout a week ago he had him a hooker over. He said she matched him on Tinder, was all proud about it. Like I believed that."

"Believed what?" Raven said, stepping out onto the connected balcony that ran to all the rooms on the second floor.

"A woman, pretty as you and just about as young, matched your fat old dad on Tinder," the man said and then began sucking the tips of his fingers, one at a time.

"Look who's calling someone fat," Raven said, nodding at the man's protruding belly.

"Being fat don't preclude me from recognizing fat. Don't preclude me from recognizing a high-priced hooker. One of them ones that plays a gag. She was dressed like a church girl," the man said. He rolled the remainder of the bag and pulled a red elastic band from his wrist to bound it closed.

"He showed you his Tinder?" Trudy said. "Dad was on Tinder?"

"Sure. Just about everyone here's on Tinder." The big man

began tonguing at one of his eye teeth.

"Can you show me the profile?" Trudy said.

"Dad *would* get a hooker," Raven said and stepped back into their father's apartment.

"No, I'm not on Tinder," the man said.

"But you said—"

"I'm on Grindr." The man waggled his eyebrows but quit quickly; Trudy didn't seem impressed. "They went to the Starbucks on Wilson. He told me that, too. She wanted to go to that one specifically, even though it's got to be the oldest in the city."

—

"Not a prostitute, no," the Starbucks barista said. She remembered the overweight middle-aged man and the beautiful young woman from eight nights ago, recognized Dennis from the picture Trudy had shown. "I think she was a famous lookalike, but I don't know who. Know what I mean? That's why I remember her at all."

"Maybe. Is she on here?" Trudy held out her cellphone, the phony Tinder profile she made with her father's photo was open on all the available women in the area.

"Could be she does commercials?" the barista said as she swiped by woman after woman. "You know? Not for real famous, but famous-ish?"

"Maybe?" Trudy looked at the vacant table where the barista had seen her father sitting and wondered why this beautiful woman had chosen him and what she'd done with him, if the two things were indeed connected.

"Oop, there she is."

Trudy snatched the cellphone and studied the little photo on her screen. The woman was totally as beautiful as the neighbor, and now the barista, had said. Her profile said she was from the city, but she didn't dress like it. She had on a plaid shirt and a jean skirt that was long enough that the hem didn't make it into any of the pictures. And in all three photos of this woman—Maggie V.—she wore that same plaid shirt and jean skirt. In the final one, she stood in front of a big red barn, behind her were the letters MIS, the remainder of whatever that word was had been cut off.

"I know I know her from somewhere," the barista said, snapping the fingers of her right hand in front of her face. "Pretty sure it's a commercial."

Trudy exhaled enough air to puff out her cheeks. She swiped right.

"Can I get you anything?" the barista finally asked.

—

The burner phone had beeped fairly steadily with Tinder notifications. Maggie liked to see who wanted to meet her, even if they meant nothing and would never, ever meet her. Though, this last one had her frowning. She and her mother were on a short trip to town for party supplies when the notification that a man she'd already met swiped right with a new account.

Impossible.

It couldn't be the man called Dennis.

But it was freaky enough that she put down her window and let the phone drop from her hand. It bounced three times against asphalt before falling into a swampy ditch. Crises averted.

—

Trudy returned to her father's apartment to find Raven and the neighbor sitting on the couch, eating chips, and watching a movie on cable. On the screen, Arnold Schwarzenegger grabbed Michael Ironside's arms and yanked him higher on the moving platform he dangled from a moment before his head and shoulders were separated after meeting the underside of something immoveable, a floor, a wall, didn't matter. Arnold then cast away the severed limbs and said, "See you at the party, Richter!"

"What are you watching?" Trudy said as she stepped into the apartment.

"*Total Recall*," the neighbor said.

"The remote's glued to the table. Like at a hotel," Raven said, yanking on the boxy remote that belonged to the boxy Zenith on the chintzy TV stand.

"I used Goo Gone to get mine off," the neighbor said.

"Fight the power," Raven said and reached into the chip bag.

"I found her. Sort of. The barista thought she was famous or did commercials, and was not a prostitute," Trudy said.

The neighbor shrugged. "Way out of his league."

"Well, yeah," Trudy said. "Was this who you saw?" She handed over the phone.

The neighbor watched the TV for ten more seconds until a commercial disrupted the movie and he accepted the phone. "That's her. Maggie, I bet that's her real name. She looks like a Maggie."

"And you saw her here? What time?" Trudy said.

"Around midnight. Same night he had his big date," the neighbor said, crunching through a mouthful of chips—same brand as the pork rinds.

"We asked our friends coast-to-coast to try our new kettle chips," Raven said along with the commercial and then crunched a chip.

"Vermis, Vermis, Vermis, the snacks for a brighter world," the neighbor said, continuing with the ad dialogue, a little hum in his words.

"Did you see him, or just her?" Trudy said.

On the screen, about 100 hicks waved, standing in front of a big red barn with the word VERMIS in white, white letters across the front. An ad for Stay Free Mini-Pads began then; none of them spoke along.

"Just her. She was leaving. All the lights were off. I heard her come up and went out to snoop. I have these cigarettes from a...I don't smoke, but I lit one and I watched her. I think she's a hooker. Way too hot for your fat dad," the neighbor said.

Trudy couldn't argue. She had gotten all her dad's fat genes and anything above a six was a very tough pull. Maggie was an eleven.

——

"Hey, if the guys can spend all day and night in the fields, I can do a few hours helping with the decorations," Maggie said to her great-great grandfather. She was in a straw hat, a tank top, and cutoff jean shorts. She was clipping stems off flowers she and the Harvest Queen hopefuls had gathered and gluing them onto a hay wagon that would be used as a parade float in two days.

"Shame you won't do a third year," he said.

"Two's enough for me."

"And you're leaving us."

"Only during the school year. It's not like I'm never coming back."

The centenarian sighed. He withdrew his pipe and a plastic sack of tobacco from his pocket. "None of those girls is right for it," he said, yellowed dentures clamped around the stem as he dropped a match into the bowl.

"Sure, they are," Maggie said.

"Who?"

Maggie sat silently, her knees tucked beneath her and flowers in her hands. None of them were, really, and everybody knew it. They were all too soft and too thoughtful. None knew the whole truth of the position or its difficult nature. It took a specific type of woman, or a woman willing to play that specific and difficult part. Also, none of the hopefuls were nearly as beautiful as Maggie.

——

In the middle of the night, Trudy couldn't sleep, thinking about her father and the woman from Tinder. She went to the pantry and grabbed a packet of vanilla cinnamon sticks. She opened the bag and inhaled the scent. So much like cola.

"Whether its salty or sweet, Vermis is the treat that can't be beat," she mumbled around a chewed stick. She huffed at herself then. That advertisement hadn't been on air for a few years now. "Vermis, Vermis, Vermis, snacks for a brighter..." She trailed in thought. She stood still in the kitchen, gazing blankly at the baker's rack beyond the cutting board island. Her mother and Jimmy, the boy toy, were away for the weekend and had left behind the keys to the car and a debit card.

"Vermis can't be..." Trudy trailed again. She pulled her phone from the pocket of her pajama shorts. She brought up the longer shot of the Maggie person. That big red building behind her, there was something about it.

MIS; were the cutoff letters VER?

And that building, was it the one...?

She quickly searched Google, landed on YouTube, and watched the Vermis Kettle Chips advertisement. She paused it. That building was a Vermis barn. She had no doubts. Blindly, she shuffled out of the kitchen and into the connected living room. She plopped down on the couch and read about the company.

—

"What're you doing?" Raven said. She was eating a congealed slice of cold pizza from the night before.

Trudy looked around. She'd fallen asleep on the couch with one hand in the Vermis Cinni Stix bag and the other on her phone. There was a bay window in the living room that faced west, and the light was entering in a way that suggested both she and her sister had slept in until after the noon hour.

"I figured it out. That woman with Dad, it was Maggie Venandi."

"Who's Maggie Venandi?"

"Venandi, Pastor, Belator, and Agricola, those are the four families who own Vermis." Trudy lifted her hand, raising the snack baggy. "Maggie Venandi is from a billionaire family."

"Bull," Raven said. She was on her way to the fridge for another slice; she could eat anything she wanted and she never gained a pound.

"No, look." Trudy opened the Wikipedia page on Maggie Venandi. Someone had used the entire picture that Maggie had cut off for one of the Tinder profile pics. It was of Maggie and another young woman. Also cropped from the Tinder pic were their feet and the sign written in flowers: HARVEST QUEEN.

"But why?" Raven said.

"That's what we're going to find out. We're going to confront the bitch," Trudy said.

"What?"

"In Manitoba."

"Canada? Can't you just call?"

Trudy shook her head. "Can't you feel it? Dad's in real danger. We have to do this."

———

"What purpose do you have for entering Canada?" the boarder agent had asked twice, and Trudy froze. "It's a simple—"

"Hey, hi." Raven leaned over the center console. She smiled a set of perfect teeth, head tilted slightly. "Hey, sorry. My sister has these panic things."

The border agent began nodding, mouth slightly agape. He was in his 40s and trim, even handsome. In an older man kind of way.

Raven moved her left arm, which was beneath her, and pushed her breasts higher in the loose tank top she wore. "You know how girls can be." She shook her head playfully, her curly locks dancing upon her shoulders. "We're going up to sightsee. Winnipeg, Riding Mountain National Park, maybe fly up to Churchill to see the polar bears." Out of boredom, she'd studied Google Maps as they drove. "To begin, we're staying at an Airbnb in this little town just outside Brandon. Cheaper than staying in the city, right?"

Trudy and the border agent nodded. Trudy wasn't hypnotized by her sister's breasts like the border agent however, she was just freaking out.

"Have a nice trip," the agent mumbled and through they drove.

"Must be nice to do that whenever you want," Trudy said.

"Pfft, that was nothing. I bet I could've borrowed a fifty from him. A little time and he'd take me on a shopping spree," Raven said. "Probably not even illegal here. Canadians are perverts about the age of consent; about everything."

Trudy looked at her sister. "What is wrong with you?"

Raven stuck out her tongue.

—

"You're sure we can't convince you?"

Maggie looked at her uncles and aunts. Behind her, the hopefuls all had their heads downturned as if ashamed that they weren't good enough but were still willing to run.

"No, tonight's my last night as Harvest Queen. I can't. I just can't, okay?" Maggie said, biting back tears.

They were about to begin the annual Harvest Parade that would run from the edge of the community to the center of the first field the families had planted when they'd settled some 200 years ago. There was no turning back now. Life went on, and if that meant their prosperous community might falter one year, she couldn't be held accountable.

"Fine. Everybody! Take your spots," a gnarly old woman shouted—Maggie's great-great-great aunt.

—

"And just how are we supposed to find this chick?" Raven said. They'd pulled off the main highway half an hour ago and according to her phone, were coming up on Domum, a county settlement rather than a town, and home of Vermis Snack Foods. "How do you know she isn't off in Paris or something?"

Trudy had been thinking about that possibility a lot on the trek, but she needed to confront somebody, anybody who might know what happened to their father. Even if he was a rather mediocre Dad most of the time.

"Think she's going to be in the middle of the road, just waving at..." Raven trailed.

They'd come to an intersection where the asphalt ended and gravel began. A sign warned that the land was not incorporated by the province. On the same post was the word DOMUM. Beneath that, HOME OF VERMIS. Crossing by them on another gravel road was a tractor pulling a parade float and Maggie Venandi in a huge flower crown, sitting on a raised platform above several young women and girls wearing smaller flower crowns. Behind the passing float were dozens of men and women in plaid shirts, blue jeans, and well-worn work boots.

"That's her, right?" Trudy said.

"Well, I'll be damned," Raven said.

The marchers in the parade eyed the idling Toyota sedan with North Dakota plates. Another tractor and wagon appeared, following the procession. It featured two-dozen large cages. Naked men had been cramped into those cages and were smeared with dirt or shit, and blood. Steadily, the men reached through gaps in the wiring to snatch at snack food items littering the floor of the wagon.

"Was that Dad?" Raven said, pointing to the second wagon.

Trudy had already kicked open her door, though hadn't stepped out. More men and women, followed by children, trailed along behind the parade.

"Get back in the car," Raven said.

"What'll we do?" Trudy said.

"Uh, get the hell out of here?"

"No, but, Dad?"

"We can call the cops and they can come." Raven made a show of holding up her phone before dialing.

Trudy climbed back into the car. The parade was by them now.

"Hey, yeah, so these people kidnapped my dad and beat him

up and stuff. I just saw them go by." Raven listened. "In this place called Domum." Raven listened some more. "Oh, okay. See you then, I guess."

"Well?" Trudy said.

Raven lowered her phone. "Thirty-five minutes."

"But what if they're doing something to him?"

"I don't—" Raven shook her head. "He should've known. That chick is way too hot for him!"

"So, we just let them do whatever?" Trudy's whole face scrunched into an angry ball. "No, fuck that." She threw the shifter into drive and followed the parade route.

"For the record, I'm not getting out of the car."

"Why are you like this?"

"Like I don't want to get caged up by Canadian hillbillies?"

The parade had detoured from the road and was stalled in a field. Most of the locals had joined hands in a semi-circle that opened onto a dirt mound. The men from the cages were on the ground, moving on hands and knees toward the dirt mound.

Trudy winced at the pendulous sway of her father's belly and his shrunken genitals, his hairy ass and back and shoulders. "Daddy," she moaned and parked. She then snatched the keys and got out.

"Hey!" Raven said.

Trudy approached quickly. The locals didn't hear her as she put a broad shoulder down and ran through a pair of kids holding hands in the circle. They tumbled and she kept on, burning a line to her father.

"Dad! It's me! I've got you!"

She reached him and dropped to her knees. She hugged tightly around his neck with both arms. He smelled terrible, mostly like feces.

"Dad, come on," she said, leaning away to look at him.

His eyes were two milk-white orbs. Green and purple bruises haloed his temples. Many of his teeth had been broken and were jagged little chunks. Cheese Doodle crumbs rimmed his mouth like clown paint.

"What have they done to you?"

A shadow loomed over Trudy, and she turned. A big man was approaching, he wore blood-stained overalls and carried a black baton prod.

"No, wait!" Trudy put up her arms to shield her head.

The man swung the baton, pressing the trigger as he did. The strike to her elbow hurt. The electricity coursing through her made her convulse. The second strike nailed her temple and the world went black. Another man helped the one with the baton strip Trudy naked and then drape her over her father's back. The procession of naked men continued until it reached the dirt mound.

From her seat on high, Maggie said, "Our Lord, our God, dear Vermis, please accept these gifts as a show of our gratitude!"

The dirt mound burst outward and a round face with no nose or eyes, and a mouth full of tiny teeth rose to the surface. It wriggled ten feet of its soft, rubbery body topside before stretching a long grey tongue out to the first naked man. It reeled him in and began chewing, rending the flesh and bones and blood into a pink slurry. The procession moved forward.

One by one, the great worm ate, until it took Trudy and Dennis into its mouth at once. The worm shivered, perhaps in delight, perhaps in disgust that it fed on a woman. They wouldn't know until next year's harvest.

—

"I won't say a word. I mean they were family, but I'm looking out for number one here. Know what I mean?" Raven said.

A group of very old people and Maggie surrounded her after pulling her from the car. The worm remained partially out of the ground, licking blood from the grass. The rest of the locals formed a distant circle, sitting in the harvested hay field, watching—including the Harvest Queen Hopefuls in their little flower crowns, knowing tears playing down their cheeks.

"Your presence is no mistake," an old, old man said.

The other elders shook their heads.

"She's perfect," Maggie said and stepped forward. "How would you like a position with the Vermis Snack Food company?"

"Uh, what?" Raven said.

Maggie lifted her large crown and set it on Raven's confused and terrified head.

"Harvest Queen comes with many benefits, your highness." Maggie bent to take a knee, as did the fogeys surrounding them. "We're a multi-billion-dollar organization."

"Benefits?" Raven said, a grin creeping onto the left side of her mouth. "Like, what Kind?"

COME STRAIGHT HOME

(2015)

It wasn't fair, not even close. He'd always been good, always did his best. His parents said it wasn't grounding—he had to understand that, they worried, it was just safer.

It sure felt like grounding.

"You comin' or what, Pas?" A small boy in dirty blue jeans and a stained white tee looked over his shoulder. His name was Mikey Rivers, his mother died a year earlier and his father wasn't big on laundry.

Pascal's parents told him it was cancer, told him to be nice to the boy despite his grubby nature and his underachieving. Told him it was such a sad thing to have a mother die.

Pascal grunted to his friend, "Yeah, cool it, 'kay?" He was only nice to Mikey because his parents told him to be, even if doing so contradicted what they told him a day earlier.

"Pascal, now I know it's not fair, but you need to come straight home after school," his father said, eyebrows lifted in the *I'm serious, pal* angle.

"Just until everything settles," his mopey faced mother added.

Pascal thought about the satisfaction of storming to his bedroom and slamming the door, it had nothing on his current satisfaction. Defiance was a drug.

It was the rundown part of town, the area where the buildings crumbled on top of luckless hobos and rusty rebar shot from the cement like permanent weeds.

"How far we gotta go?" Pascal asked.

Mikey had promised him a great surprise, something ultra

cool. Pascal didn't really care what it was, only wanted to challenge the curfew. Still, he felt a twinge of worry; his parents would be mad—he'd push it, but only so far. Also, he had chapter work to do on *The Thief of Always* before Friday and he liked to do that work right after he read, so the information was still fresh. He'd finished the third chapter at lunch.

"What, you gotta get home to mommy?" Mikey said.

He brought up the thing everyone pussyfooted around whenever he wanted to end a discussion. Nobody liked a dead mother or a motherless child. Both were nasty topics.

Pascal followed through the gravel paths between the dilapidated buildings. He looked at his watch, should've been home 20 minutes ago. He'd follow for 10 more minutes, at most, and then circle home before his parents really grounded him; maybe even took away his computer or his PS4.

Their voices echoed around in his head. "Do you understand why it's so important?" his mother had asked through the bedroom door he'd slammed. "We only want you to be safe," his father had said, voice next to his mother's.

"Leave me alone!" he'd shouted. So they had.

He came out at breakfast, sleeping off his anger, his mother sat at the table about to fold out the paper, his father fussed with the coffee maker.

"Another one, another one!" she yelled stabbing a finger into the front page.

Pascal's father rushed to her side and read. "You remember, straight home," he had said to Pascal, a good boy considering turning bad to teach a lesson in fairness.

"Just up here," Mikey said, it had grown cooler, closing in on night.

Pascal thought it might still be all right, he'd have time to see what he'd see and get home before total dark.

Ahead, a doorway stood amidst the rubble, everything around it fallen and broken. It was pretty cool that the door remained when the building fell, but hardly cool enough for the trouble.

"That it?" Pascal was indignant.

"Just a sec." Mikey stepped to the door, rapped 10 times, counting under his breath as he did, and after the 10th, turned the doorknob. "Comin'?"

Pascal nodded, amazed by the door. It no longer led to nowhere.

Acid jumped from his gut to his throat and his mouth dried, slack and open. He had a bad feeling about going through. A bad feeling about the damp pale walls inside. A bad feeling but followed the boy nonetheless. There were worse fears than parents, or schoolwork, curfews, and creepy doors. There was rep, there was looking like a wussy in front of a tough kid like Mikey Rivers.

They stepped inside and the door slammed shut behind them. "Follow me, best part is down here," Mikey said as they continued on a gentle slope.

The temperature rose around them, the soft clay walls dripped with sweat and something metallic filled Pascal's nostrils. It was familiar, but impossible to finger.

"What is this place?" A quiver danced in Pascal's words.

"Why, you scared?" Mikey said—the taunt half-hearted. He quickened, leading the way through the hall into a wide cavern full of pale figures lounging on chairs, children chained from the ceiling in their underwear, scabs about their flesh, jaws dangling, unconscious.

"Why?" Pascal whispered, understanding that this is what his parents had meant.

Straight home.

23 missing children. 19 empty children returned, breathless, lifeless, exsanguinated. That was the word his father had used. "Exsanguinated, I can't think of anything more horrifying. Pascal, promise me, you'll come home right after school."

Mikey turned to his friend. "They said they'd bring my mom

back if I got enough of my friends."

Three pale and smiling creatures approached, they didn't move like normal. They glided inches above the floor, eyes wide, licking their black lips, horns jutting from their skulls glowing cold blue and hot red.

Just what his mother had said, "...monsters, to do that to children, absolute monsters."

Pascal looked at Mikey and then over his shoulder, two more figures approached from behind. "I can't—"

"I'm sorry, but they told me I could get my mom back," Mikey whined. He took three steps away from Pascal and the encroaching figures.

"You promise us you'll come home right after school," his father had said, demanded.

"Promise us," his mother had seconded.

It wasn't grounding, but it felt like grounding, but it wasn't. It was for his protection, his safety, he understood that now, wished he meant it when he'd answered their demands with, "Mom, Dad, I promise. I swear. Straight home."

DESCRY ONE

(2016)

It was cold enough that steam clouded from their bluish lips, puffing upon every breath, even within the insulated hull of the small craft. Marxsen glared at the horizon and wondered at what speed the planet spun, even wondered if it had stopped spinning as some cosmic joke played solely on her and her partner. It would take only a small spike in solar radiation to rejuvenate the system's reservoir.

There was little else to do but to wait.

—

"March nineteenth, twenty-one twenty-one, this morning our guidance system faltered and we strayed from the course. We'll need to wait for the next sunrise. I fear that may take some time. Moordon Three is a massive and barren planet. Officer Janelly assures me..." Marxsen said.

The voice of her partner cutting into her daily log transmission. "A day, two days max!" Janelly wore a smile in the words.

"...that it won't be long. We have sufficient power to heat the hull for several days and the water will last well beyond any thoughts of a worst-case scenario. We have food enough to enjoy two meals a day for nine days. Hopefully Janelly is correct..."

"I am!"

"...in anticipating our wait period. Officer Alena Marxsen of Descry One, over for today."

—

Marxsen watched the sun on the horizon and realized that her partner was correct. Indeed, they spun and yes, it was a day. But how long is a day exactly? A day is a revolution, a spin on the planetary merry-go-round. A day has nothing to do with the human measurement of time.

Marxsen spied Janelly, the woman's sleepy face rested motionless, yet still, somehow, it taunted and teased. Jaw clenched, Marxsen opened and closed her fists, using the cold atmosphere to quiet her angry muscle motions.

The watch on her suit beeped, Marxsen regarded the time and noted, *an hour 'til transmission, you've lived for another snack, ha!* The frosty food did little to entice, but it sustained. Marxsen bit down and chewed, thinking about the sun hiding somewhere over the distant horizon.

—

"April first, twenty-one twenty-one, it's been thirteen days..."

"April fools! Joke's on us, hardy-har-har." Janelly stomped in tantrum.

"...since we'd lost sufficient power to fire the engine. Spirits are low, but it can't be much longer. If it is, we'll surely starve. We've begun a rationing of one meal per day each, but even that won't cover a future of any substance. I've sent out pings, though I fear they've been lost in the vast blackness. All we can do is wait and..."

"Wait and nothin'! This junk ship screwed us and no we're going to die on this stupid dead rock!"

"...hope that we'll meet the sun in time. Alena Marxsen of Descry One, over for now."

—

While Marxsen ate, she imagined bison steaks, and hamburgers with pickles, pizza, chocolate bars, sugar coated dates, and salted nuts. If she ever got home, she'd eat a buffet of junk. Marxsen also wondered what might happen if she did get away. She wondered how the Association would receive them.

She considered the possibility that it might be better just to freeze where they are, let her transmissions explain the situation; should anyone ever find the vessel. Should anybody wonder.

—

"April eighth, twenty-one twenty-one, it's been twenty-one days since the system malfunctioned..." Marxsen took a deep breath as she listened to her partner yell.

"Don't matter, don't matter! I'm hungry and we're going to die! This is futile, turn that damned thing off, don't waste your energy," Janelly reached over to slap at Marxsen's transmission button.

Both did what they could to avoid tears. Still, tears came when they wanted and Janelly seemed poised to flood the hull.

Marxsen felt done with Janelly, but continued, "...and left us off track and away from this quadrant's sun. Without the sun's radiation, we cannot manage any real comfort, we can sustain four degrees above zero for the next three weeks. After that we'll freeze..."

"Won't matter without food, now will it?"

"...to death. Our rations are down to three meals. We've begun splitting a quarter ration packet per day and I have to admit it is not easy and I want nothing more than to ready the entire package and gorge," Marxsen checked her shaky tone and continued with forced professionalism, "but I feel any day now the sun will fly overhead and bring with it the energy needed to..."

"Won't you just shut up?" Janelly shouted.

Marxsen stared across the small space with fire in her eyes.

"...to uh, damn it...Alena Marxsen of Descry One, enough for now."

—

Marxsen swallowed a mouthful of water and counted. It was 10 minutes until her daily transmission; if nothing else, she held onto the routine. She'd made it a lot longer than she expected. She'd never imagined surviving beyond 30 days.

The blankets over her body did little and slush ran down her throat with every sip of water. At just above zero degrees, she could just barely keep the water from freezing and life in the hull survivable.

—

"April nineteenth, twenty-one twenty-one, one month now; it's the thirty-second day. We are cold, but spirits have risen. Don't you think, Janelly?" Marxsen looked to her partner. Janelly kept her frosty expression. "No matter, we've set aside our troubles and now endure in quiet and peace. I've lowered the temperature and we've stretched the rations, shouldn't run out now, not for a long while."

"I stare out the hull window and wonder if the sun will ever come. I wonder if any of you remember we're out here. Do they remember that I was once a woman with a future? Behind closed doors commanders wished me well, swore I'd become someone and now I wonder, will they still think so? That is, if the sun ever comes and the system enlivens. I guess I'll worry about that if the situation ever comes.

"Although the spirit here is brighter than it was just days ago, I still get gloomy. Space is a lonesome place, even with Janelly so close by my side. I feel the cold fingers of loneliness poking and prodding, reminding me of..." Marxsen shook her head, checked her creeping unprofessional tone, the kind of tone men in the academy held over women, *emotionally unfit, irrational, blah, blah, blah.* "Excuse me, transmissions of a personal nature demand discipline. Therefore, I welcome a mission to remove me from the helm of this ship. I am no longer fit. Officer Alena Marxsen of Descry One, over for a million times forever, zippity-do-da, tip your server, eat your greens, mind your mother."

—

In her head, Marxsen counted down. Pressing the button was her only remaining chore, her final duty, her last link to a lost sanity. *Five, four, three, two, one,* "May fourth, ninety-billion after one, plus two. My breath has put a white blanket on everything, I feel like Frosty the Snowgal. I think if I keep it up that it might really snow in here. That'd be something. Don't you think, Janelly?"

Marxsen smiled at her partner, frost rode over her face and her eyes have clouded. "No? Oh well, she's been awfully quiet since she lost her tongue, but still, I hear her. She speaks the language of the snowfolk.

"Speaking of lost parts, tonight I think I'll try the meat from the back region, so far my favorite bit came from her cheeks, but variety is the spice of life and Janelly doesn't mind. Do you?"

Marxsen laughed and looked around the hull for another subject. "Oh yeah! Okay, so I didn't want to say anything until I'd finished, I haven't finished, but I can't hold it in. I've taken up sewing and made myself an over-uniform uniform. It's made of blankets and rationing packaging, très chic, ooh-la-la. Who needs the sun when you've got a needle and thread, that, and an officer buffet." Marxsen looked at Janelly, "Something to add?"

The corpse was true to her status and remained silent.

"How dare you! I worked hard on this. I should think someone like you might know better than to speak to me in such a manner. Guards, off with her noggin!" Marxsen grabbed Janelly's cold shoulder and gazed expectantly around the hull. "Where are they? Guards? Guards! You got off easy this time, next time, girly-girl, you're in for a world..." Marxsen ceased her speech and tightened her grasp. The sun, huge and blinding, raced over the horizon. "Janelly! Janelly, we're saved!" she shouted, shaking the corpse.

As the fat ball of flame rushed through the sky and filled the dark world with light, Marxsen's words catch in her throat. She'd never seen a sight so miraculous.

The panels on the roof collected the radiation and filled the reservoir in seconds. The dash and command center burst into life with a rainbow of colors.

Marxsen cleared her throat. "May fourth, twenty-one twenty-one, it is the forty-eighth day since we'd lost all but the reserve power on Descry One, we...I..." Marxsen thought it over, it seemed obvious that she should return to the Saturn base, but she wondered if there was any way that she could after what she'd done. "What do you think?" she asked Janelly; the heat pumping into the hull quickly melting the frost from Janelly's cheeks.

Marxsen nodded. "You're right, we have a mission to complete. On we go, Officer Alena Marxsen, over for now."

SHOOTING STAR

(2018)

A mosquito landed on Jessica's naked hip and readied to puncture. A breeze pushed by and she shivered, sending the little vampire away hungry. The moonlight banked blue against her soft tummy, while she lay on her back, one arm under her head, the other reaching across her chest, index and middle fingers tracing circles at the hollow of her throat. So far, it had been the greatest night of her life. 19 and as sexually experienced as she was, she had never experienced anything like this.

On her left was Tobias and on her right was Chris. Tobias was 30, wore a thick mop of coarse black chest hair—a color that matched his pubic region and legs. Chris, Tobias' husband, was 59 and had a full-body wax every month, and shaved his head five days a week; he had only brown eyebrows to show for his hair color.

Jessica knew Tobias as a senior from the school bus, years back, and had fantasized about sharing his surname. She was in the fourth grade then. She'd met him more recently at the library where, upon graduating, she carried her part-time position into full-time. They talked historical fiction and barrel-chested heroes.

"I've got one of those," Tobias had said, referring to Chris. Perhaps a bit of an exaggeration but it wasn't an outright lie. Chris was in better shape than most men half his age. In better shape than Tobias himself.

Tobias invited Jessica home for drinks several months later, and once in the home, explained that Chris had a thing. Over the years, now and then, he swung for the other team. So, almost like an arranged marriage, Jessica faced an odd proposition, told the men she'd like another glass of wine and time to think.

A week later, and out under the moon, the tent a few feet away, centering the clearing, a cold fire pit near it, she grinned and watched the sky.

"Ooh, make a wish." Tobias lifted his right hand to point at a shooting star and Jessica closed her eyes, thinking *I wish this night would never end.*

Chris pushed himself forward and stood. He wore only white ankle-high socks and tan lines around mid-thigh and high on his forearms. Stepping toward the tent, he picked up Tobias' pants and tossed them onto the outstretched man.

"Need my undies first." Tobias said this without humor, but not without joy—there was much joy in the post-coital tone. "And maybe another glass of wine."

Tobias got up then. Next to the campfire pit, a few feet into a shadow cast by the treeline was a small, greyed-by-the-elements picnic table. On top of the table was a box of cabernet sauvignon, the kind perfectly suitable for a night spent by a fireplace or a night spent swatting blackflies.

"Yes, honey. Though maybe we should hit the sack after this one. It's one minute to midnight. Hate for you to turn into a pumpkin." Chris held his cellphone out for Tobias and Jessica to see. "If we want the best worms, we need to be out early."

Tobias had his pants on. Jessica was up to her knees, dressing in reverse to the men—bra, shirt, then underwear and capris.

"He's always so worried about catching the juicy worms." Tobias nudged Jessica's shoulder with his thigh.

"Only your juicy worm, honey."

Jessica's grin widened. It was like being in the middle of a catty HBO or Showtime drama. She rose and stepped her legs into denim. The clothing smelled like bug spray. Her skin smelled like sweat and cum.

"I hope I'm not speaking out of turn here, but that went swimmingly." Chris handed a reusable sippy cup full of wine to

Jessica.

"Swimmingly? Jesus you turn into an old man when you're relaxed." Tobias accepted a cup. "But yes, I'm surprised. Much better than the sexual escapades I fumbled through with girls of my closeted youth."

Jessica blushed as the moon fell behind a cloud and enveloped the campsite in a shadow. Simultaneously, her head and Tobias' head jerked back, both being splashed by the same wave. It took less than a second to register that the wine box had fallen to the ground...though it seemed out of order, as if the moisture came before the thump of the box hitting dirt.

"Dammit, that'll stain!" Tobias had lost all the playfulness from his voice.

Jessica wiped her face and looked at her hands. Overhead, the cloud pushed on and the moon shined bright enough for her to see that the liquid was too thick to be wine, though it was still red.

"Chris?" Tobias leapt down to the side of the fallen man. His abdomen glistened, the gushy pink coil of his intestine poking out from his tanned stomach. "Chris." Tobias held the man's head, leaned in and pressed his forehead tight to Chris' cheek. "Call somebody! Call somebody!"

Jessica scrambled, her hands falling into a hot puddle as she felt around for her purse. It was there, between the table and the fire pit. She pulled her phone free: five bars, LTE. It took three full seconds for her thumb to recall how to make a phone call. *911* flashed, she hit call and lifted the phone to her ear. It rang and rang and rang and rang.

"What the fuck?" She hung up and dialed again.

"Oh, don't you leave me. Don't you dare... What's happening with the goddamned ambulance?"

"It's just ringing. Ringing...I don't...I don't know."

"Give me the fucking thing." Tobias lashed out a bloody hand and snatched the phone. "Fucking broad can't even dial the fucking police."

Had Jessica heard the slur, she would've forgiven him, tense times caused irrational reactions, but she didn't hear him. The idea that someone or something had done this *act* had her eyes scanning the blanket of black shadowy treeline.

"Pick up, you pricks!" Frustrated, Tobias fired the phone into the grass.

Jessica hurried after it—not a scratch, but it was sticky and nasty, the screen smeared pink. She located the flashlight app and moved the slider. The flash shined a great swatch onto the campsite. It looked utterly normal, nothing ominous, not so much as the eye shine from an animal. After four quick sweeps, she turned it off, the battery would last about five minutes with that app on the go.

"No. No. Nonono, don't die on me."

"Toby, Tobias, what did that to him?"

"What?"

"What did it? It's not like a heart attack or something, what did that?"

At this, Tobias straightened, looked around the campsite while his hands felt his pockets and then Chris'. Empty. "Get to the car," he whispered.

Jessica broke for the passenger's side, giving the bumper a wide berth. On his hands and knees, Tobias crossed the space like a werewolf in transformation limbo. The interior of the Mini lit upon the opening of doors. Keys dangled in the ignition.

Jessica closed her door and existed in a vacuum for five heartbeats that seemed to vibrate from her soul out. When Tobias opened his side, she nearly screamed. He looked like a horror flick serial killer, bathed in gore.

He grasped the key and turned. Jessica imagined a dead engine and a creature climbing from the woods, big claws and horns. It would smash the windshield, grab her by the throat, and snap her... The car started. The Radio barked, oddly, as they'd been listening to MP3s via Bluetooth, "*When you wish upon a star...*"

Tobias pulled the shifter to first gear and hit the gas, spinning the rear tires on the grass.

Jessica stared at the dash. Clock read: 11:59 and the station insignia was 115.9 FM.

"...makes no difference who you are..."

"Tobias, what's happening?"

They'd made it back to the main thoroughfare of the park grounds, though it was dead. No lights burned anywhere.

"...*anything your hear—*"

"Shut up." Tobias stabbed a finger into the radio power button.

Jessica's eyes clung to the red stamp left behind as she reached over and gripped Tobias' wrist. This was all so horribly wrong.

"What? What?" he asked, shaking his arm gently.

Jessica's grip remained firm. Touching was the natural course. She'd grown up in one of those families that hugged and kissed, shared and leaned in hard times. When she was a girl, her brother once broke his tibia and for days, the family huddled as if in a pre-game prayer. In the following weeks, they'd all taken turns sharing the boy's bed, simply to be near him. Jessica had drawn a comic book's worth of art on the plaster, *boy stuff instead of girl stuff,* as he'd requested.

"What?" Tobias shook his arm harder.

"No, let me." Jessica's voice was small as a child's and Tobias relented.

Through the woods and then the gate, the Mini found asphalt and it felt like the kiss of 1,000 tomorrows; they were going to make it.

Tobias groaned. Jessica rubbed higher on his forearm, his skin and hair rising to meet her palm as the blood dried to a sticky mat. A tiny village was a mile ahead, its single amber caution lamp bright over the nine buildings clustered beneath—gas and service station, one-room convenience store, breakfast restaurant, shower rentals, and five small, personal dwellings.

Outside the gas and service, an old timey telephone stall perched below the roof's overhang. Jessica let go of Tobias as he pulled in.

They looked through the window at the telephone.

Jessica then lifted her cell and dialed for emergency. Again, it rang and rang and rang. "Nothing," she said.

"You should try the payphone." Tobias reached into his pocket, absently. His gaze remained set on the half-booth.

"Why me?" She knew the answer though, damn well knew it in her core. Tobias was as scared as she was and something was out there. Maybe it was back at the campsite, but maybe not. Maybe it wasn't alone. And then what?

"I'm behind the wheel, if we have to move quick, it's easier this way."

The logic dwelled somewhere behind the cold cotton fog of cowardice. Still, it had to be one of them. Chris was up the hill in the bush, dead.

Dead.

Murdered.

"Fine." Jessica accepted the change Tobias managed to pass, a few coins spilling into the no hands land between the seats and the console island separating them. She took a breath, took another, took a third, this one deeper than the first two, and then exited the car.

As if chased, she sprinted for the telephone. Whether or not she needed to, she dumped two quarters into the slot and dialed 911. It crackled and then rang.

And rang and rang.

And rang.

She looked back to the Mini with the phone to her ear. The car fell into a shadow cast by the station.

The connection rang on but refused to link to a human being. She could see Tobias' nose, teeth, and eyes where he leaned forward in the car, watching her. His window came down and he shouted, "Forget it! Let's go!"

She hung up the phone and the change rolled out to the slot. She ignored it and hurried to the Mini. Inside seemed so safe. She hadn't noticed the difficulty in breathing or that her heart pounded a drumroll until sitting in the leather bucket once again.

Tobias pulled the shifter back and spun gravel when he slammed the stick into first. In a half-blink, the village was behind them. The next town was about five minutes up the highway, a bigger spot, had a grocery store and racetrack with slot machines, a damned police station.

Outside, the night darkened as a cloud rolled between Earth and Moon. To Jessica and Tobias' shared surprise, the lights of town were upon them quickly, not more than a couple minutes on the... Jessica squinted at the dash clock: 11:59.

What?

She pulled her cellphone free of her pocket, making a plank of her body to do so.

11:59.

How?

"Wait. Wait." Tobias spied the gas and service station, the convenience store, the showers, the restaurant, the little homes. "Wait."

"It can't be." Jessica gripped Tobias' arm above the wrist while his hand rested on the shifter ball.

Tobias put his foot down and burned through the village at triple the posted limit of 40KM/H. Then it was gone and they were in the bright moonlit night. The moon disappeared again and suddenly light was ahead of them. Tobias slammed on the breaks, recognizing a single lamp and the shapes beneath.

"How the—?" he started to say, but the glass of the driver's door shattered and something, maybe hands, maybe claws, maybe even paws, pulled him out into the night.

Jessica held his wrist. "No!"

Through the gloom, like a phantom, a metallic shine swung on a pendulous course. The bones and meat snapped and the strength pulling away evaporated, leaving only the gravity of holding an arm severed at the elbow.

Jessica screamed and instinctively tossed the appendage out the open window. Then, suddenly, she was alone in an idling car, on an unfamiliar stretch of desolate highway, with a cellphone that connected to nobody, and a clock on the dash that refused to slip into midnight. The night beyond the purr of the engine was quiet. Jessica knew she couldn't stay there in the passenger's seat, what if that thing came back?

What if it never left?

Quickly, she flung her body behind the wheel. She hadn't driven a stick before but understood how it worked. She popped the shifter into first with her foot on the clutch. It lurched forward and she slammed her foot on the gas, squealing but not stalling.

The town was right there again and she burned through, looking into the dark homes, wondering if anyone else existed in this... "No," she said. It was not the same village, it only looked the same because hick towns could be like that, simple tastes led to simple designs. If it ain't broke, don't call a city planner.

The wind buffeted hard against the side of her face, a welcome feeling as she revved the engine past six thousand RPMs while still in first gear. She looked at the shifter. It shined in the dash glow—11:59 in blue—and she stabbed her foot into the clutch and pulled the shifter to second gear. The RPM gauge fell and danced back up. The speedometer boogied up likewise, but much more slowly. She did it again into third and lifted her eyes back to the road, to the single light of the village by the campground.

"Impossible." She lifted her foot some and cruised, staring

through her window, into the homes, hoping for movement. Her eyes fell back onto the road in time to yank the wheel around a huge lump right in front of her.

She gasped a heartbeat before the Mini slammed into the side of a house. The airbag puffed out and sent the bucket seat backwards, as close to prone as the tiny interior allowed. Her teeth came together and she felt the tips of rear molars come away like peanut particles on her tongue. Blood began to seep from the inside of her cheek and she tasted the iron flavor deeper than just in her mouth.

The world was out of focus. The airbag was a comfort-less pillow before her, taking her away in blinks: her bed at home the night when she'd met with Tobias and Chris to discuss the arrangement; the gift from her father, the Serta queen sized mattress with a pillow-top; her childhood single on movie night.

The airbag deflated and the pressure on Jessica's chest left with it. A moment of clarity had her gasping an enormous gulp and her sore body jerked upright. One running light remained aglow and shined partway into a kitchen. Jessica swallowed blood and bits of teeth as she leaned, grabbing the steering wheel to hold her straight. She tried the handle. Stuck. She tried again, this time with her shoulder pressed to the door. It creaked, crow-like, deformed steel on steel. She looked back out onto the road. The single overhead lamp shined down on much of nothing. Something was out there, had to be. Whatever it was, it had snatched Tobias and killed Chris.

An ache centered her chest. She swallowed a breath that threatened to lodge itself in her windpipe. One foot in front of the other, she was out of the car and heading for the garage door only 10 feet from where she'd crashed.

Pitch black aside from where the light from the street reached as well as the shine of the single dimmed headlight pressed against the home. The garage had no windows. Instinctually, Jessica ran a hand along the wall next to the door, reeling back in a snap when she felt cobwebs.

Steeling herself, she pushed through the stringy wall and felt behind. Wood, likely once sanded smooth, but ridged with the natural grooves of time, but no switch. Again, preparing for the worst, Jessica closed the door halfway and stepped around it, feeling to keep in reach of the exit.

Another soft mat of web separated her fingers from wall, having done it once, she'd overcome most of the fear. She waved, fingertips grazing until they hit a pair of familiar shapes. Double switches. She lifted them both. The garage lit, as did the driveway beyond the door.

Jessica registered the white cotton webbing on the wall and her hand and arm but saw no spider. She turned then and looked at an absolutely normal garage. A riding mower, a snowblower attachment for the mower, a set of car stands. On the far wall hung handheld gardening tools from shovels to trowels. Oil stains and greasy buildups marred the cracked cement floor. On the back wall, above the workbench, were a small TV and a CB radio—alongside a wide assortment of nuts, bolts, and junk.

Jessica knew nothing about CB radios aside from the fact truckers, cops, and hobbyists used them. Maybe someone was listening, maybe someone was out there.

A toggle marked POWER flipped up and a red light glowed. She picked up the microphone—a rectangular thing that weighed more than she guessed before touching it. She pressed the button on the side. "Hello? Hello, is anybody out there?"

She depressed the button and listened, heard nothing. The face of the radio had dials and switches. She turned the one marked LOUDNESS to the right. A static hiss filled the garage. Next to that was a button marked SCAN. She pressed it and the hissing ceased for a second, then resumed, then ceased, then resumed as it jogged through the dead airwaves.

"Goddamn you."

She turned away, let the thing scan for eternity if it wanted to do so. Back by the light switches was a door. A normal door. Light brown veneer, shiny, with a diamond shaped window at average adult eye-level. Jessica thought her grandmother had the same door on the house she moved into after her grandfather died and she no longer wanted to live with the constant reminders in the farmhouse, but also she didn't want to live so far from the curling rink.

Jessica stepped close and saw herself in the reflection casted by the window. The blood appeared brown, it flecked her face and soaked into her top. Its importance instantly fell as she caught site of the spider on her shoulder: long spindly legs, huge knees— or where they elbows?—body like a shiny sphere. A squeal passed her lips and she swatted, turning her body away from the offending shoulder. The spider fell and balled up, playing dead. Jessica spun then, trying to see her back, feeling her neck and under her shirtsleeves.

Revulsion came on her in waves and she shuddered three times before opening the door and stepping into the home. "Hello?" she called, though if anyone was home, she suspected they would've come to check why someone had run an automobile into their kitchen.

The place was eerily dated. A Felix the Cat clock swung his tail and shifted his eyes, minute and hour hands only slightly askew—11:59, as she knew it would say. Seeing it again drove a nail into the impossible.

Her stupid wish.

"I wish tonight would end." She stood in the kitchen, staring at the smiling cat. The clock danced but time remained still. "Please, just let it end."

A crack rang out from the street. Jessica watched through the thin window sheer. A thing, seven, eight feet tall, lifted a black oblong shape from the street, holding it upright. It then swung a loose part.

This was Tobias, the swinging thing was his arm, waving.

Jessica's heart revved high again and she jerked away. That thing was tall and skinny, but beyond that, she had no idea, didn't want to know. Turning and running, she immediately had to leap sideways to avoid a Formica-topped dining set.

The moonlight and the streetlamp shined into the home enough that she saw the phone on a table resting next to a couch. It didn't fit, updated, despite it being a landline. She picked it up. The red light shined. Instead of dialing for an emergency, she dialed her parents' number.

It rang.

And rang.

And rang.

And then a voice answered, "Hello?"

"Mom?"

"Yeah. Jess?"

"Mom, I'm stuck. It's all screwed up and—"

"Jess?"

"Mom?"

"No."

"What?"

"Not Mom. Not Mom. Not Mom. Not Mom. Not Mom! NOT MOM!" The tone went higher as it grew louder, rising to a shriek.

Jessica howled, tossed the portable phone across the room. It thunked hard against a piece of furniture hidden by shadow. Too hard to be a sofa arm or a padded chair back. Too hard to be... The shadow lengthened and a figure rose, its head like an inverted triangle of matted black hair, as if the brain hid behind the jaw. When the light hit its eyes, she saw the pitting, like irregular honeycomb. The think blinked at her and the fluid spilled gently from each tiny hole. It then reached an extremity into the glow from the street—three long, metallic claws jutting from a furry hand

Jessica screamed and spun, then headed back to the kitchen. Felix the Cat continued to wag its tail and swing its eyes. 11:59.

The door banged against the garage wall. The radio hiss was painfully loud for a second before it stopped—scanning again—then a voice sang out, slow and drawling in an operatic tenor, "*When you wish upon a star...*"

Jessica turned right instead of left, for the left took her to the street where something had Tobias and the right took her into a mystery. Possible death was better than undeniable death. That much her harried mind knew without question.

The back door had a window that revealed only darkness. It swung inward. Behind her, the other door opened and she saw a different face. Lips like a gator. Beady eyes like a crab. Nose a pair of sunken holes. Skin tough and patchy like irradiated cowhide. Claws glistened on its big hand from beneath a coat of coarse black hairs.

"What do you want?" she screamed the moment before she plunged into the backyard abyss. Her feet caught and she stumbled, but not far.

Then she pitched forward as she heard the off-key singing, "*When you wish upon a star, dead dead dead no matter who you are!*" same as the voice from the telephone.

She crawled into the void. The floor beneath her tipped and she front rolled. The hill was spongey grass and damp soil, but still, it stung. The ground beneath her disappeared again and she was freefalling. Her ass landed hard.

"Ooh," she moaned and rolled into the fetal position for five heartbeats before remembering that she needed to move.

Onto her knees, she looked around, the campsite treeline was before her and she *knew* the tent, the fire pit, and the picnic table lingered behind her. Like a reset, she fell back, exhaled a pent breath, let her heart slow. She looked to the sky.

"Ooh, make a wish." Tobias' voice filled the night as a shooting star streaked by.

Jessica didn't hesitate: "I wish this night would end!"

"You don't mean that," Chris' voice sounded hurt, his hand

crossed as he turned to his side, pressing his...

Jessica screamed as the furry hand slammed claws in and out of Tobias' chest, blood and tissue splashing outward like a kid at a good mud puddle. Tobias fell and Jessica turned to Chris, who'd been next to her, unmoved by what had just happened.

He ran a sharp finger over her bare tummy, trailing up to her cleavage, stopping at the hollow of her throat. "You don't mean it, I know you don't."

Suddenly Chris was not Chris, Chris was a creature and it had draped a leg over her own.

She looked back and saw Tobias crawling toward her, his face pale, blood bubbling from his lips, blood draining from the huge cavity in his chest, blood everywhere. "You can't un-wish eternity," he said, rasping before draping an arm around her hip, pulling her tight, nuzzling the gore against her, trailing fingernails of his—no, not his, a creature's—free hand. The third creature loomed above them like a prison guard.

Stars fell from the sky, trailing long golden tails. "I wish! I wish! I wish I was at home!" Jessica wailed, eyes closed to make the magic stronger.

AROWANA

(2013)

A dab of solder looked so strange through the thick glass of the shop's magnifying lens: bulbous in the middle and tapering toward the edges. It resembled something from a 19th century mad scientist's lair, and when Norman looked from the right angle—had to be just right—the world had equal parts tall and skinny and short and fat. It was one of the few remaining highlights to his typical day.

"The little things," he whispered, as his steady fingers, wrinkled and gnarled, placed a brass pinion wheel over a pallet staff as he gazed through the magnifying glass suspended on the long brass arm.

The inner workings from the old machinery allowed the so-called high-tech devices to work without battery power, just motion. Motion was paramount. Once finished one of his perfect pieces of mimicry, he could give the device a shake, the pinion wheels spun and clicked the silent, rubber tipped stoppers into life. Then the pinion fell into the stoppers, back and forth, back and forth, until years later, worn and useless. That's when, to unsuspecting inspection, the floating showpiece died.

Norman blinked a drip of sweat out of his good eye, his skin seeped a lot lately, it wasn't just the time of year, it was the time of life. Drawing to a close, he suspected, he hoped, he'd done enough looking through that magnifying glass in that miniscule closet of a workshop. "Sixty-eight years tomorrow, got a present for me?" he asked the four barren walls, his pile of discarded watches, and the neatly stacked trays of computer components.

Overhead, a fan bellowed and rattled into life offering the

poor old man a reprieve from the stale swelter surrounding him. He turned his face upward for a moment, just a moment; it was between 5:00 in the morning and 9:00 in the evening, working hours.

"No rest for the decrepit." He snorted and looked around, he coughed for good measure, just in case. He turned his gaze back to the device.

The skin-mimic was such a good idea, so nice, so perfect; it certainly was something. He wished he'd never thought of it. He slid two camera lenses over the device's eye connectors, it was the only way anyone would ever see, but they'd have to look very hard and people never looked hard. People simply admired from a distance—people too trusting. People had to learn the hard way.

"It's your duty, Norman, your great achievement, your ultimate punishment."

The grip on the magnetic, flat-head screwdriver felt small and distant, part of him wanted to tell someone, get it over with, but the other part, the part that wanted, that needed, to survive, refused him. That was a weakness. He flexed his grasp and put the screwdriver back between his fingers.

"When you can't do your duty, you're no good to anybody, and when you're no good to anybody, you'll meet your replacement. Are you ready for a replacement, Norman?" Tired thoughts answered the question, *yes, please, let it end,* his voice answered any listening device hidden in the walls—someone always listened. "No, sir, many good years ahead."

Leaning back he almost laughed at the idea that what he said might have any effect on decisions from above, the higher powers didn't care if he was ready. He didn't laugh, that was a good clue he'd gone soft. Laughter wasn't part of his natural repertoire, it belonged to the others, those people his devices monitored.

Humans have it right, he mouthed without saying. Blasphemy, that.

With a gentle touch, he lowered a soft membrane over the

little device. It shimmered and danced under the light. "Six layers of paint on this membrane, but do they care? No, no they do not care, nobody does," he said and then lowered his voice to mimic his commander's some 30 years prior. "Now, Two-nine-nine-two-three-oh, we all do our part and you will do your part. Foreign soil is foreign soil on any planet, get over it or get replaced."

He almost laughed again, he held the snort, he held the cough.

Tweezers in hand, another membrane dropped over the device, it was almost clear, or rather seemed that way. It reflected a murky whiteness offering the eye and the mind clues that followed a designed path.

For some time, he wished someone would find his office, one of the people, the humans. They had their problems, but they did it right. Most went day to day working toward their next source of entertainment.

"Vacation," Norman mumbled. It was a word without translation in his native tongue.

He used to think about the days of his youth, before he had the idea to assist the good fight. They all used to learn so many subjects, never focusing too long on any one item. He'd barely looked at the inner workings of anything technical. A gift, a gift was what his squad captain said, it all started because he wanted to do right, do his part, but he didn't know. How could he know?

Watching the humans from a distance always made him furious; he had been so young. "Young and misinformed," he whispered and stopped working to listen for slamming doors, but nothing came. "Don't push it."

Monsters and heathens, those were the two closest translations to the schoolyard descriptions of the happy beings on the distant planet, the words stupid and small floated around, accepted descriptors on any examination. Every now and then, one of Norman's teachers or classmates might've alluded to an achievement. "An achievement by one of them, those things, some of the smartest idiots I know." He wanted to laugh again, but bit the bottom lip of his human overskin. "If the smartest idiots can slip their tongues, what hope—?" He stopped himself, it wasn't easy lately. It almost seemed at a subconscious level; he was ready to stand.

He dropped the third layer of membrane back into its Petrie dish, his spine straightened. Again, he listened for slamming doors, but none came. Those doors, those doors belonged to his nightmares, to his dreaming mind, but he knew, oh boy, he knew they'd come eventually.

Everyone cracked, sometime.

He exhaled a heavy blow. "Not just yet, but soon enough." He picked up the tweezers, lowering the third and final membrane to the device. Each device constantly recorded and sent the information above, to the higher power. Looking beyond the Earthly solar system to a place called Arae. The higher power decided life and death, days and nights, the higher power decided everything based on an unbendable set of rules.

Siding with the enemy was treason, it was public death. Laughter meant change, not just siding, or sympathizing, it was changing, no longer just wearing the overskin of man, but being of man; laughter meant bodily mutation.

Footfalls came from outside and Norman's heart leapt into his throat—*we are so similar and they are better, we are older, but they are better*. He felt a tear welling in his good eye. "This it?" he asked and the door opened, the heavy scent of animal feces and sawdust blew into the room.

"Oh, good, almost done, guess where that one goes?" George asked, Norman's latest crewman, also the newest manager of Through the Glass pet store.

"Close the door," Norman said. He didn't care where it went or who bought it and George's excitement made it less likely that he'd care, but the smell of the gerbil cages in the upper area of the show floor made him cringe.

"Come on, this could be it, we could bring it all down with this one," he said.

Norman put his attention back onto the device. It was almost done.

"No guess? Okay I'll tell you, Fifteen-hundred Pennsylvania Avenue."

Norman couldn't help it and he didn't care if it meant his death, he laughed, to hell with carrying on, he was old, he'd done enough.

George's excited face stretched and transformed into something between horror and bafflement. "The White House," he mumbled. "Fifteen-hundred...maybe it will go into the Oval Office."

Wrong, of course.

"Sixteen, Sixteen-hundred." Norman continued to laugh. "Sixteen-hundred is the White House."

"Oh...are you almost finished?" George's demeanor suddenly very serious. "You know, it's still government, I'll bet."

"Just have to fasten the fins."

"The transmitters, you mean transmitters, correct, Officer Two-nine-nine-two-three-oh?"

Norman understood then that a signal was already on its way to the higher power. "No, I mean fins. This is a fish, yeah? That's what we do, yeah? We make fish, spying fish; fish that watch humanity do it right?" Norman flung out his arm and knocked everything from his workbench. The clinking and rattling of steel and brass on concrete made George cringe, his training included mimicry, relations, and sales, not combat. "What?" Norman asked, seeing George cower away.

"Please sit until—" George stopped himself.

Norman was old and weak, but it didn't matter, George held an unreasonable fear, as if laughter made him some sort of terrorist.

"They're better you know?" Norman said as he walked past

George, who'd scurried to the other side of the workbench.

"You can't leave… Please, you have to wait. It's for your own good; you've been here too long."

"I can't leave…not without this." Norman snatched his work, a beautiful device, slender body of milky white, shimmering with a rainbow effect over its back, transmitters lining the spine, and belly, two big lenses, a beautiful work of art.

He gave the device a shake, spinning the little wheels, and tossed it into a plastic bag with water. For a moment he considered running, a sensational idea, but ridiculous. The Pearl Arowana, his device, that beautiful fish was to be his final enjoyment.

He walked through the door and took the clear plastic bag with him, dumped it into an empty tank on the viewing wall. The beautiful blue glow covered the floor, children and parents looked, slack-jawed, amazed.

Norman watched the Pearl Arowana, a fish so rare it was possible to let the little peculiarities slide…but he never would, he took pride in his ability, even if he didn't care for the ends.

A small girl stepped next to him, watching. "It's beautiful," she whispered.

"Thank you." Norman smiled at the girl's confusion.

"Oh, honey, look at that one," said a woman who looked like an elongated version of the little girl. The woman turned to address Norman. "How much is it? I have to have it."

"It's sold, but I'm sure someone could make you another. I made this one, but it's my last, of that, I'm sure." The woman's brow twisted and her lips tightened. "You won't believe me, but every showpiece fish you've ever seen isn't what you think. They watch you, look into their eyes, you'll see."

All three stared at the Pearl Arowana, the mother gave up quickly. "Sir, I don't appreciate—" she started, interrupted by her daughter.

"Mommy, look, look you can see!"

Norman knew if he wasn't finished already, then what he just said, what he just showed, was the cement slab screeching over his sepulcher.

"Oh my...what does it do? Is it watching, recording?" the mother asked.

Norman nodded.

"But for whom?" she asked.

Norman thought about it for a moment. "Does it matter?"

It was the mother's turn to think about it, her face scrunched and a light finally came on inside. "Hmm, you're right. How much is it to order? I've got to have one."

George rushed over to the woman, his sales training kicking into gear. Norman walked away, disappointed, returning to his workbench to warm the soldering gun, and began another Pearl Arowana.

"It really doesn't matter, does it? Somebody always watches, somebody always listens," he said to the lens of his magnifying glass.

DEVIL BOY

(2013)

At the front of the calm classroom, Mrs. Morrison, a stern woman with greying blonde hair and a boney frame that put corners into her skirts and blouses, chalked through fractions on the board. Roddy Dumas didn't care a lick about math, he just wanted Mrs. Morrison to plunk back down behind her desk and take a sip from her water bottle.

So much he wanted that, it had become difficult to look at anything else. The bottle teased like a video game advertisement a week before Christmas.

"Do questions nine to twelve and we'll check back at say," Mrs. Morrison looked to the clock, "at a quarter after."

She sat and got to looking through papers on her desk while the class body focused on the work. Though, not Roddy, he stared at the teacher and the water bottle less than a foot from her hand.

And damned if that bottle didn't continue its taunting.

At a quarter after, Mrs. Morrison rose from her desk. "Done yet?"

The class grumbled in unison.

"All right, five more minutes. That's it."

She leaned on her desk and looked out onto the busy class. Her eyes met Roddy's. A squint narrowed her gaze. She wouldn't ask if he'd finished his work; she knew better than that by now. They held a staring contest for five, six, seven...she lost, and in a natural looking motion, reached for her water.

She drank. Roddy's grin crept into a wide, wide smile. Her lips began to tingle immediately. She licked them, her tongue tingled then as well. Numbness invaded.

Mrs. Morrison pointed an angry finger. "Waawee! "Ooh oou lil' hasaard!"

"Speak English, I don't speak no gibberish!" Roddy bounced in his seat, cackling.

—

He'd never gone so far—tack pricks, pudding stains, cheating on tests, general disruption—but never chemical warfare. The principal looked up from his desk when the door swung inward.

"What now?"

Mrs. Morrison attempted to explain. Her mouth betrayed her, drool dribbling from the corners of her respectably painted lips.

"Roddy, explain."

"I think she has the AIDS or something," he said, his expression between mock surprise and blooming glee.

Mrs. Morrison grabbed him by the elbow before stuffing her hands into first his right front, and then left front pocket. She came out holding change, a pencil eraser with the word DICK scratched into it, and a prescription bottle of NovaGel.

"It was just a joke," Roddy said then, his glee still in full bloom.

—

Roddy's mother shouted at him while he sat before the TV, maneuvering Mario around his world. She stomped over to him and turned off the TV.

"What have you got to say for yourself?"

He looked at her, bored. "What's for dinner?"

The only problem with a week-long detention was that nobody was around to congratulate him on such an awesome prank. The attention was one of the best parts. No, *the* best part.

—

"Your grandfather is going to stay with us awhile." Sophia, Roddy's mother, kept her eyes on the cheesy macaroni and coined weenies on her plate.

"No," Roddy said.

"He'll be here tomorrow. I've blown it with you, somebody needs to be here to keep an eye on you."

"I said NO!"

"Sorry, Roddy."

Roddy picked up his plate and threw it across the room. Sophia didn't say a word. Once he'd gone, she cleaned the mess.

—

"Mrs. Morrison didn't have a clue. It was perfect. Next time I'll—"

A firm slap silenced Roddy's brag to his grandfather, Geoffrey. The boy sprinted into the kitchen where his mother was busy at the dining table.

"Call the police!" Roddy said, pointing back the way he'd come, accusingly—not so different from whenever Mrs. Morrison singled him out.

"Something's got to change around here." Sophia went back to readying the Avon orders she had to deliver. "Time you learn a lesson."

Roddy stomped to his room and slammed the door.

Geoffrey stepped in hot on his tail. "Clean this mess. You have half an hour."

Roddy forced a wild cackle. His grandfather slapped him again. Roddy laughed harder. The next slap stung something awful, but not badly enough to admit.

"Tough guy, huh?"

Roddy nodded and picked up the grey Nintendo remote.

"No, you don't," Geoffrey said and plucked the television's plug from the wall. He gathered the television and left.

This was a war.

Roddy started on the wallpaper, tearing away wide swatches revealing the faded and glue-stained drywall beneath. It garnered zero extra attention and the boy flopped onto his bed to kick the wall. The drywall denting and bowing. Within seconds, he had the attention he sought.

Geoffrey burst in, reached down, and grabbed the boy by his hair, dragging him into the hall and beyond. Roddy screamed and kicked.

"Mommy!"

"She's gone working. Just you and me, punk."

Geoffrey stopped dragging and punted the boy in the stomach at about quarter speed. Roddy squirmed and wailed; Geoffrey readied another assault. The door off the kitchen opened.

"I forgot my—you can't kick him!"

"It's for his own good!" Geoffrey booted, half-speed this time.

"Get out!" Sophia pushed her father and gathered her son to her chest.

Roddy stuck out his tongue over his mother's shoulder.

"I was trying to help you. I want my grandson to be—"

"Get! Out!"

———

Suspension complete, Roddy returned, king of the schoolyard. This was a beautiful feeling. This was a drug. This was an addiction. He was a junkie.

After school, a small girl handed a note to Roddy while he awaited his bus. "From him," she said and pointed to Geoffrey waiting in his ancient Buick.

Roddy flipped the old man the bird and then opened the note:

> *You will be better. Everybody loves something.*
> *Everybody has something to lose.*

Note balled, Roddy tossed it high into the air. He flipped his grandfather double birds this time before climbing aboard his bus.

The heaters hummed from beneath four of the seats. Roddy stared down at the vents. He hadn't eaten his bologna sandwich at lunch and decided the best place for the leftovers was between the fins of the heater. No reason beyond whim.

—

Roddy flipped through channels. A stuffy TV doctor yammered on about some damned thing. Roddy continued by. Seven channels later, he was back to his starting point—commercials ran everywhere else. Roddy zoned out looking at the man with the jet-black hair and the ridiculous white coat over a tie and button-up—as if he was seeing patients or doing real work right there in front of the cameras.

"...the diet can lead to constipation. The simplest solution is almost a bit of a treat. There's Ex-Lax, Laxettes, others too. Sugar addiction is so serious, you might actually be tempted to eat more..."

Roddy was no longer hearing the words, his mind swirling, swirling, swirling like evacuated turds in a bowl. Sophia called for supper and she shut down the tube, his mind still spinning around an idea too soft yet to grasp.

Hours passed and it clicked while he lay in bed, staring at the shadowy ceiling. A smile spread across his face and he began pumping his fists. The plan was full and perfect.

—

The bus driver held Roddy behind without letting any of the other students see, then handed him a screwdriver, a spray bottle of cleaner, and a rag.

"I didn't even sit there," Roddy said.

"No, you jammed the vents with meat and switched seats." The driver was a big man with a good sense of humor, though offered no space for bullshit—a farmer supplementing his income.

"I didn't do nothing, and you can't—"

"Principal says I can."

"You can't make me."

The bus driver smiled. "You like people looking at you. Kids always look at you. Do you think they'd look more or less if I poured water all over your pants and told everybody you pissed yourself?"

Roddy spied the man. A teacher wouldn't dare do that, but a bus driver? He accepted the cleaning supplies and screwdriver—he had big plans, so big he could take a backward step just this once.

He reached class late. He sat at his desk, hands stinking like chemicals, and tried to make as much eye-contact as he could with the other students, trading smiles and nods along the way.

A second after the bell rang, Mrs. Morrison dropped a note on his desk:

You will be better. We will take what you love.

Roddy put his thumbs to his temples and waggled his fingers like rubber antlers the second Mrs. Morrison faced away. All who saw, laughed. Roddy balled the note and trashed it. Challenges were welcome.

—

Taking the bus wasn't mandatory. It was a 40-minute walk or a 12-minute bike ride home. Since he had a stop to make, Roddy skipped past his bus line and headed downtown. He stopped in at Walgreens with the remnants of his most recent birthday money in pocket.

At home, Roddy sat on the floor in front of the TV and frowned. "Mom!"

"What?" She leaned into the living room from the kitchen.

"Where's my Nintendo?"

"Oh, uh, Nintendo called from California and said there was a recall. All the systems were breaking. I had to send it off when the man with the box came. It'll be back in a few weeks."

Roddy thinned his lips. "No. Buy me a new one then."

Sophia shook her head in tight strokes. "You know I can't afford that, Roddy."

Roddy looked at his reflection banked off the convex glass of the TV. It hit him then. "Grandpa," he said, the word hissing out like a taboo curse.

Challenge accepted. Roddy didn't love his Nintendo, it just killed time.

—

The next morning, the bus driver hummed the Mario Bros. tune.

There was a test in math, measuring triangles. Compass, protractor, both a mystery to Roddy and he answered every question with *15*. This scored him one mark of a possible 10 as the teacher was lenient up to a few degrees.

The bell rang and Mrs. Morrison spoke above the din of motion, "Tomorrow, I'm minding Mr. Abel's English and he wants me to remind you that your final book report on *The Whipping Boy* is due, and on Friday, we're joining the two classes for a Thanksgiving party. We'll bake the chocolate cake at lunch, should anyone want to volunteer..."

Roddy heard no more. The window was opening.

That night, Roddy copied the back of *The Whipping Boy* onto notebook paper and added two sentences:

I shur did like this book. The end was real good.

It was the only book report he'd ever done. It didn't matter that he'd fail. It mattered only that he handed it in and at a glance it appeared he'd done something.

"How you holding up?" Sophia poked her head into her son's bedroom.

"Huh?" he stuffed the report into his backpack.

"Thought you'd be bored. Both of the TVs conked out today. Repairman said it would take fifteen days to fix them."

"Fifteen?"

This conspiracy against him was thick.

—

There was a note taped to his hook in the coatroom at school:

You will be better. We now know what you love.

Laughing, he taped the note to his chest and walked around the rest of the day like a billboard. This was Roddy Barstool's world and they'd learn yet.

Mrs. Morrison took his so-called book report and offered a cursory glance. "I bet you didn't even bother changing the words. I told them you were stupidly lazy. The rest just think you're astray."

A note on the bus and yet another taped to his front door:

We know. You'll crack.

It was getting old, lame even. Bored without TV, Roddy cut out dinosaur heads from past-due library books and glued them onto hockey player bodies. He pinned his finished works up on his walls.

There was a note tacked to the garage door:

You will behave. We know what you love.

"You don't know what I love," Roddy said as he balled the note and tossed it into his mother's flowerbed.

At lunch, Mrs. Morrison and a gang of do-gooders fixed the cake and slid it into the oven. Roddy watched from a closet. Once the cake crew stepped out, Mrs. Morrison locked the door behind her. The cake, still mostly liquid, baked in an oven.

Roddy took a spatula and stirred in the chocolate laxatives, all 40 pieces, and closed the oven before returning to the closet until the first students started pouring in after lunch and he could escape.

"All right, settle down," Mrs. Morrison said to the class, her hands tamping the vacant air before her. "Mr. Abel's ready for us in the home-ec room, so in an orderly," the students frenzied, "fashion—" She gave up.

Only Roddy walked at a calm pace, hands in his pockets, whistling the *Super Mario Bros.* tune. The students buzzed around in anticipation. Roddy stood at the back, watching his masterpiece unfold.

As Mr. Abel bent in the fridge to grab a bowl of icing, Mrs.

Morrison pulled up tight to Roddy. "You sure do love attention, don't you, Roddy?"

He grinned at her with one side of his mouth as his eyes remained glued on Mr. Abel. Roddy put his hands together as if about to pray. Mr. Abel's knife cut through the cake.

"This is your last chance. After this, we'll take what you love." Mrs. Morrison's breath was hot on Roddy's ear.

Roddy shifted his weight as Mr. Abel passed out a slice of chocolate-coated angel's food cake.

"What happened to the...?" Roddy trailed. His mother was there by the door, with Geoffrey and the bus driver.

Mrs. Morrison shook her head gently. "That was your last chance to be good.

Sophia was crying. "I did all of this for you, you know that?"

"You didn't think we'd let you poison people, did you?" Mrs. Morrison asked.

Mr. Abel hit play on a boombox. *Whoomp! (There It Is)* by Tag Team thumped as the students bounced on sugar highs.

"Come on," Geoffrey said, grabbing the boy.

Roddy started to yell, nobody minded him the two seconds it took to cover his mouth and stick the needle in his arm. By the time they got him outside, he was unconscious.

—

Roddy awoke in a room with four clay walls. There was a toilet and shower stall in the corner, a hole in the high, high ceiling.

"Hey!"

Along one wall was a cot, along another were books and movies. Centering the third was a TV, VCR, and Nintendo. The fourth featured a small writing desk.

"Hey! What the hell is going on?"

Roddy banged on a wall, finding it so solid the only sound was the slap of his flesh against its surface.

"Hey! Let me out of—"

A basket of foodstuffs lowered into the cell from the hole

overhead. Okay, he'd play along, for now. Without other options, Roddy played video games, snacking on what was offered to him. After what felt like several hours, the lights died.

—

The following morning the food was different, and with it in the basket was a note:

> Show us how you've changed and you'll get your
> love back.

"Fuck you!" Roddy shouted, elongating the vowel sounds. "Fuck you!"

That night, the basket disappeared and reappeared with three books and three assignment sheets. Roddy laughed and held out, didn't touch the books.

He slept and awoke. The basket reappeared. It had no food, only books.

"I'm not doing it!"

Day and night passed beyond his sense of time. Roddy cried himself to sleep. The following morning, the basket appeared with only a note inside:

> Work or starve, up to you.

Days mounted.

"I'm sorry!" he'd cry and then, "You got to let me out of here!" then, "I'm gonna call the police!"

No basket lowered that day or the next. He'd eaten every crumb they'd sent down and was sobbing when he cracked the spine of *The Lion, the Witch and the Wardrobe*. He read for close to half an hour.

A basket with an apple appeared. Just an apple.

Getting it, he ate and read on. Two hours later, a full meal appeared before him. He considered pulling the basket down—it looked to be hanging only by high-test fishing line—but he no longer dared to risk anything.

It took him four days in short intervals to finish the first book and write the report. The second book was *Shiloh*, which took him three days. Understanding, he raced through *A Wrinkle in Time,* assuming then they'd let him out once through.

"Done!"

The basket lifted.

Hours later, food appeared in the basket. It wasn't over.

"I wanna go home! Please! Mommy!"

The following morning, day 25, Roddy awoke to find the basket lowered. There was a large box with a note on top:

> *You've proved you're willing. I know you're not better yet, and it would all be a waste if we let you out now. Days, weeks, months will fly, childhoods always do, only eight more years and you'll be an adjusted and contributing adult.*
>
> *Love, Mom.*

—

"Mister Dumas? A call came in. Sounds like Junior's into it again," said Roddy's newest assistant.

The secondary door of his office opened and a head popped inside, another assistant. "We're getting Johnny Spoons, you want your regular or...?"

Roddy waved his hand. "No, I need to take some of this off." He patted his belly.

In the hole, he'd grown not just in mind but in girth as well. He'd spent six years down there before his mother died and the other conspirators let him out. After that came university, honors, his choice of firms.

"Is it Mrs. Norris?"

"Uh, I think so."

"Put her through. It's not as if I have anything else to do."

At the click, the teacher began, "Mr. Dumas, your son, your son! Today he put peanut butter in the middle of the vice principal's roast beef sandwich. She had to go to the hospital. She's allergic."

"I doubt he—"

"I'm not done. He knew. This was a malicious attack! Yesterday during an assembly, she told the students of her allergy, told them so they could put a face to the no nut rule."

"But he—"

"Yesterday, Roddy Junior took a test and answered every question with the words *poop* and *boobs*. Last week, he pulled down his teacher's gym shorts. I had to explain to sixteen parents how it could be that children came home knowing the hair color, girth, angle, and dangle of their gym teacher's penis."

"I know. You suspended—"

"You may argue for a living, but I'm telling you now. This isn't court and you will listen. Last month, someone started taking apart Mr. Price's pickup truck one piece at a time. We found a pile of it in the woods behind the soccer field. Junior had Mr. Price's rearview mirror in his back pocket! I don't know what you expect us to do with him. Your son is a devil!"

That was it. No options.

"Nothing. I'll put him into a new school. You'll never see him again."

Roddy scrolled through the numbers on his cellphone. He found the contact he wanted and tapped it. The line rang, and a familiar voice answered at the other end.

"Hello, Roddy."

"How is my favorite tenant?"

"Okay, arthritis is no joke."

"Right...Mrs. Morrison, you think you can get the old hole ready? The boy's a devil."

THE THINGS

(2013)

Sparks bounced and died, bounced and died as shovels clanged off rocks beneath the dirt. Twelve men carried on just as quick as possible. The Things in the sacks moved and moaned, as if waking.

Burying demons was night work. Night was when they came out, when the world closed its eyes and ears to rational, when the historians dozed and turned away from the action.

Torchlight surrounded the twelve men and six women busy at the task. The men shoveled and the women watched the bags, ready with flames and knives. Not that it was so simple against something like a demon.

"Deep enough," Thomas Gray said, self-proclaimed leader of the party.

Those demons had climbed up out of the ground and be damned if they couldn't stick those suckers back in. Be damned in the literal sense.

The men climbed from the hole and the time was upon them. A screech pierced from a bag, writhing like snakes, clawing like a soon to be drowned cat.

"Quick now," Gray said.

Linus Crow scrambled for the bag, yanking it with fury.

"Go now. Let go. We need your grandfather," Gray said.

Crow's grandfather came to the new world with him, but didn't forget a lick of the old ways.

Crow nodded and started off.

A claw poked and two more bags followed the first into the hole. The fingers followed the claw, tearing the burlap further.

"I need a torch!" Gray shouted and two flaming torches fell into the hole. He hopped in on top of the sacks. "Tip in the dirt, do it!" Gray forced torch to claws and fingers. The sacks seemed to dance at this.

Surrounding the hole, men and women shoveled and pushed dirt in around Gray and the damned things.

"More dirt, we need more dirt!" one man said. The ground was falling, slipping like a sinkhole.

Short of breath, Crow returned with his grandfather, a leathery man with long grey hair and a puffy swollen face. The old man slipped down the lip and knelt into the gentle dip of earth where Gray and the things remained.

"Wata dat spot," he said, his voice gruff and tired. "Da sun grow patexuns. Keep way ebils." Grandfather Crow wasn't always called Crow, and his words hadn't always come out in a slurry jumble. Truth was, he was too old for all this.

Young Crow translated, "Water. We need a tree on there. Get water and a tree, that tree will keep down what needs kept down."

The group broke away, all but the Crows and Gray. The others circled a small tree, skinny and less than a decade standing. They dug quickly, but not hastily.

"Hurry! Hurry!" Gray said swinging torches at movement.

Group effort put more dirt and that little tree right where Grandfather Crow said to put it. They watered it and Gray told everyone to go home, he'd spend the night, watching to be sure the spell took.

Gray fell asleep and awoke with the sun touching everything but him. The tree had grown huge while he was out. An ugly, gnarly thing and that seemed just about right, seemed safer than the little tree, safer by a ton. Still, for the next 20 years a body from the village called Tranquility kept watch over that tree. Day and night.

—

In 1967, Tranquility grew too big for its britches and a subdivision for wealthier residents formed around Gray Memorial Park. Four large and sophisticated homes rose like dandelions around the strange, stocky, old maple tree.

By 1987, Tranquility's former wealthy subdivision became an area of older homes owned by everyday people. Gray Memorial Crescent, small park in the center, hosted family fun for the annual Hazy Days Festival, a weekend long party where hard-working folks brought their children—tire swings and plank-seat swings dangled from the limbs of the old maple tree—and set out blankets. Across town, a hay wagon bandstand provided entertainment next to the pork roaster. At the arena and community center, grandmothers sold pies and grandfathers sold shelves and model trains. Over at the fire hall, men displayed their waxed and chromed obsessions.

John tossed around dirty shirts looking for a clean one.

"Seems like fun, down there. What do you think?" Jessica asked, standing behind her husband gazing out the window to the families playing in the park.

"Seems the same as every year. We'll have kids once we can afford them. I don't want to be that dad that has to explain to his son—" John started.

"Or daughter."

"Or daughter, that she doesn't—"

"Or he." Jessica smiled, having cheap fun at the expense of her husband—a right decreed once both parties signed the marriage certificate.

"I don't want to be that dad who says, *sorry, you gotta wear stuff from the swap-meet because the mortgage is already past due.* Do I have any undershirts?"

Jessica took a breath, smiled, and walked to the laundry basket in the corner, full of clean clothes. "I don't know why you need an undershirt on a day like this anyway."

John didn't answer. It was a touchy subject. He wore t-shirts every day because he feared becoming one of those overweight men with their belly dipping just below his shirt line or being one of those guys too big to corral his ass crack. He pulled the shirt over his head, the tail fell well below his waist, and he pulled up his Levi's, tucking the tail under his belt line. He threw a Quebec Nordiques t-shirt over the undershirt and negotiated the button of his jeans.

Stress didn't help, that's what the doctor told him. Steadily, for almost two years, John gained a couple pounds per month. No matter which diet he attempted or which workout regimen he took on.

Jessica was sad for him, wanted her husband to take a break, a vacation; a month off ought to bring the stress back to zero.

The little company John and Malcolm started in the garage bloomed and continued to grow, but it wasn't as it was at the beginning and it took twice as much work just to make a profit. Also, Malcolm was a terrible partner; he had a few key ideas and after the initial success, he offered nothing but a smile and a hand to accept checks. John's best friend the snake, that's what Jessica saw, but she zipped her lips and watched her husband take the bad end of every deal.

"Maybe I should just sell, let Malcolm piss away the company, what do you think?" John asked, joining her at the window and putting his arm around her shoulder.

It was a trap, an unintentional argument landmine. "You'll do what you think is right," Jessica said.

The din outside was a little unnerving and both momentarily reconsidered the idea of leaving the quiet home.

"Hey, buddy," Malcolm said, one laneway over, sitting in a lawn chair drinking a bottle of Miller High Life. "You see these yet?" Malcolm grabbed a bottle from the cooler next to his chair and twisted the cap off with the bottom of another bottle.

"Yeah, I saw the commercials." John was fairly certain Malcolm had been next to him the first time both of them saw the advertisement, also fairly certain that Malcolm made a big deal about it then.

"Where's the family?" Jessica asked, stepping up behind John.

"Over there somewhere, doin' something. They wanted me to come, but this is about as close as I feel like getting to all those screaming brats," Malcolm said.

John stared at his friend, a little envious of his flat stomach and easy way. Malcolm had a trophy wife with a perfect body and a voice like honey. Malcolm and Nancy had four children, all girls.

"Sounds like a good idea. Well, shall we get moving?" Jessica said.

"Have fun." John threw a half-salute.

"Take your umbrella, she's gonna rain. I can feel it in my bones." Malcolm smirked and then sucked back on the beer.

John and Jessica strolled hand in hand down the steep slope onto Logan Street from Gray Crescent. Located atop a hill, the view gave Tranquility a postcard feel. Green trees, greener lawns, children playing, cars rolling and stopping, empty homes, and brimming storefronts.

"I really love it here, you know?" John said.

"I can see that." Jessica squeezed his hand.

A warm breeze smelling of meat and car exhaust blew into their faces as they made for the busy section of town. It was loud and Lionel Richie blared from the enormous stage speakers set out front of the arena. Next door was the fire hall and the car show

"Is that supposed to mean something?"

"It only means what I said."

That was a lie, and both knew it. Jessica missed the city. Small farming communities had charm, but after a while, knitting circles, watching pee wee hockey, and drinking beer in the backyard went from quaint to boring to outright unbearable in short order.

"I'm getting sick of this guy, it's like every day he's got a new song on the radio," Jessica said.

John thought, *who doesn't love Lionel Richie?*

The cars shined in the sun and different music roared from the fire hall, played just loud enough to drown Lionel so long as the listening ears fell within the vast parking lot.

"That better?"

"Uh-huh." Jessica planted a smile—Three Dog Night, something from when she was in the fifth grade. One of those great summer songs "These—" Jessica covered her mouth to hide an impending laugh.

"Johnny, John-boy, how are ya doin'? Stayin' outta trouble?" A ridiculous man in a red polyester button up, wearing three fat, painted gold ropes around his neck, one of which had an gold crucifix fastened to it with a bent paperclip. Rings on all but two fingers, and a cheap costume fedora on his head.

"Jim," John said, shaking the man's hand.

Jim was a local wack job.

"Jessica, your eyes are beautiful like an ocean morning," Jim said taking Jessica's hand and kissing the knuckle of her middle finger.

Jessica burst out laughing. "I've got to use the can," she said and hurried to the portable toilets just past a row of sparkly Mustangs and a Cadillac Ambulance painted blue.

She hadn't really had to go, but Jim was equal parts absurd and disturbing. Like a big muscular kid, prone to temper tantrums. She composed herself in the plastic and solvent stinking little room. After two minutes, Jessica returned to her husband and the weirdo.

"I'm goin' to Chicago for a Karate tournament. I think I can win. Only Kirk and Robbie ever score points on me at Master Ming's and if I really wanted to, I could take them. One of Malcolm's girls comes out to Master Ming's too." Jim was flexing his tits as he spoke.

"What?" Jessica burst into another bought of laughter. "You fight little girls?"

"No, I never hit women." Jim became very serious, stopped flexing anything but his biceps. "I only fight men, some are a little younger, but I don't hit women." The man's eyes had changed and seemed ready to burn fiery holes in Jessica's blouse.

Jessica looked to John for help. He was leaning forward to appreciate the beautiful craftsmanship of the hood ornament sailing the nose of a 1946 Plymouth.

"Jesus is my Lord and Savior, only Satan hits women; anyone who hits a woman goes to Hell and I'll send 'em there myself. What, don't believe me?" Jim looked about ready to hit a woman.

Jessica poked John in the side, he didn't turn but spoke, "Hey, Jim, buddy, we're gonna go check out some of these sweet rides. We'll talk to you later. Good luck in Chicago."

Jim's mood changed, as if someone flicked a switch. "Thanks, but Chicago isn't until October. You should come to Master Ming's. Learn to fight."

"See ya later," John said ignoring the suggestion and pulling Jessica away without another glance at Jim.

"That guy's crazy." Jessica had leaned in to whisper over the Steve Miller Band.

"That's not nice. He is crazy though, as in actually bonkers. Schizophrenic, certified."

Jessica had heard something along the lines and had no problem believing it. Although, it sounded too much like bored smalltown fabrication. "Really, I thought maybe that was all..." she started but trailed. For some reason John liked Jim.

"Really. He also thinks he's psychic. Once told me that someday soon the Catholic Church was going to fall, the Buffalo Bills were gonna win four Super Bowls in a row, and that he can pick lotto numbers, but if he buys a ticket or tells anybody, the numbers change."

"Why isn't he in a—"

"A home? Why? Come on, guy's harmless, besides, last season he told me the Oilers would take it in seven. I won five bucks. I wish I followed his other tidbit, too."

"What was that?"

"He told me Hextall was going to win the Conn Smythe, the MVP of the playoffs, but the Oilers would win the cup. Hextall won the MVP. A player from the losing team has only ever won the playoff MVP like a handful of times."

"So what?"

"Jim told me all this two-weeks into the season, it's eerie. He also told me six ways to catch a fox if I get lost in the woods with nothing to eat, and that Shih Tzu dogs are genetically closer to dolphins than they are to giraffes."

"Are you serious?"

"Yeah, he's bananas, but once in a while he hits the nail. Rest of the time what he says is so asinine you wonder if the doctors weren't asleep when they set his dosage."

"You said he's Camilla and Gordon's son?" Jessica was thinking if she and John had moved into their home only a few years earlier, they'd have been Jim's neighbors. The thought ran a shiver up her back.

"Yeah-huh." John looked up to the sky. "Seems like Jim has some psychic competition with Malcolm's bones." Big dark clouds rushed from two directions, meeting in a crash above Tranquility's auto show.

John and Jessica raced back up the hill, drenched by the time they arrived. Malcolm had moved to just inside the garage, still drinking, the roll-down door open to let his cigar smoke float outside.

"Looks like you got some time for a beer now!" Malcolm shouted.

John looked to his wife. "I'll go have one."

———

From inside, Jessica watched the rain pour over the garbage

riddled park, barren of the excitement prevalent only minutes earlier. With all the helpers gone, she wondered how many extra days she'd have to look at all the trash. It seemed nobody hit a barrel with their paper plates or soda cans. It made her feel dirty, so she took a shower. The hot water steamed the bathroom. Jessica opened the window a crack and lit a stale cigarette. She told her husband—told just about everyone—that she'd given them up for good, and for the most part, she had. She smoked once before work, once after supper, and then anytime she knew she'd get away with it.

Inhale, exhale; relaxing and even more so with the hot steam consuming her. She finished and tossed the butt into the toilet; a little wad of toilet paper weighed it down for the flush.

Before she got into the shower, she sprayed strawberry scented air freshener. Something about the way the steam mingled with the chemicals made the strawberries bloom on every surface.

Clean, shower off, John's heavy footfalls approached. He knocked at the door. "I'll be out in a minute," Jessica said, taking a few deep sniffs, searching for tobacco scent. It seemed clean. She stepped out after a quick once-over swipe and then opened the door.

"Malcolm wants us to come over for supper. Gonna have a monsoon party. Have you looked outside?" John had the ruddy cheeks of more than one beer drank, he also smelled like cheap cigars.

"Were you smoking again?" she asked.

"What, no. Malcolm was smoking these Mexican cigars. They stink like old woodstove and rotten fruit. It's weird, they're kind of sweet smelling. So, I'll tell him we're coming? I'm just gonna grab some brews and head back over. Just come over whenever? Supper at six."

His words spoken as questions didn't necessarily make them feel like questions. Jessica didn't get a chance to consider, didn't have a choice. At least she wouldn't have to cook anything.

She heard John race into the basement, the door on the old pill-shaped Maytag—an appliance they received when John's parents finally got a new fridge—rattled and hummed as the beer bottles clanged together. Jessica wrapped the towel tight and hurried downstairs. "Hey, should I bring anything?"

"Uh, I don't know. Maybe a snack or some wine or something. Do we have any wine?"

Where John was and where Jessica was, they couldn't see each other. She was leaning down the stairs and he was behind a wall.

"No, but that's okay. Wine and snacks, I can get. Tell them I'll come over around quarter after five."

"Do we have wine?"

"I said I'll get some, red and white, maybe champagne, maybe tequila or scotch, should I bring some scotch?" Jessica asked, the idea really sinking. Nights at the neighbors' never ended at supper or when the kids went to bed, they didn't end until one of either Malcolm or John passed out.

"Just bring a bottle of wine, hell, just get some spritzer; it's cheap and everybody likes it."

"I don't like—"

"See ya in a bit," John said and darted away with his arms loaded.

For a moment, Jessica envisioned showing up at the neighbors' with pork rinds and a bottle of butterscotch ripple liquor. She saw John shaking his head disappointedly and Nancy aghast. It felt good, but for no more than a moment.

—

Busy as it was only a couple hours prior made the sudden emptiness feel doubly empty. The Becker's Convenience was barren, as was the liquor store.

"Crazy out there, huh?" a middle-aged woman asked, chewing gum behind puffy pink lips. "I've never seen one like this."

"The rain's so cold too," Jessica said and took her bag from the counter.

"These must be good. I've had only one other customer since the rain started and he bought four bottles, but he went with strawberry." The woman blew a tiny bubble and then popped it.

"Wild. Everyone's okay with them, even people that don't like wine. The flavor's like they decided to make booze taste like juice, just in case."

"Teenagers drink 'em. I get that too; if it doesn't taste too boozy."

"How do you know teenagers drink—?"

The woman grinned and cut off Jessica. "Old Bobby Nash buys a ton of the stuff, that and cheap gin. Teenyboppers show him a little skin and he takes their money and returns with booze. I've called the cops, but they said that can't prove nothin' 'til they catch him in the act, but I guess he's pretty tricky and it's not against the law for Bobby to see a boob while he's out on his daily route."

"The mailman?"

"Yeah-huh." The woman began cracking the knuckles of her right hand with her thumb as a lever. "Have a nice weekend."

The rain fell harder and she had to put her foot to the floor to make it through the rolling waves coming down the hill. From behind, she heard a fantastic crash, but couldn't turn to check the sound. The Ford Fiesta wasn't great in any kind of weather, but the little car climbed the hill. She exhaled a thankful breath and eased off the gas.

Behind her, the world groaned and creaked and banged. Jessica glanced into the mirror and saw the road collapsing. A chasm collected unfortunate homes, cars, and property. The town sat dark and Jessica couldn't move.

"Holy fuck," she whispered, stuck at the crest of the hill, but not from rain. Shock had her. Then she thought about how close that had been. Tears began, and she remained stunned, unmoving.

A knock came at her window.

"Hey, are you okay?" asked a man in a yellow rain slicker, his hat looking very Paddington Bear.

His skin seemed corpse old, and wrinkled, unrecognizable, but her terror fell aside quickly and something clicked. "Oh, Gordon Roland!" He lived only two-doors down.

"What a mess, eh. You're mighty lucky, I watched you come up, it looked like it was trying to catch up with ya for a few seconds there. You were just about toast."

Jessica laughed a little and wiped at her eyes. "I'm supposed to head over...I think I'm going to go home and watch TV, actually."

"Power's out. My guess, we'll just have to quietly hope for the best up here until they get those poor folks all fixed up. I wonder how many died."

Jessica simply shook her head.

—

Jessica stepped into the garage and heard three male voices, she didn't notice the old Dodge with the peeling paint and patches of rust parked in Malcolm's driveway. Her mind was elsewhere.

"Do you know what's happened? Did you see? I just about bit it!"

"It's the end of the world," Jim Roland said, a bottle of strawberry spritzer in his hand.

"Shush, Jim, none of that. It's just a storm," Camilla Roland said, she wore a hat to match her husband's out on the street.

"I see a storm; how could I miss it?" Malcolm's voice was slurred and snarky.

"The road fell away, there's a big sinkhole cutting us off. It demolished a bunch of houses and the rain's pooling like a moat. We won't be able to get down for days." Jessica wondered why she was the only one who seemed all that concerned.

"Wait, what?" John shot to his feet, kicking over a half-drank

Miller.

"Explains the power being out," Malcolm said.

"Didn't you hear it?" Jessica shook her head in minute movements.

Nancy put her perfect hands to her mouth. Eyes huge.

"End of days. The Lord is cometh...like I said." Jim had that fierce, certifiably nuts expression: cheeks red, eyes wide, and bugging, lips in a tight pucker. He stared *into* Jessica.

"Jim, stop it, some people don't know that you're joking," Camilla said. "Did you see Gordon out there?"

"Huh. Oh." Jessica tore her eyes away from Jim's. "Yeah, he's fine, he saw the whole thing. I was driving up the hill right before it happened, or I guess, while it happened."

"Are you all right?" John asked but did not wait for a response. He touched Jessica's arm with beer bottle cold hands a second before running out into the rain. Malcolm followed, but Jim stayed.

Jessica turned her eyes back to Jim after John and Malcolm slipped from view. Jim chugged back the entire bottle of spritzer and started on another.

"Is it really that bad?" Nancy asked.

"It's bad, it's the end of days, ucka raba coritha, mora tunga neuvella," Jim said and began wagging his fat tongue around his lips and rolling his eyes.

"Stop it! Geez, Jim!" Nancy laughed nervously. "We don't need that crap and if you keep it up, I'm putting you on ginger ale."

"Ucka raba coitha, mora tunga neuvella, tordonden, tordindadada ucka," Jim said and swallowed back the entire bottle of spritzer in three gulps.

"No more!" Camilla jumped to her feet. "Don't worry, he can't hold his liquor. He gets excited, drinks and passes out after about an hour."

"Right and the government didn't put that mole on your

mother's back so the Nazis would hear her plans. Ucka raba coitha, mort tunga, tordindadadada," Jim said, slurring but dead serious, his eyes growing crazier with each irrational syllable.

"Actually, here, have something stronger and then pass out already," Camilla said, handing over a Crown Royal bottle. Jim accepted it like a challenge. He took a mouthful and lit a cigarette. "You know you don't have to act out every time you drink or just because something exciting happens. The doctor said—"

"Only God knows, the doctor's trying to poison me, he's trying to steal thoughts to sell them to the Russians."

Unintentionally, Jessica took a deep breath at the cigarette smell. Nobody said anything, but Jim continued to watch her.

The women moved to the roll up garage door and looked out. From their angle, they couldn't see anything but water moving. Jim belched from behind them and mumbled sounds that meant nothing.

"Mom," an irritated voice said—Amber, the eldest child, "the power's out again."

"Your father's playing in the rain, so once he gets back, he can look at the generator," Nancy said.

"I'll look." Jim swayed as he spoke. "Don't worry, God likes light."

"The generator is in the shed." Amber stood in front of her sisters. "And hurry, these babies are afraid of monsters in the storm."

"Monsters are coming whether the generator works or not," Jim mumbled as he walked out into the backyard.

"I'm gonna go get my emergency kit," Nancy said. "Just to be ready and safe."

Jessica gazed quietly into the darkening rainy sky.

"I never made them before I had kids, but once you have a kid you really think more clearly about things," Nancy said as she stepped to the door. "I can't even imagine my life before I had my babies."

Jessica had heard that line before, about a thousand times, whenever someone she knew had a kid.

"I can and if I had a time machine, let me tell ya. I guess Gordon had a great uncle that was nuts, doctors think it has to do with a mixture of genes and, in Jim's case, excessive drug use," Camilla said. "He wasn't born that way, but I guess his brain fell apart sometime after puberty. If only I had a time machine..."

From the backyard, the gentle rumble of the generator kicked. Three girls yelled happily, the fourth started crying. Nancy's voice carried from inside as she cooed to the wailing baby.

Gordon waved from the driveway. Camilla looked to the backdoor where Jim was standing in the rain, cigarette in one hand, rye in the other. She said, "Sorry," to Jessica and followed her husband away.

—

The generator stopped again. This time Malcolm was there to fix it. He went out to the shed with a jerry can and immediately fell into a fit of laughter.

"Hey, check this out," he said, poking his head through the backdoor of the garage.

Already soaking, neither Jessica nor John minded stepping out. Malcolm swung open the shed door and there was Jim Roland passed out, a crusty dribble of vomit running down his cheek onto his shoulder, leading into a fat pile of soggy red regurgitated mystery.

The puke coated crucifix struck Jessica as especially funny and she returned to the garage, shaking her head, laughing a grim and unhappy laugh. The damage on the street was too much to hold any sense of humor.

Malcolm convinced his neighbors to stay a little longer. Nancy made too many kabobs for just the family and they'd go to waste. They ate, but quickly. After Jessica had three kabobs and

John put away seven, they left Malcolm and his squad of girls.

The rain had slowed, but it still came down and lightning jumped through the sky. "We should've borrowed a flashlight," John said.

"Have you ever seen a storm like this?" Jessica asked.

John didn't answer and swung open the door. After crossing the threshold of the main landing, John instinctively ran his hand up the wall to flip the switch. "Duh," he said.

The house was muggy. John and Jessica moved about, avoiding corners. Lightning flashes filled the living room. John walked quickly while the image remained fresh and found his way to the everything-drawer. Amid the jumble of elastic bands, nearly spent batteries, cereal box toys, and lidless pens, he found a small keychain flashlight.

"Success." He hit the button. The dim yellow glow revealed the kitchen. "I think there's another flashlight in the basement and one in the garage—that old blue and black one."

Another flash of lightning lit the sky followed by a teeth-rattling boom. Both John and Jessica jumped.

"Jesus." Jessica hugged her elbows tight.

"You coming or do you want to check the garage?"

Mention of the garage reminded Jessica of the pie melting on the front seat. "Oh damn, I have to go out to the car. I bought a pie for the, the supper." Fear forgotten, she hurried down the carpeted stairs, feeling the familiarity as if she were seeing it. She pulled the garage door closed behind her.

She took the shady cement landscape around her car slowly. She felt for the rolling door's handle, and once she had it, swung the door up. More light let her move faster. The keys remained in the ignition. She opened the door and flopped down inside.

A bright flash filled the air followed immediately by a loud snap and crack symphony. The rear view reflected the big gnarly maple tree in the tiny park aflame. Black smoke rose like there was crude oil at its core.

"Incredible," Jessica said, pulled the light plunger and enlightened the garage.

They ate pie in the dark. Although not tired, they went to bed; nearly ten and without light or television time moved too slowly. Sleep came easier than expected for both.

—

Jim Roland rolled when lightning struck the tree but didn't wake. Four hours later, he opened his eyes and looked upon three black shapes skulking the yard. He saw them through the cracked door and thought they must be the girls, the girls carrying large umbrellas and wearing long masks.

That idea didn't fit. Jim's eyes shot wide and he kicked open the shed door.

The three strange silhouettes paused before taking to the sky. Jim flattened himself out on the floor. "Ucka raba coritha, mora tunga neuvella," he muttered and then yelled, "The Lord is my savior and the devil is not welcome here!"

Inside, Nancy lit a flashlight and pushed open her window. "Go home, Jim!"

"It's the end," Jim started, raising his hands to the sky, "the devil has sent his minions and the Lord will send His horsemen and war will wage. Take me, Lord, I am ready."

He stood, arms pointed like a Y, but nothing happened and Nancy said from the window, "Jim, go home. Maybe the world will end tomorrow, but tonight, the girls are trying to sleep."

Jim dropped his arms to his sides and scanned the dark sky. God didn't take him, not yet and that meant He had a plan. Jim knew he was to be one of the chosen to stand when the time came.

Jim decided he'd watch the houses from the park. He walked through the garage—gathered his two remaining bottles of spritzer—onto the street. The rain fell in sporadic drips; Jim lit a cigarette and sat down on the curb, watching.

—

Malcolm snored like a buzz saw. Nancy hadn't yet been able to fall back to sleep. She took her flashlight to check on the girls.

Susan came first, a tiny little ball of wrinkles and dark little eyes. Susan wasn't yet a year-old. The cradle rocked with a light touch. Nancy was careful not to wake her.

—

Kelly and Tina were too scared to scream. There was a monster in the room. Dark all over and it smelled of dirt and rot. Saliva bubbled on the scaled, elongated jaws, very similar to a baby alligator, but much bigger and not on the Discovery Channel.

The way it moved suggested, even to the girls, that it could smell them, but couldn't see them. Its long feet tinked and clicked claws against the wooden floor as it walked. The girls watched the window slide closed with a bang. They took their chance and dove under the bed to see feet and a short tail dragging behind the thing.

—

Nancy gave into temptation and poked at Susan's side. The tiny girl awoke in tears. "Oh there, there, baby girl, Mama's here," she said as she scooped and rocked the baby. "Are ya hungry?" She produced a nipple and Susan latched on.

The thing in Kelly and Tina's bedroom stopped moving to listen. It sniffed a few heavy snorts, as if weighing a choice meal against a buffet.

The approaching sound didn't register, Nancy felt in heaven, nipple in her baby's mouth. To her, that was life and if any woman lived anything but that, they missed out on something magical.

"Hungry girl," she said.

The thing stepped into the doorway and snarled a low rumbling growl. Behind Nancy, a window let in a little light; she saw the strange silhouette and reached for the flashlight on the dresser. She shot a yellow beam out to get a better look. It didn't work, the flashlight was too weak.

Another growl reverberated from the door. Nancy turned the light onto the thing just as it began running.

She screamed and put her back to it in an effort to save Susan. The baby, scared, bit down on the nipple before opening wide in a yowl. Claws tore into the flesh of Nancy's back and she stepped to the wall, her only hope. She attempted to climb through the little window with Susan pinned to her chest—they were on the second floor, but only feet below, sat a wheelbarrow full of loose topsoil.

The thing leaned forward and nipped its long jaw over her ear and she dodged to the side. A secondary attack of claws drained a fantastic helping of blood onto the floor, taking with it most of her energy. The end was there and she acted without thinking, tossing Susan through the open window.

Susan fell into the wheelbarrow, began screaming.

The thing tore at Nancy, blood and breast milk splattered the floor and walls. Nancy fell into a heap.

—

Malcolm flew from his bed, slamming his toe on the dresser, crushing two tarsals. "Sonofabitch," he whispered and hopped on one foot toward the sound he thought he heard.

Malcolm stopped in the doorway, looking to where the flashlight beam played over his wife's destroyed face. "Honey?"

Pain forgotten, he ran to the window and found nothing but a quiet night.

—

"Ucka raba coitha, mora tunga neuvella, tordonden, tordindadada ucka," Jim chanted as he ran toward the screams.

He stopped, backstepping when he saw a baby in a mound of dirt. Rather than picking up the infant, he wheeled the baby and the dirt into the shed. He slammed the door.

—

"John, John, wake up," Jessica said as she shook her husband; he let out a loud, but otherwise inoffensive fart. "Wake up."

"What?"

"Something's happened. I heard yelling next door. Screaming!"

Jessica's severity roused him and he rolled out of bed. His bladder ached and before he could say much either way, John shuffled to the can. His foot grazed something unfamiliar, he took two steps past it and then stopped, thinking about the feel. He turned to the far wall of the large bathroom. It was almost perfect black, but for a gentle glow coming from the smoky-glazed little window.

"Babe?" John said.

"Yeah?" Jessica called back, her voice much further than the strange silhouette in the bathroom. John took a step toward what touched his foot. He heard a heavy breath, a snort, and a click.

"Is somebody here?" he whispered and swung out an arm. He made contact.

A loud screech cried into the darkness and John flailed backward.

"John?" Jessica said—a screech wasn't in her husband's typical repertoire of toilet noises, not even when he sat through a really hot one.

The heated air of rotted breath wafted into John's nostrils and he stood stark, his bladder ready to burst.

"Don't," John said.

"What's going on?"

"Stay away—Ah!"

The thing leapt. John reached out and held the small leathery claws away from his throat and chest. It was strong and they fell backward, John's spine bent awkwardly over the tub's rim. He cried out and three sharp claws pierced the flesh of his stomach. His bladder released.

"Help, Jessica! Something's in here!"

She chased the cries and once she got to the bathroom, she

scanned but didn't see much. She swung open the small cupboard under the sink and found her Kotex box. She flicked her lighter.

A fresh scream erupted as she backed up, ass connecting with the counter. She understood that she saw John then—bloody and incapacitated—and kicked her bare foot at the thing. In return, its small tail swung wildly. Two more claws pierced John's flesh and he cried out again. Jessica looked around, thinking, thinking, thinking, time seemed to have sped, thinking, thinking, the world rolled along and her husband would die unless she...thinking...thinking... She turned the flame back under the sink and found an aerosol can. She let the light die for a second so she could reposition. The metal safety strip warmed her thumb as she flicked a new flame.

John screamed as the claws scratched deeper into his stomach. She sprayed. Flame danced upon the thing's back. Suddenly the creature was screaming right along with John.

John was flailing fists as Jessica maneuvered the makeshift flamethrower over the cowering creature. With wild swings, John's bloody fingers found the bath curtain and he attempted to pull himself upright. The curtain tore from the little rings and he fell back to the floor.

The thing spun and roared before it pushed from its knees, swinging a long stroke through the air. The aerosol sputtered and died. Jessica backstepped at this as the thing regained itself and approached, cocking its clawed hands, ready to strike. John leapt onto its winged-back, draping the shower curtain over the body.

"Quick! Get something!"

Jessica subconsciously ran through bathroom items.

Snapping a hole in the curtain came the thing's long snout and jaw, threatening anew. Snap. Snap. Snap. Jessica flicked the lighter and looked under the sink, bypassing a hair dryer and hair curler to grab the hair crimper; a tool her mother gave her for Christmas, but she'd only used once.

Snap. Snap. Snap.

"Come on, come on," John said, wrestling to hold the shower curtain over active limbs and hungry teeth.

Jessica waited for the jaw to snap closed and then she began wrapping the power cord as the thing's claws attempted to reach for her hand, but John's strength and body weight kept it down. Around and around the cord tightened and the thing snorted.

Jessica thought further, the bathroom couldn't help much. "I'll be back," she whispered as she ran.

She flicked the lighter every second to keep the layout in mind to move quickly. Still, she stumbled twice over forgotten ledges, but eventually reached the kitchen. With two large knives in hand, she raced back to the bathroom, tripping and scratching her neck with a blade. Up and moving. She banged her knee rounding the bathroom door.

John rolled and the thing freed an arm. Swinging the clawed fingers back over its shoulder at John, he dodged, but the sharp tips grazed his cheek. Jessica jabbed at the thing, sinking a blade. Another cry rose from the creature. She pulled out the knife and stabbed in and out three quick shots. It fell sideways and she continued to stab. After more than 20 strikes, Jessica, breathing like she'd just run the 100M dash, retrieved the lighter from her pocket. The thing wasn't dead but gasping quick short breaths through the tiny nostrils on the end of its jaw and snout. John looked almost as bad, his white undershirt busy with blood and claw marks.

—

Malcolm found two of his daughters up and crouching just inside their bedroom door. "Get dressed, we have to uh, we have to go out to the neighbors' house," he said.

The girls did not argue, for once. Amber felt her way toward the sound of her father. "Dad...?"

"Get dressed, we have to go."

"Is Mom okay?"

"Amber, now," Malcolm said, a hangover threatening to

settle. The situation demanded clear thoughts, but it was too much and he couldn't focus as the veins mapping his grey matter seemed to shorten and tighten. "Hurry." He then stumbled off to the washroom.

A box of matches and a fat red candle sat atop the toilet, his wife put everything out just hours earlier. Malcolm lit the candle and opened the lid of the toilet. He expelled the remaining beer he carried. After putting down the lid and pocketing the matches, he found a bottle of Tylenol, took six chalky pills, chewing them to let the residue pass through the flesh of his mouth, hoping that it might expedite the reaction time.

"Dad, where's Mom," Amber asked, coming into the washroom.

"Shush, she's gone, gone with the baby."

"But why would she—"

"Shut up! Go get your sisters, okay?" Malcolm was ready to smash the world. What he'd seen. Christ, he wanted to kill *something.*

Amber listened. Malcolm went to close the door to Susan's room, hiding the traces of the death. He lifted the hallway telephone and, as expected, the lines were down.

The depleted family stepped from the house to the Astro van parked in the driveway. "I need you all to be big girls for me," Malcolm said and strapped the girls in before pulling the sliding door closed.

Grunts and violent utterances escaped his lips nearly constantly as he thought about his wife and what he saw. *What kind of sonofabitch...?* And then, *oh God, she's gone.* And then, *where's the fucking baby?*

He opened the creaky driver's door. A low hum and a gentle giggle from someplace else hit his ears and he flopped into the van, closing the door behind him and pushing the thought from his mind. He put his forehead against the steering wheel and turned the key.

A thought struck, powerful and undeniable. The van still running, Malcolm swung open the door and hurried to the backyard. The hum grew louder and Malcolm placed it: the generator. At first, he thought it was a voice, but it was so obvious. Nancy was always ready, she must've run around the house switching lights off.

The baby had to be out there somewhere...*that giggle.* Looking at the little shed, the reality hit him. Jim Roland was responsible. The goddamned nutcase murdered his wife and...*what?*

Malcolm took a breath, clenched his fists, and then swung open the heavy wooden door of the shed. Gentle light poured from the doorway.

"The Lord has called and I have answered. I am the chosen!"

"Give me my daughter, you cocksucking freak," Malcolm said, grinding his teeth. He would've run over and nailed the man if he wasn't so goddamned big—fat or not—and if he wasn't so goddamned crazy about martial arts.

"Your daughter is with me. We are going to force the beasts from the pure souls, like mine and your daughter's. Is the Lord your personal Lord, your Savior?" Jim lit a cigarette, still cradling the baby as he did so.

"Sure. I'm Catholic," Malcolm said. His wife was Catholic, they got married in a Catholic Church—had to take some Catholic Sunday school classes for adults to do so. Though, he didn't buy into much of any of that bullshit.

Maybe an eye for an eye. He could go for some of that here.

"The Catholic Church is doomed, they bugger kids and the devils line the skies, they want blood, pure blood to punish the ungrateful, those who don't pray, those who don't accept Jesus. Oh Jesus, take us now!" Jim yelled, holding Susan to the ceiling with one hand. He was clearly drunk in this act, swaying some, but managing not to drop the girl. "Jesus, my Lord, ucka raba coritha, mora tunga neuvella, I want you to take this child, ucka raba coritha, mora tunga neuvella, this child is of the pure and only You know best."

"Goddamn you, Jim, give me the baby." Malcolm took a step forward.

"It has come!" Jim lowered the baby to his chest, eyes wide and gazing over Malcolm's shoulder.

Malcolm didn't hear the thing behind him and took two steps into the smallish shed. "You'll pay for what you did to my wife. You crazy motherfu—"

"Faith in the Lord Jesus will save me!" Jim set the baby into the wheelbarrow then and got into a fighting stance.

The open door creaked at its hinges behind Malcolm and he turned. A creature with a horrible face and wings stretching its back, short arms dangling to its hips, legs standing wide as tree trunks atop long crooked feet...and that lizard's head.

Malcolm rushed in reverse and Jim tried to push by to fight the thing but was too drunk and stepped on a watering can, pitched face first into the spot where cement foundation rose to meet lumber.

Malcolm registered none of this.

A great hot splash of blood covered the baby where she sat, wailing.

———

After washing up a little, Jessica dressed John's wounds—mostly superficial—by the flickering flames from a few candles and the yellow beam from the flashlight. The thing lay on the floor behind them, beheaded. John didn't ask and Jessica couldn't explain why she'd gone so far.

Perhaps a bit of ingrained horror film forewarning.

A yell echoed around the quiet night and travelled into the bathroom. "Must be more," John said, his voice exhausted and saddened, but not defeated.

"You don't know that," Jessica said, hopeful.

"We gotta help them."

Jessica said nothing and began tossing things around beneath the sink. A loud tink clatter crash stole attention. John moved the light. Red blush and cream-colored foundation, as well as a mix of unbroken containers, covered the thing's ugly head. A big swatch of foundation stood in a liquid mound over its eye, spatters of mascara freckled its jaw.

"Dammit," Jessica said.

"What were you looking for?"

Jessica found the Kotex box. She slipped a cigarette between her lips. Lit the smoke on a candle flame. She'd tell John to shut up if me made so much as a peep about...

"Can I have one?" he asked.

They'd quit together four months earlier, both smoked in secret since.

—

A knock. Gordon was a light sleeper and got out of bed immediately. He looked through a window and saw three little girls at the door. He scooped up a flashlight and jogged.

Once in the hallway, Camilla called out, "Who is it?" They'd slept in separate rooms for the last eight years. Camilla snored.

"It's Malcolm's kids," Gordon said and then as an afterthought, "Better get up."

Camilla began rustling.

Gordon made it to the main floor. He swung open the door and Amber began a tirade, "Dad made us go out to the van then he just left us there, our mom is gone somewhere with Susan and I don't know what to do, someone was watching us—"

"Hold up, come in. Who was watching you?" Gordon stepped aside and peeked out the door.

"I don't know, I didn't see them. I just knew they were there," Amber said.

Gordon guided the girls to the living room. He lit the candles from earlier. Camilla came down the stairs in a long evening slip, grey and silky.

Gordon said to the girls, "Well, you're safe now," he then turned to Camilla, "I'm going to go out and see what's going on. I think maybe there was an A-C-C-I-D-E-N-T."

"I can spell," Amber said, although not words that long.

"Be careful," Camilla said.

"Yep." Gordon donned his slicker and goofy rain hat in case the weather picked up again.

—

Jessica led her wounded husband outside, both had knives jutting from coat pockets and both had blunt beating tools in hands: Jessica a three wood and John a baseball bat.

A rumble came from Malcolm's backyard. They trailed it, as insane as that was. Jessica wondered if John was really this brave or was this something macho, a last ditch reveal for the wife?

They reached the lip of the yard and stopped, a few feet beyond the shine coming through the open shed door.

One of the things was around the side of the shed and had someone—Malcolm by the look of it—on the ground in a tangled and bloody mess. Susan cried from the shed and John broke into a sprint.

Not toward the baby, toward the fight.

John swung. The bat connected with a loud thud, the thing's head rocked forward. Malcolm groaned. The sound of his blood flowing onto the grass was eerily loud.

Jessica was slow coming, but there, and she pulled the knife from her pocket and began to jam into the thing's neck with a busy rhythm: one jab, two jab, three jab, four jab, breathe, one jab, two jab...

John took another swing and the landing fell onto a motionless form. He pulled Jessica back a step, thinking they'd done what needed done. "It's gotta be dead."

"Thou slain the beast; you must be one of God's army. Malcolm was impure, his daughter breathes, praise Jesus," Jim said raising his arms to the sky. His forehead was bloody and his eyes were pink and wide. "The Lord is with us, we are safe here!" He waved them toward the shed door.

The creature began moving, sluggishly a first. John was staring at Malcolm's drained body when he dropped the bat, withdrew his knife, and leapt onto the thing's back. The fine teeth made quick work of the leathery neck flesh.

Jessica watched a few seconds, understood, and then turned to Jim in the shed doorway. "Give me Susan."

"Blaspheme!" Jim shouted and slammed the door. "Beg for your souls, only the chosen go to Heaven."

No time for muffled nonsense; Jessica ran for the shed and kicked open the door—the frame already splintered. "Try and stop me, you crazy motherfucker," she said, sneering and holding out her bloody knife.

Jim sat on a bag of fertilizer with a cigarette between two fingers and the dregs of a spritzer bottle in his other hand. He mumbled nonsense sounds but didn't try to stop her.

"What do you think, the car?" John said.

Jessica was fumbling with the baby in her arms. It was a tough choice. The things obviously got into homes—were there more?—but could they get into cars? It felt like a bad idea. The road resembled a small mountain face, there was no way they could drive or climb down. The best hope was to hunker and wait for rescue.

"I guess, until we find someplace better," Jessica said and followed John along the property line to the front yard. She placed Susan on the shotgun seat and then dug into her pocket for her cigarettes.

"Just a second," John said, "mine are fresher." He jogged over to his LTD and took a pack of Player's Filter from the glove box.

Jessica inhaled and exhaled, she said, "Nobody lives forever, huh?" She looked at the cigarette like it was a true curiosity.

"We'll be lucky if we live through the night. I mean—"

John's words were interrupted by a sound and a shadow

swooping down toward Malcolm's backyard.

———

Thump. Camilla was already up and looking at the door. Gordon stood there outside, just stood there, he didn't motion and his face didn't ask for entry, he was blank. The power was still out, so Camilla saw only his shape, but that was enough to open the door just a crack. "Gordon?" she whispered.

A growling sent Camilla reeling backward. Gordon's dead body fell in through the door, and as she looked at her husband, something changed inside; she sat on the floor watching as a horrible creature crossed her shoe room and sniffed at the air. It turned to Camilla, its claws clicking on the cement doorstep.

The long gator-like, head leaned close to her face, she wouldn't have minded so much if it wanted her—with Gordon dead, what was left?—but it only snorted and moved along. She remained placid and empty, listening to the thing smell its way through the home.

There was a scream and Camilla looked to the ceiling as footfalls paraded the upstairs bedrooms.

———

Tina and Kelly ran into the first bedroom, they were too young to know what to do when monsters chased, too young to have watched the movies. Amber continued to run down the hallway until she reached a set of steps leading to the back—crazy old house had multiple staircases—finding the door that led into the garage.

Once in the garage, she stopped to discuss a game plan with her sisters, but they weren't there and she was alone.

Tina and Kelly had slid under a bed. The thing was in the room with them sniffing. Claws felt around the bedframe before clamping on the edge and reefing it upward. The girls screamed until their ribcages split and their hearts were removed for consumption.

Amber heard the screams and ran. It was pitch black in the

garage. One, two, three, four steps and she found the far wall. Her head struck a low shelf and she fell back, the shelf fell above her. The objects on the upper levels teetered and dropped, a thick cool liquid poured over Ambers head and she rolled aside, but not before the liquid filled her mouth and eyes.

Panic set in and she ran, eyes closed, spitting the horrible tasting stuff. She made it outside, wiping at her eyes and making too much noise.

Quickly, a creature zeroed in on her location.

—

John watched as what appeared to be Amber, covered in bright orange paint, broke through the park toward her house. One of the things chased.

"Oh God, how many more?" Jessica said from the driveway.

A door slammed.

There could be no mistake, makeup covered the thing's face as it moved with swaying ginger steps.

"They don't die even when you cut their—"

The creature tripped, made a gargling noise and its head rolled halfway between them and the house. The body stood and stumbled toward the head.

"Like hell," Jessica said, seeing one chance and acting on it. She sprinted and only slowed a notch as she bent to scoop up the head.

It's blood-slick jaws snapped at her. She pitched her arms out, like she was carrying a wick bomb from a Pink Panther movie.

"Help me!" she screamed, running toward her yard.

"Look out!" John yelled, not at his wife, but at Amber instead.

The girl went full speed into the green mailbox at the end of Malcolm's driveway. She snapped backward in a horrid whipping motion. The thing caught up.

Jessica kept running, eyes bouncing from the head in her hands and the beast about to... "No!" she yelled as the thing plunged a claw into Amber's chest. "Oh, Christ, no."

It leaned back and dropped the heart into its maw. Jessica began sprinting for the feasting creature and once no more than 10 feet away, she threw the head—like chucking an oblong watermelon with teeth—and it landed with its mouth open. It clamped onto its brethren and the feasting creature howled to the sky. Jessica was on it then with her knife out, stabbing into the feasting thing's neck; one, two, three, four, five... John joined the action thumping at its knee.

It let loose another great cry but was already down and all but finished.

—

Jim sat in the shed, speaking in tongues—what his deranged mind thought was speaking in tongues—and felt a sudden urge for a drink. He'd finished his spritzers and knew Malcolm always had beer.

In the garage, he flicked the switch and the lights powered on. The fridge was unplugged, but the beer was still cool. There was a choice and he went with Miller High life. He cracked, chugged its entirety, and then belched.

He took three more beers from the fridge and returned to the shed, he'd have to go out to his car soon, he had only five cigarettes left. But not yet. He closed the door and sat.

After lighting a cigarette, he downed another half beer. Something scratched at the door. It made him think of a cat.

On his feet—mostly steady—he swung the door. A thing stood their without its head. Jim shouted, "Devil! Ecartha, mena, notta, raba coitha, mora tunga neuvella, tordonden, tordindadada ucka," and pushed the headless thing. It stumbled in reverse and fell over Malcolm's dead body. Jim belched and slammed the door. "I am the general of His army, praise Jeeguus." Jim began tipping as the influx of fresh beer slipped a coat over his sensibilities.

Another cigarette lit, he cracked a beer cap off and took a good swig.

—

Jessica and John carved the thing into five pieces and then moved onto the next, always looking over their shoulders for another that would drop from the sky, claws poised, but it didn't come. They wore bloodbath gore from scalps to shoelaces.

"What'll we do with the pieces?" Jessica asked.

"I guess we bury them. We'll make a few holes and bury them, they won't be able to move if they can't get back together," John said, looking around at their work.

The idea of having the things in their backyard creeped them out, so without discussion, they walked into the backyard of their dead neighbors.

A cry rang out and they pitched their eyes upward, both had harmless chunks of creature in their arms. The thing that killed Malcolm stood on the roof, its head in its clutches.

"My God," John said. "It fucking found its head."

It dive-bombed at them, but dropped its head into a stone birdbath, where it bobbed and attempted to call out. The body soared over John and Jessica and into the wall of the shed. From within a slurred voice yelled, "Jesus lobs Tibernanny! I true army! Expos in sevemehmn!"

"Go in there and get the wheelbarrow, huh?" Jessica said, nodding to the shed. "That fucking guy creeps me out."

John dropped his payload to the grass. "Malcolm's got some good shovels too."

—

The sun rose and the emergency services made it up to the subdivision on the hill that had become an island in the sky. Days became weeks and nobody knew what to make of the grisly scene. Only Jim talked about devils and demons and creatures that he'd destroyed singlehandedly, but they'd return and he had to protect his mother.

Camilla was in shock but was ardent that Jim go back into care—she wasn't about to have him move home to *protect* her.

Jessica and John—as godparents, a title both always assumed to be hokey and pointless—took Susan.

———

It took time, but John and Jessica found a buyer for their home and they moved as far south as they could.

Camilla died after two years alone and her house remained empty until the Conservative Party took hold of the province and cut spending all over. The mentally unstable were suddenly stable and booted from care.

———

For the first time in 12 years, Jim Roland walked the streets of Tranquility, Ontario, and did so without a babysitter. The world had changed and he looked at the old house, ready to resume life.

The other three houses on the crescent sat vacant. He'd moved in on a Saturday, spent the weekend lonely and depressed, but awoke Monday afternoon to the rumble of machinery.

Apparently, a small group of investors purchased the land around the old park and planned to demolish the homes and build apartment buildings. A bulldozer tore through Malcolm's home and Jim watched, intrigued.

He'd gone to bed in his clothes and shoes, so he didn't even need to dress to hurry over and say hello. A man leaned against a shovel smoking a cigarette.

"Hey, I'm Jim. I was in a mental institute for crazies half my life." He held out his hand, a big grin on his face.

The man looked at Jim and then at the four rings on Jim's outstretched hand. "Ah, you own that house." He pointed across the empty park space.

Jim nodded. "What's going on?"

"Low-income apartments. Excuse me," he said and walked away.

Jim stood at the fence smoking, occasionally returning home for a can of Pepsi or a cup of coffee. He watched the excavator dig the foundations and the backyard; he watched as a dump truck took the debris away, collected the dirt and all the pieces, the things.

They wouldn't get them all, he knew that, just how he knew the Sharks would win the Stanley Cup and the score of the Super Bowl was going to be 49 to 11—which teams, he couldn't quite make out. Those evil creatures, they'd be back, someday, once they smelled something good to eat. Jim rubbed his belly and headed for home.

THE SECRET TO LIVING FOREVER

(2018)

Death was on Lance Heels' mind a lot. The sicker he felt, the more the notion of forever bubbled beneath the surface. Leaving the world. Leaving his life. Leaving his wife. Leaving their children. Gone, permanently.

Were kids bastards if they'd once had a father?

"Is it there? It is, isn't it?" Lance pressed a Samsung to his face with his right hand. A bloodied tissue was in his left. "Tell me—" He coughed, scarlet fluid climbed over his bottom lip in a throaty outburst.

"There's much to treasure in the San Juan. Might be something for you, mate." The voice on the far end of the line was a tease, but promisingly so.

"Daddy?"

Lance looked down at the doe-eyed boy. Tim was four. Lance doubted the boy understood what that blood and coughing meant. Though even at four, he suspected the kid was starting to get an idea.

"Daddy, are you okay?"

Lance said, "I'm on my way, have it ready," and hung up. He bent down to look at his son, face-to-face, ruffled his blonde hair, careful not to drop his sweat-slippery cellphone. "I'm not okay, but I will be soon."

"Lance." Silvia Heels only used his given name when angry, crying out while lovemaking, or when concerned. Concern was an ugly bug in the belly and it grew more all the time. "What do you mean you will be soon?" She'd gotten good at holding back tears.

Lance offered a weak smile, his lips shiny red. Silvia opened her mouth to speak, but the baby began crying from the nursery.

"I will be soon, I promise." No part of his plan involved telling his wife where he had to go or what the hired man had found. The Aliento de Siempre was not something to discuss until he saw it with his sick-tinted eyes. A secret until he had it in his hands.

———

"That's the Breath of Forever?" Lance stared at the wrinkled grey corpse sprung from its barrel coffin.

The two doctors on hand looked like brothers. The third man was a hired treasure hunter named Jacques.

"Nah, mate, that's the map." Jacques was a Canadian who'd spent most of his life Down Under, but came to learn the Atlantic better than the Pacific or Indian oceans. He'd studied the likely whereabouts of the San Juan for more than a year before stumbling onto a handful of clues in the ancient logs of a sister vessel. He'd already suspected what remained inside. The lore was fantastic and in a rare turn of archaic history, seemingly true. "That's why we have these gents."

The doctors were small men in white coats. Both had round glasses and brown horseshoe pattern growth around shiny scalps. "Fascinating," one said. "Truly," the other said.

"I paid for—" Lance began to bark a horrendous cough. He'd done well on the flights over to Labrador, but the damp cold sank daggers into his throat and chest as he stood in the hatchery warehouse.

"Chill, mate. You two, follow the cut line, like a cereal box."

The doctors each wielded a scalpel and cut the tight, healed-over former stitch lines running from head to foot of the little, water-greyed corpse.

Lance watched.

His cell vibrated with a text.

Where are you?

He closed his eyes, considered answering the text message,

but powered down instead.

"Incredible," one doctor said. "Truly," the other doctor said.

Intrigued, Lance stepped closer. The doctors pulled the two huge flaps of skin away from a strangely preserved corpse. The flesh stretched. Interior side up, they stood back to let the bright overhead lights reveal a series of green ink markings.

"What in the hell is that?" Lance rubbed his chin.

"They gotta link 'em, like so." Jacques pointed to the legs and then made a crossing motion with his fingers. "Link 'em, see?"

The doctors did and the map revealed itself. "Someone kept this man alive, cut hunks of flesh, drew the route, and sewed them back on. Amazing," one doctor said. "Truly," the other said.

"See? X marks the spot, that's where we find the Aliento de Siempre." Jacques wore the kind of grin a man wears when he knows his ship has come to port loaded with shiny bits from the treasury.

"What's all this then?" Lance pointed to the inscriptions along the arms of the flayed skin.

"Instructions. Spanish. Umm...only a...uh, mouthful from the...fountain...no more."

—

"Where the hell is he?" Silvia had Jacques by the lapels of his brand-new three-piece Hugo Boss suit and white Oxford.

"Lady, he was sick. Maybe it's better this way."

"Tell me!"

Jacques exhaled a heavy breath. He'd only gotten half his payday because of what went down, but perhaps he could still get the rest of it. "There's a matter of debt due."

"You damned snake," Silvia said, wishing to say more, but both Joyce, the baby, and Tim were present.

"It costs, the journey isn't cheap. You'll all need to come, have to talk him into leaving."

"He's okay then?"

"My guess, he's better."

—

Jacques figured that maybe it was for the best. The Aliento de Siempre was exactly as advertised, but it had some sticky rules. Bringing the children would let him keep the money and be free of nagging relatives. He doubted Silvia talked to anyone about what her missing husband spent money on before he'd vanished. The only reason she knew about Jacques was a check made in his name and her husband's cellphone call trail.

"Mommy, it smells in here." It did smell in the tiny submarine, and their ears had popped without release more than 20 minutes earlier as they dropped into the frosty Atlantic 100 miles off the Newfoundland coast.

"Almost there, then you can get out and walk around a bit." Jacques stared into the abyss as fish darted around the headlights.

"What?" Tim asked.

"He meant when we get back topside." Sylvia rubbed his back. Joyce was in a papoose over her chest.

"Not quite," Jacques said without turning to face his passengers.

Through the glass, a strange green glow began eating up the dark. A rocky outcropping blocked much of the light, but beneath it, was an opening. The fish avoided the shine.

"Mommy?" Tim began crying again. The expedition was hard on him and he had a strong imagination. Too strong.

"Shh, shh." Sylvia rubbed harder. Joyce began crying too.

Jacques steered the sub up under the outcropping until light washed over the vessel. He stood, stretched his back, and then began opening the overhead hatch.

"What in the heck are you doing?" Sylvia's expression was pure terror.

No water rushed through the opened hatch, though the sound of it was constant. A gentle splash and wash.

"This is your stop. Wanna see your husband, don't ya?"

"How? What's out there?" Sylvia stood to look out into the green shine. There was oxygen, and it was much warmer than expected. It smelled like low tide. The pressure had lessened.

"Your husband, for one."

"Mommy?"

"Fine, can I leave—?"

"No. I'm no babysitter. He needs to see them, I'm sure"

"Come on, Tim, let's find your dad." Sylvia guided the boy to the ladder.

"Forty minutes and I'm leaving." Jacques opened an app on his cellphone. Numbers began to count down.

Sylvia looked at her watch. It was 2:50 PM.

"Is that enough time?"

"He's not far. Just hoof the path."

—

Incredible and impossible in the same breath. The rocky floor beneath their feet was dry and the cave walls glowed green effervescence, water alive within translucent stone surrounding them. Ahead was a narrow tunnel. Sylvia held Tim's hand, leading him. She wore Joyce in the chest carrier. Joyce had gone silent.

Through the tunnel, the trio came onto an opening. It was painfully bright. Sylvia called out, "Lance. Lance!"

"Daddy?" Tim was in the shadow of his mother and saw what she did not. "Daaaah-deeee!"

Sylvia's eyes worked to level out as her ears grasped the sound of her son's voice. She squeezed the boy's hand as her eyes adjusted.

Lance was right there.

But so was a 40-foot baby with green skin and deep pink lips. The chest and abdomen were bare but for two nipples; it had no bellybutton. Its eyes glowed like radioactive milk saucers. It had no hair. Lance was in its lap. A pudgy baby hand behind him.

"Lance?" Sylvia stepped closer, slowly. Tim was tight to her leg.

"I'm so happy you came. Meet the Aliento de Siempre. The Breath of Forever. The Fountain of Youth. I haven't coughed since I sipped."

"Sipped what, Lance?" Using his name now was in concern. She could've said it 50 more times for how screwed up this image was.

"It's a little weird, but I feel better than ever. The ancient scroll said one sip will let you live two hundred years. I've had three times that, but I only sip. It's important to only sip."

"His fountain?"

"Mommy," Tim whispered into Sylvia's pant leg.

"Hey, Tim. How's my big man? Thirsty?" Lance reached for the baby's rotund belly.

"Lance, what are you doing?" Sylvia's Apple watch beeped the hour. She looked. It had already been 10 minutes.

Lance began scratching at the soft-looking flesh as if the giant baby were a dog. "It's a little weird, yeah, but it's the Fountain of Youth. Don't you want to live forever?"

The baby bounced, smiled a wide, toothless mouth. Lance slipped off its lap, a practiced descent, fingers and palms busy on the belly, itching and slapping playfully.

"Daddy?"

Sylvia looked at her watch, wondering if there was any point in attempting to pull her husband away from... "What the heck is going on?"

"I told you."

"Lance, what in the heck—?"

"I told you."

"Lancewhatinthefuckisgoingon!"

The baby wailed laughter, shaking the cavern. It then squinted, forcing a viscous greenish-white blob from its right nipple. Lance climbed up and made a cradle with his hands. The secretion was like a crystal ball. Liquid, but solid. "Sip with me, honey. You too, Tim, come here. Have some medicine with

Daddy."

Tim took a step because good boys obeyed their daddies.

Sylvia grabbed him. "No, Tim." She spun and raced back the way she'd come.

Through the tunnel. Lance's voice echoed, begging her to return.

Tears began to spill from her eyes. Joyce howled tight against her chest. Tim was in shock and silent. Around the final corner, they reached the opening.

Sylvia looked at the lapping water and then her watch. They had 23 minutes left. 23 goddamned minutes, so where was that damned...? "Snake," Sylvia hissed.

—

Jacques maneuvered the sub up to the light.

"How did you find out about this?" asked Carol, a wealthy octogenarian.

"Luck."

The hatch opened and Carol and her third husband Darrell, a spry 40-something, climbed out.

"Forty minutes," Jacques said, opening an app on his armband.

The passengers looked to the path and began walking. Jacques watched them go. Once they were beyond sight, he closed the hatch and dropped into the oceanic abyss.

The Aliento de Siempre was real, his 200 nearly ageless years was proof, but just smelling the air of the cavern brought that nasty salty, briny taste back to his mouth. It made him gag every time. He had a thermos of the stuff and he dipped his tongue into it once every few years.

—

The octogenarian followed the comparatively young Darrell into an opening. It was incredible. Insane. An enormous baby sat at one end while dozens of average-sized babies rolled and crawled around the floor, faces coated in slimy, greenish-white goop.

"Welcome," a young man said from the giant baby's lap. "I'm Lance. It's very important that you only sip. A little sip. Most get carried away after they've been here awhile." He began to scratch and tickle the bulbous belly anew.

The giant baby bounced and clapped his hands, huge baby smile on its baby face.

VISITORS

(2017)

In through the nose, out through the mouth. Peace and nature. Togetherness.

That fresh air has a way about it, it sinks in and grabs you, but you also sink into it and bask in the serenity it offers up. It's safe. It reminds a man of a world gone by.

Or it had been that way.

Camping in the woods. This time of year, clear blue-black sky and pale yellow moon, trees brimming with coos and hoots, twigs and grass alive with unnoticed motion, and us, by the smoldering fire, looking into the endless beyond with our sleeping bags pulled to our chests.

It was as it usually was, until it wasn't.

Lights hovered above us. Four dots. Green. Spaced at least two lengths of my Suburban apart. They dodged and danced, jitterbugged impossibly. Mark was in the middle of telling a ghost story he'd learned from a school library book. Bethany had already told hers; it came from a TV show she probably shouldn't have watched.

Those lights were magnificent and terrifying.

Mark went silent. I tried to speak, but there was no fatherly knowledge that extended to this circumstance. Fiction made fact.

A pressure fell onto my chest and the air whooshed from my lungs.

I blinked.

A throbbing tore up my side, I was on the ground by the river, soaked and cold and confused. What had happened, I had no clue, but the pain, the searing uncertainty of it all mingled, like poison in a well, oil on a puddle, visible, hideous.

"Bethany! Mark!" My voice was raspy, throat aching, a pain I hadn't recognized until then. "Where are—?"

I heard one thump and then a wail that pierced the quiet woods with otherworldly volume. Agony and terror the likes of which Mark should not know came through on the cry. I was on the move.

That blink, what had happened? It stole from me all the knowledge of time passed and the source of pain.

Even with the blank spot, hearing Mark, I knew he knew too much. But how much did he know? And how much more was it than what I knew?

I ran as hard as I could.

Questions boiled for answers.

Why was I wet?

Where were the rest of my clothes?

A second thump landed.

Bethany's cries were higher. I chased them, changing my trajectory only slightly because she is the baby, and Mark's additional three years toughened him exactly that much more, maybe, hopefully.

That blinked out moment, I'd come awake elsewhere, sore and then, then, screaming children. What had happened?

The voices of my children carried no words and all the words.

I scooped up Bethany, raced for Mark.

The pain was in my skin, under my skin, how?

I cradled them. "Hush. Hush," I said.

That blink and the pain and the wetness and the missing clothes, what did it mean? There was blood too. Blood in bad spots.

I stopped running and held them tight.

It was only a blink between looking at the lights and being by the river, but the sun danced around the treetops as if hours had passed. A night camping gone...more? Maybe.

Now, I look into their faces. The children wail endlessly and I think it's from fear.

"Why?" Mark asks.

It has to be from fear.

"It hurts!" Bethany says amid sobs.

The unknown is terrifying. Please, let it be that.

"Daddy, why'd they do that?" Phlegm or blood bounds up Mark's throat with the question.

Do what?

No, that can't be, they can't...

"Daddy!" Bethany sounds like she did as a toddler whenever she was genuinely hurt.

These cries, it has to be fear of the unknown.

"Why'd they do it?" Mark smears boogers onto my bare shoulder.

"How come they put that stuff in me, Daddy?" Bethany sounds so small, smaller than she's ever been.

"Hush."

The reason why we all wear bloodied underwear, are suddenly wet, have pain in our throat, pain up, up *inside*, and have bumps in our arms beneath the flesh can't be what's scaring them. It has to be the jarring of the mystery.

Has to be, because...

That blink and the landing is all I remember, but do I want to remember more?

"Daddy!"

It has to be fear of the unknown.

Has to be.

If I close my eyes and think, there's nothing there.

"Daddy!"

It can't be the other, why they scream so.

"Why'd they do it?"

I shake my head against what might be. It can't be that they remember what I do not. They can't go through this without their daddy.

LITTLE CANDIES BEHIND LITTLE DOORS

(2020)

FOURTEEN DAYS TO CHRISTMAS

The room is thick with sawdust. It lingers, hanging like a fog. Herbert Hicks doesn't look up from the pedal-powered jigsaw, even with the knock at the door. He can't. There isn't time.

"Come in!" he shouts as the tiny steel band cuts through thin wood.

The door opens with a flourish and a rush of cold, salty air pours in. This air is so crisp that it's almost a warning: *time's running out, Herbert.* The door closes abruptly and a woman shivers her entire body, huffing through a phony smile, and when that doesn't earn the craftsman's attention, she clears her throat.

Hebert keeps cutting. He has three orders due out and the chances of this woman wanting anything but one of his advent calendars is somewhere between a smidge and not a chance.

"Excuse me?" the woman says, making it a question, and a haughty one at that.

"Forgive me, but you're going to ask for an advent calendar—"

"Three."

Herbert sighs. "You're going to ask for three advent calendars and I have three orders due out, so I have to work while—"

"Perhaps you should hire help, sir," the woman says, full of indignation.

Herbert slides the board—now shaped in the silhouette of a grand house—off the saw and quits peddling his feet. "Oh, Mrs. Crenshaw," he says, not at all surprised to see her, she's the very last of Hartsmouth's upper crust to visit. "So, you need three? I thought you had four children?"

The woman bristles some. Her face is wet and the thick powder on her cheeks is becoming like white mud as the snow melts from the heat of her person. She is hideous in the way all heartless women are hideous.

"I do have four. My Martin has joined his friends, protecting our great country—"

Herbert interrupts her. "They send him to Virginia?"

"Why, yes, Norfolk. How did you know?" The surprise has knocked the chip from her highfalutin shoulder, if only momentarily.

Herbert lifts his right hand and says, "Lancaster, Welles, Thompson, Horton, Smith, Smith," counting names on fingers. He inhales deeply and lifts his left hand and says, "Smith, Johnson, Wexler, Nelson, and, of course, Crenshaw. All of your precious boys are fighting the good fight on American soil, or rather they will be, should anyone ever attack."

"Yes, and we're very proud of our Martin." Mrs. Crenshaw *is* proud, it comes through unrestrictedly in her tone.

"I bet. So, three?" Herbert says through clenched teeth.

"Yes. Will they be ready for tomorrow? I saw what you did for Mary Smith's girls and—"

"If you're lucky," Herbert says, and then adds, "One hundred apiece, paid in advance."

The woman straightens, absently runs a gloved hand beneath her damp and running nose. "Excuse me?"

"There's no discussion to be had. I'm too busy. These calendars aren't for everyone, only those who can afford them. Surely, you can afford it?" Herbert says, eyes already back on his work, hands about to join his eyes.

The woman's cheeks are bright pink beneath the white gunk. "Never in all my years has a simple chemist, handy as you are, spoken to me in such a manner. Perhaps you ought to take lessons in—"

"Pay or go away, or pay and go away, it's all work for me. I can't waste precious—"

This time, Herbert's cut off. "How dare you speak to me in such a tone."

"*Ma'am*, you're about two syllables away from being the only one of your chums not to have one of my advent calendars for your children." Herbert picks up the first of twelve fine little shelves as well as his glue brush.

Mrs. Crenshaw sniffles and spins on her heels. She swings open the door, letting a fresh helping of winter in, then slams the door behind her, sending a tinkling vibration through the hundreds of bottles on the shelves lining the workshop. Two seconds later, the door opens and Mrs. Crenshaw's head pops back inside and she says, "I'll have a pageboy deliver the money no later than suppertime."

The door closes again. Herbert pauses what he's doing to look at the last photograph of his three sons before the draft sent them to France. Happy faces. It's pale and made slightly smudgy by startled motions while the flash popped.

Happy faces no more. No Virginian assignments for commoners. No safe spaces for the poor.

He sighs and gets back to work.

Good to her word, a pageboy appears with a bundle in hardly any time at all.

"Mr. Hicks?" the young man says. His hat is rough, his jacket threadbare, and his shoes in need of a cobbler.

Herbert lifts his head. "Forgive me, my hands are too busy for pause. Is that the money from Crenshaw?" he says.

"Mrs. Crenshaw, yes, she demanded I bring it over immediately and receive a receipt," the young man says. His cheeks are ashy and his ears are filthy, suggesting he's also the Crenshaw's chimney sweep.

"Always something with her type, huh?" Herbert says and

sets aside the staining sponge. "All right, open it up and count it aloud for me."

He takes a slip of paper from a stack and a pencil from a jar. As the pageboy counts, Herbert jots down the receipt.

"Three hundred for little houses?" the young man says upon finishing his summation, obviously disbelieving, but believing at the same time.

"Advent calendars. Each calendar has twelve doors. Behind each door is a specialty candy of my concoction. The finish incorporates fine glass and brushed steel accents." Herbert is immodest about his labor, as he should be.

"Oh," the pageboy says.

Herbert grins. "Take a five for your troubles, and a handful of candies," he says, pointing to the row of jars.

The young man grins back and reaches for a jar of orange balls.

"No, not from that one. Take from the red or the blue candies. Those orange ones are for a more refined palate," Herbert says and rolls his eyes while rubbing his index and middle fingers against his thumb.

The young man nods, takes two red candies, and five dollars—a week's worth of his meagre wages. He leaves and Herbert follows him to the door, grabbing a candy for himself along the way. He looks out the window as he rolls the sweet treat around on his tongue. Down the 19 steps to the frozen street below, the town is busy in spite of the weather. People hurry about; some with dead birds hanging limp by their necks, others pushing wheelbarrows loaded with stove lengths, children throw snowballs and smoke cigarettes and pretend to fire wooden guns. A few others beg and attempt to sell matches or paper flowers. Horse carriages and motor cars zoom about the icy streets with passengers hidden away behind doors.

Herbert looks over his shoulder to the money counted out on the tabletop and acknowledges he has more than he'll ever need, seeing as he's a widower and now the father of three dead children.

TWELVE DAYS TO CHRISTMAS

The sun is two hours away when Herbert hails an old man with a horse carriage on blades. The dog riding next to the man barks twice in passing another carriage and then a dogsled team, otherwise, the early morning Hartsmouth streets are quiet. Herbert has the final three advent houses bundled with twine resting on his lap. He's been up for 48 hours and feels every second of it weighing on him now. The way the street ice shimmers sends Herbert into dizzy fits and he imagines the carriage dropping into a swell of thawed ice. Plunging into frosty depths. He has to close his eyes to fight the spins.

"We're here," the man riding the head of the carriage says. He wears sealskin everything, the texture is fine, shiny fuzz. "Need me to wait?"

Herbert comes to. He must've slipped into a drowse and shakes it off, jingling the loose buttons of his coat. "Please," he says.

The man simply nods and Herbert stomps his pick galoshes over the ice and up to the wooden stairs leading high into the home of the Winston and Beatrice Smith family—Mrs. Crenshaw sent her pageboy back to his shop, forcing him to stand in wait for her order. Herbert had felt sorry for the young man and bumped Mrs. Crenshaw up in line. 16 steps from ice to door—in the summer it would be 22 with lower sea levels, and in the spring and fall, it might only be six steps to the door, depending on the tides.

Out of breath, bundle at his feet, Herbert knocks and waits. It feels colder up here, and he huddles into his jacket as best he can while his breaths play out in great puffs like a steam engine. He knocks again and this time the flame in the copper fixture above the house numbers comes aglow. The door opens quickly and a young woman, face wrinkled with pillow treads and eyes gummy as industrial gears, squints, holding her nightclothes to her chest.

"I have Mrs. Smith's advent calendars," Herbert says.

The young woman's face brightens and she says, "Oh, thank heavens."

Herbert picks up the fantastic little houses and hands them off. "One candy for each child every day until Christmas morn," he says.

The young woman snorts and then glances over her shoulder. "The little devils will eat them in one go, my bet," she says.

Herbert leans in, a sneer raising the left upper corner of his lips. "The doors are mechanical. They won't release until the clock strikes seven on the morning of," he says.

The young woman snorts another laugh and Herbert starts down the steps.

TEN DAYS TO CHRISTMAS

Sarah, Emily, and Gwendolyn Welles watch the pendulum arm beneath the grandfather clock's face, aching for seven. They've yanked and punched and kicked and whispered swears and used their father's straight razor in an attempt to pry open the little doors. Like iron, they've proven. The seven o'clock rule has no rubber to it.

The nanny watched and snickered as the greedy children are made to learn a lesson in patience. They give her looks and threaten to tell, but once seven hits and the doors open, they forget about all else; those orange candy balls in their mouths as they sit beneath the butane flame glow emitted by the Christmas tree. Smiles play about their faces and for hours, they seem to float around the house in a sort of numb euphoria. Their parents don't notice and the help don't dare rock a good standing boat.

This morning's hard candy bounces off teeth as it rolls about closed mouths. The nanny waves her hand in front of the children's faces, but gets no response. She takes the moment to consider the advent calendars and their intricate details. Fine, so fine, it is incredible that a man trained in old and new world chemistry could manage such mastery with his hands in the Good Lord's craft. She wonders if it isn't some kind of miracle.

The nanny tries tomorrow's door and from behind a voice calls out, "Josephine!"

The nanny pops back and spins, her dress gliding unfettered over the shiny wood flooring. "Yes, ma'am?" she says.

"Are you stealing candies?" Gertrude Welles says, she's in her morning wear—a billowy dress, designed to be wrinkly and thusly easy to manage—with her fists on her hips. The expression and tone suggest the nanny ought to tread carefully enough to cross thin ice.

"No, ma'am, only admiring the fine craftsmanship," she says.

"How do you suppose that Hicks convinced the doors to run on a clock?" Gertrude asks.

The nanny had caught her master tugging on doors only the evening prior, but wisely stepped away, unnoticed. "I really cannot fathom," she says.

SEVEN DAYS TO CHRISTMAS

Herbert locks up his shop and heads toward the town square with his pockets heavy with money. Nothing's been right since his Moira passed, push that tenfold with each telegram he'd received concerning his boys. Life just isn't what it should be. It isn't fair, and he's going to do something about it

So close to Christmas, the stores and streets bustle with life. Dogs in doghouses snarl and bark at sled huskies and children teasing them with sticks. Mothers and nannies shout after runaway youths. Men laugh with drunken cheer. Centering the stalls, storefronts, and parked carriages is a 40-foot evergreen covered in dazzling butane bulbs of a handful of colors, white and red satin ribbons draped lazily, and topped off with a shining white star, accented by crumbled mirror glass and steel sliver tails.

"May I borrow this?" Herbert asks of a carriage man concerning a soapbox.

The man shrugs.

"Thank you," Herbert says and sets the box beneath the tree. He stands on it and clears his throat. A few faces turn and he tries louder, adding, "Hello, my neighbors?"

More turn and he gives the rest a few more seconds, either they'll acknowledge him or they won't.

"I want to pay your debts," Herbert says.

This gets attention and everyone in the square is looking at him.

"I mean it," he says. "I'll be here all day, bring me your collection receipts and I shall consider becoming more than only your neighbor, I shall become your friend."

Most stand agog, but a young woman drags two small children by the hands, racing toward the only apartment building in town. Another woman sets off in boots made of tire rubber, followed by an old man in a patched woolen peacoat, followed by another woman...

"Hurry now, I'll not be in such Christmas spirit come tomorrow, perhaps," Herbert says.

THREE DAYS TO CHRISTMAS

The train huffs and puffs into the station and Martin Crenshaw, William Wexler, Thomas Nelson, and Gilbert Smith stagger from the dining car, cheeks rosy with amaretto and eggnog. They're singing a bastardized *We Three Kings of Orient Are* with arms linked over shoulders.

They rent a horse carriage and continue their serenade of the town, all the way to McKinley's Pub. It's a quiet night when they arrive, but their lively presence sends word throughout the households and mothers and fathers with children on the frontlines appear, to soak in the hope offered by living, breathing boys in uniforms.

Mrs. Crenshaw hasn't been in McKinley's pub for more than two decades and is surprised that it's cleaner and nicer than the opinion she's held her entire life, despite that the same man manages the establishment as when she was a teenager. Martin orders her and the other mothers a squid shot that turns their mouths blue and their pupils huge.

The din is great enough to arouse Herbert's curiosity. He bundles himself tight and heads two doors down, a candy rolling about his mouth. He peeks in through a window and Mrs. Crenshaw sees him and immediately turns to her son. He bounds across the pub floor, narrowly escaping a thrown dart, and swings open the door.

"Have you any of those candies?" Martin hollers into the cold, his words riding a steamy puff.

"Candies?" Herbert says, though he understands fully.

"The orange candies the kiddies are dying for! From the dollhouses!" Martin says and then snatches a cigarette from the lips of a passing woman and takes a drag. "Thanks, pippin," he says and hands it back.

The woman is drunk and nearly falls when she curtsies. Herbert's seen enough. His boys should be drunk on Christmas spirits. His boys should be home to show off their uniforms. His boys should be gallivanting and flirting with soused girls in pub doorways.

Herbert charges back to his set of stairs while Martin Crenshaw continues to call after him about candies.

TWO DAYS TO CHRISTMAS

The Crenshaw's pageboy stands at the door. Herbert crosses the room wondering if he's miscalculated and his plan has hatched early.

"Mrs. Crenshaw sent me for more orange candies. For the children," the pageboy says, shivering.

Herbert steps aside and lets him in. He says, "I'm sorry. She isn't getting any."

The pageboy looks terrified. "They aren't for the children. The children won't shut up after they wear off and Martin wants candies and Mrs. Crenshaw herself wants candies. I can't leave without those candies," he says.

"There are none to spare," Herbert says and then taps his temple. "I've an idea, though." He hurries to the back and flicks the switch to ignite the butane lamps. He then begins pulling trays from a toolbox of jars. He finds the jar of dried dragon eel and lifts it above his head. "Eureka!" he says.

He spins on his heels, thinking it won't take but a few minutes to boil some sugar and pineapple powder—what made the candies so delicious in the first place—and hand over some knockoff delicacies, but when he returns to the front, the pageboy is gone, as are the two remaining orange candies from the row of jars.

Herbert clenches the dried dragon eel jar with one hand and makes a tight fist with the other. He'll need to replace what's gone. "Damn you, boy," he says.

CHRISTMAS EVE

Claire, Robert, and Rupert Crenshaw sit beneath the Christmas tree, glowing, vacant, and with puffy faces. They've been this way since 7:00 AM when the doors opened and allowed them their treats. Mrs. Crenshaw tried to swap the candies away from the children, but they were too quick and wouldn't hear her offers. Martin suggests that he take his service pistol and force that nobody chemist to brew up more of the delicious morsels, but of course he is only kidding. Of course.

At nine other homes, children are much the same as the Crenshaw trio. Languid. Sleepy. Fat with Christmas treats. Mr. Johnson calls upon the doctor to be sure their boy is okay and the doctor laughs, joking that he'd only just left the Horton's a half-hour earlier.

"The children are well-fed and have caught hold of the reason for the season, that's all. Be happy. Be proud. Be merry, my good man," the doctor says and then leaves behind relieved parents.

CHRISTMAS MORNING

The Crenshaw children race from their rooms and plop down before their advent calendars. The pageboy has the fire stoked and breakfast on, but doubts anyone will be eating until after opening gifts.

Mrs. Crenshaw joins Mr. Crenshaw on the couch at the end of the room and Martin strolls in with his hair in tangles and a hangover dulling his pallor and reddening his eyes. He sits sideways on a wingback chair with his right leg over an armrest. The grandfather clock in the corner, as well as the clock on the fireplace mantel, pass ticks and tocks before announcing the hour.

Frantic hands scramble for the top and final doors of the advent calendars. Fingers dig for candies and find darker, heavier, but smaller treats. None consider this and pop the candies into their mouths. Instantly, their faces sour and their expressions scrunch. Rupert and Robert swallow first. It's not that the candies are bad, just different, and seemingly begging to be swallowed whole. Claire manages to fight the urge for nine seconds but succumbs and swallows.

"What? What is it?" Mr. Crenshaw says, leaning forward, spying the drooping expressions on the children's faces.

Rupert is first to begin unbuttoning his pajama shirt. Robert is close behind him and Claire simply rises to make an A of her body and lets her nightie slip from her bloated frame.

"Claire!" Mrs. Crenshaw shouts.

Rupert and Robert are slipping out of their pants and breathing in heavy gasps. Claire cocks her head sideways and says, "Mama," a second before her skull cracks and a red fissure plays down her face as her skin begins peeling in great swatches.

Snap.

Snap.

Snap.

The room is alive with bones breaking. Mrs. Crenshaw is whining into the crook of her elbow. Martin is on his hands and knees, vomiting on the floor before the wingback chair. Mr. Crenshaw is standing in silent watch, bearing witness to this abomination.

Rupert's arms slide to the floor like snowmelt from a rooftop. Four long orange tentacles wiggle and squirm out from the fresh holes. Robert's ribs tear through the flesh of his abdomen, spilling his guts and organs and muscles onto the floor as eight tentacles writhe free. The empty hollows of his legs remain upright for 10 seconds before crumbling. Claire is walking to her mother with her arms out, leaning to her right. The crack has played down her chest and hooks over her hipbone to continue its course up her back. Her mouth is moving, but the only sound is the single, midnight black eye, blinking wetly behind her lips.

"Get her away from me!" Mrs. Crenshaw screams.

Nobody moves and Claire's hands reach. The right side of her face then sloughs off in slow motion to reveal the bulbous head of a giant octopus.

"Get her away from me!" Mrs. Crenshaw repeats.

The reaching hands crack and bend before falling with a gush of chilled blood, right into Mrs. Crenshaw's lap, as tentacles push their way free. Claire wraps around her mother in embrace and Mrs. Crenshaw wails to remove the putrid thing from her chest.

Martin is on his knees, aiming at the thing Claire has become. He squeezes the trigger at the exact moment Mr. Crenshaw kicks Martin's arm and shouts, "That's your sister!"

Within an hour, the 10 families have gathered and armed themselves. Involving the law would be too lenient for that bastardly chemist, so they're taking matters into their own hands. The Lancaster's maid hears this and breaks away from the home to warn those who've been financially rescued that a posse aims to kill Herbert Hicks, their mutual benefactor.

At the town square, the elite charge with guns and fine sabers, while the poor swing whaling clubs and aim harpoons. The blood is fast and running, melting the ice shelf of the street and staining Hartsmouth in a way that will never be washed clean.

Mrs. Crenshaw keeps seeing the eye behind her daughter's lips the second before she fully became and uses it as fuel, unaware that she harbors two helpings of the same medicine in her blood. For awhile, she's Annie Oakley, once she's out of ammunition, she's Joan of Arc, slashing and stabbing. She's even cut the head from Henry Horton's shoulders, carried away and striking one from her own side.

The battle lasts four minutes and change and the elites are outnumbered, out skilled, and out of luck for the first time since being born into silver cradles. Laura Stanley, a seamstress always on the wrong side of her bills, holds a pick-hammer cocked next to her ear and says, "Ain't nobody touching Herbert Hicks. Not today, not tomorrow, not—"

Glass shatters and wood splinters. The front of Herbert's shop has caved in and pushing through the mess is the biggest, brightest octopus Hartmouth has ever seen. So wide it can hardly carry down the steps to the street. So tall it has to duck beneath the McKinley's Pub sign. So otherworldly that all who can run, do, and those still alive but can't run, crawl. Everyone but Mrs. Crenshaw, she's caught in the eye shine reflected by the nightmarish bulbs of the huge creature. The massive tentacles slap the icy street, carrying the thing closer. Closer.

It leans over Mrs. Crenshaw, salty black slobber raining down on her, and says with wet, disjointed words, "En...joy...your..." *slus-slup*, "chil...dren..." *slus-slup*, "while...you..." *slus-slup*, "have...them."

The creature that was once Herbert Hicks then continues on, past the carnage, past the town where he'd lived and watched his children grow and his wife die, and finally past the ships bobbing in the pier.

Like coming home, he slides into the ocean and leaves history behind.

JOHN, AMY, AND THE LONG WAY DOWN

(2019)

The pain in Justina's side sang louder than the whipping winds, nearly as loudly as the silent distance from feet to tarmac. An incision cut deep above her left hip leaked steadily into the gauze and tape that she'd wound around her middle before heading out onto the ledge.

That bandaging had concluded nine minutes earlier. The pain was worse while she'd pulled the gauze taut, but it certainly wasn't gone now. Given the circumstances, any discomfort was almost a welcome distraction.

Telling herself not to look down did little to keep her from looking down. The atmosphere was icy against her naked flesh. Her bare feet shuffled over the rough cement ledge—a hair wider than 11 inches from wall to abyss. Pigeon shit speckled the path like Gretel's breadcrumbs. Her bare ass brushed against the white bricks. Her bare chest hung loose over the distant world, nipples shrunk into pebbles.

"Don't do it." Her words came out with steam puffs that evaporated instantly in the wind. Temperature below freezing. Naked and easing along the only available route at a minimum of 16 floors from the ground. "Stay away, you bugger."

On the far side of the first corner, Justina had kicked a crumbly dirt nest out of the way. Now, it appeared an occupant of that nest was unimpressed and seeking revenge. Just a swallow, a tiny thing.

It might as well have been a rabid eagle.

Justina pushed tighter against the wall. The bird buzzed her close-cropped hair. "Damn you." Her heart was a drumroll. The blood in her veins boiled. The sweat bubbling on her skin had begun to freeze. The distance from eye to ground only compounded the lightness of her head.

Strength, she needed strength.

"John. Amy."

The bird flew back around, a second trailing it. Claws dragged over Justina's scalp, stinging with a fresh helping of terror.

"John. Amy. John. Amy. John Amy. JohnAmy!" Saying it renewed her will to break through the fear and shuffle on.

A third swoop added six more birds. Wings and talons brushed. Justina closed her eyes and kept moving toward that window, the only one without bars since the window she'd escaped from.

"John. Amy."

She'd met John four years ago. He was a good influence on her, and she needed that. The drugs, the partying, the fast life, and the spending of two dollars to every one dollar that she made. John helped her put that wild side under control, and when Amy started growing in her uterus, it was like the promise of a good future.

"John. Amy."

The birds were relentless. Three beaks pecked at her chest and her hand shot up. Her feet and shoulders swayed. Eyes open, she looked down at the quiet street below. The salted snow had the ground looking slick as ice, hard as ice if she fell... Swooning, she pushed tight against the wall and steadied her feet before she moved another inch.

"John. Amy."

It was the internet's fault that she'd relapsed. Those ads popped up like weeds: strollers, clothes, mommy-centric gear. Those images had crumbled her resolve and the credit card stretched and she called for a limit increase, maxed it, applied for an additional card.

John asked and she made up stories.

Amy looked fabulous.

Other mommies probed Justina as to how they'd managed it all.

John sat her down, expressed his love, bared his soul, and begged her to look at what tomorrow would be if she kept it up. She'd sobbed and spoke of her childhood. He knew it all, but listened again. The stern upbringing and forever saving, her fifth-generation sneakers, worn and patched with silicone just to save a few bucks. He'd squeezed her hands as she revisited the limited meals, the empty Christmas stockings, and the birthday party refusals because her parents wouldn't spring for gifts to offer— the embarrassment of showing up emptyhanded would be too great. *I know, I know.* Kisses and hugs. *I know.*

"John. Amy."

A gust of wind whooshed and Justina whined. The swallows rode the backwash of that chill. Eight different points of contact and sensed wing-brush near misses told her beyond sight that more birds had joined the frontlines.

The toes of her right foot squished in something soft, warm, and unexpected. She lifted. Her head floated and she cried out. Eyes open again. Only six feet from that window with the dim light.

So close. Her foot fell back into the fresh pigeon shit, squelching.

If that window wasn't open...a later problem.

"John. Amy."

Justina had agreed to her husband's teary pleas, but it wasn't easy. She relapsed again. John was so understanding when those things came from Amazon. He reminded her of the successes and the decreases. The plan he'd mapped out included slip-ups because nobody was perfect and imperfections made her who she was. He loved her for those imperfections, and did she *love him enough to keep working?*

"I love you, John! I love you, Amy!"

The birds dived anew.

"Go 'way!"

Shuffling. The cold bit. The pain screamed. Her head swam. Her feet moved faster. The birds returned. Fresh tears sprouted and froze on her cheeks. Eyes open, she peeked to the window. Right there, almost within reach. Gaze dropped, a man walked down the street, a blip, a nothing, an ant on a hill.

She inhaled, ready to call out for help, but stopped. What if he was the one who'd put her in that icy bathtub? What if he cut into her side?

And why her? Who would do such a thing to *her*?

She had been in the apartment. They'd lost the house and the three of them lived in a one bedroom, Amy's crib in the living room/dining room/den. It was cramped, but it was forward motion. Justina had apologized and promised that she'd make it right some day and John said he knew she would. Told her she was capable of great things. Told her she was worth more than she knew.

She was, had to be now.

"John. Amy."

A huge gust rattled a steel corner. No birds followed, the wind too strong. So powerful that it raked her nakedness like acid teeth.

The brick changed beneath her hand and she chanced a look. The window frame. Her heart sang. She palmed the glass and tried to slide it up. It didn't move.

Her eyes closed and she turned her feet, fingers gripping the divots between bricks, tips forced hard against the rough grout. Turning. Turning. Turning. She leaned on her toes, the back of her heels reaching over the edge of the ledge, her ass hanging, her breasts pressed to the building.

The birds came back and she gasped, petrified while they

attacked. Each strike so much scarier than the last. Her feet seemed to *want* to slip and skid. Trills of adrenaline stroked her chest.

"John. Amy."

She lowered slowly, her feet arched so that her toes could carry the burden of weight and balance. She pressed against the window. Solid. She pushed and slid the pane upward.

The birds returned.

Her head swooned.

Why had she come out onto this ledge?

That steel room with the steel door. That steel room where she was bound to die if she'd stayed. That steel room where someone had cut her open for...

For what?

The glass slid an inch, two, three. Swimmy, her head suddenly tried to drag her backwards, down, down, down, and was that so bad? It would be simple, easy. The pain would dissolve and the terror would release her.

"John. Amy."

He didn't give up on her and she wouldn't give up on him. She pushed her face against the glass of the window, trailed her hands down, and felt the bottom.

The window moved up. She was going to make it. Eyes open, she stared at the lamp on the paper-busy desk as the glass slid against her cheek.

Birds slammed into her back and ass, scratching and pecking, but it didn't matter. She was numb from the cold and so damned close.

The window stopped moving.

"No. Come on."

Palms slapped upward. Each bang sent a quaver of pain beneath the flesh that rolled down to settle in her side. No change. She bent and lowered her feet, dropping a knee. The second knee came down and her legs jutted out over the street.

Nothing but 200 feet of air between her and the sidewalk.

The swallows dove one last time and she shook, pawing at glass, pawing at bricks, anything for a grip. Her left knee lost understanding of the ledge and dipped, toes skidding against the bricks beneath the ledge.

Justina wailed, and grabbed at the bottom of the window, yanking up. Much of the skin of her big toe remained on the seventh brick her foot touched. A smear of blood trailed.

Her forehead jerked inward, cracking a spider web into the window. New pain. More pain. Her body stiffened, rocking backward. The world was empty behind her.

"John. Amy."

Her toe dragged further and she jumped through the gap. The mysterious injury cried out anew and any clotting that had occurred undid and darkened the pink of the gauze.

But she landed. She was inside.

Still, inside was in the building with the steel room. Up, moving was imperative, her head went cloudy and she stumbled into the high-back leather chair behind the desk. Her flesh ached at the warmth. And she caught her breath, gazing around her. The door was wooden, with a stainless-steel handle. It slowed her heartrate.

Not steel. A nice wooden door.

A wardrobe was to her right. She rolled using her unharmed foot and opened the door. Inside were a long, black, Canada Goose parka, men's Loake boots (grey with faux-gator skin finish), and a keychain with six keys attached to a Mercedes fob.

Justina rose and donned the coat, grabbed the keys, and then fell back into the chair short of breath. She leaned on the desk taking deep inhalations and expelling deep exhalations as her eyes grazed over the paperwork. Ready, bent, she pulled on one boot, pulled on the other, but had to lean back for more air prior to tying.

Her eyes fell on the paperwork again before she bent down

once more. Loop, loop, cross, pull—

Upright, she grabbed at the top page of the short stack. She read her name. She read the words ONE KIDNEY / TYPE A-B NEGATIVE / FEMALE / 26. She read the dollar figure at the bottom of the invoice $795,655.00.

Remembered words floated across her grey matter: *You're worth more than you know.*

"John?"

Would he?

"John?"

Her issues. The money, was this the only way? How else would they get into the apartment to take her?

"John."

It had to be him. Her heart began to shatter, falling in slow motion crystal flakes. Each piece landed like a knife against a gaping wound...

A gaping wound.

He'd done this to her. He broke her heart because she was a terrible capitalist. He'd tried to have her killed.

"Amy."

Vigor renewed, Justina bent to tie the boots.

The hallway was empty and silent. She leaned against a wall and walked until she reached an elevator. She pressed the call button.

To her right, around a corner, another door opened, and two mannish voices spoke. Footfalls squeaked on the stone floor.

Justina jabbed the call button five more times.

Those voices and steps drew closer.

The parka hood went up and she continued jabbing.

The men were right there at the end of the hall.

The elevator doors opened.

"Hey, hold that."

Justina was in the box. The options made it easy for her. The 16 was lit and she poked the capital P at the bottom of the list.

Footfalls shuffled into a jog.

Justina slammed her finger into the close button twice before holding it.

"Hey!"

They were right there, but the doors were closing.

"Hol—"

Safe, safe-ish, she dropped, finger remaining against the close button, whether that did anything or not. The lights on the panels flashed steadily downward.

The doors opened onto a dull, exhaust-smelling parking garage. She reached into the pocket of the parka for the keys. They weren't there. She checked the other pocket. Not there either. Panic resurfaced.

Hands patted and tapped. Each movement refreshed the pain in her side.

The keys were at the bottom of the first pocket.

She exhaled a deep breath and hit the unlock button. Four spaces to her left was a black Mercedes CL 500 AMG. The interior was plush and on any other day, she'd moon over the luxury, get out her cell and snap some selfies to show off the experience, but this was no other day.

"Amy."

Car rolling, the stereo played The Beatles' *Here Comes the Sun*. Justina punched the power button, not the time for a fairy tale band or childish melodies.

"Amy."

It took five blocks before she recognized where she was. On Fraxa Line, she pulled a U-turn and headed for the highway. The car flew.

She parked on the street, keys in the ignition. A gift for any willing thief.

"Amy."

She entered the apartment silently. The door was unlocked. She grabbed a knife from the block in the half-kitchen. Amy gargled a sleepy noise.

"John."

He'd lied to her.

"John."

He'd lost faith in her.

"John."

He'd tried to kill her for an easy payday.

"John."

A lump on the bed, she aimed and stabbed 11 times in 11 seconds. He rolled and gargled, a sound very different from Amy's gargle. He then wheezed. The noise was wet and obstructed. She aimed higher and stabbed into his back until his movements ceased.

The knife remained jutting from his flesh like a sundial arm while the moonshine cast a glow through the ratty blinds. Suddenly spent, Justina stretched out. The spill of John was so warm. The duvet was warm. She needed warm.

Sleep was easy, but short.

The sun was up and she looked around. The truth struck her again as the throbbing in her side resumed. She turned over and looked at the dead man next to her.

She cried, "John!"

The knife came free and she rolled him onto his back. His face was bruised. Zip ties fastened his arms at the wrists, his feet at the ankles. There was a rag duct-taped in his mouth.

"John," she gasped.

He hadn't done it.

He hadn't betrayed her for money.

"John. No. No. Please."

She sobbed and Amy began crying. Justina kicked from bed, automatic, and followed the sound. The pain in her side had dulled, but still stung.

She picked up the girl and opened the bulky parka, put a brick dusty nipple to Amy's mouth. Baby latched, the need to pee took her to the bathroom. She slipped out of the coat and sat. Pain flared from the surgery wound.

Finished, she remained seated. Her mind was a mess.

What have I done?

If not John...?

The door creaked open and boots moved over the linoleum onto the old shag. "What the hell? No, it was just supposed to be—No, dammit!" The cry was wild, emotional.

Justina put Amy in the sink. A heavy towel went over her face to muffle any impending baby noises. They were there anyway, but dim.

The voice began again. "Hello. What the heck? I wanted Justina gone. Not—"

Justina stepped out, trailing the voice, not daring to breathe until she rounded the doorframe, saw the truth, and said, "Mom?"

She hadn't spoken to her mother in years, but John was a sentimental type. He believed in knitting families. His parents had died when he was in college and he needed contact, needed Amy to know of grandparents.

"Justina? How are you sti—?" The woman held a huge bulging manila envelope.

Justina grabbed the blocky alarm clock—black and woodgrain—from the '70s. John had rescued it from his parents' basement and kept it all those years. Steel and sturdy. She lifted it over her head.

"No. Wait."

The clock came down. The unsewn wound roared, but fueled Justina's rage.

The clock landed again.

For John.

And again.

For Amy.

And again.

For her.

The woman was on the floor, a great seeping dent changed the shape of her forehead. Justina huffed and wheezed, dropped the clock.

The envelope. A 12 by 16. It was heavy. Justina opened it. Thousand-dollar bills. Hundreds of them.

A gentle cry came from the bathroom.

"Amy."

Justina dropped the cash, thinking. She'd never seen so much dough. Imagined, briefly, what she could buy.

IT'S JUST A HOUSE

(2022)

Hockey stick blade reared back behind my right ear, shaft tight in my grip, I eyed the net before swinging through with everything I had. The orange ball, hard as stone from the mid-November chill, blazed past the goalie's flailing right arm, flopping Road Warrior catcher flimsy on his hand, and glanced off the corner of the post where it met the crossbar. The ball cut across the Edenville skyline and smashed through the front window of the Kircher House.

My guts sank to my feet. For the whole sum of the nine months I'd lived in Edenville—a family record as my father had to move for work, typically twice a year—that house had loomed over my neighborhood, its stained-glass windows like eyes that bored into my soul.

"That's our only ball," said a boy named Michael before swiping his Canucks Starter jacket sleeve beneath his nose.

When I looked at the building, it seemed to laugh at me. It was a Tudor house, almost big enough to meet the label of mansion. The framework was of cracked and peeling black paint. Moss covered every wall, leaving gaps where the windows stood prominent and bright. On the lawn was a faded Century21 sign with a secondary sign hanging from rusty hooks reading BY APPOINTMENT ONLY. The window the ball had smashed through was on the front door, right next to the handle and locks.

"Go get it, new kid." This came from a ninth grader named Shane Benoit who lived on the block. He was three years older than the next oldest of us playing road hockey, and we all acted like the coolness of his maturity might be contagious.

"It's locked," I said.

Everyone knew nobody had gone into the Kircher house in years, not kids anyway, because when kids went in, they never came out. Adults were immune to whatever witchery existed within—common knowledge.

My jaw dropped open, anxious to say no, offer up some of my allowance to buy a new ball, tape all the sticks in penance, mend the holes in the nets, anything to avoid going inside. Instead, I dropped my stick and started walking toward the house.

Too quickly I reached the step that rose from the sidewalk onto the property. There were stubby stone pillars that rose to my chest—I'd been about 5'3" at the time. Ivy twines wrapped brown fingers around the grey stone beneath. There'd once been a gate, the rusty hinges remained drilled into one of the pillars. As I passed between, my mind roared a continual mantra of IT'S JUST A HOUSE! IT'S JUST A HOUSE!

The cracked cement beneath me seemed tacky, as if tasting from the soles of my sneakers. Dead beetles had collected across the slightly darker square of grey where a welcome mat once lay. The door was burgundy wood with cast iron accents. The handle stuck out like an oozing cold sore. It was new, steel made to look tarnished and old, though in impossibly impeccable condition for it to plead that case.

The hole in the glass was smooth and round, almost begging for my skinny arm to reach in. I gave a quick glance back to the others who stood totem pole stiff, watching me with serious eyes and gaped mouths.

My arm refused to reach up and through that hole. "It's only a house," I whispered, adding, "You'll be cool." When that didn't work, I said, "Girls will know you're brave." That did it and I reached through. The deadbolt paddle was frosty to the touch. It turned stiffly, thumping out of its groove. As I drew my arm back, my flesh grazed the glass and a hairline cut bubbled crimson crude. A hiss escaped my tight mouth, and I rubbed at the stinging wound. My sudden anger at being hurt fueled my resolve and I turned the knob and pushed.

The door was heavy, and I put my knee against the wood. A sticky crackle from weather stripping soundtracked the moment. The scent inside was of mildew and something fishy, which made me think of the countless crayfish I'd caught in my nine years on the planet. It was dim inside. The wallpaper bubbled on the walls and there were spots where ceiling plaster had cracked. Cobwebs filled gaps on the banister and drooped from the foyer light. Otherwise, even at my meager age, it was obvious to me that this was a fine building.

The floor was stone tile and the ball had come to settle amid sparkling stained-glass fragments about five feet beyond the door. I moved further inside, my shoes crunching on glass. My left hand clutched the heavy door as I bent and reached, stretching as far as I could. So close but so far, meaning I had to let go of the door.

As I'd done as a small kid, racing to his bed after flicking off the light switch, I counted, "One, two, three," and took off. In my panic, I kicked the ball as I swung down to snatch it. Behind me, the door creaked, was in motion. By the time I had the ball in my grasp, the door had closed behind me.

Heat and light and a sluicing, smacking sound filled in from deeper within the home as I bolted back to the door. It was so, so heavy now that I could hardly budge it. The sounds drew nearer, and I couldn't help but look over my shoulder.

—

"Hey, Derek, come on in, I've got the info on your flight and room," Clarissa Jacobs said, leaning out the door of her office.

After clicking save on the script for a presentation I'd have to give in a few days, I made for my boss' office. Clarissa had always been fair and cordial, and the transparency with which she ran our division was nothing short of refreshing. There were two chairs on the guest side of the desk, and I fell into the one on the right.

"You all packed?" she said.

"Yep. Had to buy a new coat after checking the Yukon weather."

Clarissa huffed, grinning. "You'll need it on the site."

The site was a Rare Earth find in 2019, and to be fully compliant with the climate guidelines of 2022, a specific crusher/x-ray machine had had to be manufactured and shipped north. When it got there, the men at the site put it together incorrectly, stalling the unearthing of a steady supply of ytterbium, lanthanum, and gadolinium. They took the machine apart and were now awaiting one of the engineers who'd helped develop the thing to come by and monitor the construction and then process, after giving a peptalk to help motivate the crew. That engineer was me.

Clarissa handed over the plane tickets, rental car information, and emailed receipt for my stay at a B&B. "Sorry, there's no Hilton up there. This is the only place with a room available. Most of the crew live in temporary camps. Not going to lie, it's a rough spot. Folks aren't happy about being stuck there knowing they could simply blast with water instead of digging."

Hydraulic mining was not only more dangerous, was detrimental to the environment. The leftovers polluted eco systems and the act of blasting caused earthquakes. It was also what the brunt of the crew were used to—most had come from gold and coal mining backgrounds.

"Right."

Clarissa winced. "Also, you're not going to like it, but your flight was rescheduled. You leave YVR at a quarter after four."

My eyes flashed to the computer monitor turned just enough that I could read the clock on the corner. It was already 3:35 PM. "Holy, I have to get moving," I said and spun on my heels.

"Quarter after four in the morning," Clarissa said.

In the doorway of her office, I stopped and read the ticket.

"You'll get in well after six and the trip from Whitehorse is another two hours. Might as well grab breakfast before you leave the city...nothing between Whitehorse and Eden."

Frowning, I half turned in her doorway. "Eden?"

"Officially, it's County Twelve, but the locals call it Eden. I guess there are about thirty permanent residents. They live off the land and the tourism trade. No Starbucks up there."

—

Everything was bright, bright white around me when I awoke in the hospital room. My head ached and my arms were freezing from the ice packs they had strapped to me. A moan played up my throat before I recommenced bawling—I'm certain I'd been bawling and wailing before I slipped from consciousness within the Kircher House.

A nurse came to my side, hushing me and offering water. Moments later, a police officer hurried in, his utility belt rattling beneath his hard-packed gut. Both he and the nurse asked me questions and offered me things, but I continued wailing until my mother got there. She asked the nurse and the cop to leave me be as she cradled my head to her chest. Once I'd settled, I heard Shane Benoit's voice saying, "...only in there like two minutes," and "No, we didn't hear anything until he started screaming."

This brought a fresh bout of tears and wailing, though I couldn't say over what. There was a blank spot in my mind concerning what had happened. No, that's not quite right, the spot wasn't blank, it was gone, leaving behind a hungry hole that my conscious sought eagerly to fill with all the worst possible things.

When I got home, that empty Tudor seemed to laugh at me, its tongue detaching and licking at that gap in my memory, luxuriating in the jagged edges from the tear. And then, just shy of four months later, the sign on the lawn featured a bright black and yellow sticker reading SOLD. Six weeks after that, a crew of men in dirty work boots arrived with jacks and pry bars. The house was lifted from its foundation and basement. One morning I awoke to find a blessedly empty lot across the street, they'd even taken the pillars. By the end of the summer, a new house was there, a bland two-story building with vinyl siding and absolutely no Tudor angles, accents, or window styles.

Its presence was the cue for my subconscious to return to normality, at least on the surface.

—

"Air Canada Flight Eighty-one Eighty-two to Whitehorse is now boarding at Gate C Forty-three..."

My ears perked and I pushed from the padded seats in the general vicinity of Gate C43. After a brief Facetime visit with my daughter, Phoebe—currently enrolled at U of Victoria, go Thunder, and about to move out of student housing into a house with five other girls—I'd popped three ZZZQuil pills and managed to force five hours of rest out of the evening and night. It wasn't enough. For the last hour I'd yawned almost steadily, through an espresso and then through an americano. My two hopes were to sleep on the plane or wake the hell up.

The seats next to me were blissfully vacant and I luxuriated in the space. Though red eye flights tended to be a pain, they had a way of running on time and with little aggravation. All the passengers in the seats ahead of me and all those behind me were peaceful. The stewards were quick and efficient. We'd sat on the tarmac maybe three minutes before the pilot rolled up into place.

Takeoff was rocky. Upon leveling, we immediately hit turbulence. The speakers pinged and the captains voice filled the plane: "This is your captain speaking. I hate to be the bearer of bad—" The world seemed to fall out beneath us, all around me people let out little gasped yips. "Excuse me, bad news. We have a pretty bumpy ride ahead of us for the next hour or so. I'll ask—"

The bottom fell out again and my head swam. It was as if something had been pulled loose, the scab picked from the wound to my memory. The Kircher House...I hadn't thought of it in years until about a week earlier, and something about falling triggered a partial memory I'd assumed gone forever.

I closed my eyes to the shaking plane around me, seeing the orange ball in my hand the moment before I turned. My legs gave out...no, the floor gave out and I dropped. The splash that washed over me was cool and lumpy. It reeked of iron and rotting meat scents. Blackness surrounded me until a candle lit at the other end of the room. A sluicing, suckling slap of what sounded like a dog licking its chops drew closer, bringing with it the light.

I scrambled to find the lip of whatever this pool was that I'd fallen into. The flame grew, stretching itself into a pair of hands with wriggling fingers, stretching itself far enough that I saw the thing's face, stretching itself—

"Oh, goodness! I'm so sorry. Let me clean this up."

A steward stood over me with an empty cup in her hand. Orange juice dripped down my face and chest. The air had smoothed, but it wasn't exactly a leap to assume we'd hit more turbulence while I was strolling down memory lane. She began patting me down with napkins, my mind elsewhere, almost wholly focused on drudging up the face behind the hands of flame from that lost memory.

—

What had to be the truth of the matter hit while I stood at the Fox car rental desk. My memory was wildly untrustworthy and the awful burn scars on my arms were the only thing that pointed to the fact something indeed had happened inside the Kircher House. Those burns could've come from a radiator. Perhaps I'd stumbled once inside, my arm's thrusting between the steel coils of an ancient heating system.

Feeling a little better, I climbed into the four-year-old Nissan Pathfinder and pulled my cellphone from my pocket. Firstly, I connected to the vehicle via Bluetooth—I doubted very much I'd get many urban radio offerings that far north—and then opened a prior Google search to my destination. When I hit START, it directed me out of the parking lot and onto the highway where I'd drive for 160 KM without turning.

At 7:31 AM, my music stopped as my phone began to ring. The Bluetooth voice said, "Incoming call from Phoebe." I plucked the phone from the cubby behind the shifter and hit ANSWER on the touchscreen.

"Hey."

"Thank god. I had the worst dream. There was this rough looking kid chasing you with a hockey stick, shouting, 'Get the ball, new kid!' and there were these other kids behind him shouting. I thought it was like a plane crash omen or something," my daughter said, a little out of breath.

My guts crashed to my ankles when I heard her quoting Shane Benoit, but for her sake, I offered up my best imitation of a chuckle. "Sounds like some crazy dream. But, nope, not an omen; the plane landed."

"That's," she yawned, "good."

"Go back to sleep, you'll need your energy for the big move, right?"

"Yeah."

"Love you."

"Love you too," she said, drifting. "And watch out for kids named Shane with hockey sticks."

At that, I gasped. My mouth became a sticky, wet oven. "Shane?" I said.

"The other kids, they were yelling at the one with the stick, 'Make him go, Shane.' Totally silly. Nobody's named Shane in real life anyway."

This was so close to truth that it shifted my thinking for long enough to say, "Huh, I guess so," and then start into another round of goodbyes. My music returned and as Silk Sonic fumed over a woman, I considered the highly unlikely possibility that it was all coincidence.

Two dark hours into my trek over the frosty white tundra, I stopped in a village called Carmacks. The sun was still only an idea for the future, despite that it was creeping up on 9:00 AM. There was a hotel, which appeared to be the only business open, so I parked and stepped inside, discovering the alluring aroma of breakfast frying on the grill.

A trim man in a black t-shirt came to take my drink order. This couldn't be a long stay, so before I answered, I snatched the menu from between a Heinz ketchup bottle and a napkin dispenser.

"Can I get the Campfire? With coffee and water."

The man nodded. "Be about eight minutes," he said.

The dining area had a couple older men sitting at a table in the corner and at a table near the register was a young woman sipping coffee and looking like she was ready to go back to bed. While I waited, I withdrew my phone. The internet wasn't a thing people had back when the Kircher House incident occurred, so I'd never really looked into the place.

Two reception bars would have to do, and to limit the number of searches, I input everything I knew. Only 301 results came back. The first three were real estate ads. The fourth was an archival news story on the sale of the Kircher House from the Edenville Gazette. My food and coffee arrived at some point outside my notice while I read. One-handedly, I forked hashbrowns, cut sausage, and tore at an egg before shoveling it all home while I followed the name Pastor Adolf Franz Kircher, discovering only family tree sites with pay walls and a historical figure that went back into 1600s Germany.

Food finished, I sipped from my coffee refill, letting things settle in my stomach and bladder before I headed out again— there was only half an hour or so left of my trip, but no sense pissing on the side of the road, or worse, when I could sit a moment to see if it would be necessary with a toilet handy. To kill the minutes, I searched for what might've been a relative to the owner of the home that had returned to plague my mind.

The first offering that wasn't in document form was from a true crime website. The Pastor Adolf Kircher of the 1600s was suspected of sexually abusing children but was hung by his neck and then burned at the stake for cannibalizing vulnerable members of his congregation after hundreds of human bones were discovered in the man's basement—a basement full of torture devices and texts on the dark arts. Beneath the type was an old woodcut image of a Tudor style house, one that looked like any and all Tudor style houses.

"Weird," I said and finished my coffee.

Light had begun to kiss the distant horizon, and the wind had picked up, blowing hard enough that I had to halve my speed for the rest of the trip. This worked out for the best, as the smidgen of light offered to me lit the flat world enough to see a world of wildlife I did not want to hit with the rental.

Rather than check-in at the B&B, I went straight to the site. Men sat in trucks smoking cigarettes and vape pens as I pulled into the lot of the warehouse. Inside, men and women stood around a flame-throwing space heater. It was only a hint warmer inside.

"You Castle?" a big man said from behind a scraggily orange beard.

"Derek Castle." I held out my hand to shake, then we got to it.

—

We worked through lunch. When the big, shed doors opened to bring in another piece of the huge machine, it revealed a steely grey world, blown snow and ice crystals slashing across the sky like TV static. A shiver played upon the sum of my flesh—if the weather remained like this for three days, there was no way I'd catch my flight...if flights would even be going out. It was on my mind because I'd read up on the weather before my trip, storms could last weeks in the almost-arctic wastes.

For the remainder of the day and into the evening, as we put the final pieces together, I had an eye on the weather—though by 3:45 PM, full dark had again taken over. At 6:00 PM, we paraded to the cafeteria trailer and loaded mismatched bowls with lumpy, grey stew, using mismatched spoons to shovel it into our mouths. Edible was the only honest compliment I could've made and this shined another light on why the crew was in a mood. By 6:35 PM, six of us marched back to calibrate the machine so that, after I made my speech and presentation, the mining could recommence tomorrow morning.

Just before eight o'clock, sore, cold, and exhausted, I hopped into my rental, flipped on my wipers, and rolled to the destination I'd searched beforehand on my phone. A moderately large house only five minutes from the site. The structural shapes clicked in, but I was too tired to feel offput by a Tudor design, even where most of the homes were clapped together bungalows on stilts. Through the wrought iron gate and the stone pillars on either side, up two cement steps, and to the door. I put my hand on the knob as a gust of wind screamed out behind me, carrying the words, *it's just a house.*

I shook off the absurdity of the hallucinated utterance as well as the windblown snow. There was a deacon's bench by the door, and I dropped heavily to unzip my boots. Footfalls shushed down a set of stairs beyond my sightline. A man in a navy-blue bathrobe appeared. He was old, pale, and had one of those faces that always seemed familiar. On his feet were fuzzy black slippers. He had a piece of hard candy in his hand and took an extra suck before speaking.

"You're Derek Castle, yes?" he said, his accent was European, playfully tinted enough by his lilt that I couldn't immediately sense from where it originated.

"That's right," I said, my eyelids feeling weighted by sandbags.

The man nodded. "I'm Frank and this is my home. Only one room remains. It is not as nice as the others, sorry."

"Does it have a clean bed?" I stood.

"Oh yes."

"That's as much as I can worry about tonight."

Frank led me by a slim stairway to the second floor, by the common area, and through a large kitchen. He opened a heavy wooden door and pulled a string light, all the while explaining breakfast and the bathrooms. The stairs down were steep, and my luggage was awkward in the tight space. The floor at the bottom was cold, cold cement, decorated by area rugs. The walls were cement, too, and everything was immaculately clean. From one corner jutted a closet-sized room, walls of pale paneling.

"Your washroom," Frank said, pointing his hard candy stick. His finger roved to the other corner where another wood-paneled room jutted from the cement foundation. "And your room. If you need anything, I'll be upstairs."

My head bobbed in a loose nod as I shuffled into the room. A hanging bulb overhead revealed a single bed with brown sheets, a nightstand equipped with a clock and a lamp, and a bar to hang clothing. Door closed behind me, I stripped to my boxer shorts, found my charger in the front pocket of my suitcase, and plugged in my phone. The bed was springy beneath me, the coils singing a tune with each adjustment. After pulling the sheets out from an aggressive tuck, I lay back, instantly beginning to drift.

—

Black all around me, I opened my eyes. "How did they dig a basement into the permafrost...and what do they do during thaw weeks?" I said aloud.

As if startling it down, a lukewarm drip hit my forehead. I swiped it away aggressively, momentarily disgusted before I decided it had to be condensation from a pipe in the unfinished ceiling. According to the red digits on the clockface, it was just after midnight. I flipped away, stretching out. Another drop hit me, this time on my neck. I began to roll over to reach the lamp, and another drop fell, this one finding my slightly open mouth.

"Ugh, uck," I said as I spat out the tinny tasting moisture.

As I reached a blind hand out to the side table, three quick drops pattered against my scalp. When the bulb lit, I squinted against the sudden brightness. One eye closed, I looked to the ceiling. A great, gasping inhalation made my head spin. Above my bed was a dead polar bear, bound to the framework of the underside of the upstairs floor. I leapt to my feet the same moment a wet sluice sound played out like gum chewed into a microphone. The bear's abdomen open, spilling out its innards with slapping, wet smacks; organs and intestines playing out in gooey ribbons. Coated in foul smelling gore, I backed to the door. The knob was there, but it refused to turn.

For a moment, I was trapped in a disgusted, confused limbo. A second later, the bear really began to bleed, gushing out a tidal wave of blood. It was deep crimson and chunky with clots where the fluid had congealed. The awful surf was quickly to my ankles. The knob refused me still, so I began thrashing my shoulder against the door. It was like bodychecking concrete.

"Help!"

No sounds volleyed back above the din of the seemingly endless flow of blood. It had risen to my hips and still, it did not slow.

"Help!"

Up to my chest, the lit lamp bobbing along, threatening to electrocute me. I gave up on the door and punched at the panel wall. My fist smashed through with little resistance and on the yank backward, I grabbed the wood, reefing it aside. After a stance adjustment, I punched the inside of the far wall panel. It popped out, nails tink-tinkling on the cement floor beyond. The blood gushed out around me as I shimmied sideways between the wall's boney framework.

The blood had run enough that even in the much larger room, it was already back up to my knees. Sloshing with big awkward steps, I made for the stairs. Three feet from reaching them, four white balls rose from the blood, bobbing like ice cubes in a vodka Caesar. The one on the furthest right began a slow spin, eventually revealing two empty eye sockets.

"Skulls," I whispered a heartbeat before the first launched at me, biting into my shoulder. "Ouch!"

A second fired from the crimson surf and I lifted my hands to block its snapping jaws. Pain flashed through me. The pinky of my right hand was gone. Blood spirted from the nub in boiling bursts.

"Help!"

The next two skulls rose, taking a more precise approach, swooping around my head like bats. In tandem, as my left foot reached the first stair up, the tops of my ears were bitten off. Blood oozed down into the canals, invading my sinus with heat and scent. Another skull latched onto the back of my ankle and began twisting, spinning like a fan blade until the tendon popped and rolled up my calf.

"Ahh!" I shouted uselessly as I flopped onto my knees and hands.

In the moment's pause, the skulls were on me, munching away my flesh as my blood slick hands slipped from the stairs I was trying to climb. Through the gap beneath the banister, I tumbled, landing with a hard, dry smack. My hands came up to my face, my harried breaths threatening to hyperventilate my system. I remained there, fetal, knees to my chin, arms raised high, for several seconds before I realized the change.

I looked between my uninjured fingers. Dark but for the light coming from the lamp in my room; there was nothing untoward, all the blood was gone, the skulls were gone. Hands on the cool floor, I pushed myself upright, not even a twinge from the tendon the skulls had torn—hadn't torn. It had been a nightmare.

According to the clock, it was only 1:11 AM. I climbed back into bed, once again exhausted. It wasn't until I reached to turn off the lamp that I noticed about a half-inch of my right pinky was gone, the flesh healed over.

—

Breakfast was hearty: sausage, meatballs, a bowl of fabulous stew. Fruits and vegetables were a rare commodity that far north, so I questioned nothing of the offering. My mind was stuck on my finger and that horribly vivid vision. My brain presented a variety of hoops for me to jump, to explain the injury. Losing a piece of finger seemed like an impossible situation to forget, but I said nothing about it because it had to have happened long into the past given the healed flesh. Three of the crew sat at the table with myself and a young woman who was pale as the Yukon landscape. There were two empty seats, and once we all had plates, Frank occupied one of the seats with a steaming mug in his skinny little hand.

"Where's Joe?" one of the crew said around a mouthful of meat.

"He left us last night," Frank said.

Chewing the delicious, salty meat, I craned my head to look out the window. A yard light exposed the storm. It was on the tip of my tongue to ask where he went, but I swallowed the question.

"That means, Mr. Castle, if you'd like, you can move your things to a cozier room upstairs," Frank said.

To this, I couldn't agree fast enough.

—

The toilets were busy at lunch break, so I returned to the B&B, and for the first time saw it in the full light of day. It was the Kircher House, undeniably the Kircher House. My guts roiled and screamed that I find a toilet, but I was pinned in place by terror, sitting behind the wheel of my rental.

A bubble of gas slipped free, giving me a very hot, very smelly final warning. As I swallowed the terror and kicked open the door of the SUV, I thought of Shane Benoit, could hear his voice ordering me inside. On stiff legs, ass clenched, I hurried between the stone pillars, through the wrought iron gate, and up to the door. Once inside, panic replaced terror. Boots off, I bolted to the bathroom I'd seen that morning when I moved my things.

Door locked, jacket tossed to the floor, I planted myself on the cool toilet seat. The incredible rush reminded me of the bear from the night before. That dream that did not feel like a dream. That dream that stole a piece of my finger, or the memory of losing a piece of my finger. Where I sat, my cellphone rang in my pants pocket. It was Phoebe, video calling me. For a moment I considered ignoring it, but decided I'd tell her I'd call her back.

"Hey, hon, I'm kind of—"

Phoebe's voice overshadowed him. "It's harder than I ever thought, being here, but I'm—" She swiped her right hand beneath each eye and took a deep, harried breath as tears cascaded her cheeks. "I'm surrounded by—" She paused again, the tears flowing free and her chin quivering. "I'm surrounded by support, but it doesn't make the hurt of losing my friend, my support, my father any less."

What I was looking at hit me then. "Phoebe? I'm alive!" I said.

On the screen, my ex-wife appeared, crying as well. She held our daughter as I squeezed the phone tightly. It was my funeral. I was seeing my funeral. This house, this house was a fucking menace, and I couldn't be in it another minute. Toilet paper in hand, I leaned forward, only to find myself sucked back. My phone clattered to the linoleum floor. One hand on the cupboard around the wash basin, one hand on a windowsill above me, I pulled. The strain was horrible, and it only got worse when I gained a few inches of traction; my anus prolapsing and hanging below me like a horrid stubby tail. A wail left me and I fell back to the seat, the flesh below dipping into the murky waters a moment before the toilet broke beneath me, porcelain slicing into my ass and thighs. Water pooled around me as I lay on my chest, my backside humming agonized hymns. I reached for my phone, only to discover the screen cracked and lifeless. From the corner of my left eye came movement. I turned in time to see a scummy lily pad of feces swell like blown Hubba Bubba. As I jerked away, gasping in a great breath, my mouth opened wide enough for the shit bubble to launch between my jaws. Gagging, writhing, hands to my throat, I kicked around the bathroom floor. Never in my life had I tasted something so awful and yet so, so me. The bubble grew, like a squeezed water balloon, filling my sinus and throat, choking me. A moment before I could blackout, it popped and hot, hot feces blasted onto my tongue and out my nostrils and ears. Horrible, and yet, the sense of relief at its passing was familiar...until it continued. Shit hitched each attempt at breathing, causing me to cough until I began vomiting.

By the time it ceased, I lay in a viscous puddle of foul, greenish brown waste. Moving was beyond me and I closed my eyes to drive up my energy. When I finally looked around, I was upright on the can, wad of toilet paper in my hand. As I wiped, I panted at the pain of brushing against a series of very angry hemorrhoids that hadn't been there before I sat down.

—

My bags in the rental, I hadn't bothered to tell Frank I was leaving and never coming back to that awful place; somewhere in the back of my mind I'd already linked the name with Franz, as in Pastor Adolf Franz Kircher. Bowlegged, I continued my workday with the crew, monitoring and minding the slow process of teaching a new machine and its various duties to a team of individuals.

By 6:00 PM, the crew was tired but now had the hang of the machine, well enough that, since there was a moderate lull to the storm, I might drive down to Whitehorse. My phone refused to power on—the screen had only a sliver crack, and still—but surely there'd be a room, or even a flight.

As the current load was piling out in pebble form, two women began shouting. A punch was thrown. Hair was pulled. Instinctively, I hurried alongside the foreman. Seeing it too late, one of the women picked up an icy stone and pitched it. The second combatant ducked, and the stone nailed me in the forehead between the eyebrows. As I tipped back, my hardhat fell away and I landed solidly against a toolbox.

—

"Thank heavens you're awake," said a voice with a sly European lilt.

When I opened my eyes, I was looking at Frank. Muffling my vision was a wad of bandage between my brows, muddying my mind was a throbbing pain at the back of my skull. It hit me full on then, bringing with it intense panic: I was back in the Kircher house.

"I need a hospital," I said, trying to push upright.

Frank held me down. "There's no hospital here. It's best you stay put. Would you like some stew, there's plenty of Joe left."

At this, I blinked rapidly.

"Oh, don't worry, you're far too much fun to feed upon, at least physically."

Swirling, whirling, sickening, that meat we'd eaten at breakfast was human. I hadn't been able to place it because I wasn't a cannibal—not until that moment—but it had been a miner named Joe. My fists and legs seemed to act of their own will, lashing out at this little man. He popped back with surprising agility, as his smirk became a sneer.

The second I reached my shaky feet I was launched backward at the will of twisted ropes of bedding. The mattress coils fired through the padding, fish-hooking my ears, nose, and mouth. Frank drew nearer, his head swelling hugely from the collar of his shirt, his jaws dislocating as his mouth gaped enormously to reveal a tiny man on a small crocodile with an even smaller hawk riding his right shoulder. Frank's tongue elongated, reaching for my abdomen, searing my flesh, branding me as it touched.

In a craggy, rasping voice, the old man riding Frank's tongue said, "Seitterp ym, deef."

The crocodile turned its maw sideways and gathered the flesh of my left breast between its teeth before it twisted and tore down to the bone. My scream was sloppy and formless thanks to the mattress coils pulling my face wide. There was no time to dwell on the pain in my chest as the hawk perched on my forehead. I closed my eyes to the awful sensation of that beak snapping and slicing my eyelid. Blood stung with hot tendrils until I could no longer blink with my left eye. The hawk paused only a moment before spreading its serrated beak and slamming it into my eye. Dark, but I saw down the hawk's throat for two heartbeats—there were all the boys from the block in Edenville, holding hockey stick shafts with pitchfork blades over their heads as they cheered on the carnage. The cords of my eye then detached and the hawk flew to the old man's shoulder.

"Enid ot nrut ym," he said and began crawling up my chest and over my chin. "Teews eugnot."

With oily tasting hands and filthy fingernails, the old man grabbed my tongue. He brought it to his mouth, his thick, yellowy drool oozing down my throat. The first bite was not the worst. The ninth bite was the worst—he was in my throat, anchoring himself with my uvula. Blood drained down my throat, and I understood then that the house had no intention of letting me go.

—

I came to on the deacon's bench by the door. My vision was poor, a bit fuzzy. I probed at my left eye with a finger, only to discover glass.

"You checking out?" a gruff and manly woman asked from the hall connected to the foyer.

Beyond her, the house was different. A trick, I was certain. My tongue was too swollen to answer her with words, so I nodded. Boots on, I stepped through the steel door to the set of steps that led to the ground below. The house was now on stilts and had no obvious style to it. It was like most houses out there in that wasteland nowhere.

Night was heavy, but the weather was cooperating as I took the slow, slow route back to Whitehorse, the road thick with animalia—thankfully there was but one turn for my phone refused to power up. I'd lost a fingertip, my asshole ached with an itchy, sour throb, my left eyeball was gone, and my tongue felt like a slug in my mouth. The house remained heavy on my mind, but not as heavily as letting Phoebe know I was still alive...letting me know that she knew.

My tongue was normal enough to purchase a red eye back to Vancouver. Once landed, I got a ticket for the next flight to Victoria. By noon, I was on the Island in a rental car, my phone inexplicably coming to life the moment I left the airport. Pulled over, I dialed Phoebe. The call when directly to voicemail. I found Phoebe's new address amid a week-old text message and followed Google's instructions on how to get there.

A U-Haul truck took up half the street and I began looking for parking, knowing without Google's say so that I'd arrived. There was a spot about 20 yards past the truck and I took it. Thankfully, nothing had affected my feet or legs, so running was hardly an issue. Maple trees loaded with browning leaves blocked my view until I came around the truck.

"It's just a house," I whispered, pausing but a heartbeat.

Stone pillars and an open wrought iron gate led up to a Tudor house with stained-glass windows. My heart leapt into my throat as I drew closer, kicking aside a bright orange hockey ball as I walked. From inside, I heard wet sluicing and slapping sounds. They were sexual and yet brutal, as if those inside were fucking with strap-on knives. The scent was thick: briny, metallic, fetid. I paused in the doorway, trying to call out to Phoebe but finding my voice as unwilling to cross into the Kircher House once more as my feet.

PRECIOUS MOMENTS

(2019)

The Great Loudini wore a red velvet robe with a yellow rope cinching the middle, tufts of curly brown hair sprouted from just below his chin, his cheeks were pink, and his breath reeked of alcohol—cheap, strong stuff. "Come, come."

The three teens in their black leather hot pants and matching leather jackets stepped into the satiny tent at the back of the fair, swaying and bouncing like they knew people watched their butts wherever they went. The alpha of the trio was a tall girl with jet-black hair named Brenda. She brought up the caboose of the train in through the flapped tent doors, smacked a pink bubble, and then said, "We wanna talk to our men."

The Great Loudini squinted, scrunching half his face up to his right eye before making like he'd come to an understanding. "They've passed," he said, not really a question.

Tabby folded her arms over her buxom chest, made evermore intriguing by a push-up bra and a lacy, low-cut blouse. "They's passed all right."

The third one, the smallest, reached into her jacket pocket and withdrew a pack of Marlboros and a silver Zippo. She shook a cigarette free and slipped it between her candy apple lips. She then popped and lit the lighter in a single motion. "The damned Horseshoe Bunch pushed 'em over the embankment 'cause they was about to lose," she said. Her name was Tawny.

"They got theirs though," Brenda hissed underneath her breath.

The Great Loudini nodded and gestured for the girls to sit. "Three can be tricky, takes incredible effort and concentration...and fifty bucks."

"Fifty bucks!" Tabby said.

"Zip it." Brenda flopped down into a chair. "You get the fifty once we talk."

The Great Loudini shrugged. "Guess you saved us some time because I don—"

Tawny and Tabby were on him, both had switchblades pressed into his robe.

"Maybe you wanna try it from the other side, be the ghost in the séance, huh?" Brenda asked from her spot at the table and then smacked her gum. "We killed way harder men than you."

The Great Loudini actually smirked at her words before he lifted his hands slowly. "No problem. C-O-D works for me. I was just making sure I had the serious kind of customers," he said and sidled away from the blades and into his seat at the head of the table by the crystal ball. "Sit. Sit."

The girls sat. The Great Loudini studied each face quickly and decided these were the nastiest 16-year-olds he'd ever laid eyes on.

"This don't work, I'm a cut your nuts out and feed 'em to my cat," Tawny said and puffed as she leaned sideways in one of the chairs, ash falling to the red tablecloth.

The Great Loudini frowned as if he was simply putting up with the girls, like they were no real worry, murderers or not. Then, in a tone similar to asking about their grades on a math quiz, he said, "So to get even for your boyfriends' demises, you *iced* the Horseshoe Bunch, correct?"

Brenda licked her lips and stared down the yellowy eyes of the old man across the table. "That's right."

To this, the Great Loudini nodded. "Just making sure I got the right girls...or as the others called you, *them leather-wearing sluts.*"

"What you just say?" Tabby stood.

"You want to contact the other side, you will sit and take my hands," the Great Loudini said and stretched his arms out.

Tabby and Tawny both looked to Brenda. Brenda kept her eyes on the old drunk, thinking about gutting him when this was all over, contact made or not. Brenda took her girls' hands and in turn, the girls took the Great Loudini's hands.

"Ut mihi domum ad mundum vivorum. Ad me isti daemones revelare." The Great Loudini had his eyes closed and his chin turned up to the ceiling as he spoke, his voice deep and more commanding than the girls expected. "Annuntiate contra daemones revelare!"

The room began to spin and the satin walls and the velvet of the Great Loudini's robe began to crust in whitish purple crumbles—like mold mixed with dried battery acid. The girls squeezed their grips and began moaning. The light overhead burned violet before merging into hot pink and then scarlet red before winking out altogether. Dark. The alcohol and tobacco smells were gone. It suddenly smelled of mothballs and wood varnish.

"Let go," the Great Loudini said. Tawny did. Tabby did. Both kept hold of Brenda's hands. "Are these *them leather-wearing sluts?*" He lit a lamp and raised the flame to let the orange glow wash over a large room with wood accents, a huge table, and three grouchy looking women. 40-somethings in jeans and t-shirts. The Great Loudini suddenly wore a brown sport coat over a white Oxford, buttoned only one from the top.

"Who's these old cunts?" Brenda said, but it was clearly bravado.

The three women looked to the Great Loudini and then to the girls. One of the women said, "I was hoping you'd be all purple and bloated like you looked after you ate the Coon Doom poison."

The girls blinked. Tawny reached into her pocket for her switchblade, found it gone. In fact, she found she couldn't put her hand into a pocket. It felt as if it wasn't really there. "What's going on?" she said.

"Sometimes it takes a while to catch up...usually, you just need to jog a memory," the Great Loudini said, smirking over the lamp's candle flame like some hideous ringmaster.

"What do you mean?" another of the women asked.

"Sometimes, the dead don't remember dying, but once you remind them, their visage catches up. That is if they're of the deserving type. Karma is no joke in the afterlife." The Great Loudini leaned back then. "Go ahead, remind them."

The third woman opened her mouth, reminded the girls that the Horseshoe Bunch had mothers and those mothers had broken hearts and that the only way to mend some broken hearts was revenge and that the girls died writhing in pain, covered in vomit and urine, their corpses left in the sun for three days before anyone noticed them gone and went looking. "Remember?" she said, smile stretching the width of her face.

Tabby went first, her cheeks puffing like a chipmunk's, ectoplasmic vomit dripping blue-green down her chin. Then came Tawny, the vessels in her eyes all burst from the pressure of the sickness, her skin going the greenish grey of rotten link sausages. Brenda held out the longest, but blackened fluid began dribbling from her nose and her tongue began stretching out like a dead fish, limp and off-white.

One of the women—one of the mothers—sighed appreciatively and reached into her wallet. "Fifty was not enough for this pleasure," she said and handed over an additional $20. "I mean, I was all for seeing the boys again, but Barb here convinced me it would be better to look into those dead eyes once more... Never did I imagine I'd get to see these bitches die a second time."

Another of the women held out a $20 of her own. She said, "Truly a gift from God Hisself."

Barb nodded and smiled. "If I had another buck...heck, if I had another fifty bucks, I'd give you every cent."

The Great Loudini took her hand. "The money is nice, but

this gift, bringing peace and happiness to the wronged, it makes it worthwhile."

—

The hapless trio of girls watched the women leave and the Great Loudini followed them to the door. He then re-entered his parlor. "Well, come on," he said and waved for the ghosts to follow him.

The girls floated an inch from the floor, unable to speak from the shock and the degradation and the reintroduced physical deformities of death.

"Through there." The Great Loudini pointed to the satin flaps hanging over a doorway.

Brenda mumbled around her bloated tongue, "What's there?"

"Whatever you want, probably. Your afterlife." The Great Loudini shrugged, then added, "Beats hanging around here."

One by one, the girls left the land of the living.

BETWEEN

(2014)

I once met a man who stated with an air proud and curious that he could only swim after consuming a copious amount of tequila, said he didn't even need the lemon or the salt. I never saw the man in the water. In fact, I'd only met him twice, both times on land hard and dry. I'm glad I got that second chance too, seeing him the second time gave me an opportunity to demand an explanation. From what I could figure, he was either a liar or the alcohol relaxed him to the point of buoyancy.

Why I should be thinking about him in my current stressful predicament might seem strange, but at the moment, I'm not in control of my thoughts—not that anybody ever really is in control of such a thing. Besides, the tequila floater is a nice distraction and I think I know why I've put the two things together—my situation and the man, I mean.

You see, the man explained not only that he could not swim without the Mexican specialty, but also that he feared the water. It was irrational, he knew it, but couldn't help it.

"Sea monsters," he started, "do you believe that? Serpents, toothy fish, octopuses, giant turtles, dragons, and cracks."

"Cracks?" We stood awaiting a bus south to Buffalo—heading to a much further destination—it was cheapest to cross the border by way of bus and hop on an American flight down to Mexico. Back then anyway.

"Cracks," he repeated and stepped onto the bus.

A pushy woman butted in while I stood at the doorway, in her defense the peculiarity of the answer caused a stutter in my forward motion. Once on the bus, I wanted to enquire further but

I didn't see the man again. Part of me hoped he headed to where I headed, but two years passed before out paths crossed, long after I'd ended my social experiments in foreign land inebriation. It turns out people don't love Canadians with such an automatic nature as sitcoms might have the population assume. Nobody loves young drunkards but other drunkards.

In front of a store window years later, Christmas in St. Catharines, I was killing time. My shopping was long done when that man strode up next to me. Now, I am not from St. Catharines and the bus where I'd first met the tequila floater was more than an hour's drive north of any part of Niagara, but there he stood, next to me admiring the same mechanical Lego display.

A brown and red train followed a white track around a mock Central Park, a patch of plastic ice in the valley of plastic towers, little plastic men, women, and doggies staged on plastic skates. It was lovely and I'd posted there a while, cataloguing it to my memory.

"Quite a thing, don't you think?"

I turned; it was then that I recognized him. "You're the man afraid of cracks and sea monsters."

I don't think he recognized me. "Only when I look at water or look at water and haven't consumed a goodly amount of tequila," he said.

"What exactly did you mean by cracks?" The question had been a pebble in my boot, one that wouldn't fall no matter how much I shook my upturned footwear.

"The change in climate is shifting the ocean floor, cracks of cold emptiness draw in swimmers to feed prehistoric beasts." His expression suggested that he knew it was asinine, but couldn't help it, it was a fear, his very own, and sharing it didn't seem to quell his anxiety. "I once knew a man afraid of children in blue shirts."

"Oh?" Any story starting like that and trailing after an explanation involving prehistoric dinner plates had to have some kind of punchline.

"Yes," he said and I waited.

"Well, what happened to him?"

The man turned from the Lego scene and looked at me. He had a fine spackling of salt and pepper patches of whiskers jumping from his face without shape or reason. He exhaled a steamy puff, looked at his boots and turned to walk away. "He didn't make it."

That was it. I called after the man, but sidewalk traffic swelled and the tequila floater was gone, probably forever. Based on my current predicament, it seems undeniably likely that it is a forever kind of uncertainty. But, forever isn't a long time for those destined for quick demise. At least the pain is gone. Still, I'll never know.

The reason I should think of the man at such a time is just my brain frantically reaching for connections, I'm losing hold, coming unglued. Accounting in life flashes.

He spoke of fears, irrational fears and the reason I was so confused by the cracks after our first meeting was that I am afraid of cracks. Not the same cracks, but cracks nonetheless.

It didn't come to me until I found myself where I am, fine time for a life altering understanding of my psyche, but at least it came. My parents were firm believers in physical activity, both finished in the top 1,000 among participants of the 1994 Boston Marathon out of something like 10,000 runners. Not a feat to sneeze at. We used to hike a lot, we had trails running much of the property, but it wasn't at home where I first found my fear.

The three of us travelled to the Elora Gorge to tour the caves. I was six, perhaps seven. I fell behind a moment as we maneuvered the cool rock alleyways. I called out, but heard only my own voice, echoed around the rooms and caverns. I panicked and ran. I followed what appeared the only possible path and found myself squeezed into a crack in the rock wall. From there, I attempted to backtrack, but the more I struggled the tighter the rock held. I screamed and cried. My parents finally returned to the cave to look for me. It was horrible and my parents said I would have to sit in the car all day if I didn't want to continue. I sat in that stuffy old station wagon for what seemed like eternity. They were serious about exercise.

After that day, I saw hungry cracks everywhere, it dimmed a great deal the older and more rational I became, but there was always the claustrophobic fear that a crack might appear and suck me away, chew me up and swallow me.

The actual fear of cracks morphed into dying between walls, any walls. I dreamed of rooms that shrunk and squeezed around me. I still saw the cracks, but they weren't necessary to the terror.

I told myself I was irrational but that didn't do much beyond making me feel down about my faulty brain. Losing my mind was the thought, but I didn't really have time to focus in that way, not with a life to live.

For more than a year, I'd worked on the lower end of the news spectrum, the kind of stuff where I had to handle scene, sound, video, and reporting all at once. It's a tough job, but it's where everybody starts. I'd followed the usual beginner stories, human-interest pieces about fundraising and heroic pets; I hadn't even had a chance to grow weary yet. If I had, I might've quit or demanded better stories, probably wouldn't feel every wall around me all at once, wouldn't know this predicament for real, let it stay a horrid fantasy.

I was busy rounding up streeters from the giant pumpkin patch—a regular-sized patch, the pumpkins were giant. To be clear. The patch is just south of the city, very near the racetrack, cars not horses. I had three and only needed three, but I wanted at least nine streeters to pluck the best from—a streeter being a quote or two from the average pumpkin looker. It was good for the website, filled a space leading up to Halloween.

The sun had just gone down and the orange lights amid the pumpkin vines lit, I knew I was out of luck for any more streeters, but I thought I might as well shoot some night footage. It had a wonderfully eerie appeal and the haunted house would start up in just a few days, so I wasn't too worried, I'd be back doing my best fright-face soon enough. I wouldn't have argued, even if I'd gotten to be a bigger time reporter. Halloween is my favorite time of year and I quite enjoy haunted houses, the rubber spiders and blasts of air always give me a smile; I haven't yet been inside a haunted house where the walls cracked and closed in on me. Never will, I suppose.

I'd gathered all the B-roll I would ever need of the pumpkin patch and powered down my camera. It was then that I heard the swooshing racket followed by the gentle humming. I looked around and everyone appeared frozen. Their faces were hidden to me from that angle, but none of them moved, silhouetted against the glow of the orange. I turned back to my car to retrieve my camera.

Whoosh, I heard and felt a gentle breeze against my cheek.

Hmm-hmm-hmm.

I stood still and listened. Done. Gone. I turned around and saw the people moving again.

It's not exactly professional, but every Halloween, Tap Town Bar and Grill serves a pumpkin brew that I can't get enough of, well I can, but I enjoy it a lot. I'd had two with my supper before I went out to the patch. I rarely consume alcohol and attributed the strange feeling to an alcohol related brain hiccup—that trip to Mexico really threw a coat of whitewash over the party animal that used to live in my belly. Amsterdam shortly after Mexico was the icing on the vomit-coated cake.

I decided I'd stave off enjoying any pumpkin beer from then forward until after my *shift* ended. I drove home that night feeling not at all drunk, but suddenly worried I was well over my limit, despite my clear head. I slowed and inched into the city and parked outside my apartment on the north end. I let out a heavy sigh and gathered my equipment to take upstairs. Leaving stuff like that in a rusty old Toyota in the parking garage basement is asking for the proverbial *it*.

As exhausted as I was, I fell asleep on my couch before I untied my shoes. I dreamed of cracks, wind bursts, and humming, but I don't recall in what relation they mingled in my dreamscape. I awoke with a fresh hatred, irrational and strong.

The next two days I could hardly focus. I saw cracks everywhere, cracks opening around me as I walked, inviting me in where I might spend the last moments of my life wailing in terror. I could taste the damp cool rock against my face, I could feel the pressure as my bones crumbled and burst. It was unnerving and left me with a sickly pit in my stomach.

On the day of the haunted house opening, this morning if the clock hasn't yet passed midnight, I felt fine, better than fine. I felt strong and ready, as if the story about the pumpkin patch were on the Pulitzer level. They'd never give the nod to something so frivolous and I knew it was irrational, but it suddenly felt of utmost importance.

I got there early, interviewed the owners. They were proud of their haunted house and it was to be the best one yet, the same thing they'd probably explained to the camera year after year. They weren't the story and I was only killing time until the real story kicked. I recorded the masses passing in line, it was near dark when I finally went through myself. A terrible letdown. The haunted house couldn't have scared a toddler. I stepped out the back and the proprietors stopped me for an interview of their own.

"Scared the socks from my feet and didn't need to untie my boots," I said, a nice lie is better than harsh truth whenever speaking with small business owners. Folks don't buy ad space when they're mad.

They thought what I said was terrific, clapping hands and laughing, a good old time for the couple. I patted the man's shoulder and headed out to my car.

Whoosh, the sound found me, a gentle coolness following.
Hmm-hmm-hmm.

The hum off in the distance. The moon was up and near dark was pretty well complete dark. I continued to my car, every fuzzy peach hair on my neck, back, and arms stood. The dream was starting to return to me, still hazy, but that sound, that whoosh and hum combination, led to something. What something? I couldn't place it, not yet. I quickened toward the parking lot, the gravel grinding beneath my feet and I thought of all the potential cracks between the stones. Crunching cracks.

I jogged.

Whoosh.

The hum was closer and for the first time I understood that a conscious-being owned this voice. "Hmm-hmm-hmm, Peter, Peter Pumpkin Face, had a fear he couldn't trace." The voice was high and feminine, yet far from human. I'm not proud, but I screamed, and ran, the camera on my shoulder suddenly feeling an unbearable anchor. I dropped it and fished my keys from my pocket.

Whoosh, the breeze wasn't so gentle.

"Hmm-hmm-hmm, Peter, Peter Pumpkin Ears, knew the end and found his tears."

Until the voice spoke, I hadn't realized my waterworks, but I sobbed with the release of an infant.

Frantic, I pulled my keys out of my pocket and they fell to the ground. Feeling around my feet, whining and pleading, weeping and wailing.

Whoosh, the breeze was a wind.

"Hmm-hmm-hmm, Peter, Peter Pumpkin Nose, bones shivered from head to toes."

"What do you want?" I pleaded with the night sky. The moon rode enormous and orange like a massive pumpkin. The dream came back in a flash upon seeing it. I rushed double time then, sweeping my hand over the gravel. I located my keys and jumped to my feet. I hit the panic button; I'd lost sight of anything but the night and the moon. My car didn't respond and I spun, hitting the button frantically, again and again.

Whoosh, the wind that picked me up and launched me into the air had fingers. As I flew, the voice called on my heels. She was in my hair and under my clothes. Vines, hard and spiked with horrid fat fuzz.

"Hmm-hmm-hmm, Peter, Peter Pumpkin Eyes, your biggest fear is how you die."

I screamed and felt my body falling toward the earth. The ground opened. A bright orange fissure cracked. My body fell in and the walls closed over me, green vines holding me in place.

Once I'd stopped screaming, I felt the slow constriction of the cold damp earth around me, heard the bones in my feet and shoulders crushing into dust. The pain shocked me from experiencing the trauma and I was allowed to observe the walls closing around me, the whoosh and humming long off in the distance.

It was then that I once again thought about the tequila floater, then that I thought about his irrational fear, then that I thought about my own irrational fear. It wasn't a lot to consider and happened in the matter of a few seconds.

In a way, we were both silly for our fears, mine of cracks themselves and his of monsters let loose from cracks. Both on their own are irrational, but together, cracks and their monsters are something worth fearing. In these late in the game seconds of my existence, I'm starting to understand that irrational fear is worthwhile after all. Fear of things unknown.

Cracks and pumpkin patches.

WARNING SYMPTOMS

(2016)

Out the window of his grandfather's Ford, Antoine watched a world pass by that he had not seen since he was very small. The bleached yellow grass of the roadside ditches reached to the pale blue sky like malnourished fingers, boney and sharp. He held no memory beyond an inkling familiarity that chained the past to the present.

He'd seen his grandparents regularly enough to know them, recall the sweet licorice scents and the hints of farm bouquet—manure, grass, smoke, mold, and endless decay. The olfactory sum of life and death. Birth, growth, and waste, recycled.

Antoine had had a hard year. His parents split, and his mother moved him to a tiny bungalow with stained peach siding and a filthy sandbox in the backyard. The neighbor kids on both sides didn't like him because they knew his mother from the high school cafeteria. Twat, bitch, slut, were the words they used. Antoine didn't tell his mother what they said. Didn't want to hurt her feelings. Antoine was eight and knew that those words were bad things. They were negative in tone and that was plenty to understand. It was okay that his mother wanted a week to herself and it was even good to go all the way to his grandparents' place. His mother promised him that he'd eat dessert every night after supper, but grandma might make him pull beans and grandpa might make him help feed the animals. That was okay too.

Riding along the cloudy driveway, the boy listened to his grandfather hum to Abba on radio—*Dancing Queen...young and sweet and only seventeen*. His mother listened to that really old stuff sometimes because it's the kind of thing her parents played around the house. Antoine wondered if that meant that he would play the old stuff once he grew old as his mother, old as his grandfather. Old beyond imagination.

"There's my little guy. There's Mister Antoine!"

Antoine solidified his stance as the huge, warm bosom of his grandmother engulfed him. She smelled like piecrust.

"Boy, you're getting big!"

"I hardly recognized him! Geez, better than a foot taller than the Christmas card. Soon he'll be taller than his mama," Grandpa Gene said.

"Sure, sure." Grandma Mag released the boy. "Let's get ya inside, you've got to tell us all about the trip."

It was nice to be back, even if he didn't really remember ever being there. His grandparents were happy. So often his mother was sad. He never saw his father anymore.

They ate chicken with beans and taters, fresh biscuits on the side. Cherry pie closed the event. Antoine sat back and mimicked his grandfather, hand rubbing his little belly, eyes to the ceiling. Grandma Mag lit her after supper cigarette and busied herself with the dishes.

"You catch that stinker yet?"

Grandpa Gene shook his head. "I haven't seen a lick of him. Haven't seen those three others either. Too damn many kitties already."

"Maybe a coyote got them and they're not off birthing...all three were mighty fat though, weren't they? Damned things."

Antoine had no clue and asked, "What things?"

"Oh, the damned barn cats, we have too many. Folks know we feed them and drop off their cats at the end of the lane like we're the pound. Then the toms come sniffing and we get into collecting kitty cats." Grandma Mag waved her cigarette, fed up.

"Then what happens?"

"Then some have to go," Grandpa Gene said.

"Go where?"

Grandma Mag ignored the question. "You see those big bugger toms come around and you just shoot 'em. Damned things must smell the heat for miles. Only see them twice a year, like they're punching a kitty-cat timeclock."

"Punching the kitty-cat timeclock ain't such a bad thing." Grandpa Gene had come to stand behind his wife's ample rump while he bussed his plate. Hands emptied, he gave a squeeze.

"Get out of here, you," Grandma Mag scolded, playfully. "Why don't you take Mister Antoine out to feed the herd?"

—

The barn was old and the summer twilight streamed between the board gaps. Antoine carried a repurposed ice cream bucket full of brown kibble. Grandpa Gene carried a .22 rifle with a rust brown barrel and a pale brown stock. The food and the firearm did not associate well. Neither did the notion of what a tom was or what punching the kitty-cat clock meant.

High and snappy, like a cartoon chipmunk, Grandpa Gene shouted, "Here kitty-kitty! Here kitty-kitty-kitty-kitty!" He then added, "All right, pour that into those dishes and mind your hands."

Antoine barely heard the man. The scene before him was incredible. He saw two cats lazing on the lawn when he had arrived, so he knew the kibble was for the cats, but he never guessed. From between square bales and round bales, darting from the shadows, leaping down from the mows, and scurrying along from the ancient beams, cats oozed. Three dozen or more.

The hungry animals rubbed against his shins, tripping him up as he tried to walk. It was a swarm of furry wonder. Some had goopy eyes. Some had runny noses. Some had stubbed tails. Some had scabs and patches of fur missing. One had only three legs. One had a single eye. They all had mouths and all of those mouths snapped at the kibble as Antoine poured it into the dishes.

"You stay where ya are. I've got the chores in the basement.

Don't trouble the cats until the food's gone. A few might find your fingers tasty."

Antoine looked back at his grandfather in silent awe. It was a half-joke, hungry carnivores were not above snapping meaty accidents from unsuspecting hands.

"Oh, and if a real big sonofabitch comes out, mostly white with a black cap, almost big as a dog, you yell to me. There's another tom, too. I haven't seen him since the first of spring," Grandpa Gene said. "You see the big white one with the black cap or a massive orange sonofabitch, you call to me."

Antoine nodded. His mouth agape, still.

The food lasted a little less than three minutes. Some of the cats ate only a little before running away. The biggest, eldest cats stayed at the dishes, leisure feasting. Antoine sat on a straw bale and tried the catcall.

"Kitty-kitty-kitty," he said, fumbling; the words felt strange on his tongue. "Here kitty-kitty-kitty."

Like magic, despite his inability to say it well, two skinny cats ran to his feet. He stroked their backs. The love-starved animals bounced beneath his hands. Antoine was a happy boy.

—

Sunny overhead and hot. In the backyard behind the house, grandson and grandmother took up space, busy with different tasks.

"Do you name them?" Antoine asked his grandmother.

She sat in a lawn lounger with her feet in the grass. There was a pail between her knees, and a big bin of rinsed and whole strawberries to her right. On her left was a pile of leafy tops cut away from the meat of the fruit. She'd cut the strawberries into little red discs and let them fall into the pail between her knees. Antoine offered to help, but she told him that he was on vacation.

"Sometimes, the nice ones, I name them, but there's so damn many coming and going."

"Do these ones have names?"

"Not 'til you name 'em."

Both grey tabby cats. Brother and sister of the same litter. Born 11 months earlier.

"Um, okay. This is Larry and this is Carla."

Grandma Mag laughed.

—

Antoine thought that maybe he'd done it wrong. The following day when he sat in the dusty, manure smelling barn, he christened cats with all kinds of names. For hours he sat stroking and playing with the happy, barn-stinking animals. Even the timid cats came to meet him, eventually. The big tom was last and stayed only a moment before running off. It wasn't until Antoine saw the loose, former fat belly swinging that he recalled the description of the size and the cap on its head that he took to heels to find his grandfather.

"I saw the tom! Grandpa Gene! He's in the barn!"

Grandpa Gene was in the shed, sweaty, and only just returned from the field with a wagon of round hay bales. "That right?" Grandpa Gene went to the steel cupboard and retrieved the .22 rifle. "Go on and find your grandma."

Four minutes later, Antoine stepped inside the house. Like a bolt of lightning, a headache struck. His vision glazed and he saw gold strings everywhere. Hazy white light passed around him, sweet scents and jarring dissociation: confusing up from down and a hot sensation searing into his skull. The tremendous pain behind his right eye made him feel like dying. He screamed and screamed, not words, only high-pitched vowel sounds. Down, the boy dropped, writhing and kicking, trying to backpedal from the agony.

"Lord, what's happening?" Grandma Mag gathered Antoine from the floor and put him on the couch. Blood trickled from the corner of his eye and from his ear. "Lord, Jesus, Lord!"

She dialed 911 while Antoine whined and mewled. The

paramedics arrived 16 minutes later. Antoine was wide-awake and had no memory of the pain or what he'd seen. The blood ceased dripping and the paramedics saw nothing wrong with him, still, Antoine earned a ride in the back of an ambulance.

"It appears to be a freak thing. I can't see anything wrong with the boy. You're his grandparents?"

The doctor was new and Antoine's grandparents had never met him. Heard of him—the community was small enough that news of a new doctor moved faster than a party balloon in a hurricane. The discussion was short and inconclusive.

"Lord, you scared the bejesus out of me, Mister Antoine," Grandma Mag said.

"I'm sorry," Antoine said. The massive, familiar bosom again eclipsed his world.

—

On the third day, Antoine asked his grandfather about the tom. The boy was in the barn and only a few cats came around. The busy work of rolling hay bales kept the older animals skittish. The yearlings and lesser didn't yet know all the fear that they ought to.

"I shot him. Ugly business but couldn't be helped. That one had a wily pecker. Got too many cats pregnant, that tom did. Too many cats gets 'em sick. Sick cats turn with the seasons. They aren't so happy come wintertime and soon enough, all the cats are sick. Geez, some days I find two or three, rock solid and dead as Terry Sawchuk.

Antoine frowned. He knew about killing animals for their own good but didn't understand how it worked exactly. Too many questions often annoyed adults and made him feel stupid and still...

"You don't have to kill no more, do ya?"

"Might have to, sometimes it's best to get the kittens gone before they become too much trouble. It's ugly business, ugly business. Farm life is not for the weak of stomach. I know it sucks and people get upset. Those animal rights folks with the big ideas don't actually have a plan for these animals. I hear 'em on TV talking about spaying and neutering, but hell, who's gonna pay for that? These kitty-cats seem to pop from thin air sometimes. Say I let them all live, there's sure not enough food, then they get sick, and who pays all the vet bills?"

"Not you," Antoine said, catching the rhythm of the message.

"Damn tootin'. Culling is ugly, but it's the lesser of evils."

Antoine patted the heads of Sugar Bear, Whiskers, and Larry. The cats swirled like slow-motion baton streamers around his legs. A cat Antoine had never seen before moseyed into the barn. She had a loose belly and pink running down her hind legs.

"Ah, hell," Grandpa Gene said. "Do me a favor. Keep an eye on that girl. Follow her, not too close, but follow her. Find out where she's hidden her brood."

—

The task took a day and a half. First Antoine was too close and then he was too far. The cat lost him twice more, but eventually he found the kittens. They were in the back of a rotten horse trailer amid the long grass, down by the creek.

"That mama got her kittens in the horse trailer, I think. I didn't get too close," a winded Antoine said.

Grandpa Gene had been assisting with the potato cleaning and peeling in the backyard. He dropped his half-peeled tater back into the bucket near Grandma Mag's feet.

"Antoine, meet me by the creek where it's deep swamp. You know, where we caught that little rainbow trout. Gather up a few good-sized rocks."

Antoine nodded and rushed away. Grandpa Gene headed to the barn for a burlap feed sack and a length of bailer twine. At the creek, he met up with his grandson. "Hand me the rocks, one at a time." The sack wriggled by his feet and little mewling sounds filled the air. The mother cat was furious and frantically pawing at the sack. "Quick now. Mama ain't happy with me." Grandpa

Gene kicked out at the protective cat.

Antoine did as told and watched his grandpa's thick fingers wind the twine round and round before knotting the tie, twice.

"You run along now."

Antoine understood that it was the ugly business and he didn't really like how those kittens sounded in the bag. He turned and jogged a dozen steps before he heard the splash and saw his vision split into six views. White walls. Fuzzy fur limbs. Tiny pink paws. Bugging eyes. Water reached down his throat and grabbed for his lungs. The boy wailed and thrashed on his back in the long grass. The open world enclosed over him like a sopping blanket.

"Antoine? Antoine?" Grandpa Gene rushed to him.

The boy's screams gargled, all vowels. Water poured out from his lips.

"What in Jesus?" Grandpa Gene picked up his grandson and started running. "Hang on, boy, hang on!"

By the time they'd crossed the yard and reached the house, the boy peered at the sky with a vacant gaze. His breathing had stopped and Grandpa Gene cried out for Grandma Mag.

Grandma Mag knew CPR and went to work. Four heavy pumps to the boy's dry chest sent a great splash from his lungs. Brownish from bile, but clearly creek water.

The boy had nearly drowned on dry land.

"Lord, what's happening? What's happening?" Grandma Mag whined as she cradled Antoine. "Jesus, Lord."

Antoine bore the pain in his chest and his cough was harsh. He was spooked, curious. There was no memory of his fit.

—

Sorry to leave, Antoine waved from the platform of the ferry with the small cat he'd named Carla held tight to his chest. From the loading dock, Grandpa Gene and Grandma Mag waved back. It was a three-hour sail to the mainland where his mother waited for him. Farm life was too scary, his fits were even scarier, and he'd had to leave a day earlier than scheduled. They agreed that maybe a doctor on the mainland had better mental tools for diagnosing a mystery.

Home, Grandpa Gene carried the .22 on the ready and Grandma Mag carried the ice cream tub of kibble.

"Here kitty-kitty! Here kitty-kitty-kitty-kitty!" Grandpa Gene said.

The swarm poured from everywhere. They swirled legs and circled the dishes. Some stood patiently knowing the foreplay unnecessary.

"Here kitty-kit—"

The cats rolled onto their backs, mouths open, screaming voices beyond their natural chords. "Carla, come back! Wait! No! I'm here! Help! I can't swim! Help! I'm in here! Help!" Claws extended. Fur stood out as if shocked. Tails straightened. Their little noses fired liquids, snot and water mostly.

"Dear, Jesus," Grandma Mag said, recognizing the voice coming from the chorus of barn cats. "This can't be! That can't be Antoine!" The kibble tipped from the pail as her hand loosened its grip.

"Somebody! Mommy!" the cats cried out, eyes bulging wildly, pawing at the sky. "Help...please!" The voices became muddled, swishy. Water choked the cats and they spat the final voiced screams. "Help, don't leave me! No, don't leave me! No! I'm still here! Carla? I need Carla! Down with the cars! I'm with the cars, come get me! Carla, where did you go? I don't wanna drown!" The remainder of the sounds rode bubbled tones before the gargling took over and the cats suddenly ceased their frantic movement. Their little bodies seemed to bob on the barn floor, as if on waves amid the arrant straw. A final whisper trailed, as if spoken through a mouthful of toothpaste, "I saw Carla, but where'd she go? Where'd Carla go? Where'd—?"

Grandma Mag dropped the dish and bolted from the barn. Grandpa Gene stood an additional minute, watching the cats come to. Sitting proper as if trained, the furry bastards seemed to smile at him, knowingly.

Grandpa Gene ran then. This was a freak thing and had nothing to do with their little Antoine. *Couldn't!*

Phone in hand. "Sylvia? It's your mother. It's Margaret. Did the boat—? Oh Lord. Dear God. Sank? No, I'm sure he's on one of the lifeboats, too. I'm...Lord. Yes, of course... You'll call me when you know for sure. All right?"

"The ferry sank?" Grandpa Gene whispered.

Margaret hung up and turned. "Gene, pray with me."

DEATH GAME

(2015)

Chittering and chattering, squeaky like crickets and low as gong drums, the voices, song and conversation forever, filled the air. Growls and ticks, electricity and oil: the soundtrack of civilization. All that slid behind the quiet sounds, the chirps and clicks, the night creepers calling out from the tall corn. All of it piled together reached the point where it became part of the silence. Silence being the perception of calm and ease.

We always hear our hearts.

We always hear the blood flow.

We always hear both until we don't and true silence, true calm overcomes.

Visurum se mortem, ne sileas: the phrase followed her, tormented her, damned her very existence. Like the creepers in the corn, the television was a piece of the silence, always on, unnecessary, but helpful. Children generally needed guidance, so the television was a perfect parent. TV mothers and fathers became living lessons for a moral existence. Television, like breathing, like heartbeats...a constant until it isn't.

"I'm hungry," the boy whined, he was around eight.

Tia looked over her shoulder, exhaled a lungful of cloudy once tobacco, and shrugged. She wasn't a babysitter, she was just a chauffeur, of sorts. "Take a five, find a machine, and come right back."

"What about me?" The girl was angry. She was younger than the boy, but not by much.

"Share with your brother," Tia said. It wasn't exactly a paying gig, she only took payment from the bodies of murdered parents, whatever they had handy: wallets, purses, clips. She rarely had time to scavenge with impunity, never took enough to fatten her pockets.

The police chased Tia, robbery they said, kidnapping they said, murderer they said, capture they promised, and the faces on the all-day news stations screamed for her blood. Tia Ramone, wanted in connection with 49 murders, 49 robberies, and 111 kidnappings. They were way off, didn't have a clue.

Firstly, she'd chauffeured more than 200 children and hadn't murdered anyone. You can't own anything if you're dead, so she didn't rob those parents and sitters. They were dead and that money went to the next in line for as long as the kids stayed with her.

She stared out the window, puffing, anxious, listening for the children out in the hallway. She lived her life in motels, eating chocolate bars and potato chips, coffee brewed in tiny pots, never stopping long enough for someone to clue into her face and that grainy image on the news station warnings or *Unsolved Mysteries* or *America's Most Wanted.* She'd been to every continent and visited more countries than she cared to count, but only once had a camera caught her.

"How many more?"

She looked out at the moon for an answer. The moon knew everything but kept its secrets. That moon knew the past too, knew she was once just a regular girl, a girl on her way to a regular life with regular dreams, but that was then. Before.

She listened closely, stubbed out her cigarette. The children, where had they gone? She switched off the television and listened to the heightened silence. Nothing but the creepers in the corn. She opened the door and looked out to the cement walkway.

The children sat on a bench outside the room and ate ice cream cones. Tia let the door close, as long as she knew where they were, as long as the creepers chirped, as long as the silence never reached the point of only blood and heartbeat.

"Ice cream cones?" She smiled thinking about the cones she'd gotten with her mother as a little girl, but then... "Where'd they get ice cream cones?" The smile sagged into a frown.

She opened the door and looked out. The children were where they'd been, the girl's feet dangling and the boy leaned forward far enough to touch the concrete.

"Where'd you get the ice cream?"

The boy held out the five-dollar bill. "A man gave it to us."

"I told you, don't talk to anyone until we get you home," Tia said.

"We didn't talk to nobody," the girl said, she wore a clown's smile of chocolate.

"Yeah, he just asked and we nodded, we didn't say nothing." The boy licked his lips.

This demanded investigation. Free ice cream sounded like some pervert. "Where?" The children pointed to the motel office. "Get into the room and wait."

Dejectedly, the children slid off the bench and stomped into the room. Tia stepped away from the door, key in her pocket. "Don't open this for anyone."

The air was thick with humidity, a storm brewing quite literally in the clouds overhead. A storm brewing inside Tia too, she didn't like goody types, didn't care for their nature because it was rarely true. Monsters hid everywhere. There's a reason men give candy, same reason men offer jewelry and flowers.

"A trade," she said and pushed open the office door, *remember when you weren't so distrusting, so paranoid?* "That girl's long gone." The room appeared vacant. She hit the bell on top of the counter. "Hello!" she called, heard nothing, silence— blood, heartbeat, creepers, television. The bell dinged nine more times in quick succession, then she stepped around the counter into the *Employees Only* space.

An old man sat in a recliner, the television so loud it was no longer a piece of silence. Tia looked at the back of his head. It was a motionless ball of white and bald, some pervy old man working a motel thanks to a criminal record, she suspected. Guys like that had to work the edges of civilization.

"Hey!" She reached out and touched him, his body shook a little. She lowered the volume. "Wake up!" She shook him again. The place smelled of tobacco and old beer. "Hey!"

He opened his eyes, empty sockets, a gush of red poured free, he opened his mouth and let out a breath, tongue gone, a moan and more of that hot red stuff. The man was in the wrong life at the wrong time. She stared a moment longer and then clenched her fists, punched a wall.

It was all a trick to get her from the children. She had to learn the tricks as she went and no matter how many she figured out, there was always another rub. If only she'd paid attention that day two years ago, if she'd never run over that priest, if she hadn't watched the children tear away pell-mell only to fall dead seconds later. Not a day had gone by that she hasn't regretted taking that dying priest's hand and letting him whisper those words into her ear, *Visurum se mortem, ne sileas*, kissed her palm until the light flashed on her mind, and offered her an insight so horrid she couldn't help but act. So many children.

She covered the screaming man's mouth and listened, silence but for the blood travelling near her ears, the beat of her heart. Even the creepers were silent.

"Shit!"

She ran from the office, wiping her bloody hand against her pant leg, already knowing the worst was just around the corner. At her door, the keys fumbled between her anxious fingers, she heard the screams of the children. The door opened. There it was: the black cloak and the long bony fingers with shimmering blue flesh, touching the boy's chest.

"No!" Tia screamed, tears flowing.

The boy fell as if his bones were no longer interested in their duty, joining his sister on the floor, lifeless, fingers still sticky with ice cream. The shrouded figure turned and faced Tia. Here was a game as old as time, older than she'd been alive. There was no answer, no winner. She only had to play her parts: foresee, collect, and run.

"Just because you see, it doesn't mean you need trouble," said a voice as smooth as Barry White's coming from a face of paper-thin flesh pulled tight against bone and hollow cheeks, teeth, and eye sockets. "Death always wins. It's the rule of life."

Tia lunged but Death disappeared in a cloud of black smoke that trailed through the pinholes in the screen of the open window. She'd pack and leave. The police would come, and she drive until she sensed the presence.

"Visurum se mortem, ne sileas," she said staring down at the bodies.

She thought if she could save one, just one, from Death's grip, these horrors she foresaw would vanish and let her live in the loud mystery of life. Live in the loud mystery until it was her turn at true silence.

Visurum se mortem, ne sileas. See death, be the savior.

DICHOTOMY GROUNDS

(2015)

Two died on impact. Strong and healthy roots from separate, and yet entangled, family trees gone in an instant. A third involved in the collision died while the screaming sirens and the bright lights cleared a path and offered sidewalk gawkers grounds for speculation. The ambulance carted not much more than a still warm corpse. However, if his life's work meant much, he was in a better place. Being a man of the cloth suggested no less than Heaven. Two others survived, riding away in their own ambulances; to add to the chaos of the scene, there was the sixth body.

A body long cold and days dead. It almost seemed as if the corpse had dropped from the sky. A young woman with a locally familiar face. Carrie Howe's face. She had gone to see a friend named Sandi and had never showed. That face that had been on the news all week. There had been a fight with the parents, and according to the teary-cheeked mother, "Carrie was a good girl, acting out, that's all."

The girl—14 and willfully making all the wrong decisions— left the house in a short skirt and a fishnet top that showed off a fluorescent pink halter beneath. On her feet were pink heels. A search party began some 31 hours after Carrie should've reached Sandi's. The only trace had been a muddy pink pump in a ditch.

Carrie hadn't been the first girl to go missing along that stretch of HWY #16. She was the first to reappear on it, however. Though she was dead, local detectives couldn't help but to be optimistic—somewhere in that wreckage was the person or persons responsible for taking her.

The two who had made it to the hospital alive shared a wide room featuring two additional beds, both left empty due to the sensitive nature of the situation.

A frustrated detective waited outside the door, he'd been blocked from question attempts and he *needed* to get in there. Family members came and went, eyeballing him suspiciously. None stopped to speak.

—

Eliza Goodman, 31, no husband, no children, clung to life, a ghost of her former self. She'd paled dramatically, it was almost as if her body was trying to play chameleon upon the white, white sheets. Her lungs needed regular drainage even after the first surgery—surgery that should've repaired the issue. Things didn't look good.

"Look at her, I mean just look at her," Maria Goodman said to her husband. She gripped a battered brown Bible, sticky tabs jutting in a rainbow of colors along the edges. "Is it too late?"

Bryan Goodman put his hand on his wife's shoulder and pulled her to his chest. "I don't know," he said into her scalp.

Hell. Over the years, they'd discussed their daughter's fall from the Lord's embrace, and thought they'd have time to reconcile. Now, there'd be no redemption if she never awoke.

"We should've tried harder," Maria said. Tears danced down her face. "She's doomed if she doesn't wake up and beg the Lord, beg His forgiveness for what she'd said."

Bryan shook his head gently. "The best we can do is pray for His leniency."

"Can our faith carry her?" Maria swiped a tissue beneath her nose.

A machine attached to the woman in the bed next to Eliza beeped frantically and the woman leaned forward, gasping around a skinny tube down her throat. Her eyes scanned and her arms flailed with frantic swipes.

"Bryan, get the nurse," Maria said as she ran to the panicked woman.

Bryan raced out of the room, his sneakers squeaking on the waxy floor.

The detective tried to stop him. "What's going on?"

Bryan ignored him and got to the nurses' station. It wasn't far, but it didn't say anything about cardio in the Good Book, not directly anyway. He huffed and gasped, mouthing words. The nurse got the just of it and jogged past him.

The detective demanded information from the nurse. She ignored him. He stopped Bryan, this time making a barrier of himself. "Is that woman awake? Has she asked for anyone by name?"

Brian shook all over. "She's passing! Get out of the way!"

The detective couldn't risk waiting and followed the harried man inside—there was a better than average chance one of the women in the room was a serial killer, or in bed with a serial killer.

The nurse busied herself with a needle over the washroom's sink. Eliza was asleep. Brian clenched and unclenched fists. Maria read from her Bible as the panicked woman nodded along. Her greasy blonde hair crawled over the bandage on her head, falling into her eyes as she struggled against the pain.

"For...give...me...Je...sus! God!"

The beeping became frantic. The nurse raced back and tripped on a loose shoelace, spilling her forward, the needle skittered under the heat register. She yelled a chorus of near-obscenities and crawled across the room seeking the needle. The detective stepped up and put his hands on the mattress next to the woman.

"Ursula Donaldson, did you kill Carrie Howe alone?"

The woman's eyes flashed, even as she continued panicked jerking and gasping. "For...give...me...God!"

"Get out!" the nurse shouted as she jabbed the needle into the woman's arm.

Another nurse entered, then an orderly and a doctor. The detective was ushered away and the Goodman's returned to the spot next to their daughter's bed. Though it wasn't their daughter's, they'd helped save a soul.

Ursula Donaldson made it three more hours, but never regained consciousness, dying at exactly 7:00 PM. It was sad, but there was still a chance for Eliza. She'd gone in for another surgery at 6:00 PM and the doctors said it went well.

The following morning, Eliza had another surgery. Maria read aloud from the Bible; Brian nodded along with the words. They remained in the room until a doctor with three drops of blood up the forearm of his shirt came in to give them the bad news.

—

Eliza opened her eyes. She was warm and relaxed and yet, she didn't feel herself. Physically, she felt tighter and yet her muscles were loose and willing. It reminded her of high school but without all the acne. She sat in a field, her mind in a fog. The memory of how she'd gotten there was gone. She recalled being in Kate's car. Malcolm was behind her. Both Malcolm and Kate had sunburns on their backs, forcing them to sit forward in their seats. They were singing a song. But what?

Catchy as hell...and then what?

Eliza got to her feet and looked around. The grass was luscious green and full, without weeds, nary a single yellow dandelion marring the perfection. The sky was a comforting pale blue, the clouds puffy and void of color, void of rainfall threat. She brushed at her short dress, curious. She'd had the dress in the ninth grade. Fitting into it now should've felt eerie given the impossibility, but it didn't. She liked the dress and was happy that it fit again.

A ways ahead, there was a road, dark and long and smooth. She began to walk, the grass pleasant beneath her feet.

"What was that song?" she asked herself, stopping as the sound of her voice registered fully. "Hello, hello. My name is

Lizzy. Mo, mo, me, me." Her voice was light and high, higher than when she and Kate and Malcolm sang along to that damned song.

An urge took hold and she skipped toward the road, humming the tune of the song she couldn't remember. So catchy, and yet, what was it?

"Who cares about the song? How did you get here? Where is here?"

Just before the road, a patch of flowers she'd somehow missed earlier lined the ditch and shoulder. Butterflies fluttered and rubbed their feet where they stood on colorful petals. As she drew close, the butterflies took flight as if of one mind. A single beautiful creature with black circles over large blue and yellow wings remained until it danced on air toward her. It landed on the tip of her nose. She smiled and wrinkled her face. A sneeze rocked her head forward and the butterfly followed its friends.

She bent to pick an orange wildflower. Naturally, she slipped it into her hair. It seemed such a strange thing to do, and yet...

A gentle breeze put the scent of pine in the air from the forest on the other side of the road. She stepped into the gravel, ready for pain, at minimum, irritation. She found neither.

"I could walk here forever," she whispered and continued down the road.

The sun began to set behind her, and she assumed she headed eastbound. Meaning... *what should be up there?*

Before her mind could conjure an answer, a truck rolled along the road behind her. It was bright and shiny, but older, from the '90s. Eliza lifted her hand. Normally, she'd never flag a truck down, but here and now, this felt utterly right.

The truck slowed. A big Ford with a double-sized cab. A blonde woman with a thin-lipped grin sat behind the wheel. She reached over to turn down the radio and swung open the passenger's side door. Nelly Furtado's *I'm like a bird* quiet amid the tranquility when the door swung wide.

"Hello?" Eliza said as she stepped closer.

The driver pulled a denim jacket into the middle of the bench seat. "Hello, yourself. Need a lift?" The woman patted the empty seat.

"Maybe, where you going?"

"Don't know. I'm lost. I've been driving since last night and can't put my finger on where in the world I am, but it sure is pretty 'round here."

Eliza couldn't disagree. "Maybe I better wait for someone—"

"That's what I was thinking, of finding someone. Since last night, I've only found you. Maybe we can figure this out together."

"Umm," Eliza said, looking around; the urge to climb in the truck was fantastic, it seemed to tug from her soul outward.

The woman dropped her hand to the gear shifter. It had a blue and yellow butterfly inside its glass knob.

"I don't usually accept rides from strangers," Eliza said, sounding especially childish.

"Don't blame you there. Never know who'll come along."

At least it was a woman. Eliza nodded and followed her body's needs, climbing into the truck and sitting on the bouncy shotgun seat. She giggled, then covered her mouth and shook her head. She was acting so funny, almost befittingly so of the dress.

"Off we go, young miss," the woman said.

Eliza was about to say she was 31 but caught sight of her reflection in the door mirror. She was a little girl. The kind of girl who giggled and wore funny dresses and bounced on springy seats.

Something was off-putting about all of this perfection. Eliza forced her eyes to the road. The sun began setting with unnatural celerity.

"You like music?" the woman said as she brushed her long blonde hair behind her ear.

Eliza stared at the woman's strange earrings. Real butterflies stopped dead and hung stiff for fashion. "I guess."

"You like my earrings?" The woman tilted her head to offer a better view. "I love butterflies, don't you? Most girls love butterflies."

"I guess," Eliza said. Her stomach had begun to swirl in warning. This funny place, this funny her, this funny woman.

An old All-4-One song came on the radio and Eliza recalled a school dance, one from right around the time of her dress and her boyish shape. The time she let Robbie Dion feel her up. The memory made her laugh.

"What's so funny?"

"I remembered something," Eliza said. "A boy."

"Boys are trouble."

Eliza nodded to this.

They crested a hill.

"Look at that." The woman pointed through the windshield to a neon sign promising fuel and beds. "We ought to stop here, find out what's going on." The woman then offered an exaggerated yawn. "Could use a rest. I think we should stop. I'm getting," the driver yawned again, it seemed forced, "tired. What do you say?"

Eliza frowned. "I can't get a room with you." She then wondered what choice she had; she didn't have a purse, didn't have a credit card, she didn't even have her cell. She wished she'd never gotten out of Kate's Nissan.

Why did you? Dammit, what was that song?

The driver sniggered before Eliza could think any further. "A room? Uh, no darlin'. It's been fun and all, but we don't need a room. What's going to happen is, I'm going to reach over, you're going to struggle some, I'll hit you once or twice, you'll calm down a bit, but really, I'll wish you wouldn't. My hubby always liked the struggle, too. Then he'd do his thing, but he's not here, so we'll skip the sticky bit."

"What?" Eliza said, sounding small, small, small.

"See, I'll throw the seat flat and start my business. It's going to hurt, a lot. You might even give up for a while. Cry and moan for your mama and your pop. Once you're still, you'll feel a little something." The woman wheeled into the deserted truck stop as she spoke.

Eliza looked around for a weapon and found none.

"Don't worry, I'll be gentle in the end. I know how to treat a lady. I'm awfully ladylike myself. Ha!"

Eliza shook her head although she didn't quite comprehend, recognizing only that things were about to become much worse for her. The Mariana's Trench song Malcolm tried to push on her for the last month was on the radio. The woman ran her hand behind the front bench and it folded back, a smooth bed front seat to back seat.

"That's better, now, where was I?"

The driver grabbed onto Eliza by the shoulders and made to force her flat.

Eliza's heart hammered as she considered the best action. Out was better than in, as the saying went, and she tried the door handle. The woman punched her then, twice, two lightning strikes to the back of her head. Eliza wailed in surprise and pain as the woman dragged her flat, began squeezing her nubbin breasts like they were cold dough.

Physically she was a child, and perhaps mostly mentally, but the real her remained. She kicked at the window, forced her along the seat, driving her scalp into the woman's knee. The woman barked a noise, hands busily trying to control her pray. Eliza flipped and bit the woman's thigh through her blue jeans.

"You shit!"

Energy surging, Eliza jerked back and felt for the door handle. The door opened and she tumbled out. On the stereo, Carly Rae Jepson began to sing, "*I threw a wish...*" It was the song, from the car, from when they'd...crashed.

Eliza began hyperventilating in the gravel. The woman crawled across the bench seat and stepped out of the truck.

She loomed hugely, but so did the pack of elk that caused the crash and those other vehicles and the sunburns and the Carly Rae Jepson and the screeching metal. Now and then she'd blinked, saw paramedics, saw a nurse, the inside of a hospital room, a bandaged woman in another bed named...Ursula? She'd blinked more and saw her mother, her father, a man in a cheap brown suitcoat.

The woman withdrew an ugly, bulbous knife from somewhere and leaned close to Eliza. "You're gonna hurt all over before you die."

"Leave me alone!" Eliza shouted, trying to squirm away from the promise both this woman and her knife were making.

"God wants me to have you! That's why we're here."

The knife slipped across Eliza's arm just as a low, manly voice said, "I don't think so."

The knife let off and the woman backed off a step. "This is none of your business."

"I think it is," the man said. He had no fear of the knife, he gathered Eliza into his arms, lifting her with a surprising strength.

Eliza finally looked at him full on, recognized the Catholic collar, and despite her sourness toward the church, she accepted the new embrace.

"There you are, my child." The man held Eliza.

He carried her away from the lot and through a motel room door. The sound of tires spinning in gravel filled the world. The man sat Eliza on a single bed with old, scratchy sheets.

"Are you hungry?"

Feeling even smaller, as helpless as a young child, Eliza nodded emphatically as she sobbed.

"The Lord hates to see a child hungry."

The man stepped to an aged kitchenette. There was a row of cupboards and a small refrigerator. The father busied himself with a tray and what sounded like crackers.

Eliza inspected the room further, surprised by how un-motel-like it was. A worn wardrobe stood in a corner next to a ratty padded chair under a reading lamp. There was a child's desk with three images of a white Jesus above. On the desk was a thick, well-loved Bible.

"How about some music?" the father asked and without waiting for an answer switched on the radio. Carly Rae Jepsen's *Call Me Maybe* had started over. "This must be your song." There was a smile on his voice. "My song is by Tom Petty. I don't recall it from before...well, from before. It was on the radio."

Though it made no sense for her to say, Eliza said, "Can we call my dad?" Her voice was strange, stranger.

The father stepped back toward the bed carrying the tray of crackers. "In time, my son."

Eliza shook all over, wanted to shout. Everything was wrong. The father was strange. That woman before was terrifying. Eliza wasn't a boy, and she wanted her daddy! Instead, she sat in a respectable silence.

The father placed the tray over their laps as he sat next to her. Eliza looked down at the silver tray. Around the crackers she saw the reflection of the father and a small, boyish face with sad eyes, rosy nutcracker cheeks, and a bowl cut. Eliza shook her head gently, so did the boy in the reflection.

The father took a cracker and crunched.

Tears slipped down the cheeks of the reflected boy's face.

The father took another cracker, crunching it, his gaze heavy on Eliza.

It was impossible for her to move now. She'd become a terrified statue.

On the third cracker, he crunched and spoke with a breath of spat crumbs. "The Lord works in mysterious ways. You want to make the Lord happy, don't you, my son?"

Eliza stiffened.

"You do; the Lord wants those who follow Him happy. So,

you'll do as I say."

A finger touched Eliza's boy-knee and it struck her as Carly Rae Jepsen howled playfully: *that accident...I'm dead and this is, this is...* "This is Hell," she whispered.

The father unzipped the zipper of Eliza's trousers and said with his face against her neck, "How could this possibly be anything but Heaven?"

SUMMER SINGALONG

(2017)

"What's that smell?" Kat asked.

The stereo fizzed out on an electric snap. "Now what?" Wanda looked at her husband in the passenger's seat. The headlights shuddered.

It was not going well at all. Joel, Wanda, and the twins–Ally and Kat–had rolled along the gravel road, wipers swishing the downpour, branches reaching like spindly witch fingers, tickling the steel shell of their SUV. The rusty detour sign had directed them away from the happy zone of stadium lighting and smooth asphalt.

The Ford escape lost the last of its power and rolled six more feet.

Joel inhaled through his nose, added the smell to the visible symptoms. "The alternator's shot."

Since leaving the highway, it had been campfire-ghost-story-dark under the showery sky, but ahead, finally amid all those miles of darkness, there was a yard light.

Stopping in to visit a strange home in the middle of nowhere was Plan B. Wanda and Joel retrieved their Samsungs from the center console to find that neither had any service. Eyes returned to the home.

"What do you think?" Wanda asked. A silly fantasy floated home: Joel walking away only to return half an hour later with a new alternator and a pair of Mr. Fix-It hands. *Yeah, right.*

Joel turned around. "Okay, girls, we're going to run through the—"

In unison, they whined, "We're sleepy."

"Soon we'll be at a hotel with big beds and cable. Let's run for now, okay?"

Thoughts of the hotel drifted away as the giant home came into view. Great white pillars stood out front and a verandah rimmed the third floor. In the yard, a massive willow trees rose, leafless and awaiting the seasonal bloom. Wind shook limbs and the rain assaulted, slashing sideways. Two white orbs glowed atop steel posts on either side of a brick-chip laneway.

The home was dark inside.

On the porch, only feet from the door, Joel looked at his wrist, not yet midnight. "Guess we'll knock and ask for a phone?"

Wanda understood this phrasing to mean that she had to knock, just as she had to drive, just as she had to play bad guy when the girls asked for ice cream after a late supper because Joel had pointed it out on the menu.

Forward and steady, though weary of knocking so late, she lifted her hand to rap knuckles against the heavy brown door but stopped mid-swing. A placard emblazoned on thin, gold-tinted steel read: *Dr. Summer's Last Dance B&B, ring bell to summon.*

Incredible. "See this?" She pulled the rope dangling from the bell.

Ting. Ting. Ting.

It was such a tiny sound Wanda wondered what it could possibly do inside to wake anybody, doctor, manager, whoever. She knocked then. A gentle click sounded as the latch released and the door opened inward.

"Weird." Joel huddled the girls to his sides.

Wanda peered into the gloom. A giant shadow cast itself beyond the light emitting from behind the visitors. The floor looked like any stone floor. "Hello?"

No answer came. There was a scent. It was clean, with traces of rubbing alcohol.

"Maybe we better go back to the car," Joel said.

"Yeah, that's what we want to do, sleep in the car when

there's a bed and breakfast right here," Wanda said. "Hello?"

She stepped inside and her family reluctantly followed. They took turns calling out.

"Hello?"

"Hello?"

"Hello?"

Wanda felt the wall for a light switch and found a nubbin button. She pressed it and a buzz hummed through the vast space as old timey lamps came alive with soft golden glow. Straight ahead was a long harvest table equipped with 36 chairs. To their right was a library with a magnificent stone hearth. Great leather furniture and a marble table with gold gilded legs, two matching ashtray towers that stood near dark leather sofas completed the charm. To their left was a grand staircase that moved straight to the second floor before winding to a hallway and assumedly the third floor.

Closer than all that was a guestbook under a tiny light. She leaned over and read

Welcome. If late, sign in, pay in the AM.

Enjoy your stay.

"Mom, I'm tired!" the twins said, their timing off by a hair, creating a barbershop harmony whine.

"Yeah, me too." Wanda wrote her name, Joel's name, and *two kids* after that. "I guess we pick rooms."

The door behind them closed with a quiet click. Wanda led the parade. The rug on the stairs let them move in near silence. On the walls were portraits of men and women, doctors and nurses mostly. Also, landscapes: odd scenes of golden skies and burning trees, a grand building soaring amid the chaos. *Weird.*

The girls took the first room. Husband and wife took the second.

—

Ally awoke to a hand pressed against her and a forehead against her shoulder. "Get off," she mumbled. "Kat, it's too hot."

Hands slid down Ally's sides, over her damp tee, and stopped an inch below her ribs.

"Tickle, tickle," a harsh, feminine voice whispered.

The fingers dug and Ally laughed despite the fear, pain, and surprise.

"What'chu laughin' at?" Kat flipped over to face her sister. An unfamiliar and hairy spine, great spindly ridges poking from pale wrinkled flesh, shined in the dim moonlight seeping in through the cracked door to the hallway. She screeched and rolled from the bed, onto a throw rug.

From beneath the box spring, another set of slender feminine hands reached out. "Laughter's the best medicine, girly. Second only to singing!" Long fingers with trimmed, clean nails clasped onto Kat's ankles.

"Mommy!" Kat wailed as she clawed at the carpet, rolling it beneath her hands as she disappeared under the enormous bed. Eyes remained on the moon out there through the window until shadows devoured her view.

Kat laughed and wriggled, terrified and helpless. Alley screamed and thumped onto the floor.

"Tickle," one craggy womanish voice said.

"Tickle," said a second.

———

"Did you hear that?" Wanda sat up. She had fallen asleep after settling the girls next-door. "Joel." She swatted out and arm to an empty side. "Joel?"

Directly above her, beyond the hanging crystal light fixture and swirling plaster ceiling, a loud rolling called her attention. Three voices, one deep and two high, spoke aside from the almost bowling lane-like soundtrack. She waited for a crash of pins. The rolling continued as if the lane stretched forever and the balls were plentiful.

Wanda kicked her legs out from under the blanket and stood. "Joel?"

The light from the hallway glowed from beneath the door. Aside from this, she was essentially blind. Rather than following the light, she shuffled to the other side of the large room to the door that connected to the girls' room, arms out, fingers searching for a solid surface.

"Girls?"

No answer.

Panic rose. The voices from above grew louder. Words came in bursts. Wanda broke from the doorway, making for the light. She swung. The knob slammed plaster and wainscoting behind the door. The lights flickered.

On the floor, the rug was vibrant red with swimming lines of gold and black. It appeared almost endless when she began to run, passing closed doors and sepia photographs hanging on the walls. Very different from the paintings in the lobby: beach scenes, sunsets, boardwalks and, strangely, a cemetery plot featuring a small headstone and grass in various stages of sun-dried death. Wanda turned three corners before coming upon a staircase that ascended to the third floor.

A brass banister became a necessity along the steep gaps and irregularly deep steps. Her breath left her throat in huffs and the heat and humidity increased tenfold. Sweat re-dampened her already odorous clothing. It had been a long day that seemed poised to never end.

"Girls? Joel!"

Hair in a swampy bird's nest, Wanda finally reached the top of the stairs. She glanced back to nine perfectly normal steps that were anything but only a blink earlier. She ambled to a door; a light shining an aura along the edges of its frame.

"Joel! Ally! Kat!"

The smell of wet heat blasted her like an ocean side pork roast. Huffing achy lungs, she latched onto the door handle, and then jerked away. Hot. Searing. Her palm continued to cook, blistering, even with her hand pulled away.

"Dammit."

She used the tail of her shirt like an oven mitt and turned the knob.

"Oh my go—"

Hands reached from peripheral shadows and dragged her inside the room. The door slammed behind her.

—

The need to piss struck him like a champ's uppercut to the bladder. Wanda was asleep, so he snuck away like a cat burglar to locate a toilet, wearing only his boxer shorts.

Two doors down, nice and easy, he stood over an ancient porcelain throne with a high tank and copper chain flush, pissing into salty smelling water. His stomach bubbled and quickly, he ceased the flow, spun, and dropped to the seat, preparing for an emergency evacuation.

Joel moaned.

For six minutes, he switched between a Niagara Falls flow and a leaky faucet drip before his insides rested. The washroom was immense, a luxurious white on off-white with golden accents. There were strange abstract paintings of skeletons in tubs and barrels.

No toilet paper. Joel looked around and found two feet from where he sat was a second throne, a smaller tank below, a brass handle at the right side. He grunted, gave his ass a little shake, pulled the brass flush rope, and shuffled sideways to the secondary seat. He turned the lever and nothing happened. He turned it further.

"Please work."

He spun the lever full open.

A rush of air squeaked in pipes below the floor, and Joel felt a splash of water because that is what he expected. It took two seconds for the reality to force its way through the assumption.

"Ahh, ah!"

Joel leapt forward, the hot pain searing through his ass

cheeks, anus, and scrotum. Acid dripped down his thigh backs and toward his knees. His skin went from pink to red to open and gaping like a time-lapse video of maggots on a meal.

He dropped to the floor, hands over the pain. A new scream erupted as he brought his palms away with fresh torture, skin bubbling and oozing.

His only hope was the tub and he crawled, climbed in.

The water from the tap was cool, but only made the pain worse. Desperately, he spun the hot water lever and peered up at the golden showerhead. It hit him then. It wasn't water at all.

Gaze wide, mouth open, voice drowned by razor-fire liquid. His eyelids melted and eyeballs seeped, the milky fluids ran over his dissipating cheeks.

Joel thrashed against the chemical reaction scoring divots and valleys. Pits formed in his body like honeycomb, revealing clean white bones beneath. The acid running into his eyeholes gored his brain and his motion ceased.

The liquid continued to rain on the body. A tall man in white scrubs and black gloves up to his shoulders entered the washroom and closed the tub's plug. The acid rose and the pink mess sizzled, hunks of flesh disappeared like bacon fat in a pan. The tall man inhaled the burning scent and exhaled—a practicing slaughter yogi.

—

"Ally? Kat? Are you okay?" Gold-tinted shackles affixed Wanda's wrists and ankles to a rough stone wall. The girls sat together in an enormous gold bird's cage, huddled and weeping, hanging three feet from the floor.

"Mommy, I wanna go home," Kat said.

Alley nodded.

"I know, soon...your father will come soon."

Hearing it aloud made it almost laughable. Joel was not a figure of action. He lacked the necessary ovaries.

A bell dinged. The wail of the stones winding around the

ovular track two feet below the vaulted ceiling drowned much of the sound. One of the large stones was painted in swirling yellow, orange, and red, made to look something like the sun. The other was white with black and grey potholes and pockmarks about the surface. An obvious representation of the moon. The stones wound the pale wooden track below a skylight that opened onto a starless night.

Two boney, hairy women, nude with long drooping breasts like empty Christmas stockings, and coarse tufts of grey fur sprouting from their pelvises and from beneath their armpits, stepped to a short sliding hatch on the wall. Wrinkles covered the pair so fully it was as if they were humanized raisins. The hatch opened; the woman looked appreciatively at the pinkish-white payload before her.

"Nice bones, Mary," one said.

"A good fit for the doctor, Rosie," the other said.

The women carted the bundle of bones to a table below a lower end of the ovular track. One by one, they began assembling the stacked bones like a puzzle. Mary picked up something from the bundle and tossed it over her shoulder.

It was a tarnished watch, ruined but unmistakable. The slim hope Wanda held in Joel vanished. She thrashed, and in mimic, the twins kicked at the door of their cage.

"You can't do this!" Wanda said.

The door to the hallway swung open. A giant man with square shoulders and a hairline that nearly connected to his eyebrows stepped into the room. He wore white scrubs and long black gloves. He slipped the gloves off and then shed his scrubs. His chest bowed outward, his arms skinny but ropey. Scars traced ancient surgery lines over his stomach. He had a stubby penis and testicles that dipped nearly a foot between his thighs. Bones jutted at every connection. He had sparse, long, white hairs that sprouted from his wrinkled and liver spotted flesh. A face even a mother could hate, teeth stretching his lips, a long, bent nose, and tiny, close-set eyes.

He sneered at Wanda and the girls.

"Let us out!" Wanda struggled harder.

Overhead, the stones spun faster and the housekeepers smiled.

The tall man said in his earthquake voice, "Summer comes early for the eager."

The temperature in the room heightened, sweat began to drip from the rock walls, speckling the floor. Wanda felt her stunted energy draining, the atmosphere was like fire in her lungs. The girls were undeterred and fought against their cage door.

Through the skylight, an orange glow blazed and the stones spun so quickly that they appeared to become a single trailing hue. A semi-solid golden figure emerged from the light and floated downward to a foot above the table.

The women swayed, singing, "*Head and shoulders knees and toes. Daddy's bones and Mommy's nose.*" Their breasts swung like balls of a Newton's Cradle.

The golden figure sank onto the bones almost rubber-like. The sneering face of a decrepit old man began to form in that golden mist. It shook the bones, rattling, and easing in like fitting a wetsuit. The mannish face lingered upon the skull as if shot from a projector.

"Mommy!" the twins cried as they kicked.

Wanda ceased thrashing altogether, feeling the tickle of sweat rolling into her armpits. It was hopeless and they were as good as dead. She'd failed as a mother. She'd made the poor choice and she put them in danger. She—

The gate of the birdcage cracked open and the twins tumbled to the floor.

"Run!" Wanda began her fight with renewed vigor.

The gold-coated skeleton sat forward and hissed.

The tall man lumbered across the room. His arms were out, so boney and so ugly. His tiny penis was two inches of erection, his testicles bunched up like a cat's hairball. Legs pumping in spider motions.

"No, to the door!" Wanda shouted as the girls came to her.

Ally stumbled. Kat fell over her sister and the tall man had no room to slow his momentum. He tripped and his giant frame flailed forward into the stonework next to Wanda. The wall crumbled outward. The shackled pins pinged and slid. Arms and legs free, Wanda latched hands with her children and ran.

The golden figure shook Joel's skull as if it was and always had been his own calcified foundation. "I needs those soft bits!"

The women turned away from the doctor and hurried to intervene. They posted themselves between the hapless travelers and the exit into the hallway. Wanda sprinted sideways toward the verandah. She had a daughter at the end of each arm, a plan forming.

"Dr. Summer needs your eyes and thighs!" Rosie shouted.

Mary echoed in singsong, "*Eyes and thighs, eyes and thighs.*"

Wanda did not stop. She reached the door to the verandah and flung it open. Before her, willow trees bloomed orange flame blossoms that glowed like rabid fireflies. The rain had ceased and the draft was brimstone.

"Do as I say."

Wanda lifted Ally over the ledge and then Kat. The girls clung as the nurses closed the gap. Wanda watched the approach in the reflections cast by Ally's scared eyes. The girls scrambled for footing on the edge of the verandah.

Still watching, watching, watching... Waiting until she could wait no more, Wanda spun, swinging the chains dangling at the ends of her arms like headless maces.

The pins from the wall sliced through the ancient face meat of the women, sending a spray of blood out like a crimson spit-take. They toppled. Wanda gasped, unable to look away. The flesh of Mary's cheek had come loose to reveal rotten brown under layers of muscle and bone. Rosie was better, but pained and cradled her head. The pair looked up at Wanda, shaking Wanda's gaze.

Over the railing, she joined the girls on the ledge and shuffled sideways to a pillar. "You each need to take a chain from my ankle and wrap it around your hands. Hold tight and slide with your feet against the pillar."

"Mommy, I'm scared!" Unison cries.

"Just do it!"

The women rose and stumbled.

"Now!" Wanda sent a dagger stare into the girls.

All over the yard, the blossoms burst into flames sending molten kisses against their backs. Wanda nearly lost her hold when Ally swung out at the end of a chain before touching her feet to a pillar. Kat was much more graceful and managed her weight better. Still, the shackle clasps dug into her ankles, making ground chicken of her outer layers. With a continual groan humming, Wanda leaned down with her heavy legs, ready to—

Fingers grabbed a handful of hair. "The doctor needs those parts." The women sneered.

Strangely, despite the pain, that hold proved helpful. Wanda latched her hands around a pillar and let her body slide, feeling dozens of hairs come away with bits of scalp. Each removal screamed atop her head as if the strands were tongues, but it tempered the speed of descent if only momentarily. She clung for 16 feet before losing hold and dropping the remaining seven feet onto the sunbaked lawn below. Unbelieving, she gazed up at the home. It was not the building they saw when they'd arrived. The house was now crumbling and decrepit, a dilapidated structure, stretching something approaching eternally into the sky, unfit for even the lowliest squatters. The sky was burning orange. The world was not as it had been.

This was the place in those paintings.

Kat wailed from Wanda's left. Ally cried at Wanda's right. Kat had a broken leg. Ally had a sore butt. Wanda was in pain, but everything was relative.

"I need those bits," Doctor Summer's voice echoed over the crackling landscape. "Want it done right, got to..." His voice trailed away.

Wanda rolled to her feet and scooped up Kat. Ally hobbled next to her. They jogged, the only hope being some spell breaking once they crossed an invisible threshold they hadn't noticed on their way in. That, or that the alternator wasn't shot and they could carry on with the trip. Blind hopes relying on the faith that good conquered evil.

The big man was outside, long hairs reaching from his body lit like candle wicks as he ran. It didn't matter. Wanda had jet fuel in her veins. The chains clanged and snapped at her ankles and back with each step. She was above everything. The agony and misery, those were nothing, tomorrow problems. She had to get inside the Ford and demand sanity of the universe.

Key in the ignition, doors unlocked. Ally jumped in the back, leaving the door open for her sister. Wanda launched Kat onto the seat. Kat roared as the landing jarred her broken bones into her flesh, making them hump out. Ally's whine was constant, rising and dimming like a rollercoaster rail. Wanda slammed the door.

It took three seconds for Wanda to reappear and hop into the driver's seat.

The ignition had to work, *had to!*

The Ford turned over and started without the slightest cough. The lights flared and the wipers screeched on the dried glass.

It was a spell. That evil house had the vehicle no more.

Wanda offered a brief grin into the rearview mirror as she yanked the shifter down to drive. The heat increased. A scent wafted in through the dash vents. A shiver rose over Wanda's skin and her foot slid off the accelerator for two heartbeats. The harried woman straightened. She spun the volume on the radio to maximum. A childish song filled the vehicle's interior.

"*Head and shoulders knees and toes, Ally's lungs and Kat's lymph nodes,*" Wanda sang along in a voice not her own as she pulled the Ford between the flaming willow trees and onto the baked lawn.

"Mommy?" Ally whined.

"Maaawmeee!" Kat sobbed.

Wanda turned to face the twins, golden glow seeping from every orifice of her head. "Sing with me! One, two, three, *scalp and elbows, bone marrow, bone marrow, bone marrow...*"

THE MILKENING

(2014)

Curtains drawn, light peeked around the edges. Quiet, maybe, just maybe they had gone away. Perhaps it had been nothing more than a bad dream. And if it wasn't, what if they'd survived whatever mess overtook the—?

Moo!

Tears streamed down the cheeks of a young woman now huddled into herself in one of the diner's booths. She'd come in for a cup of coffee with her fiancé, had been on their way to Aurora's Landing for the small ceremony they'd—she'd—taken great pains over since picking the date. All she and her man had wanted was a pick-me-up, not a standoff, not the world turned upside down.

Moo! Moo! Moooo!

"Try the phone again, what if it's fixed? Please," she said. Her name was Laila Moore, formally soon to be known as Laila Knowlton, though that wouldn't happen now. "This can't go on forever."

Freddi Downs, a broad woman of 46 with greasy hair and a wandering eye, picked up the phone. "Don't be so damned bitchy; I tried an hour ago when I woke up, nothing." She fingered buttons and waited. The seconds raced toward a minute. She hung up and looked at Laila with defeat in her eyes. "Happy?"

Freddi had opened the Cat's Pajamas diner more than a decade ago; since, it had become something of a boy's club, farmers mostly. Drinking coffee, eating eggs, oatmeal, hash browns, and so on, six mornings a week. Money wasn't great, but it kept the heat on and it beat the hell out of working for somebody else.

"What do they want?" Laila said, sniffling around the words. She'd been in a state for close to 24 hours, beginning when she'd seen her fiancé charged, gored, and shaken to death by an outraged heard of beasts.

None of them had seen anything like it, not even on the worst days on a farm did things ever go down like this. It was insanity incarnate.

Duke Heinz, a local bumpkin, pulled back the curtain and looked out the window. His gaze met a close up shot, steam and nostrils.

Moo!

"Maybe they's got the rabbids," Duke said and let the drape fall on gravity's pull.

"Could be the diabetes," Duke's brother Luke said—dia-beat-ess.

"Could have them AIDS even," said the third of the trio, Mook.

"Will the three of you just shut the hell up?" Maureen Ringer said. She'd stopped in for an early lunch in the midst of a long-haul. Outside in the parking lot, where it might as well have been impounded on Saturn, was her rig. The payload was a shipment of fireworks.

"I concur, the three of you have yapped just about long enough for my patience," Robert Mastenn said. He was a local farmer, one with a touch more education than the norm. "I don't mean to get on you, but...I mean...just, shut it a while."

"How about you all shut up? This is supposed to be my day off," Freddi said as she rubbed her bleary, exhausted face. Earlier, she attempted to get through the alley and to her apartment in the building next to the diner, but a foursome of skinny Holsteins had been awaiting the move.

Mooo!

The sound seemed to rattle the universe within the diner.

Laila covered her ears.

Mooo!

A truck rolled into the lot and shotgun blasts rang like smacky kisses blown from an angel's palm. "Wooo, got'cha!" shouted a boyish voice. Overlapping the next round of shots, another voice called out. "Wooo, boy, you did it!"

The Frook brothers hurried over to look out the window, slapping their knees, shouting excitedly, making little sense, but appearing genuinely happy for the first time sense the mess had begun. The rest ran to the glass, joining them. The temperature of the room rose with the spirits.

Moo! Mooooo!

Cows and steers began to topple as the truck rolled loose donuts while the rest of the beasts ran in a parade of swishing tails and beshitted legs.

"Keep on shooting!" the boy behind the wheel said, smiling so widely his Skoal was visible from across the lot.

"That's Jilly's boys," Duke said.

"Sure is," Luke said.

"Damn right," Mook said.

Moo!

Down another went; Robert sighed while the others pounded tables, cheering. Unless those boys had 10,000 rounds and all the good luck in the universe, they weren't going to get through even half the county's cattle. The animals outnumbered people round those parts, and by more than a little. Killing a few was like trying to dry out the Atlantic Ocean one liter at a time.

Another good shot tumbled a beast. All but Robert cheered inside. He turned his head, listening to a fresh new sound. A lower grumble, so, so deep but rising high, like a freight train, steam whistle blaring as the engine's chaser.

Mooo!

"Oh, Lord," Robert whispered, scanning the sum of what he could see for what was obviously on its way.

Mooooo!

Thump. Crumple. Bang. Glass shattered. The truck tipped and skidded on its side. Jilly's boys screamed helplessly, one launched eight feet from the vehicle like a burger wrapper tossed during a road trip, his rifle spinning away, lost in a sea of shit speckled hooves.

"Rambo," Robert whispered. Rambo was his bull, was the biggest, strongest, meanest bull he'd ever had, and he'd had a few.

The fight was short lived. Rambo stomped the boy who'd held the rifle first, grinding him into the pavement with his forehooves with an alarmingly dexterous set of motions. The other boy crawled from the truck and tried to run across the lot to the entrance of Cat's Pajamas. Two angus cows charged from either direction as if playing chicken, veering at the last possible moment and each catching a leg with their wide heads. His body tore between the pressure like a Christmas cracker. Gore showered high and far, raining upon the diner windows in a chunky shower that send the patrons reeling away in disgust, surprise, sadness. Nobody said another word. Laila cried more.

The hours passed; outside, the moos became insistent.

"What do they want?" Maureen asked.

"Maybe they're just pissed; don't like being burgers and milk dispensers," Freddi said. "I'm about sick of serving them myself."

A joke, of course. The bovine species was capital D dumb. Nobody laughed. Nobody had laughed for more than a day.

"Why has nobody come?" Laila brought her knees to her chest and began rocking.

"Maybe nobody knows what's happening," Mook said; his brothers echoed the sentiment.

Robert shook his head gently.

Morning turned into afternoon, and Freddi awoke from a drowse to drop two baskets of fries. The power flickered when the mobile phones lost initial connection, but the juice had continued, thankfully. "If we get out of this, you all owe me for food and shelter. Don't you forget that."

It was quiet but for the roll of a lighter. Nobody had discussed it and nobody had complained. The Frooks smoked in the restaurant, Freddi even located a few tin ashtrays from the late '90s.

Robert searched the parking lot for Rambo. The beast had gone from sight, but it felt unlikely that he'd leave off; there were a lot of cows and heifers around the diner, and he'd fit right in as the herd leader.

Freddi came out of the back with two large bowls of steaming hot golden fries. Luke looked at her. "No burgs?"

Stupid, the stress so thick that laughter erupted, even Luke's brothers laughed at him.

"What's so fuckin' funny?" Luke said.

All laughed harder as they gathered around the bowls, pigs to the trough. What would those cattle outside do if they smelled their kin roasting on a grill?

At 7:00 PM, the chorus of *moos* rang louder than ever, became constant. This went on for three minutes before the power flickered and died.

"No good, no good," Laila said, wringing her hands. "We'll starve; they'll starve us." Her face had become gaunt, her hair a rats' nest.

"Won't starve, all gas. Might die without water though. We ought to fill what we can while there's still water in the lines and in the heater," Robert said. "Got any candles, Freddi?"

Freddi nodded.

"Why are they doing this, why?" Laila said, pleading to anybody and nobody.

Outside, the sun glowed like an orange ball of hatred and it dipped toward twilight.

"How is they doing it, more like," Duke said. The brothers held a short, pointless, circular conversation, reaching nothing even hinting at an answer.

The black and white Holsteins dipped their noses into the pools of blood, not drinking, instead wiggling their tongues about the sticky, clotting mess. They then charged the biggest window and Robert popped to his feet, nearly choking on a few cold fries he'd been picking at since Freddi brought them out fresh. The cattle stopped short and pressed their noses and tongues to the glass. The Frooks stepped close, watching in silent fascination. These cows hurried back and forth and back again, puddle to window, rubbing red streaks on the glass.

Maureen stepped next to Robert and shook her head. Four windows acted like a wall of glass after all the curtains had been pulled aside.

"Holy Moses," Robert said, finally pinpointing a key ingredient to this recipe of disaster.

Laila screamed.

The mooing had ceased.

"Su klim," Duke read then turned, his face scrunched in confusion.

"It's backward! God, they know how to write, oh God!" Laila pointed, her engagement ring sparkling in the twilight shine. "'Milk us,' they want us to milk them."

"That's...that...no, and fuck them," Freddi said.

"What if they let us leave? What if we...I..." Robert said but slowed himself.

Leaving would be a stretch. When did a man ever slap the asses of his heard for doing a good job, letting them free to exist beyond the pen? Never. Never ever ever. They were in a pen, living only as far as their masters decided.

"No way, we have the power if we don't milk them. They need us," Maureen said.

Settled, everyone was against Robert. The plan was to ignore them and use that as leverage—acting above the cattle also offered a sense of normality in the unthinkable situation. They closed the curtains and sat quietly for close to an hour drinking canned soda, coffees, and glasses of juice.

Only the Frooks stayed by the windows. Luke turned to his brothers and said, "Hell is they doing now?"

Laila pulled aside the drape closest to her booth. Two plump beef heifers dropped to their bellies and stared into the diner.

"Look at them go!" Mook said.

Moo! Mooooo!

A stream of small calves charged from across the lot. Their hooves stamped a terrifying tattoo upon the grey asphalt until their footfalls became muted by parading onto the larger animals' backs. Laila screamed as four of the calves burst through the glass and pounded her flat. Their pink mouths began gumming her all over while she writhed and screamed.

The Frooks grabbed two of the calves and withdrew pocketknives. One of the calves tormenting Laila spun and charge Maureen. Wide-eyed, she put up her hands but the skinny little beast bowled her over.

Mooooo!

The Frooks fared well with the blades. Blood ran and the calves cried out in pain. The mother heifers pushed their heads through the windows and called back.

Mooooo!

Maureen wrestled the calf that had attacked her, slamming her knees into its head repeatedly, doing more damage to her legs than the thick skull. Tables toppled as she and the animal rolled. The calf stood over her, poised to latch on. It found her breast and sucked through her flannel shirt. She screamed as it reefed and tugged. Maureen felt around for a steak knife, anything.

Robert chased Laila's cries. Freddi ran into the kitchen and slammed the door behind her.

Mooo! Mooo!

Their calves dead, the Frooks ran to Maureen. They stabbed and stabbed and stabbed. The calf jerked and wailed, eyes as big as full moons.

Mooooo!

The calf howled a final cry before it fell dead. Maureen still had two breasts, barely. The left breast drooped low while a halo of pink stained her shirt. She fell backward cradling her chest, the panting over the pain.

Robert lifted a calf and tossed it. It landed on its side, scrabbling to its feet before returning to Laila.

"Get off her!" Robert said.

Laila hadn't been so quiet since her fiancé died. Another calf tumbled in the window and Robert latched on, wrestling it to the stiff diner carpet. The returned calf launched itself and Laila tried to gain her feet. Its gummy mouth went around her throat. A short-lived red geyser burst from the flesh.

The Frook brothers acted quickly, but not quickly enough. Laila lay on the floor, vacant gaze pinned to the ceiling, her chest rising and falling in a rapid pant. The brothers sliced the calf to ribbons. It fell dead in time with the stoppage of Laila's breaths.

The mother heifers at the window cried out. The Frooks were on the warpath and rushed with their little knives. They stabbed for eyes, cackling madly as the heifers scattered. They pulled the drapes back over the windows, darkening the room as Robert pounded the final calf's skull against the floor until it snapped, crackled, popped, and a chunk of brain oozed free like toothpaste squeezed from a tube.

Freddi opened the kitchen door. "They dead?" She had candles in her hands.

Robert peeked around a curtain. There had to be 100 cows out there, sagging udders drooping loosely like rubber pendulums. He understood then. "That was a warning. We barely handled their weakest. What happens when they send in the steers and heifers next?"

The brothers pulled aside curtains then and their smiles slipped from their faces. Luke rubbed his chin as he said, "We gonna need stools."

———

Civil and orderly, the cows fell into patient lines. Robert sat on Freddi's plastic stepstool. He hadn't hand milked in a good many years, but it was like swimming—once there, it was there. The milk splashed onto the parking lot, mingling with blood and dirt.

With every happily sapped cow another stepped forward. The Frooks watched from the side. They'd never milked cows, goats, yes, but never cows. Turned out teets were teets were teets. Luke took another stepstool. Duke took a plastic Pepsi crate. Mook grabbed the firewood chopping block from around the side of the building. Three more lines formed. The cows remained peaceful while the men milked.

Maureen watched it all and something about it clicked an offensive instinct within her head. While the cows focused on the milking, she grabbed a lighter from the serving counter. Freddi was on the floor behind it, drunk as a Wisconsinite, bottle of Popov's next to her hand.

"Coward," Maureen mumbled as she headed out to the parking lot.

The moos were different now, appreciative, non-threatening. It was her chance. She ran toward her truck.

Mooooo!

This one was deep, powerful, rising high on its tail. Maureen got to the back door and fumbled with the handles and padlock.

Mooooo!

Robert looked around. "Maureen! Rambo!"

Maureen glanced over her shoulder in time to see the massive beast racing her way like every knockout punch Mike Tyson ever threw, balled into a single creature. She got the door open and hopped up into the trailer. She hadn't worked out a plan, not really. She flicked her lighter, revealing the crates of fireworks in their cardboard and plastic packages.

Rambo headbutted the back of the trailer, smashing turn

signals and rocking the world beneath Maureen's feet.

Mooooo!

On the roof of the trailer there were two safety hatches. If she could get up there, she could pop every damned explosive she had at the ever-growing herd. And maybe, just maybe.

She tore into the packages looking for the deadliest weapons of the arsenal. There were some good ones. Loaded with the first helping, she opened a hatch and pushed fireworks out by the armload.

Robert and the Frooks yelled at her, but their voices barely rose above the mooing. She caught bits and pieces, "up, watch, sneak, smarter," and catalogued them for later, perhaps after she led the victory parade. She gathered a seventh armload and piled it topside before wiggling herself up.

Mooooo!

The call came as she stood straight and looked around. *Clop, clop, clop,* the hooves created a hollow metallic sound. Maureen spun and saw the calves charging.

"How in the sweet motherfu—?"

The first butted her, sending her pinwheeling off the roof of the trailer like a hucked starfish. As she dropped, she saw from a new angle, and had a moment to consider the bovine pyramid built on the truck's nose; the cows had piled so calves could run topside. She landed with a wet *crack-thunk!* but shot to her feet, her left arm featuring a new elbow which dangled the lower half of her forearm like an ultra-thick udon noodle.

Mooooo!

Rambo caught her before she managed five steps. Maureen was tossed again, this time straight into the air. She swung her arms before her uselessly, barely lessening the nasty smack as her head hit the asphalt, her skull cracked open like a dropped melon, and her neck bent at a right angle.

Rambo wasn't done and made a bloodpie, rending her bones and guts in a slurry of anger.

Robert and the Frook brothers were spared from the view, but they heard it all. Rambo clopped around the side of the truck. A blood beard glistened in the moon's shine, his eyes two black blobs of death, his enormous testicles swinging proudly, a testament of his authority.

"Guess that's that," Mook said.

"Guess so," Duke said.

"Uh huh," Luke said.

Robert put his head down and focused on his task.

All night the four men squeezed teets, spraying milk about the parking lot. By 2:30 AM, cats and dogs had come to lap. Raccoons and groundhogs approached tentatively at first, but their hunger eventually outweighed their natural risk aversion.

At first light, the line ceased and the milkers returned to the restaurant. Freddi snored gently in one of the booths on the far side of the diner, away from the windows, away from Laila's corpse.

Robert, Duke, and Mook all flopped into booths. Luke hadn't yet given up on wanting a burger—if he wanted a cheeseburger, he'd have a goddamned cheeseburger. Over the gas flames, he cooked two patties of wonderfully pink meat. Done to his taste, he plated the meal.

While everyone slept, Luke sat at a table in the middle of the dining floor. The meat was rare, the blood dripping down his arms mingled with milk residue and cow shit.

Moo! Mooo! Moooo!

The calls came from all around the building. A snort and grunt joined it all. Luke stepped to the window and looked out with his burger in hand. Rambo scratched his forehoof behind him, stating intent, stating a line crossed. Luke looked around the diner, looked down at his burger.

MOOOOO!

Rambo charged at the window. Luke looked down at his dripping burger again. Finally got what was so funny, but not *ha-*

ha funny. Rambo came through and nailed Luke's chest, sending him rocketing across the room and into the big cooler on the far side. One corner of the diner fell behind Rambo. Duke and Mook charged at the bull.

"Not my brother!" said one. "Not a Frook you don't!" said the other.

Freddi jumped up from behind the counter, "I'm tryin' a sleep!" drunk as a teenager on prom night.

Rambo trampled the brothers and snorted at Freddi. Freddi remembered herself and fell back behind the counter. Rambo turned his massive head to face Robert. Robert lifted his hands as if being robbed.

Moo?

"I'll be good," Robert said.

Rambo stepped back through the broken wall.

Robert slept until the cows no longer permitted his rest. He got up and dragged Freddi out with him, gave her a crash course in milking, and they sat well into the night, the lot a murky pond of animal waste and milk. They returned to their booths after the long day, fell dead asleep in seconds.

Which was good because they have a lot of milking to do tomorrow.

NOBODY THERE

(2015)

There's nobody there. There's nobody there, the wishful mantra ran through Dorothy's head as her feet quickened.

"Stupid, stupid," she said.

The moon rode the sky bright and high, shadows by the millions draped and reached across the yard. Echoes from her footfalls told a lie. Still, perhaps they didn't; what if those footfalls weren't echoes at all? Those footfalls seemed unfamiliar and very close.

"Nobody there," she whispered and sped into a jog.

The light from the garage cast two separate and wonderful streams of yellow. She'd never been so thankful that she'd left that light on. A stark contrast to the anger that boiled, anger directed inward; she'd let her gas tank run dry only a mile from home.

Trees lined the roadsides, hills and fields beyond them. The world carried the weight of dark shrouds, shadows where anything and everything might lurk.

"Grow up, there's nobody there," she whispered and repeated the sentiment in her head. The grind of gravel underfoot, the wind whistling around her...her sensibilities guaranteed, *only wind.*

There's nobody there.

Just breathing, nothing but inhaled wind exhaled. Cracking and breaking, twigs and leaves, *animals parading the ditches, only mice or rabbits.* Still, *awfully loud for critters.*

"Nobody." Her legs disagreed with the word and she sprinted.

She tore away from the road and ran straight for the light of the garage. The breaking and cracking underfoot sounded of henchmen by the herd looking for any poor girl alone in the wrong place at the wrong time.

"Please, no," she whispered.

The garage light grew closer and her heart thumped at the nearing safety.

A hand reached and held her foot, stealing her balance. She teetered and crashed. Only a peep left her lips as she waited for the vicious hands of a night creature to spill her blood, let her soul depart.

"Please," she whimpered.

Nothing. She touched her ankle. It was sore and bits of bark stuck to the threads of cotton. A dirty root, *not a hand.* She took an easy breath and forced a weak laugh.

She rose, looked back to the darkness behind her and then to the light of the garage. Twigs snapped and the wind spoke. A root had stalled her forward motion. Still, *that doesn't mean you're alone.*

She sped, *there's nobody there, nobody,* her mantra resumed.

In a series of long strides, Dorothy cleared the grassy space to her walkway where a bulb glowed inside, her heart thankful, her mood lightening.

"Scaredy cat," she mocked the fleeting feelings.

Breathing easy, the garage light died.

The torrent in her chest threatened collapse, too much, too much. "Who's there?" she yelled as she stood in the middle of the garage. She hurried to the wall and tried the switch, *a poor time for the bulb to die, nothing more.*

She forced another laugh to show any monsters that she wasn't afraid.

The keys went from her pocket into the lock, click. The deadbolt swung and the door opened, she scurried through and closed it behind her. Her fear melted away as she spun the deadbolt closed and the light switch worked.

Her parents had not yet returned from the Halloween party. Dorothy exhaled pure anxiety.

Her room was as always. She readied for bed, changing into her pajamas, brushing her teeth and hair. She killed the light. "Of course there was nobody there," she said to the safe, dark, warm bedroom.

The moon played games on her wall, sending shadows, a face in the closet. *Was that a rattle, coat hangers?*

The fear returned. "Nobody there," she whispered and lit the bedside lamp.

The face disappeared and the rattle was never really there.

Stronger, she rolled from her bed to check the closet, empty but for laundry, textbooks, and her personal bric-a-brac.

She curled into bed and killed the light again, heart slowing and eyes aflutter. Fear was exhausting business. Drowsing, she slipped into a safe place.

"Goodnight Dorothy," cooed the mannish voice hiding behind the door.

WHEN YOU NEED IT MOST

(2018)

"You can do this; you can do this." Shane Whimmer fought back an urge to vomit.

He took a final deep breath and said goodbye to the semi-peace of the interior of his car. Too often he was back in the driver's seat after only minutes, seconds in some cases, driving to the next house. The insurance he peddled was junk and he knew it. But a man had to eat, and sometimes that meant going door-to-door, business-to-business, farm-to-farm shilling garbage policies.

Gravel crunched beneath his cheap loafers that passed for decent so long as he kept them swimming under a layer of polish. Secondhand briefcase at the ready, he walked trying to look like a confident man doing the whole damn world one great big favor every time he regurgitated the sales pitch. Sweat rode the ring around his collar and down the back of his suit jacket. It was the 20th stop of the day and 109th of the week. His confidence was thinner than the knees of a hooker's pantyhose.

A teenaged boy stood in his path wearing rubber boots and shorts, ball cap on his big round head. He was shirtless and tanned to a shade of coffee and cream. His skin seemed to pour over his middle, flabby, but not weak. Oddly loose.

A biggish boy.

Shane Whimmer adjusted his briefcase, making the switch from right to left, and stuck out his hand. The boy waved rather than shaking.

"Shane Whimmer's the name, insurance is my game. You have a mother or father around here?" Inside, Shane wished the boy was a farm orphan, feeding the herd until social services found out. *No mom and no dad? So sad.* A scenario like that sent an insurance man on his way without the pain of refusal.

He'd never wanted to sell anything, but times were tough, doubly so since Sylvie lost her job. Somebody had to pay the bills and to start, the junk insurance offered a rookie stipend for the first two months—$300 a week in times of need was nothing to moan about. And at least there was a script, so he didn't have to think it through. In fact, selling junk was best done with the grey meat set to snooze.

"My dad's in the barn doing the feeding, sir," the boy said.

"You think I might meet him? I've got something he'll want to see."

"I don't know. Dad's mighty irritable about people bugging him."

Me too, kid, me too. But I'm stuck and I'm fucked and if I don't start selling these policies, I'll lose my stipend and the hydro guys will cut the power. "I can understand that, but your father cares about his farm and his family, right? Of course he does. He'll want to have a listen to what I say." *Unless he's got half a brain. If he's got any wits, he'll smell the shit stench of CCI policies and kick me off his property faster than you can say yee haw, ride 'em cowboy.*

"Oh, all right, but you better tell him you made me."

You smell it too, don't ya? Sure, everybody with a nose smells this kind of stink. "So, where's your mother?"

"Mother's gone."

Dead, left for greener grass, at church? "And what grade are you in, boy?"

"Eighth. Dad never went to school, but he says I have to get an education."

There was promise in the fact dear old daddy skipped a proper training.

"Education is important, more important today than ever."

"Dad isn't stupid, he says he's self-educated. See he had to take over this farm because my grandfather lost his marbles and killed my grandmother and four of my cousins. Had to shoot him down. Dad says Granddad might've been off, but he started a change for the better. Dad took over the farm when he was still young, but he's smart. No, Mister, don't get it crooked, Dad isn't stupid, Dad's real smart. Smartest one ever come outta our family"

"Geez, killed your grandmother and some cousins? That's something."

"Sure is. Sometimes it's hard being related, but Dad says it's important to do your own thing even if everyone else thinks you ought to be acting a different way."

A rough dog joined alongside the insurance peddler and the boy.

"Hey, fella." Shane leaned down to pet the dog.

"Dad's in there," the boy pointed at the barn door, "and if he gets uppity, maybe just leave, don't push him."

Shane smiled weakly as the boy held open a steel door. The scent of pig manure pounded through and knocked tears from Shane's eyes. "Holy crow, that's a stink."

"Barn pigs stink the worst, but you get used to it. I wish they'd figure out the toilet."

Shane Whimmer smiled imagining a piggy on the can as he stepped inside the dark barn. He paused to let his senses adjust. There was a constant rumble of snorting, on top of the putrid stink. The boy took the lead once again.

"Might have to spray off your shoes once you're done, they're pretty dusty anyway."

The dust really clung to the polish. Shane hadn't thought it was so obvious, but the boy noticed, *didn't you, boy? If I ever sell one of these policies, I'll buy myself a half-decent pair of shoes from the Goodwill, if things really turn, maybe even Walmart.*

"Dad?" the boy called out. Shane stared down at the fat pink beasts, all eager, greedily sniffing for more. "Dad?"

"Over here!" The voice was deep, coming from within a pen.

Shane saw a filthy man, burly and hairy. A baseball cap like his son, but he wore overalls instead of shorts. Like his son, he was shirtless, lots of flab, and like his son, he had a big, fat head.

"This guy here said he has something you have to see. He made me bring him out."

"His funeral. Run along. Take a lasagna from the freezer, would ya?"

The man approached through the muck, nudging the pink beasts out of the way.

My funeral, Shane thought as the boy walked away. The approaching man's smile settled the trepidation.

The man hopped with a squishy thud over the short feeder fence. His overalls cut off at about the knees, an inch above his rubber boots. He carried the shaft of a hockey stick, the blade sawed off.

Shane held out his hand. "Shane Whimmer's the name, insurance is my game. A nice setup you have here."

The man showed two filthy palms and Shane stowed the second unused handshake away for later.

"I'm Henry Tugnutt, but I'll tell ya, I got lots of insurance, damn close to insurance poor."

"I hear that all the time and trust me, I can relate. You're going to want to listen because not having the right insurance can cost heads and tails more than these small monthly fees. Concerted Community offers the three coverages that hit home and really help when you need it most." In a swoop, Shane dropped his briefcase and pulled a leather binder from within. He flipped to a bookmarked page. "What do you think would happen to your son if you suffered a horrid accident here on the farm or out at play? Like you, I'm a private contractor, I don't have employment insurance coverage and something like that could stagger your whole operation.

"Coverage for when you need it most, that's what this is. I think we both know what would happen in the event of an injury, the bills would..." The man wasn't listening and Shane needed his attention or he was just flapping his tongue and there were nicer places to waste time. "Mr. Tugnutt, Henry, are you following?"

Henry's blank gaze slid back into view. "Insurance you say? Is that what you told my wife? Is that what you said before you did what you did?"

"Excuse me?" Shane saw Henry's eyes sink back into his head. Something was wrong with this man. Shane dropped the binder into his briefcase. "Thank you for your time!" Shane took a step back toward the door, turned, took a second step, and then tripped.

Henry Tugnutt's stick shaft had found its way between his feet.

"I ain't done with you. Like you wasn't done with her 'til you licked your fingers clean!" Henry swung the stick like a bat and the shit-coated tip smacked across Shane's cheek.

Shane rubbed the cut flesh. "What in the hell are you talking about? I didn't do nothing. I don't know your wife! I came out—" Another swipe cut Shane's argument short, bursting his lip.

"That stink'll get them piggies right hungry, they the stupid kind," Henry said.

Shane looked to his side through the rusty steel guards caked in manure. There were dozens of hungry porkers looking to munch. Henry back swung and Shane kicked out one of his ruddy loafers. He caught Henry square in the jewels.

"You bugger," Henry wheezed and took a knee.

The door was 50 feet behind him and he knew if he could get to the light of day, he'd be safe as an altar boy come Monday morning. This Henry Tugnutt was obviously as crazy as his father before him.

Up. There was a slick scramble, Shane felt a meaty paw clench on his foot, but freed himself with a donkey kick at Henry's upper half, scoring a headshot. The pigs sensed something and activity bloomed in the shitty pens. Hunger, never-ending hunger.

"Crazy, the whole works!" Shane shouted over his shoulder to where Henry Tugnutt had been, but the man wasn't there anymore. "Shit." Shane opened the door.

Gravel and dust clung to the pig pies riding his feet and legs. In the bright yard there was no sign of father or son.

If I do see the boy I'll tell him, goddammit, I will tell him!

He pulled on the driver's door handle and for a second, he thought he'd locked himself out when the door didn't open. No, it wasn't that, only another thing a few extra bucks might fix. *Nothing lasts anymore.*

The door creaked open, and then slammed closed after being thumped. The stupid mutt whimpered and growled, frothing at the mouth, bloodied where he smashed his skull against the car.

The dog found its footing and resumed its mad promenade.

"Good doggy, good doggy," Shane whispered, backing up to the trunk.

The plan was to get in the front passenger's side door. For the safety of the girls, the child locks didn't disengage in the rear unless he hit the unlock button on the fob twice. The fob dangled from the key and the key remained in the ignition.

Somehow, the small act of walking around back confused the dog and he cocked his head. Pink foam dripped as blood and craziness mingled about his jaws. Once to the trunk, Shane ran to the shotgun door, swung it open and heard a crack. The back passenger's window shattered.

"Holy shit!" Shane jumped through the open door. He shimmied in behind the wheel.

Nose pointed *in* the lane, toward the house—there would be trouble yet. A shot came from somewhere behind him. He looked in the rearview, his eyes passing over his reflection, no longer worried about a sale.

Another shot rattled the car. He lay flat on the seat and

reached for the key. The engine caught and another round rocked and pinged, a stream of light poured through the vinyl door interior. With his left hand, Shane tugged the shifter into drive and with his right, he pushed down on the accelerator.

Rocketing up the farm path was the only choice.

Could've gone in reverse, dumbass.

Too late for could haves, the front bumper smashed through a steel gate and the sound gave Shane reason to punch the brake pedal. Another shot rang through the air but missed the car. Shane slid around the seat, popped up, and drank in the scene. The gate he had opened revealed a path that wound behind the barn and silos. Another shot.

"You missed, shithead!"

A bang and a smash, his rear window shattered. He stamped the accelerator and followed the path. Out of the ditch the boy leapt, waving his arms.

"Please mister, you got to help me!"

Well, shit, kid. Shane veered from the path and clunked the undercarriage of his car on an unlucky stone.

"You should a listened! I told ya, he don't like people bugging him. You got to take me with you; I don't want to be a farmer, and I don't want to become like my dad and my granddad, and I especially don't want to end up like my mom," the kid spoke through a broken window.

There was another shot, Shane attempted to back up, but the car stalled, only two wheels still on the ground.

"Find me a ride and I'll get you out of here." Shane kicked open the dented door.

The dog barked and another shot echoed over the yard.

"Follow me. We got the others' cars back here." The boy darted around the barn.

Others, what others?

Shane followed. They cleared a corner and came to a fenced area with a shit floor.

"Oh my god," Shane mumbled. A sea of cars and trucks. "The others, like—" There were pizza delivery signs, insurance bumper stickers, mutual fund emblems, a pink Mary Kay Cadillac Escalade, and more.

"Feed got too expensive. Dad says it's okay to feed salespeople to the stupid pigs because most of them are bad for selling junk."

"Your father accused me of doing something to your mother." Shane climbed the fence.

"He'll do that. Get in," the boy said.

He'd chosen a rusty GM truck.

If I'm going to die, why not die in style? Can't trust this boy, like father like son and so on.

"No, we'll take the Caddy."

The kid shrugged and followed Shane to the gaudy, pink gas-guzzler. The dog yipped and leapt over the fence, kamikaze nose-diving under the wheel of the machine as Shane turned the key, pulled the shifter, and rolled forward. A squeak like a rubber ducky filled the air.

"Wooty," the boy said, sadly.

"Dog was fucking rabid as your daddy."

The pink Cadillac punched a hole through the fence and wheeled back onto the trail. The short-term plan involved racing past any shotgun blasts and heading out the laneway, hopefully in one piece. The long-term plan involved bringing the wrath of the law down on this operation.

"Just a dog, mister."

"Crazy mutt tried to eat me!"

"Nah, not crazy. Listens to Dad real good."

And how well do you listen?

Shane steered the machine up and around the barn, shots started to pelt the massive steel body. It wasn't a shotgun, something smaller and faster. Shane put his head down as well as his foot.

"Ugh, oh mister," the boy moaned.

The Cadillac thumped over something. The vehicle tilted and grinded. He looked at the boy. Blood spurted from his chest. Shane slammed on the brakes and reached over to the fleshy hole. Torn between self-preservation and nursing the boy.

"Don't you die, don't you—" Shane started and stopped.

The hole was real, but when he *really* looked at the boy, his expression hid behind a layer of something like rubber, but better. Shane put his hand on the boy's cheek, cold.

"You...smell...good," the boy whispered and then snorted.

It was a suit. A suit of flesh. He tugged at the boy's jaw and the flesh tore, came away. Gape-mouthed, Shane stared at the thing in his hands.

Emptied a face and wore it, kept the skull and jaw, and—

The thought died when he looked up at the pig head riding atop the boy's shoulders.

"No! No!" Shane kicked open the driver's door. He hopped down and stomped toward the road.

"Stop right there!"

Shane did.

"I'm losing it. This is stress. This kind of thing is impossible, pigs are pigs and people are people." His cellphone vibrated in his pocket, distracting his wrought and bungled mind. He reached into his pants. The vibration ceased and he let go.

"Pigs are pigs, you're right about that, but people aren't people, people are food. Been the other way 'round about long enough. Bacon for breakfast was one thing, but bacon doughnuts and bacon milkshakes and bacon yogurt, your bunch crossed a line. You shouldn't a ate my wife! I ain't going out like the rest!"

Shane turned around and looked at Henry. The man-mask was gone. He had a round pig's head. It was almost funny. Something snapped inside. It *was* all a joke, obviously it was. Losing his good job, Sylvia losing her job, him going to that seminar, finding his way to the farm where he tried to sell insurance to pigs that dressed as people. It was one of those big, shitty, cosmic jokes.

"You ain't getting me too! Ain't no bacon!"

"Sounds like you could use some coverage against that. We have policies for every kind of potential catastrophe." The phone in Shane's pocket beeped a message as he spoke. "I've got the coverage you need, Mr. Tugnutt. By god, I do!"

Henry Tugnutt snorted and lifted a pistol to aim at Shane Whimmer, man chops on the mind. A slug-like tongue reached out beneath the squat pink snout.

"Trust me, Mr. Tugnutt, you're gonna want to hear all about this. This stuff is the good stuff. Covers ya when you need it most."

Tugnutt squealed.

—

Sylvia had to call Shane right away and tell him, tell him he could leave that stinking job.

"Honey," she said to the message service, "I got it! The job at the clinic, full-time, twenty an hour. You can quit selling that bullshit insurance and come home!"

Made in the USA
Columbia, SC
25 March 2023

14155600R00439